Wallace Family Affairs Volume VII

At Last

Carey Anderson

ISBN: 0692397442
ISBN-13:9780692397442

DEDICATION

To my Crystal Chandelier although you weren't the first person to suggest this storyline, it was something about the way you pitched it that challenged me, thank you.

I would also like to dedicate this to my beautiful flower. Some friendships last forever even though you don't speak or check in daily, I miss you. Like Annette, my world was torn apart when you went to sleep

Cover design: Cover Couture

Join me on Facebook –
www.facebook.com/careythewriteranderson

Twitter - @CareyTheWriter

Blog - http://careyanderson.blogspot.com

Website – http://www.careythewriteranderson.com

Editorial – Treasures of Joy Editorial

Photography by – Carey Anderson (Inspired by Nae)

To Joyce. Thank you for joining me on this journey back to a time when love was enough to supply all that you could ever need. I hope you enjoy this introduction into the Wallace Family Saga.

Carey A.

ACKNOWLEDGMENTS

I would like to thank my baby-girl who is my life's ultimate expression of a dream realized. Thank you for sacrificing mommy time so that I could have the time to work some things out on paper.

I would like to thank my Soul Sistah #1 who has been my captivated audience since middle school. Without your love, support, encouragement, and FIRE I never would've completed Volume I or II, etc. Thank you for bringing me laughter when I couldn't get outside of my head.

I would like to thank my Sister-In-Law for taking time out of your busy family life to humor me with a read through of my latest thoughts and expressions. (SS1 & SIL THANK YOU for the trip to St. Helena where we spent the day lost in my imagination. I will never forget it, and it was exactly what I needed. THANK YOU!)

I would like to thank my dear cousin for reassuring me that my little hobby was relatable and entertaining. You are definitely a speed-reader, thank you for taking time out of your busy life to be entertained by my imagination.

I would like to thank last but not least Mrs. Laverne Dyes! Mrs. Dyes the day that you read my short story to my class changed my life. Thank you for giving me a positive outlet for all the angst going on in my life. You have forever changed my life, I am so thankful to have ever known you.

Chapter 1

Annette

"Annette!"

I'm sleep and then I hear my name being screamed out of nowhere! I climbed over Emma and I ran in the kitchen. "Yes ma'am?" I said trying to focus my eyes.

"Why are you looking at me like that!" I felt the sting of my momma's hand across my face. Then she cursed me out while I stood there holding my face. She clinched her lips, "you better straighten your face up NOW!"

"Yes ma'am," I said putting my eyes to the floor.

"Your brother is going to be home soon. Fix him something to eat! I'm going to bed."

My heart dropped, "Momma no! Please! Can I fix it and leave it on the stove for him?"

She slapped me again in the same spot, "No! Your father and brother go to work for us and how do you show your thanks? You are so UNGRATEFUL! How I ever raised such an ungrateful child is beyond me. Now don't sass me either! Make your brother a plate and I don't wanna hear nothing else about it!" Then she walked to the cabinet and pulled out her *medicine*. She had the guiltiest look in her eyes when she glanced at me one more time.

I ran in my room and put on three pairs of panties a skirt, bra, and blouse. Emma woke up and I told her to go back to sleep. I hurried around that kitchen in hopes that I could finish before Leslie got home. Leslie is my oldest brother and I don't like him! I dream about poisoning his food, and beating him until I get tired. Momma knows exactly what she's doing setting me up like this. She probably didn't wake me until she thought he was close by. When I heard footsteps on the porch my heart stopped. I was almost done with his eggs; I slid them on his plate over his hash. I pulled the sun tea out the cooler and poured him a glass. "Look at my pretty pretty little sister!" He said standing there with a smile.

I dropped my eyes to the floor, "here you go Leslie." I tried to hurry out the kitchen

"Hold on, where's the fire?" He said grabbing my arm. "Aren't you gonna keep your big brother company?"

"I gotta go to bed. I gotta go to school in the morning." I said in a low voice with my eyes to the floor.

"Oh come on! I've been down at the station all week. Shouldn't somebody in this family care enough to talk to me? I mean I send all my money here so you can have nice things."

"You send that money to momma for everybody, why I gotta be the one?"

"Cause I like you the best. Emma too little, she not ripe yet." He said putting his last fork full of food in his mouth.

"You are disgusting!" I hated him so much.

He reached out to touch my hand and I slapped his hand away. He slapped me hard and I punched him with everything I had. I started crying as I looked for something to hit him with. He wasn't getting me this time without a fight! When he grabbed me and took me into his arms I bit him as hard as I could. He screamed in pain, I grabbed the skillet off the stove and I started swinging. After I clocked him a couple of times he put his bloody hand up in defeat! I wasn't falling for it. I waited for him to back away. He looked like he thought about changing his mind and charging me.

"Annette what's wrong?" Emma said rubbing the sleep out of her eyes.

Leslie looked at her then he went in the living room to sleep with my brothers. Emma started crying cause she saw me crying. She helped me clean up the kitchen and then we went in our room. I put the dresser in front of the door, and then I laid down to sleep.

Timothy

"You're Franklin Wallace's boys aren't you?" He asked looking me up and down.
"Yes sir!" I said looking him in his eyes.
"What you boys doing all the way over here?" He cracked a smile.
"Just pay him so we can move on!" My brother Jeff said.
"No!" My brother Franky said, "Who do you report to?"
"Boy! I ask the questions here!"
Franky got out the car, "I'm not your Boy! You seem to know who I am, and yet you dare to take this tone with me! I will have your head and your badge! Now I got business to tend to on the other side of this bridge so I suggest you move out of my way."
The officer looked at his partner who shrugged. "Get out of here! He's too young to be going on these runs with you!" He said pointing to me.
"Mind your own business!" Franky said getting back in the truck. When he drove away he told me, we don't have to answer questions unless we want to. He said Pops owns the San Francisco police and anyone who steps out of line would be dealt with.
I took everything my big brother said in like it was written in gold. Franky was the oldest brother. He doesn't back down to anyone. My brother Dale is a bookworm; Pops gives him and my brother Matthew other things to do when we go out to *handle business*. There are eight of us total, five boys and three girls. I'm the youngest boy. I have two younger sisters and one older. Pops keeps their noses in books too. We all gotta get good grades in school and do our chores. For Franky, Jeff, and I sometimes we get "other" chores. Franky and Jeff used to try to say I was too little to come with them, but one day this kid Eddie was bothering my sister Martha. Eddie is supposed to be the cool kid the one everybody looked up to and all the girls wanted, but he decides to set his sights on my sister. Martha is always the sweetest; she doesn't act moody like those other two. Sometimes they're ok, and other times they're too much. So needless to say she's my best sister. Well Martha, my friend Jeremiah, and I were walking from the store. We each had a bag full of penny candy. When I saw Eddie coming Martha got nervous and said we should cross the street. Eddie was three times my size and mean looking, but I didn't care. I told Martha I would not cross the street, I told her to stay with me and she would be ok. She smiled at me, underestimating me because I was her little brother. "What are you guys doing walking around with him?" He said pointing to Jeremiah.
"We can walk with whomever we like." Martha said.
Eddie frowned, "you like coloreds?"
I frowned at Martha; Eddie was getting on my nerves. "Jeremiah is a good kid, we like him."
"You like him?"
"What's it to you who she likes? She doesn't like you, and that's all you need to worry about." I said giving my bag of candy to Martha.
Eddie started laughing, "what are you going to do little man? Put 'em up!"
Before he even realized what happened to him he was on the ground and I was stomping the life out of him. My brother Jeff came out of nowhere and pulled me

off of Eddie. Martha and Jeremiah's mouths were hanging open. "Don't you ever mess with my sister again or else I'm going to get you!"
Jeff stopped me, "what did he do?"
"He didn't do anything to her today, but he's always messing with her. Martha wanted to cross the street." Jeff looked at Martha who put her eyes on the ground. "Today he was getting on my nerves calling Jeremiah colored and stuff. I wanted to shut him up." I said taking a piece of candy out of my bag to eat.
"You beat him up like that for talking about your friend?" Then he patted my back, "I didn't know you had it in you."
We left Eddie on the ground. Later than day Mrs. Epstein came to our front door very upset. "Irma your boy and his dark friend beat up my boy!" She said with Eddie in tow.
"Come in have a seat." My momma said taking out the pitcher and pouring Mrs. Epstein some lemonade. She eyed Eddie, "I heard something about it. Your boy was telling my children that they were wrong for playing with the Barnes kid."
Mrs. Epstein looked around, "Irma think about it. We can't have our children thinking that it's ok to socialize with them. Next they'll think its ok to bring him in your house."
Suddenly my momma moved her eyes and she caught Jeremiah and I eavesdropping on their conversation from the hallway. "Tim and Jeremiah come here." She commanded. Mrs. Epstein gasped when she saw Jeremiah walking behind me.
"Irma! What if this gets out?"
"You are getting on my nerves! There's nothing wrong with my children befriending whomever they like as long as they're good people! Times are changing Shirley, and I couldn't be more relieved!"
"Fine Irma! Don't say I didn't warn you."
"And don't say I didn't warn you. The next time your stupid dope of a son tries to pick on somebody he could at least try to make sure they're the same size. That way he'll have some dignity about himself when the word gets out."
"Well! I guess I should be leaving if I'm going to be treated in such a fashion!"
"Yeah, I guess so." Momma walked over hugged Jeremiah and kissed his forehead. "You can marry anyone of my daughters when you can afford a wife."
"Momma!" I said embarrassed, and smiling at Jeremiah. I knew she said that to drive home the point, that Jeremiah is ALWAYS welcomed here.
That evening Jeff told me Pops wanted to see me in his study. All of the kids knew not to go in this room unless Pops invited you. The three of them were drinking Brandy, and there was a fourth glass. Pops told me to sit in front of the unmanned glass, and then he told me to drink. It was hot but delicious; I twisted my face as I took a drink. Franky got a kick out of seeing me take my first drink. Pops was watching me. Then he shook his head, he told Franky I was good. "I heard you had a fight today? Your momma said you beat the kid up pretty bad."
"Yes sir."
"Your brothers seem to think you have the stomach to work with us." Then he looked at me, "I don't know just yet. I'm gonna test you out. You need to remember what happens in our family stays in our family, you understand me?"
"Yes sir!"

Chapter 2

Annette

Boom! Boom! Boom! The door was banging on the dresser. "ANNETTE! OPEN DIS DOOR!" My momma's voice hollered from the other side of the door.

I didn't take my clothes off cause I knew as soon as she sobered up from her *medicine* she was going to come after me when Leslie told her what happened. I cracked the window then I moved the dresser enough so that Emma could get out or she could find her way in. Then I went out the window. Leslie was waiting outside; he yelled to my momma that I went out the window just like she said I would. I ran as hard as my legs would carry me. Leslie was fast, but I've learned to be faster. I ran to the road and beyond the bridge. I stopped long enough to catch my breath, and then I ran some more. I passed the schoolhouse; Harriet was outside helping her momma in the garden. When Harriet saw me running towards them she hopped up and told me to come. She removed the loose board that led to the space under her house. I crawled in and she put the board back. I laid on the damp ground silently crying my eyes out. I knew it was only a matter of time before my momma made her way out here looking for me. Harriet was my friend and she knew all about my family.

I used to make up wonderful stories about my family. I would imagine that my daddy was an educated Negro, well spoken and dignified. Instead of the crazy Indian man who left his reservation in search of something better. How he ended up with my momma I'll never know. Word around town is that he's got other kids. I don't know if that's true or not, but he loves women. It don't matter who she is or what she looks like. If she got two legs and a skirt, he wants her. His sons are nasty just like him. I spanked Raymond with a switch one time when I heard him telling Emma to raise her skirt to him. Even when my momma knows my daddy is wrong she covers for him. She does the same thing with her sons, but then they look at her like she could do no wrong. I don't care, I will stand up for myself and then I run away. I know she's gonna beat me when she catches up to me. And if it wasn't for Emma I would run away forever! I'm the slave at home anyways. Last two babies my momma had died just after they were born. I think her body needs a rest. She's always big and then she needs her *medicine* to calm her nerves. Her *medicine* is whatever moonshine the Walker boys have available.

I could hear my momma cursing and carrying on. Something was crawling on me; I couldn't see what it was. I decided whatever it was couldn't be worse than Leslie so I kept quiet. Leslie only came home a day and every once in a while two days. So as long as I stayed away until tomorrow I should be safe for another week or two. My momma was screaming like she was concerned for my well-being. She asked Harriet if she's seen me; and she said she's been tending to the yard with her momma. My momma yelled and said that wasn't a yes or no answer. Harriet's momma asked her why wouldn't they tell her if they see me, they knew where we lived. I guess the Thatcher girl was passing by, cause I heard my momma calling after her. Harriet came and sat against the house, she said my momma looked like she's getting big again. I whispered and told her my daddy came home about a month ago so she could be, but she hasn't said anything. Not that she normally told us when she was going to have a baby, but when I didn't have to wash her rags I knew there was a new baby coming. Harriet said mister Coleman was gonna come sit with her this evening so it would be late before I could come out. I told her to thank her momma for covering for me. Harriet said that I should consider letting someone call on me. If I was getting married maybe my momma would keep Leslie away from me. I told her I didn't want to marry some old man, or any one just to get away from my family. I wanted to be in love before I got married, like Claudette. Claudette got married this past spring and she was big already. She married the Hawkins boy who she's been sweet on since she was little. Harriet and I try to go by to call on her whenever my momma isn't mad at me so it isn't too often. Claudette is real nice and she's always happy to see us. The way she describes doing it sounds nothing like I know. She's real happy about doing it with her husband; she said he was worried about hurting her on their wedding night. I remember crying my eyes out that night, cause she made love sound wonderful unlike anything I've ever known. Leslie has only gotten me two times, and each time I thought I would die. I cried the whole time the first time, and the second time I imagined I was anywhere but in that kitchen bent over a chair, unable to fight back. I don't know why my momma thinks I like being treated like a dog. I would never willingly allow this to happen to me. Even if they don't see that this is wrong I know it is. And I'm sorry; I'm fighting with every ounce of power in my body. If I have to kill Leslie I will, but he's not going to get me again. Neither him nor any of my other brothers!

Harriet put a biscuit through the crack. She said once it was safe she would take the plate out for me in the kitchen. Mister Coleman came by and he was smiling real big. He greeted Harriet's mother and gave her money for the house. Then he gave Harriet flowers. Harriet said that he's paid for so many things in their house. He says once her momma says they can marry, she and her momma can move into his big house on the other side of town. He owns a store, and he's nice enough, but he's old and I know Harriet doesn't love him. I don't want any old man like mister Coleman. Mister Coleman told Harriet about his day, and he asked about hers. The entire time she was trying to talk he kept correcting her words. I don't know why that doesn't make her mad, but it makes me mad hearing it. Mister Coleman doesn't like me, and I don't like him. I know Harriet is fine with him, but I think he's just mean and looking for a young wife to tell what to do all the time. When he thought the coast was clear he told Harriet to kiss him. Harriet did as she was told and I wanted to throw up for her. Once he was long gone Harriet came and got me, and took me inside.

"You know your momma's gonna beat you when you go home?" Harriet's momma said.

"I'll take the beating everyday if it means that my brother can't mess with me!" Harriet's momma touched my face, "I know child. You are too pretty to be going through this. Why ain't you courting? You're going to be thirteen soon. You could get married easily."

"I don't want to get married yet. Besides my momma needs me too much around the house. She'd rather keep me around for Leslie." I said as tears poured out of my eyes. "Ms. Booker would you ever treat Harriet like my momma treats me?"

"Some folks don't know what is right. It will get better Annette, just hold on." She said kissing my forehead.

I slept a deep and peaceful sleep at Harriet's house. I waited until noon to make my way home. When I got to the bridge I thought about jumping in and ending it all. What's the point of breathing when it hurts this bad? "Why you thinking so hard?" A voice said robbing me from my thoughts, I was so gone in my thoughts I didn't see any one approach me.

A boy I didn't recognize was smiling at me. "Cause!" I said uninterested in what he had to say next.
"You look like you were thinking about jumping in." He said walking around me and talking in my ear.
"Shoo Fly!" I said swatting at him.
"Why you so mean? You too pretty to be so mean." Then he smiled again. This time I looked at him, and ooh! He was cute, but I wasn't in the mood to be bothered. My momma was gonna beat me to death when I got home. I looked at the ground. "If you tell me what it is, maybe I can help you."
"You can't help me." I said lowly under my breath, with my eyes still to the ground.
"You don't know until you try. Have you talked to God today? I may be the answer to your prayer."
"No I haven't, but you are a stranger."
"No stranger than anyone else." He laughed, and then he put his hand out. "My name's Josiah, what's your name pretty little lady?"
It felt like my heart was beating in my stomach, "Annette."
"A pretty name for a pretty girl." Then he leaned against the rail, "now tell me about this problem so I can tell you how I'm gonna fix it for you."
"My momma's gonna beat me cause I ran away from home again."
"Well you ain't very good at running away if you going back now are you?"
"No sir, I got a little sister I gotta look after and make sure she's safe. As long as I come back she'll be safe."
"Why you run away?" I didn't answer him I just looked away. "How far is your house from here?"
"Not far," I said.
"Well lets get going." I don't know what he was talking about, but he liked doing it. I peeked at Josiah and he was paper bag color with nappy hair. He had brown eyes that seemed like they glowed when he looked at you. He was really nice to me, and he didn't get fresh one time.
When my momma saw us coming up the road, she came busting out the house cursing and carrying on like she was so worried about me. She said she looked for me everywhere and she couldn't find me. Josiah told her his family was new in town and I was helping them get situated. My momma looked at him, she could tell he was lying. She just didn't know why. She asked him question after question. She didn't stop until he handed her money for all of my help. After that she didn't care who he was or what he did with me. When my momma walked away he told me to come and call on his family when I could. I watched him disappear on the road and then the feeling of my momma's switch breaking the skin on my leg brought me back. She beat me up and down the walkway in front of my house. It wasn't until Emma begged her to stop that she let up. She punched me, kicked me, you name it, she did it. Emma got the turpentine for me and I cleaned myself up. I'd still take this beating any day over letting Leslie mess with me.

****

"Where we going?" Emma asked me as we walked along the road to the other side of town.
"There's a new family in town. I wanna take this pie as a thank you."
"How much longer? I'm tired of walking." Emma whined.
I bent down, "get on."
Emma happily climbed on my back; we went over the alphabet as we walked. I saw the house just up the road. I could tell it was a big family cause everyone was out

and working on the house to fix it up. I took a deep breath and I walked towards the house. As we passed a big tree someone said, "what you want?"
Emma and I looked up in the tree and there was a boy sitting on a branch. "Josiah home?"
He jumped out of the tree. "How you know my brother?" He looked me up and down.
"None of your business! Is he home or not?" I gave him the same attitude he was giving me.
He frowned at Emma and me and then he walked ahead of us like he was mad. He stormed into the house and the rest of the kids around this house looked at us with curious looks but no one even said hello. The boy and a woman came out. She was big and mad looking. "What you want?"
"Ma'am. I met Josiah on the road the other day. He was very nice to my family I wanted to bring him this pie as a thank you." I said
Her eyes dropped to my feet, she noticed the cuts on my legs. "You in some trouble?"
"No Ma'am."
"Josiah!" She called out.
Then hurried footsteps came around the house. "Ma'am?" Josiah said before he saw me standing there. Then he smiled real big. "Annette!" Then he came and gave me a hug. "Momma this the girl I was telling you about. Ain't she pretty?"
She rolled her eyes, "like that matters to you." Then she went inside.
"That for me?" He said smiling at the pie.
"Yes, thank you for trying to smooth things out with my momma." I said with complete sincerity.
He looked at my legs, "I knew she was gonna get you anyways." Then he looked at Emma, "this must be the pretty little sister you were talking about."
Emma giggled, "Annette you told him about me?"
"Aren't you the cutest little thing. I wouldn't leave her either." Then he looked around at everyone who was watching us. "Come say hi to Annette everybody. This is my friend." Josiah introduced me to his brothers, sisters, and cousins. The boy from the tree stayed on the porch staring at me. "Luther come say hello."
"No!"
Josiah shrugged, "suit yourself." Then he asked everyone else if they wanted some pie. He invited us in and then we went in the kitchen. His momma was sitting on the chair resting while her pot of beans boiled on the stove. She looked like the baby was coming any day now. I looked at her pot and it needed to be stirred. I asked her if she wanted me to take care of it for her. She breathlessly said yes. Josiah cut her a piece of pie, he gave her hers as he gave a slice to Emma. She said my sweet potato pie was delicious. I thanked her. Luther peeked at us from the other room. After everyone got a piece Luther took the last small piece. He took the pan and marched right out the door. Their momma told me not to pay Luther any attention. She said he was nothing but trouble anyways. Emma went outside with the little ones and I stayed in the kitchen with Josiah and his momma. I was telling her all of the gossip of the families in town, and they told me about New Orleans where they came from. I asked them why they moved all the way to Kansas? Josiah had sad eyes as he said they ran from trouble. Josiah's momma said she liked me and for me to come back soon when I told her I had to go home. Then she told Josiah to bring Luther with him when he walked Emma and I home. Everyone said bye as we left. Luther was leaning against his tree with my pie tin in his hand. When we got close he handed

the tin to me and said my pie wasn't nasty. Josiah told him he was so rude. Luther didn't care. Josiah and Emma talked about everything a long the way. If I thought Emma was a chatterbox, she met her match in Josiah. Luther kept looking at me, and the last time he stopped in his tracks, as he shook his head no. Josiah smiled at him. "You were right, I shouldn't have doubted you." He said to his brother, and then he looked at me. "How old are you?"
"Twelve."
"Really?" Josiah said surprised.
"You don't look like a girl." Luther said
"I don't?"
"Thought you were sixteen." Josiah said, "you ain't even old enough."
"For what?"
"To run with us. No wonder your momma whooped you. My little girl would get it too." Luther said
"Have you heard of Hazel's? The speak easy by the pond."
"Ooh! That's for big people!" Emma said
"Hush! I am big!" I said, and then I looked at Luther. "I could go if I wanted to."
"Do you want to?"
"Yea right! Her momma would whoop her backside." Luther said
"She whoops me anyways, it's not like it matters. I just gotta wait 'til she takes her *medicine*." I moved my hand like I was taking a drink.
"Yea right, she's a kid, she's too chicken. Grown folk stuff happens in there." Luther said
I looked at Josiah, "he get on my nerves. If you'll wait for me by my outhouse, I'll go."
"Deal!" Josiah said
When my momma took her *medicine* to her bedroom. I waited for Emma to fall asleep then I climbed out the window. Josiah and Luther were waiting for me as promised. Josiah talked our ears off the whole way there. You could hear the music from Hazel's coming from up the road. Josiah grabbed my hand and he told me to come on. When we walked in the door I could hear the whispers, people were saying, "isn't that Elmer's daughter". Loose women were everywhere and men who were looking for a good time. Luther sat down and the oldest Jones girl sat next to him immediately. Josiah danced with me, when the women tried to get his attention he was not interested. Until Maybel walked in, Josiah had stars in his eyes. She was really pretty, and her hair was so nice. She moved like a woman, people called her loose, but she was always nice to me. "Josiah! How you know Elmer's daughter?" Then she looked at me, "how you doing baby?"
"Hello." I said realizing she knew who I was.
"Have you said hi to your father? He's here."
"Where?" I said looking around.
She kissed Josiah long and hard. I got embarrassed for them they were going at it so long. Then she told us to come on. We followed her to a room in the back where the men were smoking. "Elmer, look who's here!" Maybel sang.
My father had a woman sitting in his lap and a pipe in his mouth. "Annette? What you doing here?" He didn't really care that I was there.
"I could say the same." I said looking at him.
"Baby, this my oldest daughter. Annette this is baby doll." The woman giggled at me.
I frowned, "what kind of name is baby doll?"

"Don't she look like a baby doll? Well that's what I call her anyways."
"Momma needs you at home."
"She needs you more, but here we are. I'll get there when I get there. Is that why you're here?"
"No sir, I came with my friends." I gestured towards Josiah.
My daddy looked at Josiah, "you funny boy?"
Josiah didn't say anything, "he's here for me Elmer. Leave him alone." Maybel said.
"Oh," he said shaking his head. "You'll fix him, she's a pro!" Then he turned his attention back to his baby doll.
Now my momma was not a pretty woman, and she wasn't nice and sweet. The best thing that could've ever happened to her was having my daddy's babies. Everybody say how good-looking we were, but I wondered if that was why she hated me so much. If it wasn't for me Emma's hair would never be combed. This baby doll woman was pretty, stupid, but pretty.
Josiah told me to come back out to the front. Luther was walking out the door with the Jones girl. It made me mad to see him walk out. I couldn't explain it, but I'd rather him been mean to me then leave with her. Maybel gave me a jar full of moonshine. It tasted kind of funny, but everyone was drinking so I did too. Maybel seemed like she really liked Josiah, and he seemed like he liked her too. What did my daddy mean by asking him if he was funny. When it was time to go we followed the noise to find Luther and the Jones girl in the woods doing it. I had never seen it before, I know I shouldn't have looked but I couldn't turn my eyes. The Jones girl looked like she loved it, I couldn't understand why. Luther saw us coming, he stared at me while he did his business on her. Josiah had to make me turn my back, but I was still listening. It didn't even sound like that when my parents were doing it. I asked Josiah if he and Maybel do that, he got embarrassed and changed the subject. Luther sent the Jones girl on her way, and then he fixed his clothes as he walked with us. "You like what you saw?" He asked me.
"How old are you?"
"I'm a grown man little girl. I'm seventeen."
"Josiah?"
"I'm nineteen."
They were way older than me, but I liked being with them. It made me feel grown.

Timothy

"Hi Tim," Mary Jane said giving me that little smile she does perfectly.
"Hey Mary Jane, how you doing?" I said grinning from ear to ear.
"I'm good," she giggled.
"I'm going to be getting my license soon, are you going to ride with me?"
"Of course."
Then Jeremiah walked up, we were walking home together. Mary Jane's smile dropped. "What?"
"He's not going to come with us is he?"
"What's wrong with Jeremiah?" I looked at him then her.
"My daddy would tan my backside if I rode in a car with someone like him."
"I guess we'll have to see then won't we."
"See what?"
"What's in it for me."
She playfully hit me, "you're bad. I'm a good girl."

I walked up on her and whispered in her ear, "good girl in public, but I can see the bad girl in your eyes. I wanna take the bad girl out."
Mary Jane turned completely red, "TIM! You are so bad!"
"Come on! You know you want it!" Then I kissed her cheek.
"Come on Mary Jane daddy's waiting." Her little sister said.
Mary Jane looked at me like I hypnotized her. Jeremiah laughed at me as we walked away. "You gonna bust her out?"
"You know it!" I said knowing it was only a matter of time. "Teach her father to called me a hoodlum." People always call me names cause I don't back down to anyone. Most people don't like that Jeremiah and I are friends. I think they learned their lesson about bringing it up to my momma. Some people even think that my momma isn't as she appears and that she's passing for white. Pops literally beat the life out of this one guy for voicing his opinion about it. He told the guy to never mention his Queen again. All the guys who were there heard the message loud and clear. Pops paid them to do their jobs; it was none of their business what happened with my momma.
When I got home my momma was sitting in the living room in her rocking chair. Whenever momma sat in that rocking chair something was seriously wrong and she rocked in that chair to calm her nerves. She said Lady B, her nanny when she was growing up, used to rock her whenever she was upset and it soothes her soul. I didn't say anything when I saw her, if she didn't call my name I wasn't the one in trouble. I asked Martha what happened and she said momma got a letter in the mail and she's been rocking ever since. One by one we came in the door and then we huddled in the kitchen. We did our homework while we waited to see who it was who was in trouble. When everyone was home except Pops, Franky, and Jeff we knew it had to be bad. Jeff and Franky came in the door together. They froze like the rest of us when they saw momma. Momma told Franky to freeze. I bucked my eyes at Dale. Jeff got out of there lightning fast and then he listened in like the rest of us.
"Where's your father?"
"He's still working at the store. What's wrong?"
"A letter came in the mail, its addressed to me, but it says that Franklin has a son. My question is which Franklin, and who is the mother?"
Franky turned red, "momma I don't know about a baby. Who's the mother?"
"Franky I told you to be careful! Women will be throwing their selves at you every chance they get."
"Who's the mother?"
"She signed the letter as Edna."
You could tell Franky had no idea who Edna was. He tried to cover for Pops anyways. When Franky tried to pretend like he knew who Edna was momma slapped him and told him not to lie to her. Big ole hotheaded Franky hung his head and apologized while momma was cursing and screaming. Pops walked in the door a little while later, and Momma didn't even let him get in the door good. She tore into him, Pops stood there listening to her scream her head off. When she paused to catch her breath Pops asked her if she was done, momma started screaming again. Finally Pops had enough, "IRMA! Let me see the letter!" Momma gave him the letter, he looked at the letter long and hard. Then he looked at momma. "Irma this is a lie!"
"What?"

"Someone sends a letter and you fly off the handle. If this was true where's the baby? There's no return address, no way to contact this person. Recognize a setup before you start accusing people. What's for dinner?" He walked in the kitchen where we were listening in. "Clear this table, Dale and Matthew you set the table."
That night at dinner everyone sat quietly while they ate. Pops told us to come back to the store. I rode with Pops while Franky and Jeff followed behind us. Pops whistled the whole way to the store not saying much. When we got in his office, Pops exhaled. He told us to ride out to El Cerrito and see if Edna really had a baby. I didn't know who this Edna woman was, but apparently Franky and Jeff did. I thought Franky didn't know who she was. Pops said he would wait at the store until we came back. In the truck I asked Franky who Edna was. Franky said she was a side piece that Pops used to keep until he cut her loose because she was getting too attached. I told him I thought he didn't know who she was. He said he didn't remember until dinner after he thought long and hard about it. He said if Edna really did have Pops' son then the little boy should be about two or three years old.
When we walked up to the door you could smell dinner. Franky knocked very hard on the door. A woman's voice called out, "who is it?" Franky didn't respond he knocked again. You could hear movement behind the door and Franky told us to step back from directly in front of the door. When a guy snatched the door open Franky greeted him with a punch in the nose. The guy didn't know what hit him he went down. The woman screamed as she moved backward with her eyes stretched wide. "Franky!'
Franky punched the woman and she fell down next to the guy. I looked at Franky like he was a monster. Why would he hit her in her face like she was a man? "Who sent the letter Edna?"
Edna's blonde hair moved perfectly with each body jerk as she cried. "Franky!"
Franky grabbed her by her shirt like he was going to hit her again. "Franky come on! If we gotta beat somebody up, let's beat him. I don't feel right hitting girls." Jeff said gesturing towards the guy on the ground.
Franky slapped the woman so hard you saw blood spat on the wall. He busted her nose and lip with that hit. "That is a new born baby!" He said pointing to the baby bed. "You have not seen my father in almost three years! How dare you send a letter to my mother!" He slapped her again! "Nobody hurts my momma!"
Jeff kicked the guy, "did he put you up to this? Say it was him!" He kicked him again, "say it was him!"
"He's not even trying to defend her!" I said getting mad, and then I kicked him.
"Hey! Somebody is supposed to be the cool head over here!" Jeff said as he kicked the guy.
"Well it's not gonna be me! He's a punk! And punks make me MAD!" I said kicking him two times.
"Not madder than me!" Jeff kicked him real hard.
"I bet you I'm madder!" I kicked him two more times.
"Your two kicks are like my one that's how mad I am!" He kicked him again.
"I keep hearing my momma's tears spilled for nothing and it makes me MAD! That's how MAD I am!" I kicked him two more times.
"Oh!" Jeff said grabbing me as he looked down at the guy. "I think we killed him!" The guy was lifeless.
I kicked him again, "Why you kick him that hard in his head? You probably broke his neck or something."

Jeff looked at Franky who was now standing there watching us, "were we supposed to kill him?"
Franky frowned, "no! But oh well!" Then he grabbed Edna by her hair. "Forget that you ever knew my father! Mess with my momma again and that's your whole family!"
The guy on the ground started coughing up blood and he turned blue as he tried to breathe. "He's alive!" I said as I kicked him one more time for the road.

Chapter 3

Annette

She keep staring at me and it's making me mad. Even though I saw them she has to know I can't say a word. If I told people about Luther and the Jones girl, then I would be outing myself about sneaking out of the house. Why on earth would I do that? Although I don't know why she keeps laying with him when he completely ignores her afterwards.

Ms. Kay dismissed us for the day from school; I asked Harriet if she wanted to go with Emma and I to Claudette's. She said she couldn't, Mr. Coleman was coming over today after he closes his store and she thinks he's going to ask her momma for her. Harriet put on a brave face. "Do you want to marry him?"

"It'll be good for us. He'll take care of us, and I can start having babies."

"I didn't know you were in a hurry to have babies."

She shrugged, "it will make him happy. And my momma will be there to help me." She exhaled, "my momma can stop working in that lady's kitchen." Harriet's momma worked in the kitchen for Mrs. Miller. All Mrs. Miller does is talk about how horrible colored people are, but she loves our cooking. Mr. Miller has come after Harriet's momma so many times she doesn't even fight it any more. I think that's why they hide me when I run from my momma. They understand my pain.

"Annette you should let someone call on you. We could be big together and our kids could grow up together." Harriet was romanticizing the worst idea to me.

"Harriet I want to be like Claudette. I want to love the man I marry. I want to be so crazy for him that I go against my momma!"

Harriet gasped and put her hands over her mouth. "Annette you are crazy!"

"I wanna be crazy about the man I marry! I want to love him so much that I bite him for no reason!"

She put her hands on her hips. "Yep you're crazy!" She smiled.

"I want passion, fire, desire! Nothing like anyone around here knows." I said in defeat.

"I think you've made your point. Well I hope one day you come to your senses and marry a nice and sensible man."

We walked along the road until Harriet had to go left and Emma and I went right. Claudette was so happy to have company. She fed Emma real good and then she asked what we went over in class. I explained as much as I could then I got to the part I wanted to hear about. I asked her how married life was. Claudette rolled her eyes and said he drives her crazy. I put my elbows on the table and ate it all up; they had a dumb argument about who's supposed to close the chicken coop. She was venting about her argument but all I could hear was how much she loved him and I wanted a marriage just like that. "So I heard you been hanging out at Hazel's." She smiled and cut her eyes at me.

I gasped, "who told you that?"

"My honey saw you. Said you walked right past him. Who's the guys you been hanging with? I've heard stuff about them."

"What have you heard?"

"Everybody says that Josiah is *funny* but he keeps company with Maybel. And his brother Luther!" She cut her eyes at me. "He got his eye on you?"

I leaned back, "no?"

"I hear he's a dog and probably got babies all over the place from the way he runs around. You be careful around those men, you're just a little girl." Then she looked at me, "even if you don't look it."
She put dinner in the oven for her honey and then we walked to town. We walked slowly so Claudette could keep up. We went to Mr. Coleman's general store. Claudette got yards of fabric and things. Then Emma and I helped her carry it home. Along the way Luther ran up to us. "Where you think you going?"
"This my friend Claudette, this Luther his family lives on the edge of town."
"Hello pretty lady!" He said all charming.
"Don't talk to her like that. She's a married woman."
"Married women are the best kind of women." He smiled, and then he looked at me and stopped smiling. "Little girl when you gonna call on my momma again? She had the baby and she want you to call on her."
"I guess I'm coming soon." I said
"This a busy road today I see." Claudette said looking behind us.
We turned around and my father was coming. I wasn't excited to see him. Momma just lost the last baby, I'm sure she's about ready to see him too. "Daddy!" Emma said running as fast as her little legs would carry her.
"Why were you in town?" He yelled at me. I held up Claudette's packages. "Get home!"
"I gotta carry this stuff home for Claudette." I explained.
"You sassing me?" He yelled.
"No sir," I put my eyes to the ground.
"Can I help you with something?" He said to Luther.
Luther frowned at him, "no!"
"I don't want you around my daughter!"
Luther's eyes turned cold, "right!"
"Daddy what's wrong? Luther's our friend." Emma asked holding our fathers hand.
"I know his kind! You not up to no good!" Luther looked like he wanted to say a lot to my father, but he held his tongue and walked away. "Help her and then come home, Emma's gonna come with me."
I looked at Emma who was still too little to know the truth about him. The fact that he didn't care about none of us. He'd be home long enough to make my momma big, drop off some money, and then go back to his women. When I was Emma's age I loved him too, now I don't care. "Yes sir," if I made him mad he'd get me and then he'd tell my momma and she'd get me too.
Claudette and I hurried as much as she could. She thanked me for helping her and then I hurried out the door. The sun was starting to go down, I don't like being on the road alone in the dark. Lots of people disappear that way. "What is he mad about?" Luther asked walking behind me.
He scared me and I started to run until I realized it was him. "Don't scare me like that."
"Slow down, talk to me."
"Luther I can't, they're gonna be looking for me."
"You coming to Hazel's tonight?"
"You guys gonna meet me at the out house, I'll try to get away. Since he'll be there she won't be looking for me."
"Josiah has another itch to scratch tonight. It'll be just me and you." He cut his eyes at me.
I frowned, "why would I go? I don't wanna watch you and the Jones girl."

"Why would I need her if I'm with you?" I was confused, "come here."
He led me in the field behind some trees and bushes. He started kissing my neck and squeezing my butt. I couldn't believe it, I stood there frozen. When he kissed me I thought I was going to die! I didn't know why he was doing this at this particular time. When he pressed his body against mine he moaned and I looked at him, he smiled and kissed me again. "You gonna come out with me tonight?" When I shook my head yes, he told me I was a good girl. He told me to hurry home to avoid getting in any more trouble. I ran my heart out, while Luther jogged behind me. I didn't know how I felt about what just happened, it didn't make me mad, however I didn't feel anything and he was moaning like it was good to him. When I approached my porch he waved and went back the other way.
My father was in my brother's faces about something and my momma was happy in the kitchen. She had a mile wide smile on her face and she was singing. She was happy for this moment, she told me to come put wood in the stove to make some biscuits. My momma was moving around the kitchen happily and excited about her man. Emma came to help me make the biscuits. My father walked in the kitchen inspecting everything in the room. "When was the last time you cleaned around the cooler?" He asked trying to find something wrong.
"It's Annette's job to clean the kitchen." She said watching her fish on the stove.
My father's head whipped around and his long braided ponytail whipped too. "So you don't check her work? You that lazy that you gotta have Annette doing everything you supposed to do?" He said annoyed.
"No Elmer, I check her work. She's the lazy one. Sometimes I gotta beat her a bunch of times before she gets it right." She explained.
That was a lie! I have to be extra careful when I clean up cause she finds the smallest thing to beat me for. I do everything and I do everything right. She just wanna look good in front of him so she's lying on me. "So then what's this?" He said pointing to the cornmeal spot where she touched the cooler just now and it was still on her hands. My momma looked at the spot then her hands. My father reached back and slapped her. "I don't know why I come back! You ugly! Dirty! And nasty! This house filthy! If it wasn't for me, you would be worthless!" My momma kept her head down like she agreed with him. My blood boiled! Then he looked at me, "you need to spend more time tending to this house instead of running to town with some big girl in trouble or that good for nothing school!"
"Claudette married!" I snapped at him.
My momma looked like she just knew he was going to hit me. My father stared at me, and his face softened a little. "Don't sass me!"
I put my head down, "yes sir." I knew the fact that he didn't get me meant my momma would just because he didn't.
When we sat down for supper momma served my father first and then she put the rest of the food out. The animals that are my brothers dug in. Emma and I waited for whatever was left. Momma kept looking at my father with love in her eyes. My father looked at her then he looked at Emma and I. "You two should be thankful you came out looking like me. You darker than I expected, but she's a tar baby so I guess you should be thankful not to be that black." Then he looked at me. "I never thought I could make such a pretty girl with a woman like that." I wished he'd stop, when he goes on and on like this my momma gets jealous. She definitely was going to beat me, and then she'd send Leslie after me again.
"I'm pretty too?" Emma innocently asked.

"Just like your big sister." Then he looked at my momma. "Why ain't her hair combed?"
"I told Annette to do it, I..."
He slammed his hand on the table. "Annette! Annette! Annette! Are you useful for anything? These gals got good hair, you trying to make it nappy like yours! You mad cause they ain't ugly like you?" He paused for emphasis. "If and when I come back here I better see that my gal's have been looked out for. Who they supposed to marry walking around looking like you?"
"But Elmer, I do make sure they clean, and got nice clothes on. Everybody say our girls real fine."
He smiled, "that's cause they look more like me than you! Nobody believes Annette is just a girl. She's real fine! Stay fresh girl, tell all these nappy-headed boys to go shoo! They got some high yellow boys I want you to meet down in New Orleans. You ain't too dark where you can't get you one of them. Then I'll come visit you, stay with you for a spell." He continued smiling at the thought.
As soon as dinner was over my momma gave him some of her *medicine*, then she put on a record. They were in the living room drinking and carrying on. Emma and I cleaned the kitchen. I made sure the spot on the cooler was gone. I was dreading the morning because when she woke up and he was gone, that was it for me. I laid down with Emma until she fell asleep, I could hear my parents carrying on. So I knew momma was not worried about me.
I climbed out the window and I walked over to the outhouse. Luther was waiting and now I wondered what he was going to do with me. He told me he brought a lamp and a blanket and he put it in our shed. We used to keep our horse in there but we had to sell it. That's when Leslie found work. He led me by the hand, my heart was beating. I was scared but curious. Luther smiled at me and then he told me how pretty he thinks I am. I told him I didn't think he liked me at first cause he was mean. He said he wasn't sure why Josiah was friends with me. I asked him what that meant and he said that generally Josiah makes interesting friends like Maybel. I said she's really pretty, cause she is. He agreed and then he said she was loose, and has a soft spot for men like Josiah. I asked what that meant and he shook off the irritation of the thought. Then he leaned against the wall. "I'm the first boy to kiss you ain't I?"
"Yes," I said embarrassed.
"When your momma gonna let somebody call on you?"
"She's not," I said sadly.
"Don't you wanna get married?"
"Yes but not the way she wanna do it. She wants to auction me off to the highest bidder." I exhaled, "he said he wants me to go to New Orleans and find a high yellow man to marry. Same trade different scene."
"Is that what you want?"
"What's wrong with a man as dark as me?"
He smiled, "you are very pretty for a dark skinned gal."
"Is that why you be messing with the Jones girl?"
"She's not too dark, but she's loose. I needed somebody fast."
"Ain't you gonna marry her?"
"No."
"No? What about when she end up in trouble? The way you mess around she should be big already."
"The doctor tells my momma I won't make no babies on account I don't got one."

"One what?"
"Testicle, I wasn't born with them."
"You need them to make a baby?"
"In my case yes."
I thought about my little brothers when I changed their diapers. "You mean you have a ding-a-ling, but you don't have that part behind it? Does it look weird?"
"I only take it out when I plan to use it." He smiled, "but it's not weird to me. Women ask questions, but they love the no baby part."
"You don't want babies?"
He shrugged, "I can't make them so why stress over it? I get to be a lover with no strings attached. Married women love me."
"You've had a lot of women?"
"I'm a man of course I have!" He said like I should know already.
I asked him as many questions as I could. As soon as a new question popped in my mind I asked. We talked for a long time, some of my questions made him frown and then he'd start laughing. I loved this, he was smiling at me while I talked about Harriet marrying a nasty old man and then he kissed me. When he laid on top of me I started freaking out. I started fighting and telling him to get off of me. He backed up real slow. His eyes were sad, "who hurt you?"
My momma told me not to tell people our family business. So I stood up, I talked real fast as I explained I had to go before they realized I was gone. Luther didn't say anything he watched me talk my way out of the shed. I climbed in the window and shut it tight. I shouldn't have been out there with a man any ways. I put my gown on and as I was going to get in the bed Luther tapped on my window. I was embarrassed and afraid he was going to be mad at me and call me a little girl. He whispered, "who hurt you?"
"Why you keep asking that?" I whispered irritated.
"You were just fighting for your life! I had no idea you were that strong." He tried to make me laugh, but I was too embarrassed. "It don't matter, you should go!" Then I closed my window. I watched the shadow of the top of his head until it disappeared. I laid there preparing myself for my spanking in the morning.
I woke to the smell of breakfast cooking. My momma was singing again, that meant my father was still here. He rarely stayed. I got Emma up to get ready for school. When we went out into the kitchen momma told us we weren't going to school. She pointed to the grease and fork. I took Emma in the room I gave her the speech. If she screamed while momma hot combed her hair she was gonna get it. Emma didn't listen, and sure enough momma spanked her telling her to hush cause her hair wasn't nappy so she had no reason to be carrying on like she was. When she was done I tied a pretty ribbon around Emma's hair I told her to look at how pretty she looked as she tried to stop crying. My father walked in the kitchen as momma was working on my hair, silent tears ran down my face from the pain. He told Emma she looked pretty with her long hair like his. He told her never to cut it no matter what anyone tried to tell her.
When our hair was done he told us to go put on our prettiest dresses. Needless to say he was not happy about our dress options. Then he yelled at her for not making us coats last winter. Then he told us to follow him. We went to town and then some guy gave us a ride in his buggy to a house. The woman my father referred to as Babydoll came out excitedly to the porch. She was dressed real fancy. "Oh Elmer! They prettier than you said." My father beamed with pride.

He looked at us and gave us a mean look and told us to mind our manners. I held Emma's hand as we walked inside this big and beautiful house. My father took off his hat as he entered. A white man slowly walked down the stairs, I hated the way he walked. "Is this him?" The man asked Babydoll. She very excitedly said yes.
"I'm Mister Cadbury," He said to us.
"Are they here?" A snooty snotty white lady said coming out the kitchen. She put her hand on her chest. "Oh! Ruth Ann! They're adorable." She said congratulating her.
I didn't understand what was happening but I knew better than to say anything. The woman walked up to me and told me to open my mouth. She examined my teeth and then she did the same to Emma. Then she smiled at us and said we were good girls. Then they took us out back to a little house off the property. I saw Mrs. Cadbury shooting my father wanting looks when she thought no one was looking and I knew this would not end well.
After awhile I realized they were planning for my father to marry this idiot and live in this house out back. I guess it didn't matter that he was already married to my momma. What I didn't understand is why he needed us for this game. I guess my question was on my face cause my father told me to fix my face. Babydoll hurried to me, she smashed my head into her chest. "Elmer! Be nice to her! She been through so much already! Losing her momma so young!" Then she started rocking me. "It's ok baby! As soon as we get my house set up, I'll send for you and your sister before the baby comes!" What did she just say? I squinted my eyes at my father while this idiot kept smashing my head into her chest. "Meanwhile I'll send money to their auntie for them." Mrs. Cadbury said as she scoffed at our lack of appropriate clothing.
Aw! There it was! This was about money! This little house is really nice. From what I can tell Mr. Cadbury is unofficially the father of the idiot. I wonder where her momma is though. Why would she let her daughter marry someone like my father? I wonder how long my father would hang around here before he moved on. Mr. Cadbury told us to get going before it got dark and we didn't make it to town. My father humbly thanked the Cadbury's for their hospitality and then the guy who gave us a ride out took us back to town. He and the guy laughed and laughed about the Cadbury's and how stuffy they were. His friend told my father to watch out for the misses, he told my father that she's real trouble. My father laughed him off. My father carried Emma from town. "You really going to marry that woman? She really gonna have a baby?"
"Yes and yes, Annette don't nobody in this world owe you nothing. Nobody in this world cares whether you eat or starve. I got to do what I gotta do. When you start courting you make sure he can take care of you. Buy you pretty things and treat you real nice. Make sure he can afford you. You're smart and you're pretty don't waste it on some pretty guy who can't do nothing for you." Then he eyed me, "I don't like you hanging out with those Broderick boys. One is so funny he can't see straight, and the other one is always chasing skirts. Do they know you're just a gal?"
"Yes sir."
"Then I don't know why you're with them. Do they get fresh with you?"
"No sir," I held my breath.
"I don't want you running around with them."
"And I don't want you marrying some gal who don't know any better."
My father stopped walking and looked at me. "Are you sassing me?"

I put my hand on my hip, "yes sir! You only come home long enough to get my momma big. You bring money but it's never enough. You got so many children running around, I'm afraid I'm kin to everybody. One day you're going to stop coming home. She takes all her anger about you out on me. And when you come around you make things worse. Stop telling her she's ugly, you hurt her when you do that."

My father slapped me, but not as hard as he could have. "Don't sass me!" He was quiet for a minute like he was going back and forth in his mind. "I know your momma ain't right. I'm gonna bring you and Emma with me as soon as I get settled."

"You're gonna take us away from our momma?"

"And all those wild boys. She loves her sons more anyways. Like Leslie can't do no wrong." He was quiet for a minute. "Don't tell your momma about this. I'll tell her what she needs to know."

****

Harriet looked so pretty on her wedding day. Her momma looked so proud. However, I felt horrible for her two days later when she came to my house crying. She said it hurt so badly and he got mad about her voicing anything about the pain. She cried on my shoulder and said she couldn't tell her momma cause she'd be so upset that he wasn't gentle with her. I told her to talk to Claudette, she was a married woman and she loved being with her husband. I hoped she'd have words of wisdom for Harriet I felt so badly for my friend.

Claudette was my hero and I'm sure Harriet felt the same. She explained everything, from the simplest parts like kissing, to touching, to humping, to making love. She told Harriet to tell Mr. Coleman to slow down and to listen to her body to tell her when she was ready for more. I made mental notes of everything she said. When it was my turn I was going to do just like she told me.

A week later Harriet brought Claudette a thank you cake. She said Claudette saved her life.

****

I couldn't believe my momma went along with this whole set up. I don't care what she say, she big and she sitting up here pretending to be our aunt at my father's wedding to another woman. Mr. & Mrs. Cadbury sat over to the side like they were forced to be here. Mr. Cadbury didn't even shake my father's hand. He nodded at him and then they went back inside their big beautiful house.

Baby doll walked up on my momma with her belly bigger than my momma's. Her belly was so big it looked like she was gonna pop. "It's nice to finally meet the auntie that helps Elmer with his girls. You must be Rose." She didn't look so dumb as she sized up my momma.

"That's right and you Tillie's little girl."

Baby doll's eyes got big, "you knew my Mamie?"

"Un huh, sho did! Glad to see Mr. Cadbury still looking after you." My momma said with an evil grin.

"How come I don't know you?" Babydoll looked from momma to us.

"I recon now that we kin, I'll see you from time to time." Then she rubbed her belly, "after I have the baby of course."

Babydoll rubbed her stomach, "of course." Then she looked from us to our momma. "What did they Mamie look like?"

"Just like me. Elmer didn't tell you she was my twin sister?"

Babydoll shook her head no. "There haven't been twins around these parts ever. Folks would've talked about it."
My momma rolled her eyes, "that's because it was a long time ago."
Babydoll looked down at Emma, "it couldn't have been too long ago."
My momma got irritated, "well it was long enough for the gossipers to forget."
"Where your husband? I mean you big and all."
"Oh Lord Jesus child! You sho do ask a lot of questions. He away at work!"
"What's going on here?" My father asked.
Baby doll's eyes stayed glued to my momma. "She got mad when I asked her about her husband."
"Rose, my bride is kin now. Be nice to her." My father said, then he kissed his new wife.

****

"It done took you long enough to call on me!" Mrs. Broderick said giving me the baby who was almost big enough to start walking.
The baby looked at me with happy eyes, he was so cute and loveable like all their family. I tried to smile at the baby, but the truth was I was on the run again. Leslie came home in the middle of the night, and I had to fight my way out of that house. I hate being out at night by myself, but I'll take the cold scary darkness any day over the alternative. I hid in the shed this time, when I heard them leave I went in the house got dressed and then I ran in the opposite direction. I don't remember if I ran or walked here, I just remember walking up the steps and knocking on the door as the sun came up.
At first Mrs. Broderick was rambling on and on. Not really looking at me or paying attention. I guess my unnormally quiet demeanor caught her attention. "Annette baby, what's wrong?"
"Oh nothing, I'm just tired." I tried to perk up but I couldn't.
"Is somebody after you baby?" She asked watching my eyes.
I couldn't stop my tears from pouring out, as I shook my head yes. She took me to a little room just off the kitchen. It was so small I could touch each wall by spreading my hands out, but to me it was a grand palace. She brought me a few blankets and she told me to rest as long as I needed and that no one would find me here.
I slept on that hard floor like I was sleeping on feathers, I heard Luther's voice in the kitchen even Josiah's, but I stayed put.
While everyone was out tending to their chores, I came out and helped Mrs. Broderick with the family supper. I cleaned the kitchen and snuck out to the outhouse when no one was looking. I felt like a runaway slave trying to make my way up north to freedom. Mrs. Broderick kept me hidden from her family for three days; I figured enough time had passed for Leslie to be gone. I thanked Mrs. Broderick for hiding me and then I snuck out the back door. I was so busy going in the opposite direction of Luther's voice that I ran right into Josiah. "Annette? What you doing here? Where have you been?" He asked happy to see me.
"SSSHHHH! Josiah, please keep your voice down." I pleaded.
He looked at me confused, I lowered my head. "I gotta go home."
"You ran away again?" He touched my arm, "why you go back if you only gonna leave again?"
"My sister needs me, I gotta protect her."
"Who protects you?"
"I protect myself. She's not gonna beat me this time. She's too big to get after me right now." I said as if that made things better.

"If she's too big, why you run away?"
"I gotta go Josiah."
"I'm walking with you." We walked a little ways. "Why ain't you come to Hazel's with us?"
I shook my head, "I don't wanna watch Luther and the Jones girl."
"Since when that bother you?" I shrugged, "you sweet on Luther ain't you." I shrugged again. He exhaled, "if Emma was here we'd be talking while you and Luther tried to find the words."
"Can I ask you something?"
"Shoot."
"Why does my father call you funny? What does that mean?"
Josiah exhaled, "I'm not gonna share my secrets and you don't. You go first."
I stopped walking, "are you tricking me?"
"No, you share and I will do the same."
Then he led me off the road to a few tree stumps. He sat down and told me to do the same, and then he waited for me to speak. I spilled everything, keeping everything inside was killing me. Josiah hugged me and told me that I was so strong for fighting back; most folks would've suffered in silence. Then Josiah shared how he fell in love with the little boy who used to live not too far from their family. He cried when he said his friend's father caught them together and killed his friend. He said word spread fast around town and they had to move. I asked him why he's with Maybel if he don't like her. He said he loves Maybel. He said he loves beautiful women, and Maybel understands him. He said they'll probably marry soon so people will start being nice to her and start treating her like a human being. I asked him if she knew about him. He said she knows everything. I asked him if Luther really couldn't make babies. He said it was true, and then he said Luther's been telling him to come talk to me. To find out if I was ok. When I asked why, he said he thinks Luther has a sweet spot for me even though I'm just a gal.
We talked for a while more and then we walked. When we got close to my house, I told him not to come to the door cause then my momma would know where to find me. He stayed on the road and watched me walk in the door.
I almost past out when Leslie was still there. He called out to my momma that I was back. My momma came around the corner holding her belly and sweating she looked so happy and relieved to see me. Her baby was coming and she needed help. None of them boys ever helped her. "Annette, come help me." She said breathlessly as the pain hit her again. I stood frozen and shook my head no. "Gal!"
"You keep putting Leslie on me, and now you need me."
Her eyes were red as she looked at me. "I'm going to get you!"
"That's fine momma, but keep him off of me. Next time he come for me I'm poisoning all of you. Then I'm telling."
"Don't nobody care!" Leslie chimed in.
"Elmer does!" Leslie shut up. "He'll take me and Emma to Ruth Ann's, and still make you big. Who's gonna take care of you then?"
My momma fell on her knees, "oh lord! Oh lord Jesus! Help me!" She cried out from the pain. When she caught her breath she agreed. She told Leslie to leave me alone. Leslie went for the doctor while I helped momma. It was another boy, I'm tired of all these no good boys popping out. My momma said she's calling this one Preston after her uncle.

****

“Why are you avoiding me?” Luther said blocking my way.

"Cause."
"Cause?" He mocked me.
"You just want *it* like every other man. You get *it* from them leave me alone." I walked around him and started on my way.
"I talked to Josiah." I stopped in my tracks, "he didn't tell me your secret, but I think I pretty much figured it out." I stood there looking at him feeling like he was lying and Josiah told him everything. He walked up to me and touched my hair, "you too pretty to be hurt like this."
"Hurt like what?"
"So hurt that you don't know what love feels like."
"My momma loves me." I said defensively.
"Ok," he said stroking my face. "You like a bird with a broken wing. You wanna fly, but you can't. I can help you fix that wing Annette."
"You slick talking.... leave me alone!" I pushed past him and continued walking. Luther followed behind me, he didn't smile but he looked sad for me. I went to the Watkins Boys stand to buy my momma's *medicine*. I hated when they talked about how pretty I am. One time I had to leave cause they told me that my money was no good with them and they wanted another payment. When they saw I was really going to leave they called me back and gave me the *medicine*. They asked me who the *boy* was following me. I told them I didn't know, and I kept walking. As I walked past Harriet and Mr. Coleman's place the Jones girl came running through their yard. I thought she was running to Luther, but she was charging at me. When I realized she was coming for me she was almost on me. I hit her with my jug and blood spilled on the road. She was hollering and talking about I was trying to steal her man. Luther screamed at her telling her she needed to calm down, and I wasn't trying to do anything. I was waiting for her to rise up at me again. Instead she fussed with Luther and I went home.

****

Momma was sitting at the table waiting when Emma and I came home. Momma asked what all the noise was outside and I told her I beat Raymond up for hitting Emma with a rock. She told me to stop beating on her boys. Then she said she had another letter from her sister in California that she needed me to read. My momma can't read she never went to school, so she always had me or Butch read for her.

My dearest Rose,
How's Kansas? I wish you would move to California. Everything is so much faster in the city. The winters are so much better here. The kids can get better education and jobs. Your eldest boys could find work on the docks real easy. There's jobs everywhere, but if I know you. You don't want to leave Elmer. At least think about sending the girls, living in San Francisco will provide them with better opportunities. There are nicely employed Negros out here, your girls could marry well and take care of you. Please think about it. Your boys can find nice girls. It's so much better out here for us. We can walk through the city after dark and not worry about going missing. Rose consider moving, I can send you bus tickets, just say the word. If nothing else come for a visit so you can see what city life is like. I promise you'll never want to leave.
I love you big sister and I hope to see you soon.

Love,
Dorothy

My momma sat there smiling for a long time like she was thinking about it. I knew she'd never leave my father behind. I asked her if she wanted me to write her back, and she said no.

Timothy

"Hi Baby!" Lady B said giving me a huge hug and kiss on the cheek.
"Hi Lady B!" I said squeezing her back.
"Where's your momma?" She said looking around the train station.
"She's at home making sure everything is perfect for you." I said picking up her luggage.
"Your momma had me riding in style! My car was so FANCY! All the people on the train were trying to figure out who this uppity negro was. I just put my nose up like this." She put her chin up. "And then I smiled." We laughed. Lady B was really sweet and she raised my momma. My grandparents were too busy being snobs and living their lives. They had busy lives in society so they didn't have much time for my momma and her siblings. My momma was the only one who lovingly attached herself to Lady B. My momma enjoyed going to her house, and being with Lady B's family. I like watching the two of them talk and let their hair down. Momma's proper way of speaking (although she doesn't speak completely proper anyways) goes out the window and all you hear is her southern drawl. "Tim you driving now? But you not sixteen yet."
I smiled; it was little stuff like that that made me feel like I was important enough to be remembered. "Yes ma'am. I'm a good driver though, I'll have my license as soon as I turn sixteen."
She smiled at me. "Thank you for coming to get me. I'm gonna make you a cake special for you. What kind of cake do you want?"
I knew it was pointless to object. Besides I love when she makes a fuss over me. "A coconut pineapple cake."
She smiled, "good, take me to the market so that I can get what I need."
Momma always begs Lady B to move with us, but she always says she has people back home who need her. She has children and grandchildren back home who make as big a fuss over her as we do, so I guess it's ok that we have to wait for her to come visit. When we got to the market I followed Lady B around as she pointed at the items she needed. People always look at us when we're in the store together. Lady B is from the south and she's used to people treating her a certain way. I live here in San Francisco and I have no patience for anyone treating her any different than they would treat my momma.
When we pulled into the driveway my momma was on the porch and completely excited. "Lady B!" She screamed from her heart.
"Irma my baby, here I come chile hold on." Then she looked at the stairs and exhaled. "Did you guys add more stairs? I promise it wasn't this many last time." She always says that every time she comes. "Irma I'm old you gonna have to send Franky to come carry me." She laughed as she made her way up the stairs. When she got to the top of the stairs she was huffing and puffing. "Oh Lord! Thank you Jesus! I made it! Hi baby!" She hugged my momma. Dale and Matthew came down to help me with the bags. Lady B watched us bring her things in. "Irma why did you send the baby? Matthew or Dale could've come to get me."
Momma laughed, "momma there was a fight, and you see who won."

They had a good laugh together. Matthew and Dale turned red with embarrassment. "Tim is crazy!" My momma said, then I smiled at my brothers, they went back to their homework.
Momma made a huge spread of all of Lady B's favorites. Fried Pork chops, greens, potato salad, candied yams, cornbread, green beans, and applesauce. Pops showered Lady B with compliment after compliment making her blush and feel special and wanted. The nicer Pops was to Lady B, the happier momma was. The happier momma was the happier Pops was. Lady B put her cake out for everyone. As they tore into that cake she gave me mine. Franky is greedy, and even though he had a huge piece of the cake for everyone he was demanding a piece of mine before he went to his apartment. Well I wasn't sharing. Pops, momma, and Lady B were in the living room having a drink, while we were in the kitchen. "Tim I'm not playing! Give me some cake!" Franky said.
"No! You just want it cause you're greedy and it's mine."
"Tim just give him some," Martha said cause she knows how Franky is.
"No! I don't have to!"
Franky reached for my cake and I moved the plate. Franky got mad and swung his big ole fist at me. I kicked his chair and he went flying backwards. Martha and everyone else moved out of the way. Martha went to get Jeff. I moved my cake to the counter, and Franky crashed a jar against my head. I could feel my warm blood trickling down the side of my face. I cracked a plate against his head. I grabbed a knife to cut this fool open when Pops called out to whoever the trouble makers were to come in there. I grabbed my cake to make sure he didn't try to sneak a piece then Franky and I calmly walked in the living room. Pops looked at us and sighed. "You two are forever fighting! Cut it out."
"Little ole Tim did all that to you? Why?" Lady B asked.
"He won't share his cake." Franky said irritated. He touched his head, he looked at the blood. "Great! I have a date tonight."
Momma looked at her watch, "tonight? You do realize what time it is?"
Franky smiled, "yes ma'am."
My momma looked at Pops, "go away Franky!"

****

She smiled at me and I felt lightening strike my stomach. Maureen is so pretty to me. Her freckles and brown hair stained my brain; every time I closed my eyes I'd see Maureen. My dreams were filled with dreams of her, we didn't have to be doing anything special, and the fact that we were together would make my dreams come alive. Maureen doesn't say too much to me. Its the way she looks at me, she has those big brown eyes that hypnotize you. She has to know I like her cause I go out of my way to see her and be as nice to her as I possibly can. I'm not always nice to everybody cause some people just get on my nerves. Jeff and Franky can be the same way, we don't like a lot of people, but the ones we do like we're really nice to. I don't like Maureen's sister; she talks too much and is moody like my other sisters. I guess if I had to put my finger on it, Maureen is more like my sister Martha. Martha considers me her special baby. She's always taken care of me. Martha would take me everywhere with her when I was a baby. And she always made me special breakfasts, lunches, dinners, and desserts. She didn't need a special reason to make me feel special she just always has. Those other two, all they care about are their selves. They whine, cry, and work my nerves. They work momma's nerves the most too cause she's always slapping or spanking them. If a girl reminds me of Peggy and or Beth, I don't want anything to do with them. Maureen doesn't act like

them. I think she knows I like her, but I want to know if she likes me. After that I don't know what to do. I smiled back at Maureen, something not a lot of people see me do. She picked up her tray and walked towards me with a smile. I told myself to be cool, don't embarrass yourself. "Do you mind if I sit with you?" She asked.
"No," I said watching her. I told myself to calm down and to act natural.
"You're a Wallace right?" She asked with a smile.
A lot of people knew our family because of the businesses that Pops has. A furniture store, a market, and just recently he bought a car dealership. That's the stuff most people know about. Then there's the whole behind the scenes stuff that really makes Pops his bread and butter. The businesses that make Pops the most feared and respected man in all of San Francisco and the Bay. Pops has instructed me not to discuss business with anyone. Anyone who asks me about business I need to report it back immediately no matter how small the person may seem. "I am, how do you know about us?"
"My father just purchased a refrigerator from one of your stores. I saw you there, but you didn't see me."
"I saw you." I said watching her beautiful eyes.
She blushed, "you did? Why didn't you say hello?"
"Your father looked like he couldn't handle me speaking to you. Your family looks nice."
"Thank you, he may not have liked that, you're right." She looked around and her girlfriends were all on the edge of their seats watching us talk. She looked nervous, she blushed real hard and then she said, "has anyone asked you to the Sadie Hawkins dance?"
I smiled, now I was blushing, "no." I forgot all about that stupid dance. The idea of it was stupid to me until just now.
"Would it be ok? I mean do you mind. I mean if it's no trouble, would you like to go with me?" She was looking down at her tray. "I mean I know other girls want to ask you, but they're probably scared. And well I told myself, be bold! Be assertive! If he says no you will die but at least you tried."
I started laughing, "you did not say all of that to yourself over me?"
She kept her eyes down. "Yes I did, some of my friends say you're mean. I told them you're always nice to me. I was hoping that your niceness was a sign that you are actually really nice."
"I can be as sweet as pie… to you!" I said watching her.
She turned beet red, "so then you'll go?"
"You gotta put those big brown eyes on me again." She giggled cause she was so embarrassed. "You already did the hard part. It takes guts to approach someone like me. Come on look at me." When she shyly looked at me, "I would love to go with you." She laughed harder. "I'll pick you up around four so we can have a soda first."
"Ok," she said real excited. "I'm gonna go back to sitting with my friends now. Thank you Timothy."
"Thank you Maureen for inviting me."
When she walked away I exhaled cause it took everything in me not to act as embarrassed as she was. When I got home I told Martha about it. She told me I did a good job, and then she coached me on how to be. Lady B pulled up a chair while we were talking. She kept smiling at me, and then she warned me not to get fresh with the little girl. She said if I liked her I needed to be a gentleman and to be kind and patient. She said sometimes girls can be just as goofy as boys and not know

what they want. When Matt heard us talking, he happily joined the conversation although I didn't invite him. He told me to make sure I invited her to dance as much as she wanted to. Then we heard a loud scream and loud sobs, it was Peggy. As we began to spring in action we heard my momma's voice getting after her. We stopped in our tracks and slowly back up in the room. Lady B was still sitting. She started laughing at us. "I see Irma has you all trained."

"We stay out of her way if she's after somebody." Martha said.

It sound like momma had a switch, and Peggy was screaming. I don't know what she did, but she's hard headed so there's no telling. When she was still going Lady B got up and said she needed to go save her baby. Lady B made her voice real calm as she talked to momma who was upset about something. Peggy's continued crying was getting on momma's nerves so she sent her out of the room. Peggy looked like a wild animal had gotten to her. Her hair was all over her head, her nose was bleeding, and her face was red from where momma hit her as well as her legs. Martha took her to clean her up. Beth was crying and shaking in the corner with fear. Beth acts like that whenever anyone gets in trouble. Momma says she's weak, and then I almost feel sorry for her… until… she starts acting like a goofy girl again.

When I heard momma and Lady B laughing, I went in the living room. Lady B and I told my momma that a girl invited me to the Sadie Hawkins dance. Momma said it was an excuse for girls to act fast. Then she told me she'd make sure my clothes were pressed and ready for me when it was time to go.

****

When I knocked on the door, I heard heavy footsteps. A woman opened the door.

"Hello ma'am, my name is…."

"I know who you are. You're one of those Wallace boys, what do you want?" She asked still catching her breath from walking.

If she would've let me talk she would've known. "I'm here to pick up Maureen for the dance."

Maureen hurried to the door behind her with a big smile. "My baby? No way!"

"But momma, daddy said I could go!" Maureen almost whined.

"He didn't clear this with me." She barked at her daughter.

"Daddy!" Maureen yelled running in the wrong direction.

Her mother crossed her arms, "your family isn't fooling me. I know your mother is passing."

"Passing ma'am?" I knew what she meant, and she wasn't the first person to make this claim.

"Your mother is from the south isn't she?"

"Yes ma'am." I said trying to control my temper.

"She's colored isn't she?"

"I don't know what you mean." I said putting my hands in my pockets.

"Prissy! Leave him alone. Frank Wallace is a good an upstanding businessman. Go ahead Maureen. Timothy bring Maureen home right after the dance is over."

"Thank you daddy!" Maureen said kissing her father on the cheek. Then she hurried past her mother without looking at her.

Even though I just saw her at school earlier today, she changed her dress. And she put her hair down, she looked very pretty. We spent the first five minutes walking and smiling at each other. "You look very pretty."

She blushed really hard. "Thank you, I'm sorry about my mother."

"Thanks."

"She listens to gossip too much."
"So do a lot of people."
"I don't care if your mother is passing or not."
I looked at her; I guess I couldn't fault her for listening to idle gossip. "Thanks?"
She covered her mouth, "did I offend you? I'm so sorry, I didn't mean to."
I held the door open to the soda shop. "Ok." She was nervous and fidgeting. After we ordered our sodas, I explained that my momma is from the south. What a lot of people mistake for passing is just her southern way of being. Then Maureen asked about Lady B. I told her that she was my grandmother. Her eyes got so big. I laughed so hard; it took forever for me to catch my breath. Then I explained how Lady B was hired to raise my momma and all her siblings. She asked if we ever saw my mother's parents. I told her that we have, but we aren't close to them. I told her they're very stiff, cold, and high society types. Class means everything to them and my momma was their wild child.
When we arrived at the school gym everyone was looking and whispering at us. Eventually Dale and Matt arrived with their dates. Matt kept smiling at me and telling me to get her punch or get her a cookie. He said girls need to feel special and like you're thinking about them all the time. So I followed his advice and Maureen was smiles all night. When we got two blocks away from Maureen's house she stopped walking, she smiled at me. "I had a lovely time tonight Timothy."
"My family and friends call me Tim."
She smiled, "we're friends?"
"Uh! Yes, we had sodas." I smiled.
"Can I ask you something?"
"Shoot."
"Why do you," she moved her hands trying to find her words. "Are you friends with Mary Jane?"
I frowned; I was searching for nice words to explain a not so nice girl. I scratched my head, "well... See... I wouldn't call her my friend, but we're not strangers."
"She's not your girlfriend?" She asked watching my eyes.
"If she and I were steady I couldn't be here with you." I smiled.
"And we're just friends?"
"For now." I smiled again.
She smiled like I just offered her the world. When I walked her to her door her father opened right away looking at his pocket watch. "Timothy you brought my daughter home in good time. You'll be driving soon won't you?"
"Yes sir."
"It's ok with me if you take Maureen out. As long as you're chaperoned of course."
"Thank you sir." I started to walk away.
"Hold on Timothy, Maureen you go ahead in the house." He came outside the door and walked with me to the sidewalk. He scratched his head and he looked around to see who may have been looking. "I have a lady who needs a fix." He looked at me like I knew what he was talking about.
"I just brought your daughter home. You cannot approach me with this now!" I said looking down on him.
"I know my timing isn't right, but I've been trying to get an audience with your father for some time."
I told him I would contact him at his job in a day or two. Not that I blamed him for having a sidepiece. His wife was a piece of work, and I could tell she was pretty once upon a time cause after all she was Maureen's mother.

When I got home I felt deflated until I told Martha how everything went. She smiled real big as she took everything in. She said she was proud of me for being a gentleman. I asked her how I should've explained Mary Jane. She turned her eyes and told me not to discuss lose women with nice girls.
When Franky came by I told him that Maureen's father needed to buy from him. He processed for a minute, he said no. I waited for him to explain. He said he'd have to check him out, but it didn't add up that he would risk his family for a woman who was strung out. He told me to wait to see how everything fell.

****

"Congratulations Mr. Wallace you passed with flying colors." He said as he handed me my certificate.
"Thank you sir." I said taking the certificate and walking inside.
My father was waiting with a knowing smile. He could tell by my smile that everything was ok. I drove his car back to his dealership. I walked out to the back lot where my baby was waiting for me. I built Sadie's engine myself, with a little help from Pops and my brothers here and there. Just like my brothers I built my engine and restored my car from scratch. Pops said you'd take more pride in your car when you've created it. I drove it around the block a few times to make sure everything ran right within it, and now I could take it out. I picked up Jeremiah and we were off. We drove all day enjoying the freedom. I let Jeremiah practice driving on Sadie. First I told him he had to talk her into it. "Hello Sadie, I would like permission to drive you." Jeremiah said sounding completely proper.
"You kiss your mother with that mouth?" I said cracking up. "I know you can do better than that."
"You really want me to sweet talk this car? It's just a car."
"Whoa! Whoa!" I said putting my hands out to the dashboard. "Sadie, please don't hold it against him. He doesn't know what he's saying." I pretended like Sadie responded to me. "I know! I know! I'll show him how to talk to a lady. Give us a moment Sadie," then I looked at him. Jeremiah was looking at me like I was crazy. I was gently stroking the dashboard. "The cars can hear you, if you aren't nice to them they won't be nice to you. Now tap into that sweet talk your brother laid on Ernestine to get her in the family way and give my Sadie her proper introduction!" Jeremiah laughed for a minute then he cleared his throat. "Hello Sadie my name is Jeremiah. I know I just met you, but I think we could be great together." Jeremiah looked at me for approval. I shook my head yes, and I told him to continue. "Your white vinyl top is the prettiest top I've ever seen. And those wheels, girl did you get them from a department store? They look fresh out of a display window." I rolled my hands for him to keep going. I whispered that Sadie was liking it. "I can tell Tim took time to make sure your paint job was perfect you shine so bright. And your headlights! Gurl..."
I cut him off, "SADIE IS A LADY! Don't mention her headlights on the first date!" Jeremiah put his hands up, as he laughed. "Sorry, I went too far."
"Sadie, please don't hold it against him he's new to sweet talk." Then I looked at him. "You're in luck, she likes you." Jeremiah laughed at me in surprise. I shrugged, "women. They always surprise you."
Jeremiah got the hang of shifting gears, and then he drove us back home. I gave his momma a hug, made my chess move on his father's board, then I went home. Martha was the only person home. She said Franky got a new apartment today and everyone was already there.

I let Martha drive Sadie, she whipped Sadie around those San Francisco hills like she and Sadie had been born to ride together. Franky and Pops were downstairs talking when we pulled up to the Victorian styled building. The building was quiet and nicely styled. When we walked inside the apartment momma and Lady B were directing Dale and Matt, telling them where to move furniture. Discussing the placement and then telling them to move it again. My sisters were in the kitchen getting set up. Franky's place was nice, his greedy behind was going to have to walk up four flights of stairs just to get here.

****

"Hello sir, I'm here to take Maureen for a ride." I said pointing at Sadie.
His eyes got big looking at my car, "of course. Looks like you don't have a chaperone. I'll..."
I cut him off, "sir. That won't be necessary." I said daring him to argue with me.
He exhaled and called his daughter. Last thing he wanted his family to know about was his double lifestyle. His lady on the side and the stuff he did when with her. Maureen looked surprised to see me, but she smiled so big. "Go grab your sweater," he told her, as he looked conflicted about right and wrong.
She came back to the door with her sweater. "What time should I be home?" Maureen asked her father as she walked past him.
I dared him to put me on a clock with my eyes. "It doesn't matter sweetheart. Have a good time." He said in a disappointed tone. I could hear his wife questioning what he said as we walked away. Maureen's father shut the door as her mother fussed.
I opened Sadie's door for Maureen, she looked cute sitting in my car. I took her to Belmont to this fancy restaurant where they knew my family. Maureen's eyes were excited; she asked me how I could afford a place like this. I told her my allowance allowed me to do a lot of things. After dinner we walked to the neighboring ice cream shop for dessert. Maureen said this was her first time on a real date and to a restaurant. I asked her what she and her family did together as a family. She said they used to go camping at Yosemite in the summer. The last few years her father has been too busy at work to take time off. I tried not to show on my face that I knew he used his vacation time to see his girlfriend. Maureen asked me to find somewhere to park Sadie so we could talk. My hands got sweaty at the thought of sitting alone with her, but who am I to argue? I drove back to the city and I found a spot in the Golden Gate Park to park. Maureen was as nervous as I felt; she kept blushing every time she looked at me. "You got a new freckle."
She touched her face, "I did?"
I touched her face, "right here. I think you should name it after me."
She smiled, "why?"
"Because I discovered it." She smiled while I stroked her face. "You ever been kissed?"
She swallowed, "no."
"Maureen," I looked her in her eyes. "Do you want me to kiss you?" She shook her head yes. "But you're a good girl."
"It doesn't make me bad if I kiss you." She pleaded with her eyes.
"Doesn't make you good either." I put my fingers in her hair. "Besides don't you know kissing leads to other things." I looked in her eyes.
"I know, but I know you won't go anywhere I don't want to go."
I kissed her, at first she was frozen like I caught her by surprise. She followed my lead and it was exactly like I had imagined it would be. We kissed for a long time before I moved my hands from the entanglement of her hair and I let them roam

wherever they liked. When I unzipped her dress she didn't notice until I pulled it down one shoulder at a time. Maureen acted like she was coming out of a cocoon. I kissed her bra, waiting for her to tell me to stop. When she didn't I unlatched her bra and pulled it so that it fell in her lap. She put her hands up to cover up but I wanted to see her. I wanted my brain stained with her image. I moved her hands as I kissed her more then I moved to her neck. I asked her if she wanted me to stop before I latched on to her breast and she said no. You would've thought I was her suckling child by the way I stayed there. I put my finger against her underpants and she was ready. When I pushed them to the side and massaged her, she moaned loud and her face changed from pink to red as she called out to me. She was releasing and I had to be ok with that. I never in a million years thought we would get this far. Her face was mixed with love and embarrassment. I silently counted backwards trying to calm myself. This was going to hurt later but it was worth it. I kissed her again and then I smiled at her, "you nasty!"
She turned red, "sex is better than that?"
I squinted my eyes at her, "what makes you think I know?"
"Girls talk too." She said, "you and all of your brothers have reputations."
"Reputations for what?"
"For being ladies men." She said shyly.
"Maureen!" I faked surprise, "under that good girl exterior you're quite nasty!"
"Please don't tell anyone, my father would kill me."
I smiled, "I don't..." Someone tapped on the window. The windows were foggy so I couldn't see out. "Get dressed." I said, and then I rolled down my window enough to see it was an officer. "What? I'm busy!"
"Step out of the car son!" The officer said. When I did his eyes got big, "you're one of Frank's boys aren't you?"
I cut my eyes at him, "can't you see I'm busy! Make a mental note of my car. Tell all your friends when they see this car not to bother me. If this car had been rocking and you interrupted me, it would've sucked to have been you!"
"Boy, I don't care who your father is. You better show me some respect!"
"I'm not your boy. You have to give respect to get it. You want to waste my time going back and forth about this right now? Or would you like to discuss this with your chief?"
He exhaled, "carry on." He said in defeat.
I got back in the car; Maureen asked if everything was ok. I told her it was fine, but I needed to get her home cause it was late and her folks were most likely worried. Maureen scooted next to me and put her arms around me. She thanked me for her kiss. When I walked her to her door her father opened it. It was just after midnight and worry was all over his face. I told him to shut the door and Maureen would be in, in a minute. He reluctantly did as he was told. I kissed Maureen goodnight, and then I opened the door. Her father told her to be quiet because her mother thinks she's already home. Then he stepped outside. He put his arms around himself like he was keeping it together because of his self-hug. He tried to ask me if I had sex with his daughter, his eyes pleaded with me to say no. This is not a man; I tried not to laugh at him. I assured him that I cared about his daughter, and nothing happened tonight that she didn't want. I warned him not to question her about it.
Then I got in my car and I went over Mary Jane's house. I tapped on her window, when her sister came I told her to wake Mary Jane. When Mary Jane came to the window I told her to brush her teeth and I was waiting in the car. Mary Jane came out in her bathrobe and slippers. She said there was no point in getting dressed. We

got in the backseat and I pounded my frustration out on her. Mary Jane was a slave to everything I do to her. I had bigger plans than this for Maureen.

Chapter 4

Annette

"What do you want?" Mrs. Cadbury barked at Emma and I as we came up the road.
"Ma'am, my Pa Elmer home?"
"Oh," I could tell she didn't recognize us. "All you darkies look the same. Go around the back and don't bother no one." She said waving us on.
When I knocked on the door I could hear the babies crying. Baby doll opened the door looking stressed. She was big again and her two little ones wanted they momma. She threw her arms around my neck and kissed my cheek then she did the same to Emma. She begged us to come in. Emma and I got to work. Emma entertained the babies while I brought the tub in the kitchen. I made their bath water not too hot. Then Emma put the little ones in the bath while I cleaned the kitchen, mopped the floors, washed their clothes and hung them out to dry. Elmer jr and Ann have almost white hair, I guess since Baby doll's father is Mr. Cadbury these babies keep coming out high yellow almost white. Emma cut lil Elmer's hair cause it was all-wild on his head. Then she combed and brushed Ann's and put it in one braid like my father's since who knows when Babydoll would get around to combing it again. I picked greens out in the garden, and then Emma and I switched places as she's the fastest and catches chickens easiest. Once she caught the chicken I wrung it's neck, plucked it, cleaned it and baked it. Emma made the cornbread. When Babydoll got up she looked at her house and cried. She kept thanking us for everything. When it got dark out I asked Babydoll when my father normally came home, cause it wasn't safe for him to walk the roads out here at night. She looked sad and said he was close by and he'd be home shortly. You could hear Mr. Cadbury's car coming up the road. A few minutes later my father walked in the door just before Mr. Cadbury reached his house. My father looked guilty when he walked in the door. He wasn't happy to see Emma and I, and he asked what we were doing here. I told him we haven't seen him in a long time, and he hasn't sent money. He gestured towards his new family and said he's been busy.
I started crying, my momma was keeping Leslie off of me because I threatened to tell. Since she hasn't seen my father in two years she's starting not to care. I needed him to pop by, at least get a look at little Preston whom he's never seen. My father looked at me and asked if things were getting that bad at home. Babydoll told my father she wanted Emma and I to come stay with them cause she needed the help. It was like he was reading everything in my tears. Babydoll told my father I was almost fifteen and I needed a proper coming out. My father cringed at the thought of me courting.
In the morning Mrs. Cadbury asked my father where we were going. She was sitting on the porch watching us. He told her he was going to make arrangements to bring us with him. Mr. Cadbury passed us on the road in his car. When we were far from the house I told my father he was asking for it. "What you mean?"
"You been messing with that white lady." My father turned his head. "Her husband's gonna get you if you get caught."
"Guess that's why I'm not gonna get caught." He said sure of himself.
When we came up the road my momma came out on the porch with Preston on her hip. She was too happy to see my father, until he was meaner than he's ever been to her. He hit her, he yelled at her, he told her he was never gonna touch her again. When he told her he was taking Emma and I with him for good that's when she had enough. My momma fought back and told him he was not taking us. Raymond,

Elgin, Leslie, and Bret locked Emma and I in the shed. My father left saying he was gonna bring the law to free us. My brothers let my momma in the shed. She started beating on me saying I betrayed her. She slapped Emma one good time when she tried to help me. I told her to stay back. She told my brothers not to let me out. Preston and Butch came over and listened as Leslie described all the things he was going to do to me tonight. When they laughed, I asked them what was wrong with them? I was their sister and they were supposed to protect me and not hurt me. They laughed at me and listened to him go on and on. Emma held on to me crying her eyes out. After awhile we heard the ruckus coming from the house. My brothers were looking to see what the commotion was about. I kicked the board in the back of the shed out. I was too big to get out. I told Emma to run to the Broderick house and to stay there until I come for her. She cried and said she didn't want to leave me. I told her I was coming and to run as fast as she could, and not to stop for nobody. Emma crawled out and I heard her little feet running like the wind. I told myself she was safe and that I had to prepare myself to fight. I could hear my momma yelling and carrying on. Then I saw Mrs. Cadbury come out the backdoor. "You boys stand to the side!" She called out to my brothers. My father opened the door to the shed and told me to come out. My father asked where Emma was and I told him she got away.

We were almost to Mrs. Cadbury's car where Babydoll was waiting when my momma screamed out that he couldn't take her daughter. Babydoll froze as she looked from me to my father and repeated my momma's words. Then Babydoll looked at all my brothers with faces just like mine. "Elmer, they all yours?"

"Elmer! You lied to me?" Mrs. Cadbury yelled.

"If my husband lied to me, why wouldn't he lie to you?" Babydoll yelled at her, her face turned evil and she let my hand go. "You stay!" She yelled at me.

Mrs. Cadbury screamed at my father calling him a liar and a devil. Then Babydoll drove them away speeding the whole way. My momma ran in the house and my father ran after her. Butch and Leslie ran in the house to stop my father from killing my momma. I fell on the ground crying out, I was almost free! Almost! My father came outside fist all balled up and I assume since I didn't see Leslie or Butch that he beat them up too. He said in the morning we were going to get Emma and then we were leaving. Even though I knew at any point he could leave us, I was relieved to know that Emma and I were getting away from our brothers.

My father and I stayed on the porch not speaking when my momma came outside and offered my father food but he refused. She apologized for ruining everything for him, but he didn't care to hear it. Then I heard the sound of a car coming, then it sound like more cars. Mr. Cadbury came with two cars full of men. My father stood up poked his chest out and went out. I don't know what he thought he was going to do, but they beat my father until they were tired. My momma tried to stop them and got beat up some more. My father had already beaten Butch and Leslie so they couldn't help him, and the others were too little. Preston and Bret screamed from the porch, they beat my father until he wasn't moving anymore. Even though my momma was banged up she sent Raymond to get the doctor, then she told the rest of us to help her bring my father inside. My father was in pain, and the next night he died. My momma was hysterical while Leslie tried to comfort her. I started walking to the Broderick house to get Emma. I didn't know how to feel, I didn't have this close loving feeling for my father, but his death was final. There was no coming back from it, and he'd never be able to explain to me why any of this had to be. Luther was sitting by the gate waiting, I guess for me. "Are you ok?"

"Where's Emma?"
"Inside with my sisters, are you ok?"
"I'm fine, I need my sister!"
"Ok," Luther said not fighting me.
"They killed him! They came and they killed him!"
"Killed who?"
"My father! He gone! They killed him! Right in front of me!" I cried, Luther grabbed me and he hugged me. "He was gonna take us away from here, I was finally gonna get away!"
"You could still leave, we could take Emma with us and go away, wherever you want to go."
"You'd run away with me?" I asked him.
"I'd do anything for you Annette, I love you!"
When we were almost to the house Josiah and Maybel rode up in their car. He said news is spreading all over town about my father. When Emma heard my voice she came busting out of the house. She was crying and she said she thought I was too hurt to come for her. Emma screamed and fell to the ground when I told her our father died tonight. Mrs. Broderick made chamomile tea and she told us to rest and then we could think about next steps in the morning. Although I wanted to tell Luther we'd runaway with him, when Emma said she wanted her momma I knew I was going home.

****

My father's funeral was huge; lots of people I didn't know came to offer their condolences. Word got back to the reservation that my father came from. A man and a woman came to the house a week after the service. They were coming to confirm that it was true that my father was gone. Although they didn't confirm it, I knew we were kin in some kind of way. The woman looked at all of us then her eyes focused on me. She touched me gently and told me that I was strong and to keep fighting. She told Emma to stay sweet and obedient. She had a message for each one of us, like she only saw the positive in us. When she got to my momma, she started crying and put her arms around her. She told her that one-day she needed to make peace with herself and then things would get better for her. I knew my momma didn't hear her and she kept crying like she's been doing.

****

Leslie screamed in pain from me breaking his hand with the skillet. I kept swinging, and then I picked up the knife and chased him. "I'M SICK AND TIRED OF YOU! I DON'T KNOW WHAT'S WRONG WITH YOU, I AM YOUR SISTER!"
Leslie screamed for our momma to help him, but she sat staring out the window like she's done everyday since my father died. She's been no good to anyone since and she don't talk much. Emma's the only one who can get her to eat or do anything. I was still beating on Leslie trying my best to kill him when the mailman came with another letter from my Aunt Dorothy. I read the letter to my momma and she didn't respond. Butch told me to write and tell her that we were coming, all of us.
After I wrote the letter, I went to the Broderick house to tell Luther I would run away with him. My momma needed Emma and I knew she would be safe out in California. I saw the Jones' horse and buggy out front. Mr. Jones was extremely angry and preaching that God would punish Luther if he didn't do the right thing by his daughter. She was big and Luther's head was low, I kept walking like I was on my way to somewhere else. Goodbye Luther!

****

Harriet came by once Mr. Coleman got home from his store. She left her babies home with him and she sat with me holding me while I cried. I couldn't say exactly what my tears were for. The passing of my father, my last chance for freedom from these people who constantly keep me down, or my broken heart. Harriet said Luther came by the store the other day, he told her he was leaving. He said the baby wasn't his and it couldn't be. She said Mr. Jones has been looking for him since. I guess I could believe that Luther left without me. I'm forgettable anyways.
That night I laid staring at the walls, I don't know what was going through my brain either. I was just lost, and then I heard the tapping on my window. I recognized the top of the head as I went to it. Luther said he was leaving, and he wanted me to come with him. I asked him why he would leave the Jones girl when he knew she was big. He said there was no way that baby could be his. He said she was looser than he thought. He said he couldn't stay and have a shotgun wedding. He begged me to come with him. I looked at Luther for what I knew would be the last time I ever saw him and I told him to go on without me. He said he didn't want to leave without me, and he didn't want to leave me with no one. I told him whether I stayed or I went with him I would be alone. His selfishness is what got him in trouble and now he's running. I wasn't telling him he had to marry the Jones girl, but he needed to stand up and be a man. I told him that I lost all respect for him because he was running, he needed to stand and fight. I told him he could say what he wanted about my father, but he fought until he couldn't fight anymore. That didn't make his situation right or how he got there for that matter, but he didn't run away or send my momma to say he wasn't there. At least I could respect that aspect of my father. Luther shook his head like I didn't understand. Then I closed my window and I went back to staring at the wall.

Timothy

"Your brother is so nice." Maureen said smiling ear to ear.
"Thanks?" I said not knowing how many times she was going to mention how nice he was.
"How long is he staying with your family?"
"I don't know, why are you asking so many questions about my brother?" I was irritated and jealous.
"You are the man of little words tonight, I was just trying to make conversation."
To shut her up I kissed her. I don't know why it was bothering me so much that she mentioned my brother but it was. When things got too hot and heavy I backed away and Maureen was trying to change my mind. "Maureen lets wait!"
"I thought you said you loved me?"
"I do love you, that's why I want to wait."
"But you're not waiting, I know what you do." She pouted.
I was tired of having this dumb argument. She wanted me, FINE! She could have me. "Not like this though. Not in my backseat."
Maureen got excited, "I could fake a tummy ache Sunday and stay home from service. You could come over then." She had it all planned out in her mind already.
"What time?"
"Come at eight." She said happily.
When I got home I went straight for the brandy. I got a couple of ice cubes and I poured myself a drink. I told myself this wasn't going to backfire on me. I thought about how much I loved Maureen despite her family. My momma didn't like her all

that much; she said she wasn't the right fit for me. She said Maureen was a better fit for someone like Dale. The first time she said that Dale stood up and walked out of the room. My momma laughed so hard at his reaction. Even though Dale was away in college Momma still used him as an example. Pops asked what had me drinking so late at night. I couldn't find the words to express my frustration, so he joined me with a glass of brandy as well. We took out the chessboard and he kept beating me until I stopped playing emotionally. Then he told me there were certain people that mattered and certain people that no matter how hard we tried they could never be my Queen. He told me to let it go and let everything happen naturally. He said this as if he knew what I was wrestling with.

****

"Who is this guy?" Jeff said looking like he was about to lose it.
"He can't be from around here, otherwise he would know better!" I said not trying to calm him down.
"You guys James is ok." Matt said
"What would you know? How could you let this happen?" Jeff said
"Before I realized what was happening he was inviting her out for a soda." Matt said
Jeff squinted his eyes at Matt and mimicked him, "*before I realized what was happening he was inviting her out for a soda*… You are so weak! You let him run over you?"
"No!" Matt said like the idea of it insulted him. "I may not be crazy like you all, but I'm still a Wallace!" He declared.
"I don't believe you! I bet you let him run all over you!" Then Jeff started walking up on Matt.
Fear then anger went through Matt's eyes. Matt squared off; I was irritated cause I wanted to fight him. Matt brought home a friend from College and of course the guy puts his eyes on Martha. Maybe Matt was setting this fool up, it didn't matter both of them were getting beat up today. I sat there and watched as Matt gave it his all against Jeff. Matt was pretty strong, fast, and an all around good boxer. He lacked that kill or be killed instinct that anyone crazy enough to come against the three of us should have. Matt would stop if he thought you were down, and death wouldn't stop Jeff. Momma saved him though, this time he crawled away with a broken nose and a cut above his eye. Then we got in Jeff's car and went to the cafe where Martha and *James* were sitting. When we walked in Martha shook her head no, I smiled and said yes.
"Where are you from?" Jeff asked James, no hello, how are you? Anything like that.
"Michigan," He said sounding nervous, but could you blame him? Jeff looked crazy.
"I guess Matt didn't warn you before he brought you home."
"Warn me?" James eyes danced between us.
"Our sisters are off limits!" Jeff said snatching Martha off her stool.
"Why would you ever think its ok to stay with a family you don't know and take the sister out for a soda? You think we're running a brothel?" Jeff spit.
"And the best sister at that, you should've picked one of the silly ones." I said.
Jeff shook his head, "don't lie to him that wouldn't have saved him either."
"Oh, right!" I smiled at Martha.
"Jeff please!" Martha pleaded, "one day I'm going to get married!"

"Not to this wise guy! He's disrespectful and he's got to be taught a lesson." I said, "look at him Martha! This can't be mister wonderful!"
"No, but if I don't meet anyone how will I know the difference?" She pleaded.
"I'll tell you," then I hit him in the face. James spun off his stool, hit his face on the counter, and then fell on the ground. He was out cold; Jeff and I frowned at Martha.
"YOU GUYS!" Martha yelled running to James's head.
"I still don't think you hit him hard enough! I'm the oldest I get first hit!" Jeff barked.
"So you get to hit everybody and I'm supposed to sit back and watch?"
"Yes! Precisely!" Then Jeff smiled at me.
Jeff and I roughed up James real bad then we sent Matt and his college chump on their way with matching wounds. Martha said it wasn't fair, as she cried to momma about it. Momma didn't have any real sympathy for her but she listened anyways. Martha got accepted into a bunch of schools, but Pops said she had to go somewhere locally so he could keep an eye on her.

****

"Tim," she swallowed. "I think I'm pregnant." She said with her arms wrapped around herself like she was comforting herself.
I felt like someone just dropped a ton of bricks on me. I swallowed, "when will you know for sure?"
"I'm only a couple of days late, but I'm scared."
I hit the steering wheel, and then I apologized to Sadie. It wasn't her fault; she tried to warn me too. "Let's focus on graduation next week, then we'll decide what we're going to do." I said firmly.
"Are you mad at me?"
"Why would you ask me that?" I was irritated.
"You're acting like you're mad at me." She cried.
"How?" She kept crying holding herself. "I didn't want to get married right away, but it looks like we don't have a choice." Truth is, I didn't want to marry her anymore. Between her strung out weak father, and her busy body momma, I didn't want to call them in-laws. Then I never liked how her head turned whenever Matt was around. Everything in me was saying this was wrong. "I'll take you home."
"What? Now you don't want to be with me? I need you right now, I'm scared." She cried some more.
"Well what am I supposed to do? No matter what I say or how I act I'm wrong." I huffed.
"Make love to me!" She pleaded.
The thought of it turned my stomach. "I'm not in a lovie dovie place right now."
"Now you don't want me!" She cried some more.
"Maureen stop this! No matter what I say or do I'm wrong. Let's call it a night."
"No!" She threw her arms around my neck. "Please!" She kept kissing on me. "I need you Tim. I need you." If she started here I would've been completely turned on, by the mere touch of her. Right now I feel.... I feel... Setup!
I'm not a rookie, after all these years Mary Jane never got pregnant, but now Maureen is hollering pregnant as graduation approaches. "Wait a minute, hold on." I gently touched her. "What if you're not pregnant? What are your plans?"
She looked stuck, "plans?"
"Yes, are you going to work? Are you going to go to school?"
"My family can't afford school."
"So your plan is to get married?"

"Is there something wrong with that?"
I shook my head; "there's nothing wrong with that. You should try to trap a man who wants to be caught. I don't think you're pregnant Maureen, but let's give it sometime."
"Why don't you think I am?"
"This was not my first rodeo. I was very careful with you, I don't want you getting a reputation on account of me."
"That doesn't mean I'm not pregnant." She said
I smiled as I caressed her face. "You want a family with me so badly that you'd imagine you're pregnant when I say you're not. I think we need time before we marry. I don't think you're pregnant, but let's wait it out." It took everything in me to play nice.
"Ok," she said in defeat.
On the morning of our graduation I knew that spaced out look on her face meant she wasn't pregnant. I hugged her and I told her we'd discuss it later. I on the other hand was beside myself with relief and giddiness. I felt like the governor just called and granted my stay of execution.
All of my siblings came home for my graduation. Even though I didn't want to admit it, I missed Dale a lot. He has a gentler way of looking at the whole world, which was kind of nice. And our last boxing match was really REALLY good! Dale fought back harder than I ever would've given him credit for. He got respect from me after I helped him up. We came to an understanding that day. I wouldn't assume he's weak just because he didn't have killer instincts, and he wouldn't assume I was stupid because I'd kill first and ask questions later.
Maureen sat over to the side sulking as if her whole world was coming to an end. She should've been relieved, especially if she wasn't trying to trap me. I knew the truth; she wanted to start her family at the risk of ruining her nice girl image. Pops said he was going to need me full time just like Jeff and Franky. I was kind of tired of school anyways; Matt, Martha, and Dale could carry the education torch for the Wallace's for now.
I brought Maureen punch and told her to cheer up. I told her we had time to do it right. Matt came over, "momma sent over this plate for your girlfriend." Then he looked from her to me. "You two ok?"
I expected Maureen to be as withdrawn with Matt as she was with me. "No, I don't know what I'm going to do with myself now. I always dreamed of starting my family, but it appears I have to wait, getting older and older by the day." She explained.
"What are you barely eighteen? You've got your whole life to have a family. Enjoy being young." Matt said in my defense, I thanked him.
"I want to be young with my children." She said as a tear fell.
Matt looked at me, "how did you end up with a girl like this?"
"A girl like what?" She asked.
"You aren't a good fit for Tim. He's too wild for you."
"I love him," she said helplessly.
"There there," he said patting her shoulder. "The good thing about love is that you can love again."
She shook her head, "you don't understand."
"Make me understand." He said taking a seat.
I debated whether to stay or leave. In the end I was honest with myself, I didn't care anymore. So I walked away, eventually momma called me over, she was squinting

her eyes at me. "You broke in the Lentz girl, and now you're sicking her on your brother?"
I opened my eyes wide, I didn't think of it that way. I guess that's what I was doing. "Momma..."
She slapped me hard, through clinched teeth she said. "Take her home! What's wrong with you?"
"Momma? I wasn't...." She slapped me again.
"Don't fix your mouth to lie to me! You know I know better. TAKE HER HOME!"
"Yes ma'am." Maureen was smiling again and really enjoying her conversation with Matt. "Maureen I gotta take you home." I said
"Already? I could take her home." Matt volunteered.
I wanted to say yes, but I looked at momma who looked at me like I better not. "No, I gotta take her home." Then I whispered to Matt, "meet us out by Sadie and you can ride with us." I nodded my head towards momma.
Matt nodded in agreement then he made his way around the party and eventually out the gate towards the front. I took Maureen around to everyone to say good-bye. I couldn't find momma anywhere so we went out to the front. Momma was sitting on the front steps. "Come give me a hug goodbye suga." Momma said to Maureen. She cut her eyes at me. "I came out here looking for your brother. Guess he's still inside?"
I shrugged, "I guess so."
"Drive safely," she said watching us get in the car.
"Psst! I'm back here. Don't look." Matt called out.
I laughed, "what are you doing?"
"She was coming so I hid. Let me know when the coast is clear." Matt laughed.
When we turned the corner Matt sat up excitedly. "You're gonna get it when you get home."
Matt smiled at Maureen, "Tim do you mind?"
I looked at him in my rear view mirror. "Can we talk about it later?"
Maureen smiled real big as she looked back at Matt. When we got out of the car, Maureen was happy again. I asked her if she really wanted to do this. I didn't like it. She told me that she honestly always had a crush on Matt but he was so much older than her, she never thought he'd look her way. I asked her what would've happened if she was pregnant? This morning she thought her life was over because there was no baby. She shrugged and said Mother Nature knows better. I chewed back my reaction to hit her. Hitting her wasn't gonna change anything, and it wasn't gonna make me feel better. When I got in the car Matt said we needed to clear the air immediately. In the end I told him I didn't want to see it. I knew I couldn't give her what she wanted, but my brother! I was volatile for the rest of my party. I told Jeremiah about it and he couldn't believe it. I asked Martha if I was wrong for feeling some kind of way about it. She said I wasn't. The three of us sat on my porch kind of stuck in our own thoughts.

****

Immediately the humidity hit my skin. It was hot and sticky out here. There's no way the south would be ideal living space for me. Pops took his hat off fanned his head, and then put it back on. We walked down the stairs off the plane. Momma's daddy was sick and her family sent word. I needed to get away from the Bay anyways, so I volunteered to go with Pops. All my siblings were at home; I was going to have my parents and Lady B all to myself. Exactly the getaway that I needed.

A driver greeted us inside, I didn't like it. This grown man was calling me sir. There's no way I would ever be comfortable with Jeremiah's father addressing me like this. Momma rubbed my hand with sad eyes as I looked around. The white's only bathroom signs angered me. I exhaled, I hated being here already. The driver took us to our hotel first, and then he took us to my grandparent's house. Their house was huge; they'd consider our San Francisco house a little shack. The man at the door recognized momma, but it looked like he had to restrain himself from responding. Momma gave him a hug anyways and she told him she was happy to see him. His eyes looked sad, as he didn't respond. "You haven't changed one bit." The woman in the doorway said.
Momma nodded a irritated nodd, "Mischa."
"With the way you've always acted I would've sworn you married a high yellow man!"
Pops stared at his sister in-law. "You have something to say to me?"
"No, come in out of the sun." We walked in the door. "Who do we have here?" She said looking me up and down.
"Tim Ma'am."
"Don't ma'am me. I'm your auntie Mischa, come give me a hug." She said holding her arms out. As she came in for her hug Pops grabbed my momma's arm as she showed her disapproval. Aunt Mischa held the hug too long for my liking and she wiggled her body against me.
Pops had a disgusted look on his face. "Mischa! Don't touch my son like that again."
"Oh I'm just teasing." She laughed but no one joined her.
"Irma?" A woman called out.
"Ingrid!" My momma said hurrying to her other sister.
"I knew you'd come." Ingrid said.
"Franklin, good to see you." My Uncle Howe said extending his hand for a shake. "Irma, Vladimir is upstairs with our folks. You should take your family up."
Momma froze, "no one said Vladimir was gonna be here!" She looked at Ingrid, "WHY DIDN'T SOMEONE WARN ME!"
"Irma calm down, that was so long ago. Surely you can't still have feelings about all of that!" My Aunt Mischa said.
"Tell him to look for his missing toe and then you tell me if he's over it!" Momma said.
"Our father is sick, surely you can let bygones be bygones for now?" Uncle Howe said.
Momma grabbed Pops hand and she took a deep breath. She took a step then she stopped. "Ingrid keep Tim with you. I don't want to have to go to jail for killing Mischa!" Mischa laughed my momma didn't.
"Come with me child." Ingrid said putting her arms out to hug me. She hugged me then she took me in a sitting room. "Which one are you?"
Annoying but I let it go. "Timothy ma'am." She moved her eyes around like she was trying to place me. "I'm the youngest boy. There are two sisters under me."
"Oh I see, and you're the one who just graduated?"
"Yes I am."
"Good for you. What university will you be attending in the fall?"
"I'm going to take some time off and then go back to school."
"No! No! No! You have to go right away otherwise you won't go back. I'll have to talk to Irma about this."

Aunt Mischa walked in the room. By the way she giggled I knew something was mentally wrong with her. I frowned at her still. "Let's show him the house. Is this your first time here?" She asked me.
"I've been here before." I said watching her.
She laughed a nervous laugh, "what did your momma tell you about me?"
"What makes you think she'd waste her time talking about you?"
"Timothy! Hold your tongue that's your aunt!" Aunt Ingrid said.
I cut my eyes at both of my Aunts. I sat back on the couch and took a deep breath. We sat there quiet for a long time. I don't like high society prissy prissy people. No wonder my momma got away from here as soon as she could.
When I heard the sound of anger in Pops's voice I hopped to my feet. My aunties followed me out of the room. Next thing I knew a man was falling down the stairs and my momma was tearfully trying to calm Pops. My momma told me we were leaving while her sisters asked what happened to Vladimir. As he laid at the bottom of the stairs everyone ran to help him. Pops put his arms around momma and he focused on her. Howe hollered at Pops saying that he was an uncultured common street thug. Pops's only concern was momma and getting her out of that house. In the car momma kept crying on Pops's shoulder saying that her family hates her. Why would they call her all the way out here just to rehash old wounds? Pops told her that she didn't need any of them. He told her we have a wonderful family and they're just a part of her past. Momma said she needed Lady B. Pops told momma she needed to go lay down and then he and I would go get Lady B for her. Seeing my momma so upset about her family upset me. I don't know what's going on, but I do know your family should be those that you trust and love. Pops and momma went in their room for a few minutes. I could hear my momma crying, something she rarely did. I wanted to go back to that cold and stuffy house and burn it down with everyone inside. Pops came out the room with fire in his eyes. I could see the wheels of his brain turning. We asked the driver to take us to Lady B's address. People were looking to see who was coming as we drove up the road to Lady B's big house. Lady B owned a former plantation. There were smaller but nice houses spread out all over her land. She had a farm and her fields looked beautiful and ripe. When Pops and I stepped out of the car Lady B's son came off the porch with a huge smile. "Cousin!" He said loud and proud to Pops. They hugged just like family would. "Momma said you all were coming out. Good to see you! Come in! Come in!" He said.
When the driver stayed by the car, I asked him if he was coming. He was standing there looking confused and stunned. Everyone told him to come inside as well. Theo brought us lemonade, the best lemonade ever! Lady B was in her sewing room. She stood up as soon as we walked in the door to hug. When she didn't see momma with us she asked Pops how momma was holding up. Pops told her that momma was asking for her. Lady B's eyes turned sad. She said she would be ready to go in just a minute. Then she looked at Pops, "Frank, I know those are her kin. I don't understand why she would come all the way out here for them. They don't know love in that family. The only ones that's halfway right is Ingrid and Howe, and I said halfway!"
Pops agreed with her, "Lady B. I'm with you, but Irma has love for them even though they never showed it back. I tell her all the time that she has us, and she doesn't need them." Pops said showing his irritation. "That family will not treat my Queen like this and continue to prosper."

Lady B touched Pops shoulders, "vengeance is mine says The Lord. Have faith Franklin, God will deal with them."
Pops frowned, "I can handle this God has enough on his plate." I could tell he was forming a plan.
Lady B made her voice real tender, like she does when momma's upset. "Franklin baby. God blessed my baby, no all of us with you. You love my baby unlike anything she's ever known; you are so good to her and to us. Look around, my family is together and we're strong." Thomas stood taller with a smile. "You take care of my baby and the ones she loves. You are a blessing to all of us. God will handle that family. You just keep loving my baby like she needs you to. Don't worry about them."
Pops looked at Lady B, "with everything that family has done to you." Pops's whole body twitched, "I keep hearing Irma crying. No! I'll rely on you for prayer, but I'm thinking about it."
Theo smiled at his momma, Lady B exhaled like she tried. She grabbed her purse then ran down the list of to do things around their land to Theo. She told The to tell everyone to prepare a big meal for us tomorrow. I looked at the driver and he looked as confused as I did. What did my momma's family do to Lady B? Why was my momma so upset? Pops had that look in his eyes, either someone was gonna die or they were about to come up missing an important limb. Lady B kept trying to calm Pops the whole way to the hotel. I knew there was no point, I was waiting for instruction. When we got to the hotel momma's eyes were red and puffy. Momma held on to Lady B who rocked her and told her everything was ok. Pops told me to stay in the room when the hotel manager came complaining about Lady B using the front door with us. Momma said her father still hates her. Lady B told momma she was a woman ahead of her time. Momma told Lady B she hates the south! She hates the prejudice, she hates it down here. Lady B told her to never hate her roots, to embrace them and grow from them. Lady B told her she was so proud of Irma and that she had a nice life. A wonderful husband, a beautiful family, and lots of love in her life. Momma calmed down a lot in Lady B's arms.

****

"All I need you to do is to find out what the family business name changed to and I will take it from there." Pops told me.
"I have a feeling you're going to tell me that my Aunt Mischa is my mark." I looked at my father.
"She's the weakest link." Then he exhaled, "as you can see she's not right in the head so be careful."
I frowned, "I would never!"
Pops put his hand on my shoulder. "Don't kill her when she gets fresh with you. That family is not right. She doesn't know any better."
I relaxed; I thought he was saying I would go for something like that. "Oh."
Then Pops smiled, "it's ok if you have to kill Vladimir though."
"Pops, what happened?"
Pops ran his hand over his head. "He used to come after your momma. Her parents never believed her. They beat Lady B numerous times for saving your momma cause that no good would lie. They don't approve of your momma's relationship with Lady B. They're evil!"
I didn't need to hear anything else, I was ready. The driver and I chatted a long the way. He was a law student driving cars to pay his way through school. In the nicest way he could, he asked if we were passing, cause he never met white folk like us

before. I told him we're not all bad. He told me that his family will never believe him when he tells them about us. When I arrived at the house my Aunt Ingrid met me at the door. She was surprised to see me. I told her I was thinking about what she told me about college and I needed guidance cause I didn't know what to take. She shook her head like I was sensible for coming around. When we walked into the library I saw Howe and Mischa looking down to see who was here. I asked my Aunt Ingrid how my grandfather was doing, and she said he wasn't well. She said she was still praying for a miracle. Ingrid pulled book after book, she took pride in her education and she bragged about it like it was all she had. I asked her why she wasn't married and her face turned sad. She said she was married once and her husband died. I asked her how he died and she told me to hold my tongue. I didn't like that answer but I went a long anyways. Mischa finally came in the library to find out what we were doing. I asked her if she went to college. She said she did, I asked her what courses she took. She looked embarrassed as she said bookkeeping, so that she could manage a household if she ever married. I asked her why she never married. She said it was too hard to court when my momma left. I asked her why, and she put her hands up like the answer was too painful to let out of her mouth. Someone was coming up the road so Aunt Ingrid got up to see who was coming.

I looked around then I asked Aunt Mischa for a tour of the house cause it had been so long ago that I came here. She got excited, clapped her hands. She was so proud of their television and radio room. I guess she thought I'd never seen one. I told her my family has a television, but we don't watch it often. I faked interest until we got to the office. Their books were on the desk open and everything. Berger & Drescher was clear as day on the bank ledger. I asked Aunt Mischa who Berger was, and she said it was her mother's maiden name. She volunteered that the lumber mill was under Berger Lumber, and the Tobacco fields and smoke house were under Drescher. The rest of the businesses were under the joint name B & D. I listened while she explained all of the businesses her family has then Vladimir walked in the office. He asked what I was doing there. Aunt Mischa explained that they were encouraging me to go to college. Vladimir asked if I needed money. I shrugged cause I wanted to see what he said. "See! I told you Irma came for money." To be so smart, he didn't think anything of the check he wrote me from the family account. He then started a whole lecture about managing money and that fast money wouldn't last, etc. I was waiting for him to say something, anything about my parents. I guess he picked up on my demeanor. He looked at me and said there was a whole lot of my father in me. I thanked him. Vladimir searched my eyes for a few minutes like he was hoping for a sign of weakness. I watched him waiting for him to realize he would not find it in me. He started rambling about his wife, children, and grandchildren. I didn't say anything I just stared at him. He asked me if I had a girl back home, and I said no quickly not waiting to think about Maureen and whatever she and Matt were doing. When it sound like he was offering his daughter to me I blank stared at him in hopes that he said whatever he was trying to say he was saying it wrong. Finally he stopped talking when he caught the disapproval on my face.

When I got back to the hotel I reported to Pops everything I had. Pops sat there quietly thinking about it. His mind was ticking; I imagined that he was debating with himself. He looked at me and said, “do I?” Then he looked at my momma. “Yes!"

Chapter 5

Annette

Harriet and Claudette cried something terrible when I told them I wrote to my Aunt in California. I told them nothing was set in stone yet. My Aunt had to write back with whatever answer she had for us. Harriet calmed down when I said that, but Claudette said she knew I was leaving and she could feel it in her bones. Honestly I wanted to get away from here; everywhere we went I could hear people whispering about my father. My momma only comes out of her staring spells to yell at me and blame me for our father's death, take her *medicine*, hug Emma, and hold on to Preston like her life depended on it. The wheels shifted in the house. Butch and Leslie were no good cause they didn't even try to protect our father from the white men that came for him. She said what was the use of having all these boys if they couldn't protect anyone. When Leslie tried to argue that he was strong, she pointed to his hand where his finger was still crooked from when I broke it and it didn't heal right. She told him he couldn't even whoop a girl. Leslie got so mad it looked like he was going to jump on momma, but the rest of us stood like a wall in front of her while she kept yelling at him. No matter what she was our momma and the only parent we had. I wasn't going to let nobody outside of my daddy treat her wrong. That night Leslie and Butch fought, which I know she liked cause after that she was always putting us up against each other to fight over her. I'd try to bow out as peacefully as I could cause I could see what she was doing. At night she'd cry and cry, sometimes even her *medicine* didn't help. We had to start selling things around the house just to get by.

When the mailman came he had a huge smile on his face as he slowed his horse on the road next to me, right next to my house. "How you doing today young lady." Mr. Williams said.

"I'm fine sir," I said not looking directly at this white man.

"Y'all got another letter from California." He said happily to me.

My whole face lit up, "really?"

"Yes, make sure your momma gets it." He put the letter in my hand and hurried off.

I thanked Mr. Williams as he continued on his way. I liked Mr. Williams; he was always nice to us. My momma was standing on the porch looking mad with her hands on her hips. I didn't know what I did now, but I was in trouble for something.

"You shucking and jiving for the white man now?"

"No ma'am, he…"

"Oh so now I'm a liar?" She spit at me, "you see what they did to your daddy and you wanna be smiling at them. Dancing for them!"

"That was Mr. Cadbury, Mr. Williams has always been nice to us."

My momma jumped off the porch and chased me. "DON'T SASS ME ANNETTE! AIN'T NO WHITE PERSON NICE! THEY'LL HANG YOU FROM A TREE JUST LIKE ANYBODY ELSE!"

"I'M SORRY MOMMA!" I screamed as I ran for my life.

My momma stopped running fell to her knees and started screaming. Asking God why! Even though I knew she was going to get me I ran back to her and I hugged her. I kissed her cheek and wrapped my arms around her as I cried as well. That didn't stop her from beating me; I knew she was still hurting from losing my father so I took it. When I finally caught my breath, I got up and picked up my schoolbooks and the letter from Aunt Dorothy. My hand was shaking from the pain in my legs and arms that had been beaten until she decided to stop. I handed the letter to Butch as he came in the door; Emma was helping me clean up.

"Momma! Aunt Dorothy said she can't send tickets for us all at once to come. She sent enough for Me, Annette, and Emma to come now. As soon as I get a job, you and the rest can come. She said once we're all out there between me and Leslie we should be able to afford to get a place for our family."

"Why Emma and Annette gotta go?" Momma asked.

"She say she got a job lined up for Annette when she get there. Emma can help out with the chores around her place." He said.

She shook her head no, "Emma's all I got. Take Annette she ain't fresh no how, someone would have to be blind, and deaf to want her."

I looked at Butch cause he knew I wasn't going without Emma. There was no way I was leaving my little sister out here to become victim to my stupid brothers.

"Momma, Aunt Dorothy has a good plan. She say, we could all be out there come Spring, but in order for things ta work out it has ta go this way. Please momma! I gotta get outta here! If we stay, I'm gonna end up on a tree, please momma. If you say yes, I promise you won't ever have ta work. I'll take care of you." Butch pleaded with her like only he could.

I couldn't understand why he was helping me. Only thing I could think of was he was scared to go alone, and he knew I wasn't leaving Emma behind. Momma looked at her son with love in her eyes and she said yes. She told him to take care of Emma and to protect her with his life.

The next day instead of going to school I went to Claudette's house, and she cried again as she told me she knew this was going to happen. She told me to write her letters every day if I could. She said city life was much faster than what we were used to. I went by the Broderick house and I thanked Mrs. Broderick for everything she's ever done for me. She told me she was happy I was getting away from here. She told me to write her as well; so that Josiah could write me once I arrived. When Harriet saw me coming she started crying, I told her to stop all her crying before this baby came out like a crybaby. I told her that her husband would finally be happy to be rid of me. She told me to go by his store in the morning on the way to town and she would have somethings for me. I thanked her for everything, for every time she hid me from my momma, and for never treating me different when she knew the truth about my family. Then I went to the school house, I told Ms. Kay that Emma and I were moving to California and I needed our papers to get into school out there. She put our papers in an envelope and then she told me she was jealous and she wished she was going. She told me to watch out for strange fast talking men.

That night I braided Emma's hair and I told her that we were going to have to be brave for momma. Emma was scared to leave momma, but she was even more afraid to stay here without me. I packed what little clothes Emma, Butch, and I combined had in one suitcase. I snuck and took one of momma's pictures in the drawer of my father. We left some of the money with my momma for food and anything else she would need until we could send money, and then we got up early and got on our way. When we got to Mr. Coleman's store he was so happy to see we were leaving. Harriet packed meals for us, and a whole suitcase full of fabric scraps that Mr. Coleman didn't need so that I could use them to make whatever Emma and I needed. She even packed crotchet and knitting needles and yarn. I was so moved by my friend's love for me that I hugged Mr. Coleman. He acted like I had a disease but I didn't care. I told him to give Harriet my love and I'd write her as soon as I could. I was the last to walk out of the store and I bumped into Emma who was stuck. When I turned around she was staring at Babydoll, who was standing there with all three of her kids. She had sad eyes as she tried to look past us. "Hi Emma!" Little Anne said.

"Y'all never come to town this early." Babydoll said real low with her eyes to the ground. "I been meaning to…"

"I HATE YOU! I HATE YOU! YOU LET YOUR DADDY KILL MY DADDY!" Emma screamed at her.

"Hush now! There was nothing I could do. Mrs. Cadbury was carrying on and she wouldn't calm down. I begged her not to tell him, but she didn't care!" Tears ran down Babydoll's face. "She told Mr. Cadbury that he forced himself on her." She cried harder.

"Are we supposed ta feel sorry for you while you still live in they house? You eat they food! Your kids got nice clothes. Your clothes real fine too. Our momma cry all the time cause she missing her husband. Her kids don't eat. You never came to check up on us. You don't care! Nobody feel sorry for your high yellow tail." Butch said

"I'ma call on your momma today." Babydoll said

All three of us shook our head no, "don't go to our house. Momma will kill you!" I warned.

Babydoll switched arms with her baby, "do you think you could come by to help me out?" She asked me.

I looked at her like she had to be joking. I grabbed Emma's hand and my suitcase and I walked away. Butch said something else to her that I couldn't hear and then he came along with the other suitcase.

****

Immediately I felt like we stood out as we stepped out the station. I hadn't seen my Aunt Dorothy since I was little, but she recognized me immediately. She excitedly hugged each of us, and then she told my brother to load our bags on top of her car. It was really fancy. All the cars out here were fancy. Everybody was dressed really fancy too. Even my aunt looked fancy. I felt ugly and dirty looking at everyone at the train station. Aunt Dorothy looked at Emma and I, she smiled real big. "I forgot Elmer made such pretty babies! You two are gorgeous! And Butch look at you, you're all grown up now. Kathryn is fixing dinner, y'all hungry?"

Emma and I looked at Butch to say; momma would never let us tell anyone we were hungry. My friends would feed Emma and I would always pretend like I wasn't all that hungry even when I was. "Sho nuff!" Butch said proudly.

"WOW!" Emma and I kept saying, as we looked out the window of the car at all the buildings. I couldn't believe there were actual cable cars going up and down the streets just like we read about in the books at school. There were all kinds of people everywhere, colored people, white people, and people I've never seen before. I swallowed really big cause I didn't know how to act in a place like this. Aunt Dorothy parked in front of an apartment building and she told Butch to bring the bags up. "Whoa! I feel like I'm gonna roll in to the water!" Emma said trying to balance herself getting out of the car. We were on a steep hill.

Aunt Dorothy laughed, she said after awhile we wouldn't even notice the hills anymore. "Hey Dotty!" A guy called out from the top of the hill as he happily walked towards us. Aunt Dorothy got excited. "Ok now, this is Rufus. He's a good friend of the family!" She said smiling real big.

"Is this them?" He said smiling at us.

The first thing I noticed were his eyes, they were so green they looked like snake eyes. I never seen nobody with eyes like that, not even the white people. Emma grabbed my hand and kind of hid her face. "Yes Rufus I want you to meet my nieces Emma and Annette, and my nephew Butch. Butch is gonna go with you in the morning to the docks."
"Good to meet ya young fella! Good to meet ya."
Butch didn't say anything he stared at Rufus like me and Emma did. Rufus smiled at us. "Oh!" Aunt Dorothy laughed, "tell them how you got eyes like that."
He looked at me, "I robbed a cat!" Then he smiled harder.
"Those eyes make you look scary!" I said.
"You should see them when I get mad, they turn red."
Emma gasped and buried her head in my shoulder. "Rufus! Look at you scaring the baby."
"Aw sweet thing don't be scared. I'll stop pulling your legs." Then he looked at Aunt Dorothy, "I know you cooked."
"Kathryn did today." She said gesturing for us to come along.
Rufus took a suitcase from Butch and then he followed us. We walked up the stairs to the second door on the right. Aunt Dorothy called out that we were here and you heard excited chatter and movement. Aunt Dorothy's girls came into the living room. They looked fancy too. She introduced us to Kathryn, Jean, and Wilma. The girls said hello and then she said her son would be home from work shortly. She fixed his plate and then she put it in the oven. Then she fixed Rufus's plate, just like momma would make my father's plate. Rufus sat at the head of the table like the husband. Emma and I looked at the plates of food Aunt Dorothy made for us. I didn't understand why she fixed everybody's plates, and we all got good amounts of food. Emma and I were used to only eating was left after our brothers just about ate everything up. Emma looked to me to say it was ok to eat. Butch dug into his plate, and they kind of sat there and watched him eat in horror. I immediately felt embarrassed but I didn't know why at first. Butch barely used his fork and he chewed with his mouth all open. Aunt Dorothy tried to ignore it for a minute then she put her fork down. As nicely as she could she told Butch to slow down and to chew with his mouth closed. I watched her girls who sat straight up at the table and they used their forks as they ate all proper. When Rufus or they momma asked them a question, they finished chewing then they answered. My momma would've smacked me for not answering right away. This was going to be totally different. Aunt Dorothy said tomorrow her girls would show us around the city and where I would be working with Kathryn. That night Aunt Dorothy gave us new toothbrushes and the pajamas she made for Emma. She told Kathryn to give me a gown. Butch slept in the living room on a cot, and her son Booker slept on the couch. He was so tired when he came home he said hi, ate dinner and then he went to bed. Emma and I shared a bed in the room with our cousins. Wilma and Emma hit it off immediately, and I listened as Kathryn and Jean went on and on about the boys they were sweet on. They asked if I had anybody back home, I said no even though I thought of Luther. I wondered where he went and what he was doing. When it got late I heard they momma and Rufus carrying on. When I asked them if they momma was gonna be big soon, they didn't understand me. It felt like I was speaking a different language. Kathryn said, "Oh you mean pregnant…" then they said not as long as Rufus takes care of business. When I asked what they meant, they shrugged and said that's what they momma always said. I asked them where they daddy was and they shrugged like they didn't know the answer.

In the morning it was COLD! Emma and I stayed on the bed shivering, once the oven got going the whole apartment warmed up. I asked them what kind of summer had cold mornings? They said I would get used to San Francisco weather. We could hear the baby crying next door. I told them this whole experience was like something from a book. Houses stuck together. I couldn't understand the difference between houses and apartments out here, everything is stuck together. I told them school had just started back home, and out here we still had a few more weeks. They asked where our school clothes were and I told them I didn't have any. Then I told them about the fabric that Harriet gave me. Jean said she'd share her patterns with me and help me make some clothes for Emma and I.

When we got to the hospital we went straight to the kitchen. Kathryn introduced me to the head mistress. She told us that Bubba ran the kitchen and she was his assistant. She stared at my eyes like she was looking for something. She explained that since I was the new girl I would be cleaning dishes, mopping the floors, stuff like that. I said ok and looked at all the people moving quickly around. When we got back to the apartment Aunt Dorothy had a very big smile on her face while she hid her hand behind her back. She told Emma to come to her then she gave her a baby doll. Emma screamed with excitement, cause the only doll she had before was the sock doll I made her that momma threw away because she said it was foolish. Wilma told her to come play dolls with her. Aunt Dorothy told us to all come sit first. Her voice sounded all nice and loving, it made me nervous cause I didn't know what she was going to say. She told us that they were excited to have us with them. Emma reached for my hand she was as nervous as I was. She went over the expectations for all of us, not just Emma and I. She said we were all expected to be well behaved at all times. We needed to get good grades in school and do our parts at home. She went over our chores with us. She said even though we weren't with our momma we were not allowed to be loose and fast. She told us to act like our momma and daddy were right there. Emma immediately burst into tears. No one told my Aunt that our father died so she had no idea of what she said. I held Emma and rocked her in my arms. Everyone was concerned, I put my hands over Emma's ears and I told them that Elmer died. Everyone covered their mouths and rushed to Emma to hug her. Emma and I looked at them like they were weird. We weren't used to giving and receiving love outside of each other. Kathryn and Aunt Dorothy made dinner while Jean helped me pin dresses for Emma. When Jean asked about me, I told her that Harriet gave me what we had. I said Emma's already gonna talk and act different than the kids at school. She needed new dresses more than I did. Jean's eyes watered and she said I was a good big sister. She told me I could wear her dresses. Especially since I didn't have enough fabric to make anything for me. I wanted to say no, but my two dresses that were very worn weren't going to cut it.

****

I had a conversation with Emma after breakfast. She was very nervous about starting a new school. Fortunately Wilma would be there and she wouldn't be alone, but she was scared. When we walked to school their elementary school was first, I hugged Emma tight and I told her she was going to be ok. Emma and Wilma walked into the yard hand in hand. Jean went to the left at the corner to her middle school, and Kathryn and I went to the right. As we waited for the light to change I looked at the huge school and swallowed. School for me was a one-room building. One teacher for everyone, for all subjects. This was scary, and there were all kinds of kids here. Colored kids, white kids, and I don't know what the other kids were. Kathryn introduced me to her friends, and then they showed me around the school. I tried not too talk too much because everyone was so proper and fancy. I felt like the stupid ugly duckling. In my first class I sat in the very back. I needed to see how things went in here. The classroom was not segregated, immediately I noticed the colored kids and white kids who appeared to be.... *Friends*? A boy with big teeth kept looking at me and smiling. I turned my eyes from him; I don't know what his problem was.

At lunchtime while Kathryn and her friends talked I looked around at all the kids. A lot of them I wanted to ask them where they came from. My world only consisted of white and colored, I wondered what their stories were.

By the end of the day I felt like I was on system overload, and I was so happy I survived the day. Jean was in charge while Kathryn and I went to work. Bubba and the head mistress told Aunt Dorothy that Kathryn and I were wonderful additions to their staff. They appreciated that we came ready to work and they never found us sitting around. We were always hard at work and making sure that everything was done so that the kitchen could close on time and everyone could get home to their families a lot earlier.

Timothy

My momma was leaning against the doorway to the TV room looking like she was in a daze. Pops was watching momma for a response. I stood in the hallway waiting. My momma asked if everyone got out safely. Pops said everyone was safe and sound between Vladimir and Howe's homes. Her parent's house caught fire and burned down. They were even able to get my grandfather out in time. Momma told Pops she didn't know how to feel. She said bad news keeps coming. "Did you know they lost their lumber business? Their tobacco fields went up in flames, fires keep following them. Ingrid said in her last letter that they think one of their employees stole all their money. It's sounds to me like someone has it out for them." Momma said as she searched Pops's face for an answer.

Pops watched momma, "your family has wronged a lot of people. It doesn't surprise me one bit that they're in trouble."

Momma went to Pops and climbed in his lap just like she would Lady B's. She wrapped her arms around his neck as she kept kissing him. Pops looked at momma with so much love in his eyes. I stood there remembering what it felt like to love someone. I exhaled and walked away. I poured a drink of Brandy then I stood in the living room stewing in my thoughts. "Hello! Tim?" Beth said waving her hands in front of my face. "Are you coming with us or not?"

"Where are you going?" I asked already annoyed with her and she hadn't done anything.

"The fabric store, Maureen picked out a pattern Monday and her momma's gonna make our dresses."

I swear Beth and Peggy make me rethink my whole no hitting girls promise to myself. I chugged my drink and I put the glass in her hand. "No!"

"Oh come on, you were Maureen's first crush, but they fell in love." She sighed like she thought the situation was romantic.

"Pops!" I called out walking back towards the TV room. "I need to find my own place." I spit.

"What's the matter son?" Momma asked still cuddling with Pops.

"Your daughter gets on my nerves. I can't take this! I tell him I don't want to see them together so now he marries her! So every time we're together as a family I gotta see them together?"

Momma sat up, "what did you think would happen? That girl is ready for a husband and family. Your brother is almost out of school and wanting more as well. I tried to warn you. Later on that girl is going to feel some kind of way about being passed around this family. As for today she thinks she's in love with Matthew."
"I didn't think he was serious." I said in defeat.
"Wait until it's your turn. Reason and logic will go out the window. You won't care about details either, all you will know is how much your love for her burns inside of you." Momma said.
"You coming to the store with me?" Pops asked.
"Should I meet you there, I need to leave now."
Pops looked at momma then they kissed deeply, he told her he would be back later. Pops told Beth that momma would take them and then I followed him to the store. Mae was patiently waiting in his office. She got so excited when she saw Pops. I opened the door and I excused us. I asked Pops to walk with me. We went back out towards our cars. I leaned against Sadie. Pops waited for me to gather my thoughts. I told him I didn't understand, he loves momma. I just saw them together; I didn't understand why Mae was here. Pops was quiet for a minute looking for words. He said my momma was his Queen and no one came before her. He said there were certain times, and especially if she interacted with her family, that she would shut down. He said he couldn't fault her for shutting down because she's been through a lot. Meanwhile he still had needs, he said he wasn't proud of what he does, but.... Pops told me to come back inside so we could discuss business. Mae was out on the sales floor looking at the new appliances. In Pops's office we discussed real estate. Pops said it was a good idea for me to start investing. He said for me he wants to open a trucking business. He went over how he plans to structure the business. As he explained everything he kept reminding me that when I went back to school I needed to focus my studies in mathematics cause I was going to need it for planning and strategizing. Meanwhile he said I could have an apartment in his building a block over from Jeff. He looked me in my eyes as he told me to buy my own property right away, cause he was giving that building to Matt as a wedding present. "You mean they're going to live out here?" I tried to pull back my anger.
"Tim stop being stupid! Pull your head out of your butt and look at the big picture! Matthew is going to practice law out here, especially for the family, and for prestige. He'll work at a firm or two and then he's going to start his own practice. Everyone works for the benefit of the family." He looked at me, "now I know you feeling some kind of way about his bride, but didn't you breakup with her?"
"Yes sir."
"Do you want her back? Carrying your brother's child and all."
I frowned, "no!"
"The moment you realized her legs would spread for your brother after she's been with you, you were done with her. Those two are going to have a lot of problems, you dodged a bullet. Stop acting like your brother took her, you didn't want her anymore. Suck it up!" Then he looked at me. "She wasn't your queen. When you find her you won't let her go."

****

"This is our kid brother Tim. Tim that's Natalie." Franky said
"Nice to meet you." Natalie said staring into my eyes. "Tim your eyes are beautiful!" She said
"I'll say thank you for my momma cause she made them."
"How come you the only one with eyes like that?"

"My brother Dale, and two of my sisters have eyes like this."
"There are more of you? How many are there total?"
"You ask an awful lot of questions." Franky said cutting his eyes at her.
"Sor-ry!" She said putting her hands up and returning to her drink.
Jeremiah walked past with his girlfriend Katie. She was a real sweet girl, and he was crazy about her. Jeremiah was going crazy cause Katie is a good girl. She is determined to wait until their wedding night. Jeremiah needed a job so that he could afford a wife. He almost cried when I offered him a job with my trucking company. He's been saving his money to buy an engagement ring. Tonight is the night. Look at him looking all goofy with his nose completely open. I bet he drops the ring. Jeff leaned over; he asked what was up with Jeremiah. I told him that he was about to propose, and he yelled no! He said we have plenty of time for that. I told him that Jeremiah found his Queen and the time was now. Jeff still said that Jeremiah was crazy. We spent the rest of the evening watching Jeremiah's every move. Forget the band and everything, Jeremiah was our show. He was so nerved up that he kept making clumsy mistakes. Jeff and I couldn't breathe we were laughing so hard. Even Franky chuckled a couple of times. It was pure comedy watching him. When he pulled out the ring box from his jacket pocket he fumbled and dropped the box. I guess that counts as dropping the ring. Katie didn't seem to notice, she had stars in her eyes for Jeremiah. When he opened the ring box Katie screamed and said yes before he could get the words out of his mouth good. Katie jumped around screaming and fanning herself while she cried. Jeff and Franky shook their heads as they tisked at him.
"Franky baby, you gonna marry me?" Carol asked.
"You've already given me everything what I need to marry you for?" He said unmoved.
"We're getting older, you keep coming back. Maybe we could have a couple crumb snatchers. You know you love me." She said unaffected by his candid response.
"I like to have other women." He offered as another reason.
"I know that." She said tapping her cigarette. "You like your liquor, you like your whores, you even have a thing for dark meat. I know you Franky." Then she took a drag on her cigarette. "I already know. You won't marry me. You'll marry that little red head who's been chopping at the bit."
"I'm not getting married!" Franky said irritated with the conversation.
"That's alright Franky. I'll still have you even though you're gonna make that mistake. Younger isn't always better."
"How about you? Do you want to get married?" Natalie asked me.
"I guess so, but I can't get married just because. I want what our parents have." I said.
Franky blew air, "you want a crazy woman like momma? She drives Pops crazy!"
I smiled real big, "just like that!"
"Jeff?"
"Like Tim, I'll get married when I find my queen. Not a moment sooner." Jeff said

****

I rolled my eyes as I sat there watching Maureen vow forever to my brother with their child growing in her belly. Everybody was so excited and acting like I was irrelevant. Jeremiah tapped my shoulder and pointed to my brother and his bride.

They were taking their wedding picture and she was looking at me. I squinted at her to tell her to cut it out. She was getting what she wanted, a good guy, a husband, and a family. Her father Mr. Lentz was looking at me too, but he was in need of a fix. He even slid his mistress in amongst the guest. I told Mr. Mercer to supply Mr. Lentz for a small wedding present. Mercer came back Lentz and his mistress did not.

Funny how Prissy Lentz was concerned about my momma passing until my brother knocks up her daughter and agrees to pay for the wedding. Now I'm watching this fake woman run around kissing my momma's butt. She's even trying to play up nice to Lady B. Momma and Lady B keep looking at her like they can see right through her.

Maureen keeps looking at me and it's annoying. When I was about to blow, Franky put a beer in my hand and told me to walk with him. I told Jeremiah to come along as well. We walked outside of the reception hall and stood over to the side. Franky asked how business was going. Jeremiah and I said it's brand new but it was going. I asked how his furniture store was doing. He said it was going ok. Franky looked around then he leaned in. "I'm in trouble."

"Trouble?" I raised an eyebrow. Franky bows down to Pops only.

"She won't marry me, now she won't see me." He said with pain in his eyes.

"Who are we talking about?" Jeremiah asked

"Carol?" I asked

"No!" Franky said frustrated.

"The red head, what's her name?" I couldn't remember.

"Raynel!" Franky spit. "She's pregnant and she won't marry me talking about marriage would make my life more difficult."

Jeremiah and I looked at Franky in amazement. "Franklin you love Raynel?"

Franky threw his bottle at me and I ducked. "Didn't I just say that? Don't ask me dumb questions."

"Whoa! Whoa! Franky don't take your frustration out on poor Tim. We didn't know your heart could be open like this." Jeremiah said trying to calm Franky.

"You're not going to give up are you?" I asked him.

"Her father called me a white devil saying that I forced myself on her." He exhaled, "I've been in love with her since we were kids. I would never look at her in a way that made her uncomfortable. I need to tell momma about the baby, but you know what she'll do. Her father isn't backing down, momma would make this worse."

"Maybe you don't tell her until you've sorted everything out. Why did you get Raynel pregnant?"

"What are you saying to me?" He wanted to hit me.

"You schooled me on what I needed to do to take care of business. You loving Raynel and this baby don't sound like an accident."

Franky deflated, "this is exhausting!"

"Her father is angry, colored folks got it hard enough trying to survive out here. To find out his daughter was running around being loose is one thing. To find out it was with a white man is another thing. I know slavery is over, but things haven't changed all that much. I know your family isn't like the other white families around here, but you're talking about a man's daughter. He's going to hate you. And he's not going to make it easy on you. Raynel's a good person, she..."

"DON'T YOU THINK I KNOW THAT! I'M TRYING TO MARRY THE WOMAN! I DON'T WANT HER OUT HERE ALONE."

"Franky yelling at me isn't going to change the situation." Jeremiah said

"I don't know what else to do."
"I could try to talk to Mr. Johnson for you. I doubt it will do any good though."

****

"Wrong! This is how this is going down! If you want to continue to buy from us you pay the agreed upon price. You can go somewhere else if you like, but you'll be back guaranteed!" Pops told Mr. Danza.
"I will kill them."
"Mr. Danza, I don't bargain. If the Mercer kid has one hair out of place on his head you will watch everything you love disappear! What kind of man punishes a child for a world he has no clue about? Return the kid NOW!" Pops pounded his hand on his table.
Mr. Danza said something in Italian to one of his men. The man returned with the very frightened Mercer kid. His mother ran to him crying as she picked him up. Pops picked up his phone. Then he told the person over the phone that Mr. Danza was working against their arrangement trying to set up his own family. I saw the fear in his eyes, I reached for my gun, and Jeff told me to hold on. I shifted my weight, Franky told the men around to bring it in. Mr. Danza's men were brought in by gunpoint. Pops told one of his men to give Mr. Danza the phone. Then he stood up, smoothed out his suit jacket. Mr. Danza yelled at his boss. Pops told us to come. Pops told Mrs. Mercer and the son to come along. Mr. Mercer drew his gun. As soon as we walked out the door guns started blasting. Franky stopped he said someone fired back. Pops told him to call him, he was going home. Jeff told me to take the family to the car. We sat there waiting for Mr. Mercer. Jeff and Franky walked him out, he had been shot. Franky told me to do the final sweep and he would take the family to the hospital. Jeff told me to go to the right and we'd meet up on the other side. A couple of bodies dropped as I made my way around. When I got to Jeff the outside was swept. Mr. Danza's chair had knocked over and he was fighting to hold on. "Aw! Tim! He's suffering! Poor guy kidnaps a kid, threatens death to his boss. Comes against the Wallace's like he has balls of steal! Now he's struggling... Just die so we can leave!" Jeff said.
I could tell he was going to try to hold on as long as he could. When he turned grey I told Jeff to go check on the Mercer's at the hospital. I called Pops when Danza took his last breath. Then I made my way to the hospital. I drove wondering how I would react if someone took my child. When I got to the hospital I asked where Franky was as I watched the Mercer kid eat like he was starving. They said he had to take someone home and he would be right back. The Mercer kid said that Danza's men were mean to him and they didn't feed him. They had him over night. Mr. Mercer was going to be ok, and Pops was going to have to relocate them and set them up with a backup plan. Mr. Mercer loves his family and only worked for Pops originally as a temporary answer to his lack of employment. The money became good and he forgot about his exit plan. Pops keeps saying one day we're going to walk away from what he calls the side business. We keep opening all these businesses as our exit plan for the family one-day. One day the Wallace's are going to all be straight, as for today we gotta do what comes next and prepare for tomorrow.

Annette

"I understand but the kitchen is closed." Bubba said explaining to someone on the phone. Eventually Bubba hung up the phone all angry. He took off his apron and said goodbye as he walked out of the back door. He was done with today.

The Head Mistress was wiping down the counter when a big white man walked in the cafeteria. I guess the Closed sign didn't apply to him. His eyes said he was mean and he walked right into the kitchen. He looked at the swinging phone cord then he looked at the Head Mistress and asked what happened to the man who he was just talking to. She very nervously said he left. "Mr. Mercer was just admitted, I need a sandwich or something."
The Head Mistress may know how to yell at us, but she was shaking in her boots just by the look of this man. He was a young man a lot younger than her, but you would've sworn he was her daddy by the fear he put in her. "MR?"
"I need a sandwich you don't need my name."
"Um. um!" She swallowed.
His patience was thin he didn't have time for her fear. His eyes swept the room and landed on Kathryn. She started shaking just like the Head Mistress. I exhaled cause there was no one else there but me. He looked at me. "Can you please give me a sandwich?"
I thought about giving him a hard time, but that would just be a waste of time. I wanted to go home and the sooner he was satisfied the sooner he'd leave and the sooner Kathryn and I could get on the bus and go home. "Fine," I exhaled. "But only cause you said please."
He frowned like he didn't realize he said please. "Thank you." He said, "where's the man I was talking to?"
"He went home to his family." I said
"Mr. Mercer has a family. The sandwich is for his wife and child."
I grabbed more bread out of the refrigerator, and I made an additional sandwich. I grabbed a tray and I gave him fruit and pop with the sandwiches. "I'll come up and get the tray in a minute, what room is it?"
He looked at the tray, and then he looked at me still looking big and mean. "Thank you, 479."
"Un huh, hurry up. I'm tired I wanna go home." I said shooing him away.
When he was definitely gone the Head Mistress acted like she was going to yell at me, and I told her what were we supposed to do. The guy wasn't going to take no for an answer. I needed to get home to finish my homework. When we finished cleaning up the Head Mistress said she was going to count the trays in the morning and if that tray was still missing she was docking my pay. Kathryn volunteered to do the final wipe down and wait for me in the kitchen. She told me to hurry so we didn't miss our bus. I took the elevator up to the fourth floor. I broke out in a sweat as I saw all the white men standing around room 479. I instantly thought of my father and I felt like I wanted to cry. I gritted my teeth and took a deep breath. I could cry about this later. Most of the men looked at me as I approached, I said excuse me and then I knocked on the door. A white guy opened the door, he smiled at me. "Is this her?" He said opening the door wider so I could be seen.
"Yes," the mean guy said waving for me to enter. He pointed to a woman, "this is Mrs. Mercer." The woman was sitting next to the bed holding her husband's hand. Her sandwich was on the tray still.
The guy touched her, "thank you so much!" She said tearfully. Her little boy was sitting in the corner scarfing down his sandwich like he was starving. "It has been the most traumatic day. You are an angel! Bless you!"
I felt embarrassed, "you're welcome ma'am. May I please have your tray? I need to return it to the kitchen and hurry so I don't miss my bus."

"Oh of course." She said taking her sandwich off the tray. Then she opened her purse and took out a five-dollar bill, and handed it to me.
"No thanks. I gots to go." I said backing away with the tray.
"Franky make her take the money." Mrs. Mercer said giving him the money.
I hurried out the door and ran to the elevator. Fortunately it hadn't moved since I took it last. I ran to the kitchen. I put the tray on top of the other trays and then I told Kathryn to hurry. As were heading for the door, his deep voice scared us and we screamed. "Don't make me chase you!" Kathryn and I froze in place. He walked in my face. "Take this money or you will make me angry!" He forcefully put the money in my hand as he watched my eyes. "Now come on."
"Sir?" I said not understanding.
"You missed your bus on account of us, I'm taking you home." He said as he walked through the door.
I looked at Kathryn cause I didn't know what to do. She put her nails in her mouth, and then she grabbed my hand with her free hand. "It's ok we can wait for the next bus."
He looked even madder, "I don't have time for this. Get in the car shut up, I'm taking you home!" I frowned at Kathryn, but she told me to come on. He opened the passenger side door to his two-door car. Kathryn and I crawled into the back seat. He got in the driver's seat, "where do you live?" When neither Kathryn nor I spoke, he growled. "I know I told you to shut up, but you gotta speak to tell me where you live."
"Then we gotta shut up again right?" I said
He locked his eyes on me, "how old are you?"
"Sixteen almost seventeen."
He exhaled, "little girl! Don't play with men, where do you live? I gotta come back here."
Kathryn looked at me with big eyes, she whispered that my mouth was going to get us in trouble, and then she gave him directions to our place. He got out of the car and opened the passenger door for us to get out as Rufus and Butch were walking up from work. He looked at them then he thanked me again for helping the Mercer family. Then he got back in his car and left. Butch looked at me like I did something wrong, I felt like I was in trouble. As soon as we walked in the door Rufus was flapping his gums to Aunt Dorothy. Butch was brewing in his seat as I told my Aunt what happened. "HOW CUD YA HELP ONE A DEM? YA SEEN WHAT DEY DID TA US!"
"Butch, the little boy was hungry. They gave me money."
"Which she refused at first, until he made her take it." Kathryn said
"You refuse the money?" Aunt Dorothy asked, "and what did they do?"
"Yes, I wanted to get home, but he made me take it anyways." I looked at the room where Emma and Wilma were playing dolls, "my father." Then I swallowed air. Then Butch went on his whole rant about how he wishes he could kill all white people and they're evil and not to be trusted. Aunt Dorothy said it wasn't fair to judge a whole race based on the actions of some. When Butch tried to argue, Aunt Dorothy countered that she has friends who are white and they are very nice people. I could tell by the look in his eyes as soon as Momma came he was going to tell on me. I thought about how she acted behind the mailman, she was gonna beat me good.

****

We were sitting in the kitchen eating breakfast when everything in the room started shaking. Emma and I screamed and ran under the table to take cover. Emma wrapped her arms and legs around me as we screamed to the top of our lungs. I wondered why no one else was panicking and why they weren't taking cover. Emma and I sat on that floor feeling ridiculously dizzy. When we stopped screaming I noticed that everyone was laughing. Aunt Dorothy asked us if we were ok as she tried to hold back her laughter. Emma and I frowned at them; we didn't know what was so funny. Jean said that was only probably a three pointer on the Richter Scale. I told her it didn't matter what scale they put it on the ground should not move! The rest of the morning they kept laughing whenever they had flash backs. Emma nor I thought it was funny.
"Thank you Mr. Lakshman, that is wonderful!" Aunt Dorothy said. She closed the door excitedly. She said the landlord said my momma could have the apartment next door when the family next door moved out this summer. I tried my best to smile, I felt bad because suddenly I didn't want my momma to come. Aunt Dorothy hugged me mistaking my sad eyes for missing my momma. I liked the peacefulness of my Aunt Dorothy's home. We went to school, did our homework, chores, and work. Booker and Butch would run the streets on the weekend. All of us girls would explore the city of San Francisco. Emma and I saw our first movie. Our favorite place to go was to Playland on the beach. The first time we went Emma and I kept saying, "WOW!" We had never seen anything like it. Roller coasters, merry-go-rounds, and a Fun House. There were so many people here too. People from all over the place came here.
I was enjoying my ice cream sandwich while I waited on the bench outside of the merry-go-round when it felt like someone was looking at me. I looked around at all the people who weren't paying me attention. I was looking until I saw him approaching me. Panic hit my stomach and I held my breath. "Are you here alone?" He asked directly, no hello. No how are you.
"No," I said looking for my sister and cousins.
"Here!" He dropped money in my lap and started to walk away.
"What is this for?" I said in shock.
"For helping the Mercer family when everyone else was too afraid."
"You can't keep doing this." I said not touching the money.
He looked at me, "I can do whatever I want." He reached in his pocket, "what's your name little girl?"
"Annette."
"I'm Franky, your newly appointed guardian angel. When I see you, I will do as I feel. You have no idea what making a couple of sandwiches did for that family. So just shut up and take the money. You run your mouth too much!" He dropped more money in my lap and then he walked away.
I gasped at the forty dollars I was holding. I neatly folded the money and put it in my bra. He is probably the weirdest person ever! He got one more time to tell me to shut up; I don't care if he is white. It makes me mad when he says it. He lacks social skills for real; I don't care how scary he seems.

****

I looked at myself in the mirror. I loved all my new dresses. I've put all my money from work in the bring momma out here jar. I've used the money my angel has given me to buy new patterns and fabrics for all of us. I've stocked the cabinets and freezer with food. I bought Emma and I shoes for school and after school. I've sent care packages to Harriet, Claudette, and Mrs. Broderick. It wasn't until Aunt Dorothy pointed it out that I realized I hadn't sent my momma anything. Part of me didn't want to because she would hate anything I sent her, just because it was from me. And the other part honestly didn't think of my momma when I wanted to do nice things for the people I love. I love my momma, but she's never been nice to me. I watch Aunt Dorothy with her children and it hurts. I'm hoping that when momma comes that she's missed us so much that she's changed. I can tell by the letters she sends through Raymond she's not worried about me. She addresses her letters to Butch, and she tells him to hug and kiss Emma for her. She doesn't ask about me or say anything to me. I admired my dress one more time then we left for school. I asked Emma if she wanted to send momma anything. And she excitedly said yes. Seeing her enthusiasm saddened me more. How come I don't feel like that about my momma? What's wrong with me? When we got to school Buckie came immediately. "Annette you look beautiful!" He said with dreamy eyes.

All I could do was stare at his teeth. They were so big no wonder everyone called him Buckie. "Thank you Buckie."

Kathryn was grinning at us like she knew something we didn't. "Morning Buckie."

"Good morning Kathryn." Then he adjusted his glasses as he looked at me. "Annette are you going to Playland this weekend?"

I looked at Kathryn. "We don't have definite plans to go, but we may end up there."

Buckie smiled bigger revealing more teeth. "Will you ride the carousel with me?"

I looked at Kathryn and she was shaking her head yes at me. "We'll have to see, what time will you be there?"

"I normally finish all my chores by lunch time. I'll be there after one on Saturday."

"Ok meet us there at two." I said

Buckie jumped with excitement. "Can I carry your books for you?"

Kathryn giggled as she hurried away. "Buckie, you don't have to do that."

"But I want to," he said taking my books out of my arms. "I like your hair like that."

I touched my freshly pressed hair, "thank you."

Buckie went on and on about everything he appreciated about my appearance. By lunch I couldn't blush any harder. No boy has ever gone on and on about anything with me before. Buckie is harmless so I know he's not trying to fast-talk me. After school a girl marched up to me. "Stay away from Buckie!" She said real mean. Kathryn put her head down and told me to come on. I asked her who the girl was; she said Stacy has had the biggest crush on Buckie since they were little. I exhaled cause I didn't want to fight over a boy.

Saturday morning we rushed through our chores ate lunch and then we caught the trolley to Playland. Buckie was waiting just like he said he would be. He had the biggest smile as he rode his horse next to mine. A girl waved to him while we were on the ride. When we got off the ride Buckie introduced his sister Katie to everyone, and then lastly me. She told him I was prettier than he said. Emma frowned and looked at Buckie. "You can't be my sister's boyfriend you got four eyes and big ole teeth!"

I gasped while Buckie and his sister laughed hard. "Emma! Hold your tongue!" Emma folded her arms and turned her back to us. Wilma huddled with her as they talked about something. Buckie said it was ok. Then Katie's boyfriend and his brother came over. Katie introduced us to her boyfriend Jeremiah and his brother Hezekiah. We had a good time running around Playland, and then we hung out on the beach. Hezekiah kept looking at me, and trying to get me to smile at him. I wouldn't do it, that would be rude and mean. They caught the trolley with us to make sure we got home safely. Buckie excitedly told me he'd see me at school Monday.

Timothy

"Tim is the man of little words tonight." Natalie said

I looked at her, Jeff started laughing. "Try being more interesting and maybe I'd want to talk more." Natalie served one purpose. The least I could do is let her eat first, but tonight I wasn't feeling up to all of this. I was ready to go home and say forget it all.

"Fine, I'll shut up!" She put her hands up like she surrendered.

Jeff tapped me, "look who it is." He said pointing at Jeremiah and his small group coming into the restaurant.

It was only the four of us in our big booth; Jeremiah and his party could easily squeeze in with us. I stood up and called Jeremiah over. "Join us," I tried not to plead. If I had to talk to this girl any longer I might strangle her. Katie, Hezekiah (Jeremiah's brother), Katie's brother, and two girls slid in.

"Everyone this is my best friend Tim, Tim this is Katie's brother Basil but we call him Buckie. That's Kathryn and her cousin Annette."

Everyone said hello, I looked at Jeff and I could tell he was thinking the same thing I was. "Your teeth!" I couldn't hold it back.

Buckie was a good sport about it though, "that's why they call me Buckie." He smiled.

"Smile for me one more time, do you got big gums too?" I said

"My gums are normal, thanks." Buckie said still laughing.

I looked at the Kathryn girl who was sitting next to Katie, she was cute. Then my eyes swept past her cause I needed a minute to figure out if I really saw what I thought I just saw. I made Buckie keep talking so I would have an excuse to look in her direction. This woman was beautiful and even better; she didn't carry herself like she knew it. "So what's the group dynamics here? Katie this is your little brother?" I asked trying to figure out if this girl was here with someone or what.

"Yep my brother."

"So you brought your brother to chaperone, Jeremiah brought his brother, where do these angels come into the story?"

"I'm here with her," Kathryn said pointing to her cousin.

"I'm here with Buckie." Annette said.

I frowned, "you're robbing the cradle?"

"We're the same age, we'll both be seventeen soon." Buckie said.

I whistled, "little girls didn't look like that when I was in school."

Jeff snapped his fingers, "I know you." He pointed at Annette.

She looked embarrassed, "you know me?"

"YES! When you called her an angel I placed her." Jeff said to me. "She's the one from the hospital. She's the one that made the sandwich for the Mercer's. Remember Franky called her an angel too." Then he looked at Annette, "I was the one who opened the door for you when you came to the room."

Annette looked completely embarrassed, "I'm sorry there were so many white guys around that door, I don't remember you."

Jeff's smile dropped, "I'm not white."

Her eyes moved around the booth, "you're not?"

Jeff put his hand out towards mine. "I tanned yesterday. I'm a toasted almond color." Annette put her hands up to her face to cover her embarrassed laugh.
"Ahem!" Natalie said, "I'm Natalie." She flashed me a look like I was rude for not introducing her.
"So.... what's your name again?"
"Annette."
"Do all white guys look the same to you?"
She looked at her cousin, "I'm sorry. I didn't mean to offend you guys. You seem nice enough. I was just saying that I didn't focus on anyone other than the boy, his mother, and Franky."
"You remember Franky?"
"How could I not? He comes in big and mean like he's going to kill somebody. He makes us let him give us a ride home, and now he keeps popping up out of nowhere and disappearing again." She wouldn't let her eyes focus on me. I needed her to see me and then decide if she liked what she saw. I knew the answer would be yes, but she wouldn't look at me. So I got quiet.
When eight o'clock rolled around Annette up popped out of her seat like it was on fire. She told Kathryn they had to get home. Buckie said he would ride the bus and trolley with them. I volunteered to drive them. Natalie looked at me like she couldn't believe it. Annette said no, and Kathryn frowned at her. I got up cause it wasn't up for negotiation. I started walking towards the door. "No, please…" She forgot my name, she got frustrated. "I'll get in even more trouble if you take us home."
"Why would you get in more trouble?" Katie asked.
"Because I can't keep having strange men bringing me home. My Aunt is going to be upset."
"No, it will be ok. I'll explain everything." Kathryn said.
"Butch will tell my momma," she tried to tell her cousin under her breath.
"Oh, well Mr…" Kathryn said to me.
"Tim."
"Mr. Tim, can you drop us at the corner? That way if we see your brother he can keep driving."
"Good thinking, I like that idea." I said
Annette bucked her eyes at her cousin, "time is wasting. If you don't take the ride you're going to be late." Buckie chimed in. I had forgotten about him.
When Annette agreed in defeat Natalie stood up to come. I had forgotten all about her too. In the car Annette nervously looked around, she still hadn't focused on me. This was different, I was used to girls falling all over their selves acting like Mary Jane, Maureen, shoot even Natalie when they met me. Annette barely took in the fact that I was driving them home. When we got to their corner Annette looked out each window before she agreed to get out. Kathryn smiled at me and thanked me for the ride. I focused on Annette as I told her it was no problem. "Maybe next time we can hang out at my place, have dinner, and play cards."
"Sounds good," Buckie said. I forgot about him again.
Annette was the person I was talking to but all these add-ons were speaking up. As the three of them walked away Annette thanked me and then they walked on.
Natalie stared at me the whole way home. I was on her before we made it in the door good. I couldn't stop thinking about Annette, her shy little embarrassed demeanor was a complete turn on. In my mind I was with Annette tonight, even though I was between Natalie's legs. I hopped up cleaned up and hurried Natalie to

the car so I could take her home. "Over a colored girl? Really Tim?" She said looking at me in disbelief.
I was thinking about Annette when her question brought me back to the moment.
"What?"
"I thought Franky was the only one with a thing for dark meat!" She said as she angrily got out of Sadie slamming the door.
"You just mad cause it ain't you!" I drove away apologizing to Sadie for the slammed door.

Chapter 6

Annette

"Good! I'm glad everyone is here." Aunt Dorothy said as everyone hurried around in their normal morning routines. "I'm going to write to Rose today and tell her that we can send for her in a couple months. I talked to Mr. Lakshman and the apartment will be ready by then. We may have to all bunk here together for a week or two." Emma and Wilma cheered while Butch enthusiastically agreed. My heart started pounding. Momma coming meant I was going to be beaten again, who would be happy about that? I didn't say anything; I finished making Emma and Butch's lunch.

I was quiet all the way to school; Aunt Dorothy's news killed my spirit for the day. Buckie was waiting on the corner for us when we approached the school. "Good morning Annette you look beautiful." He said greeting me with his normal praise.

"Thank you," I said without my normal blush.

"What's wrong?"

I exhaled, "nothing."

Buckie looked at me, but he wasn't convinced. He took my books from me and we walked to our first period class together. Stacy's friend kept looking at me whispering to another girl. Normally I ignore them, but today my spirit was already troubled and I didn't need any help to continue down this wrong path. Just as I was about to say something the teacher told them to stop talking and to focus on their work. I took my books from Buckie and then I took four steps away from him towards my next class. "Didn't I tell you Buckie was mine!" Stacy called out from behind me and then she pushed me. I spun around with my book and hit her in the face. I hit her in the head again with my book, which knocked her into the wall. I kept kicking her up against the wall. I guess she thought I was going to be a push over, although she started this fight she was not prepared for my wrath. Her friend tried to push me and I turned my attention to her. Fear was in her eyes as she turned and ran as fast as she could from me. I tackled her to the ground and started hitting her in the face. It took two teachers to pull me off of her. And even then I was jerking my body trying to get free. I wasn't finished, and beating these stupid girls was making me feel better. They brought me in the office kicking and screaming. I calmed down when I saw the extremely scared looks on Kathryn and Buckie's faces as they came to the office with my things. They were getting ice and towels for Stacy and her friend's faces. They called the negro counselor Ms. Abbey to come talk to us. She was big and mean looking, she told us to go into her office. "Who are you?" She said looking at my face like she was studying it.

"Annette Cooper ma'am."

"She's my cousin Ms. Abbey, she's staying with us until her momma moves out here in a couple months." Kathryn said

Immediately my anger came back, but I didn't move. Ms. Abbey looked at me, "I didn't know anyone in Dorothy's family could be so wild. But then again you all don't go to service so I guess the calming power of the Lord isn't in you." She exhaled, "what was this fight all about?"

"She pushed me, after she's been threatening me for some time."

"She pushed you?" Ms. Abbey squinted her eyes.

"I almost fell, she was trying to knock me down. If I would've fallen she would've done the same thing to me as I did to her." I spit at her.

"Watch your tone little girl, I'm not one of these students." Ms. Abbey warned me. Then she looked at Stacy, "why did you push her?"
"I told her to stay away from my man, Buckie is mine!" Stacy said tearfully.
"They're fighting over you with teeth like that and four eyes?" Ms. Abbey said in surprise.
"NO MA'AM! I AIN'T FIGHTING OVER HIM! I WAS FIGHTING BECAUSE SHE PUSHED ME!"
"And she pushed you over him, so you were fighting over him!" Ms. Abbey snapped.
"No I ain't!" I snapped back.
"Annette!" Kathryn said in surprise that I would sass an adult.
"I'm not going to sit here and argue with a child. What you need to think about is how this little fight could affect your ability to graduate. Last thing we need is for these white folks to come complaining about all the Negros constantly fighting and causing too much trouble here. I don't care who likes Buckie and his big teeth you all need to get it together. He's not the only boy in this school. Find someone else!"
"Tell them to leave me alone and you won't see me in here!" I spit at her. Ms. Abbey got out of her seat, she slapped me hard. Buckie and Kathryn grabbed me to try to hold me back, but I was up out of my seat and in her face. "YOU AIN'T MY MOMMA! YOU WILL NOT PUT YOUR HANDS ON ME! YOU SEE WHAT I DID TO THEM! OLD OR NOT I'LL COME FOR YOU TOO!"
"Oh you think you bad now! You sure you wanna tangle with me? I'll have you expelled from this district and you'll never graduate. You'll be mopping floors, and clearing tables for the rest of your life." She growled at me.
"Keep your hands off of me, I don't want to have to tell you again."
Ms. Abbey looked at the ceiling and counted backwards out loud. Then she sent Buckie and Kathryn back to class. She sent Stacy and her friend home on suspension for the day. She called my Aunt Dorothy to come get me. Aunt Dorothy came in the office with big eyes, "Annette, honey what's going on?"
"This one has got a mouth on her, and her temper is really bad. You need to bring her to service, she needs Jesus!" Ms. Abbey said matter of factly.
My Aunt looked at her, "Jesus ain't stopped your boy from getting that little girl in trouble and leaving her to raise that baby on her own. Abbey don't go there!" Ms. Abbey looked at her real angry. "Annette is very sweet and loving, I haven't had any problems with her this whole time she's been with me." Then she looked at me, "what's wrong baby? What happened?"
The calmness and loving tone of her voice made me bust out into tears. "Stacy pushed me so I beat her. Her friend pushed me too, so I got her too. She slapped me and got mad because it didn't make me scared of her."
"Abbey! Don't ever put your hands on my kin!" My Aunt warned her, "we haven't scrapped in a long time. Do it again and see if I don't come for you." Then she looked at me. "What's wrong baby this isn't like you?"
There goes that loving tone again. I cried my eyes out like she just beat the mess out of me. My Aunt put her arms around me and told me it was going to be ok. I thought about telling her about everything that happened back home, but my momma would get me once she found out. Ms. Abbey said I could come back tomorrow if my attitude was better. I cried all the way home, and then I laid on Emma and I's bed crying and crying. My Aunt brought a cup of tea in for me. She told me she had to go to work, but she wanted to remind me that it was not ok for me to sass adults. She said she needed me to hold my tongue out of respect for her.

She told me to always tell her and she would handle the person. Then she told me she knew I was missing my momma, and just hold on cause she would be here in no time. I didn't say anything, I cried some more. She closed my door and then she left for work. A little while later I heard Rufus and Butch come in the door. They were talking about a woman and how pretty she was. Butch and I hadn't had any problems since we've been out here, but my Aunt has always been around. I don't trust him no further than I can spit on him or any of my no good brothers. I laid there not moving until I knew they were gone. I don't know why they came home in the middle of the day, but as long as they left me alone I was fine. When Emma and Wilma came home I was going to say something when I realized they weren't alone. I heard at least one more voice. I listened as I realized it was a little boy and he was trying to convince Emma to kiss him. I cracked the door and I saw Wilma and another little boy wrapped up in each other's arms kissing and touching. While Emma was about to give in to this little boy. I snatched the door open and the little boy with Wilma took off. I grabbed the little boy with Emma and I started beaten his tail as he ran out the door screaming. I got Aunt Dorothy's belt and I chased Emma and Wilma around that apartment beating their tails. I told them it was not ok to run around here like some loose fast tail girls. They said I could beat them as much as I needed, but they begged me not to tell Aunt Dorothy. I made them promise never to do anything like that again, they promised with complete fear in their eyes. When Jean got home she asked what was wrong. The girls looked at me wide eyed as they told her nothing.

When Kathryn came home she said everyone at school was talking about my fight and how I took on two girls and beat them stupid. The girls sat there with big eyes as Kathryn explained the whole fight to them. The way she told the story it sound like I had super human strength. She said a whole lot of girls started being nice to Buckie because of the fight. I exhaled cause those stupid girls were going to pump his head up and make him too big for his britches and those teeth.

****

I just finished washing dishes and it was time to go out and wipe down the tables again and bring in the dishes that were accumulating out there. Kathryn was sweeping and I was collecting dishes. "Let me help you with that." He said

I looked at him; I was trying to remember his name. "Thank you."

He smiled at me, and started collecting dishes. When I started wiping down the tables he stood next to me. "Do you have plans for this Saturday?"

I frowned, "not sure yet."

"Y'all should come over my place like I said before."

Kathryn was standing over to the side moving her broom in the same spot, watching us with big eyes. "What's your name again?"

"Tim," then he smiled at me again.

"Tim, you should really talk to Buckie." His smile lessened a little. "I don't know why you want us to come over anyways. We don't know you."

"Buckie your boyfriend?"

"Why does it matter to you who Buckie is to me?" I wasn't in the mood for whatever this was. All I could think about is if my momma finds out about this.

"Annette, I want to be your friend." He said watching me.

"I don't need no white guy friends. My momma will beat me." I said honestly. My comment wounded him, and I immediately felt bad for saying it. "Look Tim, I can respect the fact that you got a colored friend, but everybody isn't like you and your

friend. I get enough beatings as it is, my momma would blow her top if she saw me talking to you."
He smiled, "where's your momma? I bet I could change her mind."
"I know you couldn't."
He touched my hand and I jumped, "look Annette. I just wanna be your friend. I'll set everything up with Jeremiah so that you all can come over Saturday. I'll even entrust my beloved Sadie to Jeremiah so he can bring you over. We'll have food and play cards. So that settles it then? Great! See you Saturday." He patted my hand, waved to Kathryn, and then he left.
Kathryn hurried over, "what did he want?"
"He wants us to come over Saturday to play cards." I said feeling confused.
Kathryn cut her eyes at me, "is he sweet on you?"
"Please! He's white; they don't get sweet on us. Maybe he wants me to be his maid or something." I said shrugging it off.
The next day at school Buckie met us at the corner like he always does. He informed us that Jeremiah wanted us to hang out with him at his best friend's apartment. I told him we'd have to bring all the girls cause Aunt Dorothy wanted the apartment to herself this weekend to be with Rufus. He said that was fine and that he and Jeremiah would come to pick us up at one o'clock in the afternoon.

Timothy

Martha came over Friday night and started cooking for me. I thanked her over and over again for doing this for me. Then she told me to sit down at the table with her. I smiled at my big sister thinking she was going to give me words of wisdom or something I could draw from. She put her hand on my hand, and then she gently told me she's met someone. My insides turned into fire immediately. No guy was going to run over my sister, she was precious to me and no one would ever be good enough. Martha said she would appreciate it if I would allow him to come over tomorrow while my friends were over so that I could meet him and give her my honest opinion. I continued to go off for a good thirty minutes while she sat there and patiently let me go off. Then she calmly asked me again. "I don't like it Martha!"
"He's a good guy, you'll see. He comes from a good family, and I really care about him. Please Tim!" Martha pleaded with me like only she could.
"Fine! But I'm going to tell you now, that I don't like him already." I said in defeat. Martha gave me a big hug and kiss, and then we finished cooking. She told me how they met and all the things she liked about him. From the sound of him, he sound like an ok guy. I was waiting to get a good look at him.
The next day Jeremiah came over in the morning. He was excitedly talking about his wedding. "I need to ask you something." He looked embarrassed. "I'm worried about the wedding night." He bowed his head, "I don't know what I'm supposed to do. I'm afraid I might hurt her."
I smiled, "you sure you don't want to ask your old man?"
"All he said was," he cleared his throat to sound like his father. "You're a Barnes! You know what to do." Jeremiah looked at me, "he told me nothing! I don't know what to do."
I got a pencil and paper. I drew stick figures on the paper. "This is you, and that's her." Jeremiah was embarrassed but he wanted to know more than he wanted to hang on to his embarrassment. I explained that he wanted her to be ready and to want it as much as he did, but that was tricky cause as a man we want it all the time.

I told him he had to kiss her good let his hands roam freely everywhere and pay attention to the places that he touched that she gave him a reaction to. I told him the hardest part is conveying your passion without scaring or hurting her. I told him that he wanted it to be good to her, and if he successfully did that then she'd be on him and he'd have to ask for a break more than he would have to talk her into it. He smiled saying he liked the sound of that. Since their wedding was only months away he needed to start building the fire in her now. I told him when he kissed her goodnight to put passion in the kiss, and every once in awhile to surprise her with a grab on her butt, cup her breast, a kiss on her neck. With the stick figures I showed him where to touch her and how. He asked questions like he was preparing for a quiz, I was very proud of my pupil, he was catching on quickly. Since I didn't have a little brother, I imagined this is what it felt like when my brothers had these conversations with me.

I gave Jeremiah the keys to Sadie and then he started laughing. He said that Hezekiah was going to come later; he said that his brother was sweet on Annette and he felt tonight he'd be able to let her in on his crush. My smile dropped. "He likes Annette? Why?"

"What do you mean why? You seen her haven't you? That little girl is beautiful! She's down to earth; I can see why he likes her. I told him that it wasn't ok for him to take her away from Buckie though."

"Jeremiah, sit down." He did, "Hezekiah can try, but I like Annette."

Jeremiah looked at me with big eyes, "but you only met her that one time."

"I know! I can't stop thinking about her. I went by her job and told her personally about today before I mentioned it to you."

"Does she know you like her?" He asked with his mouth hanging open.

"She hasn't even looked at me yet." I said in defeat, "she said something about her momma beating her."

"She's from the south, who knows what she's been through out there with white people. I know for a fact she doesn't think you like her."

I frowned, "how do you know that?"

"Why would she think that you do? You're white, she's colored. She doesn't strike me as the kind of girl who gets lost in fantasies about white men." Then he laughed, suddenly he stopped laughing and he sat up straight. "What about Buckie?"

"What about him?" I said looking Jeremiah in his eyes.

"Tim, that's Katie's brother. If he goes crying to her cause you took his only chance at happiness with a girl that's going to put a strain on our relationship."

"What do you suggest? I'm not worried or concerned about Buckie Beaver! She doesn't even like him like that."

"How can you tell, she accepts his invitations out."

"Pay attention to their interactions. Yea she likes the attention but only to an extent. Watch, she's not overly concerned with what happens with him. She's just being nice, I need her to see me." I smiled, "once she sees me…."

Jeremiah huffed, "what do you want her for? This is a sensitive subject but I guess now is as good as any." He sat up straight and looked me in my eyes. "You need to be sure you want this to happen. I don't say anything when I see you running over the Mary Jane's and Natalie's of the world; but it would make me feel some kind of way watching you roll over a colored girl. We got enough problems, please don't be the white man to add more to the list."

I put my hand on his shoulder, “I understand what you’re saying, but you forget one thing.” Jeremiah looked at me. “We’re brothers, I don’t see color when I look at her. I don’t know what it is about that girl, but I liked her immediately.”
“Probably cause she pretty and she ain’t look at you first.”
“Could be. I didn’t know she was just a girl when I fixed my eyes on her. Maybe she comes over here today and I realize I didn’t see what I thought I saw.”
“Or maybe she comes over here today and you realize you’re in big trouble.”
There was a knock at the door, and Martha happily danced to open it. I could hear her laugh, Jeremiah looked at me and I rolled my eyes. Martha walked in proudly, “Timothy this is Sebastian. Sebastian this is my brother Timothy and his best friend Jeremiah.”
I stuck out my hand, “how you doing I’m Jeremiah.”
“I’m Timothy,” Jeremiah said.
Sebastian looked confused for a minute and then he started laughing. He had the dorkiest laugh ever. “Good one guys. Nice to meet you both.”
Jeremiah smiled at me, “I’ll be back with my fiancé and the gang.”
I told Martha to leave us, and I invited Sebastian to sit. I stared him in the eyes and he stared right back. I hit him with question after question. He had good answers for each one, and he even asked me some good ones in return. I hated to say I liked him so soon, so I told Martha he was ok for now. She threw her arms around my neck and thanked me. When Jeremiah returned with the group, my entire house lit up when Annette walked in the door. Her little sister looked just like her, I decided that if her little sister liked me then she’d put in a good word for me with her sister later. All of the girls were in the kitchen, so I asked Emma and Wilma to play cards with me. Wilma happily accepted my invitation, while Emma kept her eye on me. I asked them if they knew how to play go fish. They said yes, so that was our game for a few rounds. Then Wilma suggested we play "I declare war”. Emma kept looking at me and cutting her eyes at me. “You want something.” She said looking at me.
“Am I that see through?”
“You’re white of course you are!”
That made me laugh, “ok so what do you see?”
“Your guts and stuff.” I laughed harder, “I don’t know, but you want something.”
“You don’t like me because I’m white?”
“My momma’s gonna be mad!” She said shaking her head.
“About what?”
“About this. Not too long before we came she whipped Annette real bad cause the mailman was talking to her.” She said.
“Did she like the mailman?” Wilma asked.
“No, he gave her the mail and momma got her. Momma’s mad cause the white men came and killed my daddy. I wasn’t there, but sometimes Annette looks at his picture and cries. Which is why I don’t understand why we’re here. I thought Annette would hate white people too.”
“Maybe Annette realized that those bad men who did that to your daddy is not all white men.” I said feeling horrible.
“I guess so, we have friends at school who are white. They seem ok.” Emma said.
“What about me, do I seem ok?”
“You want something.” She eyed me.
I smiled, “I do dont I.”
“What?” Wilma said as she and Emma leaned in.

"I want to be your friend so that Annette will be my friend."
"Why you wanna be friends with Annette for?" Wilma asked me looking at me out the side of her eye.
"She seems like a really good friend to have. I don't have a friend like her. Can't we all use new friends?"
"I guess," she looked at her cards. "So you want to be my friend?"
I shook my head, "yes."
Wilma and Emma smiled at each other. "We noticed that you have a television, a radio, and it smells like a cake somewhere in that kitchen." Wilma said sniffing the air.
I laughed, "yes I think there's a chocolate cake in there."
"Can we watch your television, play your radio and your records, AND have as much cake as we want?"
"My records too?" I said still laughing.
"Only if you have something good." Emma said.
"I think I got some Etta James, Jackie Wilson, and Big Joe Turner."
"WOW!" They said together.
When I put the records on, everyone started dancing. Martha pulled Sebastian up and he turned completely red, as he couldn't do any of the steps that Martha was trying to do. Annette stood in the kitchen watching as I danced with her cousin Jean who looked at me with big eyes as we danced. When Jeff came over he brought Franky with him. Instead of dancing they immediately wanted to know who the guy was dancing with Martha. I introduced Sebastian and I told him it was sink or swim time, I couldn't help him. Franky was about to get in Sebastian's face when he saw Annette and froze. He asked me what she was doing here. "I invited her." I said.
Franky looked at me, "you invited her?"
"Yes," I said watching his eyes. Franky exhaled and adjusted in his seat. "How are things?"
"She left last night." He exhaled a tortured sigh.
"What about the baby?"
"They're sending her to a doctor out there." Franky swallowed air. "I gotta go." He stood up.
"What about Sebastian?"
"Let Pops deal with him." Franky said standing up to leave. He walked in the kitchen put money in Annette's hand and then he left.
Annette came out to the table and sat down. "He's your brother?"
"Yep."
"Why doesn't he ever smile?"
"You mean like this?" I said pointing to my smile.
She didn't smile back, "why does he keep giving me money?"
I watched her eyes she was looking at me but she wasn't seeing me. "You want the truth?"
"Now why would I want a lie?"
"He noticed your shoes." She looked embarrassed as she tucked her feet under her chair. "My brothers and I are very observant and we notice a lot of things that other people probably wouldn't notice right away." She started bouncing her leg. "Look, it's not a big deal. You have no idea what your kindness to the Mercer family meant to them and to us."
"All I did was make a couple of sandwiches." She said shaking her head.
"You could've said no, you always have a choice."

"What's so great about the Mercer's?"
"My Pops and Mr. Mercer's father were old friends. They're like family. They went through some pretty traumatic stuff that day."
"I saw the little boy eating the sandwich like he was starving."
"He was, if it weren't for you we would've had to have gone to someone's house and he would've eventually eaten. You saved everyone an extra step when you didn't have to."
"Oh," She said then she smiled.
Buckie came over and asked Annette to dance. She said ok, and then she kept her distance as she politely danced with him. Jeremiah was looking and I pointed to them showing him what I meant. Jeff warmed up to Sebastian. When Hezekiah came Annette avoided him even more than she did Buckie. Hezekiah finally caught on to the fact that Kathryn was open to the idea of him and Annette wasn't. He quickly adjusted to the idea of Kathryn as a consolation prize. I told myself to be patient, Rome wasn't built overnight.

Annette

"Emma remember how I promised to keep your secret?" I said, Emma shook her head yes. "I need you to keep a secret for me."
"Ok," She looked at me with her eyes stretched.
"Please don't tell momma about our new friends. She wouldn't understand, you remember how badly she beat me for taking the letter from the mailman?" Emma shook her head yes. "Imagine what she'd do to me behind this."
"Why does momma come after you like that? I'm going to ask her not to when she comes."
"Emma don't make momma mad at you on account of me. She still loves you and she protects you from our brothers."
Emma's eyes watered up, "why did she let Leslie hurt you?"
My insides screamed, "you know about that?"
"I heard what he said to you when they locked us in the shed. Then I remembered all those times you were running from Leslie. Is that why you won't let Buckie kiss you?"
I hadn't thought of it. "I guess so, but nothing inside of me wants to kiss Buckie. Did you want to kiss that little boy?" Her eyes got big. "You've kissed that little boy before?"
"Yes but, he's my boyfriend and you're supposed to kiss your boyfriend."
"Says who?"
"Wilma, she kisses her boyfriend all the time."
"Emma, don't follow after her. That girl is going to end up in trouble."
"I liked kissing, it felt good."
My eyes stretched, "it did?" I didn't even feel anything good when Luther kissed me. It was just something that happened.
"Yes," she waited for my reaction.
"Don't do it Emma. You're going to end up in trouble. I don't want momma coming after you like she comes after me."

****

My heart was pounding as my momma and brothers approached us. My brothers were all looking around the same way we were when we got to the station. Momma's eyes were fixed on Emma as she stretched her arms out and told her baby to come give her a hug. Emma ran full speed screaming "MOMMA!" the whole

way. Momma hugged her then she hugged Aunt Dorothy. Butch went over for a hug, and I followed behind him feeling like the bald headed stepchild. Butch hugged my momma and I hugged them while they were hugging. When momma saw my aunt looking at her she told me to give her a hug too. I didn't care that she did it cause her sister was watching, I enjoyed the first hug from my momma since I could ever remember. Momma said we all looked fancy. Emma told momma that I've been making her so many fancy dresses. Momma looked at me and smiled, then she said it was her turn. I got excited, my Aunt Dorothy smiled. She told momma her girls were at home making dinner. Preston walked up to me with a small version of my father's face and put his arms up to me. Even though he was almost too big for me to pick up, I picked him up and loved him up. Momma said it was starting to rain pretty heavy back home. She said they made it out just in time. I immediately thought of Harriet, Claudette, Josiah, and Mrs. Broderick. Everybody squished into Aunt Dorothy's car and then she took us to her apartment. Mr. Lakshman was next door talking to the tenants as they prepared to move out. My Aunt introduced my momma, even though he didn't say it, he was looking between my momma and her sister wondering how they were related. My momma stopped smiling, her feelings were hurt. My aunt didn't even notice. My aunt proudly brought my momma inside her two-bedroom apartment. My momma looked around with her nose turned up. My Aunt excitedly called her girls in to meet momma. Momma looked them up and down like she wasn't impressed. All my brothers on the other hand looked hungry. I screamed inside, this was not a good idea. When it was time to eat all the smacking and slurping was driving my Aunt insane. She told all the boys to stop then she told them like she told Butch how they should eat. Momma didn't like it. "Who made this?" My momma asked moving her macaroni and cheese around her plate.
"All the girls stayed behind to cook dinner remember." My aunt said.
"You should've let my girls do it, everything is so bland." She said turning her nose up.
I looked at my aunt with sad eyes; I could tell she was regretting everything in that moment. "Next time you can spend your money and then prepare it any way you want. I happen to think my girls did an excellent job. Especially cooking for such a large family."
Momma smiled cause she knew she upset her sister. "Oh it's fine. I was just saying."
When Booker and Rufus came home my Aunt forgot she was irritated and stood to introduce them. "Rose this is Rufus!"
"How y'all doing, it's nice to finally meet you." Rufus said
"How long y'all been close?" My momma asked
"Oh it's been for some time now. Years ain't that right Dotty?" Rufus said
"Sho has," she said with a smile.
"Why ain't you married?" Momma asked.
"Rose!" Aunt Dorothy said
Rufus frowned, "you ask a lot of questions that ain't none of your business. Where's your husband?" He said looking around at all my momma's kids. "Oh that's right he ain't here no more. Got your kids running scared of white folks instead of standing like human beings. Worry 'bout your own life before you start ruining your sister's."
"You come in here with eyes like white folks, of course you gonna defend them." My momma said.
He bucked his eyes at momma, "even with these eyes I'm purer African than you are. Stop poisoning your kids with your backwards thinking. All white folk ain't

good, but they ain't all bad either. Same goes for coloreds. Honestly, I don't know if you're good; but from what I see of your children I don't think you are."
Momma looked at me, "what did my children do?"
"They run from white folk! Hello! I just told you. And I don't care that y'all came from the south where most white folks is evil. I know there are some good ones out there too. Stop being mean cause you mad at the world."
"You would be mad too if they killed your husband or father right in front of your eyes." Momma said then she started crying real hard.
My aunt hurried out of her seat and hugged my momma telling her it was ok. Rufus said it still wasn't right then he took the plate my aunt made for him and he left.
At nighttime while we were all changing I told my cousins with sad eyes to be careful around my brothers. I told them to always be prepared to defend their selves cause they were sneaky and mean. Emma was blossoming just like I was when Leslie got me. Needless to say I was paranoid. Fortunately it was summer and Aunt Dorothy got all the boys except Preston and Bret jobs. Preston and Bret helped Mr. Lakshman around our building and a few of his other properties.

****

The Head Mistress told Kathryn and I we could go home early because they were over staffed. I was happy cause I wanted to finish momma's fourth dress. Momma loved the first one so much that I was excited to keep making them for her. Franky still appears out of nowhere, gives me money, and disappears again. I've been using that money to buy everything for momma. When momma puts her new dresses on she actually smiles in the mirror, then she wants to go to the market or somewhere. She even walks a little different in the dresses. Like maybe she feels a little fancy too. I'm just happy that she lets me do anything for her and that she likes what I do.
When we walked in the door Wilma, Jean, and Emma were sitting on the couch with their eyes stretched. Just as I was about to ask them what, I heard my momma carrying on like she used to with my father. I was confused, "who's in there?"
"Momma and Mr. Lakshman." Emma said looking to me to respond.
I opened my mouth but nothing came out. I tried to gather my thoughts but I couldn't. I looked at Kathryn for help. "Where are the boys?"
"Cleaning the yard." Jean said.
"Let's go for a walk." Kathryn said.
I put my arms around Emma and Jean. We walked a few blocks over to the park and sat on the swings. Franky's car pulled up and he walked over to us on the playground. "Why aren't you at work?"
"Too many people today, they sent us home."
"Who are you?" Emma asked.
"Franky."
"You know Tim?"
"That's my kid brother."
"Why don't you smile?"
"Cause."
"Cause what?"
"Cause I don't got much to smile about."
"Tim smiles, and he laughs too."
"That's him, I'm different."
"I bet I could make you smile." Emma smiled at him.
Franky exhaled put money in my hand and walked away. At least he didn't tell me to shut up this time. Emma asked me if he was sweet on me, and I told her no, but

he was weird. Kathryn asked me what I did for him to keep giving me money. I told her I guess because I felt sorry for them, he feels sorry for me. Kathryn cut her eyes at me like she didn't believe me. So I asked her when I could've done anything for him, she's with me everywhere I go. She said except for when I kept getting sent home for beating on people. I frowned at her and said Aunt Dorothy picked me up each time and I stayed in the room until they came home. It hurt my feelings that Kathryn would think I would do something like that. I guess if she's looking at my momma right now she might wonder. Jean said my momma and Mr. Lakshman were talking about the rent for next door. She said she went to the bathroom and when she came out her momma's bedroom door was closing then a few minutes before we came the noises started. I wondered why it was ok for my momma to lay with a white man but she beats me for looking at them.

****

"Shut up Rose! My girl's hair is just fine." Aunt Dorothy yelled at momma.

"Ok, ok. I was just saying that your girls can't wear their hair like Emma's cause she got good hair like her daddy. Even Annette's hair is better than there's."

That's how they been fighting these days. Aunt Dorothy's patience was growing thin with momma. Momma was always comparing us, and dividing us.

Momma would pick fights with aunt Dorothy and Rufus all the time. When Rufus would get on momma's case real bad momma would cry and ask Aunt Dorothy how she could let Rufus talk about her family like he does. Rufus keeps telling Aunt Dorothy that she's trying to drive him away just because momma don't got nobody.

When I can I sneak next door and I still slip Aunt Dorothy money. I tell her I love her and I'm so sorry that my momma is causing her so many problems. Every time I do that it's like Aunt Dorothy remembers how things were before my momma came.

I don't know what he did but Aunt Dorothy kicked Raymond out of her house. Then she took me for a ride with her, she was so angry. "You didn't want your momma to come out here did you?" I put my head down cause I didn't want to say anything against my own momma. "How did your daddy die?"

"He was messing with a white man's woman."

"What did your momma have to do with that?" I put my head down again. "Annette tell me."

I started crying, "I can't! You and momma argue too much. You'll accidentally say it, and she'll know it was me. It's me even when it isn't me. Everything is my fault."

"You know why? Cause Elmer loved you best. She didn't like her man loving any girl more than her."

"My father loved Emma, he didn't love me."

"Yes he did Annette! He had a selfish way of showing it, but he did. The girls told me how you warned them about your brothers." She looked at me, I sunk in my seat. She started crying. "YOUR MOMMA IS EVIL!" My Aunt screamed from her heart. "I've made so many excuses for her on account of she's my only sister with the same momma and daddy. When people told her she was ugly I took up for her. When momma put me in school I tried to teach her what I learned. I've always loved my big sister no matter what she did to me. I can't do this no more. She's trying to make you all hate one another. She trying to drive my man away. And I know what she does to get the lower rent." She looked at me, "what she do when she found out about the guy that Butch was having a fit over?"

"She beat me. I begged Emma not to tell her about Buckie's friends, but that won't matter in a minute."

"Why?"
"I think Buckie and Stacy are going to get together soon. I never wanted to be more than Buckie's friend."
"Well, make sure you have fun at the wedding this weekend. You can be friends with whomever you like. Don't let your momma taint your view of people individually."
"Auntie, I'm sorry my momma hurt you."
My Aunt started crying hard. "I'm sorry you gotta have such a momma."

****

"Oh Annette! You look so pretty!" Aunt Dorothy said.
Kathryn and I barely worked this morning. It was the only way to get out of the house without my momma ruining the fact that we were going to Buckie's sister's wedding. I made Kathryn and I's dresses special for today. Katie said she was having her dream wedding. I bought the prettiest accessories and everything. I left everything at Aunt Dorothy's and she brought it all to us so we could get ready here at the hospital. "Thank you," I said cause I did feel pretty.
When Kathryn came out in her dress, my aunt and I clapped for her. She looked really pretty as well. "You two mind your manners, Annette keep that temper in check."
I smiled, "yes Ma'am."
She gave us a ride to the fancy part of San Francisco to this big and beautiful house. Aunt Dorothy said she's never been to The Seacliff area before either. All the houses around here were big and fancy too. Each house looked like it was stretching to look at the water. We definitely weren't in our Hunter's Point neighborhood. It didn't even seem like we were in San Francisco anymore. Hezekiah and Buckie were waiting out front for us. They hurried to the car and then they pleaded with my Aunt to stay as long as she could. Hezekiah said his parents wanted to meet Kathryn's parents since they were getting so serious so fast. Aunt Dorothy fortunately always looks nice. She put on some lipstick then she patted her hair. There were beautiful decorations everywhere and ceremony chairs set out in the yard. There were a lot of people here. I could tell which side was Jeremiah's kin cause Franky's family was over there too. There was a small debate over where we were supposed to sit. Hezekiah said Kathryn was his guest so we should sit on their side. Katie said we were her guests so we needed to sit on her side. In the end the bride put her foot down and the groom made it so. We took our seats then Franky came over. "Hello I'm Franklin." He said almost smiling.
"I'm Kathryn's momma. I'm Dorothy."
"I would've thought you were her sister." Kathryn and I looked at each other, Franky has teeth.
"Oh go on!" Aunt Dorothy blushed.
"Your daughter and niece are real good friends of the family. They're always nice and sweet."
"Thank you Franky." We said in unison.
"Well I hope you enjoy yourself. Ms. Dorothy please save me a dance." Franky said as he walked away.
"Oh these are real good white folk you got here." Aunt Dorothy said still smiling.
"Momma Franky's never that nice to us. He tells us to shut up all the time." Kathryn said.
Aunt Dorothy smiled, "that's good too. Y'all probably need to shut up." Then she laughed, we smiled.

When it was time for the ceremony to start Jeremiah and his best man Tim took their places in the front next to the man performing the ceremony. Tim tapped Jeremiah and nodded in our direction. Jeremiah smiled then he turned his attention to the procession. The cutest little girls came down the aisle dropping flower petals. Then the bridesmaids and their escorts. When the maid of honor made it to the top of the aisle. She stepped too eagerly and her foot got caught in her dress and she fell over ***timber*** like a big ole tree on top of the guest sitting next to the aisle. Tim and Jeremiah looked like they were suffering cause they were trying not to laugh. Tim's brother Jeff ran out the yard cause he couldn't keep it together. Once they established that she was ok, she slowly limped down the aisle. I looked away cause it was hard not to laugh too. Katie was a beautiful bride and Jeremiah looked so proud to take his wife. After the wedding I heard Katie telling someone she begged her maid of honor not to wear her glasses, she couldn't see and that's why she fell. Hezekiah's parents came over praising Aunt Dorothy for raising such a nice girl. When they left Aunt Dorothy asked Kathryn if things were more serious than she understood between Kathryn and Hezekiah cause his parents did make it seem like their wedding was next.

"Hello, your girls are breath taking. I had to make my way over to say hello." The white lady said.

"Thank you, this is my daughter Kathryn and my niece Annette."

"Oh so you're Annette." She smiled at me. "I've heard so many wonderful things about you."

I pointed to my chest in shock, "you've heard about me?"

"Yes, you're the angel that helped the Mercer family. And the angel that saved poor Sebastian from my oldest child Franky. If it weren't for you Martha wouldn't be engaged right now. Her brothers are very protective of her."

"You're Mrs. Wallace?" Kathryn asked

"Oh yes, where are my manners. I'm Irma and all those hoodlums belong to me."

"Irma I've heard what the girls have said. How do you keep those boys in line?" Aunt Dorothy asked.

Mrs. Wallace pointed to a man, "My King rules with an iron fist!"

I liked how she called him her King. Mrs. Wallace and Aunt Dorothy hit it off right away. You would've sworn they were old friends. Her daughter Martha came over and gave me the biggest hug and she kissed my cheek. She showed us her engagement ring, she was so excited. Her fiancée Sebastian sat over to the side with her brothers that we hadn't met yet. Martha introduced us to Matthew and Dale. Matthew introduced me to his wife and son; he was the cutest little muffy cheeky baby. His wife kind of stared and barely said hello. I didn't know why she was looking at me like that but I shrugged it off. When the music started The bride and groom had their first dance and then everyone eventually joined in. I danced with Buckie to a couple of songs then his momma asked him to come help move the chairs to make the dance space bigger. Tim came over and asked me if he could cut in. I said yes even though I was wondering how Buckie would feel about me dancing with his brother-in-law's friend. Tim looked at me and told me I looked beautiful. I smiled and said thank you, he's always looking in my eyes, and I always look away. Its like he's trying to hypnotize me with those hazel things. I don't know why he does that so I kind of keep my distance. When the song was over the bride and groom cut the cake. Buckie asked me to get him a piece of cake. I looked at him like I didn't understand what was wrong with his hands and feet, but I told myself to be a good sport since I saw Kathryn bringing Hezekiah a piece without him asking. It was like everything Hezekiah did Buckie had to do it too. Tim brought me punch, and it was right when I was feeling thirsty. I thanked him and then I drank it. When the night coolness rolled in, Tim took off his jacket and put it on me while everybody was talking. Buckie didn't notice until Hezekiah followed Tim's lead and put his jacket on Kathryn. Buckie asked who's jacket and Tim told him he gave me his, then he went back to what he was saying. Buckie was helping cleanup as we saw the bride and groom drive off in a new car, a wedding present from Mr. Wallace. I was looking up at the house thinking about how amazing it must be to live in a house like this. Tim asked me if I wanted a tour of the house. I said yes and then I looked for Kathryn, she was already walking back into the yard with the rest of the group. Tim looked at me and smiled he told me he doesn't bite. I took a deep breath and said ok. When he touched my hand electricity shot up my arm and I quickly took my hand back. I told him I needed to put his jacket on. Then I followed him up the stairs as I put my arms in the sleeves. When we walked in the door the first thing I noticed was the rocking chair, it looked really nice. He said it was his momma's chair. He walked over to the mini bar and reached for the brandy. He asked me if I wanted a glass. I hadn't had a drink since the last time I went to Hazel's back home. My mouth watered a little. I asked him if his parents would be mad if he gave me a glass. He smiled and said of course not, as he poured a glass for me. He asked me if I wanted ice and I said no. He took a swallow of his drink and then he waited for me to do the same. It was smooth and velvety better than any moonshine I tasted back home. I smiled as I shyly asked him to pour me a little more. I wanted to savor my drink while we walked around this house. The house was big; it had four bedrooms, a television room, a sitting room, and a big office for his father. Each room was huge, I laughed when he exhaled and said his old room betrayed him. It was all pretty and girly in that room. He said it used to be a man's room. We were looking at the view of the water off the kitchen window when Mrs. Wallace came in. She smiled at us real big then she asked me what I was drinking. I got nervous and told her that Tim said it was ok for me to have some Brandy. She said she didn't know I liked to drink. She said next time I came over she'd make us some mixed drinks with a kick. I smiled because she wanted me to come back. Then Tim said he wanted to show me the garage and basement. Mrs. Wallace said if we weren't back in five minutes she was coming to look for us. Tim exhaled like he didn't like the comment, but he wasn't crazy enough to actually say anything. I hesitated before I went down the stairs to the garage, I didn't want to have to hit this fool if he got fresh with me. He was a gentleman and I appreciated that. When we went back out in the yard, Buckie asked where I went. I told him I saw the house. He was irritated and he asked me if I was sweet on Tim. I looked at him like he was ridiculous for asking me such a crazy question. Maureen stood over to the side openly watching our conversation. I rolled my eyes at both of them and I told him he needed to get a grip.

Timothy

"MY NAME IS MARY JANE! GET OFF OF ME!" She yelled.

"What?" I said moving off of her like she asked.

"MY NAME IS MARY JANE, WHO IS ANNETTE?" She yelled.

I started laughing, "did I call you Annette?"

She pulled the covers up to her neck. "Yes," she said like she was going to cry.

"Sorry?" I laughed some more.

"Why are you laughing Tim? This isn't funny!"

"The whole situation is funny to me. Guess I was lost in the moment."
She sat up still holding the covers around her chest. "I have never felt so cheap in all of my life! How dare you do this to me!"
I frowned, "did you think I was in love with you?"
She looked at me and cried harder. "All these years Tim. Really?"
"You are not going to make me feel bad about this. You were fine with being second when I was with Maureen. What if I would've married her?"
"You mean instead of your brother?"
I laughed to try to calm myself. "Don't push me!"
"Or else what? You gonna hit me? You might as well."
"Worse! I won't let you have anymore of this sweet loving."
She didn't expect me to say that, she tried to hold back her smile. "Tim! I'm serious!"
"I am too! You'll be looking high and low for me trying to get my loving. I'll hide, you won't find me. You'll be walking up and down the street calling out for me everywhere asking where did I go. *Tim's Sweet Loving! Tim's Sweet Loving! Where are you? Where did you go?*"
She giggled, "so I guess you don't want to marry me?"
"I'm not the marrying kind. This is my life, bachelor pad. Work, and my family."
"I want a husband."
"Well then I suggest you go find one."
"What about you?"
I looked around the room, "I just said I'm not the marrying kind."
She exhaled, "so who's Annette?"
"She's not anyone yet."
"Another one in your harem?"
I shrugged, "you want me to take you home?"
"Why can't I spend the night?"
"No one spends the night with me. Do you want to finish or I can take you home."
"The mood is gone, take me home."
"Ok," I pretended not to see that she was hurt because I didn't beg her to stay.

****

"Tim, I need to ask you something man to man." Buckie said baring his big ole teeth. "Why do I keep seeing you every where Annette is? At the wedding you gave your jacket, you brought her punch, you showed her around your parent's house."
I exhaled and spun around in my seat. "You came down to my place of business to ask me about a girl?" Then I stood up.
Buckie swallowed, "yes."
"What difference does the answer make to you? I know you seeing that Stacy girl on the side. Why don't you let Annette go?"
"Annette is my girlfriend, and I think you're trying to take her."
"Annette doesn't want you."
"Oh and you think she would want you?" Buckie laughed sarcastically. "Her momma would skin her alive if she even thought about you."
I remembered her saying something like that. "Lookie here big teeth, when you become a man you will learn that this tactic doesn't work. First of all you don't come to a man's place of employment accusing him of trying to take your woman. The only way she could be taken is if you don't have her. Second, if you felt disrespected in some kind of way, I'd expect you to make your point. All this talking and accusations stuff will just make me mad, and you don't want to meet my

temper." I saw the fear in his eyes, "besides. You about to get with that Stacy girl who's got it so bad for you that she gets suspended for fighting over you. Why are you trying to hold on to Annette? She don't want you like you hoping for."
"Annette is a cold fish!" He said in frustration.
"Aw! There! There!" I stood up. "You's a little boy, she's supposed to be cold to you." I patted his shoulder. Then I moved him towards the door. "Hear me when I say this to you. Come down to my office.... No! If you ever come to me with this nonsense again, I'm gonna have to hurt you. I don't like being interrupted at work with foolishness. Got it?" I opened my door and pushed Buckie and his teeth out of my door. I needed to plan for fuel, trailer pick-ups, shipments, things like that. I didn't have time to be worried about this little boy's insecurity.
After work Jeremiah thanked me for not hurting his brother-in-law who was too stupid. I asked Jeremiah if he honestly thought Annette would go for me. Jeremiah shook his head and honestly said no. He said her family was against white people and it would take a lot for her to ever look at me as anything other than a friend. And I would have to work really hard just to become her friend.

****

"I don't want some big monstrous sized building. No more than six units each. I want houses as well. Find me a neighborhood that's selling pretty well. I want to eventually own a block of houses." I told the realtor.
"Ok, so here's a question for all of you. Are you set on owning only in the city?" He asked.
"I own a lot of property out here. First find a house for my daughter. Then I'll focus on branching out." Pops said.
"I'm open to where-ever, your office will manage the property for me anyways." Franky said.
"I agree," Jeff said.
"I second that," Matt said.
"Third!" Dale said, "However I want to buy open lots, residential and commercially zoned as well as residential properties."
"Lots?" The realtor asked.
"I'm going to be an architect. I'm going to need land to build on."
"You know," Pops sat up. "You could buy condemned buildings and houses with the intention to tear them down. You may get the lot a lot cheaper that way." Pops looked at the realtor, "add condemned properties to my list."
"Timothy would you like to focus on San Francisco only?" The realtor asked.
"Initially yes. Eventually I'll move out of here."
The realtor looked at my momma and Martha. "And you want at least a three bedroom home?"
"Yes sir, a nice sized backyard. Not too far from my parents." Martha blushed, "my husband and I want to start our family right away."
"You're trying to get him killed!" Franky said, while the rest of us frowned at her.
"Oh hush up, your sister's getting married. She's going to have babies and I know each one of you know how babies are made. Get over it, it's happening!" Momma said
Franky looked at me, "this is all your fault!"
"Fine! I'll take the fall for Martha's happiness." I said putting my hands up.
All of my brothers looked at me, "and if he hurts her?"
I looked at Martha, "I'll take care of him personally."

"None of that will be necessary. Sebastian is a good guy." Martha said, my momma patted her hands.

Chapter 7

Annette

"Annette we need to talk." Buckie said like he was choosing his words.
"What do you want? I'm working."
"I don't think we're going to workout."
I frowned at him, "why did you think we were a couple?"
Buckie's eyes got big. "You didn't know you were my woman?"
"I don't know what would make you think I was. You never asked me to be your girlfriend. Cause if you had I would've told you no. I thought we were friends."
"Is that why you wouldn't let me kiss you?"
"I'm not kissing on some big tooth boy just for the fun of it!"
Buckie looked mad, "well Stacy wants to give things a go. So I'm breaking up with you to be with her."
"Again, you ain't never asked me to be my boyfriend so I don't care." I said walking away.
"Besides, now that I'm out of the way you can decide which Wallace boy you wanna lay up under."
I stopped walking and turned around, "what are you talking about?"
"It's clear as day that you sweet on at least one of them. Maybe you gonna do like that girl at the wedding and play with both of them until one marries you. I'm not trying to end up dead so I'm thru with you."
"What are you talking about? I could never date a white man!"
"That's what you saying right now, but I know you will. They gonna chew you up and spit you out like everyone else. Watch!"

****

Leslie hurried in the door not looking at anyone. He went in momma's room and shut the door, like he was going to take a nap.
"Why you always go next door to take a shower?" Momma asked.
"I like the soap Aunt Dorothy uses." I couldn't say that I didn't trust my brothers not to mess with me or come for me while I was vulnerable.
"So buy some of that soap and bring it here. You always running over to my sister's house you gonna wear out your welcome."
Then someone knocked at the door loud and hard. It was a white police officer, "does Leslie Cooper live here?"
"Who wants to know?" My momma said real mean.
"The San Francisco Police department that's who."
"What for?" She said looking meaner by the minute.
"For the rape of Leigh Ann Betts."
"Rape? Rape? My son didn't rape nobody!" My momma yelled.
I covered my mouth, I sat on the couch. I knew it was true, and I knew my momma knew it was true too. That's why she was getting so mad. "Step to the side ma'am, we need to search your home." The officer said.
My momma tried to close the door on him while she yelled to Leslie to run and told me to come help her.
I was torn cause I wanted to let the officer in cause I knew it in my heart that it was true. I ran to the door but my heart wasn't in to helping her. The officer pushed the door open and he hit my momma hard with his club. I backed away with my hands up. The officer came in swinging. Then I heard Leslie screaming from outside. I

saw clubs going up in the air and Leslie's screams. The officer inside was mad cause momma closed the door on him so he started hitting my momma with his stick. I screamed and begged him to stop. Momma wasn't screaming anymore or moving. The officer looked around the room at my little brothers and then me. He got up to come get me and I ran, I ran out the door down the hallway and onto the street. The officer was on my heels as I got to my corner. I was screaming for my life. Rufus and Butch called out to the officer as he hit me in the arm and knocked me on the ground. Rufus jumped in front of me and put his hands up to plead for me. "What did she do?" Rufus yelled.
"She.... Was.... Interfering!" He said trying to catch his breath.
"No sir! Not this girl!" Rufus pleaded, "she's a good girl and does as she's told." Rufus pleaded while Butch walked towards the apartment. People were coming out of their houses onto the street to see what was going on.
The officer looked at everyone who was coming out. "Tell her to stay out of police business." Then he hurried back to the apartment.
Rufus touched my arm and I screamed in pain. He said it looked broken. He told me to come so he could take me to the hospital. He asked me what happened. I told him as he helped me up, and then down the street. He said I can't listen to my momma. He said she could've gotten me killed. When we got to the building they drug Leslie's bloody body out and threw him in the police car. Aunt Dorothy was trying to ask questions, but the officers wouldn't answer her. Aunt Dorothy asked Rufus to help her bring my momma out she needed to go to the hospital. Momma's mouth was bloody and her eyes kept rolling around. Aunt Dorothy rode in the back with momma holding her sister and crying. When we got to the hospital they took momma in right away. They had me sitting and waiting, Rufus stayed with me while my Aunt went with her sister. Rufus let me cry as I kept thinking about his words. My momma was gonna get me killed, and I doubted that she would care. The doctor came in and looked at my arm. He confirmed it was broken and then he said they had to set it. I thought I was going to pass out from the pain. He said I was going to need to wear my cast for six weeks. As I stood up Tim and Franky snatched the curtain. Franky always looks mean and mad, but it was scary to see the same look on Tim. "What happened to you?" Tim asked angrily.
"A police officer broke it." I said through my tears cause my arm was still hurting.
"Which one!" Tim barked.
"Why?" Franky asked.
"I didn't get his name." Then I put my head down. "They came for Leslie. My momma tried to stop them, she asked me to help her. He knocked my mom out then he chased me. My uncle saved me." I said.
"So you saw him? Could you point him out?" Tim said to Rufus.
"Yes," Rufus said looking confused.
"How's your momma, and your brother?" Franky asked.
"Leslie wasn't moving, my Aunt is with my momma. But you can't go see her!" I pleaded.
"Why not?" Franky asked.
"She don't know y'all my friends. She'll get me." I pleaded.
"I'm your Aunt's friend too."
"Annette are you ok?" Tim looked in my eyes with concern for me.
"Yes I'm just worried about my momma." I said.
"Can you go with us sir?" Tim said.
"Where am I going?" Rufus asked.

"You're gonna point the one out who did this." Tim said with fire in his eyes.
"Come on, we'll take you to your momma." Franky said as he gently helped me off the bed.
Rufus took us up to the next floor and in room 228. My momma's head was all wrapped up. Aunt Dorothy tried to smile when she saw us. Franky and Tim gave her hugs. My momma looked at them then she looked at me. Franky explained that they were going to find who did this to us. They were almost out of the room when Rufus said my friends were pretty standup guys. Everyone looked at him like he was an idiot. My momma looked at me and repeated that they were my friends. I knew as soon as she could she was going to beat me.

Timothy

Jeremiah came to work with a sad face. I told my best friend to go in my office as I addressed everyone on the floor. I gave the driver's their schedules for the day, and then I gave the foreman's on the floor their instructions. I looked up at my office and I saw my best friend looking sad. I took a deep breath then I went up to the office and shut the door. I poured him a glass of brandy, and he declined it saying it wasn't noon yet. I told him it was twelve o'clock somewhere and to take the drink. He gulped it in one drink then he kept looking down. I told him to stop stressing about it, it just wasn't time yet. Katie was upset because she wasn't pregnant. Every beginning of the month it was the same thing. "I don't know what to do, maybe I'm doing it wrong?" He looked at me in hopes of an answer.
"I doubt that, it's just not time yet. You guys should just relax and let nature take its course. Its gonna happen."
"I hope you're right. Her mother keeps asking her where her grand babies are."
"You let her get away with that?"
He put his hands out, "it's Katie's momma. When I say something Katie gets all upset. Her father and I have had lots of words behind the things his wife says to my wife. Maybe, I'm stressing her out."
"You're trying to find some reason this is your fault. Maybe it's nobody's fault, maybe you're just not ready yet. Be patient, watch pretty soon you're gonna have more kids than Mrs. Wallace." I smiled.
He started laughing, "I don't want that many kids. You guys got a whole tribe." He laughed, and then he sat up. "Katie said that Buckie broke up with Annette. He says she was heartbroken and pleaded with him not to leave her." He gave me a look.
"Which means she probably broke up with him and he's trying to save face." I laughed.
"Right, but I don't think you should go after her. At least right now."
"I'm not insensitive. I'll wait the proper day of mourning before I go after her." I laughed again.
Then the foreman knocked on my door, I told him to come in. "Mr. Wallace this is our new hire Avery Glickman."
"Hello, this will be the only time you interact with me. You report to your foreman, who reports to Mr. Barnes here." I pointed at Jeremiah, "he'll tell me everything I need to know." Then I waved at my foreman to shut the door.
Franky came in the door just before it closed with an about business look on his face. I asked Jeremiah to excuse us. Franky said Annette was in the Emergency room, but he didn't know what for. I stood up immediately, he tossed me the keys to his car, and we rode in silence to the hospital. The orderly who called Franky approached us. He told him that Annette had a broken arm and that there was a man

with her. Annette looked so small sitting on that bed. We took her to her momma and then we rode to the police station. Her uncle Rufus was in the back seat looking nervous. Franky told the clerk he needed to speak to the Chief. When the clerk came back he asked us to follow him as he showed us to the Chief Phillips's office.
"We have a problem!" Franky said as he walked in the room.
I told Rufus to have a seat; Phillips stared at him for a minute. "We sure do, you can't walk into my office with him!"
"This is Mr. Rufus," Franky said. "His niece and sister in-law were attacked today by one of your men. I WANT HIM!" Franky said.
"You can't take the word of some colored guy!" Phillips said.
Franky looked at me. "How about this!" I said touching his family portrait. "I'll go to your house right now, break your daughter's arm and then you tell me how you feel about it! I want him NOW!" I growled.
"Where did this take place?"
"Hunter's Point," Franky said.
"The Leslie Cooper case?" Phillips bucked his eyes.
"That's my nephew." Rufus said.
Phillips put his hands up. "That fella raped a young lady in her own house. She gave us an accurate description of him and where to find him. He resisted arrest."
I looked at Rufus, he looked embarrassed. I could tell he didn't know what the charges were. "I'm waiting for the part that explains why his mother and sister were beaten." I said.
Phillips opened his door and called four of his officers to his office. They looked like they were having a good laugh about something as they walked in. Rufus stood up, "that's him! That's the one!" He said pointing at the third one to enter the door. The officer frowned at Rufus. Phillips asked them to tell him what happened when they accosted Mr. Cooper today. The first officer said O'Brien went to the door, while he and his partner went around the back in case Mr. Cooper tried to run away. The officer said Mr. Cooper climbed out of the window and tried to run. They said he was fighting them until they put him down. Franky asked what they meant by down. The officer speaking said that they had to make sure he didn't run away.
"I'm waiting for the part where you explain his mother and sister." I said.
"The woman was hostile and defending her son. She tried to protect him; I forced my way into the apartment. When I saw my partners had her son, I roughed her up a bit to teach her some respect." O'Brien said nonchalantly.
"You gave her a concussion!" I said, O'Brien shrugged. I smiled to chew back my anger. "What about the girl?"
"She was in the wrong place at the wrong time. She was a fast little critter though." O'Brien chuckled.
I felt something pop inside of me. I smiled, "she was a fast little critter huh?" I moved closer.
"Hold on Tim!" Franky said with the same evil look on his face. "So you positively apprehended the right guy?"
"Yes, the victim positively identified him." Phillips said.
"Does this sound right to you?" Franky asked Rufus asking about the character of his nephew. Rufus put his eyes to the floor. "Fine!" Franky said angrily. "You killed him?" He asked the first officer.
"He was breathing last I checked."
"Go check him again!" Franky growled.

The officer left and when he came back he said they needed to call the hospital cause Mr. Cooper was having difficulty breathing. “Franky, my boys were doing their job. He was a criminal and the streets will be safer with him gone.”
Franky looked at me to say it was my call. “Try to save him!”
“What?” The officer said.
“That’s Annette’s brother try to save him!” Then I looked at O’Brien and smiled again. “I wanna talk to my friend! The rest of you have work to do.” The officers looked at their Chief and he told them to do as they were told. Then I looked at him and I told him to get out as well. Phillips looked like he wanted to say something but he knew better. He got up in defeat. Rufus adjusted in his chair to look at O’Brien. “So that critter that you referred to.” O’Brien looked confused. I felt his jaw crack as I hit it. “She happens to be very precious to me!” I hit him again and he went down. Rufus’s mouth was hanging open as he moved his feet so that O’Brien wouldn’t fall on them. I beat this sorry excuse for a man all over the office. Franky sat there watching like he was making sure everything was done to his satisfaction. When I tired of beating on him I pulled out my gun. Franky touched my arm. He told me to let him suffer; he was going to die either way. He asked me why would I end his misery early, he had a point.
Chief Phillips started cursing; he was really upset when he saw his friend. I shrugged, “this critter wasn’t fast enough.” I made them wait before they called the hospital.
Then we took Rufus back to the hospital, Rufus remained quiet the entire time. We got to the hospital right after the doctor told Annette’s momma that her son died. Annette didn’t cry, she watched her momma cry. I could tell by the spaced out look on her face her brother’s death didn’t affect her.

****

"So let me understand why you're upset." Pops said leaning back in his chair. "Your boys killed a man, a clearly guilty man so I'll give you that." Pops looked at Chief Phillips and Commissioner Daniels. "Please explain to me how a woman and her daughter ended up in the hospital?"
"The woman was obstructing police business." Daniels spit.
"So you arrest her. You don't put her in the hospital with a concussion. Explain the girl?" They were quiet, "your man told my sons she was in the wrong place at the wrong time! THE WRONG PLACE AT THE WRONG TIME?"
"Your sons killed an officer!" Commissioner Daniels said, "he was a good man with a family."
"Clearly he wasn't good!" Pops looked at me, he put his hands out to tell me to remain calm. "Your man went too far."
Daniels shifted in his chair. "Mr. Wallace, an officer was killed. We cannot have this!"
Pops looked at him long and hard. "So tell me how differently this would've been handled if this family wasn't colored. What if they were just trash?"
"That kid's death was an accident!" Phillips said.
"And so was O'Brien's," I put my hands out. "I didn't mean to kill him."
"I saw how you hit him." Phillips said.
"I didn't know my own strength, so sue me!" I said smiling.
"This is not funny son! There's nothing to smile about!" Daniels barked.
Pops narrowed his eyes at Daniels. "You dare to take this tone with my son?"
"Mr. Wallace I think we're all emotional about this whole situation." Phillips said.

"Right, but what I don't understand is why you're here." Franky said, "it's over and it's done. But yet, here you are. All the talking in the world is not going to bring your man back."
"You can't kill cops!" Daniels said.
"Tell your men to keep their hands off what's mine and we won't have any more problems!" I said looking Daniels in his eyes.
"The Cooper family is yours?" Phillips asked.
"The women are, and the Hill family that lives next door. OFF limits!" I said.

Annette

I could hear Rufus going off through the wall. He snatched their door open and then opened our door. I was still on the floor, Emma was crying and rubbing my head. This is the second time momma has beaten me. Every time she thinks about Leslie or my father she starts crying then she says I keep bringing white people to kill her men. Emma begs her not to get me, but even Emma can't save me. I try to take it but I'm getting tired of getting hit on.
Rufus looked at me then he got in my momma's face. He said Leslie was her fault; she shouldn't have aggravated the situation like she did. Momma told him to mind his own business. She said I needed to learn how to stay out of trouble. Rufus and my momma argued for a long time. Preston brought me some tea to help me calm down.
I laid there wondering how she fixed everything in her head to blame me for Leslie. I was a victim of Leslie, if anything it was her fault. He never learned that he couldn't mess over females without consequences bigger than a broken finger. Knowing what he did to me how could she doubt his guilt?
I got off the floor and sat on the couch my back hurt, and I just got that cast off. Rufus was still arguing with momma trying to defend me saying that I was a good girl and she needed to leave me alone. I thanked him for trying with my eyes, but I knew this wouldn't stop until I moved out.

Timothy

"Hello pretty lady," I said smiling at Annette.
She shook her head, "no! Please go away!" She said with tears coming to her eyes immediately.
"What's wrong?"
"Every time my momma thinks about you I get beat again."
I saw the bruises on her arms and neck. It looked like she had been in a fight. "Your momma did all this?"
She started crying, "Please Tim! I can't be your friend anymore." She said continuing to wipe down the tables.
I felt like I had been shot, her momma don't like me just cause I'm… White, she knows nothing about me as a person. She has no idea of what I've done for her daughter or all that I would do for her. "I don't want to cause you anymore problems." I exhaled, "you've been through enough." She shook her head in agreement with me. "How will I get your graduation present to you?"
"Present?"
"I have to get you something for your graduation."
"Please don't Tim, my momma!"
"What if she doesn't know it's from me? You know what, don't worry about it. I'll take care of it."

"Un huh, please go Tim. Her heart is broken about my brother. It don't take much for her to get after me. I can't be your friend." Then she hurried away.

Annette

Kathryn, Raymond, Jean and I were approaching the house. My momma was talking to a lady on the stoop and she was smiling real big. "Y'all say hi to Mrs. Henson. She just moved out here from Oklahoma."
We all said hello as my momma introduced us. "Rose, this is your daughter?" She said with her eyes stretched real big like she couldn't believe it.
"Yep, but if you think she's something you should see my youngest daughter. She's really really pretty."
"Oh Rose I'm speechless over this one. She should meet my boy Rudy." Then she laughed, "they could marry and then we'd be kin."
My momma smiled, "Rudy the one with the real good job?"
"Yep, his job so good he could take care of all of us and all the babies they would have." She raised her eyebrows at my momma. Then she looked at me again. "Who you lay with to get her hair like that?" Then she laughed.
"Gurl! I found me an Indian man straight off the reservation. All my kids got the same daddy." She said proudly.
"That's why she's so red." She said staring at my face. "I see it now. She got those cheekbones, kind of flat face. I bet if you dress her up like an Indian she'd look just like them." They laughed; I didn't see what was so funny. "You got you a bunch of mixed babies. Good for you! I need some of that in my grand babies."
"When you want him to meet her? If he want her he can have her." My momma said like I wasn't there.
Kathryn grabbed my hand cause tears started pouring out of my eyes. I'm not a puppy that you just give away.
"Let me check with Rudy, probably this Sunday. Can she cook?"
"Yes, Emma's a better cook though."
"Have her make us dinner, make..." She stopped cause she noticed my tears. "Why you crying honey?"
"You don't even know him and you're planning to give me away!" I said to my momma.
"What's wrong with you? You don't want to help the family?" Momma said not seeing the point in my tears.
"He could be mean, you don't care."
"Oh hush up my son is not mean. You'll see, I raised him right." Mrs. Henson said
"Go inside and fix your face before I give you something to cry about!" Momma said through clinched teeth.
Kathryn rubbed my back and told me it was going to be ok and to be brave. I told her she said that cause she was going to marry Hezekiah whom she chose and I was going to let my momma auction me off to the highest bidder.
Momma woke me up early Sunday morning. She made me clean everything and then she told me what to make. She told me if I didn't do a good job she was going to beat me. When dinner was ready she told me to shower and put on my dress that she laid out for me. She made sure my dress was pressed and clean. She sent everyone else next door and she told me to stand next to the couch so I didn't get wrinkled. I was tired; I had a long day already. When they knocked on the door my heart started pounding. I felt like it was auction time and he was coming to get a good look at me. Mr. & Mrs. Henson walked in the door first. They were all smiles

then I heard their son. "Mrs. Cooper I hope you like whiskey." He said handing her a bottle.
"Yes I do. Thank you!" Then momma closed the door.
Rudy looked stuck when he looked at me, and I felt kind of stuck too. I expected Rudy to be ugly. Just because of the way this was happening. He hurried over to me, "it's nice to meet you. I'm Rudy." He said grabbing my hand.
"Annette," I said looking at his eyes.
The parents stood there smiling at us. Momma told us to come sit at the table. Rudy helped me bring all the food, and then he opened the whiskey and poured some for each of us. I looked at my momma when he poured some for me. She was fine with it. I pretended like this was my first drink. I was surprised that I was enjoying our dinner. Rudy raved over my food. He asked what my plans were after graduation. I told him I was going to look for work. He told my momma I should go to school. He said educated Negroes produce more educated Negroes. He told her the only way we were going to get ahead was by educating our children and ourselves. That settled it I was now going to college. Rudy kept staring at me smiling. Then he told everyone he thought his momma was exaggerating about my looks, he was happy that she underestimated me. I blushed really hard. Rudy was cute and well spoken, nothing like anyone I would imagine my momma picking for me. I was pleasantly surprised.

****

"You are so beautiful!" Rudy said staring at my face like he was lost.
"Thank you," I said blushing.
"I wanna marry you."
"You do?"
"Yes! You're beautiful, you're still pure, and you can cook and clean. You're almost perfect." I tried to keep my face even; thanks to my brother I wasn't pure. "The only thing is that I need you to get your education. I can't have no dumb wife."
"Are you saying I'm dumb now?"
"No, but you can stand to know more. We all can. I'll help you with your homework. I have a plan for us. You wanna hear it?"
"Of course."
Rudy sat on the couch excitedly gesturing with his hands. "Oh wait," he touched my hand. "Annette will you be my girlfriend?" My heart was pounding as I said yes. He smiled then he leaned over and kissed my lips. "Since we're boyfriend and girlfriend now." He smiled at me, "we'll get engaged before you graduate from college. I'm not telling you when though." He smiled. "We can marry after. I can't wait to get in to you."
"In me?" I didn't like the sound of that.
"Making love to a beautiful woman is going to be wonderful!"
I calmed a little, "making love? A man hasn't ever touched me in love."
"Your daddy never hugged you?"
"When I was little, one day he stopped."
He scooted closer to me. Then he gently touched my cheek. "This is what a touch from love feels like." He smiled.
"You love me?" I looked at him with big eyes.
He blushed, "I guess I jumped ahead of schedule huh."
I felt this before. I thought about Luther, he touched me like this. I hadn't thought about my friends back home in a minute. I wondered where Luther was and how everyone was doing.

Momma peeked out the kitchen at us and she smiled. If we were at the Henson place his parents wouldn't let him sit this close to me. Guess that's why lately he comes over here more.

****

I was surprised my momma said yes when Rudy asked to take me out. She suggested that we double with Kathryn and Hezekiah. Rudy wasn't happy about the chaperones but he played along. Rudy had dinner with my family, and then the four of us silently rode to the soda shop. Kathryn introduced Hezekiah and Rudy. Immediately Hezekiah held an expression like Rudy stunk. "Where are you from?" Hezekiah asked

"Oklahoma."

"Why you move to San Francisco?"

"I got a really good job offer in Berkeley. My momma always wanted to live in San Francisco so I brought my parents along. Where your people from?"

"Here! We've been here for a long time."

"Good for you." Rudy said looking around the shop.

"So it sounds like your job is better than mine. I work at the ship yards in Richmond."

"I guess it sounds that way."

"So are our sodas on you?" Hezekiah joked.

Rudy didn't see anything funny. "No! I don't pay the way for grown men."

"It was just a joke, lighten up."

Rudy exhaled and looked at his watch. "We better get a move on it if we're going to make it to the show in time." He said swallowing the last of the soda we were sharing.

Kathryn mouthed to me to ask if Rudy was mad, I shrugged cause I didn't know. When we got to the theater Rudy waited until Hezekiah paid for their tickets before he paid for ours. When we walked into the lobby Hezekiah asked Kathryn if she wanted popcorn and candy. Kathryn smiled and said yes. Rudy shook his head and said that was a waste of money. Then he reminded me that we ate dinner at home with my momma before we came. I guess he was stressing the point that I shouldn't be hungry. Hezekiah looked at Rudy like he was wrong, and then he told me I could have some of their popcorn if I wanted some. I declined of course. In the movie I held Rudy's hand. He shook his head when Kathryn and Hezekiah started kissing. Then he asked me to move over a seat with him like my cousin had a disease or something. I refused to move, and he didn't like that, but ask me if I cared. Rudy was getting on my nerves being so cheap. All I hear about is how good his job is, and how well he could take care of me. By the way he's Penny pinching I can't tell if he's just cheap or they exaggerated how good his job is.

As we walked out of the theater Jeff came over to say hello. Rudy stood there analyzing their interaction. "Who's this?" Jeff said to me.

"This is my boyfriend Rudy." I said proudly.

Jeff frowned, "boyfriend? What happened to Buckie?" Then he and Hezekiah laughed.

"Buckie was never my boyfriend!"

"Nice to meet you I'm Jeff." Jeff said putting his hand out to shake Rudy's.

Rudy exhaled like Jeff was beneath him, "Rudy."

Jeff frowned then he looked at me. "He's not cool sis, call me when you need me."

"Call you? Who are you?" Rudy said in an indignant tone.

"I'm Jeff, and I don't like you."

"You don't have to talk down to me because I'm colored. Maybe you need to speak that way to him, but I comprehend English quite well."
"Why you gotta..." Hezekiah said getting angry as Jeff stopped him.
"I wasn't talking down to you, and I never talk down to my cousin." He pointed at Hezekiah, and then he said. "You've got a huge chip on your shoulder that's going to land you in trouble, if you don't get that fixed." Jeff looked like he was trying to calm down. "Annette I'll check in with you later on." Then he walked away with his date.
We rode home in silence. When we pulled in front of our apartment I started to get out. "Hold on Annette." Rudy put his hand out then he turned to Hezekiah, "I believe you owe me gas money."
"Rudy!" Kathryn said.
"Rudy seriously?" I was completely embarrassed. "I'll give you money for gas."
"You're going to pay for a grown man who has a job?"
"You would've spent the same gas if my momma was in the car instead of them. You don't have to act like this."
"Well if that's the case you should pay me back for the money I spent tonight if you're in the habit of paying for grown men!"
I got out of the car irritated; I let them out the backseat. "I'll be right back with your stupid money!" I slammed his door and marched to my apartment. I was slamming doors every time I went through one. Momma came out of her room hollering until Rudy knocked on the door. He explained that I was mad at him. I shoved money in his hand. "This should be more than enough to cover everything. Now get out!"
"What is going on?" Momma yelled.
"I guess I embarrassed her." Rudy said giving me sad eyes.
"Yes you did! All everyone talks about is how good your job is. Well it cain't be that good if you so up tight you cain't afford gas no where!"
"Can't! The word is can't!" Rudy corrected me.
"Get out!" I yelled.
"Annette! Calm down!" Momma yelled at me.
Rudy noticed how I didn't utter a peep when my momma spoke. "I do have a good job, but if I pay for everything for everyone I'll never have money for us for our future."
"Annette you wanted him to treat everyone?"
"No ma'am, but he volunteered to drive tonight. Then after everything else he asked Hezekiah to pay for the gas."
"Hezekiah was riding he should've volunteered to chip in." Momma said.
"Right, some people don't have good home training." Rudy said, "and that white man was talking down to me." Momma squinted her eyes at me. "Ma'am would it be ok with you if I apologized to Annette alone?"
Momma touched Rudy's shoulder. "Of course sweetheart." Then she turned to walk back in her room. She told Emma to go back in our room. My brothers were all pretending like they were sleep in their various places.
Rudy led me back out. Kathryn and Hezekiah were kissing outside her door. Rudy rolled his eyes and led me out to his car. He leaned against his hood and he pulled me close. He gestured with his head back at the building. "I don't like him, he's sneaky." I didn't say anything, "I'm sorry Annette. People always come looking for handouts from me just because I'm making something out of myself. I don't want to be used."
"That doesn't excuse you being so cheap. I've never felt so embarrassed in my life."

"I will never pay for anything for a grown man. Each man should pay his own way!"
"Next time don't volunteer to drive then. Hezekiah could've driven."
"Deal!" He said rubbing my shoulders cause it was cold. "Give me a kiss, before your momma comes looking for you."
"I don't feel like kissing you."
"Kissing is a form of affection Annette."
"And I haven't met a guy who didn't want to kiss me. I don't feel like kissing right now."
Rudy put his lips on mine anyways. When he started licking my lips I backed away from him. It grossed me out. I said goodnight and then I went inside. Momma was waiting by the door. She slapped me hard, "what white guy?" There was fire in her eyes.
"It was Hezekiah's friend momma." I said holding my face.
"Oh," she said searching my eyes. "Go to bed!"
When I got in the bed Emma looked at me. "Was it Tim?"
"No, Jeff." I said exhaling.
"Tim's family isn't like other families. I wish momma could understand that."
"Me too."

Timothy

She walked up to me with her eyes on the floor. "Hello Tim," she said like she was disappointed in herself.
"Good afternoon Mary Jane, you're looking well."
"Thank you, I miss you." She said still not looking at me.
"Isn't that nice, it's good to see you."
"I need to see you," her voice pleaded.
"Would you like to eat first?" I asked pointing to a chair. She exhaled and smiled, and then she kissed my cheek and sat down. "But there's one thing. Apparently today is a missing Tim kind of day. I saw Natalie here earlier, I think she's working up the courage to come over and speak. If you can't handle it I suggest you walk away."
Mary Jane exhaled as Natalie walked over. "Is this one of your sisters?" Natalie asked.
"Heavens no!" I said laughing.
"Hi I'm Mary Jane," she said trying to assert herself.
"Is this your girlfriend?" Natalie asked.
"I don't have a girlfriend. Mary Jane and I have known each other since school days."
"Really?" Natalie said reading Mary Jane. "Has Tim always been a bad boy?"
"The worst!" Then Mary Jane laughed.
Natalie looked at me, "cute kid. So, Mary Jane," she said taking a seat. "Are you entertaining our friend this afternoon?"
"Yes."
"Does that mean I get to have him tonight?"
Mary Jane exhaled, "if you can't beat them!" She shrugged, "I guess so."
"Look at it this way darling, at least we know who we're sharing with." Mary Jane still looked a little bummed out. "We should exchange numbers and get together sometime."
I laughed, "you two are some kind of special."

****

"This is what you're giving her?" Franky asked.
"Yes, I think she'll like it. Her sister said she sews all the time. So I'm giving her this top of the line-sewing table and machine. Pops had it special ordered for me. You don't think she'll like it?" I asked
"She'll like it, there's nothing romantic about it." Franky said.
I exhaled, "I know. I'm restricted to this space for now." I could feel my frustration. "I'm wasting my time, but I don't know what to do."
"Maybe you should move on." Franky said, but I knew he was talking about himself.
He's got men combing the south looking for Raynel. He found out that she ran away from her family as soon as she got off the bus. We don't know if that means she had the baby or not. "I don't want to move on. Not yet anyways."
Franky exhaled, "Christy's pregnant."
"Who's that?" I asked
"Little miss red head." He exhaled
"You're a baby making machine." I joked.
"It was an accident, oh well."
"You getting married?" I asked.
"Her name's not Raynel. I'd marry Carol, before I'd marry this girl."
"What's wrong with her?"
"She's not my Queen," he said in defeat.
Jeff walked in the door, "what's that?"
"A graduation present for Annette. You think she'll like it?"
He shrugged, "I'm not a girl. I couldn't tell you yes or no." He turned his chair backwards and sat in my face smiling. "Speaking of Annette, I saw her the other night."
"Ok?"
"She was on a date.... With her boyfriend!" He smiled real big.
"HER WHAT?" Franky and I said in unison.
Jeff looked at both of us standing over him. "Um, I understand why he's upset." Jeff said pointing to me. "What's it to you?" He asked Franky.
"I've been looking after that little girl longer than you two knew she existed. She reminds me of Raynel in a lot of ways." He said.
"You sweet on her?" Jeff asked.
"She's a little girl!" Franky barked.
Jeff looked at me and then back at Franky. "That's not a yes or a no."
Franky stood up, "I don't have time for these childish games!"
"It's ok Franky J! You don't want to admit it to us that's fine. Just don't pull a Matt and marry her." Jeff said motioning for him to sit. "Let me tell you about this guy."
"Why?" Franky barked.
"Cause I don't like him, that's why." Jeff told us what happened. The way he mimicked the guy was hilarious. He said he talked to Hezekiah about him and he said that the guy and Annette argued because he's so cheap. "Apparently he's got the nod from her momma, but check this out. He won't marry her until she graduates from college."
"Is she going?" My heart started beating fast. "Pops told me to go back to school as well."
"Yep, SF State."
"I'm enrolling now!"

Annette

"It's about time you two came up for air. I was wondering if you were going to end up in trouble." Kathryn said washing her hands.

"My momma really likes Rudy. She has us together all the time." I said blushing.

"I see. Do you like him?"

"Of course I do."

"I just asked cause you always saying what your momma thinks."

"Momma is so happy about us, she's nice to me even. It feels so good to see her smile at me and be happy about me."

"I understand, I don't know how you continue to love your momma after all she's done to you."

"She's my momma." I said not knowing how else to explain.

"I think Hezekiah is going to ask me soon." She giggled.

"Are you ready to be a wife?"

"Yes! It's hard enough not giving it away now. All I can think about is how good it's going to be."

"Am I crazy for not thinking about stuff like that?"

"No, girls aren't supposed to think about stuff like that. I can only tell you stuff like this. My friends would paint me up like a harlot if I told them."

Wilma and Emma walked in the door looking suspicious. "Where have you been?" Emma's eyes bounced around the room. "We were helping a teacher after school." Wilma said calmly, but I knew it was a lie.

I looked at Emma, something was different but I couldn't tell what. I finished up with Kathryn then Emma and I came home. Momma looked at Emma the same way I did. After a couple of days when Emma and I were going to bed momma came in our room. She looked Emma up and down, and then she went out of the room. Emma looked at me nervously, I asked her what was wrong and Emma said nothing. Momma came back with the belt and started beating Emma. I threw my body in the way to protect her. Momma pulled Emma from under me and started beating her some more. "You wanna be fast! You supposed to save yourself!" I looked at Emma and I screamed no. Emma kept saying she was sorry. "How could you disrespect me like this? Your daddy would be so hurt!" Momma said lowering her head and crying hard. Emma cried, momma asked her who the boy was. When Emma acted like she wasn't gonna tell, momma started hitting her some more.

"Hezekiah!" Emma yelled in defeat.

"Kathryn's boyfriend?" I gasped.

"We're in love. He said he's going to marry me."

"Emma you're only twelve."

"Back home girls my age get married all the time." Emma cried.

"Emma?" I asked her through tears, "what about Kathryn? She's always been good to you. She don't deserve this." I pleaded.

"We weren't trying to hurt her."

"When?" Momma said between sobs.

"When what?" I asked.

"The baby Emma! When?" My momma said getting angry again. She got up quickly picking Emma up. She dropped her on her back on the floor. Then she picked her up and did it again. I screamed for her to stop. She told me to shut up, and then she punched Emma in the stomach a bunch of times. "You not gonna do this to me!" Momma yelled, then she made her stand up and she kicked her in the stomach so hard that Emma flew into the wall next to me. I covered Emma with my body as momma kept trying to beat the baby out of her. I was trying to save her, but it was too late.

Chapter 8

Annette

I held Emma in my arms; she didn't go to school for a whole week and I stayed home from school and work to take care of her. She kept crying and asking how momma could be so cruel? I told her when she gets married one day she was going to be a wonderful momma. We said we would show our children love. She finally stopped bleeding and momma told her the worst was past. She told her that she couldn't see that boy any more and she better not tell a soul. Emma looked at momma with fear in her eyes. Momma told me to go to the market to get groceries for dinner. I was waiting for the bus or the trolley whichever came first when I saw Hezekiah trying to look casual as he saw me. He was going to have to walk past me. My blood boiled, Hezekiah was older than me by almost two years, and Emma just turned twelve. When he got close he looked at me and nodded at me. I punched him in the face and I kept hitting him. When he fell I jumped on him and kept punching him. He was yelling at me to stop. I was calling him every name I could think of as I kept punching him. I've been fighting men all my life; he was not ready for me to hit him like I was. Whether I was a girl or a guy he wasn't ready for me. "Kathryn loves you! How could you do this to my family? My sister is a little girl! I HATE YOU! YOU GONNA TO DIE IF I HAVE ANYTHING TO DO WITH IT!"
Booker pulled me off of Hezekiah.
Then he asked what was going on. I looked at Hezekiah to say, he kept spitting blood from his busted lip and trying to catch his breath. I spit at Hezekiah and I ran to my Aunt Dorothy's apartment. Kathryn was lying on her bed reading a book. She went from relaxed to alarmed as she saw my tears. "Annette what is it?"
"I'm sorry!" I cried.
"What?" She asked me shaking her hands.
"I'm sorry!" I cried again.
"WHAT?" She screamed at me.
Wilma came in the room wide eyed looking at me. "I beat on Hezekiah."
Kathryn deflated, "no you didn't." She said almost ready to write me off until my tears kept coming. "Hezekiah got beat up by a girl? Why?"
I looked at Wilma, "tell her!"
Wilma looked like a deer caught in headlights. "Tell me what?"
Hezekiah came bursting in the apartment yelling at me and angry. Booker was telling him to calm down. "Tell her!" I told him.
He glanced at Wilma, and then he swallowed. "Baby she's lying!"
Kathryn's eyes bounced from me to Wilma to Hezekiah. "About what?"
"Don't lie Hezekiah." Wilma said.
"Lie? To me?" Kathryn pointed to her chest, "but you're my sister!"
Wilma put her head down, "I'm sorry."
"FOR?" Kathryn yelled.
"Emma's pregnant." Wilma said sadly.
Kathryn looked at Hezekiah with pain in her eyes, "what does this have to do with you?"
Hezekiah exhaled, he debated with himself then he exhaled again. "You weren't my first choice. Before I knew what was happening...." Booker hit Hezekiah so hard you heard it. Hezekiah flew backwards, Booker started punching on Hezekiah while Kathryn stood there screaming and crying. My momma and everybody came over from the noise. Momma immediately slapped me and started to come after me.

Until she saw Emma trying to tend to Hezekiah who was trying to get up. Momma started going after Emma and Hezekiah grabbed her hand before she could knock Emma good. He growled at her and told her she would not hit her. Emma cried and told him the baby was gone. Hezekiah deflated for a minute it looked like she stabbed him, then his eyes turned evil at momma. He squeezed her hand and then he threw it backwards. He told Emma to get up. Momma was screaming at him and hitting him, but he marched Emma out the door. When momma started charging at them, they took off running. Even though Emma only had house shoes on she ran with Hezekiah. Momma was telling Booker to go after them, but he was tending to his sister who was sitting heartbroken on her bed. Wilma stood to the side looking so guilty. Kathryn screamed at her and asked her how come she never told her. She was her sister! Wilma didn't seem to care all that much about how the situation affected Kathryn. Momma came back in the door frantic cause she didn't know which way they went or what was going on. Everybody tuned momma out which made her mad, everyone was looking at poor Kathryn. Aunt Dorothy and Jean came in the door with big eyes. Momma screamed everything at Aunt Dorothy. Jean immediately rushed to Kathryn to comfort her. Aunt Dorothy volunteered to take momma to Hezekiah's folk's place.

Kathryn kept crying and crying. When momma and Aunt Dorothy came back in the middle of the night, momma was still crying. Aunt Dorothy said Hezekiah called home to tell his parents that he and Emma were running away together to get married. Hezekiah said he wasn't going to let momma treat Emma like she treated me. He told his parents he had to protect her. His folks told him Emma wasn't old enough to get married. Hezekiah said he was almost to Mexico, and they would get married there. He said there was no use fighting it cause it was happening. Aunt Dorothy told me to go home as she held her baby in her arms. All my brothers were sleep and unconcerned about any of this. I tried to go to my momma to comfort her, and she threw her shoe at me and told me to get out. I laid in my bed feeling empty; I had been looking out for Emma since I was six years old. This was the first time ever I didn't have to watch out for her. I cried to myself then I realized that Emma had what I wanted. I didn't want the drama and the mess, but I wanted to love someone so much that I threw caution to the wind. I had so many questions for Emma, I cried when I thought about never seeing her again.

Timothy

"Thank you for taking me to the airport." Franky said with nervous energy. "What should I bring her?"

"I'd bring her flowers, and a bear for the baby, maybe a baseball mitt." I said

Franky exhaled, "I can't do the mitt. That would hurt too much. It'll make me think about the time I won't have with them."

"Why won't she come out here?"

"She say she won't let me throw my life away by marrying her. That's when we start arguing. It took a lot of convincing for her to let me come see our son. She say he looks just like me." Franky shifted in his seat. "This is like a nightmare you know? I can't marry the woman I love, and everyone is asking me why I'm not marrying the girl I barely know. If I tell momma now about Raynel, she's going to make this situation worse."

"You say that, but maybe momma could help convince Raynel that coming back is the thing to do. You could have your wife and family."

"What happens to Christy?"

"She could have the baby, give it to momma and go on with her life." I said like it was that easy.
"She actually told me that I was her big fish. That I'm supposed to take care of her for the rest of her life just because she has my child. This is why you shouldn't get drunk before sex. Accidents can and will happen." Franky said irritated.
"Well think of it this way, when she has that baby its gonna hurt. Especially if its a boy and he got your head. She'll never walk the same. She's gonna pay for every dumb comment she makes."
"She makes it hard to demand that Raynel come home."
"So what's supposed to happen when you go out there?"
"I'm still going to try to convince her to come home. If she's set on staying and I know her, she's stubborn. I'm going to make sure she has everything she needs. There's nothing I wouldn't do for her or give her."
"Aw! Franky has a tender side."
"Cut it out!" Franky said looking out the window. "I thought love was supposed to conquer all, all of it!"
"LOVE MAKES NO SENSE!" I blurted out. Franky stared at me waiting for me to explain myself. "She won't even look at me! After all this time all she sees is that I'm white. She won't let her eyes see me."
"So forget her and move on."
"I CAN'T DO THAT! DON'T YOU THINK I'VE TRIED THAT!"
"I understand…" He said.
'NO! I DON'T THINK YOU DO! YOU HAVE A CHILD WITH THE WOMAN YOU LOVE! SHE THINKS SHE'S PROTECTING YOU BY STAYING AWAY! YOU'VE KISSED HER! YOU'VE MADE YOURSELF VULNERABLE TO HER! SHE WON'T EVEN LOOK AT ME!" I hit the steering wheel. "Oh I'm sorry Sadie, I didn't mean to hurt you!" I rubbed the dashboard.
Franky blank stared at me, "Sadie?"
"Yea! Sadie! Don't act like you didn't name your car."
"Tim, you just apologized to the car."
"Sadie has feelings too."
"It's a car!"
"It's my Sadie, probably the ONLY BABY I'LL EVER MAKE! SHE DRIVES ME CRAZY! YOU KNOW WHAT I'M GOING TO DO? DO YOU?"
Franky nonchalantly stared at me, "what?"
"I'M GONNA DROP YOU OFF! THEN I'M GOING OVER HER MOTHER'S HOUSE! I'M GOING TO TELL HER TO SHUT UP AND I'M TAKING HER DAUGHTER. THEN!!! THEN, I'M GOING TO TRAP ANNETTE IN THE CORNER UNTIL SHE OPENS HER EYES AND SEES HOW MUCH I LOVE HER!"
Franky stared at me unmoved by my tangent. "Why do you love her? If she hasn't looked at you, she hasn't even showed you the real her."
"I love her for the same reasons you do." I stared at him and dared him to tell me I didn't know what I was talking about. He looked down then he looked straight ahead. "You're not Matthew, I can trust you?"
Franky exhaled, "I'm not Matthew. I'm Franklin the second and I'm on my way to meet Franklin the third. That's all that matters to me."
"Good!" I said.
After I dropped Franky off I didn't feel like going home alone so I drove to Jeremiah's house. He just pulled up at the same time as I did. He looked whooped

and disturbed. I asked him what was wrong and he shook his head as he walked inside of his house. “My brother!” He went straight to his liquor cabinet. “Join me in a drink!”

“It’s that bad? Where’s Katie?” I said looking around.

“No! Not like that! She’s out shopping with her mother. Hezekiah is on his way to Mexico.”

I frowned, “Mexico? What for?”

“He’s getting married.”

“Why wouldn’t they do that here?”

“He’s not marrying Kathryn. He’s marrying Emma.”

I gasped, “the little girl? You’re pulling my leg?” I couldn’t believe he was serious.

“I wish I was. Apparently they’ve been messing around for some time. Some how her momma found out, and she beat on Emma. When Hezekiah found out, he took her. They’re on the run right now.”

“What about Kathryn?”

“She wasn’t his first choice.”

“That’s cold.”

“Mrs. Cooper was at my parents house acting a fool, until they called. Emma wouldn’t come to the phone to talk to her momma.”

“How’s Annette?”

“I don’t know, devastated I’m sure. You know how much she loves that little girl. Maybe now that her sister’s gone, she can start living for herself. You know? Her momma is a real piece of work, the way she walked up in my parent’s house. I get it, she was upset about her daughter, but she ain’t right."

"I enrolled at SF, I'm in almost all of her classes this Fall."

"Do you really think being in her classes is going to change things?"

I shrugged, "I gotta go to school anyways. I might as well have the pleasure of looking at her while I'm there."

Jeremiah exhaled, "let's switch gears. Avery is a very good worker; he's smart and everything. However, I get the impression that he has a problem reporting up through me."

"You wanna fire him?"

"Not yet, but the moment I have confirmation he's out of here! I just thought you should know."

"It's your call, once school starts you're going to be running everything basically."

"Driver number fifteen is making a pickup at the Napa airport. Pops is expecting delivery in a couple hours."

I looked at my watch, "good. Break down and dissemination should happen shortly after that."

Jeremiah picked up papers. "We need to discuss this grocery store chain. They want to hire us."

"What you think of the proposal?"

"We'll need to ramp up more drivers and buy more trucks. Even with that you're going to make a killing hand over fist." Jeremiah said happy for me.

"How about this? I'll have Matt go over the contract. If everything is everything we'll reorganize. That contract is your baby, I want you to pocket the profits."

Jeremiah fell into his chair. He put his hand over his mouth as he frowned. "Do you know how much money we're talking about?" He pointed at me.

I smiled, "yes I do! Think about it Jeremiah, you have been nurturing this whole deal. You've done most of the footwork."

Jeremiah eyed me, "what's the catch?"
I smiled bigger, "nothing! You could help your family."
Jeremiah sat back connecting the dots. "My family, which is now Annette's family?"
I laughed, "oh would you look at that!"

Annette

I excitedly read my congratulations letters from my friends out loud to Rudy. He showed no interest in my letters but I read them anyways. Everyone back home kept saying how proud they were of me. Mrs. Broderick said that Josiah and Maybel just had another baby. She said they had a little girl and they call her Annette. I was so honored, I cried a little. Rudy sat there looking at me annoyed. He was irritated cause he was kissing on me, and then he stopped of course when my momma entered the door. She gave me the mail, and then I saw my letters. I guess Rudy expected me to want to kiss him when she left again. Honestly it felt better to me to read my letter than to let him slobber all over me.
There was a knock at the door. I happily and quickly opened it. Katie and Jeremiah were standing there. I invited them in.
Katie asked me how Kathryn was doing. I told her that Kathryn is still really depressed. I told her it took a lot of convincing to get her to come out for her graduation. She went to the ceremony and then she got back in her bed. My Aunt says she's going to send her to her father for a change of scenery for a while. Although I didn't want my cousin to leave, I hated seeing her in pain like she has been. Emma hasn't called home once; I get updates about her from Jeremiah. They got married in Mexico. Hezekiah got a job in San Diego, and Emma's in school. I wondered if she was scared being all the way out there with no family, no friends, no one but Hezekiah. He was in the same boat so I guess as long as they had each other it didn't matter.
"We have your graduation present, it was too big to bring to the ceremony." Jeremiah said looking me in the eyes.
"You got me something?" I said completely surprised.
"Jeremiah," he said sticking his handout to Rudy.
"Oh I'm sorry, this is Rudy. Rudy this is Jeremiah and his wife Katie."
"Hello." Rudy said watching everyone.
"Can you help me bring in her gift?" Jeremiah asked him.
Rudy exhaled and then he got up. As soon as they walked out the door. Katie ran and put her hand on my ear. "It's from Tim." She had a huge smile on her face.
I frowned, "why would he buy me anything?"
"Gurl, that man has got it bad for you!" She said fanning herself.
"No he doesn't?" I was confused.
"Yes he does! Don't tell me you didn't know?" She looked at me in disbelief.
"But he's white, he's always with white girls."
"And he wants you!" The shock on my face tickled her. "You really didn't know?" I shook my head no. She put her hand back up to my ear. "You can't tell nobody I told you!" She looked at my face for confirmation that I swore to keep quiet. "He got the policeman who beat your momma up and broke your arm."
Panic struck my stomach, "no he didn't! Don't say that!"
"Tell me you didn't see murder in his eyes when he came for you at the hospital?"
"It ain't true! I'm not nobody! Stop pumping up my head...." Jeremiah and Rudy came in carrying the most expensive and beautiful sewing machine and table. I've

seen it in the department store a few times. It can do all kinds of fancy stitches and it's electric, Aunt Dorothy's was old and you had to pump manually with your foot to work it. I covered my mouth in shock. Katie smiled at me and asked me where I wanted it. I made room for it in my room. Then Jeremiah invited us out for ice cream. Rudy was reluctant to go until Jeremiah said it was his treat.
"This sure is a fancy car!" Rudy said taking in the car.
"Thank you, it was a wedding present."
Rudy looked confused, "you guys give fancy gifts and you receive them as well?"
"I guess you could say that."
Jeremiah told us to order whatever we wanted. If we wanted food and then ice cream that was ok as well. I expected Rudy to decline and stick to ice cream and then a small cone or something. I was in shock again when Rudy ordered a burger and fries for himself, and then he asked me if I was going to eat. I tried to take the irritation off my face, but it wasn't working. I ordered a simple ice cream cone and then I looked at Rudy. He shrugged and said what, like he didn't get it. Jeremiah and Katie tried to pretend like they didn't see my irritation. After he ate his burger he ordered a big sundae. I couldn't even look at him; he knew this was Hezekiah's brother. He had to know they heard about how cheap he was. Had us sharing a soda that at the time seemed romantic, but now I know he was being cheap. Everything at the movies and after, now this. The more I thought about it. The more I knew I couldn't see forever with him. When the bill came he didn't even try to offer anything. He sat back happy and satisfied. On the car ride back to my house he told Jeremiah he had a good time and we'd have to do this again sometime. I looked at him telling him to shut up with my eyes. Katie gave me a hug and told me to bring Rudy by sometime so we could all get better acquainted. I waited until they drove off and then I went completely off on Rudy. I told him I've never eaten so good when I've gone out with him. I kept going and going. He was trying to talk but I wouldn't let him. He was getting frustrated but I didn't care. When he couldn't take it anymore, he slapped me. I grabbed my cheek in shock. "LET ME TALK!" He barked at me.
Before I could ask my hands what they were doing I had him up against the fence unable to defend himself. "DON'T YOU EVER IN YOUR LIFE PUT YOUR HANDS ON ME!"
Rufus grabbed me and spun me around. Rudy moved out of the way looking at me like I was crazy. He had no idea all of that power existed within me. People were laughing at him as he walked away.
Rufus was cracking up as he told Aunt Dorothy, Booker, and her girls what he saw. Kathryn said I was crazy for fighting a man. Everyone sighed when we heard the banging on the door. Rufus snatched the door open, "Rose! Leave her alone!" He said in my defense.
"THAT'S MY DAUGHTER! You need to mind your own business!" Then she looked at me. "Get over here!" She said through clinched teeth. When I came she hit me upside my head hard. "What is wrong with you? You gonna run that boy away, and you can't do no better than the Henson boy!"
"Rose! That's not true!" My Aunt said in my defense.
"Mind your own business. You can't even give one of your nappy-headed girls away."
"At least mine weren't stolen before they even understood what puberty is." Aunt Dorothy said.

Momma got angry and started to charge at my Aunt. Booker jumped in front of her, he told her she was not going to hit his momma. Momma screamed to me to help her, I couldn't move. She was going to beat on me either way. I wasn't going to fight my cousins or my Aunt who has always been good to me. Momma looked at me in disbelief when I didn't move. She yelled at my Aunt until my Aunt kicked her out. Aunt Dorothy and my cousins wouldn't let me go home. I could hear my momma next door going off, I kept apologizing to them for bringing all the chaos to their house. Aunt Dorothy told me to come sleep with her. She rubbed my back while I cried. Then she told me stories about my parents. She said she was the one who caught me when I came out. She said she put me in my father's arms. She said she never seen him smile so big in her life. She said when I was a baby he was always kissing on me and carrying me around. He was so in love with his first babygirl, it made my momma mad; and that's when she started acting ugly with him. That's when he stopped coming home every night. She said every time he came to the house he came for me, she said that drove my momma insane.

I took a deep breath, and then I told her about how life was at home for me. When I told her, what momma let Leslie do to me she cried. I even told her about all the times I snuck out to hang out at Hazel's and drink moonshine, and smoked cigars and cigarettes with my friends. She said Emma was doing the same thing I did, just in a different way. I told her how my father died, I cried hard for a long time. I could still see him sticking his chest out as he knew the men where coming for him. How strong he was at first and how they wore him down. "Annette, baby he died trying to set you free. His life was his life and he didn't have to interrupt that for you. You didn't bring those white men there. Those white men came as a result of the choices that he made. He was coming to set you free, but you let your momma put you in a cage. Do you like Rudy?"

"I do for now, but I can't see spending forever with a man who's so selfish and cheap. Being nice to him keeps my momma off my back."

She rubbed my shoulder, "I understand child, but one day you gonna have to live your life for you. I forgot how evil Rose could be. She stay trying to make you guys mad at each other and put you guys against each other. She so angry at the world. Growing up they called her all kinds of names, always told her she was ugly. And you know I love my sister, but she's not beautiful to look at. Over the years she's let her bitterness about life and the way things are turn her into the person you know. She used to be a wonderful big sister. She used to take care of me like you took care of Emma." The mention of her name took me right back to tears. "Don't worry sweetie, your sister will be ok. She's got your fighting blood in her. That situation is wrong, but Wilma put her up to it."

I looked at her, "what do you mean?"

"Hezekiah liked you, and you weren't trying to give him the time of day. Wilma manipulated the whole situation to where before the two of them knew what was happening they were falling in love." My Aunt sighed, "Wilma's got a whole lot of her daddy in her, rest his soul. Kathryn and Jean's daddy," she put her head down. "He's married been married and his wife ain't gonna die like he told me all those years ago. He married an older woman for her money, so he says. Promised the world dressed real nice, bought me pretty things. I was young I didn't know no better. I had a son who needed things, and he gave them to me. He still sends me money every month."

"Who's Booker's daddy?" I asked.

Her eyes turned real sad, “when our daddy left, our momma got married again. He came for me one day. I ran away to Rose for help. She helped me, took care of me. She even went and caused problems at our momma’s house on account of me. That’s why I can’t understand how she could turn around and become just like our momma?”
“Did anybody ever come for my momma?”
“I suspect so, but she don’t talk about it. Only thing she ever talked about was Elmer! She was in love with him the first time she met him. She took good care of him and showed him love when he seemed like he was hurting for it. He was kind of mean to her, but he was sweet to her too. He was the only man to ever want her. I don’t know how she’s messing with Mr. Lakshman. That little skinny homely man.”
“Maybe that’s what they have in common. Every time she laid with my daddy she had a baby coming. I don’t know what she's doing different now.”
My Aunt looked at me, “you don’t know about condoms?”
I shook my head no; she explained how they worked and what they’re used for. I told her I’ve never been interested in having sex. She rubbed my arm and said she understood and she used to feel like me until she met Kathryn and Jean’s daddy. She said all he had to do was look at her and her clothes would jump right off her body. That made me think of Claudette, she made it sound so good, but not good enough to want to do it. I knew I wasn't ready. I asked her why she and Rufus weren’t married. She said he had a wife, but she died. She said he can’t bring himself to remarry although its like they’re married a lot of the time. She said regardless they’re a family.
In the morning I got up made Rudy a pie and then I went over his house. Mrs. Henson said Rudy didn’t go to work today cause he got in a fight yesterday with some random guy, and he needed a day to rest and get his spirit up. When I went to his room his door was cracked and he was staring up at the ceiling. I knocked gently on the door as I pushed it open. Rudy looked over his head and then he jumped up when he saw it was me. “I made you a pie,” I said as nicely as I could.
“Annette I’m sorry! I’m real sorry! It was all my fault.”
“It was wasn’t it.” I smiled.
“I promise I won’t act that ugly ever again. It was just that they bought you that fancy present, had that fancy car. It didn’t seem like they needed to hold on to their money like we do. You were right; I was taking advantage of their generosity. I’m sorry for ever touching you in any way other than with love.”
“Ok,” I said as I let him hug me. “Well here’s the pie you don’t deserve. Get dressed and come to my house so my momma will see that we made up.”

Timothy

"How did it go?" Momma asked
"She graduated, I couldn't say anything to her though. Her family was everywhere."
"Why does it matter where her family is?"
"Her momma don't like White people, she beat on Annette every time she catches wind of anything with us."
"After everything y'all done for that family?"
"Annette don't know about none of it."
Then the maid Carlotta walked into the kitchen. "Excuse me Mrs. Wallace, did you move the vacuum?"

"Oh yes honey. It's in the front closet I told Peggy to put it back. I'm gonna get that girl."
When Carlotta walked away I smiled. "A white maid momma?"
"You know how I see myself, this white skin is a cover up for who I really am on the inside. I don't know how Lady B isn't my real momma."
"Is she coming soon?"
"Yes, and she's gonna be so tickled to see that I gots me a white girl cleaning my toilets." Then she laughed real hard.

****

I couldn't stop smiling, "so she like my gift?"
"Timothy she loved it!" Katie said, "you should've seen how surprised she looked. I hope you don't mind that I told her it was from you."
My heart started pounding, "did anyone hear you? I'm not trying to get her in trouble."
"No one heard, but I could tell she was touched."
"Her boyfriend was there." Jeremiah said smiling.
My smile dropped, "oh yeah?"
"He's an idiot! She was so mad you could see steam coming out the top of her head. Hezekiah said he told him he don't pay for no man, but he had no problem with me paying for him. He's cheap and an opportunist. Her momma like him more than she does, I can tell." I tried not to smile at the crack in the pot of their relationship.
"Then he gone say that we needed to get together again. Of course he's going to say that if I'm paying."
"He did? Then we gotta do that, but at the perfect time!"

****

"Excuse me Mr. Wallace a colored man and woman want to come over to speak to you." The host pointed to Annette's aunt and uncle. I smiled and told him to bring them over and to bring chairs for them.
"Who's coming?" Natalie asked
"Friends of the family." I said not really paying her attention. I gave Ms. Dorothy a big hug and kiss on the cheek, I hugged Rufus.
"Oh no honey we didn't want to intrude on your evening we just wanted to say hi when we saw you."
"Nonsense you're eating with us."
"Colored ain't really allowed up here." Ms. Dorothy said.
"Then they should never allowed my family up here!" I laughed, they laughed with me. Natalie was staring at me. "Oh yeah, this is Natalie." She really was an after thought.
"Nice to meet you." They said to her.
"They're joining us?" She looked at me.
"You got a problem with that?" I had no problem with dismissing her. Natalie sucked her teeth and looked away. "Ms. Dorothy you gotta try their lobster! Talk about melt in your mouth!"
"I've never had lobster, where is it?" I pointed it out on her menu. She dropped the menu her eyes were bulging. "You see how much it cost?" She tried to keep her voice down. "We didn't come prepared to spend that kind of money."
"Ms. Dorothy you are my guest here. Order whatever you like. Matter of fact Rufus would it bother you if I order for you two?"
Rufus hesitated, "I guess it's ok."

I waved the waiter over. I ordered all the house specialties. Oysters as appetizers, Caesar salads, surf and turf, and I told the waiter we'd select our desserts later. Then I told them I wanted over flowing champagne glasses of their best bottle. Natalie looked annoyed, but I didn't care. Neither one of them had ever had champagne or any of the items I selected before. Ms. Dorothy didn't really like the oysters, but Rufus loved them. Watching her take her first taste of her champagne was rewarding. Natalie sat over to the side brewing but I didn't care. We enjoyed the jazz show and our meal. Ms. Dorothy and Rufus were so grateful for everything, they kept saying thank you.

When we got back to my place I felt so good about myself I didn't need to touch Natalie. I told her she could stay until I got sleepy then she'd have to leave. "Your mom really is passing isn't she?" Natalie searched my eyes for the truth.

"Get out!" I said not feeling the need to answer her question.

"I'm trying to understand your soft spot for coloreds."

"Get out Natalie! You're going to ruin the good feeling I got."

She started crying, "Tim I need to understand! I love you! I would die for you! Anyone colored come around and you forget about me. Why?"

"If you love me you love all of me! You love who I love! You love what I love! You don't!"

"Yes I do!" She argued.

"No you don't! You were so embarrassed to be sitting at that table with us. You see people and you see color. You need to look at people as just that, people! You only love the white part of me, you don't love who I love. My queen will love people for who they are, not for the color of their skin!"

"I can change!" She cried.

"If you have to change, then it's not in you to love me."

Annette

Rudy needed to take his father to the hospital. He came and picked up momma and me. Preston pleaded with us to bring him, Rudy only agreed to let him come cause we needed to hurry. Rudy asked my momma to drive his car to take me to the bank. He needed to deposit his paycheck but he couldn't do both. His momma was too upset to ask the doctor all the right questions. When we pulled up to the bank momma told me to let her see his check and his bankbook. She may not know how to read, but she knows numbers real good. Her eyes got big when she looked at his check. His job was as good as his momma said it was. Momma started licking her lips as she looked at everything. Then she told me to make the deposit. They recorded his deposit in his book and wrote down his new balance. I was happy that Rudy trusted me with his banking. I also could see how being so cheap has made his account grow so big.

When I got in the car I could see the wheels of her brain turning. "When y'all gonna get married?"

"He says not until I graduate."

My momma's eyes got big, "from college?"

"Yes Ma'am."

"I can't wait that long. Butch is sweet on that girl. She gonna end up big and then they gonna get married. Then what's gonna happen to me?"

"I could pitch in more."

"How can you? I take your whole check from the hospital."

I wasn't going to mention the money Franky still makes me take. "I could get another job."

"Work two jobs and go to school? When are you supposed to have time for Rudy? You'd lose him for sure." She was thinking, then she started shaking her head like it was the only way. "You gonna have to open your legs. Then he'll have to marry you."

"Momma!" I said glancing back at Preston who was quietly listening.

"Momma what? You ain't fresh no how, go on ahead and do it."

"Momma, please." I started crying.

"Shut up Annette! Sometimes we gotta do what we gotta do. You think I open my legs to Mr. Lakshman cause he makes my love come down? I can barely feel him, he's white. If I didn't do that we could never afford to stay there. Poor Butch does all that he can to provide for us, but he's getting tired. He needs someone of his own. Unfortunately he don't want you."

"Unfortunately?" I said through my tears. "Momma he's not supposed to want his little sister."

"Shut up! You don't know nothing. Now you're going to give it to Rudy. Give it to him good! Make him scream your name. Then you'll get big and he will marry you and take care of us."

"Momma Rudy's so cheap, I don't think he would take care of you."

"He will when I have to come stay with you. You won't let your momma be homeless on the street and what can he do about it?" Momma shook her head. "Yes, this is our plan."

"But momma he thinks I'm a virgin. When I open my legs he's gonna know I'm not."

"A what?" She yelled at me.

"He thinks I'm fresh."

She slapped me, "don't use those fancy words on me." She drove thinking, "I'll figure it out. You just get ready."

****

"I'm gonna miss you. Write to me as much as you can." I said hugging Kathryn and Jean goodbye.

Their daddy was sending for both of them. They were going to be gone for at least a year. We had a whole crying Fest at the train station. I was going to miss my cousins.

Booker got a girl name Phyllis pregnant, so they got married and live a few blocks over. It was just Aunt Dorothy, Wilma, and Rufus next door now. Wilma always sneaks boys over, and I always tell Aunt Dorothy. One day Aunt Dorothy says she's tired of all of the fighting and chasing Wilma. Then she stopped caring. Aunt Dorothy and Rufus go away on the weekends now, they falling more and more in love.

Momma keeps making me sit in the bathtub. She tells me to make the water real hot and then she puts Epsom salt in my water. I had to stop pressing my hair cause it kept going back from all the steam from the water. She says Rudy's not going to know the difference when he goes in. I guess it doesn't matter that I don't want to lay with Rudy. He's all right, but he kind of grosses me out sometimes. I don't even like kissing him. He drools! Gross!

He came over extremely excited. "You ready for school tomorrow?"

"Not as excited as you are."

He sat next to me and gently held my hands. "Annette we are that much closer to being man and wife."
"But what if I don't find a job right away?"
He frowned, "a job?"
"Yes a job, isn't that why I need to go to school?"
He shook his head, "no. I'm going to take care of you. I just need you to have the education. I don't want my wife to work."
"So tell me why I need to go?"
He explained that he has a plan for his life. He wanted a beautiful educated woman, two sons, and a successful career. I asked him what if he had girls. He said it was impossible. His family was all boys. He has all brothers, and nephews. He said with all my brothers we should have all boys. I reminded him that I'm a girl and I have a sister. He shushed me and told me it was genetics. The more he talked the more I knew I couldn't do forever with him. I didn't know how but maybe we could marry, he move my momma in. And then I could run away.

****

"Well, well! Aren't you a pretty little thing?" He said blocking my path. This guy was big, white, and rude! Every time I tried to step around him he cut me off. "What's your name pretty little lady?"
I exhaled and then I looked at him. "Move outta my way!" I said through clinched teeth.
"Ooh pretty little lady's feisty! I like conquering the feisty kind. Pucker up and give me a kiss!"
I backed away from him then I walked fast in the opposite direction. This guy has been bothering me since school began. The first time I saw him he told me to get on my knees cause he had a lollipop for me to suck on. I guess when I wasn't flattered by his request he decided that sideways compliments was a better approach.
I went home and cried to my momma and Rudy. Momma pretended like she cared and Rudy said I had to just ignore ignorant guys like that one.
Between this big guy and seeing Tim everywhere, I was filled up to my neck with white men. I've resorted to rolling my eyes at Tim whenever our eyes meet. He acts like he likes it, that man is off if you ask me. He can't be up to any good no more than this big guy. He just has a different approach.
It was a nice Fall day and the San Francisco weather was actually nice. I had a few chapters left in my book and then I'd be done and I could finish my paper. I decided to sit under a tree in the main courtyard. I was on the edge of my seat, Elizabeth just stood up to Mr. Darcy's Aunt. I was so into my book I didn't pay attention to who came and who went. Elizabeth slammed her bedroom door and then coldness ran through my hair and down my face. This big guy was pouring his milk over my head and people were standing around laughing. I hopped to my feet and started screaming at this guy. He told me to shut up and then his big ole hand went across my face and I stumbled backwards. I kicked him and followed with my book. He was about to hit me again, when Tim came out of nowhere. Tim picked up this big ole guy like he was little like Preston and threw him up against the tree. The guy didn't stand a chance Tim was big and angry. He kept beating the guy until I begged him to stop. He asked me if I was ok, and I shook my head yes while milk still dripped off my chin and hair. Tim ripped the big guy's shirt right off of him and he gave it to me to wrap up my hair. Security came and Tim explained what happened. "Eddie is a bully and he needs to be expelled. His behavior today goes against the school's code of conduct." He told the guys.

The security guards didn't argue, they helped the guy up, and then they took him to the office. I thanked Tim for defending me. I told him I couldn't accept his offer for a ride home. So then he suggested that he asked Katie to come get me. He waited with me until she came to get me.

When I got home I told momma and Rudy what happened. I thought Rudy would be outraged and ready to defend me. Instead he told me to remain peaceable and to not let this event stop me from progressing forward. I don't know why his lack of outrage upset me. Then I thought about it, what was he going to do? I beat him up before, so could he ever be a match for a man?

When he left it surprised my brothers and me when momma felt some kind of way about Rudy's lack of anger. She told us our daddy would've never let anyone put their hands on her no matter their color. Momma told me to stay in the good side of the nice white people at my school. I told her that would involve me interacting with some of them to show I was a team player. She said as long as it was for school it was ok.

Timothy

As soon as Katie drove away, I had Sadie take me top speed to Pops's store. When I walked in the door Mae was on her knees and my father was relaxing watching her head bob. He looked at me and then he told me to give them five minutes. Mae didn't even stop to see who opened the door.

When Mae walked out of Pops's office he was still sitting in his chair totally relaxed with an almost smile on his face. This scene was not helping my anger.

I told Pops I wanted Eddie Epstein taken OUT! Pops didn't say anything; he sat there watching me. I told him how Eddie's been harassing Annette and what he did to her today. "Sit down son."

"No! I want him to feel the pain!" I barked.

Pops stood up and walked around the desk. "You and your hot head! Everyone can't die because they look at someone you love crooked. You've already killed a cop, now you want this kid killed like you didn't do enough damage beating him up in front of everyone? Calm down and use your head! You took care of him, it's over!" Pops said

"How could you say that? This is my Queen we're talking about!"

"Your Queen? So her momma stopped having a fit about your presence in regards to her daughter. This girl has had a conversation with you? Does she even know how you feel?"

I got frustrated! "She's my Queen! I've said it, it's going to happen!"

"How do you know?"

"I know it the same way you knew about momma!"

"Tim you can't let your heart take over your reasoning. Look at the board, slow down and think. You've already beaten this kid twice. He's never gonna bother you or what's yours again. You got him son, calm down!"

I sat down, he had a point but I still wanted to yell at him. "Lock your door! Nobody wants to walk in here and see all that!"

Pops smiled, "you need to learn how to knock."

Annette

"Annette Cooper?"

"Yes sir?"

"I'm pairing you up with Lauren Salvo." He pointed at her.

Both of us looked each other up and down. I couldn't tell if I was gonna have problems with this white girl or not. "Hi."
"Hi."
"You wanna go to the library?" I said cause she was just sitting there looking at me.
"Sure," we walked in silence.
When we sat at the table she started staring again. "Why are you staring at me?"
"First of all cause you're really pretty. Second, I've never interacted this up close and personal with a colored person. How about you?"
"Not this close." I said. She looked like she was analyzing all of my features.
"You're still staring!"
"Whenever I make a new friend I look at her to see what a guy might like about her. There's so many features to choose from with you. Your cocoa skin, those almond shaped eyes, the richness of your brown eyes, those high cheekbones, you don't really have a negro nose."
"Thank you I think?"
"Now look at me," she lifted her chin and posed like I was taking a picture. "I'm beautiful! Go ahead, admit it. If you were a guy you'd want permission to date me." She smiled while she held her pose.
"Definitely! I'd be your midnight lover." I laughed, "you are crazy!"
"Glad you noticed. Now who's the guy?" She nodded behind me.
I turned to see Tim smile at me. I rolled my eyes. "Tim, you wanna meet him. Maybe you two could hit it off and he could stop looking at me."
"Oh yes! I don't know why you wouldn't want him to look at you. He's cute."
"He is?" I hadn't really ever looked at him. I turned to him and waved him over.
"Tim this is my new friend Lauren. Lauren this is Tim."
Tim looked around, "is it ok to speak?"
"I told my momma I'd have to interact with all kinds of people for school. Rudy had to convince her, but it's ok to be friends."
"Rudy?" He said sitting next to me.
"My boyfriend." I said asking Lauren what the goofy look was for with my eyes. She shook her head as she smiled.
"You've wounded me!" He said holding his chest. "I'm supposed to be your boyfriend, not some other fella."
I laughed, "what?"
"One day Annette." He patted my hand. "What are we working on?"
As we worked on our assignments Lauren kept flashing me goofy looks.
I exhaled, adjusted in my seat, and went back to the beginning to start over because apparently I wasn't getting it. Tim stopped reading and asked what. I told him my reading for chemistry made no sense to me. He clapped his hands together and said chemistry was his middle name. He scooted closer to me to look at my book. That's when I noticed his cologne. It wasn't strong but it smelled good. For the first time ever I looked at Tim. He wasn't pasty, he definitely walked around outside in the sun. His hair is kind of blonde brown and curly, but he kept it short and neat. His eyes sparkled especially when they lock on you. He had a slight mustache like he shaves it off with his beard. His face was smooth, and dare I say he's cute? No handsome, cute is for boys. Tim's definitely a man. In that moment I wondered if Katie was pulling my leg. I think he's just a nice guy, I doubt he'd ever really look at me. As if he heard my thoughts he stopped talking and looked at me with a slight smile. I turned my head, then I asked a question about the reading and he continued

explaining. And he's smart too! I looked at the time and I had to get home. Tim offered us a ride, but Lauren had her own car. He looked at me and smiled, then he asked me if we could study together tomorrow too. Lauren said yes before I could respond. When we got in her car she went on and on about how he was looking at me, and he paid her no real attention. She said he had a crush on me. I asked why she gestured so wildly and she said she's Italian and it's in her blood. She offered to pick me up in the morning for school. I thanked her and I gave her my number so she could call me when she was on her way.

When we pulled up to our apartment my momma and Rudy were outside talking. I introduced them to Lauren. Momma was only pretending to be nice, but I could tell Rudy thought she was pretty. Momma noticed it too.

Timothy

I parked all up on the sidewalk. Jeff came out of his house. I had the biggest smile on my face. I did a flip on his grass. Jeff stood there waiting for me to say what. "I need to keep a journal. Today goes down in the history books!" I said then I did another flip.

"You better cut that out before you break your neck. Is it Annette?"

"Yes!" I said excitedly hopping up to his porch.

He opened the door for me. "Did she kiss you and where? Spare no details!" He said handing me a drink and preparing for a good story.

"Better than that! She looked at me!" I stared off smiling to myself.

"What?" Jeff said not amused.

"She looked at me man!" I was excited.

"I'm looking at you. Does that turn you on too?" Jeff said sarcastically.

"You don't understand. All this time she's never taken me in. Her eyes glossed over me. Today while I explained chemistry, we were having chemistry!" Jeff looked at me unimpressed. "It's happening man, I'm excited. She's going to be Mrs. Wallace! She'll have all my big head babies! Most importantly she's going to love me!" I started laughing hysterically.

"How do you know she wasn't looking at you and thinking that your older brother Jeff is more handsome?"

"PLEASE! You may have that debonair thing down. But! I've got her eye! Watch! It's happening!" I couldn't stop smiling. "I LOVE COLLEGE!"

Chapter 9

Annette

"School is closed tomorrow, does your mother know?" Lauren asked
"No, how about your father?" I asked her.
"Nope, I say we run away. Let's do something fun to let our hair down. What do you say?"
I got butterflies in my stomach, "like what?"
Tim cleared his throat, "is this a girls only trip? I wanna go."
Lauren smiled at him, "I bet you do. Of course you're invited, otherwise I wouldn't have brought it up in front of you. The hard part is figuring out what we could do."
"I heard about a place where they have mazes in San Jose by the farms. We could go there." Tim suggested
"Sounds fun, but we gonna spend all day in the mazes?" Lauren said thinking.
"How about this? We'll drive up the coast and have a picnic somewhere secluded. Then if we feel up to it, we'll head to the mazes on our way back." Tim said
"Whatever you two say, I've never been outside of San Francisco."
Both of them stared at me, "you mean you've never seen the redwoods? Or the Geysers? Or the freaking wine country?" Lauren said looking at me in disbelief.
I shook my head no, "we caught the train here. I saw some nice places along the way. My first time going to a beach or seeing the ocean is here."
"Tim! Tim! Tim! What are we going to do about this? This is a crime and a shame." Lauren said
Tim was staring at me for a minute with a smile, "this is going to be fun! We should do things outside of school more often. Like we started to years ago." He said
"You know my momma won't like that. She wants me to spend as much time with Rudy as I can." I said looking away.
Tim didn't like that answer, "bring him a long. I wanna get a good look at him anyways."
"We'll see. What should I bring tomorrow?" I said
"Just your sense of adventure and fun. I'm gonna ask Jeremiah if he can get away tomorrow." Tim said
"Is Jeremiah single?" She asked
"No, he's married."
"So you're gonna be foaming at the mouth all day over Annette, then you're going to invite a married couple? I don't want to be a fifth wheel." She pouted
"I could ask my brother Dale to come. He could probably use a day away too." He said not denying her claim about me. I couldn't believe it.
"Dale, what's he like?" She asked
"He's a good guy."
She frowned, "pass! I don't want some tender foot gentleman. I need.... I need..." she thought about it. "I need a man who is a gentleman, but knows how to handle an Italian woman. Someone who will appreciate my beauty and not be intimidated by it."
"What about Franky?" I asked
"No, he's got a lot on his plate right now. Maybe Jeff could come, but this don't sound like his type of party." He said
"What's wrong with our plan?"
"First of all he don't like being set up, Picnics are definitely not his style. There's a lot of things we do in the water, but staring at it ain't one of them. I can ask him. If

he say no, I'll bring Dale. Dale would be better than no one, especially on such short notice."
"Deal!" Lauren said.
That night I had a dream that momma let Leslie in my room, but then he turned into Rudy. I had to beat him until he stopped moving. I woke up sweating and afraid to go back to sleep. Fortunately it was a few minutes before I needed to get up anyways so I got up like I would for school. Lauren called me to say she was on her way like she always does. When I walked up to her car she was smiling. "Annette you're so predictable. I knew you would wear a dress today. Do you own pants?"
"I always make dresses." I said touching my dress
"I brought a pair of pants and a blouse if you wanna try them on."
I've never worn pants before. The idea tickled me and I couldn't stop laughing. Where will I try it on. "We'll stop here," she said pulling into a cafe parking lot. "Let's go in the bathroom and see how you like it. If you don't like it you can put your dress back on."
I pulled the pants up under my dress, and then I took off my dress and handed it to Lauren over the stall wall. I put the white top on and I immediately felt naked. It was so open. The neckline was box shaped only the straps to hold it up. I've made dresses with this neckline before, but I always make a jacket to go with them. The pants stopped mid-calve, and they were baby blue color. I walked out of the stall feeling vulnerable. I fidgeted with my hands, "how do I look?"
"Oh my goodness Annette! Look at that body! If I didn't have my own curves I would be completely jealous. You look beautiful! I bet you Tim turns red, how much you wanna bet?"
"Why would he do that?" I said looking in the mirror.
"Because his nose is completely open for you. He wanted to go get lost in the mazes with you so he could find a corner to kiss on you all day." She laughed
"Me? That's hard to believe."
"I don't know why. Look at you, you're beautiful and he appreciates your beauty."
"You're pretty."
"Thank you, and I know it. I think he likes your humility about your looks." She put her hands on my shoulders and stretched her eyes. "Listen to me, he's watching everything you do today. So be nice to him, smile, and talk to him. BUT DO NOT! I REPEAT DO NOT! Let him get fresh with you. You have a boyfriend at home, don't forget that. Today you're playing hooky. And when you walk, walk like this." She demonstrated a sexy walk, "you want him to look every time you walk past him. Try it." I mimicked her walk, "oh my goodness Annette! Tim's going to pass out when you walk past him. I never knew you had a caboose like that under those dresses."
I looked at my butt in the mirror, "is it big?"
Lauren stood next to me and pointed between my butt and hers. "Mine is nice, slightly big for a white girl. My momma used to say my bottom comes from the Sicilian side. Yours," she pointed to mine, "comes straight from your roots!"
"Is it too big?"
"It's perfect for you. You ready? Or do you want to put the dress back on?" She said hiding it behind herself.
"This feels so weird, but I'll try it." I said
Lauren clapped her hands then we got back in her car. When we pulled up to the school's unusually empty parking lot Tim was leaning against his car with Jeff and

Jeremiah. Katie was hanging out the window talking to them. "Which brother is that?" Lauren asked
"That's Jeff."
"He's delicious! I think I'm in love!" Lauren joked.
When I stepped out of the car, just like Lauren said, Tim blushed. Jeremiah kept bumping him and he took a moment to get it together. "We should leave your car here." Tim said to Lauren.
Lauren marched right up to Jeff and extended her hand to him introducing herself. Jeff was tickled by her boldness and he kissed her hand introducing himself. As we drove up the coast Jeff rode in the front with Tim while the rest of us rode in the back. Katie loved the pants and we talked about stores and fashions, I don't know what the men were talking about if anything at all. We stopped at a local deli and got sandwiches, potato salad, and fruit for our picnic. It was nice to be with men who didn't make you feel bad about every penny you spent, even though I was still watching how much I spent.
The woman who owned the deli was kind enough to wash off the fruit for us. When we got to the beach the men set out the blankets for our picnic and I noticed the couple of bottles of brandy they had in the trunk. Katie said she didn't like alcohol and Lauren had never tried it. I asked Tim if the bottles were for today, and he shrugged and said they could be.
When we initially sat down to eat, it was awkward and everyone was quiet. Jeremiah decided to share what it was like on his first date with Katie. By the end of his story everyone was laughing. We told Lauren about their wedding and when her maid of honor lost her footing. We laughed so hard. We really relaxed when Tim opened the Brandy. Lauren loved it, Katie tasted Jeremiah's and she said she still didn't like it. Tim was definitely paying attention to everything I did. I was watching him the same way. He was funny, and definitely silly, however he could be serious as well. In a lot of ways he reminded me of Luther. I didn't know if that was a good thing or bad just yet.

Timothy

I went to Jeff's office and I asked him if he could take the day off tomorrow. He eyed me and asked me what for. I told him the whole story how I had the day off, and this was going to be the first time doing anything with Annette outside of school, and I needed to bring someone so her friend didn't feel left out of the loop.
Jeff frowned, "I don't like set ups, they never work out."
"I told them you wouldn't do it. I was just asking so I could report back that I did. I was going to ask Dale anyways. Even if he don't like her. He'd have a good time." I said
"What she look like?"
You're asking a man who stares at Annette all day to pay attention long enough to another girl to tell you what she looks like." Jeff tilted his head at me. "She's this tall, about the same height as Annette. She's a brunette, good body, Italian and proud of it, she's pretty but she's no Annette."
"Is she any fun?"
"She actually hasn't gotten on my nerves once, so I think that's a yes."
"What the heck, I'll go! I could use a day off." Jeff said
I told him I'd pick him up in the morning. I swung by Jeremiah's place as they were packing their things to get ready for their move into their new house. They didn't have a move in date yet, but the paperwork was moving along swiftly. Katie was

thankful for the break; she said Jeremiah wasn't really all that much help in the packing department.

In the morning I was excited but I didn't do any flips, it was too early for that. Katie packed a basket of fresh made muffins and a couple thermoses of coffee. She said we couldn't have any until Annette arrived. When Annette got out of the car, I felt heat rush over my entire body. As usual she was beautiful, however today's attire was a lot more revealing of her curves. She still had a nervous demeanor about herself, but I could tell she liked what she was wearing. As Sadie soared down the coastline the girls chatted in the back about patterns and things I would never care about. Jeff looked at me and raised an eyebrow. I asked him with my eyebrows what that meant. He pointed his eyes towards the backseat and then he raised his eyebrow to me again. That meant Lauren wasn't half bad, knowing my brother he's writing her off as a little girl. Jeremiah leaned forward and asked us to talk about something manly before he ended up on the same period cycle as the women sitting next to him.

When we got to the deli before our final destination Annette brought her purse out of the car. I gently grabbed her arm and asked her what she was doing. She looked confused as she asked me if we were getting things for lunch and I said yes. I told her she never reaches for her purse for anything when she's with me. She smiled an embarrassed smile and then she apologized. I told her there was nothing to apologize for. Then she asked me what was her limit and I told her the sky. She laughed a yeah-right laugh and then she browsed the store looking at the prices of things and putting them back. Then she asked what kind of sandwich I liked, and then she ordered two. I liked how she kept remembering to consider me whenever she picked something. That's it; this girl's a keeper.

As we sat on the beach eating our lunch and sipping on brandy everyone kind of split off into pairs. When I heard Jeff laugh, I knew he was enjoying himself and he'd be in no hurry to leave. I looked at Annette who was staring off at the water.

"So what do you think?"

"I think the Ocean is beautiful and I don't know how I ever lived so far away from it." Then she looked at me, I could get use to her eyes taking me in. "What other things are there to see in California? I live in San Francisco, and I've walked the Golden Gate Bridge, is there really more?"

"There's a lot more. I'll show you everything I know."

"So gang what do you say? A cook out at our place next weekend?" Katie asked the group.

"Sounds good to me." I said.

"What do we want to eat?" Katie asked.

"FOOD THAT TASTE GOOD!" Jeremiah said.

"Tim should choose," Annette said.

I looked at her, "what do you know how to make?"

"You ask for it and I'll make it." She smiled.

"Oxtails and rice, black eye peas, greens, yams."

"Ox what?" Lauren interrupted.

"You've never had southern cooking?" Katie asked Lauren.

"No, I don't know what any of those dishes are." She looked intrigued.

"Sounds like it's a plan." Jeremiah said.

Annette smiled but I could see a little worry in her eyes. I asked her what was wrong and she said she had to think of a way to get away from her momma and Rudy for this. I told her to tell them she had to meet Lauren for study group. She smiled and said ok. Annette and I sat there talking about nothing but it felt like everything. This girl has no idea how much I want to take her and lay her down on this sand, I don't care who sees. Lauren asked about the mazes I mentioned earlier, and I told her she shot down my maze idea. She smiled and said she changed her mind. When we got back in the car Jeff rode in the back with everyone and Annette moved to the front seat. I told her I liked her outfit, and then she told me how Lauren said she was predictable and brought it for her. I asked her if she liked it cause I loved it. She said she felt a little naked; I smiled and said that was part of the appeal. In the mazes I followed Annette around watching her walk, she said I was no help to her as she tried to find her way out. All I could do was laugh. When we ran into Lauren and Jeff kissing in a corner, Annette accused her of being a hypocrite. Lauren reminded her that she didn't have a boyfriend at home and she could kiss whomever she wanted. The four of us eventually found Katie and Jeremiah kissing in a corner as well. The women eventually discovered the way out the maze.

****

"Hello Mr. Wallace, we weren't expecting you today." The foreman said walking along side me as I walked to my office.

"You never know when I'll pop up, let Mr. Barnes know I'm here." I said taking my seat.

I looked at all the mail piled on my desk; I exhaled at the thought of going through and reading all of it. All I wanted to do is spend time with Annette and to continue on the path of our growing friendship. Jeremiah walked in with a huge smile. "They got in this morning." He said.

"Good, their apartment should be ready in a week. I'm having it painted right now for them."

"Emma is very adamant about not seeing her momma. She doesn't want her to know she's back out here."

"Can you blame her? If she could do that to Emma what has she done to Annette?" I asked out loud.

"She sounds completely crazy and ruthless." Jeremiah shook his head, "Hezekiah will start on Monday." Then he exhaled, "Avery."

"What about him?"

"He's not out rightly doing anything. I can read him, he's up to no good."

I hit the intercom button on my phone. "Avery please come to my office."

"What are you going to say to him?"

"Not sure yet, lets see where this goes."

When Avery walked in the door he did not look at Jeremiah or in his direction, he focused on me. "You wanted to see me?"

"Yes, I'm hearing wonderful things about you on the ground floor."

He smiled, "thank you."

"I would like to know if you have a problem with upper management?" Avery frowned, "I could beat around the bush or get straight to the point right?"

"Right."

"I'm hearing good things about your work ethics, etc. I'm troubled by your disregard for the management here."

"Honestly, I don't know how you could trust a colored man to run your business. They aren't to be trusted."

"Why do you say that? Have you witnessed something I should be aware of?"

"The way he's structuring the whole grocery store lineup, he's doing it like it's a separate section. I was up next for a driving position but with the way he's doing things I'll still be here on the docks."
"Oh I see, so you were part of the planning committee involved in the entire deal from start to finish. You know what my company's agenda will be?"
"No, I only know what I see."
"Exactly!" I said, "you only know what you see. You have no idea of how we've planned to execute this service." I put my finger up, "watch yourself. If you can't respect this man." I pointed to Jeremiah, "then you can't respect me. And I have no tolerance for being disrespected. Since Jeremiah feels you're a good worker you won't lose your job today. If you can't work for this man, then you can't work for me. I suggest you look for other employment or risk that one day you could be fired for insubordination. Do we have an understanding?"
"Yes sir." Avery said standing to leave.

Annette

"HELLO! ANNETTE!" My momma was hollering at me. I was off in daydream land again. I can't seem to get Tim out of my head. I'm always wondering what he's doing? Who he's doing it with? If he REALLY likes me like Katie and Lauren seem to think. I've written about him to Harriet and Claudette, I just couldn't seem to think of how to put in the letters that he's white. I mean it shouldn't matter right? Momma mentioned that the boys needed school shoes and so I volunteered the last of my money stash to get them what they needed. No one said thank you or even paid attention to the fact that I gave them everything I have. My momma asked when her new dress was going to be ready cause she was going to be going out with the Henson's and she wanted to wear it with the hat I bought her some time ago. I told her I was almost done. Truth is she's been eating more lately and I would've been done but I had to let the dress out and add more material at the last minute. I planned to focus on her dress after our errands but instead she dropped off my brothers and then she brought me over to the Henson house for dinner. I stopped listening when they started talking about white people this and white people that. "I thought college was supposed to make you smarter? I swear she been staring off and not focused much these days."
"Aw! That's ok, she's probably daydreaming about Rudy and when they get married." Mrs. Henson said with stars in her eyes.
"Is that how you were when we were courting?" Mr. Henson asked his wife.
"Oh yes! I was so in love. My momma said I was no good for helping around the house no more." She smiled, and then she looked at my momma. "Rose how was it for you when you met your husband?"
My momma smiled real big, "it was like nothing I knew before. He was pretty for a man and he love me. He take me down by the pond and tell me all about his life on the reservation. He cry with me, talk about how nobody love him. When I tell him I love him," momma's eyes rolled in her head at the memory. "He didn't know what to say. He kiss me, then he say we have to get married right away. I can't believe it! This pretty man want me. Everybody say I's ugly, everybody say I's big for no reason. This pretty man love me still. I got big right away!" My momma smiled at the memory.
Mrs. Henson smiled at momma with stars in her eyes. "All your children beautiful, it must feel good."

"Yea," then she cut her eyes at me. "But the white man keep taking everything I love away from me. They took my Elmer, they took my Leslie, thank goodness Butch got a colored girl, or else I lose him too."
"That's what they do, any way they can keep us down they will!" Mr. Henson said Rudy sat there silent watching me and drinking his drink. I plug my ears when they start generalizing. And I know better than to speak against my momma and say that my father and Leslie died because she allowed them to get away with everything.
"So Rudy when can we start planning this wedding?" Mrs. Henson said excitedly. "I need to give the family notice so they can all come out for the wedding. I keep making checklist so that when you say it's time Rose and I can get started."
"Annette and I have a plan momma. We'll let you know when I give her the ring."
I could've not been sitting here for the way they go on and on. Rudy asked my momma, when his parents weren't listening, if he could walk me home. I saw my momma watching how many drinks he had. She smiled real big at me when she said yes. Then she said goodnight to his parents and he told his parents he was walking us out. Momma walked straight out to Aunt Dorothy's car, that she let her borrow for the day cause her and Rufus were staying in, and left. "You've been distant lately." He said staring at me.
I shrugged, "must be my classes. They're very interesting." And that was the truth. I was learning a lot, somethings were completely fascinating to me. I never thought of myself as an artist, but it turns out I have a talent for landscapes. One day I'll master the art of detail to draw a decent face. Meanwhile, I'm learning so much about the things I can actually do.
"Is more happening at that college than your new found knowledge?"
"You mean like being harassed by idiots?"
"Are they all idiots?"
"If they're harassing me then yes!"
He stopped walking and looked at me, "you are so pretty! I can't wait to get married. On our wedding night you're not getting any sleep. You better show me that you're worth all this waiting! Make sure your momma tells you what to do so you can give it to me right." He was drunk. "First I'm gonna drink buttermilk from those juicy…" He licked his lips. "Perhaps you could let me get a little sample." He said grabbing my breast.
The warmth of his hand in the cold air made my skin crawl! I slapped his hand away. "Keep your hands off of me!"
"Ooh! Don't get mad! I don't wanna meet the wrath of Annette!" He laughed, "come on baby. You looking all-fine in that dress, just let me rub against it. You don't have to let me in, please!"
"Go home Rudy, you're drunk!"
"No! I got to walk you home." Then he smiled, "I bet your momma would be ok with us sitting in my car for a little bit. I wanna taste them!"
I was done with this conversation, "go home Rudy!" Then I ran away from him. I left him standing by his car looking at me confused.
I stood outside my building catching my breath. I grabbed my composure then I walked inside. I got a glass of water out the faucet. Momma came in the kitchen, "so?" She said with wishful eyes.
"He wouldn't do it. I asked him to get in his car, and he said no. He just wanted to drool in my mouth."
"Did his pants grow?"
I looked at the floor, "I don't know what that means momma." I honestly didn't.

She huffed, "when a man gets ready, his pants grow. Pay attention to all these boys around here in the morning."
"I leave before everyone gets up, I'm sorry. I didn't know."
"Next time reach down and rub it. You gotta be careful cause you could hurt him though. Better yet put his hand down your dress. Once he touches you nature will take over."

****

"Ok, now they're just showing off!" Rudy said staring up at Jeremiah and Katie's new big and beautiful house.
"Wow! It's something ain't it?" I said smiling at the house.
"Isn't it." He corrected me.
"Stop doing that, if I'm wrong just let me be wrong." I fussed.
"What? What did I do now? Seems like I can't do anything right these days." Rudy fussed back.
"Stop correcting my words, if I'm wrong let me be wrong. Let me ask you how to say something. If I don't ask don't offer!"
"You better fix your tone! This is not how you talk to your man! You better show me some respect."
"And you better show me some respect!"
"You heard me!" He said in a threatening tone.
"Or else what?" I said daring him to ever think he could hit me.
"Or else I'll break up with you and let you explain to your momma why I'm gone!' I didn't say anything when he said that. "Yea like I thought! I don't gotta hit you, all I gotta do is tell your momma and she'll get in that butt for me." He chuckled to himself.
I took a deep breath and I told myself to be calm and not bash his head in. Jeremiah's new house was BIG and definitely fancy. Tim was already here of course, and I saw Lauren's car as well, amongst other cars. I introduced Rudy to Mr. & Mrs. Barnes. Tim, Lauren, and a white girl I didn't know where in the living room talking and drinking. "This is Rudy, you've met Lauren. This is Tim, and I don't think we've met." I said sticking my hand out.
"Mary Jane."
"Nice to meet you, I'm Annette."
Mary Jane's entire body jerked and she looked at Tim with fire in her eyes. Tim stepped forward and shook Rudy's hand, "it's nice to finally meet you. I've heard a lot about you."
Rudy looked at his hand, "I wish I could say the same. I think I've heard about everyone except you two." He said pointing between Tim and Mary Jane. "Honey why is that?"
I frowned at him, "what do you mean?"
Katie came to me super excited, "can you come with me?"
"Gladly!" I said walking away from Rudy.
She led me up the stairs; "I've got a surprise for you. I hope you'll be pleased." She led me to the room at the end of the hallway and then she slowly opened the door. I felt like I burst into flames as I saw my sister standing there looking at me. I put my hands over my mouth to stop the scream that almost cried out of me. Emma was crying and so was I. I wrapped my arms around my little sister and I squeezed her as tight as I could. I kept rubbing her head and kissing her as we cried in each other's arms. I missed her so much everything in me ached from the sight of her.
"What are you doing here? I thought you were in San Diego?"

"Hezekiah got a good job back out here, so we came back. I missed you!" Emma said crying.
"I was so worried about you!"
"I'm so sorry for making you worry. The opportunity to escape momma presented it's self and I had to go."
"I understand, I understand!" I said still rubbing her head.
Katie smiled and closed the door giving Emma and I a chance to talk and get caught up. Emma said she still has nightmares about momma beating her like she did. Emma said she didn't know how I was still at home, or how I was still with Rudy. I told her how momma doesn't talk about her anymore. She tries to act like she never existed. Emma said eventually she would go make peace with momma, but for right now she was still too hurt. She said they decided to wait to have a baby, she said right now she's enjoying being a wife. I asked her what that was like, and she said they have their challenges but she loves being a wife. I told her that Kathryn and Jean moved to the south to be with their daddy, Booker got married and has a family, and Wilma was completely loose now. Emma said Wilma wanted Hezekiah to break her in for the pure drama of the whole situation, but she was angry when she found out they were in love. Emma shrugged and said it worked out for the best. Katie brought us food and we talked and talked and talked. Emma said I needed to come back without Rudy, she said he's a stooge for our momma. I couldn't argue that. Katie came back and she said Rudy was ready to go. I told Emma I was coming back tomorrow.
When I came downstairs Rudy was fuming and Tim was watching him. Rudy told me it was time to go, and he marched out the door. Tim told me to hold on cause he wanted to walk me out. I told him I didn't think that was a good idea, so he asked Jeremiah to come with him to keep him calm. The three of us walked out, Rudy was already in his car with the engine running waiting. Tim opened the door for me then he stood in the way so I couldn't sit down. "You know her momma's got a real bad temper?" He said looking at Rudy.
"Your point?"
"Depending on what you say, you could set her off and then Annette would have a hard time dealing with her."
"What's it to you?"
"What Annette feels I feel. I can see you wanna get home so I'll get to the point. Everything her momma does to her, I'm gonna do to you. Watch what you say!" Tim said staring at Rudy.
"You're threatening me?" Rudy scoffed.
Tim shook his head, "Threats are for people who can't back anything up. I'm making you a guaranteed promise. You seem like a smart man, you understand what I'm saying to you?"
"Why do you care?"
"Because I always have." Then Tim got out of the way so I could sit. "Drive safely." Then he shut my door.
When we drove away, I smiled to myself. "You sweet on him?"
"Why would you ask me something like that?"
"Cause you've mentioned everyone but him, and I saw the way you looked at him."
"I didn't look at him in any particular way. I've mentioned him before, it just goes to show how much attention you pay when I'm talking. He's my friend who beat up the big guy for pouring milk over my head. I guess he feels like my protection now." I was driving home the point that Rudy doesn't make me feel safe.

When we pulled up to my building I started to get out and then Rudy grabbed my arm. "Hold on, I've been meaning to ask you something." I looked at him. He gestured around, "what's happening here? We go from your mother personally chaperoning us to; No chaperone, no curfew, and I swear whenever I come over for dinner your momma's trying to get me drunk." I didn't say anything. "It's like your momma keeps setting the scene for something to happen but you're gun shy."
"We have a plan, why does anything else matter?"
He sat back in his seat. "White people are interesting aren't they?" He smiled, "I had no idea you were surrounded by such beautiful women. It should be against the law." He chuckled to himself.
"What are you saying?" I asked staring at his face trying to control my temper.
"Your friend is beautiful, and that girl Mary Jane!"
I punched him in the face. "Are you a dog now? You want every female you see!"
Rudy flinched at me like he was going to hit me back, but I knew he knew better.
"Stop hitting on me! You are so violent!" Then he looked at me, to my surprise he lunged on me kissing me all over and touching all over me.
Suddenly I was back in that kitchen fighting for my life. I kicked, I screamed, I scratched him. "GET OFF OF ME!"
He backed up, "you don't want me?"
"We have a plan!" I said through tears. "Why would you change it now?"
Rudy's face was angry. "That guy is circling like a shark. He wants to taste you."
"That doesn't mean he gets to!" I couldn't stop crying and shaking. I got out of the car and stormed up the stairs. I knocked on Aunt Dorothy's door. Wilma opened the door for me, and then she went back to her bed. I laid on the couch and silently cried myself to sleep.

Timothy

"There he is!" Hezekiah called out as he approached me.
"Good to see you how are you?" I said
"Great! I'm absolutely great." He smiled big.
Emma came out and hugged me as well. She was anxious to see her sister. I told her that Annette would be here shortly. I relaxed with Jeremiah's family, everyone was so proud of Jeremiah and how well he was doing. Katie's face turned sad while she was talking to her mother in the kitchen. No doubt she was giving Katie a hard time about not having a baby yet. Jeremiah immediately saw his wife's sadness and then the argument began. Jeremiah threw Katie's parents out as he held on to his wife who was in tears. He told her that there wasn't anything wrong with her and that it was all his fault. He said he was the reason they didn't have a baby and he was sorry for hurting her like he has.
I looked at the time and it was time for me to pick up Mary Jane and meet Lauren. I decided to bring Mary Jane cause it would be obvious if I was there alone. Besides part of me wanted Annette to see that someone else wants me. Mary Jane was excited cause I rarely invite her out anywhere. Lauren followed us from the cafe to Jeremiah's house. Mary Jane seemed startled when she saw Jeremiah and all his family. "You invited me to come hang out here?"
Lauren frowned at her, "what's wrong with you?"
"It's a bunch of colored people." She whispered.
"Oh yeah, what color?" Lauren laughed.
"You're Italian right?" Mary Jane asked her.
"Your point?" Lauren looked annoyed.

"How does your family feel about you being seen with them?" She nodded her head to the house.
Lauren's eyes hit the ground for a minute, "who cares? I'm my own woman. Katie and Annette are becoming my best friends. They understand what I go through with my family, they get me. I don't like girls like you. You try to act like you're one way in front of people, and then you're totally different when you're alone. I bet your father thinks you're still wholesome and pure." Then she looked at me, "while I can see that you've given everything to Tim. Stop hiding who you are. I'm not saying you should walk around like a whore, but stop acting like you're too good for PEOPLE! These are good people!" I smiled at Lauren.
Didn't matter what Lauren said, Mary Jane still saw herself as too good, until. Until her eyes landed on Rudy. Suddenly she's shy and bashful, and his eyes were rolling around her body like he couldn't believe it. Mary Jane immediately connected the dots when Annette introduced herself. I didn't feel good about her hurt feelings but we were already here. It was happening. When Katie came and took Annette upstairs, I invited Rudy to sit down. "Would you like something to drink?"
"What do you have?"
"You name it, they got it. Jeremiah has a full bar." Lauren said
"Well if that's the case, I'll have a double single malt."
"A whiskey drinking man huh? Mary Jane baby can you get this man a drink?"
Mary Jane half smiled as she got up to get his drink, Rudy's eyes followed Mary Jane for a few minutes. Then he looked at me, "how do you know Jeremiah?"
"We've been best friends since we were kids. How do you know Jeremiah?"
"I met him through Annette." He said watching my eyes.
I smiled, "Annette's a smart girl. You should be proud to be on her arm."
"She's proud to be on mine." He said still watching me, "what do you do?"
I smiled, "I work with Jeremiah, he runs the facility."
"How does it feel to report to a Negro?"
"It's only right, look at this house. You see the car he drives, and I get to be his best friend. I'm very happy for him."
"What we talking about?" Jeremiah asked as he sat next to Lauren.
"Tim was telling Rudy how he works for you." Lauren said
Jeremiah smiled, "is that right?"
"Did you pull some strings to get him the job?" Rudy asked
"Tell him how you talked me up to the owner, how you begged and pleaded for me to get the job." I laughed.
Jeremiah was cracking up, "You are crazy."
Rudy sat back and watched us for a while. He kept looking around looking for his woman, but she was nowhere to be found. Jeremiah asked Rudy what he did, and he said he was part of a science team in Berkeley. As he used words he thought we wouldn't know to describe what he does, I blurted out, "you're a lab assistant? You hold the beaker and hope the acid doesn't splash on you during their experiments."
"That's one way of dumbing down what I do."
"You say dumbing down, I say telling it like it is. Same thing, different way of saying it."
"And you do what exactly?" He asked me.
"I push paper around."
"You're not even a driver?" Rudy laughed.
"I've driven before, but its not required anymore." Then Mary Jane, Peggy, and Beth walked back in the room. I introduced them to Lauren and Rudy. Rudy's eyes

lingered too long in Peggy's direction. "You are some kind of bold to look at a man's sister like that."
"Like what?" He tried to play innocent.
I stared him down, cause I wasn't playing with him anymore. Jeremiah got up and walked away. Lauren sat there with a smile taking everything in. Rudy asked Jeremiah where Annette was cause he was ready to go.
I wanted to rip his throat out! When they drove away Jeremiah had to convince me not to follow them home. My gut told me he would try something.

****

"When do we get to meet your son?" Jeff asked Franky.
Franky exhaled, then he mumbled something. Then he looked at us. "Women! When I told her about Christy she says she's not coming. Talking about I already have a family out here. I told her I haven't touched Christy since the night she got pregnant, but she don't care. This woman drives me crazy!" He growled.
"How are things with Lauren?" I asked.
"She's a cute kid. Her father is crazy! Her father is very religious and says it's a sin for her to consider me because I'm not of their faith." He scoffed.
"So you see her anyways?" I asked.
"Of course I do!" Jeff said, "I tried to leave her alone, but she comes for me so what can I say?"
"You can say no, this is a man's daughter you're talking about?" Franky barked, we stared at him.
"What's up Franky?" I asked
"What if I end up with a daughter one day? I don't want men treating her like we've done a few." He said
We all sat back, I hadn't thought of it that way. I didn't like Mary Jane's father so I paid him no mind. I never met or thought about Natalie's. I know Annette's father passed away, but I doubt he'd want me around his daughter if he thought like her mother does. No matter how I try to qualify it, if I tell my daughter to do something and some young fella came around telling her different… "Wait a minute!" Jeff blurted out breaking our silence. "Before I go jumping off the Golden Gate to end my guilt, where is this coming from? What have you done?" Jeff said looking at Franky.
I looked at him, "is Raynel pregnant?" I asked sitting on the edge of my seat.
Franky looked away, "you didn't?" Jeff said leaning in.
Franky huffed and puffed, and then he shot out of his seat. "Listen!….."
"OOH!" Jeff and I said in unison.
"Tell me you didn't?" I said.
Franky hadn't looked at us yet, "I don't know yet. My life is spinning out of control." Franky rubbed his head, "she wants to move to Harlem. Fine…" then he rubbed his head. "LOVE IS FOR THE BIRDS!"
"Franky, you did it on purpose?" Jeff asked, "does she know?"
Franky shook his head no, "I'm… I'm… Normally I have everything figured out. I know exactly what to do all the time. You know this about me." He looked to us for confirmation.
Jeff and I shook our heads in agreement. "I know, I always come to you for advice."
"Yeah normally you give great advice." I said.
"Then why couldn't I talk myself out of setting her up? It's like how many babies will it take for her to come home. I wanna see my son every day. I want to come home to her. See her face at night when I go to bed, and in the morning when I

wake up. She's so stubborn, if she thinks she knows the right way there's no talking her down."
"Sounds just like you."
Franky squinted his eyes at me, "I am not unreasonable!"
"Sounds like the only time you think she is unreasonable is when she doesn't give in to you."
Pops walked in his office with Matt, "what are we talking about?"
We were silent for a minute, "how many kids do we think Matthew will have? Will you have more kids than Mrs. Wallace?" I smiled.
Matt smiled, "it sure looks that way." He shrugged, "I don't care. She can keep having babies until her body gives out as far as I'm concerned."
"Isn't that nice!" Jeff said
"Business," Pops said redirecting our attention. "Matthew came to me with a brilliant idea. Tim with your trucking business flourishing like it is, I think this one should fall under your umbrella." Pops and Matt explained the need to start an investment firm. He said our bank accounts sit like sitting ducks if the Feds should decide to turn their attention towards us. We went over the structure of the company and how silent we would be, but still vitally important. Pops said we needed a name that was outside of our own. We shoved names for a while. Then I suggested Cooper Financial, after Annette. Franky said no. Pops was quiet for a minute, and then he went back to the name. He said he liked it. Franky said eventually I'm going to name everything after Annette. I smiled at the thought of it.

****

"Momma this is our friend Lauren, and you remember Annette." I said introducing them.
"Of course I do." She said walking towards Annette with her arms stretched open, "how are you doing sweetheart?" She said giving Annette a hug, "you never came back over so we could have cocktails."
"I'm sorry, things got so crazy, but I can come over now. I'd probably have to bring Lauren with me, but I could come."
"Nice to meet you." Momma said giving Lauren a hug, "well aren't you pretty."
"Thank you, and nice to meet you as well." Lauren said
Momma told me to go do something with myself and then she took the girls into her television room. I went to Pops's office and sat with him and Dale for a little while. I could hear my momma laughing loud and carrying on. Pops looked at me and smiled. "Sounds like your momma done made new friends."
"Who's here?" Dale asked.
"Friends from school, you wanna meet them?" I asked him.
Dale and I went in the television room with the women. Matt and Maureen had just arrived with their son and Maureen looked like she was going to burst any day now. As soon as I walked in the room her eyes stayed on me. I introduced Dale to Lauren and Annette. "So this is the brother I could've been in love with?" Lauren asked. Dale looked at me. "We were going on a picnic and she didn't want to be the fifth wheel. I suggested asking you to come, but I guess my description of you made you sound too kind hearted."
"Its a crime to be a gentleman?" Dale asked her.
"No a gentleman is preferred, but I think I'd be too much woman for you." She flirted.
Dale looked at me, "this is that Lauren?" I nodded yes, because Jeff had mentioned her a couple times. Dale smiled at Lauren, "a gentle man can handle any kind of

woman who comes along. You ladies say you want a gentleman, but all of you want the outwardly bad boy. It's ok darling, one day you'll learn that seeing is believing. You would've been happy with me, but now you're waiting. Nice to meet you Annette." Dale said then he went back to Pops's office.

Annette

Emma sat on the bed and kind of hopped up and down, and then she smiled at me. "This will do nicely."

I frowned at her, "Eeewwllll! Emma do you really like doing it?" I asked her.

She shook her head happily, "I love it!" Then she got up and I helped her put on her sheets and bedding. "This place is nice isn't it? All these new furnishings, I still can't believe it."

"How are you two paying for all of this?" I asked, "this apartment is fancier than ours. We struggle to make the ends meet."

"Hezekiah is working for Jeremiah. He pays him real good too. Katie and I picked out all this furniture as wedding presents. Hezekiah's family is real good to us. His momma demands respect, but she don't beat on everyone like our momma. She don't even expect her children to take care of her. I guess cause she got a husband who take good care of her. Momma acts like I never existed?" She asked me with sad eyes, I shook my head yes. "That's fine! She killed my baby, I can be dead to her too." Emma went to the kitchen and started fidgeting with stuff in there.

"Annette why you don't runaway? Why you stay there and let her hurt you like she does?"

"That's my momma, the only one I got. I know she ain't right, but I want her to love me."

Emma started crying, "I know! I feel like that too. I'm so **MAD** at her right now! I never thought she could do that to me. I knew she'd be mad, but the way she hurt me was evil! She ever kick you like that?"

"She punches me, kicks me, throws me on the ground up against the wall. You name it; she's done it to me. I just never thought she'd do it to you." I exhaled, "now she want me to open my legs to Rudy so he can make me big and have to marry me. She don't want him to wait until graduation."

"What about Tim?"

"We're just friends."

"You may be his friend, but he got it bad for you. He always has." She smiled.

"A guy like Tim is not looking at a girl like me. I saw the girl he was with at Katie's place. She was really pretty."

Emma frowned, "Annette am I pretty?" I said of course, "Am I prettier than that white girl?" I said of course again. "Not that it's a game, but you got her beat hands down. He keep her around for maintenance only, he would never marry her. I think he's been waiting on you. Think about it, how old is he?" I told her I wasn't sure. "I think he and Jeremiah the same age. I think he's in college to be with you. He's real sweet to you and he's cute too." She gave me a knowing smile.

"He is handsome isn't he? I don't know how I never noticed until now."

"You let momma blind you to good people. I say you open your heart and let love in. It's your life Annette. Momma needs to live her own and leave yours alone." She had a point.

"Since when you get so smart?" I smiled.

"Since I started thinking like my big sister." She smiled back, "give Tim a chance. Forget about momma."

****

Tim came in class and took his usual seat next to me. "Where's Lauren?"

"She's sick."

He smiled at me, "does that mean I get to have you all to myself today?"

"I guess so," I smiled.

After class Tim grabbed my hand and told me to come on. Every time he touches me I feel something. It always makes me jump. "Can you call in sick to work tonight? Lets ditch the rest of our classes today." His eyes pleaded with me to say yes.

"I can't, I need the money."

"Is that the only thing standing between us having the day... Money?" He looked at my eyes.

"That and Rudy." I said moving my eyes.

Tim stepped in my face and touched my hair. "Annette, I'll give you the money for your wages today." He looked at my eyes, "I can tell you don't love Rudy. Break up with him."

"I can't, my momma..."

"Annette you're spinning your wheels, wasting time with him. I love you, and I think you like me. I need your attention so you can fall in love with me too." He kissed my lips gently.

"But Tim! You're white!" I said feeling confused.

"Only on the outside, I promise that's the only part." Then he smiled at me and kissed my lips again. I felt tingling in a place I never felt it before when he kissed me. "Please Annette."

"Ok," I heard myself say. Then I puckered up to kiss him back.

We went to the pay phone and Tim gave me a nickel to place my call. I coughed and told Bubba to tell the Head Mistress I was sick and I wasn't coming in today. Normally I came to work even when I was sick. One time Bubba drove me home cause I was burning up with a fever. He said he was happy I didn't come in and he'd see me when I felt better.

Tim led me by the hand to his car; he opened the door for me. And then he hurried to the driver's side. "Sadie you and Annette have not been formally introduced." He said rubbing the dashboard. "This is the girl I've been telling you about...." He acted like they were having a conversation. "I know she's prettier than I said, but there aren't enough words to describe her... Ok.... Ok..." He cleared his throat. "Sadie wants to know what took you so long?"

"So long for what?" I asked smiling.

"So long to come around, she just reminded me that I've been in love with you since the first time I met you."

"Why do you say you're in love with me? You don't even know me." I blushed.

"I know you Annette, you just don't know me yet. So where would you like to go?"

"I have no idea, surprise me!"

He smiled, and then he drove. We drove over two bridges and then we were in beautiful country looking land again. There were farms at first and then vineyards as far as the eye could see. Tim said we were in wine country, and then he pulled off the road up the driveway to a winery. There were people out all over the vineyard of all colors working on the grounds. Tim opened my door and a white man walked out to greet us with two glasses of wine. "Bon jour!" He said handing over the glasses.

"Thank you," I said smiling.

"How are you?" Tim went in for a hug. "I believe you know my family. They come out here whenever my grandmother visits. Franklin and Irma Wallace."
"Oh yes! I know your family! Come in! Come in!" The man said to us. "Brad! Bring out a platter for this beautiful couple!" He said to his almost teenaged looking son.
Mr. Barbeau was from France and he spoke with an accent. His wife spoke very little English but I could understand that she thought I was beautiful. The family took us on a tour of the grounds and the delicious wine kept pouring. Mr. Barbeau pointed to a construction site to the side. He told Tim that his father funded the building of a new wine cellar. Mr. Barbeau explained that he inherited this vineyard from his father and one bad winter almost ruined their business. He said Tim's parents came out with his grandmother and his vineyard was the first to greet them warmly with open arms. He said that Tim's father is a silent investor, and with his financial backing the vineyard is thriving again. Tim looked proud hearing all these wonderful things about his father. The son kept staring at me and blushing when I looked at him. Then he gave me a bouquet of flowers he picked for me in the yard next door. I thanked him for the flowers.
When we got in the car Tim put his arm up on the seat. Then he told me to slide in. When I did he kissed me gently at first then he opened my mouth with his tongue. It had to be the wine, because I've never been kissed like this. I melted into the kiss, even though the tingling I was feeling down there confused me. We sat there kissing for a long time! Tim pulled away from me. "GO BACK OVER THERE!"
"What?" I asked with a smile.
"Woman! You...." He started to scoot next to me, and then he backed up. "I hear you Sadie! I'm cool!" He looked at me, and then he hopped out the car. He started doing jumping jacks real fast. Then he got back in the car breathing heavy. "I have to calm myself! You make me CRAZY!" He blurted out.
I had my hand over my mouth. "Tim, you're crazy!" I laughed.
"As a fox over you foxy lady!" He chuckled.
Then he drove holding my hand. I kept looking at him, how could a man like this think anything of me? My heart kept speeding up. We crossed a bridge and then we drove through a town on the waterfront. There were Colored people and white all living, working, and walking together. I asked Tim where we were, and he said this was Richmond. It was like San Francisco but the houses and buildings weren't stuck together and without all the hills. He drove through the town to an even smaller little town on the hill by the water. He said this was Point Richmond. Then he pointed to a hotel, "Hotel Mac."
I looked at the fancy people coming in and out. "We're going there?" He shook his head yes. "Will they let me in?"
"This is Richmond California, not Richmond Virginia. Of course they will, especially since you're with me." He held my hand as we walked into the hotel. The host said there was a little bit of a wait. Tim asked me if I wanted to wait and I happily said yes.
We sat down and this chubby white man smiled at us. "How y'all doing?"
"Hello," I said and Tim said the same.
"You sure are purrtyyy! Daisy ain't she purrtyyy?" He said to his woman.
"Oh yes-sum purrtyyy indeed! How you get so lucky?" She asked Tim.
Tim smiled, "I ask myself that everyday."
"How long y'all been married?" He asked Tim.
"About six months now." Tim said smiling.

"I can tell you two are in love! It's all over you!" She said smiling at us. "Never let passion die you hear me? Look at your man today and make a note of the feeling. Never give that up! Life tastes richer when you got love like you two got!" She said chewing on her gum and popping it.
The host came over to show the couple to their table. "Sonny if it's alright with you. We'd like to wait for a table that will seat the four of us nicely."
"Is that ok with you?" Tim asked me. I smiled and shook my head yes.
When our table was ready we sat with this man and woman who were from Texas. They were nice and really accepting of me. During our dinner for the first time I didn't feel like the lower class colored girl. Tim wasn't correcting my English or even bothered by the way I spoke. We had so much fun with this couple; the guy Walter gave Tim their number. He told us the next time we came to Richmond to look them up.
When I got in the car Tim put his key in the ignition but he didn't turn the car on. "Annette," he turned to face me so I did the same. "Thank you for spending the day with me. Thank you for letting me kiss you. If I died tonight I'd be a happy man because of you." I blushed hard, "I know it's too soon for you to hear me say this again, but I love you! I'll wait for you, but you don't love him. Get rid of him."
I thought about momma and I got sad. "My momma is going to try to kill me. She needs me to marry Rudy."
"Why?"
"Cause he has a good job." I said sadly.
"I could have a good job."
"Yeah but she thinks he's going to take care of her when we get married."
"That cheapo?"
"I know, that's what I said. She don't listen to me. She got it set in her mind that this will work."
"Do you want to marry him?" He asked watching my eyes like he was looking for truth.
"No, you're right. I don't love him, but I do care about him."
"Of course you do. You wouldn't be with him if you didn't care. But!" He scooted closer to me. "I'm in love with you! I want you! I need you! I'm exhausting myself right now trying to control myself!" He said like he was aching.
"You don't even know me." I said looking away from his stare.
"I know you! Come out with me tomorrow. I'll take you anywhere you want to go."
"We have to go to school, and I have to go to work."
"No we don't! We're educated, we graduated from high school. I can cover your wages from the hospital."
"How can you do that? Do you even have a job?"
He exhaled, "you're right. We need to go to school, but I can cover your job. Quit your job and spend that time with me."
"But my momma will know. When I get my check I give it to her and she put it in the bank."
"Tell her they changed the system and you have to give her cash because they gave you a raise. She'll like that. I'll hand you cash every week and you hand it to her."
"What about Rudy?"
"Breakup with him."
"I told you she will kill me if I do."
"When she sends you out with him come out with us. I'll bring Mary Jane or Lauren and he will be happy." Tim said.

"Ok so how long we gonna do this?"
"Until you're ready to love me."

Timothy

Lauren looked from me to Annette then she put her book down. "Ok spill it, what did I miss!"
Annette blushed and looked away. I smiled, "what are you talking about?"
"Look at how close you two are sitting. Don't make me chase you spill it!"
"We ditched school the first day you didn't come. We had a really good time." Annette said bashfully.
Lauren screamed and the librarian shushed her. "Am I gonna be an anty soon?"
I started cracking up, "no and shut up! Nothing like that happened." Annette said completely embarrassed.
"Annette do you like Tim?" She asked bluntly.
"Yes, now shut up!"
"Tim, do you like Annette?"
"No, I love her. I told her that."
Lauren balled up paper and threw it at Annette who still had her head down cause she was blushing so hard. "We rode to school together this morning and you didn't say anything! Did you two kiss?" Neither one of us answered. "I hate both of you so much! Don't keep secrets!"
"I don't ask you what you do with Jeff." Annette said
"That's because I tell you the little bits you don't see. Besides I haven't seen Jeff in a month. He's probably tired of me."
He wasn't tired of her; he keeps trying to say she's a little girl to stop himself from caring as much as he does. Mister, I don't need anyone is breaking down. "You should call him." I said stirring the pot for my brother.
"Or maybe I should call Dale."
Now she was probably joking, and my response could've been a lot calmer, but she struck a nerve! "Lauren if that's the type of woman you're going to be, forget you ever knew me or my brother! Every man in my family is handsome and has a lot to offer any woman he chooses. What we don't have time for is females who choose to thump on each of us until she finds the melon she's looking for." I glared at her.
Lauren turned red, "Tim, you gotta know I was just kidding. I would never!"
"Your joke wasn't funny!" I said trying to shake my irritation.
Annette shifted in her chair. "I'm sorry." Lauren said putting her head down.
Annette shifted again, I finally looked at Annette and she looked like a lioness about to devour her prey. "What?" I said looking clueless.
"Whew!" Annette said fanning herself.
Lauren lifted her eyes to Annette and then she started cracking up. "You like that didn't you?"
Annette kept fanning herself while she smiled. "Whew! Shut up Lauren!"
I couldn't help it, I laughed out loud. The librarian kicked us out like she has to once a month at least.

Annette

"Annette I don't know if I can forgive you for missing my wedding." Martha said
"I'm sorry, things were so crazy. Please tell me you have pictures." I said sipping the cocktail Mrs. Wallace made for me. It was fruity and with a definite kick.
"Momma where's your picture book?" Martha said getting up slowly.

"Sit down enjoy your cocktail I'll get it." Mrs. Wallace said.
I looked at Martha's stomach, "are you nervous?"
She rubbed her belly. "A little but I'm more excited. I never thought I'd get to be a mother cause my brothers wouldn't let anyone get next to me. You have no idea how badly they've behaved. You know what never made sense to me. All the stuff they were trying to protect me from they've done to girls too. It wasn't fair, but now I get to love a man and feel loved in return all thanks to you."
"Why do you...."
She came busting through the door like a red ball of fire. "MRS. WALLACE????????" She walked into the kitchen with a baby. She dumped the baby in my arms. Then she looked at Martha, "YOU'RE BROTHER IS THE WORST! HE HASN'T COME TO SEE THE BABY IN DAYS!" She said lighting a cigarette.
"Christy please don't light that around me I can't stand the smell of them." Martha said
She looked at me, "go change him." When I looked at her confused she barked at me, "GO ON!"
Martha's eyes turned black as she slowly stood, "who do you think you're talking to?"
"The maid of course! Your mother said you finally got one a long time ago."
Martha slapped her HARD twice! "GET OUT!"
Mrs. Wallace came back in the kitchen with evil eyes. She put the photo album on the table. The baby started crying and I started rocking him cause I didn't know what was about to happen. Mrs. Wallace grabbed a fist full of her red hair and calmly drug her to the front door. "Martha asked you to put the cigarette out! How dare you walk in my house talking to anyone like that regardless of who you think they are! Don't come back until FRANKY calls you!" Then she slammed the door. I expected her to be mad and calming down when she came back. Instead she smiled at me and took the baby from me.
"Who was that?"
"This is my grandson." Mrs. Wallace said bouncing the baby and getting him to calm down.
"Franky's married?"
"Nope, he knocked her up and won't marry her." Martha said.
"I think he's quietly courting someone away from all of this noise. I just wish he'd hurry up and bring her home so he can get settled already. I wanna see all my children settled and happy." Then she smiled at me. "So what do you think of today's cocktail?"
"It's delicious as usual." I smiled
"Annette honey can you explain this to me cause I don't understand what you and Tim are doing?" Mrs. Wallace asked.
"Momma!" Martha said like she wanted her to leave me alone.
"Mrs. Wallace...."
"Annette! I done told you to call me Irma or if you must you can call me momma, but Mrs. Wallace was my mother in-law." She smiled.
I smiled, "momma we're getting to know each other."
"What's to know? He loves you, you love him. Get married and make me some more grand babies."
"I got one right here for you momma!" Martha said pointing at her stomach.

"Yes you do sweetheart." She said smiling at her daughter. Then she looked at me, "but I want more! I want a bus load of grandkids and I want them to all know me."
"I would love to have your grand babies, but my momma ain't so understanding."
"What you mean?"
"My momma isn't as loving as you are. She's never really liked me. She wanna give me away to a boy from around the way. I don't know what to do."
"She don't like my boy?"
"She'd never give him a chance." I said sadly.
Irma looked mad.

****

I never knew kissing could feel so good. At first when I saw Tim I'd wait for him to kiss me. Sometimes I'd go home disappointed cause he wouldn't even try. So I started kissing him, something I thought I'd be embarrassed to do. It feels too right to be wrong so I go for it. When I'm not with Tim I'm thinking about when I'll see him again.
Every time Rudy tries to make plans with me, I tell him I have things to do for school. It's true cause I've had paper after paper due. I have high markings in all of my classes so they can't say I'm lying about the time I need for school. Momma still thinks I work at the hospital, she got so excited when I told her they gave me a raise. When I bring home the money she puts it directly in her bra. Then she asks me about Rudy, I try to give her good excuses for why I haven't talked to him, but she gets mad anyways. Then I try to leave. At night sometimes I sleep on Aunt Dorothy's couch. Momma has gotten so used to me sleeping over there that sometimes she doesn't look for me.
One night Lauren and I accidentally fell asleep on Tim's couch. I think we all woke up as the sun was coming up. Tim dropped me off so that Lauren could hurry home. I was frantic as Aunt Dorothy let me in. She smiled and told me to calm down. She said I should've stayed and that she would've covered for me. Then she told me that I was such a good daughter, I should be allowed to have some fun. She said to let her know my plan but she'd cover for me. I was so surprised when she said it, but my momma and Aunt Dorothy argue so much. I honestly think she's tired of my momma and wants her to move away.
Tim stopped kissing me, "have you broken up with him yet?"
I put my forehead on his as I looked down. "I don't know how. I'm scared to do it, cause he's gonna tell my momma. Then she's gonna come after me."
"Even if you show her this?" He held out a ring box. "Tell her I've asked you to be my wife."
I blinked my eyes fast and hard. I had to be dreaming. "What is that?"
"What does it look like?"
"I've only seen that type of box in the theater. This can't be real."
"Annette, I've loved you from the first time I laid eyes on you. I need you here with me every single day. Please be my wife." He said from his heart.
"But my momma..." I started crying cause I wanted to say yes, but I knew my momma would kill me first literally.
"I'll put your momma in a nice apartment or house if you want. Say yes." He pleaded.
I felt like I couldn't breathe. Tears started pouring out of my eyes. "You can't have a wife who doesn't work."
He looked at me confused, "what are you talking about?"

"I can't have sex! I... I..." I swallowed. "You need a wife who enjoys laying with you. I panic every time the thought crosses my mind."
Tim deflated, "Annette. You're supposed to say yes and then we work out all the details." He grabbed my hand. "There's nothing wrong with you, you're fine."
"I would die knowing that you're unhappy. And I know what men want, so there's no point."
He put his arms around me and he exhaled deeply. "This is not how I envisioned this going."
I felt horrible, "I'm sorry. I should go." I tried to get up.
He hugged me tighter, "most virgins think they don't work or something like that, cause they don't know what to expect." I didn't say anything cause I was afraid to tell him I wasn't a virgin.

****

I was waiting for the bus when a car slowed as it approached me. I recognized the car, it was Franky. "Get in."
I looked around fortunately it was early. I got in the car. "Thank you Franky, you didn't have to stop."
"Why don't you drive?"
"I don't know how, I don't have a car. Between the bus and trolley I don't need a car really. What are you doing up so early?"
"I had a long night."
"I met your son, Fernando is so cute."
"I heard about that, thank you." He exhaled. "Tell me something, you love my brother?"
"Yes, I've never met anyone like him." I said honestly.
"Why you turn him down then?" He looked at me.
I exhaled, "he deserves better."
Franky frowned then his voice rumbled like it came from his feet. "WHAT SENSE DOES THAT MAKE? He loves you! He wants to marry you!"
I jumped; the deepness and emotion in his voice startled me. Franky never shows emotion, to me anyways. I didn't know where this reaction was coming from. "It makes complete sense, and the reasons are none of your business!"
"MY BROTHER LOVES YOU! HE DOESN'T WANT ANYONE ELSE! YOU'RE REALLY GOING TO BE THIS SELFISH?" He barked at me.
I hit him upside the head, "what's wrong with you? My reason for saying no is not about me. I want to be his wife! I want to share my life with him! I don't want him to be miserable behind being married to someone like me."
"You should let him manage his misery, if he's chosen you the rest shouldn't matter."
"You don't know what you're talking about. Who would want a marriage like that?" I said not wanting to explain any further.
He pulled into my school parking lot. "Look, I'm not going to pretend like I know first hand what it's like to be Negro in America cause I don't. I do know that love doesn't see color, and if you two are willing to make it work the world shouldn't matter."
I looked at Franky, he was emotional. I could see sadness in his eyes. He wasn't talking about me and Tim. "Who is she?"
Franky exhaled real hard and his eyes turned red. "She's carrying my child again and she still refuses me! Stating that she doesn't want to make my life harder. Every time I leave her I die a little."

I sat there listening as he explained his situation. He's in love with a colored girl, and she refuses to marry him because she doesn't want him treated badly on account of her. I could tell he wanted to cry, but he's such a brick wall, I knew he wouldn't.
"You can tell me to shut up if that will help."
I caught him off guard and he chuckled. "I do that a lot don't I?"
"You used to all the time, not so much lately." I smiled, "you should laugh and smile more often."
His smile dropped, "I have nothing to smile about."
"She loves you Franky. No woman wants to raise babies alone or live in secret with love in her life. You want to scream it out at the top of your lungs. Only love could carry a woman through something like that."
"I don't want her to do it alone. I want her here with me."
"Then don't give up, keep fighting for her."
He smiled, "you hit me."
"You weren't making any sense."
"Take your own advice and don't give up on my brother. He loves you Annette."
"Ok."
Franky leaned in for a hug so I extended my arms to hug him. He kissed me instead. My heart stopped beating, I thought I was dead. "I'm sorry!" Franky said immediately. I got out of that car so fast. Franky ran and caught me. "I'm sorry! I'm sorry!"
"Why would you...." I looked at the sadness in his eyes. "There's more to that story." I said begging the love to leave his eyes.
"I'm sorry! You didn't do anything wrong, I shouldn't...." Then he screamed a frustrated yell. A few passing students looked at him.
"Why are you scaring the students?" Tim said walking up with a smile. He hugged me then he looked at my face. I tried to smile but I couldn't. Tim spun around, "you didn't?"
"Walk with me," Franky told Tim.
I didn't know what to do so I went to class. I wished Lauren was here. I was fidgeting in my seat when class began. Tim snatched the door and he came in angry and determined. He gently grabbed my arm and told me to come with him. My heart was beating so hard, I was afraid he was going to blame me. I didn't know. Tim put me in his car, when he shut the door he rocked the car and growled. I started crying immediately. He calmly walked around the car then sat in the driver's seat. He growled then he looked at me. "No one kisses you except me, do you understand me?"
"I didn't know he was going to do that. I honestly..."
He cut me off, "I know. He told me. I don't blame you." Tim started his car. "I can't go to school today. I need to relax."
"Did you eat? I can make you breakfast." I volunteered.
"That wouldn't be too much trouble?" He said gripping the steering wheel.
"Baby, of course not!"
When we walked in the door, he dropped his keys on the table by the door and he deflated. He went in his room and fell on his bed face down. I took his shoes off and I told him to relax. He looked at me and smiled as he laid on his bed. I went in the kitchen and got busy. I made him a simple breakfast and then I brought it in to him. He sat up excitedly as I gave him his plate. I made eggs, sausage, and toast. His reaction made it seem like I just put a turkey dinner in his hands. I kissed him quick then I went back to the kitchen to clean up. I was cleaning his skillet when he

put his arms around me, and kissed my neck. I smiled then he kissed me again. I turned around and put my arms around his neck. We kissed for a long time, then I told him to let me finish the dishes. He told me to go lay down and he'd finish cleaning up. I assumed we were going to take a nap so I took my shoes off and then I laid on top of his covers on his bed. Tim started kissing me again, when he touched my breast I internally argued with my panic. I told it to back off, but when he laid on top of me I was back in that kitchen. I was kicking, crying, and screaming. Tim pinned me down and told me to open my eyes. His eyes were big and red. "Who hurt you?" He asked just like Luther did. Only Tim wasn't letting me go until I answered him.
I cried from the bottom of my soul after I told him about Leslie. Tim held me and told me I was safe now and I didn't have to be scared. I fell asleep crying in his arms.

Timothy

"I don't know what happened with you two, but you need to cut this out." Dale said looking between Franky and I.
"Where's Pops?" Franky asked.
Pops came out of his bathroom washing his hands. "I'm here, now I wanna know what's going on."
Franky looked in the opposite direction. "Pops, its nothing. Can we drop it?" I said.
"You two have always been fighting. I thought that stuff stopped when we became adults." Dale said.
I thought about it, and Franky has always demanded what was mine. He was always trying to muscle his way to get my stuff from me. That's why even though we said it was over, I keep getting mad over and over. I started cursing, no one said anything they sat there quiet as I went completely off. Franky looked at me sarcastically, "a cake Tim really? You're reaching." So I reached out and hit him in the face. Franky is fast and strong, he saw my fist coming but he didn't move. Pops looked at us, "stop." is all he said and I paused almost in the air. "Call Matthew down, set up the boards." All of us groaned. None of us were leaving for hours. This was going to be a marathon chess match until Pops drove whatever point he was trying to make home.
"WHO'S FAULT IS IT?" Matt growled coming in the door. "Pops, I got a family now. I can't come down here whenever you feel like torturing us!" Matt fussed.
"Shut up! Tim play Dale, Jeff play Matt, Franky you play me." When everyone was sitting he turned the thirty-minute sand glass timer over. Dale came out safely and I went straight for his queen. Dale saw my anger as weakness until I checked him. I was upset, but capable of thinking. When I played Matt I admit I was playing emotionally, but I was mad at him too. I loss, then I had to play Franky. "Mister no emotion expects me to believe he got carried away with emotion!" I barked.
"You think I did that to you on purpose?" Franky said with no emotion.
"Everything is a calculation with you. It's hard to trust you when we talked this out. You're just another Matt in different clothing!"
"A Matt? What did I do?" He said turning his attention to me leaving his game.
"I tell you I don't want to see you date her, so you marry her. She's always looking at me, watching my eyes like there's supposed to be something still there for her. You think I like walking around knowing intimate things about my brother's wife?"
"Tim!"

“Don't Tim me, it don’t matter. Now you’re married and having baby after baby together FINE! I finally find what I’m looking for. I’m in love! And this big Bluto looking fool makes a move on her!”
Everyone looked at Franky; he sat there with no emotion staring at me. “I met her first!”
I turned the table over, “is that supposed to matter?”
“It matters. I met her first! I was taking care of her, watching over her. Then here you come. I didn’t make a move cause I had nothing to offer her. I’ve cared about her since before you knew she was a live. I did not mean to do what I did. I told you that!”
Pops looked at Franky, “when are you going to come clean about the Johnson girl?”
Franky slumped, “I want her to choose me. You wouldn’t understand.” Franky said
Pops pounded the table, “I’ve got a grandson that I don’t know. A grandson who carries my name, and I don’t know him! If your momma finds out about this from someone other than you she’s going to get you.” Pops threatened.
“I’m working on it.” Franky said
“What was Annette’s reaction to this nonsense?” Pops asked.
“It was all me Pops. She was completely clueless and I doubt she even suspected.” Franky said.
“She didn’t suspect it!” I said.
“Do we need to take out the gloves or is this over? I mean we can’t do nothing about Matt thinking it was a good idea to knock up your ex, I take my wife down south and you kids lose your mind. Its a wonder Peggy and Beth didn’t get knocked up too.” We all blank stared at Pops. “Matt we gotta take your father in-law out.” Pops said switching gears.
“WHAT? Why?” Matt asked.
“Loose lips sink ships!” Pops said.
“What about Maureen?” Matt asked, you could tell he wanted to plead for his father in-law on account of Maureen.
“She has you, and that thing she calls a momma. He died a long time ago, as far as his family's concerned, she’ll be ok."

Annette

Lauren collapsed on my shoulder crying her eyes out. I rubbed her back cause I know how it feels. You're mad cause it happened, it hurts, but then you feel guilty for being angry. Lauren's daddy blackened her eye again. She doesn't even know why this time. I rubbed her back while she cried. She caught me as I walked in the door. I pretended like I was talking to Rudy even though I didn't say his name. Then I hurried right back out the door before my momma could ask me anything. Lauren called me from a pay phone around the corner. She met me at the bus stop, and then we went to Emma's. Emma brought Witch Hazel and then I put it on her eye. She said she was tired of getting beat on. I told her I was in the same boat. "Let's get a place together." She said.
"Your daddy would disown you for living with me."
"He's already disowned me for not being pure. At least I won't be at home."
"I don't have a job, how would I pay rent?"
"Oh yea, that's a good point." She was thinking. "Emma could we stay with you?"
Emma laughed, "no single women around my man sorry."
Lauren smiled, "good thinking. I'm going to have to remember that."
Then she smiled at me, "we could ask Tim."

"It's bad enough he wants to be with me. People would really talk about how he's living in sin with the colored girl."
"We gotta think of something. You gotta get away from your momma before Rudy tells on you. I can't live with my daddy anymore."
Emma smiled, "Jeremiah said the building owner is going to be looking for a manager pretty soon. You gotta take care of the tenants and the building but the rent is included in your wages."
"How come you not doing it?" I asked.
"Hezekiah is making good money. We're going to buy a house. We need more room for when the baby comes."
Lauren and I stared at her, "no fair! You're younger than me!" Lauren shouted.
"I thought you guys were going to wait?" I said
"This baby said it wants to come now." She smiled.
We hugged, and then I thought about Katie. I felt sad for her, tell Katie before you tell the others. She's going to need a minute, ok?"
"Ok" Emma said.

Chapter 10

Annette

I was trying to run through the house to get a few things and get out the door before momma went in on me. I was hoping she wasn't home or was busy with something else and didn't notice me. She had my sewing machine out in the middle of the living room, poor Preston was standing there shirtless waiting for her to finish making his shirt. "Annette!" She said as soon as she laid eyes on me. "Where have you been?"

"School and Katie has been tutoring me to help me out with some things. I actually need to grab something and then go."

"No! No, the whole point of you going to school was to get you closer to Rudy. You haven't seen him in weeks."

"I know momma, but what if I could get a job good enough not to need his money? What if I could take care of all of us on my own?"

She looked at me and then she started laughing, "that school is making you dumber not smarter! You too stupid to ever be better than laying on your back." I looked at Preston who stood there smiling at me.

"My Professors all say I'm real smart and I can be anything I want to be."

She slapped me, "who you gonna believe? Professors who don't know you? Or me, the woman who brought you into this world. Took care of you when you had no one else. Stop listening to those fancy stories and do as I tell you!"

There was a knock at the door and she told me to go answer it. When I opened the door a white woman was standing there with her two boys. She looked scary and mean. "Look at her face, study it good!" She barked at them while they frowned at me.

"May I help you?" I asked her.

"Who is it?" Momma asked me.

"I don't know," I said looking at this woman who looked like she hadn't slept in months.

Momma snatch the door open wider, "yes?" Momma said.

The lady pointed at momma, "you're the mother aren't you?"

"Who you looking for?" Momma asked putting her hand on her hip.

"The parents of Leslie Cooper, that's you isn't it?"

"Who wants to know?" Momma asked.

"MRS. O'BRIEN!" She said like we should know who she was.

"How can we help you Mrs. O'Brien?" I said.

"How can you help me? How can you help ME!" She slapped her chest! "I wanted my boys to get a good look at the faces of the monsters who created that monster!"

"MONSTER! MY BOY AIN'T NO MONSTER!" My momma yelled.

"He stalked that poor Betts girl, waited until her father left and then he raped her! He deserved everything he got!" She yelled, "my poor husband came here to arrest your boy and your savage son killed him! That's why they killed your monster!" She yelled.

Rufus and Aunt Dorothy opened their door. "What's going on?"

"Did you help him?" Mrs. O'Brien accused all of us. "I don't know how the rest of you are walking around unharmed and my poor husband is dead!" She cried.

"Ma'am, I don't know what you were told, but the only person who died here was my brother. He tried to run away and the police beat him to death." I said

“YOU NO GOOD NIGGER! ALL OF YOU LIE! I’VE SEEN THE POLICE REPORT! I KNOW HOW MY HUSBAND DIED!” She screamed at me.
Rufus stepped into the hallway, “who’s her husband?”
“I’m Mrs. O’Brien!” She yelled.
Rufus’ eyes got big, “ma’am I know you’re not going to believe us. A white man killed your husband because he brutally beat on my niece and sister in-law. Your husband broke her arm and broke her head.” He said pointing between my momma and me. "Your husband died at the police station at the hands of a white man.”
I looked at Rufus like I didn’t understand what he was saying. “LIES! YOU SEE HOW THEY LIE!” She said to her son.
“Think about it ma’am. If we killed a cop, we’d all be dead.”
She started crying cause she knew it was true, but she didn’t want to believe it. It was easier to hate us and to teach her sons to hate us. She reminded me of momma.
“It ain’t true!” She backed away with her sons. “it ain’t true!"
I asked Rufus what he was talking about when they were gone. Rufus said I didn’t need to worry about it, and that I was safe.

****

"Good morning Annette," a student at my school said he slowed down to walk with Lauren and I.
"Good morning Harvey."
"Can I talk to you for a moment?"
"Harvey do you know Lauren?" I asked because he didn't even acknowledge her.
"Hi," he said uninterested in talking to her.
Lauren started to walk away and I grabbed her hand and I interlocked my fingers with hers to tell her not to leave. "What do you want?"
He looked at our hands. "Are you messing around with Timothy Wallace?"
"How is that any of your business?" I asked him annoyed.
"Look, I just think you should know who you're messing with. Annette you're a beautiful young lady, very smart, you could go anywhere you want. That family is not to be trusted."
"Bye Harvey!" I said turning to walk away.
"Annette! Why would you want a white man when you can have anyone you want?"
"Oh I see! That's what this is about!" My body instantly was on fire with anger. I pointed my finger in his face. "I happen to want Tim and I don't care if you or anyone else has a problem with that! You don't know me or anything about me. I don't know what you've heard or think you've heard about the Wallace's but I don't care. They're good people and they have always been good to me! Not that it's any of your business! Don't you ever come speaking sideways to me about my family again! Or you won't have to worry about the Wallace's, you'll need to watch out for me!"
"You go on then, don't say I didn't try to warn you when they chew you up and spit you out. There are lots of bodies in the SF cemetery behind that family."
I rolled my eyes and marched away holding Lauren's hand and dragging her a long.
"What do you think?" She asked me.
"About what?"
"Do you think the Wallace's are dirty?"
"Define dirty!"
"Don't get mad, we should make sure we're paying attention. I love Jeff, you know I do. I don't understand some of their dynamics. Where does Franky fly off to all the

time? How can he afford all the women he's got. Jeff doesn't really answer my questions about his business. Who knows what those other two do. Has Tim told you what he does for money? He told Rudy he works with Jeremiah, but he's always with us, and he pays for everything."

I knew that Matt is a lawyer and Dale is an architect, but I didn't exactly know what Tim does for a living. I really didn't care; as long as I could work I was fine. "Don't let him plant seeds of doubt in your head about our men. Nothing he could say could make me stop loving Tim. As long as he loves me, I don't care about the rest!"

Lauren was quiet for a minute. "I don't want to end up like my mother. Stuck with a man she doesn't love who tries to beat love into her and kills her. I'd rather die on my back in the biggest mind blowing orgasm ever!" She laughed.

"SSSHHHH! Someone might hear you." I said looking around embarrassed.

Lauren smiled, "I know what we're doing tonight."

"What?"

"Yea what are we doing tonight?" Tim said

Lauren and I jumped, "how long have you been there?" Lauren asked.

Tim looked angry, "long enough. Long enough to see that fella what's his name approach you. I heard everything." Then he smiled at Lauren, "you're nasty."

"Thanks Tim!" She smiled.

"So you were saying about tonight?"

"Have you heard of Francine's in downtown San Francisco?"

Tim smiled, "yes. You want to go there? That's where grown up stuff happens."

"Now I want to go more." She said.

"You're going to need a dress." He said to me.

"I have dresses." I said thinking of all the dresses I've made.

He looked at Lauren, "can you two go shopping?"

"Can you ask Jeff if he can make it?" She asked.

"He's going." Tim said then he put his arm around me as we walked to class.

After class Tim gave me money so we could go shopping. I kissed him goodbye, he said he'd pick us up at Jeremiah's house at eight o'clock.

Lauren took me downtown to the department store. People looked at the two of us and ignored us. Then a middle aged white woman approached us. Lauren told her we were going out tonight and we needed cocktail dresses and we needed to look amazing. She asked what our budget was and I told her the sky. She had the models come out in beautiful dresses. Lauren and I kept picking the same dresses to love. Lauren said she wanted to try on the green dress. I picked the black dress. The woman gave us shoes and all of the accessories to complete our looks. When I came out the dressing room in my just above the knee length sheath dress with white gloves, small hat, and red wrap I felt stunning. Lauren was standing in the mirror, she screamed when she saw me. She said Tim was going to die from the sight of me. The sales lady walked around and then she said I looked perfect. I told Lauren I liked her green dress with her cream-colored sweater, gold shoes and accessories. We told the saleslady we'd take it all. Her eyes got big; she took everything and packaged it up for us. She watched my eyes when she gave us the total. I took the money out of my purse and happily paid for it. She seemed relieved that this wasn't all a ruse. She told me her name was Delores and to come back directly to her next time we were in the store. Lauren had lunch and she asked me how it felt to be able to pull that much money out of my purse without feeling like I was giving the woman all the money I had in the world? I told her it was an amazing feeling cause

I'm used to not having. Lauren said she was too. "Do you think I should dye my hair blonde?" She asked me, "I was blonde when I was little and I miss it."
"How does that work? One morning you wake up and your hair is brown?" I asked
"It gradually darkened. The important question is will being blonde enhance my beauty or take away?"
"Maybe you should try on a wig to see if you like it first."
"Good idea, tomorrow we're going to the wig shop." She said as she laughed.
When we got to Katie's we told her about our experience in the store. She said the next time we go all the salesgirls will be stepping over each other to wait on us. She said the same thing happened the first time she went. She said now she only deals with the person who was kind enough to wait on her. We laughed when she mimicked the other sales people's sad faces. Katie started coughing and it was nasty. She said she had the flu about a week ago, and the cough was still here. Then Katie showed us both of her closets full of clothes. Lauren said we could've come shopping in her closet. Katie held on to her smile, she said shopping makes her feel good whenever she thinks about her empty womb.

Timothy

"The girls want to go to Francine's tonight." I said to Jeff.
"The girls meaning Lauren too?" He asked, I didn't say anything, that was a dumb question. "You know Franky's going to be there. I think you two should clear the air before we get there."
"There's no need, we can be civil." Then Franky opened Jeff's door.
His eyes went straight to me, "Timothy." He said acknowledging me.
"Franklin," I said watching him.
"I didn't expect to see your car outside."
"The girls want to go to Francine's tonight." I said.
"Consider it done." He watched me.
"You going to be there?"
"Do you want me to be there?"
"I'm asking you if you're going to be there is there any other way to say that? As long as we have an understanding." I watched his eyes.
"You're my kid brother, what's there to understand?"
I looked at Jeff, "I gave Annette money so she and Lauren could go shopping. Jeremiah is going to meet us downtown."
"DOWNTOWN? Why can't I wear a suit I have in my closet? What's wrong with the suit I'm wearing now?" Jeff spun around in his suit.
"I will shoot you if I have to look at that vest all night. Stop being frugal, and let's treat our women to a night they've never seen before."
Franky said he'd meet us there. We went downtown and bought new duds, Jeff suggested that we hire a driver since we were going all out.

Annette

Jeremiah came home with a garment bag and a shoebox. We sat on the couch so he could show us what he bought. Katie lit a cigarette, the way she inhaled it made it seem so soothing. I asked her if I could try one, Katie asked me if I was sure cause it was a bad habit to have. She gave me a fresh cigarette holder with a cigarette in it. She lit it for me and when I exhaled without choking all them stared at me waiting for an explanation. I told them I used to sneak puffs on my father's cigars and when I went to Hazel's everyone did it. Lauren asked to try mine and she choked and gagged. She shook her head and said she didn't see the appeal. Jeremiah said he didn't know how Tim would feel about me smoking so I put the cigarette down. We started getting dressed around six-thirty. Jeremiah went in one of the spare bedrooms so that we could get ready with Katie's vanity. When we heard voices downstairs we knew Tim was here.

Timothy

We got dressed at my house and then we made our way over to Jeremiah's. "What do you think about me letting Lauren manage my building?"
"She know you're the owner?"
"No, but you know she needs to get away from her father. I'm not ready to pop the question yet, but I feel like I need to rescue her."
"I asked Annette to marry me."
Jeff's mouth fell open, "why are you just now telling me this? You haven't been dating... Wait a minute! Don't her momma think she's still dating that other fella?"
"I didn't say there weren't complications. She gave me a soft no."
"WHAT THE HECK IS A SOFT NO?"
"She's not ready."
"That's the kind of stuff that gets women choked! If I'm putting my heart out there for her and she rejects me.... I'm not responsible." He shook his head.
"Momma would skin you a live if you raise your hand to a female. Besides I know Annette loves me and she wants to be with me. It's that same thing that I love about her that's keeping us apart. As amazing as she is, she thinks I deserve better."
"So what are you going to do?"
"Convince her that my life's happiness rests on her acceptance. She's going to say yes. I just need to be patient."
Jeff blank stared at me, "faithfully patient?"
I shrugged, "of course."
Jeff and Jeremiah started cracking up. "Yea right!"
"I think I can do it!"
"You'd be the first. Even Matt couldn't let his wife get off the table good from delivering their son, before he was on someone else. I don't think even Dale could do it."
"I don't mind being the first. I've gone this long."
"How long?"
"It's been months." I said trying to ignore my pent up frustration. When we walked in the door Jeremiah was posing and trying his best to put on a happy face. He was overly silly all day. "What's wrong?" I finally asked.
"Emma's pregnant," then he laughed.
Jeff went to the bar and poured drinks for all of us. "How's Katie?"
"She got sick immediately, flu or something. She's coming around though. Oh and Buckie's getting married, so I'm sure there will be more babies to be had." He gulped his drink.
"Eeewwllll! More buck teeth in this world?" Jeff said, "you know their children will look like they've been beaten over twice with the ugly stick. His four eyes, buck teeth, and let's face it Stacy is UGLY!"
Jeremiah and I cracked up. "With parents like that the child would have no choice but to be beautiful." Jeremiah said, "no offense. Tim have you seen Annette's momma?" I shook my head no. Jeremiah stuck out his hand to Jeff for another drink. "She's as ugly as she sounds. Annette and Emma get their coloring from her,

and a couple features, but I would've never thought women that beautiful came from her."
"You're scaring me!" Jeff and Jeremiah laughed hard at me. "What do her brothers look like?"
"Never paid them no mind. I can't really tell you."
When we started complaining about waiting our women glided down the stairs. My soon to be bride is beautiful! I loved what she did with her hair, I loved her whole outfit. When I hugged her I grabbed a hand full of her beautiful bottom. I watched her face to make sure she wasn't offended. She smiled approvingly and then her bottom became a magnet for my hands. That dress showed off the body of a woman, my chocolate Goddess. Her neck tasted like the sweetest cognac and I was drunk from drinking from it all night long. Annette accepted all of my affectionate touches, holds, and grabs. Who wouldn't want this forever?

Annette

The three of us posed in the mirror like we were taking pictures. Lauren said we deserved to be on the cover of a magazine. I laughed at the thought of it, but I knew I was looking good. We practiced our sexy walks for awhile. Then we heard the men calling up to us. Katie said we could all sleep here after the club. Her only request was that we wash the bedding afterwards. I swallowed the fear of her implications; I was irritated with myself for reacting so nervously. Katie told us to come on; she said they had been waiting long enough. She led the way and I brought up the rear. Each of their eyes filled with approval and excitement. The men looked so sharp in their suits, shawls, and hats. We screamed with excitement when we saw the driver waiting by the car. You should've seen the look on the white driver's face when we all walked out. Jeff reminded him that his tip was determined by his attitude and the level of service he provides. I've never ridden in such a fancy car before. When we arrived at the nightclub picture girls were all around the floor. There were tables all over with small candles in the middle. The carpet was red and all the furniture was dark colored. Cigar and cigarette smoke filled the air. There was a live band of colored musicians playing music. And small dance floors on either sides of the stage. Jeff led us to the table on the side that was slightly elevated so that everyone could see us. Franky and little miss red head were already sitting at the table. They introduced us, "they're going to sit with us?" She asked Franky.
"This is the Wallace table, they're Wallace's." Franky said nonchalantly.
She nodded in the direction of Jeremiah and I. "They aren't Wallace's."
"They're more Wallace than you'll ever be." He snapped at her.
Christy took a drag on her cigarette as she looked around the room I guess to see who was looking at us.
"You know you're trying to give me a heart attack." Tim said in my ear, I smiled. "You stop my heart with one look."
I put my eyes down while I blushed uncontrollably. We ordered drinks and enjoyed the night. Franky would not look in my direction for anything, while Christy kept staring at Katie and I. After she drank enough courage juice she spoke to me. "I wanna apologize for the way I acted. No one wants to be mistaken for the maid. I was so mean." She said shaking her head.
"Ok," I wasn't going to say it was nothing or lie.
"You are really pretty!" She said like she was shocked.
"We all are!" Lauren said irritated.

"You're not on the same level." Christy said
"Wow! Should I be insulted or enraged?" Lauren spit
"Calm down! I'm saying that for a colored girl…"
Franky cut her off, "STOP! Stop talking, you sound so dumb right now."
"Franky!" She whined….
"UGH! Kill me now!" He said walking away from her.
The rest of us followed Franky out onto the dance floor. A slow song came on; I looked at Tim nervously as I said I've never slow danced before. He smiled and said he was happy to be my first. I put my head down and he lifted my chin to look at him. He put my arms around his neck, and he pulled my body in close to his, then he put his arms around my waste. He moved to the slow rhythm and I followed his lead. He kept staring at me and grinning, "you're not anything for a colored girl. You are the most beautiful woman I have ever laid eyes on in my life. I knew you were too beautiful to be anything other than beautiful inside as well. Say you'll marry me, I'll give you anything you want."
I put my head down again, "I want to be your wife Tim. I can't let you do this to yourself. I'm broken, and I don't think I can be fixed. What kind of life is that supposed to be? You'll be miserable, and I'd never forgive myself."
"Do you love me?" He said staring at me, I shook my head yes. "Look at me Annette, do you love me?" I said yes, "then that's all that matters. Say yes."
I put my head on his chest..

Timothy

Everyone was drunk and happy when we got back to Jeremiah's. Jeremiah paid us no never mind as he followed his wife into their bedroom. Jeff carried Lauren up the stairs; I led Annette to our bedroom. Her drunken state seemed to relax her and she was open to my advances. As long as we were standing she was fine. As soon as we laid down, she closed her eyes and the demon in her nightmares scared her. My baby couldn't remember that she was here with me. She couldn't remember that I love her. She was fighting for her life screaming for her daddy to save her. She wouldn't calm down until I moved off of the bed. Then she wrapped the blankets around herself tightly and fell asleep. That night she cried in her sleep and she fought no one. In the morning her hair was wild and she was hung-over. She asked me why I was on the floor. When I told her what happened last night she cried. She told me to stop asking her to marry me, and that I deserved better. I got up and paced the floor trying to think of how to convey my feelings without scaring her. I tried to hold my voice back so that I wasn't yelling at her. "There is no one more perfect for me than you! If you're trying to tell me that I will spend the rest of my life as a depressed bachelor then fine! You are the only woman I will marry! You are the only woman who will carry my child! You…"
She cut me off, "would you ever leave me to fend for myself?" She watched my eyes with tears in her own. "I don't want to trust that you love me, that you will protect me, and then you let me down."
"Annette I would never leave you, why would you ask me that?"
Tears silently fell from her eyes. "I used to be so happy to see my daddy, I would hug him and kiss him every time he came. My momma would be so happy when he came no matter how mean he was to her. When he was around we ate good, he'd whip my brothers into shape, and we had a family. Every time he left my momma would get angry with me cause…." She looked around the room. "My Aunt Dorothy told me how much he loved me. I didn't want to believe it. If he loved me

he would've stayed. As I get older, I'm trying to understand the things a child couldn't. My daddy became my father when I couldn't deal with how much he let me down. Rudy says he loves me, but I don't believe it. He loves looking at me; he loves all the things he thinks he's going to do to me. He's never just sat and talked with me like you have. You act like you know me before I feel satisfied that you do." She looked around the room. "A woman came to our door the other day. Her heart was broken cause her husband was dead. She told her boys that we killed him. I didn't know what she was talking about. Then Rufus told her a white man killed her husband and she didn't want to believe him." She looked at me.
"Who was her husband?"
"She said she was Mrs. O'Brien." She watched my face. "That was the name of the officer who broke my arm." I didn't respond. "Did you kill him?"
"Did I come to you and tell you that I did that?" I asked her, she shook her head no. "Don't listen to gossip."
"Tim that's not a yes or a no."
"You will always be safe with me. No one touches what is mine, and gets away with it."
"Yes or no."
"Don't listen to gossip." I said changing the subject.

Annette

Emma held out her arms while I measured around her waist ."I suspect you'll get about this big around. Just in case you blow up I'll make your dresses hang nicely."
I looked at Emma and she was all weepy and trying not to cry. "What's wrong?"
"I WANT MY MOMMA!" She collapsed on my shoulder and sobbed loudly.
"Your momma?" I was shocked, surprised, and confused.
"I don't know why, but I just need my momma!"
Hezekiah came out of their bedroom annoyed. I looked at Emma and he exhaled, "you don't need her you got Annette!"
"HUSH UP! Annette is my sister not my momma! Until you made me dirty my momma ALWAYS.... LOVED..... ME!" She cried.
"Maybe you should wait until you have the baby to resolve stuff with momma." I said
"No! I need my momma there, this thing is going to rip me apart with his big ole biscuit head like his daddy." She said while she cried some more.
"Stop talking about my head. Its normal sized." He said
"Your head is big, I don't know how your momma recovered from your delivery." She cried some more.
Hezekiah looked at me, "she been like this all day."
I looked at my sister, no matter how much she played grown up, she was still just a little girl. "Take me now!"
"Emma, we should..."
She cut him off, "NOW! I said!" He stood there like he wasn't gonna move. "I'm not playing with you! If you don't take me I won't do that thing you like no more!" She said through clinched teeth.
Hezekiah sucked his teeth, "aw man! Come on Emma! What if she tries to attack you?"
"You will be there to protect me!"
"I gotta stay???"

"I know you did not think you were going to drop me off at the curb! Put your shoes on! We're going!" She commanded.
"Emma, if momma finds out that I knew you were here and I didn't say anything. I'm dead."
"I'll tell her I ran into you at the market, and you convinced me to come make peace with her. You get to be the hero." She said excitedly.
I was sweating bullets the whole way over to momma's house in the cold San Francisco air. Rudy's car was out front, and I wanted to run away. There was nowhere to run to Aunt Dorothy's car was gone. Emma held onto Hezekiah's arm like she was afraid for her life. I opened the door slowly as I heard my momma going off with my name in her mouth. "Speaking of the devil! COME HERE!" My momma yelled at me.
"Momma, I want to show you what I found." I said still opening the door so she could see who was behind me.
"I don't care what…." My momma grabbed her chest when she saw Emma. "My baby!" She gasped. She started to rush towards the door and Hezekiah moved like he couldn't read her and he was on guard. Momma stopped in her tracks, she put her hands up. "Come here baby!"
Emma ran to her crying and they hugged and cried real hard. Momma kept pushing her hair back and kissing her forehead. Telling her how much she missed her, how miserable she's been without her. How sorry she was. Rudy on the other hand was staring at me with pain and disappointment in his eyes. He stood up, and marched to my face. "Where have you been?"
"School, working, nothing new." I said cool as the breeze.
"This is ridiculous! I don't see you anymore."
"You're the one who wanted me to go to school. Be careful what you ask for next time."
"I was talking to your momma and I think we should get engaged soon. I don't see the point in waiting all that much anymore. We just won't start having babies until you graduate."
"You were talking to my momma? Rudy who does that? Who plans someone's life with someone through their parent?"
"You haven't been around." He shrugged.
Momma was holding Emma but she was giving me evil eyes. "That is not a license to do something like this. I don't…"
Momma cut me off, "Rudy! She's hanging around all the white devils. She needs to switch schools, they're brainwashing her!"
"Momma! My friends are not devils." I said hurt cause her resolve hasn't changed.
"I agree Ms. Rose, she's getting too attached to students there." He said smiling at me.
I didn't have to stand around and listen to this; I turned on my heels and walked out the door. When I heard my momma coming after me I ran. I ran like Leslie was chasing or like that police officer was trying to kill me. Momma may have been fast back home, but she wasn't used to walking let alone running these San Francisco hills. She tired out real fast and she screamed profanity at me. I kept running until I couldn't hear her anymore, and then I walked holding myself and crying. Rudy pulled up on me and hopped out of the car, I looked to see if he was alone. As soon as he was in firing range I punched him in his mouth. I kept hitting him in the same spot, all I could see was red. I screamed at him and told him he was a coward and he could marry my momma since they were so compatible. Rudy's head kept

jerking backwards and then he charged me pushing my shoulders up against the building. He screamed at me to calm down when I tried to kick him. He reared up like he was going to hit me, "please give me the reason!"

Rudy turned to see Tim standing there with the most serious expression on his face.

"This is my woman, you need to mind your own business!" Rudy barked at him.

"She is my business! Take your hands off of her before I break them and you never hold a beaker again!" Tim said.

Rudy reluctantly released me, and I ran to Tim and I put my head on his chest. Rudy looked at us like he couldn't believe it. Tim kissed me long and hard all the while keeping his eyes on Rudy. When I glanced at Rudy he looked like he wanted to cry. "Here's what you're going to do. Get back in your car and you can report to her momma that you couldn't find her. I think I already made you a promise. And I don't forget promises. If anything you better try to talk her momma down, you hear me?"

Rudy rolled his eyes and sucked his teeth, "whatever." He huffed.

Tim walked up on Rudy and punched him so hard without even drawing back. Rudy's body went up in the air and flew backwards from the force of the punch. "Do you hear me now?"

Rudy was dazed and looking like he was drunk. The tingles spread all over my body and I couldn't help myself. I kissed Tim as deeply as I could. He allowed me to kiss him and then he told me to get in Sadie. He walked over to Rudy and said something else to him and then he got in the car with me.

I asked him how he found me. He said he was supposed to meet us at Emma's and when we weren't there or at Katie's he decided to drive to my momma's house just to see if he saw Hezekiah's car. He said he saw me walking and then Rudy's car pull up. He said he stayed back to see what was happening. He looked at me and smiled, and then he said I handled myself pretty well on the battle line. I snuggled into him and I told him he made me feel safe.

****

I pounded on his door. Tim opened the door with sleep in his eyes. "Annette? What's wrong? Come in! Come in!" He moved out the way so I could enter. He closed the door then he held me while I cried. "Your momma?"

"She said I'm spending too much time with you! She came after me when I said I wouldn't give you up." I cried into his chest. "I'm sorry for the hour, I had nowhere else to run to."

"SSSHHHH! You always run to me you hear me. You go ahead and take my bed, I'll sleep in the other room."

"I can sleep in the other bed, you don't have to give up your bed." I said

"Nonsense, go ahead." He led me to his bedroom. He was about to walk out the room while my eyes pleaded with him. "She hit you?" He said looking at my face.

"Of course!" I said like that was a no brainer.

He hugged me and I held onto the hug. Until Tim started hugging me I didn't realize how important hugs were. I buried my head in his chest and cried a little. I was tired of being hit on, tired of being treated like I deserved all the crap she was giving me. Tim was my only real happy thought these days. "Go to bed Annette." He said like he was tired.

"Will you sleep with me?"

Tim exhaled, "I get in that bed with you, I'm not going to sleep. You're not ready for me." He kissed my forehead.

I felt bad, "I'm sorry about that. Can you stay until I fall asleep?"

"You need a shirt or are you going to sleep in that dress?"

"Shirt please." He gave me a shirt and I went in the bathroom.

When I came out the bathroom he looked at me then he turned his head. Then he exhaled as his pants started growing. I covered my mouth and laughed. "Great! Now I'm up!" I got in the middle of the bed and pulled the covers up to my neck. He crossed the bed and pulled the covers back. "Look at me," I did. "What's my name?"

"Timothy."

"Do you believe that I love you?"

"Yes!"

"Do you love me?"

"Yes!"

"Do you honestly think I would ever do anything to hurt you?"

"No!" I said looking in his eyes.

"Why did you come here tonight?"

"I needed to go where I felt loved and safe."

His face softened. "You wanna go get married?" He asked sincerely.

"Tim you can't have a wife who doesn't function right." I said feeling bad about myself.

"Annette you work, I promise you do." He looked around, he put his soft pillow under my head. Then he kissed my lips, my neck, my chest, and my stomach. Then he got in front of me opened my legs and kissed me down there. I gasped at the feeling of his warm mouth. I didn't know what he was doing to me but I didn't want it to stop. Air left me! I kept my eyes open so that my mind wouldn't make me flip out again. I couldn't control my breathing and then my body started jerking. I kept tingling down there when Tim came up to kiss me. When I started to close my eyes he told me to open them and look at him. He opened his nightstand and pulled out a condom. I got nervous and Tim told me to look at him. I watched him put it on then he kissed me. Keep your eyes open, it's me. Then he kissed me until I relaxed, I was still tingling. He watched my eyes and he let it touch me. My eyes got big and he told me it was him and to keep my eyes on him. I took a deep breath and he waited. He pressed in a little, "Annette I love you so much!" His voice calmed me. I told him to keep talking to me. He pressed in a little more and it hurt a little. "I love you so much!" I melted, I looked at him with wide eyes and repeated that he loved me. I held on to him and scooted away a little each time, I was uncomfortable. I loved this man, I wanted to get past this. Tim's mouth opened wide when he was all the way in. I laid there afraid to move cause I felt him in my stomach. Tim took a deep breath before he moved. His breathing was now as heavy as mine. "You are a virgin!" With that one statement I cried but it was like he set me free. The tingles I felt down there spread through my whole body. Tim moved slow and easy, air left my lungs and I had to hold on to Tim to catch my breath. I started throbbing in the best way ever! I couldn't be still I kept pulling Tim in closer and closer. When I kissed his neck he lost it with me. Tim held on to the condom as he backed away from me. There was blood on the condom and he told me not to move. He came back with a warm towel. He smiled at me, "you were a virgin."

Timothy

I laid there stroking Annette's face. Trying to chew back my anger from the bruises her momma put on her. I put the ring I bought Annette on her finger and I told her not to take it off. Annette cried when she actually looked at the ring. I kissed her forehead and rubbed her back. "Baby, I need to be honest with you right now." Fear

entered Annette's eyes. I rubbed her back some more and I kissed her. "I've never been in this deep before. I'm looking at these bruises and I'm battling my internal rage! No one puts their hands on you!"
She kissed me and started rubbing my head. "Thank you for loving me enough to get angry. The only person to halfway defend me was my father, and that was only when he was around."
"Tell me about him, you don't talk about him much."
Annette gave up information like it was bubbling over inside of her. I found it interesting that her momma was ok with marrying a man who was not Negro, but her children could not.
When we finally got up, I told Annette we should share our news with my family. Annette put on a brave face, and when I asked her what was wrong she said telling someone made it real and that made her nervous. On the car ride over I told her that I was going to teach her how to drive cause she needed a car. Annette slid over and put her head on my shoulder while I drove. Matt was taking the new baby out of the car as we pulled up. He proudly waived us over to meet his baby girl Jennifer. Matt didn't hold her like he held his son. She was his little heart, and he was so proud. Annette told him the baby was beautiful and he proudly said thank you. Momma was anxiously waiting on the porch for her newest grand baby. As soon as Matt handed her to momma, she went to her rocking chair. Pops took pictures of momma and the baby, then all of us. Maureen was in the kitchen drinking coffee. When she saw Annette and I her eyes immediately went to Annette's hand. The smile she once held was gone.
Beth noticed the ring as well and broadcasted it to the entire house. For once her big mouth didn't get on my nerves. Dale and his girlfriend congratulated us. Dale and his girlfriend came with similar news, they were also expecting. We were celebrating when Franky and Whispers, one of Pops's men, walked in the door. Franky's expression let you know this was about business. I excused myself from Annette, then I walked into the office.
As soon as the door closed Franky went in, one of my trucks was hijacked and ten kilos of product were stolen. Whispers said it was a very well thought out and executed plan. I asked if the driver was in on the job, Franky said he's being watched to make sure. However, so far it didn't appear that way. We discussed forward movement when Jeff got there. Pops congratulated me again on finding love, but he told me he needed my head back in the game.
Franky adjusted in his seat, then he curved his words. "Peggy's pregnant."
It looked like someone shot my father. "HOW COULD YOU LET THIS HAPPEN?" He yelled at us. I assumed the guy was some unsuspecting fella like Sebastian. He had no idea who Franklin Wallace is and he thought he was messing over on some goofy dame. I was dumbfounded when Franky said the father was one of Jeff's men. Jeff was as surprised as I was, but surprise wasn't sparing this guy from the wrath of my family. "Bring Peggy home! Get rid of him!" Then Pops thought about it, "better yet. Take him to the warehouse. He's mine!"

Chapter 11

Annette

Tim proudly introduced me to "Whispers". This man was tall and dark like my momma. He didn't look like he's ever smiled a day in his life. I smiled and told him it was nice to meet him, he didn't smile back as he told me the same. Tim told me when I was ready to go home, Whispers was going to take me, he apologized for having to leave, but he had family business to tend to. I asked if I should go home now, and Tim said I didn't have to. Then Jeff came to Tim and said that it would be best if Whispers took Lauren and I back to her place. Since Lauren didn't drive, Whispers would drive us. We were having dinner at this really nice restaurant in the downtown area. We just saw a lovely play at the theater and then we came to have dinner.

I invited Whispers to sit with us, he sat but he didn't relax. He was watching everyone around us and taking everything in. "Is Whispers your birth given name?" I asked him

"It might as well have been." He said without any further disclosure.

"Would you like to order something to eat?" Lauren asked him.

"You two enjoy your evening, don't worry about me." He said continuing to look around.

The way his eyes shifted from person to person made me nervous. "Are we in danger?" Lauren stopped eating and looked at him for his answer as well.

"No," He said still looking around.

"You're looking around as if we are." I said

He put his eyes on me, "you're safe with me. Please enjoy your meal."

Our waiter came out and paused a little when he saw Whispers. He asked where Jeff and Tim were and we told him they had to leave. Before the waiter could open his mouth to say something else Whispers handed him money for our table. Then he showed us outside to a car that was waiting for us. There was another guy driving the car. They drove us to Lauren's apartment in the building she manages. We didn't tell them where she lived, but they seemed to know. I was nervous for Tim to come back, and tell me what was going on. After a few hours there was a knock at the door. When I opened the door Whispers had Tim's sister Peggy with him. She was crying hysterically. Whispers said nothing he kind of handed her over and then walked away. Peggy's hair was all over her head. Her dress was torn, she looked like she had been in a fight and she did not win. She fell on my shoulder deeply sobbing. I hugged her and brought her to the couch that I was making up to sleep on. Lauren put on the teapot. I asked her if she was ok and she shook her head no and sobbed harder.

When Tim and Jeff came they looked big and angry. Peggy had finally calmed down and she was staring off not saying anything. One look at her brothers and she started sobbing all over again. Tim told us to go into the bedroom. Lauren and I did as we were told. Lauren tried to listen at the door, at first I was telling her to come away from the door. Then curiosity got the best of me and I wanted to know what was going on as well. I couldn't really hear too much they sounded muffled. I asked Lauren what she thought was going on. Lauren said a lover's spat gone wrong. She said Peggy was probably dating a fella and he probably hit her, and she called one of her brothers before she thought of the consequences. We sat in that room speculating for a long time. Then it got quiet out there. Lauren cracked her door then she opened it. They were gone again.

Timothy

It was cold and I was ready to get back to my woman. Pops was in there going completely off. When it got completely silent, Franky brought the black bag out dragging it on the ground, he said everything was ready. Pops walked over to his car, changed his clothes and threw his disposable clothes on the bag. Franky went over to his car, changed his clothes and brought his old clothes to the bag. We put their old clothes in the aluminum trash can next to the dock. We walked out to the edge of the dock, I unzipped the bag while Jeff held it up, then he emptied the contents into the Bay waters. We waited an hour making sure none of that guy floated up and then Jeff and I went to our cars and changed. Jeff poured the kerosene and Pops struck the match.

Pops proceeded to say that we were all relaxing too much, and there was no excuse for letting something like this happen. Then he told Jeff and I to bring Peggy home. Jeff and I rode in silence. As soon as Peggy saw us she started screaming and crying. She told Jeff and I that we weren't any different. She said she loved him! Jeff told her that she knew better than to try any of this. He said if she wanted him and she really wanted this to work she would've let him come to Pops like a man. Peggy screamed anyways, she didn't want to hear anything or reason. If he was on the up and up he would've stepped forward before it became a scandal. Jeff assured her that the guy didn't care about her. Peggy pointed around the room. "If that's the case the girl who occupies this apartment means nothing to you!"

"That's different!" Jeff growled

"HOW?"

"HER FATHER'S NAME IS NOT FRANKLIN WALLACE SR AND I DON'T WORK FOR HIM! THAT FELLA WAS USING YOU, AND YOU'RE TOO STUPID TO SEE IT! IF HE LOVED YOU, KNOWING WHO WE ARE HE WOULD'VE COME TO POPS LIKE A MAN!" He said

"BUT POPS WOULD'VE SAID NO!" SHE CRIED

"THIS IS WHY I'M NEVER HAVING KIDS! YOU DUMB DIZZY BROAD! OPEN YOUR EARS AND LISTEN! HE WAS PLAYING A GAME WITH YOU! HE'S GONE! SHUT UP! MOMMA'S WAITING FOR YOU!" He said

In that moment either Peggy remembered she was pregnant, or she finally realized we knew. "NO!" She tried to run.

Jeff gave me an irritated look, then he threw a couch pillow at her and she fell into the wall. I helped her up then I firmly grabbed her arm. "Let's go." I said

"Tim please!" She pleaded.

"Pops told us to bring you, so we're bringing you." I said

"THIS ISN'T FAIR! YOU GUYS AREN'T ANY BETTER!" She yelled trying to get away.

"It doesn't matter." I said picking her up.

I sat in the back of Jeff's car with her so she didn't try any fast stuff. When we got to the house momma was standing on the porch. Peggy was still trying to fight.

"Margaret Anne CUT IT OUT! Bring your tail up these stairs right now. Don't make me have to come down there!" Momma warned.

"Momma no!" Peggy cried

"I promised Peggy if I have to come down there!" Momma warned. Peggy cried the entire way up the stairs. "Now get in there the doctor's waiting for you."

Peggy jumped up and down, "Please momma! Please don't do this to me!"

“Do what to you? Save your life? You’re too young, you don’t have a husband! You shouldn’t start your family until you have a good foundation! Now quit stalling and get in there!”
“But Momma….” you heard the sound of momma’s hand, but she moved so fast you didn’t see it. Peggy flew backwards.
“I told you to get NOW GET!” Momma pointed inside the house.

Annette

"Annette this is Lady B!" Irma said proudly. "She's the closest thing I've ever had to a mother. Momma this is Tim's fiancé."
She looked me up and down like she was dissecting every aspect of me. "Nice to meet you baby." She said staring at my face. "Where are your folks from?"
"Kansas," I said waiting.
"Did you live near a reservation?"
"Yes."
"That explains your features." Then she smiled at me. "What difference does it make? Nice to meet you honey." Then she gave me a hug. "Tim is my very special baby. You make sure you're always good to him."
"Yes ma'am." I said, then I looked at Martha. She smiled at me real proud.
"What are you making?" She asked us.
"Momma wouldn't let us help with dinner so we're making cookies for dessert." Martha said proudly.
"Sounds delicious. Where's Tim?"
"Momma he's working, Annette comes over to be with the family." Irma said
"Is your momma here, I'd like to meet her?" Lady B said
"No ma'am," I took a deep breath. "She don't know about me and Tim."
"WHY?" She yelled startling everyone except Irma.
"I got a different kind of momma, my happiness is not her main concern." I said
"I want to meet your momma!" She said through clinched lips.
"Yes ma'am," I said
"Wash your hands! We're going right now!"
Panic ran through me, "yes ma'am." I went to the television room where Lauren was playing with the baby. I stretched my eyes at her. "Tim's grandmother wants to meet my momma, can you give us a ride?"
"Of course," Lauren said giving the baby to Peggy who was sitting over to the side looking depressed.
When Lauren followed me in the kitchen Lady B looked at her. "Where are they finding all these beautiful young ladies?" She asked Irma.
I was having little panic attacks all the way to my momma's house. I hadn't been home in weeks, and I was going to show up wearing a ring that I've been hiding from her.
Aunt Dorothy was getting out of her car when we pulled up. My heart leap for joy. I happily introduced Lady B and Irma to her. Aunt Dorothy raved about Tim. She said he was such a gentleman, I wished we could stop here. Raymond came down the stairs and stopped when he saw me. I smiled then he ran inside. Next thing I know my momma came storming out cursing and screaming. She didn't even notice that I was with people. She slapped me hard and as she raised her hand to hit me again Lady B grabbed her hand. "WHAT IS WRONG WITH YOU!" She yelled at her while Irma looked like she was going to pounce if my momma turned on her momma.

"THIS IS MY UNGRATEFUL DAUGHTER! MIND YOUR OWN BUSINESS!" My momma yelled
"SHE IS MY BUSINESS!" Lady B yelled back as she threw her arm at her. "Get a hold of yourself! Why would you come out the house beating on this child like that?"
Momma squinted her eyes at Lady B, "who are you to question me about my child?"
"Your daughter happens to be engaged to my grandson!"
I swallowed and ran behind Aunt Dorothy.
"She is not! She's gonna marry the boy I picked out for her."
Lady B looked at me with sad eyes. "I'm sorry honey. I guess I needed to see for myself."
"See what?" My momma growled at me.
I saw my traumatic life flashing before my eyes. "I..."
"Rose! I'm leaving!" Aunt Dorothy blurted out. "I can't take this no more. The way you treat Annette is horrible over something she has no knowledge of or control over. You forgave Emma, but this child can't get no love?" She shook her head. "You don't need her to marry that Henson kid. As long as your legs stay open to Mr. Lakshman he hasn't and he won't charge you no rent. You been pocketing all the money these poor kids been breaking their backs to give you. You should have a nice little cushion saved up."
"What?" I looked at my Aunt who has no reason to lie to me and I hoped she was. "Whenever they needed anything," I pointed to my brothers who were all watching from the stairs. "We had to pull together to make it happen. You've been sitting on money all this time?"
"Get in the car and leave here Annette. There's nothing for you here." My aunt said, "I'll send word to Tim to let you know where I end up." She hugged me and then pushed me to the car. My momma started cursing and screaming. My aunt told me to look at her and not to listen to any of the things my momma was screaming at me.
I started to get in the car then I thought of my picture of my father. I couldn't leave it behind. I got out of the car and I slowly walked towards my momma, Lady B was right on my heels. Preston stood up, "don't go Annette. Please stay." He cried.
I took him by the hand and we went inside. I sat him on the bed, pulled my big purse and I put my things in it like the perfume, bracelets, and clothes Tim bought me in it. I told Preston I had to go cause momma keeps hurting me. I told him I loved him and that he needed to continue to be a good boy for momma. I put my picture under the lining at the top of my dress just in case momma went through my purse. I wanted my box of pictures but I decided to have Emma bring it cause I knew momma would destroy it if she had the chance. I told Preston I would see him at Emma's house or something but I had to leave. I told Lady B that Tim bought the sewing machine that my momma moved out of my room into the living room. She told me to leave it. When we walked out of the apartment my momma was still cursing and carrying on trying to get to Aunt Dorothy while Rufus blocked her and would not let her past. When she saw my bag she snatched it from me. She said everything in that apartment was hers and I was stealing. I started crying thinking of all the things Tim bought me in the bag. I cried for her to give it back. Then she opened the bag and took out my perfume. She knew it was a gift, she smiled at me and threw the bottle down and it shattered. I lost it! I charged my momma, I hit her in the face two times before I realized what I just did. My momma fell on the

ground, and I felt my heart stop. I screamed as if I wasn't the person who knocked her down. Momma's eyes rolled around for a minute, then she started trying to focus. "I'm sorry momma! I'm sorry! I didn't mean it! I'm sorry!" I said rocking her. "Get off of me, you ungrateful disgusting WHORE!" My momma yelled as she came to.

My Aunt Dorothy grabbed me and told me to get in the car. Rufus handed me my bag. Then he made sure I got in Lauren's car before my momma got up. Irma threw her arms around me and she squeezed me. She kept kissing my forehead and apologizing. When we pulled up to the house Lauren and Lady B got in the back seat with us. Everyone put their arms around me and cried for me. I felt selfish for needing every moment of this. Tim wasn't here and I needed affection. Irma told me to come inside and she'd make us some cocktails. Lauren said she knew it was bad but she had no idea. I took out my picture of my father. I told Lauren if my momma knew I had that picture she would've killed me. Lauren said Emma and I look a lot like our daddy. I knew she was trying to be nice. I wished I could say my momma was beautiful, but that wasn't the case. Irma brought us glasses with tall drinks in it. Then she told me to follow her. She took me up to her bedroom and shut the door. She told me to have a seat on her bed then she went in her closet. She brought out a picture box and she sat next to me. She took a big gulp of her drink and then she exhaled like that swallowed just gave her the peace and calmness she needed. She showed me pictures of her family. She said she grew up in a family like my own. She said the only difference was their color and that they had money. She pointed to one of her brothers and she said he used to come after her all the time. She said he came for her and all her sisters, but he liked to get after her the most because she was the only one who fought back. She said she fought back so much that she shot his toe off with her daddy's gun. She said that didn't stop him though, it just made him meaner. I asked if her parents knew and she said they acted like it was news to them every time she told them, but they never did anything to stop it. She said her father was obsessed with Lady B. She said he swore he hated colored people, and he was cruel to them. However, it took a sudden accident that handicapped him for him to lose the strength to try to come after her anymore. She said they would try to protect each other as much as they could. Irma said family pain and dysfunction knows no color. I didn't go into detail, but I told her about Leslie.

****

Every time I cook for Tim he has the most appreciative response. Even though I technically live on Lauren's couch, I spend most of my time between Emma, his momma, and his place. I told him we can't live together until we're married.

So we go to school, Tim normally has to hurry off to work, so Lauren and I study together. Then we hang out with Katie. Emma's normally up under her momma but every once in awhile she comes up for air and we see her. I try to have dinner done or close to done by the time he comes home from work.

I was putting the finishing touches on my smashed potatoes, while green beans simmered in the corner. My steaks were marinating and waiting to go under the broiler. My dinner rolls were done, and I planned to throw them back in the oven as he walked in the door so they'd be hot.

Someone knocked at the door, I wondered who it could be this close to dinner. I opened the door and a white girl stood there gasping at me. "Can I help you?"

"Is Tim home?" She asked looking me all over.

I didn't like how surprised she looked when she saw me. I took a deep breath. "Who wants to know?"

I could see the indignation flash across her face. "Tell him to come to the door to see."
I slammed the door in her face. I didn't have time for games. She started banging on the door and screaming. I took another deep breath then I snatched the door open. "May I help you?"
She tried to push her way in the door. "Tim it's me, Natalie!" She yelled into the house.
I pushed her backwards, she stumbled a couple of steps. "I'll tell him Natalie stopped by." Then I slammed the door again.
She banged on the door for awhile then she left. Seeing this very pretty white woman demanding anything of Tim made me angry. It made me angrier that she automatically disregarded me as no one. Like he couldn't possibly be with me or something. I paced around the kitchen trying to calm myself. When I looked at the clock it was 4:37pm, when I looked again it was 6:34pm. Tim is normally home by 5 to 5:20'ish. When 7:49pm rolled around I put all the food in the garbage. I got in my car and drove angrily to Lauren's. "Sis is that you?" Lauren called out from the bathroom.
"Of course!" I snapped.
"Ok well, turn your back to the bathroom. We didn't know you were coming home." She giggled.
"Don't nobody care about your cheeks!" I snapped again as I turned my back.
Lauren giggled as I heard movement and then her bedroom door closed.
I picked up my books to try to fill my brain with anything other than the sounds of their love making. I sat down in the hallway in front of her door. I was focusing all my anger on my school work. Lauren came out; she said Tim was on the phone. I walked in the door and hung up the phone. Then I told her I wasn't there. When the phone rang again I picked it up, hung it up and then I took it off the hook. Lauren looked at me with a the question on her face. I put her phone back on the hook and it rang immediately. "Hello?"
"Annette? What's going on?" Tim barked into the phone.
"I'm mad!"
"Clearly, but why?" I didn't answer, "I'm coming to pick you up." I hung up.
I went downstairs and waited in the lobby for him. When he pulled up, I got in the car. He leaned over to kiss me and I leaned away from him. He looked at me like I was already working his nerves. We rode in silence back to his house. I sat on the couch like a visitor. He turned on the light and went in the kitchen. I guess he didn't see that I threw everything in the trash. It still smelled like dinner was waiting.
"Annette!" He yelled when he looked in the trash after he searched the oven for his plate. "Why did you throw my dinner away?"
I hopped up and got in his face. "YOU DIDN'T CALL TO SAY YOU WOULDN'T BE HOME! I AM NOT AN AFTER THOUGHT! I DON'T HAVE TO COME HERE AND MAKE YOU DINNER!" I yelled.
"YOU THREW AWAY MY DINNER BECAUSE I DIDN'T CALL TO SAY I WAS RUNNING LATE?"
Tim was beyond angry and hungry, and I didn't care. My feelings were hurt! "I THREW AWAY YOUR DINNER BECAUSE YOU DIDN'T EVEN CONSIDER ME ENOUGH TO TELL ME THAT YOU WERE RUNNING LATE. LIKE I DON'T HAVE OTHER THINGS TO DO WITH MY TIME."
"THAT IS THE DUMBEST THING I'VE EVER HEARD!" He growled.

"OH SO NOW I'M DUMB? NOW I DON'T MAKE SENSE? CALL YOUR MOMMA, I BET YOU SHE COULD EXPLAIN IT TO YOU!"

Tim stood there staring at me. I could see anger all over him. "Fine! I'll call when I know I'll be working later." He was still angry. "Can I please have a sandwich or something?"

I looked around, "you expect me to make it?" I pointed to my chest. "I made an entire meal. I'm not making a sandwich!" I said taking a seat in the kitchen. Tim spun around on his heels and jerked and slammed the refrigerator door and cupboards as he made a peanut butter and jelly sandwich. "Yes, thank you. I'll have one too."

"Stop messing with me Annette!"

"I'm not kidding!"

Tim kicked the refrigerator and I know it hurt, but he refused to show it. He put my sandwich on a plate and sat it in front of me. "Your sandwich madam!"

He sat down and took an angry bite out of his sandwich. "You had a visitor today." He could've cared less. "She said," he looked at me like he had to watch my lips say her name. "Her name was Natalie." He watched my face. "Why would she come here demanding to see you?"

He swallowed, "I don't know. I haven't talked to her in awhile."

"Who is she?" I watched his eyes.

"Ancient history," he watched my face.

"How ancient?" I growled.

He put his sandwich down then he leaned in. "She's nobody for you to be worried about. My goodness! When you're in a mood you're in a mood! Where's the calendar?" He said standing up.

I gasped and then I threw my sandwich at him. He frowned I threw my plate, and then I ran. He chased me into the guest room. He slammed me on the bed asking me what was wrong with me. "Are you messing around?" I started crying as soon as the words came out of my mouth.

"NEVER!" He growled with hurt feelings.

"She was pretty! Just like that other girl! I will not compete for you!"

He sat on the bed and put his arms around me. "Annette, they don't compare to you! I love you! I want you!"

"She was really pretty!"

"You're gorgeous, and I now see a little crazy." He laughed, "I like that though."

"Don't treat me like an after thought. As soon as you know you're not coming home right away call me." I said hiding my face in his shirt.

"Ok, but I have to warn you that sometimes I can't call. You have to trust how much I love you."

"Why wouldn't you be able to call me? You're sitting at a desk."

"Sometimes I have to go out in the field. If something happens out there it may delay my arrival home." Then he kissed me.

"You taste like peanut butter. Get away from me." I said playfully.

"Kiss me," I shook my head no. "Kiss me!" He demanded as his hands went all over me. "All I could think about all day was getting home to you, and this is how you greet your man? Plates flying at my head!" He chuckled, "kiss me!" I gave him a peck. "Open your mouth!" We playfully drove each other crazy for a while before he went in. Heaven knows I love this man!

Timothy

"So, what do you think?" Dale asked proudly showing me the house he built in Oakland.

I looked around at all the features, the crown moldings, the hardwood floors, the archways, and the French door windows that opened to a small deck too small for anyone to sit on. This house was nice and full of character. "I like it."

Dale explained in detail all of the characteristics of the features of this house. "I've got plans to build more like it. For right now, I've got to renovate these apartment buildings to generate some cash flow."

"Right, and my office on the dock." I was moving part of my business over to the Oakland docks. It made sense to have trailers ready for hauling next to the docks and train yards on the East Bay side. Jeremiah has the grocery chain moving a long as a well oiled machine. He needed more space and this move would provide that.

"Right," Dale said exhaling at the house.

"Are you nervous?"

"Husband and Father is a big role to have. I want to be good at it you know?" He said

"I do know."

"Do you and Annette argue?"

"All the time," I laughed. "Nothing ever too serious, or nothing I can't handle. She got a temper like momma. The other night she threw my dinner away because I didn't call to tell her I was running late." I laughed hard. "As annoying as it was, I liked that she felt some kind of way immediately. She didn't take it in and keep it to herself. I knew where I stood immediately, and I knew how to fix it."

"Blanche doesn't yell, and I got to pay attention to know whether she's upset or not. She's not like momma; I don't know how I feel about that. I always thought I'd have someone as feisty as momma."

"Don't worry, you could have a girl and all of momma's personality will come from there. Watch!"

"What if I have a son? What if he's like you guys more than he's like me?" Dale said

I put my hand on my big brother's shoulder, "remember the only difference between me and you is that I show no mercy and you do. You're a Wallace man, we bow to no one! We do what comes next. Your son will be just like you, and he will always look up to you."

Dale smiled at me like he needed to hear that. We continued walking around the house, and I kept seeing Annette in every corner we turned, in every room of that house. I asked Dale when he was going to put it on the market and he said soon cause his company needed the money. I told him to let me know when he did cause I wanted to bring Annette to see it. I told her that my company was going to move on this side of the bay and we discussed moving so that I could be closer to work. She was hesitant about leaving the city where all of our family was, but I told her we would visit on a regular basis. I was hoping that this house or a house like it might be the selling point for her. Either way I need to continue buying properties on that side of the Bay anyways.

As Dale and I had lunch I looked across the street at a building. A young guy was outside painting the main entrance; it looked like he took pride in every stroke of paint. Curiosity wouldn't let me let it go. After lunch Dale and I went over to the young guy who had Jazz playing on his radio. He smiled excitedly as he explained that this was going to be his little nightclub called the "Jazz Room!" I immediately liked the sound of that, and he invited us in to take a look around his small club. I told him that I was soon to get married and I may need to convince my bride that Oakland was a good place to live. I told him a Jazz Room was a good start.

Gus asked why we would leave the city when there are talks of building a stadium for our football team? I simply said business and he understood. I told him we'd create buzz about his spot in San Francisco, and he got excited. He told us when opening night would be, and I told him I'd bring a nice sized group with me. Gus looked a little nervous as he stated that his family would be there and he hoped we didn't have a problem with it. I looked at this small possibly colored man and told him there would be no problem.

Franky brought Carol, and all my other brothers brought their women, Martha and Sebastian came, along with Pops, Momma, and Lady B. Beth and Peggy stayed behind with the children. This was Annette's first time going to a jazz club and she was extremely excited. Gus had his best table set up for our group. It was a little cramped, but that made things cozier. The line to get in was long and down the street. Telling Franky to spread the word meant telling all of San Francisco. All of San Francisco was here and eagerly waiting to get in. Pops told me Gus was in over his head and that he needed help. With that I knew that meant we were going to help him. A look of relief and excitement spread over Gus's face as he approached our table. He brought his wife over, a beautiful and animated Hispanic woman. She sat with us for a while and we had a good time.

In the car Annette kiss me, "thank you for such a nice evening. I love being out with music don't you?"

"I do," I said enjoying her touch as I drove over the bridge.

"Gus's wife is pretty isn't she?" She asked me.

"No one compares to you." I said kissing her forehead.

"Good answer Mr. Wallace." She smiled, "sometimes I wonder what a man like you could see in a girl like me."

"I thought all those poems I wrote you explained all of that."

She kissed my cheek, "I thought you were just trying to sweet talk me. I guess I should sit down and reread them. You sure your opinion hasn't changed of me now that you've had me?"

"Now I love you more!"

"Why is that? I don't know why I expect you to turn around one day and hate me."

I put my arm around her, "because that's all you've known your whole life. I think we're both used to fighting, which makes for some pretty interesting times with us don't you think?" She giggled, "I can't wait to grow old with you. Have all of our grandchildren around us, and relax with you by my side. That's what I call a plan for happiness."

"Tim," Annette said as I got off the freeway by my house. "I need to go to Lauren's."

I shook my head no, "I need you tonight."

"Tim," she said like she didn't want to have this discussion. "We're not married yet, we can't get comfortable doing it whenever we feel like it. We gotta wait."

"We won't do anything, I just need you in my bed." I said knowing I was lying.

"You promise?" She said weakening.

"Yea sure," I said turning into my garage. When we walked in the door the power was off. I looked out the window and the block was dark again. I lit candles in the bedroom, PERFECT! Annette brought brandy in for both of us. She went in the bathroom and put on her nightgown.

When she came out the bathroom she smiled shyly, "you promised."
"Actually I said yea sure."
She laughed, "Timothy!"
I gestured for her to join me in the middle of the floor. "Dance with me."
"There's no record playing, no power remember."
"Dance with me," I said holding my hands out. When she joined me on the dance floor, I pulled her body in to mine. I told her to keep those eyes on me, and then I kissed her. I have to be patient with Annette, although this wasn't our first or twentieth time, each time I have to make sure she's ready for me. I can't ever assume that she's ready, she has to be ready. I kissed her neck and silently begged her to let me in. When I laid her down her big brown eyes looked at me with so much love. I put a condom on and then I slid into the gateway of heaven. My wife!

Annette

"I don't understand what the problem is!" Irma said staring at the woman like she was daring her to say the reason why is because I'm colored.
"Um! Mrs. Wallace, um!" The woman shuffled papers around on her desk.
Her boss walked in and the woman exhaled. "Aw Mrs. Wallace how is Big Franky doing?"
"Everyone is well Charles, but your assistant is trying to tell me that my son and daughter can't marry here." She looked at him, "she's mistaken isn't she?"
He sat on the corner of the desk. He exhaled like he was about to explain something. "Well...."
"Right! I know she's mistaken. Because if my husband and I felt like any member of our family wasn't welcomed here," she shook her head. Then she exhaled, "well then all the Wallace's would have to pull out completely. I'm thinking about how badly that would affect your little country club. I guess that's your problem and not mine. I mean that if my misunderstanding isn't a misunderstanding." Then she waited for him to respond.
He exhaled, and then he asked his assistant for the appointment book. "When were you thinking?"
"You have to ask my daughter, she's the bride." Irma said pointing to me.
"Spring time." I said quietly watching how Irma threw weight around. I wondered if it was just her money that got her so much respect.
Irma told them they needed to give me their top options package, and they needed to give it to her at a discount for the misunderstanding. Then she warned him that there better not be anymore.
We went to the dress shop and they had beautiful dresses, I went to the sale rack and started looking through the options. Irma watched me for a minute then she asked me what I was doing. Immediately I felt embarrassed to say that I was looking for the cheapest dress. The shop owner swallowed as she approached us. Irma asked her about the latest fashions. The woman pulled out a book and pointed to a lot of dresses that were all the rave in England and France. There were no prices in the book so I sat there with my eyes stretched. Irma told me to pick out the ones we liked and then we'd narrow the selections down. The shop owner pointed out dresses that she thought would look good on me and she told us why. To say I felt overwhelmed is an understatement. We picked out three dresses for the shop owner to order. She said she'd keep the two I didn't pick as samples for her store.
"Momma why are you doing all of this?" I asked Irma once we were in the car.

She took a deep breath then she looked at me. "Of all of my daughter in-laws we come from the most similar backgrounds. You give kindness and you want it, but I know how it feels to be suspicious of folks generosity. I'm showing you love, and I'm giving you kindness just like Lady B has done for me all of my life. I'm not colored so I can't say I know how it feels to be you. In this family you are not colored. In this family you're Annette. You are loved for all the things that make you special. My baby was brokenhearted until you came along. My baby who's never had patience, is learning it waiting for you. He's growing up to be just like his daddy and I couldn't be prouder. You are a special part of this family. And if it takes a few pennies to make you happy so be it."

****

Since Dale and Blanche were getting married so fast she couldn't find a wedding dress in the store she liked. We discussed designs and I volunteered to make her dress. Blanche's momma was so grateful. She kept hugging me and thanking me. I would smile at them and wonder how strangers to me knew how to give me what I was dying for from my momma.

Emma has stopped trying to bring momma around. Momma gets so angry when she mentions me. When Emma had the baby, I had to wait a whole month before I could come by Katie's house to meet my niece. Emma doesn't want to be home alone with the baby, and I'm relieved that she's leery about having her daughter around Butch, Raymond, and Bret. Every time I come over Katie has the baby with her while Emma sleeps or cooks for them. Katie is so in love with the baby you'd swear the baby was hers. Emma was irritated with momma cause she expressed her disapproval for how dark little Kiah was going to be. Emma said Hezekiah told her to pull back on going over there as much. So whenever Emma feels the emotional pull of momma she leaves the baby with Katie. Katie has made so many little hats and outfits for the baby.

Sometimes it seems like Kiah is looking for Katie more than she is Emma. I mentioned it to her, but Emma shrugged it off and then she started grilling Hezekiah about where he went after work. Those two fuss and fight so much since she's had the baby. Emma's paranoid that he's going to mess around on her. Jeremiah tries to give his brother pointers; I can see that momma is filling her head with doubts about Hezekiah. I don't understand why Emma listens to her. If the shoe was on the other foot momma wouldn't have done anything. I reminded Emma that we went to our father's wedding to another woman with our momma. My little sister let's my momma get in her head anyways. I have to remind myself that's she's only fourteen.

Timothy

"I DON'T HAVE THE PATIENCE FOR THIS!" I growled.

"California state law requires that trucks hauling a load must stop at the scales. Our highway patrolman pulled your driver over when he bypassed the scales. I…"

I cut him off, "What you're doing is stalling. Tell me what I need to know, where is my truck? Where's the driver? Put all the rest of your fluff in a report that I'll read later!"

Pops and Franky walked in while I was on the phone. I wrote down the information the officer gave me. I didn't trust this guy no further than his voice carried over the phone. Pops sat down, "let it go son."

"They have my truck, they have your product!" I said trying to calm myself.

"Tim stop moving so emotionally! I will get my product and the driver is fired anyways." Pops said.
Franky said the product was safely concealed and he was going to send Whispers in to retrieve it. We alerted the buyers that there was a day delay. He said since we're normally on time this one day delay should be ok as long as they get to dispose of the driver. Franky went over the plan with me. He said we were going to have to personally drive part of the distribution to Los Angeles. He said that buyer couldn't wait on our delay and he's such a good customer that we can hand deliver the product this time. Franky asked if Annette was going to come or if I was going to bring someone else. "I have to go? Why can't Jeff go? Annette doesn't have anything to do with this. Nor does she know about this aspect of who we are."
"Jeff is handling business here, you're loyalty is to your family first. You don't have to bring her. You can bring someone else." Pops said.
"I can do it alone," Franky said watching my eyes.
"I don't want you out there without someone to have your back!" Pops told Franky. "Tim, I'm happy for you son. Believe me, no one can be happier for you. However, you can't fall apart on me son. Your soon to be wife needs to make an informed decision about who you truly are. She's going to have to understand who you are and decide for herself if she wants to be with you."
"We leave at five," Franky said turning his eyes from me.
Panic ran through my mind at the thought of Annette possibly leaving me or not wanting to be with me. I can't live without her! Pops and Franky left after a while. I sat there drumming my pen on the desk trying to figure this puzzle out. How do I make all the pieces fit without losing my wife? I drove to momma's house, Annette and momma were in the television room watching TV and drinking. They were having a good time making each other laugh with stories of things my western raising didn't exactly allow me to grasp. I asked what they were drinking and then I poured them another white Russian, and I made sure Annette's was heavy on the vodka. I took Momma's throw blanket off the back of the couch, and then I asked Annette to take a ride with me. She smiled and cheered as we drove across the Golden Gate Bridge. I took the second exit and we drove down the road that led to a residential area along the beach. Even though this side is still a public beach, we had the beach to ourselves. I told Annette to walk with me. She kept saying how beautiful the bridge was to her and she needed to try to draw it for her friends back home. I took off her shoes and then I led her on the sand away from Sadie with the blanket in my arms. I could see the affects of Annette's drink taking their toll on her as she tried to focus on my words. I told her how much I love her, and how she's always safe with me. I told her I needed her to take a trip with me in the morning. Annette asked about school, and I told her we needed to miss the rest of this week. She didn't like the idea of that, but she couldn't exactly focus on everything I was saying. "I don't want to wait for the wedding. I need you to have my baby now."
"What? No Tim, spring will be here before you know it." She said trying to grab some clarity.
I kissed her so deeply her head spun, "school has barely begun. I don't want to wait." I said feeling on her body.
She laughed, "did you bring condoms?"
I kissed her deeply, "Annette. I have never loved anyone like I love you. Forgive me for being selfish. I will spend the rest of our lives making this up to you." I said as I made contact skin to skin. My plan was to make this as enjoyable as possible for her; I did not plan on feeling as if I've lost control over my soul. Nothing about

this session of lovemaking was like anything I've experienced before. Every grind pulled my soul in closer to hers; I couldn't help but watch her reaction to the orgasm I gave her. Even her climax seemed different. When I blew my top, I felt like my mission had been accomplished. Immediately I felt guilty. When we got home, I put Annette in the bed and then I packed our bag. I discreetly packed my guns in our bags and on my body. Like I always say, *you never know where the day may lead you.* I kept waking Annette up and giving her water to drink. I fell asleep with her in my arms, I whispered my apology and promise to make this up to her.
When Franky saw Annette coming out to the car, he looked at me for an answer. I looked away from him and then I volunteered to drive first. Annette climbed in the back with Carol; they leaned in opposite directions with their pillows and proceeded to sleep. "What did you do?" Franky asked me pointing his eyes to me.
"We aren't that different." I said feeling guilty.
Franky looked back at Annette who was completely knocked out. "That wasn't necessary, all you had to do is talk to her. She's already on your side."
"How was I supposed to explain what she's about to see? I couldn't risk her walking?"
"She's dependent on you for everything, where would she go?" He asked.
"She's a smart girl, she's determined, and independent she could figure it out. I couldn't risk that." I said, then I changed the subject.
Halfway through we stopped at a rest stop so that Carol could use the bathroom, so Annette when too. Annette and Carol definitely weren't friends; they seemed tolerant of each other at best. Franky took over driving while I got in the back with Annette. She said she barely remembers where we're going. I told her Franky was throwing a party and we had to go. Franky looked at me in the rear view mirror.
"Why are you throwing a party way out here?" She asked Franky.
"Different market." He replied.
Carol smiled, "she doesn't know you're the *Candy Man*?"
"Tim keeps secrets." Franky said.
Annette didn't say anything she took it in and then she watched the scene change out the window. "Oh my goodness! Who's house is this?" Annette said as we entered the gates of Franky's house.
"Mine for now, but I'm going to sell it." He said
"Why on earth would you sell something so beautiful?" She said admiring the driveway.
"When I bought it I was spending a lot of time out here. I barely come out here anymore. I can have *CANDY SHOWS* from a suite the same as I could from my house and less clean up."
"What exactly are we talking about when you say candy like that?" She asked.
Franky looked at me. "She's here, prepare her for what she's going to see."
"Let's let them unpack the car. I'll show you around." Carol said to Annette.
I looked at Franky who was huffy. "What's the latest from Raynel?"
"Why are you asking me about her?" Franky huffed snatching cases out of the trunk.
"You're telling me to be upfront with my woman like you live by this creed yourself. Everything with me and Annette goes back to Raynel for you."
"Nothing's going on with her. She thinks this baby was an accident. That's it that's all."

I smiled at him, "and your guilty conscience is eating you alive!" Franky huffed and walked away from me. "So I guess that means the conversation is over." I said as I shrugged.
I took one of the cases into my bedroom, and then I found Annette and Carol on the grounds. Annette was admiring the garden while Carol talked about the celebrities that have partied here. Annette didn't care about that, she loved the look of the grounds. I exhaled again because this was definitely my Queen. When we walked in our bedroom I kissed Annette with everything in me. Annette smiled at me then she took in the bedroom. "This place is amazing, it's a shame that he's going to sell it."
"Would you want a house like this?" I asked to see what she would say.
"No, my only job would be cleaning it everyday. This is too much house." She said laughing me off.
"A house like this comes with the idea of maids. I wouldn't expect you to keep it up." I said
"And what kind of children would come out of a house like this? I love your parent's house because it was just enough room for all of you. I want down to earth children." She said entertaining me.
"Annette, we could have a house like this. Do you want it?" I asked watching her. She laughed until she saw I was serious. She was quiet for a minute. "No," she said lowly.
"Why not?"
"I like that you still drive the car you built when you were sixteen. I like that your house now is nice, but it's not flashy." She swallowed, "I know where my momma stands with you. If she thought you had money her tune would change, and then one day I might forget who she is. Until one day it came slapping me in the face."
"I'm not Rudy, your momma can't bully me."
"But she can and does bully me." She swallowed, "I kind of like this time alone just you and I. No negativity from her. She would tell me that being on my back was the only way I would have a man. I can hold my head up high and say that I have a man who actually loves me for me. He's gonna marry me, and not because I trapped him or tricked him." She walked up to me and put her arms around my neck and kissed me. "I love you so much and I thank you for choosing me. Thank you for waiting for me. Thank you for putting up with me. Thank you for giving me the space to see how much you love me."
Instead of being moved, I felt guilty by her little speech. "Annette...." I held her hands as she smiled and waited for me to find the words. "Tonight is going to be different. The house is going to be packed with a lot of Hollywood's finest, actors and actresses, singers, musicians, movie directors you name it."
"Really?" She said watching my eyes.
"They're coming for the *CANDY* SHOW."
"Why do you guys keep saying it like that?" She asked.
"Stay by my side, this is not the type of crowd I can afford for you to wander off in."
She looked between my eyes, "is it dangerous?"
"It can be, the appearance of two spoken for fellas is easier to play down than two bachelors. I didn't want to bring you because of the risk of danger. However, I'd rather not have you doubt me in this space of our relationship. I know you think of me and my family one way. There's a lot more to us than meets the eye."
"Like?" She said sitting on the bed.

"Pops and I own the company I work for. My primary objective in going back to school was to be near you and to hone in my statistical planning for my business."
"You don't work for Jeremiah?" She clarified.
"I didn't tell that fool I worked for Jeremiah. He assumed that when I said Jeremiah ran the floor. I let him run with his assumption."
Annette was quiet for a minute. "Did you kill that officer?"
Ugh! Why does she keep asking? "Do I look like a killer to you?" She lowered her eyes at me to say, do you want me to answer that? "Annette, stop asking me that?" She put her hands up, "fine Tim." She looked around the room. "What's that?" She pointed to the case.
"*Candy*," I said watching her eyes.
Her eyes stretched, "can I see it?"
"As long as you promise to live sugar free."
"I promise," she smiled.
I opened the case and I showed her the powder and the liquid. I told her people will be doing lines and shooting up all over the house. She asked why would we bring them here to do that. I told her that's why Franky wants to sell. That way we can leave when it's time to go.
Annette said she felt underdressed and I told her that only the pretentious guest would be dressed up. People started trickling in around seven, by nine the house was packed out. People were smoking, swimming, singing, dancing and having a good time. I didn't have to remind Annette to stay with me. Her hands were glued to my arm. The only time she got a little star struck is when she met an actress she admired. Her movie came out last year and it was a big success. She chatted with Annette for a little while telling her that they didn't use her actual singing voice in that movie. She was really down to earth. She was here with a Producer friend. Like Annette she stayed on the arm of her friend. Franky provided the buyer with what he needed for the show tonight and his supply for later, and then the buyer made his way around the party making new "friends" and making sure everyone had what they needed. Just when I felt the party would be uneventful screams came from the bathroom upstairs. I told Annette to stay with Dorothy, her actress friend, and I would be right back. I figured they could talk about movies or something real quick. I ran up the stairs as Franky told the dizzy dame who was screeching to shut up. She thought Mr. Lanthrop was overdosing, but he was fine. Franky told them they had enough and it was time for them to go. Franky asked where Annette was, when I said downstairs he told me to go. When I came down the stairs Dorothy's friend was pulling her away as I see someone standing too close to Annette. Annette's eyes were to the floor like she was trying to calm herself before she yelled at this guy. My ears felt hot, right as his slimy finger slid down her arm I grabbed his hands.
"Why are you touching her?" I said squeezing his hand.
"I didn't know she belonged to you. I was going to take this little trick home with me." He smiled revealing his yellow and brown teeth.
I took a deep breath his choice of words was making me angry. "It's time for you to go!" I turned to the crowd, "PARTY'S OVER! GET OUT!"
"I need someone for tonight." He said completely high.
"That's not my problem. Get going."
"Unless," I looked at him in disbelief. "You want to share. Bet that's the sweetest chocolate milk ever!" He reached for Annette's breast.
The look on my face told Annette to backup and she did. I kept telling myself this guy was high and to calm down. However, in my mind the scene kept replaying

with his hand extended towards Annette. Franky pulled me off of this guy and he told someone to get the guy who was now crying on the floor in a puddle of urine and blood. "I thought that stuff was supposed to give them superhuman strength." Franky said trying to make me laugh so I'd be cool.
Annette watched me while I told Franky I was cool. Then we made sure everyone was gone. I sat at the piano, and then I told Annette to sit next to me. Her eyes stayed fixed on me, but I couldn't tell what she was thinking. "You want me to play you something?"
"What can you play?"
"Whatever you like."
"Surprise me."
I spread my fingers like I was going to pound out Mozart and I played chopped sticks. Annette chuckled, then she asked for a specific song. I told her that was a good choice. I spread my fingers again and then I played chopsticks again. We heard a splash in the pool, we looked up and through the glass Carol was standing naked with her back to us right before she jumped in the water.
Annette frowned and looked at me; as soon as I saw the cusp of a cheek I knew it was bad. I put my eyes back down. Annette asked me if Franky was naked too. I told her I didn't know, but unless we wanted a peep show we should go upstairs. Annette smiled at me and then she looked back out at the show. I kept my eyes on her face. I didn't know if this was a test. "You don't ever like to watch?" She asked like her mind went somewhere far away.
"Not my brother," I said like she was crazy. Although if she were Jeff we'd be sitting here rating them on technique, approach, style, and duration.
"Of course not your brother. Is it weird that I like the sound of it?" I shook my head no. "Not so much the woman's sound cause they fake it too much." Then she turned to me. "I love when you talk to me, it's like you're speaking from your heart. We can't have a full on conversation in that space. I'm in your arms and you kiss me ever so gently as you call me your good girl as I'm doing something very bad." She rolled her eyes like the thought of it was turning her on.
I sat up straight, "you wanna take this upstairs?" I asked hoping she said yes.
She gave me an evil grin. "Or...."
I wiped my mouth from the drool that almost escaped. "OR?" My voice cracked.
"You go upstairs, get what you need. Then meet me out in the garden." I tried not to slump cause I didn't bring condoms with me. She watched my eyes, "what?"
"I forgot my condoms." I said deflating.
Annette slumped, "how could you? Tim!"
"One time won't get you pregnant." I said trying to talk her back into it.
Annette was shutting down before my eyes. "I don't want to risk it. Your momma is ordering dresses from Paris for me. I don't want to be fat on my wedding day."
"It doesn't matter." I said trying to chew back my irritation. "Let's go stroll the garden anyways." I said wanting to escape the sounds of my brother and Carol.
Annette took one last look out towards the pool, and then she followed me. "Last night was amazing, the parts of it that I remember." She sighed.
I sat down on the grass and looked at the garden with only the moonlight to illuminate it. "Sit down, and take this in with me." Annette hesitated, but like the good girl she is, she didn't recognize that this was a trap. She sat next to me and I kissed her, then I pulled back so she wouldn't recognize the ambush. "Would you ever want to live out here?"
"No," she replied quickly. "It's too hot! I've grown to like the coolness of the city."

I smiled, "it's hot in the south."
"And you see I don't live out there anymore." She said wiggling her neck.
"Do that again."
"What?"
"The neck thing," I said trying to do it.
Annette cracked up laughing, "you mean this?" She said wiggling her neck again.
"Yes!" I exhaled, "that is so sexy!" She laughed harder. "Do it again," I said moving closer.
"Oh no! Not if it's sexy, I'm not trying to turn you on right now." She protested.
"Too late, your sexy snake ways have opened me up girl. I gotta have you." I leaned in to kiss her neck.
"Tim! Come on, we gotta be responsible."
I moaned in her ear and she closed her eyes. "Let's make a deal." She shook her head yes. "Just the head."
"What does that mean?" She asked already succumbing to my request.
"I'll show you," I internally told myself to be cool.
I laid her down, took off her panties. Kissed the gateway to heaven. Annette gasped as she felt me. "You feel! You feel!" She said looking at me.
"Feels good doesn't it?" I said trying to remember my word.
"Give me just a little bit more." She begged. When I did she gasped, then she repeated her request. No trickery needed she asked for more until there was no more of me to give. When I collapsed her body tensed, "TIM!" She said pushing on me, "you didn't!"
"SSSHHHH! We'll think about that later." I said trying to calm her.
"GET OFF OF ME!" She yelled, her hair was all wild with grass laced in it. "How could you?"
"I'm sorry, I got carried away." I said not moving.
"Tim, no!" She cried. "I explained all this not too long ago."
"Blame me, it's my fault." I said feeling almost horrible.
"Trust me! I'm going to." She said, "can I get up please?"
"In a minute," then I worked her again like we didn't just finish. I love watching her face as she responds to what I'm giving her. She always looks so surprised, especially this time as she came again. I kept her long leg up, until I felt satisfied that my seed hit the mark.
I fixed my clothes then I stood, I helped Annette up and then her legs wobbled. I picked her up and then I carried her upstairs to our bedroom. As soon as Annette's head hit the pillow she was out. I laid there thinking until I heard Franky and Carol come up the stairs then I closed my eyes.

****

I heard soft sounds of a window breaking. I was up and at the door in record timing. I cracked the door listened and I heard the sound of scurrying. I silently cursed, why does anyone ever think this will work? I got on the bed, I kissed Annette's face as I stroked her head. When her eye opened I told her to be quiet and to keep her eyes on me. The closet wasn't big enough in this bedroom. I told her to get under the bed and not to make a sound. Annette's eyes were big as she did what I told her to. I took a deep breath, then I opened the door, and shut it behind me. Franky came out at the same time. We walked down the stairs and three guys were looking for the money from last night's party. I turned on the light and they charged immediately. The house was already a wreck from the party, and this fight was insuring that everything was completely trashed. This guy hit like a mule and for a moment I

could've sworn I had wings cause I was flying. I hit the wall hard, I needed a minute to grab my composure cause the room was spinning. Now these guys were probably high, and they were professional. Then I had to ask myself, "self?"..... "Yes Tim?"..... "Why are you fighting these guys?"..... "Good point self!" I was surprised Franky didn't come down holding. 1, 2, and I took three to the ground but not fatally for now.
"It took you long enough!" Franky barked at me. As he spit blood.
"Since when you come empty handed?" I said catching my breath.
"Since I thought you had it." He said
"Well I thought the same thing."
"You're the one who says, *you never know where the day might lead you*, then you play these games!!!!" Franky was irritated to say the least. We walked over to the guy who was still rolling on the ground. "Who sent...." Franky looked at me. "How he going to answer any questions if you shoot him in the face?" Then he shot him to put him out of his misery.
I was about to say something when we heard a woman's scream.
Franky and I raced to the top of the stairs to see Carol fly across the room. I took two steps backwards to look at my bedroom door. I put the gun in my pajama pants waist in my back, then I went to the door of my bedroom. I opened to see a guy holding Annette with his hand over her mouth. Everything around me got dark and quiet. "Give me the money or she gets it!"
Franky walked over to the room. "Let her go!"
"I said…"
Franky cut him off. "Let her go and I won't get pissed off. You're going to die, it's a question of how painfully!" Even in the dark I could see the hysterical look on Annette's face. The guy tried to say something else and Franky and I went in on him. Annette didn't scream once, it wasn't until Franky pulled me off of the guy saying I was only tenderizing the corpse at this point did I stop. "Carol! Call the police!" Franky called out.
Then we turned our attention to Annette who was standing there holding herself. I wanted to say something but there were no words to explain this. The police came fast, and they took pictures of everything. Franky told them we had a party and these guys came to rob us. Which is basically what happened. Franky said he brought his girl out here to show her some fun in the Southern California Sun. I was holding Annette and kissing her. A few of the officers looked at me like I was crazy as I openly showed love and concern to my wife. I silently growled at them, and they turned their eyes. We grabbed our bags and we went to a hotel.

Chapter 12

Annette

When I opened my eyes Tim was watching me. He was laying there with his arm around me. We laid there silently for a long time, not saying a word. Then I exhaled, "thank you." Tim watched my eyes. "So many bad things have happened to me in my life that most times it feels like the next thing is just one more thing." I took a deep breath so I could speak beyond my tears. "Rufus risked getting beat on himself to stop that officer from hurting me." I cried a little into the pillow, "until then I never knew someone would step in to save me. I didn't know you Tim. I didn't know you! I'm not saying I wished him dead, but thank you for caring."

"I didn't mean to kill him. I got mad, and then he was having a hard time breathing." He said, I kissed him. "You're not scared of me?"

"I honestly don't know how I feel right now. I'm trying to process everything. My head is spinning you know?" He shook his head yes. "I'm battling with myself inside. You're crazy, but who isn't? I don't think you'd hurt me. I'd only be lying if I said I didn't wonder if your temper could ever turn on me. What if I make you mad? Would you kill me?"

Surprise and hurt flashed across Tim's face. "Annette, please! You should know right now how much you mean to me. I would never harm you. Please remember it's me. I'm in love with you, I would never hurt you."

"That's what you're saying now, but what about when you get tired of me. When we aren't new to each other anymore? Seems like my breathing makes my momma mad at me. She gave birth to me and after all of that I'm the stray dog she kicks around. That's my momma I gotta take that from her. I refuse to let anyone else hurt me."

"You don't have to take that from your momma."

"You would hit your momma?" I watched his eyes.

His eyes bucked, "**NO WAY**! She's crazy! I know she'd kill me and all I could do is be dead."

"Exactly!"

"What I'm saying is some people we gotta love from a distance cause we know about their ways."

"My point is my momma is the only person who gets a pass when she behaves like that. I won't let you hit on me."

"I've never, and I would never! You're hurting me by implying that I would ever do anything like that."

"You're too good to be true. Normally when something seems that way it ends up being that way. My mind is racing right now, I don't know what to do with you." I said rolling on my back and staring at the ceiling.

"What are you saying to me?" Tim said trying to hold back his anger.

"I don't know what I'm saying. You and Franky are *Candy Men*; this is the life you lead. Did you bring me in so I would fall hopelessly in love with you, and then I take the fall when the police come after you? Why did you bring me here?"

"You freaked out about me coming home late, like you wouldn't have been upset about me going out of town for a few days. I didn't know how else to tell you about all of this. I'm trying to show you all of me."

"If I have babies with you, are my sons supposed to be *Candy Men* too?"

"No, our children won't live like this."

"So why do I?"

"You don't, but I needed you to know."

"This is too much Tim." I said turning my back to him and crying. "I don't know if you're trying to use me or if you really care."
"I care! I told you, and I keep telling you how much I love you!"
"You're just fast talking me. I'm not going to jail for you."
"If I were using you why would I marry you?"
"My father married my momma then he married baby doll. Who knows how many other women he married around town as well. Marriage doesn't mean anything." I cried harder.
"Annette! Don't fall apart on me. I know last night was scary, but it's over. Think about it, you know I love you. You know my heart, the rest is nonsense." He yelled. I laid crying not responding. Tim turned me over and I kept my eyes closed while I cried. "That's your problem! Whenever you close your eyes you forget that it's me you're dealing with. Open your eyes!" I kept my eyes closed as I cried. "Open your eyes Annette!" I refused and Tim kept yelling at me.
There was a knock on the door, Tim snatched it open. "Why are you yelling?" Franky asked him.
"What do you want?" Tim barked at him.
"Stop yelling at her!"
Tim growled, "don't tell me how to deal with my woman! You have no idea of what's happening in here right now!"
"Tim get a grip! This isn't you, you're gonna scare her away."
"Did I ask you for your advice?" Tim growled at Franky.
"Come talk to me." Franky told him not backing down.
"No! I'm talking...."
"You're talking but is she listening. I'm trying to stop you from repeating my mistakes. Come talk to me."
Tim went out the door and I laid there crying. What if they're trying to set me up? What if none of this is real? I laid there thinking as hard as my brain would let me. Tim doesn't change up no matter who's around though. He wouldn't confirm or deny anything about officer O'Brien. If it was for show he'd have told me right away or made sure someone told me. I don't think he put Katie up to telling me either. Why would she go along with his little scheme? He did sound broken up about it. I don't want to be used or left behind. I'm so confused!
Tim came back in the room. He drew a bath for me and then he put me in it. He told me he'd wash me if I needed him to, but he needed me to get dressed. I washed up and then I waited until he got in the shower. Then I opened the room door. Franky was standing there, he smiled at me, I frowned at him. "Tim said you were going to try to run when he got in the shower."
I rolled my eyes at him, "are you trying to set me up?"
"For?" He stopped smiling.
"I don't know a *Candy* bust? I don't know."
"Why would we show you everything, how to point the finger back at us and then set you up?"
I looked around the hallway, that was a good point. I know these Wallace's are smarter than me, this could be a trick. "I don't know! Shut up Franky!" Then I slammed the door. Tim was standing in the bathroom doorway with his towel around his waist. My eyes went all over his body. "You can't argue with Franky!" He said as he tried to hold back his anger.
"Why?"
"Because you only care about me that much!"

I didn't think of it that way. "Am I the little colored girl who will do anything for you?"
Tim put the suitcase on the bed to get his clothes. "You're not the little colored girl or anything else! You're my wife! When you're with me you see me as the white boy, is that my descriptor?"
"No."
"Do you even love me?"
"Of course I do! It's not hard to believe that I love you."
"But it's hard to believe that I love you? Why?"
"White men don't love colored girls!" I blurted.
Tim stared at me with the most hurt expression. "How could you say that to me!"
"Cause I'm scared!" I was being honest.
"And I'm not? You are the first person to truly love me. Or at least I thought so. Maybe I'm just a white boy to you."
"Stop trying to turn this around on me. I left my momma's house to sleep on my friend's couch for you. I'm trusting you to provide for me! I'm trusting you to protect me. I allow you inside my body! You have no idea what that's like for me. To allow you to touch me the same way someone hurt me, and then interpret that as love. Don't give me that! You're hiding something!"
His face twitched, "Annette, sit down."
"No! I'm not stupid, tell me while I'm standing."
He pulled on his clothes fast and then he laced up his shoes. "I knew you were going to freak out. I needed reassurance that you couldn't run too far." I watched his eyes. "I didn't use a condom on the beach either."
I grabbed my throat. "You're trying to get me pregnant?" Tears poured out of my eyes. "Why?"
"Don't leave me Annette! I love you! I mean it from the bottom of my heart. You're my wife!" He made me stand up and he hugged me.
I looked at him, "you really want me? Nobody ever wants me."
"I want you, I need you, and I have to have you!" He said

Timothy

We rode home in silence. Carol wore shades the entire time. The guy did a number on her face. Carol was dealing with it the best way she could.
As soon as we got home seems like Franky flew out to be with Raynel. She was due any day now and he refused to miss the birth. A little over a week later he called me extremely excited. It's another boy, and Raynel finally agreed to come home. Franky was talking so fast and excitedly. He told me to go into his place, rid the evidence that a female has ever stepped foot in there and change the locks. I couldn't ask my sisters for help, so I asked Annette, Lauren, and Katie. Katie asked if they could set up the nursery, and Franky said it was fine. He said as soon as they could travel they were coming.
The girls asked a ton of questions and for some reason they seemed to think this whole set up was romantic. Of course I didn't tell them that Franky did any of this on purpose.
When they arrived at the airport, Annette and I waited at the gate for them. Franky was carrying Franklin III and Raynel had the new baby in her arms. I hadn't seen Raynel in years, one look at her and I knew why Franky was gone. Annette smiled really big when she saw her. "Timothy be the first to meet my son Franklin III!" Franky said with so much pride.

The little boy looked at me with my brothers face. "Nice to meet you, I'm your uncle Tim." Then I looked at Raynel. "It's good to see you again."
"Tim! Look at you all grown up!" She smiled real big at me.
"This is my wife Annette."
"Soon to be," Annette said taking Raynel's baby bag. "It's nice to meet you."
"Franky she's prettier than you let on." Then she rolled her eyes at him. "I have a feeling there's more."
I looked at Franky, "I told her everything." Then he looked at both of us, "and this is my wife Raynel." Raynel held up her ring hand.
My brother and I hugged, "either way momma's gonna get you anyways right?"
"Right!" Franky chuckled.
When we got to their house, Katie, Lauren, Jeff, and Jeremiah were waiting for us. Franky proudly introduced everyone to his sons.
Ice shot up my spine when I heard a car door close. I glanced out the window and Pops and momma were randomly popping by. Panic hit my soul as I cursed. "IT'S MOMMA!"
Everybody started screaming and running in every direction.
"Go open the door!" I told Jeff as I tried to hide in the closet.
"Not me! Not me!" Jeff said trying to steal my hiding place.
"Where did Franklin go?" Raynel said as she stood in the middle of the floor panicking and not knowing what to do.
"Hit the floor!" I told Raynel.
"I can't! Your momma already saw me." She said frozen in her spot.
Everybody cursed! "You know what I don't appreciate?" Everyone was still scurrying as my parents approached the house. "How I'm going to get in trouble and this is not my deal!" I said.
"Man up! Man up!" Jeremiah had to say to all of us as we were three cowering grown men.
"There is no manning up when it's momma!" Jeff said as we all laughed.
The doorbell rang and my heart fell on the floor. "Ok, ok.... Franky you gotta face this sooner or later."
"LATER!" Franky called out from the kitchen.
I took a deep breath, I can do this, I told myself. "I'll do it." Raynel stood in the middle of the floor looking at me with scared eyes. I opened the door. "Hi! Hi momma! Hi Pops!" I said blocking the doorway, "what brings you by?"
"Did I see the Johnson girl through the window?" Pops asked.
I panicked, "I didn't have nothing to do with it. It's not my fault!" I yelled.
Momma jumped, "what's going on? Move out the way boy!"
I moved out the way, and then I ran behind Annette and Lauren who were cracking up from the couch. My parents walked in the door, momma scanned the room. She smiled real big when she saw Raynel. "Are you the reason my son's been...."
Momma's eyes landed on Raynel's ring. "FRANKLIN!" She yelled. Pops put his hands in his pockets. Franky came out of the kitchen holding little Frank. Momma screamed to the top of her lungs. Franky hung his head and came to momma and handed over his son. "HOW COULD YOU?"
"Momma we told him to tell you, we're innocent." Jeff said coming out of the closet with his hands up."
"You knew about this?" Her neck snapped.
"Pops knew too! That's right if I'm in trouble all of y'all in trouble too!" Jeff said.

Pops popped him upside the head. "Irma we...." The baby started crying. Pops looked at Franky, "ANOTHER ONE?"
"I'll go get him." Raynel volunteered as she ran up the stairs.
Momma pointed her finger at Franky, "you've got a lot of explaining to do." Then she looked at little Frank. "Hello baby, I'm your Nana." She said kissing and hugging him. Little Frank melted into momma and smiled for the first time since I've met him.
"Irma I didn't know there were two!" Pops tried to explain, but momma wasn't letting him slide. After Franky explained all the men except Jeremiah and the babies were in the doghouse. Pops kept smacking Franky upside the head for getting him in trouble. Franky was so happy, I doubt any of that mattered to him. Even Franky's gestures were different; it was like he was teasing me with his wedding band. I think Jeff was noticing it too. It was one thing that Matt and Dale were married. Franky though?

Annette

I tried to stop my hands from shaking but I knew no matter what it was the point that I tried, I knew this wasn't going to change anything. I wrapped my pies, and then Irma and I drove to my momma's apartment. Sitting outside of her building I tried to control my emotions. I wanted to come and once and for all make peace with my momma. I wanted her to come to my wedding, I wanted her to love me just like she does all of her other children. I told Irma I would be right back. When I told her what I wanted to do, I could tell she wanted to tell me not to, or that it was a waste of time. Instead she helped me make my pies, and then she told me she was coming with me. I couldn't stop my hand from trembling, some how I found a way to knock on the door. Little Preston open the door and his whole face lit up when he saw me. "ANNETTE!" He yelled as he hugged me so tight. If only this was my momma hugging me like this.
He opened the door and Emma, my momma, and a woman I've never seen before were sitting on the couch. It looked like they were having a good time. Momma's smile and happy disposition disappeared as soon as she saw me. A tear ran down my face, I already knew this wasn't going to go well. "I made you a pie, I hope you like them. I made enough for everybody."
Emma sat forward on the couch and she said she could smell them and they smelled delicious. I couldn't take my eyes off of my momma. My momma said she needed some money, I opened my purse and I gave her everything I had in my wallet. She took it and put it in her bra, then she rolled her eyes. "So, you hate me so much, that you let the white man blind you into thinking he could ever love you!"
"Momma I don't hate you, I love you very much. I can't help who I fell in love with. I don't love him cause he's white, I love him and he happens to be white." I pleaded.
"Oh, so I's stupid. I don't know the difference. You ran over there to those white people happy to be their house dog. I's tryna marry you off to a good, respectable, educated black man, but you's too good for him."
"Momma that's not what happened at all."
"SHUT UP! Cause of you, he run off with that white girl who only want his money. Now Mrs. Henson heart so broke we can't be friends no more. You are selfish Annette!"
"But momma the Wallace's aren't bad people, they…"

"EMMA!" My momma clinched her teeth, "don't sass me!" Emma immediately stopped talking and put her eyes to the ground. "Did you open your legs to my husband? Is that why he was so in love with you?" The room spun, my heart broke, and I stood there crying looking at my momma in disbelief. How could she EVER think something like that? She pointed at me, "this one is so fast. She went after her brother Leslie! He would come home for a couple days, and he would have to sleep outside sometimes cause she was always all over him." I looked at Emma who was now crying cause she knew that wasn't true.

"Momma?" I cried from my broken heart.

"Don't momma me, I stopped being your momma the day you got my husband killed! I don't know what I ever done to you to make you so ungrateful! Thank you for the pies, but you got to get out! Don't come back here no more. I can't stand the look of you!"

I turned and ran out the door, Irma was waiting right outside. She immediately put her arms around me and walked with me crying. She rubbed my back as she put me in the car. She drove up a hill behind the Cow Palace and then we parked at the top in an open field. I cried hard as she rubbed my back. "Don't take any of the things she tried to poison you with to heart. Some people don't know how to love Annette."

"She hates me, my momma hates me!" I cried harder.

"Don't focus on her. She's miserable so she wants you to be miserable too. Focus on all the things you do have. You've got your health, You're smart, You're Beautiful, You got a good man raised by the best momma on this western side of the country! She don't matter Annette!" She said rubbing my back.

"But she's my momma!"

"I'm your momma, and I love you! Now come look with me." We got out the car and it was a beautiful and clear day. She told me to look around and take in the beauty of the day. To appreciate the fact that I'm here, and that by simply breathing I bring so much joy, love, and peace to so many people's lives. Irma talked to me so long I eventually was able to laugh, but all I wanted was Tim. I wanted him to come home and hold me.

"Momma," I swallowed. "I think we need to move the wedding date up. I don't think we're going to make it to spring."

She looked at me, "what's wrong?"

"Can I be honest?" I said scared she was going to be mad.

"Of course," she said watching my face.

"Now that I know the difference, I don't want to go back to condoms." I was embarrassed.

She laughed, "why you think I got so many kids? Ain't nothing like being skin to skin. Let's call the country club and see what we can arrange."

****

"I can do your hair for your wedding." Raynel said.

"Like what?" I asked her.

"However you like. You should've seen some of the fashions coming out of Harlem. Hhhmmmm!" Lauren and I smiled, while Katie and Emma stared. "What is wrong with you guys?"

"It's the way you talk. I need to talk like you." Lauren smiled.

Raynel touched her mouth, "how do I sound?"

"Everything sounds like sex coming from your lips. I bet you Franky gives you whatever you want." Lauren teased.

Raynel blushed, "he does actually."
"How do you do that?" Lauren asked like she was going to take notes.
"I don't know, I've always spoken this way." She said still blushing.
"Those sleepy eyes, full lips, how could he not fall in love with you?" Then Lauren leaned in, "how did you fall in love with Franky?"
I gasped at Lauren's nosiness but I leaned in to hear Raynel's answer. "Franklin has always been very sweet to me. When everyone else has always thought he was mean, I always knew he was sweet and gentle. My parents were never going to approve of us together, so I convinced him that we needed to hide. I told him to date those other women." Then she shook her head as she slipped into yesterday. "I didn't mean to give it away though. One perfectly timed kiss, at the perfect moment to make me forget my daddy and the Christian way I was raised. I was hooked after that. " Lauren and I hummed like we knew exactly what she meant. "I thought my world was coming to an end when I found out I was pregnant with little Franky." I rubbed my stomach as she said that. "My daddy," she cried. "This man who taught me life is precious and should always be celebrated wanted to send me to a doctor out by his sister to take my baby away." I got off that train a stop sooner than I should've and ran for my life. This lady Ms. Parnell gave me a job in her shop. Taught me how to do hair, and treated me like a daughter. One day I was sweeping and Big Ole Franky walked in the shop with so much love and concern in his eyes. I cried and I held on to him as I cried. There are moments in my life I will never forget, like that kiss, making love to Franky, and the moment I introduced him to his son. My daddy said color matters to everyone, I guess he never truly knew the Wallace's."
"Yea but they did the same thing to Peggy." Emma said.
"What do you mean?" I asked.
"Emma, Beth told you that in confidence." Katie said.
"I'm only telling them, it won't go further than here. You all promise?" We all agreed. "Peggy was dating one of the men that worked for Jeff. When her father found out no one has seen the guy again, and they had a doctor come for Peggy. They may know love, but they know hate real well too."
"Whoa! My daddy beat on me until he was satisfied that there would be no baby." Lauren said.
Emma's eyes filled up with tears, "my momma did that to me. That was the only time she's ever come after me like that. She looks at Kiah the same way she looks at Annette. That's why I leave her with Katie. She don't even ask me about her." Emma said crying.
"That's not your baby?" Raynel asked Katie.
Katie coughed hard, "she's my baby. But she's not my baby."
"I'm a little girl, what I know about being a momma and a wife?" Emma said repeating the venom my momma's been pumping her head with.
"Emma no, you know…" I said.
"No I don't. Hezekiah's running the streets, doing who knows what!" She spit.
"Emma, he goes to work and he comes straight home. I know, I checked." I said.
"You don't know! He's trying to take my youth away from me. He doesn't want me to be young and free!" She cried.
"Momma doesn't want you to be a happily married woman. Please Emma, don't let her change the way you know right to be."

"It's right that I finish school, get good grades and maybe one day I can get a good job where I can take care of myself instead of relying on him to take care of me." Emma said

"What about the baby Emma? Kiah needs you."

"She don't need me, she has Katie. She act like she don't even know me anymore." Emma said like her heart was broke.

"All you gotta do is show her some love, she loves you Emma. Don't give up on your baby!"

"Annette I can't be nobody's momma right now. I'm a little kid myself." She cried.

"What about Hezekiah, you guys are in love." I cried.

Emma shook her head, "he..... he.... He's a man. He running around anyways! Now he won't have to hide it." Emma stood up, "I don't appreciate you trying to make me feel bad about my life Annette!"

"I'm not trying to make you feel bad, momma is telling you wrong. Don't walk away from your baby, you'll regret it. Don't walk away from your husband, momma wouldn't have walked away from your daddy for nobody."

Emma's eyes turned evil, "but he died because of you!" My body jerked, and Emma stormed out of the room and out of the house.

Nobody said anything, cause they didn't know what to say. One by one they put their arms around me as we all cried.

****

All day I've been feeling like I'm coming down with something. At the grocery store I had to stand still and take a minute to gather myself. Lauren asked me if I was ok. I told her I needed to sit down for a minute. She asked me if I was catching one of Katie's many colds. I shook my head and said I didn't know. I didn't feel good at all. Lauren brought me a paper cup full of water, and it was refreshing and cool. It seemed to do the trick, and even though I broke out in a sweat moments ago, I felt fine now. Lauren said I was weird and we finished all of our shopping. As we walked out of the store Butch walked towards me like he knew I was here. His face was not friendly as he walked up on me. "Momma told me what you said to Emma!" He yelled in my face.

I exhaled, cause if momma said it there was no truth to it. "What did I say?"

"Who is this?" Lauren asked in my defense.

"Don't worry about it.... DEVIL!" Butch literally spit at Lauren and she backed up.

"Butch, don't act like that. She's my friend!"

"You can't be friends with Devils! You so busy running behind them you can't see straight!"

"What did I do? Why are you mad at me?"

"You cost momma her only friend out here! You choose to be with the likes of those people, and then you make Emma break up with a black man who's willing to do right by her."

"Butch! I didn't do any of that!"

"Are you standing here with her?" He spit at Lauren again. "Then as far as I'm concerned you did it all!" Then he looked at me with cold eyes, "stay away from us Annette! If I find out you've gone by momma's place again.... I'm not responsible for what happens to you!"

"Butch!'

"Matter of fact, if I see you again I'm not responsible." Then he turned on his heels and walked away from us.

Lauren’s eyes were big as she looked at me. I cried as we put our groceries in our cars. “Are you going to be ok?” Lauren asked me with tears in her eyes for me. “Yes,” I said. I gave her a hug, and then I got in my car. I sat there staring at the steering wheel while Butch’s words floated around my brain. Lauren tapped on the window then she opened my door and gave me a hug. She told me to call her to let her know I made it home safely. So I did, then I started making dinner. All the smells invaded my nose at once. I didn’t have time to turn anything off. I ran to the bathroom to throw up.

Timothy

When I opened the door the smoke from the kitchen poured out, I left the door open. The food on the stove was completely burnt up and the fire was still going underneath them. I turned off the fires then I surveyed the room. One chair slightly in the path of the kitchen and the living room was out of line, but nothing else. My eyes were burning from the smoke but I opened my ears. I was actually home about an hour earlier than normal, where was Annette. Then I heard her crying, she was in the bathroom and the door was open. I crept up to the bathroom and Annette was on the floor crying her eyes out. She screamed when she saw me, "WHAT ARE YOU DOING HERE?"

"Why are you trying to burn the house down?"

"I'm sorry I'll clean everything up." She said going to the sink.

I opened all the windows in the house. "What's the matter, are you sick?"

"I need Ginger ale my stomach is acting up."

"Let's let the house air out. Let's go out to eat."

Annette was quiet the whole car ride. I know she's still upset about her momma so I try to cheer her up. "I smell like a chimney!"

"You're fine," I said looking at my menu.

"What would you know? You're not the one stinking up the table."

I looked at her over my menu. This attitude was getting old. "Go ahead and cry." I said watching her face.

"WHAT?"

"I know you're upset, you start snapping instead of crying. Just let it out so this snipping and snapping can stop." I returned my attention back to my menu.

My ears started bleeding from all the colorful words she proceeded to throw at me. I sat back trying to chew back my anger. "ARE YOU HAPPY NOW?" She said as tears flew out of her eyes. "I'M PREGNANT! I HATE YOU SO MUCH!" I stared at Annette in shock. I had no right to be shocked, but as soon as she said it I was. "OH! SO NOW YOU HAVE NOTHING TO SAY! I WANTED TO WAIT!" Then she started crying so hard she couldn't speak.

I stood up and hugged her. I put my arms around her and I apologized, "you're right. I am selfish! I am ungrateful! What was the other part?" I asked kissing her forehead again.

She held on to me as she cried. "We can't stay here, we have to move."

"A new start, and a new beginning."

****

“I LOVE THIS ONE!” Annette said holding on to my arm and jumping up and down.

I looked at Dale, “you heard her. She likes this one.”

“What the lady wants, she gets.” Dale said putting the keys in my hands. “We’ll go over the paperwork tomorrow.”

“Thank you DALE!” Annette said as she twirled in the middle of the living room.
“A brand new HOUSE! Who gets a brand new house the first time they buy a house?” Annette sang.
“I can ask my sisters to help pack up the house with you.”
Annette stopped twirling, “Tim! I was not kidding I don’t want anything in our new house that was around when you had all those other women around.”
“Annette, that’s my whole house.”
She smiled, “I know! I want all new stuff. I’ve never had the opportunity to decorate and I think I could be good at it. I want to make the nursery pink.”
“What if its a boy?”
“PLEASE! I’m having a little girl, and she’s going to have you wrapped around her little finger. Daddy please!” She batted her eyes at me.” Prepare yourself for the letters from the department stores. The girls and I are going to go crazy!”
“Annette!” I don’t know why I was protesting but I was.
“Deal with it, it’s happening!” She skipped down the hall. “I want to have my Aunt and Uncle over as soon as we have furniture too.”
Annette holds on to her Aunt and Uncle for dear life, they’re all the family she has these days. Our wedding was coming up in a week from today. Every time Annette thinks of it she cries. She said she couldn’t believe that her momma wasn't going to be there. Since we suddenly moved the wedding up none of her friends from back home could make it. What she doesn't know is I reached out to her friend Harriet. She's one of my many surprises for my bride. I followed Annette around the house as she's the happiest she's been in a minute. I know getting her pregnant on purpose was selfish, but I DON'T CARE! I did what I felt I needed to do at the time. I refuse to apologize to anyone, except this crazy lady for my choice. I know it wasn't fair to her, but it was too risky not to.
I asked Annette if she wanted anything from Pops' store. She smiled and said she was hitting every store.

****

Jeremiah and I pointed at her. "That's her!" We said at the same time, as we approached this little chubby girl who was looking around the train station like she was on another planet.
"Mrs. Coleman?" Jeremiah said.
She smiled real big, "yes sir. You must be Timothy." She said to Jeremiah.
Thunder stolen, immediately I knew she didn't give her friends back home very many details about me if she assumes that Jeremiah is me. I reached for her bag, "actually I'm Timothy ma'am. It's nice to finally meet you, I've heard so many wonderful things about you."
She bucked her eyes and blinked real fast. "You're the Timothy Wallace marrying my friend Annette Cooper?"
"Yes ma'am," I smiled at her.
"Things sho are different out here!" She said then she smiled at us. "Are you his hired hand?" She asked Jeremiah.
"Hired hand? I don't think so. This is my best friend since I was a little fella." He said.
Harriet unintentionally stared at me. I knew she was looking for something that said I was possibly passing. I smiled at her and let her take me in. "You wanna ask me something?"
"Are your people from Louisiana?"

"I'm not creole if that's what you're asking." She looked embarrassed, "Harriet I love Annette very much and we're so happy you could make it. She's going to be so surprised when she sees you. Thank you so much for coming."

"You're going to stay with my wife and I." Jeremiah said proudly.

When we got to the house Katie had the baby as usual. Hezekiah was there waiting for us. "Harriet this is Emma's husband Hezekiah and their daughter Kiah. This is my wife Katie." Harriet smiled real big then she picked up the baby. She asked where Emma was. Hezekiah nonchalantly said she was at her momma's house. Katie showed Harriet to her room.

Hezekiah asked me if Kathryn was coming to the wedding. When I said yes his eyes turned sad. He said Emma leaving him was pay back for breaking Kathryn's heart like he did. He almost fixed his mouth to say he was going to miss my wedding behind running from that girl. I let him work it out; I told him missing my wedding wasn't an option.

Once I saw everything was taken care of at Jeremiah's I told them I was going to finish up at the office. When I walked in the door, as usual Avery was inquiring about the driving position that needs to be filled. I told him I hadn't made a decision yet, and I would keep him informed.

My desk was just about clear when my foreman knocked on the door. "Mrs. Wallace is here to see you." He had a goofy look on his face, but I didn't pay it any mind until...

She walked in the door and shut it behind her. I felt all the blood rush to my face.

"What do you want?" I lowly barked at her.

"Why do I have to want anything? Why couldn't I have come to congratulate you?" Maureen asked.

"Congratulations should only come from people who mean it."

"You didn't mean it when you congratulated Matt on our marriage?"

"I never congratulated my brother, and I don't speak to you."

"Tim why do you act like you hate me?" I cocked my head to the side at her. "It's been hard, I have two little ones. Then my father up and dies out of nowhere." She got emotional. "I miss talking to you. I...."

I picked up my phone and started dialing. It rang once, "this is Matthew Wallace how may I help you?"

"Your wife is in my office crying!" I growled into the phone.

Matt was quiet for a minute like he was processing my words. His voice was low and angry. "What does she want?"

"She wants to know why I act like I hate her. Come get your woman!" I said then I hung up the phone.

"Why would you do that?" She cried.

"I don't know why you came here."

"I'm still in love with you Tim!" She blurted out.

"That sounds like a personal problem." I growled telling myself to let it go. Not to remember that she even said that.

"We were in love! You don't feel anything when you look at me?" She pleaded.

"Disgust!" She fell back in her chair as she cried. "I don't know what kind of family you're from, but the Wallace's do not play these games. You are MARRIED to my brother. He has to live with his choice to lay with you behind me. As for you, the moment you went for my brother sealed the end of our relationship. I am marrying the woman that I was put on this earth to love."

She made a face while she cried. "Annette is from a different world. Marriage is hard enough; she won't be viewed as white. You will be viewed as colored. That's a hard life to have, why would you choose it?"
"After all this time you haven't put two and two together. Annette and I are from the same world. I don't know where you come from."
"Annette is cute, but....."
I cut her off, "MY WIFE IS GORGEOUS! Stop lying to yourself!"
"That's enough for you?"
I looked her in her eyes. "Annette is my everything! I never have and I never will love another woman like I love her. I don't know why you're here! The sight of you makes me want to vomit! I don't know how I ever let you suck me in with your innocent pretenses. I should've looked at your parents and walked away from you. Your father was so desperate to meet my father that he offered you up to me as his sacrifice! Youth blinded me from what was happening."
"Tim it's disrespectful to speak of the dead!" She said putting her hands up.
"RESPECT! RESPECT? What would you know about respect? By coming here you have disrespected my entire family who took you in despite yours and you! You've disrespected my brother who loves you. You've disrespected me, who could careless about you. I like Christy more than I could feel anything for you. You've disrespected yourself and your family!"
Maureen sat there crying. "I still love you! I'm sorry if that makes you angry."
"Angry would mean I still care. I'm disgusted, and insulted. Matt is going to get you." I said going back to my paperwork and ignoring her tears.
She kept talking but I wasn't listening. She could've said my hair was on fire and I wouldn't have known it.
My door flew open as an enraged Matthew stood in the doorway. I was going to say come in and shut the door, but Matt charged his wife picking her up by one hand and slapping the life out of her. I shut my door then I tried to tell Matt to calm down. He kept shaking Maureen asking her why she would ever think this was ok. I could understand his reaction, but I didn't want to see it. "Matt please take your wife home." I asked him calmly and quietly.
"GET UP!" Matt barked at her. "Your father dying does not give you license to behave this way. Keep it up and you will join him!"
Even I looked at my brother with big eyes on that one. By the look of him I didn't think he was making an idle threat.

Chapter 13

Timothy

This morning the birds were singing louder, the sky was clearer. And my momma and Lady B prepared a feast before they ran off to Annette. Jeff walked in the kitchen rubbing his eyes. He looked at me and smiled. My bachelor party was one for the history books. Jeff left the club with the stripper; I didn't expect to see him so early. "You're up early?" I said handing him a mug.

Jeff exhaled shaking his head. "I'm not getting married just because all of my brothers are." He barked

"Who said you have to?"

"No one!"

I laughed at him, "you're going to run from her. Just like that other girl." I snapped my fingers trying to remember her name. "I can see her face!"

Jeff took the coffee pot off the stove. "Edna!"

"Right! You gonna keep switching directions until she tires of you. Edna's married with how many rug rats now?"

Jeff cut his eyes at me. "I will cut you on your wedding day!"

"What's wrong with Lauren?"

"Nothing, she's a little wild, but so am I. She's a little girl!"

"She's a year older than Annette."

Jeff exhaled, and then he sat down. He put his fist up like he was warning me. "When we talked about it she brought up my extras. Then she admitted to having a few of her own. Who does that?" He looked at me like he was waiting for my answer. I opened my mouth and he put up his fist again. "She's too wild!"

"But that's what you like about her. You want to tame the unattainable."

"She's a wounded cat, I'm trying to help her and she scratches me."

"Give that pussy some catnip first! She'll let you pet her and anything else you want to do to her." I cracked up.

Jeff didn't, "I can't stand you!"

"Stop acting like you don't like her dysfunctions. You thrive off stuff like that. I'm not telling you to marry her. Just stop acting like you don't like it." I said

"That's what you do?"

"Annette appreciates everything I do for her. We argue cause she's never had this. Shoot! Neither have I! I love being her night in shining armor. Embrace it Jeffy!" I smiled real big.

Jeff didn't smile, "I can't stand you!"

Franky walked in the door with both of his boys. He frowned at us as we watched him fumble with his boys. "You see me having trouble!" He barked.

I took the baby; both of his boys were serious just like their dad. No smiles and they looked at you like they were trying to figure you out.

Matthew brought his entire family and he told Maureen to get in the television room. Pops asked him why he was talking to her like that. Matt hadn't calmed down yet, and I didn't tell anyone so they were surprised when he told them. You could tell Pops felt sorry for her when he told Matt to go easy on her. We all looked at mister no mercy in shock.

When we got to the country club the staff was hurrying around making sure everything was set up perfectly. The harpist arrived and was getting instruction from the director. Momma looked so pretty in her dress. She said Raynel did her hair, she asked if we liked it. We loved it. Maureen took her seat with the kids; she looked like she was on the verge of tears the entire time. I was talking to momma when Christy marched up to us with Fernando. She was fussing cause she didn't understand why she wasn't invited to our wedding. Momma took the baby and then she told Christy to leave before she got on momma's bad side. Christy moved fast as she walked away. Momma took Fernando to Beth and Peggy who already had little Frank and Ethan. Little Frank and Fernando stared at each other for a long time. Momma snapped pictures of them looking at each other.

Annette

"Baby! It's your wedding day! The last day that is all about you until the day you die." Aunt Dorothy said smiling at me so proud. "Timothy is a GOOD man. He loves you so much! I am so happy for you, he's exactly what you need and deserve. Don't hold back baby, that's your man. Give him all the love you have to give and know that you deserve all the love that he has back. You two were made for each other, embrace it and live in the love." She said brushing my hair.

Aunt Dorothy was EVIL! She's been showering me with love all morning making me cry this whole time. Irma had me lay down with ice and cucumbers on my eyes to reduce the swelling, but Aunt Dorothy had to keep talking to me. Making me snot all over myself. I promise I'm going to pass a long this kind of torture to my daughters, it's only right.

Kathryn and Jean came to my rescue telling me about their father. Jean has a bow and it's getting pretty serious. She said her wedding may be next. It got uncomfortable when Kathryn asked about Emma. I told her the truth. She said it didn't make her feel better that everything blew up in his face. She said none of it had to be. I told her I admired her strength, cause I would not be so calm if it were me. When Raynel came in the room Kathryn and Jean were stuck on the way she spoke just like everyone else. She pulled my hair back, parted the side to give it some style. Then she pulled it all back into a low bun.

Irma and I fussed about my dress, she demanded that I wear a white dress, and I said I felt like a fraud. Then she brought Lady B in on the discussion who said in Africa we wear colorful dresses so we could wear any color dress we wanted. I happened to fall in love with a white dress, so Irma won this round. My dress is sleeveless with a lace neckline. The bodice is heart shaped under the lace. There was a belt at the high waist and the skirt was straight and full. At the bottom of the skirt, which hit at my ankles the lace from the top was there again. Martha gave me her shoes that went perfectly with my dress. I had wrist length lace gloves. And at the last minute I found the most perfect little fascinator hat. Instead of the big veil, this hat was a small oval and the lace from the hat dramatically swept over my left eye. Everyone dotted their eyes at me. Raynel made sure everyone's hair was right before we went to the country club grounds from our dressing room. My wedding colors are ivory, gold, and brown. All my brides' maids have brown dresses with gold accessories and ivory gloves, shoes, and hats. The grounds were decorated nicely and my gold accents sparkled everywhere.

Timothy

I got butterflies when momma came to get us to tell us it was time. I excitedly took my place with Jeff, Jeremiah, and the rest of my brothers standing at my side. I heard Jeff stop breathing when he caught a glimpse of Lauren. Her hair was blonde and her eyes were locked on Jeff. He tried to move out of the way of her stare by shifting his weight from one leg to the other. Pops watched them with the most amused look on his face. When I saw Annette my heart sped up, there was my wife. She didn't run away at the last minute or look like anyone was forcing her down the aisle. I don't know why I kept bracing myself for her to run away or announce that she was secretly in love with Franky and she couldn't continue to fake her love for me. Ridiculous I know, but nothing this good has ever happened to me. When I felt myself about to give in to any type of female reaction inside of me and make myself the subject of every joke my brothers and father would come up with in the future. Annette noticed her friend and broke character from the poised bride to a screaming and excited friend. Her reaction was priceless and exactly what I needed to get it together.

Annette

My Uncle Rufus smiled the most fatherly smile as he extended his arm to walk me down the aisle. He kissed my cheek and told me I was breath takingly beautiful. I smiled and thanked him. There were Wallace's everywhere, so my people stood out. As we were walking I caught a glimpse of someone who looked like Harriet. I did a double take and that fast I forgot I was walking down the aisle in my own wedding. I screamed and let go of Rufus. I leaned over Hezekiah as I hugged Harriet. I kissed her on her cheek. Everybody was cracking up laughing at me and my reaction. The only thing that could've topped Harriet being here is if my momma and sister were here. I took a deep breath then I put my arm back under Uncle Rufus's arm. Tim was still laughing as I got it together. I mouthed, "thank you!" And he said, "I love you!" Everyone said "aw" when he did that. It was a bright and sunny San Francisco day. We got married on the country club grounds and Tim wrote his own vows for me. I was embarrassed that he didn't tell me to do the same but I loved every moment of it.

Timothy

"My life changed forever when you walked into my heart. The hardest thing I've had to do is wait on you to see me. Wait for you to accept me, wait for you to know that my love comes from a genuine place created just for you. I promise that I will always love you! No one could ever mean as much to me as you do. I will always protect you; I would die protecting you from anything and anyone. I love you more than this existence could ever discover the words to explain. You are the air I breathe and the reason I continue to live. I will exhaust every atom in my body in service to you." Annette was in tears, and then she told me I cheated by not telling her to write her own. I kissed my bride in complete and total appreciation for everything she has done for me and all that she will.

Annette

Tim and I took tons of pictures, and then I introduced Harriet to everyone there. She told me that Tim sent for her. When we were alone she leaned in, "you never mentioned that he was white."

"I didn't think it mattered."

"I embarrassed myself trying to ask him if he was high yellow."

"Harriet you didn't?" I gasped.

"He didn't seem mad, but please tell him I meant no harm. You should've told me."

"I'm sorry," I said. "Can I tell you a secret?"

"Of course." She leaned in.

"I'm pregnant," I said halfway embarrassed.

"Is that why you moved the wedding up?" She asked with big eyes.
"No, but I knew it was going to happen sooner than later. I wanted to look like this and not like my water was going to break at any moment on my wedding day. My daughter's not going to know I was pregnant today. I don't want her to get any ideas."
"Good thinking." Harriet exhaled, "it's like a different world out here. I wish I could stay longer. My momma isn't doing all that well and Mr. Coleman cain't stay away from Hazel's these days." Harriet sighed, "he don't really touch me anymore. He cain't do it as much as he used to. He gets mad at me like it's my fault. Honestly I'm thankful for the break. Six kids in seven years is a lot. My body needs this break." She faked laughed. Then she leaned in, "do you like it?"
"It?" I clarified, and she shook her head yes. I shook my head and rolled my eyes. "YES!"
"How does he compare?" She whispered.
"To?" I said trying to remind her of who I am.
"Luther," she said like she just knew I didn't tell her.
"You think I did it to Luther?"
"Isn't that why he was going crazy when you left? He said he was coming to find you. When you never mentioned him I figured you turned him down."
"Luther came to San Francisco?" I was shocked.
"Yes, he told Mr. Jones that the baby wasn't his. Turns out the Jones girl was messing with the Sutton boy. Baby came out looking like his twin. Her daddy made them marry and now she look mad all the time. You know that Sutton boy ain't all there. I don't know why she lay with him in the first place."
I smiled, "Luther stopped running? Good for him."
"He said he was coming to rescue you. He left before your momma did, or right after. I can't remember." She sat there quiet for a minute. "Make sure you send me your wedding picture. Everyone's gonna die when they see how fancy you are now."
I smiled, "thank you. I never had Luther."
Her mouth fell open, "he was in love with you like that and he never got a taste? Wow!"
"Like what?"
"He picked up work everywhere he could. Everybody knew he was coming to California for you."
"I never saw him."
"He came back after awhile, but he wouldn't talk about it with anyone. His momma didn't say or ask anything in her letters?"
"Nope," I said looking at Tim who was calling me to the dance floor. "My husband is calling me. I'll be back." I said happily joining him on the dance floor.
Lady B called out, "that's right! Show them what your grandma showed you to do! Go head Tim! Go head!"
We laughed, and then Tim told people to join us on the dance floor. "Who were you two talking about?" Tim asked watching my eyes.
"Harriet thought I messed around with a boy back home. She says he came out here looking for me, but he never found me." I said looking at him.
"I could tell you were talking about a fella. You're all mine, you snooze you lose." He said kissing me.
"I got a question for you. Your sister in law is a mess today. She never talks to me, always stares, and today she's falling apart."

Tim exhaled, "I dated her first, and then she decided to jump ship for Matt."
Light bulb! "That's why you put Lauren in her place that day?"
He nodded, "and why I wanted to kill Franky. We discussed it! I wanted to rip his head off. None of that matters now. You're my wife forever and ever! I love you and will love you with every breath in my body." He said using his eyes on me.
"I don't understand why you love me this much." I said putting my arms around his neck and kissing him.
I looked at the couples dancing around us. Irma and Pops, Lady B and Matt, Hezekiah and Kathryn? They were talking while they danced and I got a sinking feeling that their dance was a mistake.

****

"Where is Emma? I wanted to get a look at her at least once." Harriet said zipping up her bag.
"My family's not talking to me." Saying it hurt.
"Since when does that include Emma?" Harriet said not looking at me.
"Since now I guess. She doesn't want me to say anything against her walking away from her family. So she's not talking to me." I rubbed my arms cause I felt empty.
"You are brave Annette. I can honestly say that California is different from Kansas. Wait until I tell Claudette about your husband. Who's ever heard of a white man marrying and loving a colored girl like this? You left your family to surround yourself with all these white people. They're very nice, I've never seen anything like it."
"Tim and I are in love. Remember when I told you I wanted to bite my man?" I said.
"Yes, I remember thinking you were crazy." She giggled.
"I bite Tim all the time!" I said proudly.
Harriet laughed, "maybe I'll have that with my second husband after Mr. Coleman dies."
"You think about your husband dying?"
Harriet frowned at me; "Mr. Coleman was a old man when he came calling. I was comparing notes with Claudette."
"Oh lord! I can imagine how that went." I smiled.
"She can't get enough of her honey even after all these years. Mr. Coleman and I do it, but not like them." Then she looked at me, "you can't get enough either?"
"Not a fair question."
She frowned, "but your pregnant."
"Yes, but I got married yesterday. It's not like I've had the chance to lay with my husband without fear or guilt. I love what we've shared so far, but I'm not on the married level that you two are yet. Tim wanted to marry me before anything ever happened between us. He would've waited for me. I guess I kind of forced his hand stating I wouldn't marry him because I couldn't lay with him."
"So you had sex to prove you could lay with him? You could've waited."
I exhaled, "I know it doesn't make sense or sound right, but I wouldn't have married him unless I knew I could lay with him."
Harriet shook her head, "it doesn't make sense."
"You know how my brother hurt me." I sat on the bed next to her. "You were the first person to tell me I wasn't crazy for thinking there was something wrong with the things that happened. Even though every time Tim touches me my body tingles over. I still freaked out when he got next to me. I told him I was broken and he had to prove to me that I was wrong. Not just the first time, but also every time Tim was

patient and gentle with me. It wasn't until maybe the fourth time that I realized that my brother didn't know what he was doing, or maybe he went in the wrong place so that he wouldn't get me pregnant. I was a little girl who barely knew the difference between the front and back. Tim telling me I was a virgin," I shook my head and rocked. "I thought my brother made me dirty. Tim showed me I was clean. All my guilty, and unworthy feelings about Tim's love for me vanished. I know the technical way to do it is the way you and Claudette did it, but I needed this."
Harriet put her arms around me like she always has. "Annette, my momma is getting sicker and sicker. She's not close to dying yet, but when she does. I need you to come hug me." She said from her heart.
"Of course I'd come!"
"You promise?"
"Harriet, you have my word! I promise!"
She exhaled, "let's get to this train station. So I can get home. I know Mr. Coleman is having a fit."
"Harriet! He wasn't ok with you coming?"
"Girl no! Since he can't do me, he's afraid someone else will. He tells me to write down what I need from town. He asks the kids who came by while he was gone. He's a mess."
"Harriet be nice to that old man. Don't kill him with stress."
She smiled real big. "There's a thought! Good plan!" She laughed I didn't. "I was just kidding."
"You know there's truth in a person's joke."
"I know! I know!"

Timothy

"Thank you so much for bringing Harriet out. That was such a wonderful surprise." Annette said laying her head on my shoulder as I drove us home from the train station. I kissed her forehead. "Her husband never liked me, he's really going to hate me now. She left without him being ok with her leaving."
"What?" I shook my head, " that was not a good move. You wouldn't do that to me would you?"
"Like you would ever try to stop me from going somewhere!" Annette chuckled.
When we got to the house Annette took out suitcases to start packing for our honeymoon. We were leaving the following night. I asked her to sit on the bed as I took a deep breath then I got the folders. Annette sat on the bed looking at me. I explained that I had my will changed to name her as the beneficiary to everything that I have before we were even officially dating. She put those big brown eyes on me again asking me if I was crazy. I kissed her and said that it hadn't been proven either way yet. Then I gave her the Cooper Financial papers. Tears started pouring out of her eyes as soon as she saw the company letterhead. I told her this was her company and she never has to work again. I explained that the company has performed better than projected. Annette listened to everything as I told her how the company was setup. She asked me questions as she processed everything.

Our honeymoon was beautiful, we went to Canada and spent a week at Niagara Falls. I wanted to take my bride away from the ignorance of the states where we would be celebrated as a couple. Rather than deal with the stares and amazement of our neighbors in other states. No matter where we went, everyone kept asking me the same question, "how did I get such a beautiful wife?" At first it was funny, by

the end I had to start asking people if they've seen me? And when they would say yes, I would tell them the answer should be obvious then.
When we came back we went straight to Pops' car dealership from the airport. I told Annette to pick out any car that she wanted. Of course my bride wanted to pick the simplest car, but I wouldn't stand for it. This was a wedding gift. I made her take the fanciest car on the lot.

Annette

I can't get enough of my husband! He's the air I breathe! My heart! My soul! Now that the house is all decorated and I'm happy with the way it looks, I don't like to leave it much. Whenever he can, Tim comes home for lunch and me. Tim says I take all the life out of him, but I can't help it. I want him more and more. I finally noticed a difference in my stomach so I guess the doctor was right about a baby being in there. I've help my momma and the doctor deliver so many babies. I can remember momma's cry every time the baby didn't cry when you smacked it's bottom. One baby cried after the second smack, but she so little and she was gone by the morning. I tell my doctor about all of my momma's babies and how scared I am. She's a nice older lady, she listens and then she tells me I'm going to be ok. Irma goes with me. Sometimes Martha and Lauren come too. I can't believe I'm gonna be a momma. I'm going to have a baby of my very own to love and take care of. Tim told me to stop insisting that this baby is a girl before I end up disappointed. Then I noticed that he was hoping for a boy. So our playful banter began, back and forth. Whoever came up with the best reason why the baby would be one sex over the other got to choose the dinner for the next night.
The difference between Oakland and San Francisco is so crazy. It's not nearly as cold here as it is there. People are friendlier over here and the neighborhoods are really mixed up. There are people from all sorts of backgrounds and countries out here. I feel really good about moving here, even though it means I have to travel to the city to see my family and friends.

****

"Hi Kiah! How's auntie's baby?" I said picking my niece up. Even though this was definitely Hezekiah's daughter, she looks a lot like Emma too.
Katie was in the kitchen making tea. "She's getting big isn't she?"
"She sure is. I like what you did with her hair." I said admiring her bows.
"Thank you, she's such a good baby. I wonder what yours will look like." She said
"I'm thinking this baby should look Asian just to throw everyone off." We laughed
Katie and I were making each other laugh like only she and I could. Katie straightened up. "Stacy had the baby."
"And?" I said hurrying to sit down on the stool so she could tell me everything.
Katie shook her head no, "that's definitely Stacy and Bucky's baby."
"Girl, boy? Cute?"
Katie stopped moving and looked at me. "How you gonna ask me that? You've seen the parents!"
I covered my mouth with my free hand while I cracked up. Kiah looked at me like she was trying to figure out what we were saying. "That's your brother!"
"Bucky's teeth! Stacy's face!" She shook her head. "No one said that baby was cute. They just said," she put her hand up to her chest and pretended like she was looking down. "OH!" She said like she was scared. "That's a baby alright!" We cracked up.
The doorbell rang; Katie came back with Emma in tow. Emma paused when she saw me, I could tell she was debating internally. "Where's your car?"

"I got a new one." I said
"You want me to leave?" Emma asked.
"I don't have a problem with you Emma. Why are you mad at me?" I asked.
She shook her head, "I'm not mad at you."
"I'm going to go upstairs. Do you want me to take the baby?" Katie said.
"No you can stay." Emma said, she walked up to Kiah. She said, "hi," to her, like she was a stranger. Kiah looked at her long and hard. Then she looked at me. I told her to go, and then she went to Emma. "I let momma ruin everything!" Emma said as tears ran down her face. I bit my tongue. "You know Hezekiah and Kathryn been writing each other letters?" She looked at me.
"I didn't know," I bit my tongue again.
"He's talking about moving out there to be with her. She's trying to steal my man back." Emma said like she was angry.
"Who told you that?" I asked
"Wilma told me about the letters. Last time I saw him he was talking about moving away. So I asked him what about the baby? He said if I didn't care, why should he!"
I turned my eyes to Katie and she silently tried to tell me to calm down. "Emma! When are you going to start thinking for yourself? You know first hand that momma lies, but you let her talk you into ridiculous stuff. Then you know Wilma means you no good and you still listen to her. Your husband has been begging you to come back and you only pay attention when someone else has his attention. So what if you're a little girl, you're a momma and a wife act like it! Nobody told you to get with Hezekiah in the first place!"
"Wilma did!"
"The blind leading the blind! Is anyone supposed to feel sorry for you right now? If you want your husband, get your family back. Fight for it! Stop acting like you're a rejected victim! You chose to leave them. They're going to move on. They're not going to sit on pause waiting for you. You can get mad at me for telling you the truth if you want to, but it had to be said."
Emma cried, "it was too hard! I felt like I was messing everything up. I want Hezekiah back, but it was too much with the baby." Emma looked at Katie. "You are a good mother. You hug her and kiss her like Annette has always done for me. I can't give her that right now. Please don't hate me!"
"Emma! You gave me a beautiful baby to love and take care of. Why would I hate you?"
Emma cried, "cause I can't do it!"
"Kiah is fine. Does this mean you're leaving her with me?" Katie tried to hold back her excitement.
"If Hezekiah will have me back, and be ok with leaving her with you. I need to take one thing at a time."
"Momma's not gonna be happy about this." I said
"Mr. Lakshman is courting a white lady. Momma thinks she's going to have us put out. So she's freaking out about money." Emma swallowed, "I gotta get away."
"Is that why you want Hezekiah back?" I asked
"No, I'm leaving momma's house regardless. I can go to school and rent a room downtown. I love him, and all of this started because we fell in love."
Katie immediately started coaching Emma on what to say and how to say it. She told her Jeremiah and Hezekiah aren't that different in nature. They're good men, and they love hard. I called Tim and told him where I was, so that he wouldn't be

worried. Emma was staring at me real hard. She asked me why I looked weird. I smiled and waited for her to catch on. I asked her what made me look weird. She started to say that my face was fuller. She screamed and congratulated me, and then she rubbed my stomach. She asked for details about my wedding. She said she made the mistake of telling momma when the wedding was and there was no way she could even sneak out to get a peek at us. Katie told her there were no blind brides maids, Emma looked disappointed that she missed Harriet.

Jeremiah and Hezekiah walked in the door talking about their day. Hezekiah almost gasped when he saw Emma. You immediately saw him put a wall of emotional protection up. His eyes said he was happy to see Emma, but his mouth was mean and hurt. Emma looked like she wanted to run at one point, but Katie mouthed to her that he was weakening and to keep going. Emma served him his dinner, and she listened to him whenever he said anything. She rubbed his head like Katie told her to. Hezekiah was trying to be strong, he even barked at Emma. He was amazed when she took it. Then they went out to the backyard to talk. They left the door cracked so Jeremiah and I shamelessly sat by the door to listen. Hezekiah confessed that he and Kathryn spent *time together* after the wedding and they had been exchanging letters with Kathryn, and that he was considering divorcing her and moving away. Like Katie told her to, Emma accepted everything he said. She let him tell her how much her walking out on their family hurt him. He said he knew she was young, but he didn't think she would leave him. Emma kept apologizing for hurting him. Tim stuck his face by mine so he could hear what was going on. He scared me, and almost made me give away the fact that I was listening. When Hezekiah broke down and said he missed his wife, as Emma was about to leave. I looked at Katie who was rocking the baby to sleep with a smile on her face. When they started kissing all of us frowned like it was disgusting and turned away.

I told Katie she was amazing. She smiled and said she knew her man, and Hezekiah wasn't much different.

****

"What's wrong?" Tim asked looking at my face.

"The baby doesn't like coffee so I can't drink it. I got a little headache." I squinted at the morning sunlight.

"What should I do? You wanna take a sip of mine and see if the sip is enough to get you through?"

I smiled, "no. There's something else you could do."

"That won't work," he chuckled.

"It worked last time."

"Say what girl?" Tim chuckled, "I made love to a sick woman?"

"Yep, I think I should call you King Midas! Your golden touch cures everything with me." I teased.

"You love gold woman," Tim said laughing.

"Yes I do Goldie, come on Goldie give me some. Cure me!" I pleaded.

Tim laughed harder as he played hard to get, "no. I don't wanna lay with a sick woman."

I fake coughed, and then I kissed him. "Come on baby, your touch heals me."

"You are little miss can't get enough these days." Tim smiled.

"I hope it's not the pregnancy. All I want right now is you on top of me. Me on top of you. You next to me. You behind me," I moaned. "Your hands all over me. You…" Tim was smiling from ear to ear as he listened. "You are so beautiful!" I said looking at my husband.

He gasped, "Handsome! I'm handsome Annette."
"Still means you're beautiful. I don't know what I did to deserve a man so beautiful! Every time I think about you my body tingles. I can be thinking about how you like your eggs and there it goes. You washing the cars, mowing the lawn, anything that references you and my body is on sizzle. When I was a little girl I said I wanted to love my husband like I love you. That's why I didn't want to be married off like Harriet. I always wanted what Claudette has. Even when she talked about her fights with her husband all I heard was how much she loved him and I wanted a husband like that of my very own. Not that I actually thought I would get one. I never imagined all of this for my life. A man who loves me for real."
"What about the guy from back home?"
"Luther was the bad boy who had me sneaking out the house to hang out with him. I used to watch him and the Jones girl do it out in the woods. Or him and whoever, now that I think about it, that was kind of messed up. At the time it was all new so I'd watch. I didn't want to do it myself, but I was always curious. Luther was gonna rescue me and then his ways caught up to him. His touch never felt like yours, but he was the first person to touch me in a loving way. His touch was like Rudy's. I knew he cared about me, but there was always something missing with both of them."
"Like?" He asked taking everything in.
"I don't doubt that Luther loved me. I actually believed him when he would say that he did. Luther seemed like he was always running from something. I didn't trust him to not run from me one day. Rudy wanted to control me. He liked to look at me and think of all the disgusting things he wanted to do to me. He wanted to tell me how we were going to be, I was supposed to swoon because he was with me. Seeing him bow to my momma was a definite turn off. When I told him about that guy at school, his reaction was cowardly. It didn't even seem like he cared. Even if he couldn't beat that guy, the fact that he wouldn't stand up for me was a turnoff."
"So why me?"
"For one, you stood up for me when no one else would. I like that you never forced yourself on me. You were always there and you let me come around to the idea of you on my own. Whenever you could, you would ask me questions about myself and listen for my answers. You think I'm pretty not just for how you want to lay with me, but like you've looked into my soul and fell in love with me inside. I always wanted this, I never thought I would have this." I smiled at him, "even though you're a *candy man* and all. I guess no one's perfect."
He smiled, "does it bother you that I'm white? Tell me the truth."
"Only when I think of my momma. Do you sometimes wish that I was white?" I asked.
He frowned, "NO! I couldn't imagine you any other way."
"Did you know you would fall in love with a colored girl?"
"No, but I am so happy you are. I can finally be myself. I told you I don't feel like I was born in the right body. None of my family for that matter. When I was little I used to get so confused by my momma calling Lady B momma. I thought she was my real grand momma for a long time. Then I used to wonder why my skin wasn't browner. I thought our curly hair was because momma and Lady B weren't telling us the truth. We didn't listen to music the way the kids at school did, we were always different. I wasn't looking for a colored girl in particular. The moment I saw you that was it for me." He sat up and looked at me. "It took you forever to see me! AGONY!" Then he plopped back down on our bed. "If we had to rewind time the

waiting would drive me even more crazy now cause I would know what's waiting on the other side." Then he kissed me. "My wife."
"When did you realize we were in love?" I asked.
"I was always in love with you. I was waiting for you to catch up."
"I knew it the first time we were alone. You were silly, but always good to me."

****

"Momma?" I called out as I walked in the house.
Peggy came out of the television room. "I'm the only one here." She came and gave me a hug. "How are you feeling?"
"Today is a good day, what are you doing?"
"Watching a little television and then I was going to finish my book." Peggy looked around nervously. "Can I talk to you?"
"Sure, but I'm meeting Lauren in a little bit. We're going to a museum, you wanna come?" I asked.
"Ok," then I followed her into the television room. Peggy fidgeted with her hands as she tried to decide what she wanted to say. Then she blurted out that she was pregnant AGAIN, and she was afraid of a repeat of last time. Since no one officially told me what happened, I had to play dumb and ask her what happened. She told me about the guy before this one and how he "went away" as she put it. She said her parents wouldn't let her keep the baby and she was afraid they wouldn't let her keep this one. I asked her about the father, she turned her eyes to the floor as she said he was a sailor, and he's gone. I put my hand on my stomach, and then I asked her why did she do this? She started crying as she said she didn't know. All she knew is that she didn't want to lose her baby again. I was mad at her for telling me. She begged me to help her, and I told her I had no idea of how I could possibly help her. She told me to get Tim on our side and then he could talk her parents into letting her keep the baby. I felt bad for her, cause I honestly didn't think her plan was going to work.
When we met Lauren for lunch, she kept asking what was wrong. When Peggy finally told her, Lauren said she regretted asking. At least now we were stressed together. That night when I couldn't sleep, I tearfully broke down and told Tim what Peggy told me. He jumped out of the bed like it was on fire. He was beyond angry, and he called his parents. I tried to tell him not to cause it was two o'clock in the morning. I've never heard Tim's father so angry before. He called back a few minutes after we got off the phone, Peggy and Beth weren't home. Tim's father said he was calling everyone to find them and bring them home. Tim was angry saying that his sisters have always been goofy girls and causing nothing but trouble. Tim kissed me and told me he would be back. I told him it was the middle of the night and he couldn't think he would find her at this hour. He said he had to try.
Tim didn't come home until the afternoon. He said no one found them; we went over his parent's house. Irma was a mess, she was angry, she was hurt, and she was worried. On the car ride home Tim's mouth fired off a mile a minute going off about his sisters and how goofy they've always been. "Seems like no matter how the parents try to stop it, they end up pregnant again. My sister, yours, I wonder if it would've been so bad to let them have the baby in the first place. Being a parent isn't easy which Emma learned and Peggy's going to learn. Some lessons in life have to be learned the hard way."

Timothy

"We wanted to welcome your family to the neighborhood." The elderly woman said holding a dish in front of my face. "I hope you like banana nut bread."
The aroma slapped me in the face. "Yes of course!" I said taking the dish from her. "Would you like to come in?" I said walking towards the door.
"If it wouldn't be a bother. Your wife moves so fast whenever she comes home, I didn't have a chance to introduce myself. I just wanna say hello." She said.
I called out to Annette when I opened the door. She said she was in the kitchen. I told her we had a visitor. Annette came out of the kitchen with her little apron on. Her little belly had grown from this morning, and she looked absolutely angelic and adorable. "Annette this is Mrs. Tucker she lives across the street. She brought us banana bread, smell this!" I said inhaling the aroma.
Mrs. Tucker looked stuck for a minute, "oh this is your wife? I thought the blonde was your wife."
I frowned, "me with a blonde? Never!"
"She means Lauren," Annette said watching Mrs. Tucker's face.
Mrs. Tucker stood there trying to regroup and we weren't helping her. "Do you want your bread back?" I held it out to her.
She swallowed air, "no. I'm sorry. You know this kind of thing doesn't happen. I don't mean to be rude." Annette and I looked at her while she tried to take her foot out of her mouth. "You young people surely do have a way of trying to change the world. I have a son about the same age as you all. He thinks he's going to be the next heavy weight champion. He trains all day and night sometimes." She said proudly.
"What's his name maybe I heard of him?"
"Liam Opp!" She said proudly, "he's my son from my first marriage. Next time he comes home you have to come by and say hello."
"Sounds good."
Mrs. Tucker took another look at Annette then she took a deep breath. "Well, I'll let you two get back to your evening. Your supper smells lovely."
"Thank you," Annette said watching Mrs. Tucker.
I locked the door behind her and then I went straight to my wife. I said hello to the baby who was growing by the minute then I kissed my beautiful wife. Annette told me not to bring stray cats home anymore.

****

"Welcome to the Grand Opening of **The Place Where Jazz Is Played**! In addition to the house band, we have a performance by a local Bay Area Jazz singer Mr. Calloway." Everyone applauded. "So let's get this show started!" Gus said as everyone applauded.
The band started playing and Gus came directly over to our table. He and his wife Isabelle joined us for the evening. Annette was so happy to be here for the Opening. She said it would be a while before she could come again after the baby was born so she was trying to live it up. Momma kept the babies for Franky and Raynel so that they could be here, but there was obvious tension between them. Jeremiah came with Hezekiah and Emma, Katie stayed home with the baby because she was feeling a little under the weather. Dale came solo as well; Blanche couldn't leave the house yet. She and the baby were doing well, she told Dale to come out with us tonight. He was shocked but happy to be free for the evening.
Gus's new location was a much better fit for his club. It was still downtown, and the set up was more like a theater. The stage was off the center of the room and it was a

big circle. The white Grande piano, the entire band and their instruments, performers and there backup singers, and a little space to do a little dance captured your attention in the center of the room. On the main floor there was dinner service from the kitchen. Customer's paid extra for these close up and personal seats. Then there were mezzanine and balcony seats. The customers in these seats could go down and purchase drinks and food from the main lobby.

"Oh honey!" Isabelle said rubbing Annette's belly. "How much longer?"

I loved watching Annette lovingly touch her belly. "We got one more month and then our little bundle will be here." Annette blew air, "I can't wait to get back to coffee to kick these withdrawal headaches."

"You don't drink it now?"

"No, the baby doesn't really like coffee. I can't wait to have my body back." Annette said, "this baby is very picky about what it will let me eat and what I can't."

"It will be over soon and then you'll be a mother to a beautiful baby. What do you think it will be?"

Annette rubbed her stomach, "a girl." She said shamelessly.

I cleared my throat, "tell her what the baby was in your dream though." I smiled real big.

Annette rolled her eyes at me, and then she stuck her tongue at me. "Never mind all that. I'm going to have a girl and her name's going to be Lucinda."

"What are you going to do if it's a boy?" Isabelle asked.

"Make him give me a girl right away." Annette joked.

Sounds good to me, but I would like to have some time with my wife in between babies. I don't want her to forget about me.

The show was amazing and we had a good time. On the car ride home Annette said she was going to miss nights like tonight once the baby came. I told her our down time would only be temporary. "We can have as many babies as we want to have. Its important to me that we don't lose sight of who we are." Now I didn't see anything wrong with what I said.

Annette's tears startled me, "SHUT UP TIM! I WANTED TO WAIT! YOU COULDN'T! NOW YOU WANNA TELL ME NOT TO GET PREGNANT RIGHT AWAY? YOU ARE SO MEAN!" She cried like I said our baby was ugly or something.

"I'm sorry Annette...." I said feeling like I couldn't do or say anything right. When we got in the bed I waited for her to say it was ok to touch her. Which of course meant she cried at me for not automatically knowing to comfort her. I couldn't take the water works, so I had to dig deep and find the funniest something I could think of. The element of surprise was on my side and my wife couldn't stop laughing. She thanked me for the laugh.

****

"Franky's here," Jeff said sneaking a rib off the grill.

Annette bucked her eyes at me as she brought the next tray of prepared meat out to me. Raynel was behind her carrying the last tray and she was frowning. Franky came out the door behind them with all three of his boys.

"Hello Tim," Raynel said as she put the tray down. She looked upset, and by the look on Franky's face I could tell their frowns had something to do with Christy. She did not take the news of their marriage well at all. She's been causing them problems as much as she can. Momma's gone after Christy so many times that Christy won't come to my parent's house anymore. Raynel still hasn't reached out to her family, she purposely avoids anywhere that she thinks her family will be. So Franky has Dale building a surprise mansion for Raynel in Walnut Creek. I saw the plans and their home plans to be amazing.

"You-who! Tim!" Mrs. Tucker called from the gate to our backyard. "Can I introduce you to my son?"

Annette looked at me and then she took her seat next to Lauren. "Sure, come on in."

Mrs. Tucker entered the yard with the proudest smile as her big corn fed looking son followed her. He was bigger than solid Franky. "This is my son Liam!" She said like she was showing off a masterpiece.

"Nice to meet you, I'm Tim. These are my brothers Jeff and Franky, our wives are over there." I pointed to the girls. Jeff shot me a look like I was giving Lauren ideas.

"I'm a boxer!" Liam announced.

"I would hope you're not big like that for nothing." Jeff laughed.

"Nice little house." Liam said looking around the yard.

"Thanks," This guy wasn't very smart.

"Liam is in training right now. He has a fight coming up in San Francisco, I told him all about you and your family."

"I told my mother that men bring their dark girlfriends to fights all the time." All three of us stared at him; I don't know what point he was trying to make. "She wants me to invite you to my fight."

"Thanks?" Jeff said

Liam looked at Jeff, "you talk too much! I don't like you!"

I cheesed at Jeff really big, his smile disappeared and irritation settled in. "SO! Who cares who you like!"

"Let's go mother!" Liam said firmly grabbing his mother's little arm with his big ole hand.

"Oh Liam, be nice. I was hoping you could get along with the new neighbors." She said weakly.

"Let's go!" He commanded his mother, who helplessly did as he told her.

"Liam hits his momma." Franky said watching them cross the street.

"Strike one, why he don't like me? That's strike two." Jeff said annoyed.

"I guess we were supposed to fall all over ourselves over him." Franky said.

"I dont kiss no man's butt!" Jeff spit.

"Calm down, he's gone. We know you're not a sissy." Franky said.

Chapter 14

Annette

The doctor says the baby is coming any day now. Irma comes over every morning most times before Tim leaves. She gets breakfast going, feeds her son. Then she lays in the bed with me singing whatever new silly song she's come up with for the day while she rubs my head. I never had this from my own momma, so I eat it up. Irma said this is what Lady B did for her, her momma never did any of this either. We talk about everything while she shovels delicious food down my throat. I asked what I was about to go through, cause I was scared. She said the first baby is the scariest because you don't know what to expect. She said she thought she was gonna die when she had Franky. She said he was born big, she rubbed my belly and told me to remember that all mothers have delivered at least one baby and then some decide to do it again. She didn't lie and say it wasn't going to hurt. She told me I was strong enough to get through it.

Tim watches me like I'm a ticking time bomb. If I so much as scrunch up my nose he panics. It was cute at first, but now it's a little bit over the edge. So I do stuff to mess with him. If I know he's staring at me while I sleep I suddenly stick my tongue at him. He laughs and then he mellows out for five minutes, then he's up tight again.

"Its almost over sweetheart, the baby is almost here." Raynel said rubbing my stomach.

My due date came and went, I wanted this baby out of my body. I'm tired of dropping things and not being able to pick it up. "I don't know how you did this twice and by yourself each time."

"The Lord gave me the strength to bare it." Raynel said looking off. I rubbed her hand cause I knew she was thinking of her family. "I drove past my daddy's house. Everything is still exactly the same there." She exhaled, "how long do you think I have to play stranger to my family? I want my children to know my family too."

"I know what you mean. Do you worry about your kids being spoiled?" I asked

"YES! All the time! Franky don't seem to get it though." She said like it's a touchy subject.

"Tim and I talked about it, our children will always have what they need. I want them to work for the things they have. I don't want them to know about the money."

Raynel sat next to me and lowered her voice. "Franklin and Irma are going to sell their house."

I stretched my eyes, "why?"

"It made sense, in a way, to have that big fancy house when they had all their kids at home. With Peggy and Beth on the run, it's too much house for just the two of them."

"With all these grandkids coming at once pretty much, don't they think they're going to need all the space?"

"The space, yes, but that house and neighborhood is too fancy. They standout too much, all that old money around there."

"Irma has been here just about everyday and she hasn't said anything." I said

"Her focus is you and the baby when she's here. Act like you don't know nothing about any of this when she tells you."

"Of course, who told you?" I asked.

"Franky of course." Then she squeezed her hands together. "He's still messing around with that red head."
"Franky is in love with you."
"Her hair is all over him whenever they get together. I know I started this whole messing around thing. Somehow I actually convinced myself that if we got married it would be different."
"What does he say when you confront him about it?"
"He doesn't even try to lie about it anymore. He just looks at me like I'm crazy. I've cursed Franklin from the bottom of his feet to the top of his head. His ears should still be ringing from my beautiful combinations, but it doesn't matter. I could invent words to say how I feel but it doesn't matter. I gave up my family for us. He can give up other women. Maybe I'm not pretty enough, or its because I'm colored maybe he still feels like he needs to have someone white."
"Try talking to him instead of cursing him." I said not knowing what else to say. Of course I wanted to say that all those things she said were crazy. What I do know is that Franky is in love with her. I don't know if he feels like he still needs someone white, or if he feels like Raynel isn't enough. I have my suspicions that he still sees Carol as well. "This is what I do know, the times I've seen Franky with other women which were all before you two were married. They were just there; Franky has so much pride in being with you. He loves you Raynel and it's all over him. Nobody likes Christy, she's a trouble maker, and her mouth runs away with her."
"Then why does she have his son? She obviously meant something to him for him to give her what he's given me! She can't just be anybody." She said tearfully.
"Fernando was an accident." I blurted.
"Does Franklin make mistakes? He might think I don't know, but he gave me both of my boys deliberately. He's too smart to suddenly come up dumb. I don't want to spend my life competing with some white girl for my man's love and attention."
"Raynel you have Franky's love and attention."
She looked at me, "I don't want to share!"
I couldn't shake my afternoon with Raynel off my mind. When Tim came home I kept looking at him. "What?" He asked watching my face.
"Sit down let's talk this out." I said patting the couch next to me.
"Ok," he said taking a seat. "Talk what out?"
"Franky and Raynel are having problems." Tim watched my face. "Raynel knows he's cheating on her..." Tim started to say some thing but I cut him off. "I don't want to confirm or deny with you the validity of her facts. I want to talk about us."
"Ok," he said like he was happy not to discuss his brother.
"So I told you before you could never hit me. We're clear on where I stand with that. I know you would never, but just so we're clear if you ever did I'll kill you. Settled?" I looked at him, "good that's settled." Tim started laughing. "It would break my heart if after all of this, all that we've been through and will go through if you even thought you needed someone else. I don't care what color she is, both of you DIE! Are we clear?"
Tim laughed so hard he turned completely red. "Crystal clear baby. You're more than enough for me anyways. How would I have the strength to run around?"
"I'm about to pop over here. Our fun time will be suspended for a while. Remember, I will kill you! I'll circumcise you first. Then as you heal, I'll pour salt on the wound and then acid on your chest. I'll watch you die a slow agonizing death!"
"Sounds like you've put some thought into this." Tim said no longer laughing.

I shook my head, “nope. I just came up with that. It would kill me, I don’t want to share. I don’t ever want to feel like Raynel does.”

Timothy

"What gives Franky?"

Franky rolled his eyes then he walked away. I followed him to his home office.

"She knows about Christy."

"Knows what?" I was lost cause apparently I was the only one who didn't know.

"That I still see her sometimes." He said sitting in his chair.

"Why would you still see her? She causes you two so many problems."

Franky exhaled, "I love my wife! I will never love another woman like I love her." He exhaled, "she's a good girl. Too good sometimes."

I squinted, "what do you mean?"

Franky leaned forward, "there's certain things she won't even try because she says good girls don't do them. I do EVERYTHING for, on, and to her. If anything goes outside of her scope of what a good girl does she won't do it. You know me, it don't get much nastier than me. Do you know how many people would die behind my frustration if I try to pull back who I am? My wife can't do certain things, fine! What she's not understanding is that if she won't do them, there's always someone else who will. Oh!" He raised his voice a little. "She's telling me we need to downgrade and move to a smaller house. It's too late to call off the new house. She's going to blow a gasket when I tell her we're upgrading."

"Just sell the house."

Franky glared at me! "Sell the house? You saw the plans! It's my dream house for my dream woman and our dream family. I'm not selling the house. She better stop with the attitude before I knock her up again." He laughed to himself.

"How is pregnancy supposed to make her happy?"

"I want a little girl, she owes me that much!"

"How does she owe you anything?"

"Because she's married to me!" He said like it was simple.

"Franky, I got Annette pregnant on purpose."

Franky smiled, "I know!"

"How do you know?"

"I know you, you and Jeff are just like me. I know!"

"Although she loves me, I think she's heart broken about it. She saw her life going one way, and I changed everything. Raynel loves you; she defied her father and let you in. How do you repay her? You play God and make her go against her family. She had to rely on the kindness of strangers until you found her, and what do you do? You knock her up again. You got her tip toeing around San Francisco, hiding from her family. When do you bend for her? When do you give her what she wants?"

"Downgrading? Me?"

"Annette doesn't want a fancy house either. I can do without the big fancy house as long as I have my Queen! Compromise Franky."

Franky rocked in his chair, "I can't!" He said in defeat. "Pops is moving all the distributions under me. I have more mass to cover them. I'm going to have to beef up security. A simpler house is too vulnerable."

"It's not impossible Franky."

"For me it is."

"What about your wife?"

"She has to deal with it."

Annette

I wiped myself and as I got up to get off the toilet something fell in the toilet. Immediately I panicked thinking maybe it could've been my baby. When I looked in the toilet it looked like a big wad of snot. I flushed then I washed my hands.
"Momma?" I called out as I walked back to my bed.
"Yes baby?" Irma said holding the spoon she was using for our dinner.
"There was something that looked like snot in the toilet, what does that mean?"
She frowned at me, "did you flush it?"
"Yes, it looked nasty. I was using the bathroom. I wasn't going to show you everything." I said embarrassed.
"Sounds like the baby's about to come. Get your rest tonight, the baby's almost here."
Her words hit their mark, and I was uncomfortable and in pain. My stomach kept tightening and untightening. When the pain would stop I would fall asleep, and then the pain would wake me up again. Irma didn't go home, she stayed right there in the bed with me. Whenever I woke up so did she. Poor Tim brought a chair in the room and he would pop up every time I awoke. When Irma said it was time we went to the hospital. She told Tim to call everyone from the waiting room. She already warned my doctor to alert the hospital that she was coming all the way in with me. I kissed my husband goodbye, as he had nothing but worry for me on his face. I told him I would be back with our daughter. My last attempt to get my plea in for a girl. Tim humored me and chuckled a little, but he was worried for me I could see it all over his face. The nurses shaved me, and then they gave me an enema. Not my idea of a perfect day, but Irma said it was all normal.
As the pain became worse and worse Irma kept saying it was almost over and to hang on. The pain felt like lightning on top of the contractions I was already having I was now experiencing another pain that was almost familiar. The doctor held up the baby and she said it was a boy. I had a flash back of looking at my momma's baby and saying to myself another useless boy. As they cleaned my baby up I heard the doctor explaining that even though they cut me I still tore, and the rip went down pretty far. They gave me a shot of something else to help me relax as I laid there while my doctor stitched me up. They gave the baby to Irma to show to the family. I thought about all the people in the waiting room. I wanted my momma, I now understood what Emma must've felt. I started crying because my momma wouldn't care about my baby. She'd probably spit at my baby like Butch did at Lauren. I couldn't hold back my tears, and one of the nurses left to go get Irma because I was crying so hard. She didn't ask me what was wrong; she put her arms around me and hugged me.

Timothy

Pops put his hands on my shoulders, he told me everything was going to be fine. I hated being out here not knowing what was going on in there. Annette was back there because I decided that I wanted to start our family sooner than we needed to. Martha and Sebastian brought the baby and they waited with us. In the morning when momma came from the back with the biggest smile on her face, I felt a little relieved. She wouldn't give me the baby until Pops was ready with the camera. As my momma put the baby in my arms she said, "Timothy Wallace meet your first born son." My heart leap for JOY! I have a son! A namesake, a smaller version of

me. He looked at me like he was taking me in. Momma kept smiling and kissing me. She kept saying he was beautiful. I felt a little emotional when I handed my son to my best sister. Martha looked at him and said it was me all over again. I asked momma how Annette was doing, her smile weakened. She said the baby is a big baby and Annette would be fine, but she was in a lot of pain. I looked at the baby and I asked him what he did to my wife.
The nurse brought me to Annette's room. She said as soon as she was out of recovery they would bring her in. I sat in the chair, I was about to close my eyes when I realized the nurse was lingering. "Your wife is real pretty."
"Thank you," I said waiting for her to get to her point.
"Your boy is real handsome, just like his dad." She said waiting for my response.
I sucked my teeth and leaned back in my chair. I wasn't going to entertain her comment with a response. I hadn't looked at this woman longer than knowing she was there. This was not the time or place for this type of nonsense.
When the door started opening I stood up, Annette's face was so sad. My guilty conscience tugged at me again. Everything is such an emotional experience for Annette especially during this leg of our relationship.
Momma asked if we had a name for this little guy. Annette looked at me, "Junior of course."

Annette

When they brought me out of recovery, Tim was waiting for me in the room I was assigned to. His face looked so sad when he saw me, I didn't have to tell him that I had been crying. He seemed to know and to know why. When he thought I was sleep I listened to him talk to the baby. He introduced himself and told the baby how much he loved him and how happy he was that he was here. He told the baby that he knew that he was going to be a momma's boy just like Franky, but he would try his best not to let him be a "sissy". A nurse woke me to tell me to try to feed the baby. When she took him from Tim she asked how such a big boy came out of me? The baby was almost nine pounds. I told her it was all the food my momma made for me. She looked confused when I nodded to Irma as I said that. It took a couple of frustrating tries, but we got the baby to latch on. We were having a good old fashion stare down. I couldn't decide who the baby looked like. His hair was curly but there wasn't much of it. He was looking at me like he was trying to figure me out just like I was doing to him. Tim sat on the bed with us; he asked me if I was ok. I was honest when I told him I was scared. I was afraid that my son would be another no good boy just like my brothers. Tim looked at me and kissed my tears. He told me I was going to be a wonderful mother and there was no way I would allow my son to be anything like that. I exhaled and I told him I hoped he was right.

Timothy

It seems like everywhere I go, these females can smell that it's been a minute since I've had some. That or I never truly paid attention to how sexy I am. Each time I get away I tell myself that was a close call.
Annette is running on autopilot. She takes care of the baby, and she runs from me. Every time I come in for a kiss fear shows through her eyes. She has no reason to fear me, so I have to assume I said or did something that unknowingly put her in a bad place. I get my quick smooch and then I move out of her way. Sometimes she looks like she wants to talk to me, but she changes her mind. I am dying over here! I miss my wife from every angle possible. She's not talking to me; she won't let me

hold her! Sometimes I watch her sleep just so I can have alone time with her. When my frustration mounts too much, I literally feel like something is going to pop in my head. I go out back and have a cigarette to calm my nerves.

****

"Good morning Timothy!" She called out to me.
"Good morning, what do you have for me today?" I said walking up to her cart.
"Coffee and a sticky bun." She said with the biggest smile.
"Thank you Ruby, you always take care of me."
"Timothy why doesn't your wife make sure you eat before you leave for work?"
"She just had a baby. Our son was a lot bigger than her body was prepared to deal with. She's getting better, besides my momma makes sure I eat."
"Momma? You from the south?"
I chuckled, "no ma'am but my momma is."
"That wife of yours better get it together. You're too handsome to be walking around here going without for too long."
"My wife is fine, I have no problem waiting for her." I said proudly.
She watched my face, "Un huh." Then she looked behind me, "hurry up and get inside. White trash and the rest coming." Ruby said full of disgust.
The dock walkers are what we called them. I wonder if these girls ever sleep. They don't come everyday or even every week, but when they come all you hear are whistles and catcalls. They come in high heels, dresses or pants, and little tops. They walk around saying hi to the men looking for dates. To look at them they don't seem unclean, but knowing what they do for a living there's no appeal. A lot of these idiots go for it though, on the days they come I keep my eyes focused straight ahead. I don't need any distractions or irritations. I thanked Ruby for the bun, and then I headed for the door. "Tim!" I heard someone call out.
I spun on my heels and fire turned in my stomach. "WHAT?"
She hurried over to me, "I wanted to congratulate you on the birth of your son." She tried to smile.
"Why did you come here? You know I'm going to tell Matt you're here!"
"Tim, please!"
"Please what? I don't know how you found out about the location anyways."
She walked closer to me, "is there anything I can do for you?"
Even though she tried to give me an innocent look her actions enraged me. I grabbed her shirt and swung her around. "YOU DARE TO DISRESPECT ME LIKE THIS? YOU DARE TO DISRESPECT MY WIFE! MY FAMILY!" I caught myself as I reared up to knock her. I let her go and I took a deep breath. "I'm calling Matt!"
"Tim! Don't!" She pleaded.
I could feel fire shoot out of my head. "Have you been sniffing your father's powder? Of course I'm telling! The only reason you could've possibly came here is to get his attention! I don't keep secrets from my family!"
"Only your wife? She doesn't know about us!"
"There is no us! She knows who you are."
"She...."
"Maureen! I swear! If you don't get in your car right now, I'm going to forget how I was raised..."
She tried to run up on me, before I could stop myself I backhanded her and I heard the blood from her busted nose as it hit the ground. Maureen screamed and I was furious! Maureen stumbled backwards holding her face. Ruby hurried over with a

napkin for Maureen. This dizzy broad would rather bleed all over herself than take a napkin from a colored woman who was only trying to help her. "Miss Ruby," I reached in my pocket and I gave her everything I had. "Thank you for trying to help, but she's beneath you. You go ahead on, I'm calling her husband to come get her."

"Tim!" Maureen said holding her face and crying.

I turned on my heels, I asked the foreman to help the lady who was bleeding outside. I took a deep breath then I dialed Matt's number. "This is Matthew Wallace."

"Matt!"

"Tim?"

"I busted her nose." I felt horrible. "She tried to rush me to kiss me, and...." Matt hung up.

I took a deep breath, and then I called Jeff. He hung up at the same part that Matthew did. I went out back by the water and I took out a cigarette. I needed to calm down. I was angrier with myself for actually looking at her this time. I didn't like the confusion that settled inside of me. I love my wife, I love my family! I'm not going to willingly be this stupid. All Annette knows is hurt and disappointment; I want to be the one who changes it all for her. I'm the reason she's all tore up right now, how selfish would I be if I cheated. I know what my brothers and my father do, I'm different.

When I finished my cigarette I walked around to the front. Jeff was holding Matt back, and he was struggling to do it at that. Matt was beyond enraged as he tried with everything in him to get to his wife. Maureen was shaking she was so scared. I stayed by the doorway, when I saw Pops's car slowly approaching I exhaled. Pops calmly got out of the car and approached my brothers. He told Matt to calm down then he told Jeff to let him go. Pops told Maureen to ride with him. He told Jeff to calm Matt down before they came to meet them. Then Pops calmly got in his car and slowly drove away. I told the foreman to make everyone get back to work. Matt was in Jeff's face yelling at him like he did something wrong. Jeff held no emotion in his face as he watched Matt yell his heart out. I stayed by the door imagining how much it hurts to love a woman who is in love with someone else. Not that I understood why he loves her so much, the way they began is not the way she and I began. I never asked him why or how, I just knew they were together and they were in love. When Matt finally broke down and cried Jeff hugged him and I came in for the group hug. "I'm sorry I hit your wife, I should've ran."

Matt started laughing through his tears, "you running from a girl? I'd pay to see that!"

"No admission necessary, come to my house when I'm on Annette's nerves. I run for my life."

"Then what's Franky's problem?"

"He's foolish, he stands there and takes the hits." I said, we all laughed.

"You alright?" Jeff asked Matt.

He shook his head no. "No," then he exhaled. "She hasn't been right since her father died."

"I mean no disrespect, but I have to ask. Is she using?" I watched his eyes.

Matt fell against his car, "I don't know. Something's going on isn't it?" He said in a defeated tone.

"Are you going to tell Annette about this?" Jeff asked.

"Did I tell her about the last time?" I said, "she's not herself right now. That could be the straw that broke her back." I looked at Matt, "what are you going to do?"
"After I choke her almost to death, I don't know."
"Annette says there's truth in a person's joke."
"Guess that means I'm not joking." Matt frowned.
"Why do you hit her?" Jeff asked.
Matt put his hands out, "stuff like today. It's getting out of control. I can't live like this."
"Momma's gonna skin you alive!" Jeff said.
"I know," he exhaled. "My back is up against the wall. What do I do? Divorce her, and never see my kids?"
"That or risk momma coming after you. What if Maureen was your daughter?" I asked.
Matt shook his head like he understood. "None of this has to be. I don't want a divorce!" Matt yelled.

Annette

"Annette! He's beautiful! Momma needs to meet him." Emma said as she looked down at him.
I sighed, "momma don't care about Kiah. Why would she care about Timothy?"
"Kiah is Katie's baby." Emma said matter of factly, as if she forgot she's her momma. "Timothy is so cute. How could she not love him?"
"How could she not love me?"
"I think she's changing. I told her about your wedding, and your new car. She looked like she was proud that you're doing so well." Emma said.
I blank stared at Emma, "you mean she started thinking of how she's not benefitting from my situation."
"How you feeling?" Emma said watching my face.
"The doctor said my stitches are just about healed. I don't feel ready for my husband at all." I swallowed.
"Is Tim getting anxious?"
"Not yet, but I think he's just being a good sport about everything. I feel broken, and the thought of anything going on down there is a turn off. The baby ripped me from front to back."
"Tim's going to wait for you to be ready." Emma said like it was a no brainer as she played with the baby.
Emma wasn't getting it or understanding what I was saying. I pulled my knees into my stomach and looked out the window. My body looked like I got in a fight with a cat and I lost. My stomach looked like a deflated balloon covered in stretch marks. My breast, hips, and tops of my thighs had them too. I lost a lot of weight the two weeks I was in the hospital, but I still had a lot to go. I didn't feel very pretty, and I didn't want Tim to see my body. It seemed like having the baby ripped the bandage off my old wounds. It depressed me to wonder how I was going to have my little girl without laying with my husband.
Katie came back in the room with Lauren. Lauren kissed my forehead then she watched my face for a minute. She sat next to me and put her arms around me. When Raynel came with her little ones, they ran straight for the back door to play in the backyard with Kiah. Ethan is an itty-bitty thing running behind his big brother trying to keep up. Emma went in the yard with the babies before she had to go. Katie was admiring the baby and I couldn't fake my lack of enthusiasm.

"What's wrong?" Raynel asked
"I feel dead inside, I don't have anything for Tim. I don't know how to pick up my life and go from here." I said in a monotone.
"It's been more than six weeks, your doctor hasn't said it's ok?" Raynel asked
I shook my head, "Timothy tried to rearrange everything down there. I'm almost healed."
"Tim is good he hasn't complained as far as I know one time." Katie said.
Raynel rubbed my head, "baby you're going to be fine. Maybe you and Tim don't make physical love right away, but you can talk. You can tell him what's on your heart."
"What if he thinks I don't love him anymore?"
"As long as you're talking he'll know that's not the case."
I looked down at myself then back at Raynel. "This body is not sexy. He couldn't possibly want me."
Raynel looked offended, "Tim loves you and you just gave birth to his son. I didn't look like this before I had little Frank. It's only natural to feel some kind of way about their possible reaction. I was skinny before. Now I got stretch marks everywhere and this dress is not a size six. Franklin's first words to me were how beautiful I am. His physical response to me hasn't changed either."
"How do you feel now that Franky is putting on some weight?" Lauren asked.
"It's only natural that he'd start picking up weight once he stopped running the streets as much." Raynel said.
I exhaled, "I guess you're right. I'm just scared."
"Of?" Katie asked.
"So many things. What if he's not attracted to this train wreck of a body? Now that I'm completely open what if he decides he doesn't love me anymore? Even though I've threatened his life, what if he cheats on me anyways? I'd rather not go through the head-trip if he's just going to end up with someone else. It would be easier to kill him now."
Lauren laughed until she realized I was serious. "Annette honey, you're just going through the baby blues. I promise this will pass." Raynel said.

****

Tim kissed my cheek goodbye like he always does in the morning. There was nothing different about the kiss but my heart was pounding so hard I had to sit up. The doctor gave me the all clear a week and a half ago, but I wasn't ready so I said nothing. Tim hasn't asked once what the doctor said. At first I was relieved but now I'm wondering why he doesn't ask. I fed Timothy then I bathed him. I know it's because I'm his momma but I think my son is the most handsome man ever created. No man will ever love you like your son. Or at least that's how I feel whenever Timothy looks for me. I can't believe I'm a momma.
The sweetest victory was when I could fit a summer dress I had put to the side. I decided me and the baby needed to drop by Tim's office and surprise him. I've never gone down there and I figured now was as good a time as any. I told the guard I was there for Ace Trucking and Shipping. I parked next to Tim's car and then I got my bag and the baby. I took a deep breath then I walked towards the building. A truck passed behind me and the driver whistled, I was surprised when I saw it was a white guy but I kept walking. When I walked in the door men were everywhere working hard. A guy walked up to me, "how may I help you?"
"Is Tim here?"

"Yes, whom may I say is here?"
"Mrs. Wallace."
"Right this way ma'am." He said leading the way. The guy knocked on Tim's door. I heard him tell Tim that Mrs. Wallace was here.
"What?" Tim stormed out with fire in his eyes that vanished as soon as he saw me. He got the most surprised and excited smile. "Annette!" He said coming in for a hug. "This is my wife!" Tim said proudly. The guy looked confused and then he hurried away. "Come in, come in." He said taking the baby from me.
The guy was talking to other guys on the floor. They all looked up at me in amazement. "Why don't you have my picture up?" I asked as I looked around.
"I handle all kinds of business from this office. I'm not going to advertise my weakness." He said smiling at the baby. "You look good, how do you feel?"
"Thank you, I feel a little better."
"That's good." Then he started playing with the baby.
I took a deep breath, "I know I threatened your life, would you really be crazy enough to test me?"
Tim pointed his eyes at me, "explain." Like he wanted to hear me out before he went completely off.
"That was some reaction to hearing your wife is here. Does someone else come here posing as me?"
Tim exhaled, "no. The last time one of the misses Wallace's came by out of the blue it was my sister in-law and Matt was not too happy." He cut his eyes at me, "you came by here to catch me doing something?"
I rolled my eyes and looked around the office. Tim stared at me for a minute, and then he kissed the baby. He told me he needed to get back to work as he stood up. I was about to stand my ground when his phone rang. Tim answered it, he barely said hello when the person on the phone started talking. Tim's eyes turned even more serious. He told the person on the phone to secure Jeff's house and that we were in route.
Tim told me to come and we got in my car. As we went over the bridge Tim touched my hand. "Something's going on with your momma."
"What?" I said as I nursed the baby.
"I don't have the details yet. Emma called Jeremiah hysterical looking for Hezekiah."
"Why did you say to secure Jeff's house? What does that mean?"
"That's where you're going to be until I figure out what's going on."
"Ok," I sat there quietly.
"You don't trust me?" He asked like he couldn't believe the answer.
I didn't say anything, I held on to Timothy. Whispers was walking around outside Jeff's house as we pulled up. "Your boy is getting big." He said to Tim.
Tim smiled proudly, "healthy and strong like his father."
Lauren came outside, "what's going on?"
"The police have been called to Mrs. Cooper's apartment. Once the officers arrived on the scene they called in they're waiting for direction." Whispers said.
"Who is it?" I asked.
"I'm not sure."
"Lauren can you watch the baby for me?" I asked her as I handed Timothy and the diaper bag over.
"Of course," she said looking between Tim and I.
"Where are you going?"

"You're taking me to my momma's house." Tim started to say something and I shot him a look. There was no way in the world he was going to tell me I couldn't go see about my momma no matter how horrible she is.

Tim put his hands up and turned to walk towards the car and I followed.

When we pulled around the corner to my momma's street, I saw the police cars outside by my momma's apartment. Tim pulled behind the police car and we got out. My heart was pounding. I grabbed Tim's hand, my hands were sweaty. My momma and that woman that was here before were outside arguing. Butch was sitting in the back of a squad car. An officer walked up to Tim and started reporting. He said Butch and his girlfriend got into a fight, he said the woman said that my momma was provoking the fight. When they came to arrest Butch my momma went off. None of the officers touched her, but Butch's girlfriend keeps insisting that they arrest my momma too. He said they're both claiming that the other person hit them. I asked where Emma was, and the officer said my momma's daughter left when they showed up.

My momma was cursing and carrying on when she saw me out the corner of her eye. Her face was so evil when she saw me. I also know she didn't know why I was here. Butch saw me, he started screaming and acting like he was going to bust out of the police car. The girlfriend took everything in as she watched. "Momma what's wrong?"

"She's been messing around on your brother!" My momma spit, "I saw you and that high yellow boy kissing and everything!"

Now I wasn't going to believe my momma cause she's lied on me in my own face. This girl looked me up and down, crossed her arms and slowly said, "SO!"

It seemed like everyone stopped talking and looked at her like *what did she say?* "Why are you here?"

"SO? SO? WHAT DO YOU MEAN SO?" Butch screamed from the back of the car. He was trying to get that door open so hard the whole car was rocking.

"Butch already knows about him. He knows he's not the only guy I see. Your ole raggedy momma is just mad because your brother has been spending his money on me and not giving it to her. She kept pushing him and until he got too angry."

I put my hand out, "please don't talk to me about my momma like that. Use your words." I said rather peacefully.

"Well its not like I'm lying or something! All she does is sit on her fat butt all day taking all the money her kids bring home. She don't cook or nothing any more. Oh but wait, there is one thing she happily gets off her fat butt to do." She said evilly.

I blew air, "ok. Ok, they've got Butch in the police car. You can leave now, it's over."

"I'm not leaving until someone hits her. She started all this and its only right."

"Hits my momma?" I looked at her like she was crazy.

"Yes! Hits her! She needs at least one good knot up side her head to match mine." She said pointing to her forehead.

"Can't you take her away for trespassing or something?" I asked the officer nearest me.

"She's standing on a public sidewalk, she hasn't gone inside the residence." I could tell they were waiting for an excuse to take momma in too. She probably, no I know, she gave them a hard time when they came for Butch. They'd like nothing better than to take her in too.

"Why do you care anyways, I heard all the stuff she said about you. After hearing how she talk about you to me and your sister, I know half of it can't be true."

"Please stop, just leave! I'll talk to my momma."
"She's not going to listen to you. The only way someone like her learns is if you speak they language." She said hitting her fist into her hand.
"I don't care how wrong she is, you can't be that dumb to threaten someone's momma in front of them!"
"That's alright, bring your little fast tail on. You need your tail BEAT!" My momma said squaring off.
"No! You are not going to fight my momma." I turned to the officer, "can you take her home?"
The officer looked at Tim who wasn't looking, he was talking to another officer. "It's a public sidewalk."
Butch started rocking the car real hard and then I heard contact. I turned to see the girl punching my momma in the stomach. All I saw was RED! I snatch the girl up by her hair. I punched her in her face then I kicked her. She started tumbling down the hill and I took off to stop her from rolling only so I could beat on her some more. "YOU WILL NEVER PUT YOUR HANDS ON MY MOMMA!" Just as I was about to dive on her Tim grabbed me and held me back.
"ENOUGH!" Tim yelled, "TAKE HER IN FOR ASSAULT!"
"What about him?" One of the Officers asked.
"Process him if you have to, don't touch him!" Tim put me behind himself, "Clear these streets. DO YOUR JOB!" The officers did as they were told. "Annette why did you let her provoke you?"
"Tim! She hit my momma!"
He raised his eyebrows, "she did?"
"YES!"
Tim hugged me then he kissed my face. "I'm sorry, I didn't know. You want me to tell them to let her go? You can beat her up as much as you like?"
I smiled, "no. Thank you for offering." Then I kissed him for the first time since our son was born.
Tim stared at me for a minute, "stop it woman. You are not ready for me." He smiled.
I looked at my momma who was watching us from the sidewalk. Then I looked at the car, Tim signaled something and the officer opened the door and took Butch out. They took the handcuffs off of him, and then the officers drove away. Tim and I walked towards momma and Butch. "Momma are you ok?"
Momma's eyes stayed stuck on Tim. "Yes, I'll be alright."
"This is my husband Timothy. This is my momma and my brother Butch."
"Mrs. Cooper, Butch." Tim said acknowledging both of them.
Butch looked the other way like he was too pissed to say anything. I pushed him hard, "I HATE YOU! TIM JUST GOT YOU OUT OF THAT POLICE CAR! YOU KNOW THEY WEREN'T GOING TO TAKE YOU TO JAIL! YOU COULD'VE ENDED UP JUST LIKE LESLIE! YOU SO HUNG UP ON THE COLOR OF HIS SKIN THAT YOU CAN'T SAY THANK YOU FOR SAVING ME? TIM NEXT TIME LET THEM DO WHATEVER THEY WERE GOING TO DO TO HIM! YOU THREATENED TO HURT ME THE NEXT TIME YOU SAW ME ANYWAYS!"
Tim stared at Butch, "he did what?"
"You sent the other white men away to put this one on me? I don't lick no white man's boots!"

"Butch! It's not licking anybody's anything to say thank you. Now right is right, he just saved you. You should thank him." Momma said watching Tim. Butch put his hands up and walked back inside. "I didn't know he threatened you, I'm sorry sweetheart."

I knew she was lying, especially when she put the sweetheart at the end. I looked at Tim, "let's go."

"I hear I have a grandson I need to meet?" She called out as we took a couple of steps away.

Tears filled my eyes as I looked at Tim; I knew she wasn't being genuine. I knew she wanted something, but I also wanted her to at least see the baby once. "Yes ma'am"

"What's his name?"

"Timothy."

"Bring him by one of these days, I want to see him."

"Ok," I said then I turned to keep walking with Tim.

Dollar signs danced in my momma's eyes as she saw us get into my car. She stood there until we drove away. Tim was quiet the rest of the evening. We got the baby then we went home. I heated up the leftovers and then I fed the baby. When I put him down for the night, I was so nervous my hand was shaking. I put a nightgown on that actually fit, and then I walked around the house. Tim wasn't inside; when I opened the back door he was leaning against the house smoking a cigarette. He looked like he was trying to calm his nerves. He looked at me but he didn't say anything. I asked him when he started smoking. He said he started smoking again when the baby was born. He said it was never something that he did all the time, but from time to time he'd have one. I took it from him and I took a drag on it, then I gave it back. He smiled and asked how come he never knew I smoked, and I told him like him I only did it every once in a while. Then I kissed him again. He looked at my gown and then he asked me what was going on. I told him the truth, that I was scared. He told me he could wait if I needed him to wait. I apologized for accusing him earlier, he thanked me.

That night instead of making love like I thought he needed to, we talked. In the morning Tim patiently made love to me. It was like losing my virginity again, it was better. Again my man patiently waited for me.

Chapter 15

Timothy

The rules are driving me crazy! I'm trying to be patient with this woman, but there's only so much patience that anyone can exert! I have to pretend like I'm blind seeing her body through Braille. This is ridiculous! She completely shuts down if I even look like I'm going to look at her body. It wasn't that big of a deal at first, but it's getting worse and worse. I will not live in this blind world forever!

"Tell everyone to go home." I told my foreman.

"REALLY! You don't have to tell me twice." He took off excitedly as he gave the workers the word. He came back deflated. "Avery's still in route, he should be here in a hour." He sighed, "then his truck has to be inspected. Can I wait for him in your office?" He asked trying to man up.

"I'll wait for Avery, you go ahead and go." I felt sorry for the poor sap. I could spend that time working uninterrupted and I would still leave early. The foreman said an excited thank you and then he took off before I had a chance to change my mind.

I called the flower shop by my house. I gave them specific directions; I wanted a huge floral bouquet with bright happy and exotic flowers. Pops' friend Marcos opened a new deli not too far from our house next to a pharmacy and drug store. Since it was hot out I knew Annette wouldn't have dinner started yet, and we loved the food from this place. I called in an order, and then I planned to go to the liquor store and pick up the most expensive cognac they had. I plan to get my wife drunk and make her show off what she's been blessed with. With all my planning the time flew by. I grabbed my jacket and keys when I heard Avery's truck pull in. I had no doubt that when I told him everyone was calling it quits today he would move that much faster to get home to his family or whatever he had.

Avery looked tired until I told him that everyone knocked off and as soon as we finished his inspection he could go home as well. I had the checklist in my hand as I was going over the truck. "Anything eventful happen during your route?" I asked as I looked at the truck.

"No, it was a pretty standard day." Then he kind of stood there looking at me. "I saw your wife the other day when she came by."

I smiled and turned my eyes back to my clipboard. "My wife is one of a kind!"

"She is pretty for a colored girl." He said looking at me for a reaction.

I stopped writing and I looked at him. I took a deep breath to calm myself. "You know this whole talking thing is going to upset me, I can see it coming. What you need to remember right now is that I am your boss and I can fire you if you piss me off. Don't get on my bad side Avery." I growled at him.

Avery stood up straight, "I'll let it go because you're my boss. All I was saying is that seeing your wife made everything come together. I guess Barnes is her brother or something, its ok what's a little nepotism if you can't use it to your advantage?"

"Didn't I tell you to stop talking? I'm not the kind of man who repeats himself!" I was regretting letting my foreman go home. Then I stared at Avery cause I was trying to calm myself from dumping his body right off the dock. Then I thought about the clean up and how long it would take me to dispose of his car. It would eat away at my time with my wife. So for the sake of the romantic environment I was trying to provide he lives today. When Avery tried to apologize to me as we were walking out I told him to shut up, and get out of my face.

I picked up the cognac, and then I went to the deli. Marcos was so happy to see me when I walked in. He said his daughter Rita was getting the last part of my order together. When the other customers were gone and we were alone. Marcos leaned in and said he was going to need to increase his quantity for his portion of the distribution. He said his clientele was growing. I told him to follow normal procedure and to call it in.

Marcos's daughter Rita had the biggest crush on me. It was cute to see. I honestly think she's a little boy crazy at such a young age, but who am I to say anything to Marcos about how he's raising his daughter. She packed all of my things, and then her father told her they never charge me. So I gave her a nice tip for being so helpful and generous. She turned red blushing so hard. I thanked Marcos and then I went to the florist. When I saw the bouquet I knew I was scoring big tonight.

When I walked in the door Annette was in the family room putting the baby down for his late afternoon nap. "PERFECT TIMING!" I thought to myself. When Annette turned around and saw everything I had, I saw her melt immediately. I told her to come to daddy, and she smiled. She excitedly took the flowers from me and I put the food in the refrigerator. I poured both of us tall drinks and then Annette walked in the kitchen in a nightgown. I smiled, the nightgown was nice, but I was ready to see my wife in her birthday suit. I gave her the glass I poured for her, and then we went in the bedroom. Annette asked why I was home early, and I told her I couldn't wait all day to get next to her. I needed to be with my wife. She smiled as she took another drink. When Annette finished her glass, she put it down then she got on top of me and kissed me. I let her undress me, and when I pulled at her gown she seemed to sober up and stop me. She put the condom on me and then she mounted me. Annette was extremely excited already and she proceeded to take control and work those hips on me. I pushed her gown up so that I could look at where our bodies connected. Annette slowed down a little when I did that. She frowned at me like I distracted her. I kissed her and then I rolled us over, I pushed her gown up and when I saw the slightest hint of her stomach, she freaked out. She has too many rules and all my frustration was back. That fast my whole vibe was ruined, I told her I would rip all of her clothes up and make her walk around this house naked, which sound like heaven to me. Annette wasn't hearing me. UNTIL…

Annette

"You're being ridiculous!" Tim yelled

"Oh I'm being ridiculous? We'll see who's being ridiculous in a week!" I said crossing my arms.

"Listen to me little girl! What difference does a week make? I just did almost four months cold. You think a week is going to matter to me!"

He had a point but I didn't care. "It will if I have anything to do with it!" I yelled, and then I stormed away.

Tim followed behind me, "it doesn't matter!"

"It does matter! I asked you not to, and you did it anyways!" I said trying to close the bathroom door on him.

He put his hand in the door. "I will rip up every piece of clothing you have in this house if this is the way you're going to act. You are my wife! You just gave birth to our son! I have a right to look at my wife's body!"

"NO YOU DON'T! It's ugly, I asked you not to look, and what do you do? You look anyways!"

"Annette you are beautiful, why do you have to act like this?"

"I KNOW WHAT I USED TO LOOK LIKE! THIS AIN'T IT!"
"I like your body better now!"
He insulted me, "you like my body now Tim? You like it because I would be too ashamed to show it to someone else? You like the security in knowing that I'm ugly?"
Tim threw his hands up, "so what are we supposed to do, blind fold me every time we make love? I'm not going to stay under those hot covers, its summer for crying out loud!"
"That's not a bad idea." I said.
"This is bigger than you! I'm telling you you're beautiful, and you're making me feel like there's something wrong with me for feeling and thinking that way. I don't know how to convince you other than by telling you and showing you. If I got to rip every piece of clothing in this house just so you'll understand me then so be it!" Tim said turning on his heels and marching back towards our bedroom.
I don't know why I thought he was bluffing, the look in his eyes should've been confirmation enough that he wasn't playing. It was quiet for a minute and then I heard the sound of cloth ripping. I screamed and ran in the bedroom. Tim was in the closet and that fast he had a nice sized pile of shredded clothes. I screamed at him and begged him to stop, but he kept going. I threw a shoe and conked him upside the head. Tim acted like he didn't even feel it. I screamed and pleaded, "ok! Ok! You made your point!"
"I don't believe you!" He said grabbing another dress. He watched my eyes as he shredded it with his hands.
"OK! What do you want me to do to prove it?"
He reached for another dress, "strip!"
"Strip? You must be crazy! I ain't stripping!"
"Fine!" He reached for my favorite before the pregnancy dress.
"NO TIM! PUT IT DOWN! I'LL DO IT! I'LL DO IT!"
He held the dress up, "you'll do what?"
"I'll take the gown off! Don't hurt my dress!"
"I hear you talking, I don't see you stripping!" He moved like he was going to rip it.
I yanked off my gown; I wanted to go hide under a rock as Tim stood there looking at me. "Can I have my dress?"
His eyes turned serious when he looked at me. "This dress means more to you than I do?"
"No! Of course not!"
"Then why would you do for this dress what you wouldn't do for me?" I had no answer for that. "You better kiss me before I get angry!" He warned. I kissed him and he dropped the dress. He picked me up and took me back to our bed. "We didn't get to finish anyways." He said kissing me and then picking up where we left off.

Timothy

When I laid her down I could tell she wanted to hide from my eyes. I looked at the marks that my selfishness left on her body and I kissed them. I thanked her for having my child, and for loving me enough to carry me in her body. I put on another condom, and I went in slow and tender at first and then long and deep. I would not accept Annette focusing on the fact that she was naked before me. She was going to get in to this if it meant I had to stop myself from blowing my top every time. I did everything I knew to get her right to the point where she was about

to explode and then I looked at her body and then I'd kiss her deeply again. When Annette's eyes rolled in to her head I knew I had her. Annette grabbed on to me and screamed as she lost it, her rhythm sped up and now I lost it. Covered in complete sweat we laid there giving in to our bodies who now took over and made us render every last good feeling we had to give.
Once I caught my breath, I told Annette I didn't want to see her in clothes anymore. I told her she was a walking masterpiece and I wanted to enjoy the sight of her daily. When she didn't respond, I moved my hips bringing her orgasm back and then she had no choice but to obey my every command.

Annette

"That's YOUR husband who I see coming and going everyday?" She asked me in disbelief.
"Yes," I said watching her face. I was telling myself to count backwards and not to immediately react to what she was saying.
She put her hand on her chest. "That's amazing!" She said taking me in long and hard.
"What's amazing about it?" Lauren asked her.
"I've heard about white men loving colored girls, I just never seen it before. You two get a long so well."
"How would you know how we get a long?" I asked even though I was already over this conversation.
"Everybody in this neighborhood knows when my parents argue. It's very rare that they contain their arguments to inside the walls of our house. Over time everyone ends up arguing outside. For the length of time you've lived over here, you should've had one fight out here at least once. The only thing I've noticed is that you two have a lot of visitors all the time. I thought she was the woman of this house." She said pointing to Lauren.
"Why me?" Lauren asked.
"Because its obvious that her husband is the man of this house. He just doesn't seem like the type to be married to a colored girl."
I frowned at her, and then I looked at Lauren. Lauren turned red and she was angry. "You are rude and ignorant! I don't know why you came over here to be rude like we have to tolerate the way you're talking. It's not ok, and I need you to leave before I can no longer calm my inner self and I have to mop the floor with you!"
My neighbor flinched like she couldn't believe Lauren was responding to her like that. "I didn't mean to offend you…"
Lauren cut her off, "but you did. I don't know why you're still here either. If I have to tell you to leave one more time." She warned
My neighbor swallowed then she walked back down the street.
"Lauren, you're so violent." I teased my friend.
"Please, I saw that look in your eyes. She only had a small window to escape through before you lost it."
"You know me so well." I said rocking my baby in my arms.
Lauren looked at Timothy, "he's such a good baby. When are you going to get started on the next one?"
I exhaled like the thought of another baby was too much right now. "I want to prove to myself that I can get my body back first. It will never be the same of course, but I want to know that I can do it size wise."
"What do you mean?"

"I've got horrible stretch marks everywhere. I'll never look the same naked again. Tim makes me walk around naked as much as he can to prove to me that he still loves to look at me if not more than now that he did before."
"He makes you walk around naked?" She asked like how does he do that?
I smiled, "my man knows how to make me do anything he wants." I smiled at the thought.
Lauren put her fingers up to her ears, "keep talking move past it. I almost got a visual." She laughed, "I got something that will help with the stretch marks. It won't take them away, but it will help fade them."
"I'm desperate, I'll try anything."
"Interesting neighborhood," she said looking around.
"It's funny to me how everyone assumes you are Tim's wife, it couldn't possibly be me."
"Girl please, Tim is cute and all. If they saw Jeff they'd know there's nothing better."
"Matter of opinion." I said cause Jeff wishes he was as handsome as his little brother.
"Yep, I'm glad our opinions swing the way they do." Lauren said.

****

"Go ahead child, he's going to be fine with us." Lady B said taking Timothy's little jacket off. "Lady B's got some mashed potatoes for you. You're going to love them!" She told Timothy. Timothy looked at her plate with wanting eyes. He didn't care that his momma and daddy were leaving, he wanted the food.
I kissed Timothy on the forehead and then I took Tim's hand. I was too excited when I could finally fit into my pre-pregnancy dresses, the ones I had left anyways. I decided to work harder to lose weight especially since my husband was determined to look at my body. I hated being embarrassed and that's all I ever was. Lauren gave me some Shea Butter cream mixture to put on my stretch marks, well my skin altogether. My stretch marks are still there but they changed from red to barely noticeable. I could get used to this body that other body was hard to deal with. Even though Tim seemed to prefer me with the weight on, I didn't like it. I felt like he was lying, when he's never lied to me before. We went to Lauren's place for pre-dinner cocktails; Jeff was going to meet us here. The three of us chatted like we used to when we were all in school. I dropped out last year, and Lauren was in her senior year. She was excited about graduating; she was accomplishing a major goal of hers. When Jeff came he said Dale and Franky were going to meet us at the restaurant. I noticed that Jeff looked a little off, but Lauren didn't. She made Jeff's drink without even looking at him. She handed him his glass, as she was about to walk back to me, when he grabbed her hand. "Lauren Salvo pay attention!" Jeff said holding on to her hand. "I hate being set up, and when Tim asked me to come along that day as soon as I saw you, I knew I was in trouble." Lauren looked at me for confirmation. I shrugged, cause I didn't know this was about to happen either. "I went to speak to your father, but he slammed the door in my face. So I'm going to take that as a none verbal yes." He chuckled, "Lauren Salvo will you marry me?"
Lauren put her hand over her mouth as Jeff got down on one knee, "you want to marry me?"
"I need to marry you! I have to marry you! I can only marry you! Please say yes!" He said.

"Yes!" Lauren said then they kissed. Jeff put the ring on her finger and Lauren scream hysterically. They kissed again and then she ran over to me so we could look at the ring together. Tears poured down her face, "he wants to marry me, **ME**!" She kept saying like she couldn't believe it.

Her ring was gorgeous and I was so happy for her. Tim came and put his arms around me as we watched them freak out over the proposal. Lauren and Jeff took turns saying how they couldn't believe they were engaged to be married. They were talking to each other like they were talking to other people. Tim and I laughed at them so hard. Dale, Blanche, Martha, Sebastian, Raynel, and Franky were waiting for us at the table. All of the ladies did the *I'm so happy for you* dance. While the men congratulated Jeff. I now understood why it was so important for me to be here. When I told Tim I wasn't in love with the idea of leaving Timothy behind, Tim insisted that we needed to get out tonight. Plus he said Lady B needed time alone with him just like all her other great grandchildren. I looked at Lauren who was still in shock about Jeff's proposal. She kept looking at her hand in disbelief. When the conversation at the table distracted everyone I asked Lauren why she seemed so shocked about the proposal. She said she's never thought any man would want her forever. She said it seems too good to be true, and she was in shock. I rubbed her hand and I told her I knew what she meant. The good vibes were so strong tonight-even Raynel and Franky had to give in and succumb to them. Those two were still at odds, they loved each other. Seems like their love for each other was their last agreement. Champagne was flowing and drinks were coming. We ate good and enjoyed the night. I felt eyes on me so I looked around the restaurant, a man was looking at me and he was beyond angry. Tim looked over when he saw me looking. His smile dropped and his face immediately became angry. His brothers noticed his change and looked over as well. They all stood at the same time and walked over to the table. Sebastian asked what was going on and I told him I had no idea. The guy looked familiar, but I couldn't put my finger on why he did. The four of them chatted for a few minutes then the guy left and the men came back to our table. It seemed like they sobered up real fast and the good times left. They were now in work mode having silent conversations with their eyes across the table. My breast told me it was time to get back to my baby anyways.

When we got to the house Timothy was knocked out in Lady B's arms. She was sitting in Irma's rocking chair rubbing his head. I asked her how he did, and she said he was fine like I should've automatically have known that. Tim and his brothers were now in the office with their father. Lauren was still freaking out about her ring. It was just after one in the morning when the doorbell rang. Everyone stopped moving and froze in place. Franky came out the room fast to get the door. He told all of us to go to the television room. We did as we were told; there were boxes everywhere from all of the packing. We shut the door and then we waited, Pops came to the door and he told Irma to come. I heard Irma scream, and then tears. We looked at each other, Lady B looked completely concerned and she stayed with us until she couldn't stay any longer. When she walked out she left the door open and we could hear Irma and possibly Pops crying. I looked at everyone and we all had the same scared looks on our faces. If Irma was crying someone was going to die, literally. Martha went out to her parents, and then I could hear her crying as well. Lauren and Raynel looked at me, I peeked my head out the door and Franky looked at me. He came in the room with red eyes, he told Raynel they were leaving as he picked up both of his sleeping boys. Raynel asked no questions she did as she was told. When they left Tim and Jeff came for us. Jeff's eyes were red as well. He kissed Lauren deeply then he led her out. Tim took Timothy from me; he asked me if I had everything and then we walked out. Pops was sitting on the sofa leaning forward with his head down while Martha held on to him and cried. Irma was in Lady B's lap like she was a big ole kid, both of them were crying. Tim's face was cold as he walked past and we walked out of the house. He didn't say anything in the car, and then he laid Timothy in his crib. He walked in the room talking, he said they found Peggy and she's in Fresno, she just gave birth to a little girl. He said Beth was in the hospital; some guy she hooked up with beat her up pretty badly. His parents were too upset to drive out tonight, but they were leaving in the morning. Tim told me to pack enough clothes for a week, just in case. He said he and his brothers had to go handle business once his momma and Lady B came home.

Timothy

When we got to my parent's house momma was holding the baby. Peggy was sitting next to the rocking chair watching them. My sister has always been goofy and silly to me, but watching her as she looked at her child I knew she has done some growing in the time she was away from us. I couldn't tell with Beth, she was still depressed about this guy.

The way she explained the situation to us last night was that she was dating this nobody of a guy. Someone from San Francisco who knew of our family knew this guy. They told the guy that her mother was passing. Filled with rage that he had been dating a colored girl he came to their room at the hotel they were staying in and beat her up badly. I guess the person forgot to tell this idiot other IMPORTANT factors about our family. Like that my momma wasn't passing, but she didn't act like any of the other white folks around here, and that when it came to the Wallace's no one messes with us.

Peggy gave Pops all the information she could about Miranda's father. Pops put a private investigator on to find him. Peggy didn't fight Pops on it; she didn't seem to have much fight left in her. She was out there in Fresno with no one to provide for her, and then all the emotional breakdowns that come with being pregnant. I know how off and on Annette was; I can only imagine how taxing the whole situation was for her.

Pops, my brothers and I loaded up in the car. Pops sat up and looked forward the entire time that Franky was driving. We went directly to this fella's house and sat outside watching the house. We spotted the car that Beth described then we waited for him to come out. Meanwhile Pops pointed out each one that he wanted laid out on General Purpose. We followed this idiot to his job, he ran around the market like he owned the place. Flirting with all the skirts as they came through his checkout lane. Pops bought some food, and he went through his lane. He tried to joke with Pops, but his cold stare made him shake in his boots. About an hour later Franky went through his line and did the same thing, then Jeff, then me. Each time he cowered a little to the side. Which just made us all madder. When the guy got off work he went by the hotel where the girls were staying. He quickly came out, I guess when they told him that the girls were gone. We went back to his house and waited outside.

When he came home he noticed our car out front. In true cowardly fashion he went inside and came out with five other guys. "Can we help you with something?" The Biggest one said walking up to the car.

Pops got out the car and stood up tall to look the guy in his eyes. "I'm Margaret's father." Pops said.

"Who?" The big guy said.
"Peggy, Beth's sister;" the coward said from the back of the group.
"The mulatto dame?" The big guy said.
"Yes," the coward said.
"What do you want?" The big guy said.
"Him!" Franky said standing on the other side of the car leaning over the top.
The big guy laughed, "what do you want old man? My brother will lay you out."
"Old? I'm an old man?" Pops said looking around.
"That's what he said." Jeff said.
"I've come for him, and I'm not leaving without him. If you would like to join his fate, be my guest." Pops said.
"It looks like there's four of you and six of us, you don't want this fight old man." The big guy said laughing.
Pops looked at me, "we're going to need his keys. Bring him and his car."
When I walked towards the coward the big guy took his eyes off of Pops to address me. Pops hit him so hard you saw his face cave in. The big guy went down and this so called fight was over in less than five minutes. I put the coward in his trunk, Jeff got in the car with me. "Let's get out of this heat and back to the Frisco Breeze!" Jeff said excitedly.
I maneuvered around the bodies laying in the street as we drove away. "So…" I smiled at him. Jeff gave me a toothy grin back. "You're going to join the ranks of the married men."
Jeff couldn't stop smiling, "I feel dumb." He laughed, "she wants to have my babies and junk."
"And you want to give them to her don't you????" I teased.
Jeff cracked up, "SHUT UP!" Jeff adjusted in his seat. "Who would want to willingly live out here?"
"They definitely picked a place we wouldn't have looked for them."
"Fresno is not off the map anymore."
I was quiet for a minute, "so we're Mulatto?"
Jeff adjusted in his seat, "is that why we got so much rhythm?"
"So what if we were?"
"That would be one more thing for me to love about myself. Who cares what they think?"
"My thing is, why hurt her because you think she's colored?"
"That's ok, he's about to get his."
And he did. The coward found himself driving on the bridge high under the influence. He was so high he drove off the bridge into the Bay waters after being severely beaten.

******

"Aw! She loves her Uncle Tim." Peggy said looking weepy at Miranda and I.
"All my nieces and nephews love me." I smiled at Miranda who was smiling and looking up at me.
"Pops tell you he found her father?" Peggy asked with pain in her eyes. I nodded yes. "He's married with a family. I didn't know he was married when we got together, but it's not like I asked either."
"So now what?"
She looked at the floor, "there's this guy from school. I ran into him the other day at the market with momma."
"What guy?" I frowned.

"Relax Tim, Pops has met him and he's ok with it." She said as if that would calm me.

"So what! I haven't met him. Pops met him? So what, it's serious already?" I spit.

Peggy's eyes filled with tears, "you love me enough to get angry about me? I always thought you only loved Martha this much. I never thought you would love me enough to get angry about what happens with me."

I looked at Annette who was sitting in the corner rocking our son to sleep. She smiled at me and told me to talk to my sister by nodding her head. "You're my sister and my little sister at that. Of course I care what happens to you, and who the guy is in your life."

Peggy scooted a little closer to me. "You never really hugged me, but you always hug Martha."

I exhaled then I put my arm out. Peggy happily scooted under my arm with happy tears pouring out of her eyes. "When do I meet this guy?"

"He's coming to dinner."

"With everybody? That's ambitious."

"Martha and Annette said if I get you on my side, then you could help me."

Annette started laughing. I looked at her, "you knew about this? How could you betray me?" I joked.

One by one my brothers arrived with their women. Matthew arrived with his kids and a different woman. No one said anything; I think we were all confused. Momma stood next to everyone, she didn't move right away. Raynel and Annette invited the woman into the family room. I stood there hoping momma didn't tell me to leave. I was nosey and wanted to know what was going on. I hoped Matthew didn't follow through on his promise and actually kill Maureen. The look on momma's face was new as she stood there staring at her son for a minute. Then she asked him where Maureen was. He said she's in the hospital very matter of factly. Momma cut her eyes at him and asked why she was in the hospital, for how long, how come she was just now finding out about it, and who was this new woman. Matt couldn't stand momma's glare, he looked up at the ceiling and then back at her. He said Maureen started using trying to cope with the loss of her father and the ridiculousness that is her mother. He said she kept getting too sick trying to clean up, so she needed to go to the doctor. He said since she's been at the hospital she's been having mental episodes. The doctors moved her from San Francisco General hospital, to the Napa State Mental hospital. He said Maureen's doctor wasn't making it sound like she would ever be healthy enough to come home. Matt chewed back emotion as he said that to momma. Momma showed no emotion when she asked who was the other woman-playing momma to her grandbabies. Matt said he went to Law School with Truvy, and they lost touch for a while once he set his eyes on Maureen. He said she's been a huge help with the kids. Momma asked what was supposed to happen to Truvy once Maureen was released from the hospital. Matt said he doubted that she was getting out, and he'd cross that bridge once he got to it. Momma was not giving him any sympathy. She was angry, she said if he needed help with his kids he should've come to her. Then she looked at him long and hard. She stared him in his eyes for a minute then she asked him if Maureen was really crazy or was he done with her and he stuck her somewhere to make his life easier? Matt took a deep breath and he told momma he wouldn't do that, he said he loves his wife very much. I paid attention to his very lawyer stance as he spoke with momma. Although he was telling the truth, it was a spin on the truth. Momma looked at Matt for a long time, she wasn't buying it either. Momma walked up on

Matt, she popped him upside the head and then she pulled his ear to bring him down to her level. She yelled in his ear telling him that she told him not to go behind his brother in the first place! She asked him what did he think was going to happen? She said she couldn't believe he would stoop so low, just so he wouldn't lose. She kept hitting him upside the head as she went off on him. I inched my way out of the room before she found a reason to be mad at me like I had something to do with this. I was still trying to get used to the new house, although it was big, it was different. I went into the family room; Truvy was cute, not as pretty as Maureen. I wished my nephew and niece were old enough to say whether she was as nice as she seemed. I could tell Annette didn't have a good read on her either. She wasn't overly conversational with her, but she hadn't crossed her arms to say she was intolerant of her either. Everyone was moving around like they weren't paying attention, but we all knew we were watching everything she did. Peggy excitedly showed her friend Thomas to the family room. I held back my laugh as I looked at the completely harmless fella standing before me. He was so harmless he didn't mask his nervousness one bit. Jeff was shaking his head no, Dale even kind of frowned at him, Franky looked like he couldn't believe what he was looking at, and Sebastian was happy to have someone on his level. Peggy brought him to me and proudly introduced him. I looked at him and then I said hello, and then I decided to cut my sister some slack. She had been through enough emotional traumas. This guy wanted her even though she had a daughter. As long as he didn't turn out to be a pervert or violent Peggy could have him.

****

"It's about time I got a chance to put my eyes on this little one." Mrs. Barnes said taking Timothy from me. "Why didn't you give him his own name? Why does he have to live up to yours?"

"This is my first born son, a reflection of me. Why wouldn't I happily give the forever proof of my love for my wife my name? Timothy will be his own man, but he will only be who he'll become because I am his father."

Mrs. Barnes smiled at me, "you're such a romantic Tim. Do you still write Annette poetry?"

I leaned in, "every chance I get. I'm saving it for when I'm in trouble." I smiled.

She smiled, "she probably reads them already and you just don't know."

"I doubt it, but maybe I should think of a better hiding place than the back of our closet huh?"

"You should come talk to me when you can. I'll tell you when you need the help." Mrs. Barnes looked at Timothy, "I can see both of you in his face, but its like he has his own look."

"Annette says he looks like her father a little."

"What does her momma think?"

"She hasn't seen him yet. Annette's not ready." Mrs. Barnes shook her head like she understood. She admired Timothy for a while, and he sat there eating it all up. My boy is such a ladies man. The way he looks at women is like he's checking them out. Figuring out how to make each one feel beautiful. Timothy isn't as brown as his momma. He's a caramel to butterscotch brown. His hair is a mixture of Annette and I's. I have curly hair, but I keep my hair pretty short, Timothy has a little more of a fro than I do. Annette says I can't cut it until he's a year old or else I will ruin his hair. At first I thought she was trying to trick me, so I asked Lady B. Mrs. Barnes gave Timothy back as she went to Buckie and Stacy as they walked in the door. She took their baby from them and then she walked on.

When Stacy spotted Annette she made a beeline over to me. When she put her hand out to say hello to Timothy, he moved his hand before she touched him, then he laid his head on my shoulder. "Your son is so cute," Stacy said. Then she looked at me. "He doesn't look white though. You sure he's your baby?" Immediately my eyes searched for Annette. She was talking to Katie and Lauren, holding Kiah not paying us any attention.
"Stacy you shouldn't say stuff like that, if my wife hears you I doubt she'll be nice about her response."
"Ain't nobody worried about your little wife." Then she turned on her heels.
I called after her and I told her not to do it. The idiot didn't listen. Stacy marched up to Annette telling them how cute Timothy was. Annette smiled and thanked her. I shook my head internally telling Stacy not to do it. I watched Annette's face as she genuinely smiled at Stacy and then her smile suddenly dropped. I exhaled, Annette put Kiah down and then I saw Stacy's feet flying in the air. I thought Katie would try to stop Annette from harming her sister in-law, but Katie stood there shaking her head and coughing. Katie picked up Kiah and moved her away from them. I told Katie to look after Timothy as I went to save the idiot. Its not like Stacy didn't know what Annette was capable of and this was a surprise. No this idiot went in knowing, maybe she thought someone would save her. Buckie came rushing over asking what was going on as I picked my wife up. Annette told Stacy to think before she spoke and if she kept it up she was coming for her when there would be no one to stop her. I tried my best to hold back my laughter. Stupid Stacy must've forgotten what a hit from Annette felt like, she was quiet the rest of the time she was there, and nursing her banged up face.

Annette

"I have a telegram for Mrs. Annette Wallace." The messenger said
I signed his paper then I took the envelope.

Annette,
Momma held on longer than I thought she would. She's on her final leg; please come as soon as you can. I have room for your family and Emma's.

Mrs. Harriett Coleman

I picked up the phone and I called Tim at work. I told him we needed to go right away. He said he'd come home in just a minute. I was packing again, but I was so worried about Harriet. Her momma was all she had, her father left before she was born and it's always been just her and her momma. I called Emma and I told her about the telegram, she had just gotten home from school. She said she would talk to Hezekiah and then she'd call me back. I was talking to Emma on the phone while I nursed Timothy when Tim walked in the door. He kissed me then he asked me if Emma and Hezekiah were going. I shook my head yes, then I continued talking to Emma. When she and I got off the phone, Tim sat on the coffee table in front of me.
"How long do we need to be out there?"
"I don't know yet."
"Would it be ok with you if I finish up some business out here, then I'll join you out there?"
I felt a little disappointed, "how long will you be?"

"I may need a week, the timing for this couldn't be worse. I've got some task to take care of and then I will be right there."
I pouted, "a whole week without you? We've never been away from each other for that long since we got together. Should I wait for you?" I didn't want to go without Tim.
"No, Harriet needs you. You go ahead, and I'll be right there."
Suffering from separation anxiety, I was all over Tim all night. I wanted and needed my man as much as he could hang with me. He seemed to be right there with me though.

Timothy

Annette and I hugged and kissed until it was time for them to board their plane. I told her I was coming as soon as I had a good stopping place at work. My foreman was going to be in charge, however Jeremiah and Jeff would take turns coming by to check things out. "I can't believe I'm going without you." Annette said.
"Me neither, but Harriet needs you. I'm coming as soon as I can." I kissed her forehead.
"Call and let me know when you're coming. Everything is a lot slower there and…" Annette shook her head. "I'm nervous, it's like I'm going backwards in time. I don't know what to expect back there with all the civil rights changes that's been happening. I hope things are better but I don't know."
I kissed her, "you're arriving by daylight and a driver is taking you directly to Harriet's. It's going to be ok."
"Hurry soon," she kissed me.
I kissed my son, "you be a good boy and look after your momma." Timothy shook his head yes. Emma and Hezekiah waited by the gate for Annette.
I watched them board the plane, and then I stood in the window watching the plane take off. When the plane took off I watched it until I couldn't see it anymore. I exhaled then I went to my parent's house. Momma and Beth had just finished making breakfast. Momma said it was cute how I pouted behind missing my wife already. I tried to pull my lip back in, every time I focused on something else it would pop back out. I ended up staying in the city all day. When Jeremiah got off work, I went by his place. Katie and Kiah were doing their girl thing around the house while Jeremiah and I spoke. Avery was fired, but I was trying to determine if I should just give him his pink slip or if he needed a visit as well. As usual Jeremiah was trying to talk me out of violence.
Jeremiah's division was doing so well, that we had request for estimates from four other grocery chains for exclusive business. Jeremiah and I went over the plans for expansion, he said we would need a bigger yard than the San Francisco office could provide. He had location suggestions, estimates for new trucks, and new staff. Jeremiah is a great businessman, and is always on top of what needs to be done. Because of his help I could focus on my portion of the business, and also keep my eye on Pops's distributions. Fill in for my brothers wherever they needed help in their businesses, and keep an eye on our affiliates.
When I got home Annette called me to tell me that they made it to Harriet's. She told me she missed me already. I told her the house was empty and cold without her. I told her I might go stay at a hotel just to make it through, but she told me she wanted to be able to reach me when she needed to. We talked for a little while and then we got off the phone. When we hung up the phone rang again. I thought she called me right back because she forgot something. "Hello?"

The person was quiet for a minute. “Can I speak to Annette?” The woman’s voice said.
Immediately I knew it was Rose. “She’s not home.”
“Do you know when she will be home, it’s kind of important.”
“How can I help you?” I asked not wanting to tell her where Annette went.
“Can you ask her to call her momma as soon as she can?”
“I sure can, she will not be able to get back to you for a while. Is there anything I can do for you in the meantime?”
“No, I’ll wait for her to call me back.” She said sounding irritated.

Chapter 16

Annette

When the engines on the plane started to fire up Emma and I grabbed hands, neither of them had ever flown before; and my first time was for my honeymoon, so the experience was new. Timothy watched my face, and so I tried to keep a brave face even though I was nervous. He put his head on my chest and rubbed my shoulders. I kissed my little man's head and then I relaxed. Emma kept saying she couldn't believe we were going back. Only the love of a good friend could ever convince me to come back to this place. Hezekiah put his arm around Emma, and then he kissed her forehead. He asked her if she was ok, and she slowly shook her head yes. Timothy happily ate most of my food on the plane and then fell asleep. As we were grabbing our bags off the carousel a guy walked up and grabbed my bag. "I'll take this for you ma'am." Then he smiled at me.

I screamed when I realized it was Josiah. "Oh my goodness look at you!" I said with the biggest smile.

"Claudette said to look for the fanciest looking people at the airport and she wasn't kidding. Look at you all! Who's this little guy?" He said towards Timothy.

"This is my son Timothy."

"Where's his daddy?" He looked around.

"He's going to come in about a week, he couldn't leave when we did."

Josiah smiled real big, "there's my pretty little girl! Look at you all grown up, this must be your husband. Nice to meet you, I'm Josiah." Then he looked around, "I thought you had a baby too?"

"Oh, we left her with my sister in-law." Emma said matter of factly, "but I have pictures of her."

"Maybel is in the car, when you can you have to come over the house to meet all of our children, especially little Annette."

Now it was the thing that Josiah and I had only talked about before, but now that I've lived in San Francisco I can see it all over him. The way he gestured, the way he stood. Even the way he walked with that slight switch. I smiled at my friend who has tried to save my neck so many times, and I thanked him for coming to get us.

On the car ride to Harriet's it was like old times. Emma and Josiah chattered the entire ride. Hezekiah looked at Emma in amazement with how much her mouth was running. Harriet came out on the porch as she saw us approaching, she ran out to the car. She ran to my door and snatched it open. I was barely out of the car good before she had her arms wrapped tightly around my neck as we cried. I kissed her cheek and I kept rubbing her head as we stood there rocking. She told me she thinks her momma was waiting for me. Harriet hugged Emma the same way, and she thanked Josiah and Maybel for bringing us. I followed Harriet in the house and her momma was in the dark room off the living room.

"Momma, Annette's here. She came just like she said she would." Harriet was crying to her momma.

Mrs. Harris opened her eyes and she looked at me. She smiled real big when she saw me, "oh Harriet she fancy. Just like you said." She said just above a whisper.

"My husband is sorry he couldn't come out immediately. He's trying to make it as soon as he can."

"Oh honey its ok. I'm just happy I got to see you again looking good and healthy. You got love in your life, you wear it well. Where's the baby?"

"He's with Emma and her husband outside, he'll be in in just a minute."
"Sit down honey, tell me all about California? Harriet said the Golden Gate Bridge isn't really gold?"
I told them about every place I could think of. When Emma came in the room, she's the natural chatterbox so she described everything so colorfully. Hezekiah sat there listening to Emma like she was describing a place he had never seen, not the place he's lived in all of his life. Mrs. Harris told me that Timothy was beautiful, and that he was such a good boy. Timothy sat quietly with us, Harriet said anyone of her kids would've fussed and acted up by now. Timothy kept looking at my face. I think he was concerned for me. I used the phone and I called home collect. I told Tim I wasn't sure that Harriet had a phone or not. I gave him the number and then I put Timothy on the phone to talk to his daddy. Tim asked how it was going and I told him Mrs. Harris was disappointed that he wasn't here, and that she doubted she could wait for him. He asked me to send his condolences and that he would be here as soon as he could. We pouted over the phone about how much we missed each other then we got off.
We stood in the kitchen cracking up watching Hezekiah go out to the outhouse. He was definitely a city boy; he was swatting the fireflies and all the other bugs away in the most hilarious dance. Hezekiah refused to drink anything with his meal cause he said he was not going back out there in the middle of the night. Harriet's kids thought Hezekiah was hilarious and that we all talked funny. Their country accents were amusing to us, but Hezekiah kept asking Paul to repeat himself cause he mumbled and talked low. He had a little raspy voice and he would say funny stuff. The rest of the kids would laugh and Hezekiah would ask him to repeat himself. When Mr. Coleman came home his eyes darted around at the children then us. I was trying to do the math in my head cause he didn't look that old when I left. He only spoke to Hezekiah and then he took his plate upstairs. I asked Harriet if he was ok with us being there. She said he was fine with it, but it wasn't like he had a choice either. Hezekiah went upstairs and got Mr. Coleman to come out of his shell. Eventually he came downstairs and chatted with us. We took over two of the kid's bedrooms, I was happy to have Timothy with me, but I couldn't wait for Tim to come.
In the morning we sat in the room with Mrs. Harris. Emma was brushing her hair as we all talked about nothing when we heard the front door. "YOU WHO! ANYBODY HOME?" I recognized the voice and I came out the room holding Timothy. "Oh Annette he's beautiful!" Claudette said putting her hands out to hug me.
I touched her belly, "weren't you the same way when I left?"
"Un HUH! Big, and loving every drop of it. I can't stay off my honey!" She said proudly. "Why aren't you big with baby number two yet?"
I modeled in front of her, "I had to get it back together before I went in for another." I smiled.
"You sure don't look like nobody's momma." Then she smiled at me, "I wish you weren't here under these circumstances. I want you to be happy when you meet all my kids."
I hugged her again, "me too. I'll be happy when I see your babies."
"Look at you, looking all fancy. You don't look like you even came from here. And your honey… Ooh! He's a fine white man. Are all the men in California like that?"
I smiled proudly, "only in his family. It's a different scene and a different way of doing it, but in the end it's all the same."

Emma came out and hugged Claudette. She proudly introduced Hezekiah to Claudette, and they started talking about him like he wasn't standing there. "Emma he's a fine young man!"
Emma smiled proudly, "thank you! I caught him myself!"
"Did Annette tell you what to do?"
"Nope, I heard it all from you."
Claudette gasped, "what?"
"Just because I was little didn't mean I wasn't paying attention when you all talked about sex." Emma smiled.
"Emma you were taking notes? Did they work for you?"
"He's standing here satisfied ain't he?" Emma said proudly, Hezekiah blushed and then he slowly backed away. He took Timothy from me and then he went back in the room with Mrs. Harris.
"So now that you've gotten a couple years of married life under your belt answer my question. Can you get enough?" Harriet asked with big eyes.
Everyone looked at me for my answer, "I love my husband very much. And he's very good to me." I said feeling weird about talking about Tim this way.
"Annette it's just us, you know we share everything. Is it true that white men are small?"
"I can't speak for all white men, but mine isn't lacking." I blushed.
"Now that we're all married women, I can dish the real real talk!" Claudette said.
"The stuff you said before wasn't real?" I asked in disbelief.
"I'm sure you've figured out that there's so much more to talk about. My honey tells me when I'm pregnant, before I know it myself. I honestly think he keeps me pregnant cause he loves the feel of it." Claudette laughed.
"I don't know, it's pretty good without the pregnancy." I said.
"True, it's a lot easier to grab your ankles for sure." Claudette said.
I never thought four women could sit around and talk about sex all day. Leave it to Claudette to keep it going. Every time Hezekiah came in the kitchen he blushed and walked right out. Poor thing was afraid to come for food. We gossiped about people around the way. People who moved away and the new people who came in. When Mr. Coleman came home, we went in the room with Mrs. Harris and let the men hang together. That's when Hezekiah came and said Mr. Coleman wanted him to come to Hazel's with him. Emma shot up and said she wanted to go too. They asked me if I wanted to go and I shook my head no real fast. Everyone laughed at me.
Until that very moment I didn't think of the possibility of seeing Luther while I was out here. I did not want to go there and chance running into him. I wished Tim were here.
Mr. Coleman wasn't happy about Emma insisting on going with them during their male bonding, but they left anyways. I rocked my baby on the porch as we watched all the fire flies dance around outside. I forgot about the beauty of the evening in the south, everything gets really quiet and you hear everything the way it was intended to sound. Crickets, birds, and wild life. I told my baby how much I loved him and how happy he made me. He was so mild mannered sometimes I wondered how he could be Tim or I's son. Being out here holding my baby did make me think of my father. Timothy looked like him a little bit to me. In that moment I wondered how Babydoll and her children were doing. I wondered if I would get a chance to go out that way. I didn't know how Emma would feel about going with me. I was sitting there rocking Timothy when I heard a car coming up the road; it was coming kind

of fast like something was wrong. When the car pulled up fast and came to a screeching stop Harriet came out with me. Emma called out that it was Mr. Coleman. Harriet ran to the car quickly. Hezekiah and someone else helped Mr. Coleman out of the car. He could not walk on his own, and after a few steps although they were helping him his body jerked and Mr. Coleman fell to the ground holding his arm. Harriet fell down to help to hold him as he laid on the porch. "The doctor told us to bring him home and he would meet us here." I knew that voice. I sat back down in my chair and I started rocking Timothy again.

Harriet pleaded with Mr. Coleman not to go right now. She said she needed him and she was losing her momma. Mr. Coleman told her that he loved her and then he slipped away. I gave Timothy to Hezekiah as Emma and I went to Harriet who was hysterical. She was telling the lord this was too much, and she couldn't bare all of this at once. We held her and rocked her; I focused on Harriet, although I could feel Luther's eyes on me. The doctor came and said that Mr. Coleman had a heart attack. The town mortician came and picked up Mr. Coleman. I never looked at Luther once that night, knowing he was there made me nervous.

****

Lucille, Harriet's oldest, took charge of all of the little kids. They had the house ready for callers as they paid their respects for Mr. Coleman. So much food kept coming. People who were real sad, and a lot of his family came by as well. A cousin asked Harriet if she was going to sell the store. When she said no, and that she would run it, they laughed at her. Emma and I frowned at them. Just as we were winding down from Mr. Coleman's services, Mrs. Harris couldn't hold on any longer and she passed away as well. Harriet laid down and she couldn't get up for two days. Harriet was trying to be strong, but she kept saying she needed just a moment of weakness as she cried and cried. I couldn't help but think about how many times this woman saved me from my family. I told Harriet we needed to go see the store. I asked Emma and Hezekiah to make the arrangements for Mrs. Harris just like we did for Mr. Coleman and then Timothy, Harriet, and I walked to town. I asked her to show me her store. The store was pretty big and everything was nicely displayed and put away, but it was all very old fashioned. I told her about Pops's department store in San Francisco. I told her she needed to upgrade her General Store to look more like a Department Store. As Harriet's mind switched gears and she listened to my ideas she started to come to life again. I told her I would talk to Tim and Pops about sending her appliances to sell, new fabrics, patterns, and anything I could think of. Harriet said no one around those parts could afford fancy equipment like I was talking about. I told her she could rent them out. Harriet looked at me in amazement as she listened. All I was really doing is telling her what Tim did with his trucking business. How they leased their services to companies and collected payments monthly. She said she could handle the money, but she didn't know how she would afford the inventory. I told her I would talk to my husband about it. I told Harriet how her simple act of kindness when she gave me what Mr. Coleman called scraps to make dresses for Emma when we got to California saved us. I told her we didn't have clothes and all I had was what she gave us. I told her that getting her store up and running was the least I could help her do.

We were looking at Mr. Coleman's books when a woman started banging on the door. I went to the door wondering who on earth it could be. I opened it and surprise spread across my face. It was Babydoll, and she looked upset. She stared at my face for a minute like she was trying to place me. "Annette?"

"Babydoll?"
Surprise spread across her face, "no one's called me that in years. I need to talk to Mr. Coleman." She was trying to look past me.
I could hear Harriet approaching slowly; she had Timothy in her arms. "He passed away a few days ago, no one told you?"
"NO! NO! NO!" She screamed like it broke her heart. "No one told me anything! How did he die?" She cried out loud.
"He had a heart attack at Hazel's and then another right as he got home."
"No! No! No! This can't be happening."
Her attack was heavier than the loss of your friendly grocer. "Did you have an account here?" It was kind of late for her to be here. Most of the stores were closing up.
As Harriet opened the door wider to get a look at Babydoll she said, "we were close."
The look on Harriet's face as she looked at her scared me; I took my baby from her. "To my husband?"
Babydoll put her head down and backed up a couple of steps. "I…"
Harriet lunged on her. "YOU'RE THE REASON HE HADN'T TOUCHED ME! HE WAS MY HUSBAND! HOW COULD YOU?"
I didn't do anything to save Babydoll; I stood there watching as Harriet beat her up and down the walkway. Luther pulled up in the car and pulled Harriet off of Babydoll. Harriet was cursing and screaming as she tried to get back to Babydoll to continue trying to rearrange her face. As Babydoll slowly stood up, I noticed the baby bump in her belly. I looked at her with tears in my eyes. That woman was so lost! Babydoll limped away holding herself and crying. Harriet was sitting in the chair crying her eyes out. She said in the back of her mind she knew it wasn't just the moonshine that was calling her husband to Hazel's.
Luther stood there staring at me while I talked to my friend. "Hello Luther." I said tired of him staring at me like I wasn't real.
Luther swallowed, "I hate that you're married."
Harriet's mouth fell open, mine did too. "No hello, how are you, how have you been? You just dive right in?"
"You're supposed to be my wife!" He said still staring at me.
"But I'm not, and I love my husband very much."
Luther put his hands up like what I was saying tasted nasty. "I don't care about how much you think you love him. I had your heart first."
I frowned at him, and then I looked at Harriet who was still sitting there with her mouth hanging open. "Why are you here Luther?"
"Because I love you, I can't understand any of this."
"I'm sorry you feel that way. I think we should stop talking."
"STOP TALKING? YOU'VE NEVER TALKED TO ME! YOU LEFT WITHOUT SAYING GOODBYE TO ME! EVERYONE ELSE GOT A GOODBYE EXCEPT ME!"
Timothy sat up straight in my arms and he frowned at Luther looking like his daddy. "Luther please stop yelling in front of my child?" Then I looked at Harriet, "we need to go."
"Annette please talk to me! Don't act like I'm nobody!"
"You were the grown man sweet talking a little girl. Doing it to other women and letting me watch. You may have cared about me, but I know no one could love me

like my husband does. It's pointless to sit here and talk about whatever you felt for me."
"FEEL!!"
"Whatever Luther, I'm married and in love with my husband, there's no point to this conversation." Then I looked at Harriet, "let's bring the books back to your house we can look at them there. It's going to be dark soon we should get going."
"I came to give you all a ride home."
"Thank you Luther," Harriet said before I could turn down the offer.
When Harriet and I put all the bookkeeping books in the car, I understood why she was so quick to accept the ride. These books are big thick and heavy; it would've been murder to carry them. I held on to Timothy and I didn't utter a peep in the backseat. As soon as we got to the house I called Tim collect at work. I told him about Harriet's store and my ideas. Tim said he'd bring catalogs to show Harriet appliances and things. Then he asked me what was wrong. I told him I really missed him and I couldn't wait to see him. He didn't believe that was the only thing wrong, but he didn't pressure me about it. He told me he was coming in a day and a half. I told him I couldn't wait to see him. We talked a little longer then we got off the phone. Emma came in the kitchen with wide eyes; she said Luther wanted to talk to me. I shook my head no and then I sat at the kitchen table. I held on to Timothy as if he was my last connection to Tim. I rubbed his head and then he fell asleep.
Luther helped Harriet bring her books in the kitchen. Hezekiah walked in, "Hey Luther..." Then he looked around. "You're back?"
"I need to talk to you." Luther pleaded with me.
Hezekiah sat down at the table while looking at Luther. "No, it's not a good idea."
"Annette!" Luther said like he couldn't believe I wouldn't go with him.
"I'm a married woman. If what you have to say is important it can wait until my husband is here."
Luther pulled a chair close to me. "Um! Her husband is family to me. I'm gonna need you to come on this side of the table." Hezekiah said with bass in his voice.
Emma and I looked at Hezekiah in shock. Hezekiah didn't take his eyes off of Luther. Luther sat there for a minute like he was debating what to do. "Luther, please leave or move."
"Annette, what did I do that was so wrong? Why are you mad at me?" He said as he walked around the table.
"You're acting weird. I haven't seen you in years. Since I left and you're acting like I never left. As you can see, I moved and I moved on. Was I supposed to wait for you to stop running?"
"I stopped running. I've been here waiting for you. Except for when I came to California looking for you."
"YOU CAME TO SAN FRANCISCO?" Emma blurted.
"Yes, I came I saw you. Both of you, and you looked so fancy. I saw you talking to that big white guy, and I saw him give you money. So I got a job to show you I could and would take care of you. Then I saw you out, on a date with that uppity looking colored guy. I came home. I asked my momma to ask you for permission for me to write you. When you didn't respond, I sent a letter. Nothing! Then I hear from Claudette that you got married, and to a white man? Why wouldn't you talk to me? What did I do that was so wrong?"
"I didn't know all of that. Outside of my letters to your momma, Claudette, and Harriet I didn't let my mind think about here too much. Your momma didn't ask me anything about you. I never got a letter from you. I'm sorry you feel some kind of

way about my life, but it's done. I wouldn't change what's been done. I love my husband very much. I'm convinced that no one could ever love me the way he does." Luther started to respond. "I'm sorry Luther. I didn't know you would ever stop running, but what's done is done. I couldn't change it now even if I wanted to." Luther looked at me for a long time. I could see his broken heart so I looked away.

Timothy

"How are you doing today sir?" I said to the gentleman as he got out of his car. He looked at me suspiciously. "I'm good and you?"

"My name is Timothy Wallace, I was wondering if we could discuss your duplex. I'd like to make you an offer."

Mr. Lakshman walked up to my window, "an offer?"

"Let's go discuss it over pie just up the street here."

He agreed and got in the car. We went up the street to the little cafe. "You want to buy my duplex?" He asked eyeing me.

The waitress came and asked what we were having today. I ordered the blackberry pie alamode and coffee. Mr. Lakshman ordered apple pie with a slice of sharp cheddar melted over the top with ice cream on the side and coffee. "Yes, but I would like to make the sale as transparent to the tenants as possible."

"Transparent? How?"

"Maybe I could pay you to look after the building for awhile."

"You want to buy my building then you want to pay me to look after it? What gives?" He asked trying to read me.

"I'm married to Mrs. Cooper's daughter. I understand that your bride is changing somethings." I looked at him.

"Can I be frank with you?"

"Within reason, we're talking about family here."

"Mrs. Cooper is good at what she does. If I had it my way, I would die underneath her. I can't explain any of this to my wife, how would I? She wants me to kick her out or make her pay rent."

"I'm not telling you to continue seeing Mrs. Cooper, but I guess that's your business. I would like to make sure she's taken care of. So, I'd like to buy your duplex from you at market rate, and then I'll pay you to manage the building. It's neither here nor there to me, how you explain it to your wife."

Mr. Lakshman's eyes got big. "But my building is paid for."

"Good, so that means you'd pocket the profits. Where should I have the paperwork sent?"

"Can I come by? I'd rather my wife didn't know about this."

I gave him Matt's card. "I'll have my lawyer give you a call when everything is set up."

****

"This place is amazing!" I said looking out the big window that pretty much covered the wall. Dale was finishing up Franky's house. Franky's reaction to the house was bitter sweet. His dream house was not turning out to be his dream come true.

"Thanks," he said in a deflated manner.

I looked at my big brother, he wasn't his normal self. "What's wrong Franky?"

He took a slow deep breath keeping his eyes on the landscape. "She's not pregnant, it worked twice before. I don't know why it's not working."

"I didn't know you two were trying for another baby." I smiled.

"She's not I am," my smile dropped. "She's becoming more and more distant from me. It's slipping away; I don't know how to fix it. She's going to hate this house, while I love it!" He sighed, "I thought it was every girl's dream to marry a rich man and live in the lap of luxury?"
"Annette said she doesn't want spoiled little rich kids."
"They're our children. What's wrong with spoiling them?"
"Our house was nice, but not this nice. Do you know how many kids you'd have to have to make this place relevant? Talk to your wife, explain your initial intentions. Tell her everything. Fight for your wife!"
Franky looked at me, "this house will just be the straw that broke the camel's back. If there was no Christy or any others maybe we could work it out. Either way I'm losing."
"How are you introducing things to her?"
Franky looked at me, "she's not open to it. She don't want me behind her, she say she want to look at me. She won't get on top, good girls don't do that. She had to be drunk to enjoy me kissing her. Forget about her doing it for me. No variation! NONE! Me on top of her, and now she don't even enjoy that. I love her, BUT I'M BORED STUPID! I'm wrong for asking for more, for bringing it up!" Franky shook his head, "I love Raynel! I don't...." He swallowed, "I'm losing her!"
Franky looked like he wanted to cry, but even his tears knew better than to betray him. "Let the house sit, you don't have to move in right away."
"We're going to have to move soon. We're gonna be sitting ducks." Franky moved away from the window.
"Franky, you're getting fat." I said looking at my brother.
"Thank you, I had no idea that everything on my body is getting bigger. I was standing here wondering why I felt heavier on my feet. Thank you for pointing out the obvious!" He snapped at me.
"Raynel's not afraid you're going to smash her to death? She should want to get on top just to save her life." I teased.
"You play too much Tim!" Franky said cracking a smile.

****

Butterflies raced around my stomach, I couldn't wait to see Annette and Timothy I missed them so much. I grabbed my bag off the carousel and then I headed for the front. Since I was able to get an earlier flight I needed to take a cab to Harriet's house to surprise them. When I stepped out the door a fella approached me with a sign that said Tim Wallace. "Franklin Wallace sent me." He looked me in my eyes.
"Why?"
"Please call him from the pay phone inside." The fella said.
I went to the pay phone and called Pops. He said Berger and associates have been trying to rebuild through an Arnold Cadbury. He told me to find him and let him know how. He said the Berger Empire needs to be destitute. He wanted me to find out if we needed to buy this guy out or if he goes down with them. He said Tomas would be my driver and back up out here. When I got in the car I looked at the map while Tomas drove. We only got lost a couple times, but we made it to Harriet's house. Kids were outside playing in the yard. When I got out of the car I heard Annette scream and then she came bursting through the door. She jumped off the porch and on to me. She kept kissing me and kissing me. She said I was the best surprise ever. I had to control myself cause everyone was looking at us. That didn't stop Annette from kissing all over me. I took a deep breath then I waived hello to everyone. My son was jumping up and down happy to see me. I couldn't properly

say hello to anyone cause this crazy lady had her legs wrapped around me and she was kissing me all over. So I picked up my son and gave him a hug and kiss. Then everyone came and hugged me around Annette who shamelessly would not stop kissing me. I introduced them to Tomas as my driver. He said he was going to get a room at the hotel in town, but Harriet wouldn't hear of it. She told him he could sleep on her couch. When Annette finally came up for air I gave Harriet a big hug and I told her I was sorry about her family. She cried a little then she switched gears and asked for the catalogs that Annette said so much about. Harriet invited us into the kitchen. She and Annette made our plates, and then Annette sat in my lap and fed me. Emma laughed at her and said she had it bad. Harriet said people were going to talk about her having two white men in her house and her husband wasn't even cold yet.

That night I had to put Timothy to sleep cause Annette was impatient and she wanted to get to our time. Timothy was telling me about all the things he saw at the pond. All the animal noises he learned, and all the fun he's had with his Uncle Hezekiah. Annette laid on the other side of Timothy with the most annoyed look on her face. Timothy finally talked himself to sleep, and Annette jumped on me. I told her we couldn't do it right next to the baby. She was about to have a fit. It tickled me that she was as anxious as I was. I thought she would be talking me down. I told her the bed was too squeaky, every time we wiggled our toes it made noise. I dropped the big blanket on the floor and Annette pulled me on the floor on top of her. No convincing, no encouraging, my wife was ready. I told her I needed to get a condom out of the bag, and she told me there was no time. Before I could get my whits about me she took me in. I could hear the hallelujah chorus as we connected. I guess this is all the down time I was going to get between babies. I had to cover Annette's mouth cause she seemed to forget we weren't at home and that we had a sleeping toddler up in the bed. I loved every moment of it, my wife loves me and she misses me.

In the morning Annette could focus again. I sat there listening as she went over options with Harriet. My wife was very patient with her friend as they went over everything. Annette told her she was going to need an electrician on standby as she offers a lot of these appliances that were too modern for some of the homes. She told her she was paying for upgrades in the store as well. When Annette told her everything she wanted to do, Harriet's eyes got big and she asked me if all of that was ok with me. I told her of course it was. Tomas took us to "town" and Harriet proudly showed me her store. This place looked sad and very low income. The bar across the way caught my attention. I asked who owned the bar and Harriet said Mr. Cadbury. I asked her if she meant Arnold Cadbury and she said yes. Annette watched my face but she didn't say anything. Annette wanted to set up this store like Pops's department store. I told her it was a good idea, but in order for the general store not to stand out like a monstrosity they needed to at least upgrade the appearance of the adjacent businesses. Annette pulled out the phone book.

"Does Arnold Cadbury own any other businesses down here?"

"He owns almost everything down here." Harriet said looking at Annette.

"What?" I asked Annette, she shook her head like she was trying to shake off the bad feeling.

Hezekiah and Emma walked in the store all smiles. "I just showed Hezekiah where I was born. The house is still there. Like it's waiting for me or something."

"You wanna live here?" I asked in shock.

"Maybe in a few years, we could bring Kiah out here and start over." She smiled at Hezekiah.

Annette looked at me, "I do not want to live here. I'm not leaving the Bay." She said as a guy walked in.

"What's wrong with Kansas? You too good?" He spit.

I looked at Annette and her eyes showed a flicker of pain. "I live a different life outside of everything here. I don't want to come back here to relive what I've grown above." Annette said then she looked at me. "Luther meet my husband Tim. Tim this is Luther."

Luther looked me directly in my eyes as if he was looking for any signs of a sissy, as I did the same. "I would shake your hand, but I don't want to."

I smiled at him, "you're a bigger man than me. I don't know that I could stand here and deal with it."

He tried to stand taller, "you may have her now. The moment you mess up, I will always be right here waiting!"

"Prepare to die a old and lonely man then." I said still smiling.

"Your smile makes me mad!" Luther said honestly.

"That's what it's supposed to do." I said still smiling. I knew I was teasing him. I pointed my son at him. "Did you meet our son, a bond that will never be broken walking around in flesh and blood."

"Ha! Ha! Ha! I don't like you!"

"Yes you do, and you're mad that you're not me. It's ok, we can be friends anyways."

He wanted to hate me, wanted to have a reason not to like me. How could a man not be cool with a man? Sneaky and deviant fools will hide who they are. He was simply putting it out there. "What just happened?" Emma asked.

"Nothing, we're cool. Just like other people before him who wanted my woman but had to bow down to the fact that she's with me." I said then my eyes glanced at Hezekiah. Annette saw my glance and she frowned at Hezekiah. Harriet and Tomas looked like they were watching a movie scene. "You know any electricians around here?" I asked Luther.

"Besides myself, there's a couple. Why?"

"Come talk to me." I told him, as I took him around the store. I told him about all the upgrades needed. Once he stopped trying to find fault with me, he put his work hat on and discussed the project. I asked Harriet what she thought about a sign that lit up at night. Her eyes got big, I asked Annette to sketch my idea. I explained while Annette sketched, Harriet told her she never knew Annette could draw. Annette humbly told her she could only draw abstract stuff like this she could sketch and she learned how to do it in school. Then she said that Timothy was going to be the artist. Even though he was only two years old his pictures for a two year old were really good. I could tell Harriet thought she was just saying that because it was her son. Seeing is believing for some folks. I told Harriet she was going to need landscapers, and permits to upgrade most of the shops and stores over here. I told her to give me a list of the owners and I'd go talk to them personally. Annette looked at me again when I said that. I told Harriet that people would travel far and wide if they think that destination will have what they're looking for. I said if they travel across counties and they see this town looking like this they will turn around. The best business is word of mouth. Harriet sat on her stool a little overwhelmed. "How soon can I get that list?"

“Everything on that side of the street Arnold Cadbury owns.” She said handing me the short list.
Emma’s breath turned to fire, “WHEN DID THAT HAPPEN?”
“Some time ago, maybe a little after you all left. Mr. Cadbury needed to generate some cash flow some of his other businesses went belly up. He don’t have money like he used to. I guess that’s,” she sighed like it hurt to say. “I guess that's when Ruth Ann started befriending my husband.” Then she cut her eyes at Luther. “You knew didn’t you?”
“You two were married it wasn’t my place to get involved.” Luther said plainly.
“That’s so unfair! So mean! Cruel! You let that old man run around on me.”
“That was your husband! It wasn’t my place.” He said matter of factly.
“Does she have babies?”
“Harriet please!” Luther said not liking being on the spot.
“Ruth Ann? As in Babydoll?” Emma spit again.
“Yes,” Annette said quietly watching everyone.
“What am I missing?” Hezekiah asked.
“THE WOMAN WHO GOT MY DADDY KILLED WAS SLEEPING WITH HER HUSBAND!” Emma screamed.
Hezekiah went to Emma and held her as she cried angry tears. “Who is she to Arnold Cadbury?” I asked Annette who looked like she was remaining calm by being quiet.
“She’s his daughter.” Then Annette turned her head and looked for something to change the channel on her mind.
I looked at Tomas, he nodded at me. “I’m going to go talk to the other owners.”
“Just find out if they’re open to the upgrades and then we’ll go from there.” I said, and then as he got to the door I called out, “find out who owns this land too.”
Luther was watching Annette; she went over to Timothy and asked him what he was drawing. Then he looked at me, he knew I was watching him. “Are you passing?” He asked me as he stood in my face.
“Why does everybody ask me that? That’s the only possible explanation for me being in love with that woman?” I said insulted.
“Yea,” he said not apologizing for his accusation.
“I love her because of who she is. Both of my parents are white, but the nanny did raise my momma and she instilled in her love and respect for all people and my momma passed that thinking down to her children. I don’t not trust you because you’re colored. I don’t trust you because you want my woman. Keep your friends close and your enemies closer.”
Luther smiled, “at least we’re on the same page.”

****

When I reported to Pops that Arnold Cadbury was not only going down, but he needed to die a slow and painful death he was all ears. When I told Pops this was the man who killed Annette’s father in front of her, I could hear Pops’s hand hit the desk. He said this world was too small, and then he asked how Annette was holding up. I told him she was a mess. When we came home one night she couldn’t pull it together she sat in the rocking chair on the porch and cried her eyes out. She told me the whole story of how her father died, I never thought about what it would do to a person to helplessly watch their father being murdered. Annette felt guilty about the whole thing like it could’ve actually been her fault that her father died. I could tell by the way she told me she battled with this thinking all of the time. I

reassured her that it was not her fault that he died. Nothing has made me want to go after someone like hearing her story.
So I told Pops my plan and he helped me see it from a few other angles. He said he was sending two more guys. He said they would stay in a hotel. He said he didn't want me seen with them as they were coming in for blood. He said I needed to tell him when they needed to strike and they would go in and do specifically as he directed.

Chapter 17

Timothy

"Everyone is on board except Mr. Cadbury." Tomas said

"Figures! Guess we should drop by his house." I said knowing I wanted to see where he lived anyways.

"The Mayor has some questions about the renovation also."

"Perfect! Can you go warm up the car? I'll let my wife know we're leaving." When I walked in the bedroom Annette was still sleep. Timothy woke up as I walked in. I put my finger up to tell him to be quiet, then I kissed Annette's forehead. She opened her eyes; I asked her how she was feeling. She's in denial and it's my job to humor her. I pretend I don't know why her headaches are back. Or why she's suddenly tired. She doesn't want to be a burden or slow down. She's ready to go home so she's trying to suck it up. She said she was fine as she sat up. Timothy kissed her cheek and she melted. I told my son to look after my woman and I'd be back. She asked where I was going, and I told her I was going to handle business. She sat up straight and looked me in my eyes. I looked away and then she called me closer to her. She kissed my forehead and then she told me to come back safely. I promised that I would.

We drove through town and right on the edge where the houses got big and plantation like there it was. I could tell that once upon a time this house was really nice. It was in desperate need of paint and the grounds needed a good going over. As we pulled up a woman came out of the door. "May I help you?" She said as Tomas and I got out of the car.

"We're looking for Arnold Cadbury, is he home?" Tomas said.

Her eyes bounced back and forth between us. "You all not from around here are you?"

"No ma'am, we're visiting from California. We've come to discuss business with Mr. Cadbury." Tomas said.

"Please come in Mr. Cadbury will be home shortly." She said gesturing towards the house.

"If it's alright with you, we'll wait outside until he comes. We don't want to disrespect him."

A little boy came around the corner. "Can I wash your car for you sir. I don't charge much, whatever you can spare."

"WHO ASK YOU TO COME AROUND HERE BOTHERING MY GUEST! GO ON GET!" Mrs. Cadbury screamed.

I frowned at her, "it's fine."

"I don't know that we'll have time." Tomas said.

"I'll have my sisters help me, we can work real fast." He said anxious for a yes.

"You live here?" I asked him.

"My family lives around back." He said looking at me with my wife's eyes.

"You gotta do a good job, he likes his car to sparkle."

"Yes sir! I'll go get my sisters and the soap." He said then he ran away.

Mrs. Cadbury squinted her eyes. "Are you two the ones that have been trying to fix this place up for that colored woman? I've heard about you."

"What have you heard?"

"That the widow's husband wasn't even cold and you y'all been spending nights over there. Sounds like you two got a weakness for midnight lace." Neither one of us responded to that statement. "Darkies can be good for something some times."

"Do you know if your husband would be interested in selling his portion of the land in town?" Tomas asked, "he hasn't responded to my letters."
"He ain't selling!"
The kids came back with buckets of water and rags. The girls had long singular braids. The oldest had slightly curly hair and the youngest hair was straight. I wondered what they momma looked like cause they were all very fair. The kids got to work moving fast around the car. This was not their first time washing a car.
"Can I ask you why? Even though he sells us the land he can lease the spaces for his businesses. We put money in his pocket, make all the upgrades, and everything will be like new."
"Nothing is that simple, you two are up to something."
"Yes, we're trying to help a widow provide for her rather large family. While putting some money in this town."
"Like I care if darkies live or die!" She huffed. The little boy flinched when she said that, but he kept moving. A woman was walking up the road with two little ones.
"YOUR KIDS ARE OUT HERE BEGGING FOR MONEY AGAIN!" The woman kept coming.
Then a car passed her on the road and pulled behind our car. He looked back at the woman, and then at the kids cleaning the car. "What's going on?" The man asked.
"They're slaving away on their car begging as usual. Ruth Ann is just getting back, and they wanna save the Negros in this town one colored person at a time." She said sarcastically.
The man looked at us, "we got us a couple of nigger lovers?" He said looking me and Tomas in our eyes. "How I know you two not some octoroons trying to save the colored nation?"
Tomas got mad, "if I..."
I put my hand up to calm him as I did my best to keep my own composure. "Money is green and no matter what color I am, green always spends the same way."
"I don't like the idea of coloreds owning the property that I do business on."
"Suit yourself, whether you sell or not the renovation is moving forward. Everything around you will look brand new and the white man's side of the street will look run down and ancient. You can pretty much guess how that will affect business. You'll shut down anyways."
Mr. Cadbury rolled his eyes. "Where have you been?" He said to the woman.
"I went to...."
"To go lay on your back some more! You're no good just like your mother!" He barked at her.
She put her head down, "no sir. I took the baby to the doctor, he not well."
"He better be paying for it, I don't got money to spend on you."
She started crying then she looked up at the woman, "you ain't tell him he died?"
Mr. Cadbury stood up straight, fear showed all over his face. "When he die?" His eyes darted at us.
"Arnold, let's discuss this inside." Mrs. Cadbury said reaching for her husband.
"We're not selling!" He said then he slammed the door.
All the kids dropped their rags and ran to their momma and hugged her while she cried. "I'm sorry sir, we'll be finished in just a minute." The boy said.
"What's your name son?"
The little boy frowned at my kindness like it was foreign. "Elmer Junior sir."
I looked at the momma, "you're Babydoll?" She looked tired and lonely.
"Where did you hear that name? My husband called me that."

I looked at Annette's brother and sisters and I felt bad that they had to live with that tone around the Cadbury's. “That’s what they said your name was in town.”
She looked at the house, “why are you here?”
“We were trying to get Mr. Cadbury to sale us his land in town for the renovation, but he’s so worried about the color of the skin of the people he’d be leasing from.”
“My father doesn’t own land in town.” She said angry.
“He doesn’t? Everyone said he does.” Tomas said.
Babydoll looked at her kids and then she moved closer to us so we could hear her. “Mr. Coleman owned that land already. They traded my father’s use of the property for me.” A tear fell from her eye.
Tomas turned red, “he’s your father!"
Thinking about my own momma I looked at Tomas. “Its a different kind of father daughter relationship. Mr. Cadbury will never openly say he’s her father. Just like Mrs. Cadbury will never openly say she loves colored men. They know it, and everyone else does too. The parental bond has limits here.”
“You colored?” She asked me.
“On the inside.” Then I looked up at the window and Mrs. Cadbury was looking. “Can I trust you?” She shook her head yes as she tried to stop crying. “Do not tell them what you told us. Make up anything you want, but don’t tell them I know. If you can keep this secret, I will make sure you and your children are taken care of.”
“What that mean?” She asked wiping her face.
“Prove to me I can trust you and you will find out.” I said, I put a few dollars in her hand as I shook it. “Give this to your children tonight for the wonderful job they did on his car. Don’t tell them I have a feeling they’ll take it from them.” She tried to smile through her tears. “Elmer, look at the sparkle on this car. You all did an excellent job!” I smiled, then I handed the boy a handful of coins.
“OH WOW! THANK YOU!” Elmer said with big eyes. “Thank you mister! Thank you!”
“Make sure you share evenly with your sisters, they did their share of the work as well.”
“Yes sir!” He said with big eyes.
“How much is that?” The oldest girl asked.
“I don’t know, we gotta go count it. Come on!” He told his sisters as they picked up everything with huge smiles on their faces.
Babydoll said thank you and then we went to the Mayor’s office. We had him pull up the property ownership records and sure enough Mr. Coleman owned everything that Mr. Cadbury pretended to own. After Tomas and I explained how much their city stood to gain from the renovation he assured us there would be no problems with inspections zoning etc. I used the Mayor’s office phone while he and Tomas went for some brandy to celebrate. I told Pops everything. I told him to tell his men to look alive cause now that Mr. Cadbury knew that Harriet owned everything I didn’t put it past him to try to hurt her to gain control. Pops said he was telling his men to move in tonight. I told him to put someone on the house as well. I had a bad feeling about Mr. Cadbury.
The Mayor was so excited about all the possibilities; he could’ve cared less that it was a colored woman who was making all of his happen. He was just happy that it was happening. He told us he wanted to meet Harriet, to pay his respects to the young widow and to let her know that if she needed anything all she had to do was call him. So we told him to ride with us to the house and Tomas would bring him

back. "I don't think I could ever get used to these pitch black roads at nighttime." Tomas said.

The Mayor sniffed the air, "smells like somebody is barbecuing."

I looked at Tomas and he stood on the gas. The car bounced around on the dirt road. As we came around the hill I could see that something was on fire in front of Harriet's house. All I could see was red! "What is that?" Tomas asked.

"Oh no!" The Mayor said as he looked in horror.

"Stop the car!" I told Tomas. I went in the glove box and pulled out my gun.

"Do you think that's necessary?" The Mayor asked.

"How you gonna ask me something stupid like that? Do you see that burning in the yard? Their white sheets are brighter than the fire. STAY HERE! Ask me another stupid question and I'm going to shoot you!"

Tomas got his shotgun out the trunk and he put bullets in his pockets. As I hurried through the field I could see Pops' men closing in as well. I got their attention then I told them to go. I could hear the children crying, and then I saw a man dragging Annette out of the house. Another brought Emma as she was kicking and screaming. "Mrs. Coleman! We need you to sign those papers immediately or your friends here will die!"

One of the men were telling me to wait, then I saw Annette hop to her feet and punch the guy so hard he fell backwards. Two guys started to rush her and I started shooting. Bodies were dropping left and right. I ran to my wife and her lip was busted. Even though the guy was dead I still kicked the life out of him. I wanted him to stand up and try to hit me. When all six of Pops' men came in I told them to get rid of the bodies. I went to the one who was once standing like he ran this intrusion before he was shot. I lifted his hat and it was Mr. Cadbury, the bullet had gone through his head. I got water from the well and I put out the fire and dropped it all over the ground where blood had spilled. When all the bodies were gone, I told them the Mayor was in the car. "The bad men ran off when they heard the gun shots, everybody got it?" I looked at Annette who was still shaking and I put my arms around her. "It's ok, you're safe."

"You should've at least let me beat that man up some more before you killed him!"

I took two steps backwards, "Annette…"

Tears started pouring out of her eyes, "it was vengeance for my father! They came the same way before!"

"And those men will NEVER come again! Baby it's over!" Annette held on to me as she cried. Tomas brought the Mayor. "Where's Timothy?"

"He should be sleep, I had just laid him down and came back downstairs when they came."

I hurried in the house, "did anyone go upstairs?"

"No!" Annette said as she hurried behind me.

I opened the door, and Timothy was knocked out sleep on the bed. He slept through all the noise. As the Mayor went through his whole speech about how nothing like this would ever happen at the Coleman home again Luther and Hezekiah came home. Emma started screaming at Hezekiah asking him where he had been, and that it wasn't safe for colored men to be out on the roads after dark! Hezekiah looked confused and he said he was working downtown with Luther. He didn't understand why she was so upset. Harriet told them about the men in sheets who came, but they ran away when they heard the gunshots. Hezekiah hugged his wife and apologized for not being here to protect her.

Annette

I looked around with satisfaction at the complete and total transformation of the town. Everything looked more modern, there were flowers, lights instead of lanterns, there was an actual sidewalk instead of the old wooden and dilapidated walk way. Electricity flowed through each store. Harriett's General Store was the crown jewel of the downtown area. Pops sent all of her inventory, using Tim's trucks and drivers.

Emma and I helped her display everything just right. She had high quality fabrics and prints, and new in-fashion patterns. Beautiful sewing machines, washing machines and dryers, you name it she had it.

Across the street where the bar used to be was now the Good Eats restaurant that the Broderick family came together to run. Babydoll opened an actual candy store, although Emma refused to acknowledge her, I gave her some pointers and I convinced her that in addition to the candies she made, she had to sell candied and caramel apples. It took Harriet a minute to come around, but once Babydoll explained everything they introduced the children as brothers and sisters. I introduced myself to my little brother and sisters. I watched how little Elmer looked after his sisters and brothers and I exhaled. He wasn't like my other brothers.

Emma and I were silent partners with Harriet on the purchase of the land and the leasing of the storefronts to the businesses. Tim paid for advertising, and I paid for the renovation of my best friend's house. Luther wired the house cause Mr. Coleman had the electricity rigged up some crazy kind of way in the house. The biggest and most expensive part was the indoor plumbing. It was a big ordeal but none of the kids knew how to act when it was done.

Immediately people from all over started flocking to the downtown area. Most of them came just to look at everything, but that meant more traffic and people. Most people fixed up their homes because people would pass through and see them as they made their way into town.

Tim made sure all the necessary paperwork was sent home, so that we would have everything we needed for our taxes. Once I was satisfied that everything was good and my friend was taken care of. I told Tim I was ready to go home.

Chapter 18

Annette

Saying goodbye again to my family and friends for the second time was hard. Ask me if I'm excited about going home? I couldn't wait to get back to my life. To get back to my own house, and to make love to my husband in my own bed, because I had to have him I settled for the floor, but I wanted the comforts of my soft bed again. When I get home, I'm going to the doctor to confirm whether I'm pregnant or not. I think I am, but I'm not sure. Tim hasn't seemed to notice just like with Timothy, men can be so clueless sometimes.

Tim wasn't clueless about Luther though, he made sure he kept him busy and right under his sight at all times. It didn't go unnoticed by anyone that Tim was present every time Luther came around. For whatever reason he liked teasing Luther. Luther would get mad, but what could he really do about it? Last night he told me in front of everyone to come back to him the moment Tim messes up. Tim laughed so hard at him, I looked away. What was I supposed to say to that?

Everyone waved goodbye from Harriet's house as we drove away. I wasn't going to miss these dirt roads and these older than dirt cars. I couldn't wait to get back to my life in the city. Timothy waved goodbye to all the animals. As we drove through town for the last time I thought about how it looked when we arrived and how it looked now. Thanks to us our friends were going to live better lives. The whole city was benefitting from our generosity.

I told Harriet to beware of the men who will come for her money. She was going to be very well off now, and there were going to be men coming to take advantage of that. I thought about my father when I told her that. I told her how he married Babydoll for the money, and when it stopped coming like before how he was about to move on. I told Harriet to focus on her kids and a good man would come eventually.

I held on to my man as the plane engines fired up. The whole flight Emma and Hezekiah were in a deep conversation. It didn't look like they were arguing, but they were talking about something. I laid my head on Tim's shoulder and I kept softly kissing his neck. I know it wasn't easy on him being away from his business all these months. I appreciated the fact that he made it work for me and he didn't complain once. Timothy sat next to me looking out the window and drawing on the paper the stewardess gave him. When we landed in San Francisco I looked at the cold and smiled. I was home. As we walked off the plane our family was all there waiting for us. Katie said there was a fight over who was coming and in the end no one agreed so they all came. We all went back to Pops and Irma's house for dinner. When we walked into our front door I smiled so big. My house is a lot smaller than Harriet's but to me it was like I was walking into a Grande palace. It was nice putting Timothy in the bathtub with hot and cold running water. Tim unpacked our bags while I got Timothy ready for bed. "I think you're ready for a big boy bed, what do you think?"

"Yes!" Timothy said with a smile.

I rubbed my baby's head and he fell fast asleep. Tim was downstairs sorting all of our mail.

"Now that we're home I need to tell you that your momma called." He watched my eyes.

I sat down preparing myself for him to say that another one of my brothers died or something. "What did she want?"

"She wouldn't tell me, she didn't want to speak to me at all." I nodded my head cause I knew that was right. "So I did some digging." He sat down, "Mr. Lakshman's wife was putting pressure on him to make your momma pay rent or put her out." Of course she wouldn't have called to apologize for all that she's done wrong. She needs me so she calls. "So I bought the duplex from him and I'm paying him to manage the building. This way his wife can get off his back about the rent, and your momma permanently has a place to stay."

"Thank you, thank you for taking care of her even though." I said swallowing.

"So that we're clear, she does not know we own the building. So if she tries to tell you that she has nowhere to go, you know that's a lie."

"Maybe I should look into buying her a house." I said

"Why would you?" He said trying to pull back his irritation. "She's fine right where she is."

"It's my momma Tim."

"That apartment was good enough when there were too many of you there. It's good enough now."

"We can put my Aunt and Uncle up in a house, but my momma has to stay in an apartment?"

Tim looked at me like I wasn't making any sense. "Your Aunt and Uncle genuinely love you and will be there for you. Your momma will only use you."

"Don't talk about my momma!" Tears poured out of my eyes. "My momma isn't like Irma or Lady B, but she's my momma. How you gonna tell me I can't do for her?"

"Annette you know your momma doesn't mean you any good. What message are you sending her if you break your back to give her everything, when you know she would rather you have nothing."

"I don't expect you to understand!" I got up and stormed out of the kitchen. I knew he was right, but it still rubbed me some kind of way when he was telling me I couldn't do better for her. Right or wrong she was my momma. I came out of her; she nursed me as a baby. How dare he say anything.

I expected Tim to come and try to smooth things out. When I woke up in the middle of the night he wasn't in the bed. He slept on the couch, and then he left in the morning for work. I went over Katie's so that Timothy and Kiah could play. Plus I needed her to keep Timothy for me while I ran to the doctor's. "Katie you done lost a little weight, what you been doing?" I asked.

"Nothing girl, just running behind Kiah. I'm so happy you're back Kiah was asking about you and Timothy."

"She didn't ask about Emma?" I asked with sad eyes.

Katie shook her head. "She don't know her no more than she knows Lauren or Raynel."

On the way to the doctor I couldn't understand how momma could turn Emma on her own child. I love Timothy so much, and there's nothing my momma could say that would make me feel it was ok to be away from him.

"Congratulations Mrs. Wallace you're pregnant." My doctor said, fear hit me immediately. "Relax child you've been through the worst, each baby is different. Make sure you get exercise and eat well."

"I knew those headaches meant something." I fussed.

When I got to Katie's house Stacy was there with her daughter. I wasn't in the mood for her and if she said anything out if line baby or not I was going upside her head.

"Girl, our kids play so well together I wouldn't be surprised if we don't end up family later on." She said jokingly.

"Eeewwllll! They're being raised as family. I will beat Timothy's behind!" I was trying to be nice.
"Like they won't know they ain't blood." She laughed at me. "It's not like you have him calling us uncle and auntie. Give it time; Timothy will be a grown man. He's not going to be doing everything his momma tells him."
I could feel my blood boil. "My child will be.... WHY AM I ARGUING WITH YOU! MY SON WILL NOT MARRY YOUR UGLY DAUGHTER!" I crossed my arms and dared her to say something.
Katie tried to stop it but she couldn't help it. She laughed loud and hard. Stacy looked like she wanted to cry, but I was telling the truth. I told Katie I had to go before I could feel bad enough to apologize.
When I got home I called Aunt Dorothy and I told her I was home. They were coming over for dinner and to see us. Uncle Rufus gave me a big hug, and he told me he heard about what I did back home. He said he was so proud of us. I melted into his hug; I took it like my own father was saying it. Aunt Dorothy was spoiling Timothy with hugs and kisses. He was eating it all up, that little boy.
When Tim came home he looked like he forgot we were having company tonight. He kissed my cheek like usual, but there was no spark in his kiss. He was a natural chatterbox with my aunt and uncle though. I felt myself getting more and more angry. I don't know why but I was. I was reaching for the salt and Tim and my uncle started laughing about something. It made me mad, and before I could catch myself I threw the saltshaker at Tim's head. He moved of course, like he knew I was going to do it when I didn't. "Annette!" Aunt Dorothy said in shock.
Tim tried to hold back his smile, which made him grin as he continued to eat his food. "I'm sorry auntie, he gets on my nerves!"
"Telling you the truth makes you mad!" Tim said still smiling.
"I would never tell you, you couldn't do for your momma!"
"But my momma ain't your momma there's no comparison." He said matter of factly. I threw the pepper at him and he moved again. "You're just making a mess that you're going to have to clean up later." He smiled then he took a drink of his brandy.
"I HATE YOU!" I yelled.
"This is the same way you acted last time. You got something you wanna tell us?" He said still smiling.
I growled at him, "I don't want to tell you nothing! I hate you!"
"Annette! You should know nothing about your momma is ever worth arguing over. Always side with your man when it comes to her!" Aunt Dorothy said.
I started crying, "I want to tell her that the man and woman who killed my father are dead. I want her to have something nicer than that apartment."
Aunt Dorothy put her arms around me and let me cry. It felt good to let all those tears I was holding back out. "Telling your momma about them won't change how she treats you. My sister ain't right, and nothing you do is going to change that."
I cried some more cause I knew she was right, even though I wished she wasn't.
"She hasn't met Timothy yet and I'm pregnant again." I cut my eyes at Tim and he was smiling again and patting himself on the back. I wanted to throw something else at him.
"Oh baby! Congratulations! What a blessing!" She said now rocking me.
"I'm sorry for ruining dinner." I said
Tim blew air, "you didn't ruin nothing. They know you crazy."

I cut my eyes at him and he smiled back at me. The rest of the evening Aunt Dorothy talked me down from being mad at Tim. I really wanted to be mad at him and I don't know why. When my aunt and uncle left, Tim started getting comfortable on the couch watching television. "You're not coming to bed?"
"I don't want to sleep with you right now."
"Why?"
"I didn't say or do anything wrong. I'm not your enemy. It takes your aunt to talk you down. How do you think that makes me feel? I'm happy you finally came to terms with the fact that you're pregnant, but I've known for some time. I'm glad I celebrated our child with you before this crazy lady came out again."
"I'm sorry Tim." I said feeling bad.
"How sorry?" He said messing with me.
"Completely sorry."
"You don't look sorry."
I unbuttoned my blouse, I dropped it on the floor, "but I am."
Tim stared at my chest, "whoa!"
I shook my chest, "look who's back." I laughed.
"Come here," he said licking his lips.
"No! I'm going to bed. I guess I'll see you in the morning." I picked up my blouse and I went back to our bedroom. I looked in Timothy's room and he was knocked out. I put on my nightgown and then I got in the bed. Just when I thought Tim was going to be strong and hold out, he licked the back of my neck.

****

"Annette?"
"Yes?"
"It's your momma, where have you been? I been calling you for months."
"We were out of town for a little bit. How are you?" I asked hoping she'd pretend to be interested in me.
"Stressing! Mr. Lakshman needs me to pay rent and Butch moved out to go be with that girl."
"What! After she hit you?"
"I don't know why all my children find evil ways to hurt me! Can you believe he did that? He got his head so far up her butt he won't even talk to me no more. Raymond has a job and Bret and Preston, well they do what they can."
"Momma you could probably get a job at the hospital...."
She cut me off, "ain't nobody gonna hire me if I can't read!"
"I could teach you, it's not hard." I volunteered.
"How is that supposed to help me today? I need money can you help me out or not?" She barked at me.
"Momma I'm pregnant please don't yell at me."
"You gonna push out another demon spawn?"
I gasped, "MOMMA! My children are not demons."
"Unless you got some sense and started messing around, they are."
"After everything my husband has done for you, why would you say such evil things about him?"
"He ain't never did nothing for me!"
"Momma! How you gonna say that? Didn't he save Butch?"
"My son ain't never needed to be saved by no white devil!"
I couldn't take it anymore I hung up the phone in her face. She could talk about me as much as she wanted, but I would not tolerate her talking about my husband!

****

"Why my son gotta be the one? I don't want beavers in my family anymore than you do." Raynel said cracking up.
"I'm saying, watch your son around that thing. She's trying to marry her daughter off into our family already." I said laughing.
"I'm glad I don't have a son." Lauren said.
"Give it time, yours won't be safe either." I said.
"I thought you were going to lay her out!" Katie said.
I rubbed my stomach, "me too."
Raynel looked at my stomach. "Franky's been trying to get me pregnant."
"If he's trying how do you avoid it?" I asked
"It's not exactly legal yet, but I volunteered to be a guinea pig for this study. I had to forge Franky's signature and everything. I take a pill everyday and then my doctor checks me for side effects. So far so good. They said the study is showing positive results and it will probably be available to all women in a few years."
"You don't want anymore babies that bad that you'd risk your health?" Katie asked trying to hold back her tears even though her voice shook.
"I don't know...."
"Raynel!" A woman exclaimed cutting her off.
Raynel looked busted, "Auntie Gidget?"
The woman rushed out of the restaurant. "Where is she going?" Lauren asked.
"To get my daddy." Raynel said trying to catch her breath.
An older man came rushing in with his keys in his hand like he didn't believe the woman. As soon as he saw Raynel he slightly jogged to her and he threw his arms around her. He was crying loud and hard, he kept kissing her cheek and apologizing. The woman stood there dabbing her eyes cause she was crying.
"Babygirl! I'm sorry! I'm sorry! I'm sorry! I know you hate me! I'm sorry! I'm sorry! I'm sorry!" He kept pleading.
Everybody was in tears, Raynel couldn't even talk she was crying so hard. She kept trying but she couldn't. "You broke my heart daddy!"
"I know! I'm sorry! Where's the baby? Is it a boy or a girl?" He asked.
"Franklin and I have two boys." She held up her hand, "I'm married."
"Ok," he said like he was accepting it. "When do I get to meet them?"
"You want to meet them?" She asked crying all over again.
"Of course I do, they're my kin." He said.
"Franklin and I can come by later."
"I can't wait!" He said hugging his daughter again. He started crying again. He kissed her forehead, "I'm so sorry!"
When he walked away she was still trying to pull herself together. "That's not the man who put me on the train."
"Losing his daughter wised him up." Katie said wiping her tears.

****

As we walked up the path to the house we could hear them going at it. Franky's voice was roaring on the San Francisco air. Raynel's combinations were quite impressive. I bucked my eyes at Tim cause I didn't know what to do. My parents didn't argue, my father yelled and my momma listened. Tim and I argued, but I didn't know what to think of Franky arguing. Tim shook his head, he told Timothy and I to wait back by the sidewalk and then he walked to the door. He knocked and then Franky snatched the door open. I could tell he forgot we were coming over. He ran his hand over his head as he tried to pull back his emotions. Raynel opened the

window upstairs, "ANNETTE IF YOU DON'T GET YOUR FANNY UP HERE!" She yelled at me. I swallowed then I walked past the men. Timothy took off to go play with his cousins outside in the backyard. All three boys were out there. When I walked in their bedroom Raynel was pacing she was so angry. "WE WENT TO MY PARENT'S HOUSE AND THAT BIG OLE FOOL SAT THERE BARELY TALKING! Can you believe that?"
"Well…"
She cut me off, "WELL WHAT?"
"I didn't know Franky was conversational until you. He was always the man of little words."
"My parents were trying to talk to him and he was one word answers all night."
"Did they talk out the bad blood between them?" I asked.
"There wasn't a chance! He was one word Franky all night."
"Did your father at least apologize to him? You weren't the only person he wronged."
I could tell she didn't think of it that way. "No, he didn't." Then she plopped on the bed, "this isn't working Annette."
I rushed and put my arms around her. "Don't say that! You and Franky are in love, you're going to have a happily ever after." I cried.
"No, my man isn't happy with me. I can't do this!"
"NO! RAYNEL! Franky loves you!"
"Then why does he need other women?" She cried.
"He don't love them, he loves you!"
"No!" She shook her head, "NO!" She stood up. "We're changing the subject. You guys came over for a nice evening." She looked around the room. Then she snatched up her brush. "Let me brush your hair."
I looked at her like she was crazy. "You not about to start raking through my head taking out your frustrations on my poor hair!"
Raynel started laughing and she looked crazy as she bucked her eyes at me. "Come on ANNIE let me brush your hair!" She made her face look crazy.
"No! You're crazy! I came over for fun with my sister in-law, but instead this crazy woman makes me cry then she wants to brush my hair. I'm going home." I laughed.
Franky walked in the room and he mouthed thank you to me, and then he hugged his wife with his big ole arms. Raynel hugged him back as she cried and apologized. Franky apologized as well.

Timothy

"What's wrong?" Franky asked Pops as he sat there looking disturbed.
"I missed a move!" Pops said angrily.
"What?" Dale asked.
"Your Aunt is coming out to visit." Pops said beyond irritated.
"Who?" Dale asked
"Ingrid!"
"So what's the plan?" Franky asked.
"I'm securing the door to my office. No business conducted from home. Also this widow needs a man. Find someone not connected, very square but not too square." Pops said, "he needs to turn her out." All of us grimaced. "They're desperate and I don't put anything past them. Jeff, you and Lauren will be double dating with her until she's open."

"Tim was the last one to interact with her. Wouldn't she feel more comfortable with him?"
Pops's face turned red, something that rarely happened. "You know your momma's family."
"Pops what happened to her husband?" I asked.
"Her family found out he was passing. Didn't matter how much she loved him, not even to her." Pops frowned, "it did but then it didn't. My bottom line is she could've ran away with her husband, tried to fight for her man. He's gone and she's there with them." Pops said angry. Normally momma was the one to get angry about stuff like this and Pops would take care of it. "Subject change real quick. Since you all have decided to bless us with grandchildren, your momma and I have decided that we need to reinstate our annual camping trips. Our family is getting bigger and the children need to see that we all come together. Matt," Pops shook his head. "I hope you love that Truvy girl cause you can't change up again. Your momma will kill you."
"I've been trying to give her space to adjust." Matt said.
"No woman likes to sit back and watch another woman get messed over. I'm not saying Maureen didn't deserve it. That stupid story you told your momma, didn't stick like you thought it would. Besides, you're trying to be a reputable lawyer scandals don't sit well with people."
"Everything is going like it should." Matt said with no emotion in his face.
"Do I even wanna know what that means?" Jeff asked Matt.
Matt looked at me; "don't fall in love with a woman who loved your brother first. It'll kill her."

****

That meeting with my family shook me. I keep looking at my wife and I wonder. Could she have loved Franky back? Franky and Raynel are on their last leg, especially since she has her family back. The time bomb is ticking. I don't want to have to kill my brother if he starts looking at my woman again.
I stroked Annette's beautiful face, "hello gorgeous!"
"Hey pretty boy!" She teased.
"Wrong on both counts, I'm handsome and I'm a man!" I smiled.
"Yes you are!" She kissed me.
"I need a minute to fill you out without you flipping out. Can you handle it?"
She smiled, "I hope it's not like last time." She said playfully raising her fist.
I exhaled, "I'm only a man. You have mood swings all the time. I'm not allowed to have one from time to time?"
"No!" She laughed, and then she rubbed my head. "What's on your mind?"
"Franky," I watched her eyes.
"I know, isn't it sad? I hope they can work it out, because I'm not giving up Raynel. I like how she does my hair. And you see what happened to Lauren's hair when she tried someone new."
"What? I thought she cut her hair on purpose." I said in surprise.
Annette laughed still rubbing my head. "No, she had to do it after all the damage happened. She says short hair is not the wedding look she wants. So, we're waiting to see how long she'll need to grow her hair back out. At least I won't be pregnant in the wedding."
"I was wondering," I looked her in her eyes. "Did anything happen with you and Franky that I don't know about?"

Annette frowned, "you are freaking out." Then she exhaled, "as far as I know I've told you everything. I didn't know about his feelings until that morning. The way I see it is that he was missing Raynel. Some how I reminded him of her."
"Did you ever feel anything for him?"
"He was my guardian angel, but I never had loving feelings for him. He wasn't gonna bully me like he did everyone else."
"You loved Luther though."
She exhaled, "he was a man and I was a little girl. I didn't know any better than to love him."
"If something happened to me, would you go back to him?"
She was quiet thinking for a minute. "Who could ever love me like you do? I know I'm difficult, and I act a fool around here. You understand me and let me have my fits. I'm not stupid I know what your brothers do, you save everything for me. No other man does that, who could ever be more perfect for me?" I smiled, "what about you? If something happened to me would you go back to that girl who came to your house?"
"Yuck! If something happened to you, I'm jumping in too. I don't want to live without you. There's only one you!"
She smiled, "what about our kids? Timothy and Lucinda are going to need you."
I laughed, "you didn't learn your lesson last time? Automatically this one is a girl?"
She grabbed my hair, "I want a girl! Can you please give me that?"
I laughed so hard, and then I put my hands on her stomach. "I don't know, I'm getting a boy vibe."
"Tim don't play!" She said laughing.
"Will you be heartbroken if it's a boy?"
"No, that will just mean that I will have to suck it up and do it again right away. I want a little girl so bad!"
"Meanwhile, you've got nieces." I said.
"And I see how you are with them. Don't tell me you don't want one of your own."
"I do, but I think about all the guns I'll need. I get tired."
"Maybe you won't need a gun. Maybe she'll meet someone like you." She smiled.
"Someone like me?" My smile dropped, "I'm good to you, but I was not good to them. I didn't even try. Our daughter deserves someone better than me."
"There's no one better than you." She said.
"True, but he's gotta be a close second."

****

"Do you have any driving experience?" I asked the young fella.
"No, but I am a fast learner." He said confidently.
I like this kid, there's something about him that seems familiar and comfortable. I saw him when I was driving in the other day. He was hitting the pavement hard looking for work. I saw my foreman trying to blow him off. The kid was giving my foreman direct eye contact standing tall and assertive. Because he wasn't being straight with him my foreman was looking everywhere but at him. So I called down and told my foreman to send him up.
The kid walked in observing everything in my office. I gave him a minute then I invited him to sit down. I asked him if he liked football. We chatted about the new stadium. Even though he relaxed some, he was smart enough to stay on point.
"I think you'll be a good fit here. I'm promoting one of my workers to a driving position and after the attrition settles there will be an entry-level position available. Are you interested?"

"YES!" He said excitedly although he did not smile.
"You have a very familiar way, do I know you or your family?"
He adjusted in his seat. "Do you know a man who goes by the name Whispers?" I nodded yes. "He is my father, but I told him I wanted to stand on my own." He explained.
I couldn't stop smiling at him, "son I understand. Does he know you were coming here?"
His eyes moved around the room. "Where is here?"
I laughed, "exactly! You start Monday. Your performance will determine how far you go with this company. I understand wanting to stand on your own, cause this business is my own. Your father is a very intelligent and wise man. Make sure you consult with him before you step. You may be happy to know whether he's stepped there before and if it's a good direction to go in."
"Thank you, I will remember that. Thank you for the opportunity. I will not let you down."
"Eugene, welcome to Ace Trucking." I said with a smile.
"Thank you sir."

****

When I walked in the door Annette was reading to Timothy and rubbing his head, while he rubbed her stomach. I smiled big as I looked at how peaceful they looked. My smile faded when I did not smell dinner, I was starving and not in the mood to hear about her being too tired to cook. I knew I was in a funky mood; Avery came to the office AGAIN causing a fuss because he was angry that he had been fired, and then he noticed Eugene. His racist remarks seemed to affect me more than anyone else there. I wanted to rip his head off, but he made sure to create this scene in front of everyone. Pops is still feeling out the law enforcement on this side of the bay. He's warned me numerous times to control my temper. Pulling back has had me in a bad mood all day. I hate bringing my mood home, but all I wanted was a home cooked meal and to go to bed. I sat down in the chair bouncing my leg waiting for them to finish their story. Annette ignored me and continued on with her love fest with our son. "Dinner?" I said as soon as the book closed.
"It was a long day and..."
I cut her off, "ALL I ASK IS THAT I HAVE A HOME-COOKED MEAL! Is that too much to ask?"
Annette blank stared at me, "why are you in a mood? What happened?"
"I came home hungry and there's no food! I'm hungry!"
"Ok, well before you have a complete melt down. We're going to your momma's for dinner."
I blank stared at Annette, "I'm hungry right now, and you want me to drive all the way to San Francisco before I can eat?"
She slowly got up and then she told Timothy to get his jacket. She walked past me without acknowledging my irritation, which irritated me more. She went in the bedroom grabbed her purse and jacket. On the way back she handed me a sandwich wrapped in foil. "Put this in your mouth and shut up. I knew you would be hungry, but you don't have to be rude about it. Don't open your mouth again until you're ready to tell me what put you in such a foul mood." She said then she took Timothy's hand and stood by the door waiting for me. She told me she was driving so I could eat my snack along the way.

After I scarfed down my sandwich I apologized for coming in the door roaring at her. Then I told her about Avery, she let me finish. Then she told me next time to tell her what was wrong and not to come in the door screaming like that.
When we got to the house my Aunt Ingrid was greeting everyone as they came in the door. She always stares at Annette and Timothy like she can't believe it when she initially sees them. Then she snaps out of it and says hello. She even hugs Annette, and I think she's fond of Timothy. She does the same thing with Raynel and her boys, Franky gets mad immediately.
Pops announced the location of our family trip and the dates. As we sat down Mr. Yeck rang the doorbell. He came with a bouquet of flowers and admiration for my Aunt. You could tell she was not used to male attention, as she acted very awkward when he complimented her dress. After dinner he invited my aunt to go for a walk around the neighborhood. When they came back Pops invited Mr. Yeck along on our trip. Momma asked where he was going to sleep, and he said Mr. Yeck could bring his own tent. Aunt Ingrid was going to share a tent with Beth.

****

"Annette this is Eugene, he's Whisper's son." I said
Annette kind of stared at Eugene like she was looking for the resemblance. "Nice to meet you."
"Likewise." Eugene pointed to her stomach, "what are you hoping for?"
Annette rubbed her belly, "a girl of course." Then she looked at him. "You got a family?"
"No ma'am, I'm a young man about town. I haven't found the right girl yet." He said
"Un huh," she said eyeing him.
I chuckled, "my wife is forever reading people."
"Stop spreading your seed. I can tell you like to fast talk women. I can see it all over you." She said rubbing her stomach.
He looked at me, "is it ok?"
"Remember you're talking to my wife."
"There's no fast talk necessary. These little girls are fast these days. I'm not intentionally spreading anything." He said matter of factly.
"Doesn't remove your responsibility to any babies you make. You hear me?" She said firmly.
"Yes ma'am. I hear you." He smiled.
Whispers's voice rumbled out of nowhere. "You need to find a nice girl and settle down."
"I will settle down when you do." Eugene said to his father.
"You don't know what I've done, I could be settled already." Then Whispers looked at us, "so everything is ready. You all have a safe trip, and I'll report back to you when you come back."
Annette stared at me when they walked away. I told her we'd talk about it in the car. Jeff, Lauren, Jeremiah, Katie, and Kiah squished into Sadie with us. Pops had a van with all of his camping gear strapped to the top of the car. Mr. Yeck asked Aunt Ingrid to ride with him, and he conveniently had all his gear in the back, so he only had room for her in his car. The look on momma's face said she was going to drill Pops with questions about Mr. Yeck as soon as they got on the road. I was happy I wasn't riding in that car.

Timothy and Kiah sat in the front with Annette and I. I let Timothy hold on to the steering wheel and he got so tickled by the idea that he was driving. Annette cleared her throat as she looked at me. “What exactly is your question?”
“Whispers isn’t married?”
“No, but as you see he has kids.”
“How many kids does he have?”
“I don’t know, but he has a lot.”
“He’s still having kids.” Jeff volunteered.
“He is?” Annette said in shock.
“Whispers isn’t ugly.” Katie said
“He’s not?” Jeremiah said giving his wife a look.
“Oh come on, just because you’re married doesn’t mean you don’t notice when someone else is nice looking.” She said.
“Yes it does!” Jeremiah said.
Everyone started laughing. Annette looked at me, “do you agree with Katie or Jeremiah?”
I looked at Jeremiah and Katie in the rear view mirror. “Trouble makers!” I shook my head; “I only have eyes for you my love!”
Annette cut her eyes at me. “You’re not telling the truth.”
I gasped, “how could you doubt me?” I said playfully.
She smiled at me, “cause I know for a fact that you may not have a reaction to it, but you know when someone is attractive.”
“How do you know this for a fact?” I asked, thinking she had nothing.
“How did you get Jeff to come on our picnic?”
The car fell silent and then Jeff busted out laughing. “She got you!”
“Huh? What am I missing?” Lauren asked.
“Girl I’m gonna tell you how they conversation went.” She cleared her throat I guess mimicking the way I speak, cause she deepened her voice and her gestures and manner of speaking were now smooth. “Jeffery I need you to come on this picnic. Lauren is cool, she cute, she ain’t no Annette though.”
Jeff couldn’t breathe he was laughing so hard. I was so tickled to know she knew me so well. “I don’t sound like that and that’s not what we said.”
“Yes you do and that was pretty close.” Jeff said laughing.
I looked at Jeff, “you’re supposed to be on my side.” I laughed then I glanced at Annette who was still smiling at me. “You just proved my point, I only have eyes for you.”
“And I proved my point that you notice when someone else is nice looking.” Then she put her hand out to Katie, who smacked it like they were tag teaming us. “So Whispers has a ton of kids, still having them, and his son is following in his footsteps. That’s too bad.” She was quiet for a minute, “Could you have kids you don’t know about?”
I sighed, “man! I highly doubt it, but I guess anything’s possible.”
“What about you?” Lauren asked Jeff.
“I will say the same thing that Tim said, highly unlikely, but anything’s possible.”
“What if someone showed up right now with a child, would you postpone the wedding? Or call it off altogether?”
“You mean postpone it longer than you have?” He snapped, and then he caught himself. “No, I wouldn’t do that. The only way we’re not getting married is if you die.”
“If I die, you could die too.”

"Death wouldn't stop me from marrying the little girl who has stolen my heart." Katie and Annette said, "Aw!" Like they liked his answer. Apparently Lauren liked his answer too cause she threw her arms around him and they started kissing.
"I guess that's something we don't have to worry about, we were each other's first." Katie said proudly.
"That's so special." Annette said smiling at them, "you two amaze me. You're so in love." She said like it touched her.
"Um, we're just as in love as they are." I said.
"But there's is different." Annette said idealistically.
"We're just as in love as they are too." Jeff said as he abruptly stopped his kissing fest.
"But their love is different." Lauren said agreeing with Annette.
Then the debate began. Some how we let these women trick us into debating over which couple was more in love. Yes, we fell for it for a while, until I noticed how we were doing all the talking and the women were sitting back and eating it all up. Jeff and Jeremiah caught on at the same time as I did. "It's ok, cause I'm the finest man that's why I'm getting married last." Jeff said.
"You might be cute, but you're not finer than my man." Annette said.
"Or mine!" Katie said.
"You're crazy Jeff is the most handsome." Lauren argued.
We sat back and enjoyed how the tables turned. We laughed so hard all the way to the Lake. After we got our tents set up it was time to eat. Even though they were trying to be polite to each other, the spark wasn't there with Franky and Raynel. Franky took all three boys with him everywhere and Raynel stayed with the girls. Dale and Blanche were fine, and Matt was doing everything in his power to try to get momma not to be mad at him. She wasn't being mean to him, but she didn't have her normal loving way about her with him. She showered little Matt and Jennifer with love and attention like she always has, but she was not happy about their dad.
All the men including Mr. Yeck and the boys went fishing. We left the girls behind to do their girlie things. In between fish bites we talked about life, poked fun at each other drank lots and lots of beer. It was no secret that Franky was depressed about his marriage. Pops asked him why he wasn't being more covert with his escapades. Franky said he wasn't putting it in her face. It didn't matter cause she knew how to read him, and it was like she could see it all over him.
Franky put his foot down, he told us he was telling her that they were moving into the new house. All of us told him that approach was a bad idea. He shrugged and said it didn't matter; he was in the doghouse anyways.
We brought our fish back and cleaned them, cooked them, and served them to our women. Fernando didn't want anything to do with the dead animals. He cried when we caught the fish and hit their heads to kill them. He hated when we gutted them and cleaned them. He wouldn't eat them, everyone looked at him like how did he come from Franky. If he didn't look just like him we would all wonder. Little Franky got the boy to calm down and man up as much as a little boy could.
At night I helped Annette down to the ground to lay on our sleeping bags. We looked up at the stars through the tent and talked about all kinds of things. How much we loved each other, my favorite topic, our hopes and dreams for our children. We were in the middle of a conversation and it was pretty late when Annette stopped talking cause we heard a moan. We smiled and then we asked each other who did we think it was. Apparently it was freak hour cause then we heard

another set of moans. One was on the right and the other was on the left. We kept moving from side to side trying to place the voices. I guess everyone heard each other and let go. The sounds of lovemaking filled up our campgrounds.
In the morning everyone was acting normal, so I stood under the tree and called everyone's attention. "I would just like to say, that family coming together is a beautiful thing. I'm loving all the love in the air right now, and the camp site wide orgy was spectacular!" I heard gasped, coughs, and chokes. "Don't be ashamed everyone, passion is important. Passion is needed, besides we weren't ashamed last night." I laughed, "I say tonight we have a competition to see who can be the loudest." I laughed.
"Tim!" Momma snapped, "cut it out! There will be no competition if I can't compete!" Everyone including myself turned green. "Un huh! It ain't so cute when I'm talking about it is it?" Momma fussed, "got me and my man stuck with all the kids while y'all out scaring all the animals away."
That night we had fun mocking animal noises and being silly. I think I embarrassed everyone enough, and if that wasn't a mood killer, momma saying she wanted to join the fun killed it for everyone.
Pops's plan worked; Aunt Ingrid and Mr. Yeck were completely open. My aunt didn't spend one night in the tent with Beth as originally planned.

****

"Hello?" I said
"Are you two coming or what?" Franky said
"We're coming! We're coming! You don't rush pregnant women."
"Hurry up!" Then we hung up.
Timothy was so excited, although I take him to the park and zoo all the time. The fact that all of his cousins were going to be there had him super excited. When we pulled up to Momma and Pops' house Franky was outside talking to Christy. I didn't like the look of their exchange, and by the look on Annette's face she didn't like it either. Franky had to know momma was watching even if Raynel wasn't. I don't know what's wrong with him but I shot him a look like he needed to cut it out. "Timothy," Christy said.
"Christy."
It was quiet, "um hello!" Annette said.
"Hi," she said unenthusiastically.
"If you can't greet my wife don't speak to me!"
"You guys are so sensitive!" She said walking to her car.
Franky turned around and walked towards the house. As soon as he hit the porch momma was all over him. Raynel was standing next to momma breathing so hard her chest was moving in and out like her breathing was labored. Both of them were on him. Matt was so happy not to be the one in trouble that he suggested that we take the kids so they didn't have to watch this scene play out.
We loaded all the children in the van and then we went to the zoo. Dale and Blanche each had a child in their arms. They were pointing out the animals and mimicking the sounds. Matt looked at the monkey enclosure. "Truvy is pregnant, I don't know how to tell momma." Matt said
"You're looking to me to tell you how?" I said bucking my eyes at my brother.
"Yes, Maureen isn't getting out. I can't divorce her, what do I do with Truvy? She doesn't deserve to give birth like this. I need momma to give her a chance."
"I don't know what to tell you. You can't marry her while you're married to Maureen. Why won't you divorce her?"

“There’s a lot of legal tape around it, let’s just say I lose a lot of control if I do.”
I squinted at him. "I don’t want to know what that means. Just man up and deal with it. Momma will get over it. Franky was in the doghouse for a long time when he showed up married with two kids, but she got over it. Just….”
Matt grabbed my shirt, “that’s it!”
“What’s it?” Matt kissed my cheek and I punched him, “what’s the matter with you?”
“You’re a genius! Thank you! Watch the kids I need to use the pay phone.” He ran over to the phone.
Annette came over. “What’s up with him?” She said rubbing her belly.
“As far as I can tell, its trouble.”

Chapter 19

Annette

Just like last time Irma was over cooking, cleaning, and pampering me. This baby caught us both by surprise when she decided that she wanted to come two weeks earlier than the doctor said she would. I was taking my breakfast plate to the sink when my water broke. Irma called Tim and it seemed like he had wings and he flew home. Timothy kept looking at me with big eyes and telling me he loved me. He didn't understand what was happening. Irma was very excited and she made him laugh and laugh as she told him we were having a baby. Tim kissed me goodbye, and I wondered if our fun this morning is what caused the baby to come early.
Now that the baby had our attention it wanted to be slow about coming. I relaxed when I heard the baby cry, and I cried when the doctor said it was a boy. Out of nowhere I thought of Rudy's comment about having two boys and I wanted to find him so I could stab him!
I didn't rip like last time, and the baby wasn't as big thank goodness. However, the doctor still had to cut me so I still had to deal with stitches. Irma brought him close to me and said, "look at all of this hair. What a waste huh!" Then she laughed. Then she told the baby he needed to come meet his father and brother. I awoke when they took me to my room. Timothy kissed me and then he told me to tell him when I was ready. Meaning he knew I was going to be determined to get my little girl now.

Timothy

When momma brought the baby out she smiled real big as she introduced me to my son. I felt a little disappointed to have been right. One look at my son and I knew it was perfect that he was here. Timothy got so excited to see he had a little brother. The baby responded immediately to my voice. Just like Timothy he knew exactly who I was and I was so happy another piece of me is here. I asked momma how Annette was doing; she smiled and said a lot better this time.
Momma took Timothy home with her while I spent the night with Annette and the baby. Annette was a lot more energetic and responsive this time. "Do you think he looks like Timothy?"
I held him up, "a little but he has his own look. He looks like me, but not the same way Timothy does."
Annette smiled, "isn't that something. I think he looks more like my father and Elmer jr."
"Are you saying that because he's lighter than Timothy?"
"No, I'm looking at his face."
"He has a sprinkle of you in his face, so I guess that could be your dad."
"Wait until Harriet and Claudette see all this hair. They're gonna call him a pretty boy."
"Just because he got all this hair?"
"He's real pretty, I wonder what his personality will be like." She said excitedly.
I smiled at her, "I love how well you're taking all of this."
Annette smiled then she put her head on my shoulder. "I was scared that my boys would be dogs like my brothers. Seeing how Elmer jr is turning out, I can see that how you raise your boys has a lot to do with how they come out. Timothy is so sweet to me, and I make sure he's always nice to girls. Between me and your momma, our boys won't be like my brothers."
"Just you and my momma?"

She bumped me, "you know what I mean. The way my father talked to my momma set the stage for my brothers to look at women a certain way. Then my momma only made things worse. Maybe Bret and Preston will turn out different too? They were little when all that happened."
"Maybe." I said, "so.... How do you feel? Momma said it wasn't as bad."
She exhaled, "next time will you come in?"
"Instead of momma?"
"No in addition. I hate going through all that and you're nowhere to be found. Your momma is good about making them keep me comfortable, but I need you."
I smiled; I didn't like the whole waiting game and not knowing what was happening on the other side. "I'll be right there."

Annette

“Good morning Mal-da-Kai!” Timothy whispered bringing a book to read to his little brother. Malachi's little eyes popped open and he watched Timothy read him a story. Malachi wants to talk so badly; he watches your lips as you talk to him. It was a challenge at first with two babies. I was out numbered, but Timothy is such a good big brother he makes things easier.
Timothy is my little helper; he wants to help me with everything for the baby. He takes his job of carefully holding the safety pins for the baby’s diaper seriously while I change him. When I bathe the baby Timothy holds the towel for me until I need it. He’s very involved in everything with the baby. He's very protective of him and he asks me why I do everything. Then I see him repeating what I've told him, he's so smart.
When Raynel brought the boys over to play with Timothy. Timothy spent a lot of that time telling them about his baby brother.
“He’s so pretty I forget he’s a boy.” Raynel said rocking the baby.
“I know, but every time I change his diaper there’s the reminder that nope, it’s a boy.”
Raynel was trying to hold on to her smile. “It’s not that I wouldn’t want to have more babies with Franklin. I just can’t do it when I know that means I’ll be trapped.”
“I’ve been trying to hold my tongue, but Tim told me you moved out. Is there anything I can say to make you change your mind?”
“Not after what happened. For a moment I was trying to convince myself that the other women didn’t matter. I know he loves me, but sometimes love isn’t enough to make a relationship work. If he has to have other women then it means that our relationship is lacking something. I’m giving him everything I have.”
“I don’t want you two to get a divorce.”
“Neither does Franklin, he said he refuses to give me one.”
“So what are you going to do?”
“He’s going to live in that big ole monstrous house. I’m moving out here with my parents, and Franklin’s going to finance a shop for me.”
“That’s a good idea, I will be your number one customer.”
Raynel tried to smile, “you’ll need to have enough babies for me to get my baby fix. This little fella is so precious! Little Franky is going to be starting kindergarten so I need to get settled for the boys.”
“How are the boys taking not being with their father?”

"They don't understand," she wiped tears. "You heard how we've been fighting. It's not fair to them to live like that. My momma has that, told you so, look all the time so I avoid her as much as I can."
"You two will get back together, he loves you. And I know you love him. This break up is only temporary, I can feel it."
"I doubt it." She said trying to shake her mood.

****

Dear Annette,
It was really nice talking with you the other day. I know you're probably surprised to receive a letter when we normally speak over the phone these days. I just don't know how to tell you, and I don't think I could handle hearing hurt or disappointment in your voice. You are the closest thing I have to a sister and we never meant to hurt you. I was lonely one evening and Luther and I got to talking. At first it was all about you and how much we love you. Then our loneliness came to the surface and before we could control ourselves it happened. Please don't hate me, but we were wedded a month ago. Now you probably understand my hesitation about you coming out. Luther is a good father to my children, and he has grown up to be a good husband thanks to you. I now know what you and Claudette feel about your husbands, and it kills me to say it, but I think Emma should come out for business. I will always love you, and no one could ever replace you in my heart. I hope you understand.

I'm so sorry,
Harriet

I stared at the letter all day, crying my eyes out. When Tim came home I showed him the letter and he helped me workout my thoughts to respond to her. I thought he would misunderstand my tears and think that somehow my tears were for Luther. I was so relieved when he understood me. So I replied the following:

Harriet,
No one could be happier than me, to know that you've found love and happiness in your life. What I'm struggling with is why our life long friendship had to end because of it. Seeing as you have already made up your mind there isn't much else to say. I will not come back out there per your wishes. I will sign over my ownership to Emma. Please keep in mind that Ace Trucking, Wallace & Son's, and all of my affiliates will also no longer be available to you. I'm sure you have vendors to replace them.

Annette ***Wallace***

****

"Annette he's so pretty." Beth said snuggling up to Malachi.
"Thank you, and he's a good baby too."
"Auntie I want to hold the baby." Kiah announced.
"Ok but you have to sit down."
Kiah happily sat on the couch, and I carefully placed Malachi in her arms. Kiah smiled so big at the baby as he watched her face as if he was begging her not to

drop him subliminally. Irma and Katie snapped a bunch of pictures as they oohed and awed the moment. Peggy and Miranda came in the door with the baby in her arms, and her pregnant belly. Beth shot up and took the baby.
"Good, I'm glad you're all here now. I picked out these three patterns, but I'm not opposed to going through the department store catalog." Lauren said excited about her wedding.
"Are we voting?" I asked.
"It doesn't matter to me, as long as you're all in agreement."
"Can I suggest as the mother that you let the department store do all the work? I know between all of you, you have some pretty talented seamstresses, but lets go with as little fuss as possible. Now, I still have the catalogs from Peggy's wedding if you all want to browse them."
"Your dress needs to be a little different." Lauren said to me.
I smiled really big, "am I your maid of honor?"
"Are you kidding? Of course you are! If it wasn't for you and Tim, Jeff and I never would've met."
I hugged her and kissed her. As soon as she stepped out of the room we started talking about her bridal shower. Everything was happening within six months. We had very little time to play around. She picked out harvest orange dresses and a buttery burgundy for me. She told us to relax and that everything would look perfect for her fall wedding. Raynel pulled Lauren to the side and she asked if she was sure she wanted to have her in her wedding. Lauren said she was positive. She said if the only way she could get her way was to put Franky and Raynel together in her wedding then so be it. Raynel later told me that her parents question her and give her a hard time about being involved with the family when she and Franky aren't together anymore. I told her to tell them they weren't divorced and to mind their own business.

Timothy

The man at the gate opened it as soon as he saw it was me. I drove up the hill admiring the trees Franky had installed. I opened the door, "Franky!" I called out. There was no response. Then I saw Franky sitting in a chair with his back to me. It looked like he was enjoying the sunlight by the pool. I opened the door to the back.
"What are you...."
Christy's head peeked over to the side. "Don't stop," Franky told her. "I'll be right with you Tim." He said a little breathlessly.
I turned on my heels and went back inside. I went over to the bar and poured a drink, then I went to the window to take in the breath taking view. "Tim, you can go out now." Christy said as she grinned at me.
I didn't like it, I walked out back and Franky was smiling in his chair. At least he fixed his clothes. "You look relaxed."
"I needed an afternoon pick me up." Then he looked at me, "I have a feeling you're going to bring me down again."
"You're selling the San Francisco house?"
"Yep! She don't want it, I don't want it. I don't want to see it ever again!"
"Why?"
"Cause she won't be there. She ran to her daddy's house when I started packing."
"You're getting a divorce?"

"NO!" He growled. "One day she's going to learn what a man needs and when she does I'll be waiting for her. I'm not divorcing the love of my life so she can marry someone else and give them what I have been begging for."
"This is an extremely big house for one person." I said looking around.
Franky rolled his eyes, "Fernando and Christy are here."
"What are you saying?"
"I let her move in." He said lowly.
"What about when Raynel finds out, or worse, momma?"
"If Raynel was taking care of her man there would be no Christy! It's my life, momma will get over it."
"If you say so, I'm not so sure."
Franky shrugged me off, "you come to talk business or just get in mine?"
We went over the plan for distributions. Our product demands have increased, so we've had to be more creative with our shipping. Thanks to Jeremiah the grocery supply and distribution division has grown. I moved a lot of my drivers over to Jeremiah since a lot of them started under him. This gave me space to put more of Pops, Jeff, and Franky's men as my actual drivers. Knowing that we have strong confident drivers provides more confidence in our moving capabilities. We haven't had to do any candy shows in some time. I told Pops I wasn't in that place anymore.
When Franky and I walked in the house Christy was laying naked on the couch by the window, trying her best to pretend like she was sleeping. I squinted my eyes at Franky. He picked up an orange out of the fruit bowl and threw it so hard it exploded on her chest. Christy gasped as she popped up. Franky kept picking up fruit and no matter where she moved he hit his target. Each time he hit her a bruise immediately surfaced. He told her to take her nasty behind in the bedroom. I asked him where Fernando was, and he said he was in school. Christy cried as she ran to the bedroom. I asked him what was wrong with her. He said he made the mistake of expressing how conservative his wife is, and she has taken that as license to be the complete opposite. He said she would do anything for attention, and then he looked at me and repeated, "ANYTHING!"

****

"Timothy! Your boys are so precious! I'm very happy for you." Auntie Ingrid said slurring her words.
I laughed, "how many of those have you had?"
"I feel great! I'm free! I got a man! A real white one this time." Then she got sad. "I still love him Timothy! That man was good to me. Better than my father and brothers. They took me away kicking and screaming." She started crying, "I didn't know about him." She threw her arms around herself spilling a little of her drink on the ground. I'll never know love like that again!"
"What about Mr. Yeck?"
"It's not the same. He wants to marry me, ME! He's good to me, but I think he doesn't want to die alone. I don't neither so..." She shrugged.
Pops noticed that her mouth was running. He moved closer so he could hear. "What made you decide to come out here after all this time? You could've found someone a long time ago."
"Vladimir wanted me to come and see how Irma was doing. He's convinced she has it out for him."
"If she did, could you blame her?"

She started rocking, "no. He got mad at me when I told him there was nothing to tell. All of you work so hard, doctors and lawyers. All of your businesses. He's up to no good! He got so mad at me he told me to stay out here. He's keeping Mischa of course, she don't know no better."
I pointed my eyes at her, "do I want to know what that means?"
She sighed, "no. My sick little twisted family secrets." She looked away. "My sister is very loving with all of you. I don't know where she got that from."
"Lady B," I said staring her in her eyes.
"Irma was like her baby. As soon as she could talk she was asking for Lady B."
"How come you weren't close to Lady B? My parents said she was just the help. In order for her to take care of Irma like she did they had to bond. My parents didn't expect Irma to turn out the way she did behind it though."
I stood there trying not to take offense to the words of a drunk person. "How could they know she would end up with such a wonderful family, right?"
She shook her head in agreement, "especially yours and Franklin junior's. Seems like you two picked the most beautiful colored girls too."
"The fact that they're beautiful doesn't matter right? Our families are still beautiful regardless, right?"
"Right," she said picking up on my tone. She looked around, and then she stumbled off to my momma who was watching us from across the yard as well. Momma was bouncing Malachi on her knee.
The kids cheered as Franky came in the yard with boxing gloves. "Let Uncle Franky and Uncle Jeff show you how it's done." He said handing a pair of gloves to Jeff. I finished the last dab of barbecue sauce on the meat then I closed the grill so the meat could cook some more. I grabbed Timothy and I spoke in his ear while my brothers boxed. I told him to go for the nose just like I showed him. Timothy stood there taking in everything. I couldn't have been prouder to see the killer instinct in his eyes. When they asked who wanted to go first, I told Timothy to go get them.
"Ok, so we got Timothy and Fernando. This is going to be good." Jeff said, "killer against killer. Remember gentlemen you're supposed to see blood. You ready?" He looked between the both of them, "GO!"
Timothy came out strong hands up and blocking, and he's only four. I stuck my chest out with so much pride. Timothy walked around in a circle like he saw his uncles just do, Fernando followed his lead. Fernando swung wild at Timothy, and Franky frowned. He swung wild again and he actually landed a good punch on Timothy. Timothy looked surprised and then he looked at me. I told him to put his hands up and go get him. Timothy put his hands up and then he rushed Fernando. He hit him with a right, left, another right, and another left. Fernando fell backwards and immediately started crying. Franky was livid! "STOP!" Franky commanded. Timothy looked at me and I smiled so proudly at him. He smiled big at my confirmation that he did a good job. "SHUT UP WITH ALL THAT CRYING BEFORE I GIVE YOU SOMETHING TO CRY ABOUT BOY! YOU GONNA CRY LIKE A LITTLE SISSY JUST CAUSE HE KNOCKED YOU DOWN? YOU'RE BIGGER THAN TIMOTHY FOR NOTHING!" Franky looked at Timothy. "Let me have those gloves." Timothy took them off and gave them to his uncle. "You're going to fight Ethan."
"No daddy, I don't want to fight anymore." Fernando said.
"Shut up, before I make you fight Franklin. You better fight for real, or I'm gonna whip you!" Franky told his son. Ethan happily put the boxing gloves on and prepared to fight. Fernando got up still crying, he took a deep breath and then he

weakly put his hands up. In one motion Franky yanked his belt off and popped Fernando. “I SAID FIGHT! STOP ACTING LIKE A SISSY!” He said with his belt still in his hand.

Fernando put up a good fight; Ethan threw heavy punches at his big brother. Fernando got a couple of decent punches in as well, but Fernando wasn’t a match for anyone. Even little Kiah laid him out.

“I want next!” Liam said looking over my fence.

“These kids can fight better than you, you might want to go back across the street before you get embarrassed.” Jeff said.

“You and me, let’s go!” Liam said inviting himself into our yard.

“Tim who is that?” My momma said annoyed.

“My ill-mannered neighbor.”

“I don’t want you guys hurting your neighbors.”

“But momma I could understand if he were a nice boy. He hits his momma!” Jeff said putting on his gloves.

“HE DOES WHAT?” Momma yelled.

Liam smiled, “she told you that?”

“She didn’t have to, we got eyes.”

“Carry on then, don’t kill him Jeff.” Momma said getting comfortable to watch.

Everyone was now watching, Liam automatically assumed that his size gave him an advantage with my big brother. Clearly he doesn’t know the Wallace’s. I told Timothy to watch Liam to see what a clown does. Dale told them to break and immediately Liam starts dancing. You heard a few of the kids say wow! Jeff was watching Liam’s cockiness with a smile. Liam told Jeff he’s been waiting a long time to do this. Liam tapped Jeff a couple times, and right when he thought he was going to knock Jeff good. Jeff blocked the hit and proceeded to hit Liam so hard he hopped backwards. Liam stood there shaking his head for a minute. Jeff smiled and waited for him to get it together. Liam wasn’t talking anymore, he was mad and vengeful. He danced around a little more and Jeff toyed with him, he kept hitting Liam and stunning him, but not knocking him out. Liam was no longer happy on his feet. He was angry and embarrassed. Momma told Jeff to stop playing with him. Jeff said, “ok momma.” With one hit Liam flew backwards and he was knocked out. All the kids said, “WOW!” Jeff put his gloves up. “What did you learn today children?”

“The bigger they are the harder they fall.” Little Frank said.

“Yes, and what else?” Jeff said holding his glove out to give someone else the floor. He pointed to Darren, “don’t hit your momma?”

“Yes, and what else?” Jeff asked looking around the kids. They all sat there scratching their heads at a loss. “Never go against your Uncle Jeff!"

****

The door was locked when I turned the knob, so I knocked. Jeff and I exchanged looks. Christy opened the door with a black eye. She was trying to look as pitiful as she possibly could. “Did you lock this door?” I asked her.

“Franky is in his office.” She said sounding wounded.

Jeff and I exchanged looks. Franky was on the phone giving out orders. We sat in the chairs facing his desk. “Close the door.” Franky said putting his hand over the receiver, and then he went back to his conversation. When he got off the phone he looked at us, he looked angry. “I hit her!” He said like he needed to get it out of the way. Neither one of us said anything. “I’m having this dream about my **WIFE** and its good! You remember what it was like when you’d have a wet dream?” We

nodded, "as I'm releasing I realize I was releasing for real. When I opened my eyes and saw the wrong colored hair I went off. I hit her before I completely realized what was happening." He said sitting back in his chair like he was still mad about it.
"Why don't you kick her out, you don't even like her." Jeff said.
"She does have some use."
"Yes, but once she's off her back then what? Where's Carol?" I asked.
"She couldn't get past the fact that I married Raynel. She's trying to play wife to some guy, she creeps over from time to time."
"While Christy is here?" Jeff said getting too excited.
Franky smiled a devilish grin, "yes."
"What does Christy do? She go knit or something?" I asked.
"NO," he said still smiling.
"WHAT?" I yelled! "You are blowing my mind right now!" I jumped on my chair. "How did you get them to agree to do that?"
He acted like he wasn't going to tell us. Then he said he let Christy watch a few times. Then one day she asked if she could join them. The way he described everything had me and Jeff going crazy in that office. Nasty Franky! He said its been over a week since he hit her. His smile dropped. He said it was going to take an army to hold him back if she ends up pregnant. I told him to prepare himself he came from fertile parents. He moved angry in his chair, "I'd lose Raynel forever if that happen." He said chewing back his emotion.
"You could always have the doctor come for her if it did happen." Jeff said.
"Have you ever done that with your own child?" Franky asked him.
"No, but I don't know why you wouldn't sleep in condoms if you knew she was going to be in your bed. She's plotting on you, and you know it." Jeff said.
"She always catches me slipping. I can't have a good drink with her around, cause I know what she's going to do. I go from the prude to the exhibitionist. Tim told you what she did?" Jeff shook his head no as he waited for the story. "We walk in the house and she's trying to pretend like she's sleep naked on the couch when she knew we were just outside."
Jeff frowned, "she hot for Tim too?"
"She better not be! Someone needs to tell her about Maureen." I said.
"My name is not Matt, she should know better than to test me. Every time she looks in the mirror she should be calling herself **STUPID**!"
"I don't know man, if momma finds out you hit her…"
"If momma knew the circumstances she'd hold her up for me. She's always asking when Raynel is coming home. I don't know what to tell her, I wish I knew. The guy Whispers put on her parent's house and the shop has been doing a good job of laying low."
"Right, down to business." Jeff said.
Pops and a few of his men went to Germany to talk to our supplier. Some new guys were trying to muscle their way in on our territory. Franky carries the weight of the family on his shoulders. If it comes down to a name, all roads point to Franky. He said he was fine with that, probably cause without Raynel he felt there was nothing to lose. As a safety precaution whenever the girls went out, someone was always near by keeping an eye on them.

****

"Tim this is Detective White, he works in the Oakland police department." Pops said.

"Nice to meet you." I said observing this man.

"Likewise, I told your father if you should run into any problems to contact me first."

"Can you do something about pesky neighbors?"

"What do you need?"

"My neighbor across the street hits his momma for one thing. Ever since my brother knocked him out, he's been a pain and annoying. He's a sore loser. I don't want the woman to lose her son completely, but I need him to leave me alone. I value my sleep, this idiot likes to rise early and disturb my household with his noise."

"Consider it taken care of, he'll live." He moved his hands around, "what about around here?"

"I will need a patrol around here, the shop, and my house."

He handed me his card. "Always call me first."

Annette

We all smiled at the little ones as they tried on their little tuxedos and dresses. Even though Malachi surprised us all and started walking at nine months old, and then proceeded to run everywhere, he was still too little to be in the wedding. This little boy is a ball of energy and Irma says he acts just like Tim when he was his age. I made running after him part of my get it back program, and it didn't take me nearly as long to bounce back from having him as it did after Timothy. Malachi is very curious, but if he sees disapproval on my face he won't do whatever it is that had his attention. Just like Timothy, Malachi loves his momma. Sometimes they fight over who gets to sit in my lap, so I set each one on either side of me and I love them up. Malachi wants to do everything his big brother does, and he gets mad when we tell him he can't do certain things cause he's too little. His hair grows fast and Tim can't wait until he was a year old so he could cut it. People always mistake Malachi for a girl, but that's just because he's so pretty. I know I thought Timothy reminded me of my father, but Malachi does for sure. Especially when I used to put his long hair in one braid like my father wore his. I would look at Malachi with tears in my eyes. Malachi would think I was sad and he'd smother me with kisses. Both of my boys are momma's boys and I am so proud. They love their dad too, but momma always wins.

We were excited cause everything was set for the wedding. I was checking our last to do things off of my list. We were all set. "Momma can I have this orange?" Timothy asked stopping at the fruit stand.

"No, put it back. We're going to have lunch right now." I said going back to my list.

"But momma..." Timothy whined.

I cut my eyes at him. "You know better than to whine..."

"ANNETTE!?!?"

I looked up and my little Preston wasn't so little anymore. "Preston!" I said with a heart felt smile.

My baby ran to me and hugged me. He was getting tall, "I miss you. Why haven't you come to see me?"

"Momma," I said hoping he understood. "Say hi to your nephews."

Preston looked at my boys and said hi. He didn't have a proud uncle moment, but what could I expect from a child of momma's? "Hi," he said.
"Hi," Timothy said, Malachi just looked at him.
"So this is where you work?" I said looking up at the name of the market.
"Yes, Butch manages here he got all of us jobs."
"What are you doing here?" Butch barked at me.
Timothy and Malachi frowned at him. "She was passing by when I saw her, be nice." Preston said.
"We don't want your business, get out of here!" Butch said.
"Don't worry, now that I know you're here I wouldn't give this place one red cent!" I said grabbing my boy's hands.
"Don't let me catch you down here again!" He threatened.
"Or else what?" I said letting my boys hands go.
"You know what!"
I walked up in his face and spit in it. "You are pathetic!"
Butch reached back like he was going to hit me. Preston grabbed his arm, "Butch! Don't!"
"Naw son, let his arm go!" Whispers said coming out of nowhere. "He's not crazy enough to try nothing."
"Who are you?" Preston asked.
"You need to ask your brother who I am." Then he looked at me, "go ahead and let the boys get bags to fill with whatever they want." Then he looked at Butch. "Go get them some bags!" Whispers didn't yell or raise his voice. The raspiness of his voice and his low manner of speaking is probably why they call him that in my opinion. Butch came back with two bags. "Timothy take your brother and get whatever you want from this store. Your uncle Butch is paying for it!"
Butch was angry but he said nothing. Timothy smiled at me as he put that orange he showed me earlier in his bag. They got fruit, cereals, and candies.
Lauren walked up, "um hello? I was waiting at the car for you. What's...." Then she saw Butch, she looked at Whispers then she clasped her hands and stood quietly. Butch got angrier when he saw Lauren. Even Preston stared at her. "Since y'all got staring problems make me a bag as well!" Whispers said. "I want your best cut steak, potatoes, and vegetables. Throw a good bottle of wine in there. The most expensive one you got. Don't try to pull any tricks either. When I get home and have my meal prepared if everything isn't top quality, I will be back!"
"I can't afford all that!" Butch said.
"But you will!" He glared at him. "I've never seen you be so disrespectful to a woman."
"You don't know my sister." Butch said shaking his head.
"Actually I do, and I know for a fact you are out of line." Whispers said.
Butch's eyes got big. "How do you know my sister?"
"That's none of your business! Get my groceries so we can go."
Timothy was happy with his bag full of groceries. I told him not to spoil his appetite for lunch. Malachi drug his bag back to the front. I picked it up for him. When we walked away I heard Preston asking Butch who Whispers was. When we got to the car, Whispers was inspecting the contents of his bag. I asked him what he was doing here. He said he had a meeting down here when he saw us leaving the store, so he followed us.

In the car Lauren said Whispers and a few of the other guys have been conveniently popping up all over the place. She said sometimes Jeff seems stressed but he won't talk about it.

Timothy

"Roar! Roar! That's how the lion sounds!" Timothy excitedly told Malachi. "This is what it looks like."

I peeked at the picture he drew out of curiosity.

It was really good; my son has a good eye for details. He had the lion's mane, the pointy fangs, and claws, even his man parts. "This is really good son." Timothy smiled proudly. "I see you've got your momma's creativity."

"When is it going to stop raining? We want to go outside and play."

Malachi looked at me like Timothy was interpreting for him. "I don't know son, once it stops everything is going to be wet. Once it stops raining we can go wash momma's car for her."

"The man at the gas station already washed the window. We don't have to wash that part." Timothy said.

I continued looking at my papers. "Did he now?"

"Yep, he told momma she was too pretty to have a dirty window." Timothy said nonchalantly.

I looked at my son, "what did momma say?"

"She said thank you. I don't like the way he talk to her. She say thank you, thank you, and he keep talking." Timothy said shaking his head.

"Does mommy smile?" I knew I shouldn't pump the child for information, but Annette never mentioned a guy flirting with her at the gas station.

"Yes."

"Does she get mad?"

"Only that one time."

"Why did she get mad?"

Timothy exhaled like he was going to explain something difficult to me. "Cause! He said," Timothy made his voice deep. "Hey baby!" Then he switched to his momma's voice. "I not your baby!" Then he went back to his drawing.

Malachi sat there watching our faces like he understood what was happening.

Annette honked her horn when she was outside. I told Timothy to watch his brother and not to let him wander outside this time. Malachi is very curious and slippery. That little escape artist scaled his crib walls and came in our bedroom one morning to watch the show. We were in our groove and Malachi walks up to the bed smiling with his hands out cause he wanted to be picked up. I could've choked him. Annette bought bells for the bedroom doors. She was so traumatized. It took some severe convincing to get her open after that. She kept getting embarrassed every time he smiled at her as if this baby knew what he was looking at.

I grabbed an arm full of groceries each trip. I looked at all the bags, "we having a party?"

"I'm going to make some pies, put them in the freezer, and daily bring one to Raynel's shop for a few weeks." She smiled then she kissed my cheek. Then she kissed my neck, and then she grabbed my butt.

"So you gonna tell me about your little boyfriend?" I watched her face for a reaction.

She laughed, "besides you?" As she put groceries away.

"Cute? I'm not little in anyway. I'm talking about your little boyfriend who washes your windows." I said putting groceries in the cabinet and watching her face.
Annette stop moving, "the guy at the gas station?" I nodded, "that's just Hector. I don't take him seriously."
I tried to pull back my jealousy. "You should still mention it, otherwise you look guilty."
Annette stared at me, "if you want me to tell you every time a man flirts with me that's all we'll ever talk about. You don't come running to me every time someone flirts with you. Shoot! You're not forth coming on a lot of things on that topic." She looked at me daring me to test her.
"I tell you what you need to know." I said feeling good about myself.
"So I didn't need to know about you busting Maureen's nose?" I couldn't control it; I know I turn completely red. "Un huh! Practice what you preach Tim!"
I walked up behind her and put my body against hers. "That was different, but here's what we're going to do. You're going to go to a different gas station unless I'm in the car with you."
Annette started to say something against what I was saying until she looked at my face. She immediately pulled back her sass. "He's just a guy Tim." She said searching my face for mercy.
"My understanding is he crossed a line. He knows your married with a family." I kissed her, "someone should've told him not to even look at what's mine!"
Annette looked nervous, "couldn't you give him a warning. It's not like you're known over here like in San Francisco." She put a box in the cabinet turning her back to me.
"If he's just a guy, why would you plead for his life?" I pressed my body against hers making her brace herself against the cabinet.
"Cause he honestly didn't know. I don't say anything when they know better. I'll go to another gas station, don't hurt him."
"You like him?"
"He didn't know better."
"Annette you didn't answer me."
"A little flattery is nice every once in awhile, but I promise he only tried to fast-talk me once. I put him in his place. After that he slips in little compliments here and there but I don't want you to hurt him." She said trying to look at me, but I wouldn't let her turn around.
"If you don't tell me about it, I will be suspicious. Tell me."
"Ok! Ok! Ok! Stop being scary! That's over! Can my husband come back to the room now?" She said trying to change the mood in the room as I allowed her to turn around.
I took a step backwards, "here I am." I smiled.
She hugged me, "I'm so happy you're here. That scary guy that looks like you was just here threatening lives. I don't like when he comes out, keep him away from me ok."
"That guy handles the candy business, sometimes he has to come around."

Annette

"Hello?"
"Annette!" My momma's voice boomed through the phone.
"Yes momma," I said knowing she was upset with me.

"You messing around on your husband?" She was accusing me, she wasn't really asking me.
I drummed my fingers on the counter. "That's what you think of me? Why do you call me at all?"
"Your brother said you had that thug fighting for you." I could hear the smile in her voice. "Does he give you money?"
I took a deep breath, "no momma. It's not like that."
"Then what is it then? No man gives a woman anything for nothing."
"He's just a friend." I said.
"Yea right! Ask him if he can give one of the boys a job."
"That's why you're calling me? It always comes down to money with you. Do you ever call me cause you love me and you want to know how I'm doing?"
"You ought to be of some use to me. You are my worst child. So disrespectful, sneaky, and devious! I should've lost you instead of my other babies. You've always been worthless to me. A waste of my husband's seed."
"So why call me then?"
"Cause each time I'm hoping you will prove me wrong."
"Momma I always happily gave you everything I had, and it was never good enough."
"Elmer is gone because of you! You owe me!"
"HE'S NOT GONE BECAUSE OF ME! HE'S GONE BECAUSE OF YOU! HE LEFT YOU FOR GOOD AND YOU KNEW IT! THE ONLY WAY YOU COULD KEEP HIM AROUND WAS TO KEEP ME AND EMMA! YOU CHOSE THEN TO STAND UP TO HIM AND IT COST HIM HIS LIFE! HE WAS WRONG FOR LEAVING US MOMMA! HE WAS WRONG FOR EVERYTHING HE DID! HIS DEATH WAS HIS FAULT!"
I could hear her crying, which I wasn't expecting. She wasn't one to fake cry, I immediately felt bad. "Elmer was the only man to love me. I should've been a better wife! I should've tried to make him happier." She cried.
"Momma you did everything you could to make him happy I was watching. I saw you, I saw it all."
"I did?" She sound surprise to hear me say it.
I swallowed, "my daddy loved you. You were his one true love. The money was getting low with that woman. He was going to find a husband for me and then you know he was coming back to you. He always came back to you." I hoped my lie made her feel better.
"He was wasn't he." She said calming down. "Then why was he making it seem like he loved you more than me?"
"He didn't mean to. Outside of sweet talking you when did he ever say anything right?" She giggled, I exhaled a little. It sound like I was finally getting my momma to love me just like she loved everyone else. "He loved you momma."
She exhaled, "you're right. I wish he was here now."
"Me too."
"Is that why you agreed to be the white people's dog? You punishing yourself over what happened with your daddy?"
I tensed up, "I'm not anybody's dog. I fell in love with my husband and we have a family because of our love."
"White men don't love colored girls! Stop lying to yourself!"
"Momma why do you do this? You can't help who you fall in love with. You've seen us, you know that man loves me."

"All I saw was you all over a white man like I ain't teach you to be better than that. You let all the neighbors see you throwing yourself all over him like you ain't got no sense. He's going to use you up and then leave you holding the bag. He...."
I hung up the phone!

****

"Mrs. Wallace is everything to your liking?" The hotel manager asked me.
I looked around the room in amazement. This room was very standard when I came by this morning. Now there's beautiful flowers, this room was setup for royalty! They brought in chairs, linens, crystal, silver, and beautiful china. They draped beautiful silks, chiffons, and tulle matching Lauren's wedding colors from the ceiling and along the walls. I looked around so excited you would've thought it was my shower. Even the piano was dressed nicely for the occasion. "It's beautiful!" The manager smiled proudly, then he told me to sample the food. It was all delicious. He asked me if I needed anything else for my party. I shook my head no. I told him I would be back with the rest of my party. When I got home Tim was wrestling with the boys in the living room. I looked at all three of them like they have lost their minds. They know I don't allow rough housing in the living room. Both of the boys took off running leaving their daddy to save himself. "Is this what you all do when I'm not home?" I cut my eyes at him.
"Um! Did I tell you how beautiful you are today?" Tim said hurrying over to kiss me.
"Un huh, Tim you need to teach them to confine their rough housing to the backyard, not in the house." I said walking to the bedroom.
"Yes ma'am!" Tim said grabbing a handful of my butt.
"Cut it out, I gotta get ready. Your momma and everyone will be here in an hour."
He looked at the clock, "momma said she was coming at 5:30."
"And you know you're momma always come early so cut it out."
Tim was fifty million arms and hands all over my body. "You came in the door looking so beautiful. I need you." He said then he kissed my neck.
I could feel myself giving in. "No Tim!" I didn't say convincingly.
He smiled at me. "I'll be right back."
"No Tim!" I whined, "you're going to make me late and everyone will know it's your fault." He continued out the room.
I ran to the shower and I made the water as cold as I could stand it. If he brought his butt in here it was his fault. Tim came in the bathroom and stripped. He screamed when the cold water hit him. I laughed so hard. "You did that on purpose." Then he kissed me.
My plan backfired; I thought the cold is supposed to make them shrivel up. "Wait a minute! Wait a minute!" I tried to find clarity. "Where's the condom?" Tim exhaled like he forgot. Then he shrugged it off and made me hit operatic notes I didn't know I could hit. Tim kissed me for a long time as he rendered everything he had to give me. The cold water didn't even seem cold anymore. Then he got out of the shower, dressed, and went back to the boys like that didn't just happen. Here I was knees weak and he was fine. As soon as I sat in front of my vanity I was mad. He got my hair wet and everything. I cursed him.
Then there was a knock on the door and it slowly opened. "It's me," Raynel said peeking her head in.
I made sure my robe was closed and I told her to come in. Raynel sat on the bed behind me blushing.

I looked at her in the mirror. My heart stopped, "TELL ME YOU JUST GOT HERE!"
"I could say that but it would be a lie." She said still blushing.
Horror splashed across my face. "Who let you in?"
"Timothy, he looked out the window before he opened the door though."
I swallowed real big, "you heard everything?"
Raynel chuckled as she blushed. "Yes."
"Don't look at me!" I said completely embarrassed.
"Let me fix your hair." She said coming to me and grabbing the comb. Then she looked at my face in the mirror, "you earn this one."
I wanted to die! Whenever our eyes met in the mirror we giggled with embarrassed laughter. Tim stayed away from the bedroom. I hurried and dressed and put on my makeup.
When Irma and everyone came Tim blushed when Raynel and I came out the bedroom. "What's wrong with you?" Irma asked him.
Tim shook his head and walked away. Raynel and I were blushing. "I got here a little early is all." Raynel said.
All the women stood there processing the scene. One by one they all started laughing. I didn't want to talk about it I wanted to go. I walked out the front door first in hopes that they would get over it. When we got to Hotel Mac in Point Richmond I let Lauren see the outside of the hotel and she smiled. When we stepped inside the Manager took us to our private room. I covered Lauren's eyes cause we couldn't trust her not to peek. Everyone gasped as the entered the room. The piano player started playing soft music and then we yelled surprise when I removed my hand. Lauren looked around in shock, and then she started crying really hard. She hugged each person and said thank you. She kept looking around the room all-night and crying. Then she stood up, "as you all know losing my momma was like dying myself. I felt all alone," she wiped her face. "I'm not proud of everything I've done trying to find somewhere that I belonged. The best thing I ever did was befriending the girl assigned to work on her school project with me." Then she looked at me, "you have no idea what your friendship has meant to me. I found a mother, and sisters. People who I could be myself with, and not feel like I was too loud or trashy. Momma, you are my momma now. Now I got all these sisters. I've got family! It means so much to me that each one of you are in my life." She fanned her face. "I'm sorry I'm bringing the party down by crying but this is heavy. You all love me, and I haven't felt that since my mother died."
That did it, we were all in tears. Even the guy on the piano looked a little misty eyed as he sat there staring at our love fest. Irma said that was enough with the water works and then she told the waiter to bring in our presents for Lauren. She started crying, she didn't expect presents. Although none of us spoke to each other, we each brought fancy lingerie from the boutique downtown in the city. Aunt Ingrid was the only one to give her a book that we dismissed at first until Lauren turned red flipping through the pages. "What is Karma Sutra?" I asked looking at the cover.
"Girl come see!" Lauren said with big eyes. "Auntie you don't need this for you and Mr. Yeck, after all you're newlyweds."
"I have my own copy." She smiled.
"I've done that one." Martha said pointing to a picture.
"Sebastian has moves?" Beth asked.
"I thought of it. I thought I was coming up with something original." She laughed.

“Is that when this one happened?” Peggy said rubbing Martha’s stomach.
“Heck if I know, I woke up pregnant one day.” Martha laughed.
Raynel had big eyes; “all of you do stuff like this with your husbands?”
“Of course!” Martha said.
I looked at Raynel’s face and it was covered in pain. Irma noticed her face as well. I told Raynel to come with me. Irma followed us out the room into the hallway. “Are you ok?”
Her hand was shaking as she cried, “Franklin!” She couldn’t talk she was crying so hard. Raynel bent over covering her mouth as she cried. “I couldn’t do it!” She cried so hard.
I rubbed her back on one side and Irma rubbed the other. “It’s ok sweetheart.” I said.
“Fornication is a sin! My momma always stressed that to us, she talked so bad about sex. She said good girls don’t do this, and good girls don’t do that. When Franklin would try stuff I would freeze up. He got so tired of being on top of me in our bed that he wouldn’t even try anymore. I pushed my husband away!” She cried.
“So you never came after him?”
“NEVER!”
“Men need to feel wanted, loved, and desired just as much as we do. It’s not too late, you could try it now.”
“Me?” She said through her tears.
“Yes, you. I told you, you guys were only on a temporary break. You will have your man back. I can try to coach you.”
“And if she can’t I know I can. I haven’t been married this long for nothing.” Irma said smiling.

Timothy

"Hello?"
"I need you to get to Franky's as soon as you can. I'm on my way." Jeff said.
"What's going on?" I asked.
"The worst has happened. Go save "Franky I'm on my way." I told my foreman I was gone and I flew up the highway and up those Walnut Creek Hills. When I pulled up to the house Christy was sitting outside on the grass barefoot holding herself crying. When I got closer to her I could see handprints on her neck, her cheeks were bruised, and that's the stuff I could see. Now I don't like this girl, but I'm not ok with him treating her like she's worse than one of his dogs. I made her stand I hugged her. I asked her if she was ok, and she said he tried to kill her. I wanted to think she was exaggerating, but I wasn't too sure about my brother. Franky stood in the doorway while I comforted Christy. I shot him daggers with my eyes and he shot them back.
Jeff flew up the hill, he was yelling as he got out the car. As soon as he saw her busted lip Jeff went off even worse. "Like it or not that's the mother of your child! You can't treat her like this!" Jeff's voice boomed.
"She's a scheming little bottom feeder!" Franky yelled back.
"If you know that why did you invite her into your home? Why were you continuing to mess with her, if you knew that she would only trap you?"
Franky stood up straight, "I needed..."
Jeff cut him off, "you! You! You! Remember that this is all because you're too selfish to do the right thing! You want this! You want that! You are getting what

you deserve!" Franky got mad and charged Jeff. They weren't punching each other but they were wrestling like angry brothers do. "Man up!"
"My wife!" Franky yelled and then he rolled over as he cried. "My wife!"
"Man up Franky!" Jeff said getting up slowly.
Christy looked more scared seeing Franky cry than she ever did seeing him angry.

****

Jeff's bachelor party was wild! My brothers, my father, and our friends all seemed to forget about their wives. At first I was trying to go with the flow, but something about looking around the room and seeing this reality didn't sit well with me. As if they knew I would resist it seemed like they sent the prettiest girl to me. I could see that willing to please look in her eyes. I grabbed my jacket and faked being drunk to leave. I drove Sadie with determination. Annette's silhouette in the bed was the perfect welcome home for me. She wasn't expecting me so she was laying in the middle of the bed. I stripped and then I got on the bed. Annette popped up as she called my name. I let her see it was me and then I made love to my wife. I have no judgment on them for how they chose to spend their evening, as for me... All I want is my wife! As if she understood where my mind was she went above and beyond expectations. Instead of falling asleep I passed out happy and satisfied with myself with a clear conscience.

****

"No matter how much you tried to fight it, she wore you down." I smiled at my brother.
Jeff didn't smile back, "it did not go unnoticed that my best man left me hanging last night."
“I needed to get home,” I smiled.
“You don’t miss the newness of a new woman?”
“Not at all,” I said looking him in his eyes.
Jeff shook his head, “one day I hope to be on your level.”
“Wait a minute, if you’re not on my level why are you getting married?”
“I love her, I want her to be the mother of my children. I’ve never had with anyone else what I have with her. She blends so well into our family. Lauren is my wife.”
“So then why aren’t you on my level?”
“Lauren and I are not like you and Annette, when we fight we fight dirty. It gets pretty bad.”
“I’m so confused,” I said throwing my hands up. “One minute you love her and you sound like me, then the next minute you sound like Franky.”
“Hey! Hey! Give me my credit; I’m never as bad as junior. If anything I can see myself being like Pops. There’s no one he loves more than momma, but he has others. You saw even Dale stayed last night. You’re just different.”
“And proud of it, I thoroughly enjoyed my unexpected night with my wife.”
Jeff looked at me for a minute, “well that’s why we’re getting married. One day we’ll be on your level. Today I’m making a respectable woman out of her.”
“She’s doing the same for you?”
“I guess so. Did you tell Annette what was going on?”
“She didn’t question me, she accepted that I was home.”
“If she ask you, don’t tell her about the party.”
“I know the drill.”
As we waited for the ceremony Pops talked to all of us. He said now he no longer has a single son to offer. He told Jeff he was proud of him, and that he has chosen a beautiful wife.

Annette

As I looked at Lauren all put together, I could see why this extra long engagement was important to her. Her bridal look was elegant and lovely. Jeff smiled with so much pride as he watched his bride come down the aisle. Franky had a surprisingly pained look on his face as he looked at his wife. I thought he would be excited to see her after these past few months. As the happy couple said their vows assisted by Tim and I, when the ceremony got to the part, "speak now or forever hold your peace." A man stood up and started yelling. Everyone jumped! "My daughter don't deserve no happily ever after!" He said very drunk. Pops moved very quickly and snatched the guy by his collar. He was almost carrying him out of the hotel auditorium. The guy was yelling and screaming the whole way. Pops slammed his body through the double doors. You saw Pops rearing back to punch him as the doors closed then you heard the punch and Lauren's father screamed in pain. Dale left his station to go check on his father. Pops came back and told us to continue. Jeff hugged his wife and she tried to suck it up, but it was visible to everyone that she was upset. So I guess that's why when they said, "you may kiss the bride." Jeff laid the longest juiciest kiss he could on his wife. It got to the point that everyone was cheering them on, and Lauren started kicking her leg to beg for mercy. She completely forgot about her daddy and her focus was back on her husband and their wedding day. After we almost lost our vision from taking so many pictures we went into the reception hall. Lauren kept thanking me for all of my help; she said her day was exactly as she dreamed it would be.

Timothy

Franky was looking nervous and sad about seeing Raynel. He was happy to see his boys and they hugged and chatted. He was dreading telling Raynel about the baby, he threatened to end Christy if she told anyone. I figured he was hoping she'd have an accident. Seeing as how she didn't lose the baby after he slapped her up I don't see the point in postponing the inevitable. Seeing the love in his eyes, I could tell he needed one last night without her hating his guts. Franky proudly escorted his wife down the aisle. After dinner all of the kids kept the dance floor moving. Lady B couldn't get over how little Malachi was and how he was keeping up with his brother and cousins. My beautiful wife and I stayed within an arm's reach of each other all night. Katie felt ill halfway through the reception, she tried to tough it out, but Jeremiah insisted that they go home so they could rest. I volunteered to bring Kiah home, but Hezekiah said that he and Emma would be happy to bring Kiah. Hezekiah was tired of playing uncle to his daughter, and Emma was fine with things the way they were. Annette said Emma and Hezekiah argue about it all the time. I told Annette I didn't understand, and she said every time she tries to understand she remembers that her momma doesn't make sense.

Chapter 20

Annette

I could smell Tim before I saw him. As Tim came in for his normal kiss hello I pulled away. "What?"
"You've been smoking!" I covered my nose.
Tim moved his eyes around, "that's not new."
"It's new to my nose today. Please go brush your teeth, wash your hair in the shower. The smell is making me nauseous." I said holding my nose and stomach.
Tim eyed me, "well hurt my feelings then." He said walking away.
"I'm sorry," I called after him.
"Yea, yea!" He said from the hallway.
Lately my nose is very sensitive, I would think I was pregnant but I haven't had a headache and I've lost a little weight. My skin is glowing and I feel great until I smell something disgusting. Which makes going out difficult because there are so many smells in the world that I've never noticed until now. Tim keeps asking if I'm pregnant. I had a period last month, it was very light, but I had it. With Timothy and Malachi no period, no caffeine, and those awful headaches. Plus with Timothy I gained a lot of weight, I gained with Malachi but not like Timothy. And! I was always sick, the only time I feel sick right now is when something hits my nose wrong. I made an appointment with my doctor anyways just to be sure.
"Congratulations Mrs. Wallace, you're going to have a baby?" My doctor said smiling.
"But! I feel good, I haven't had one headache? Are you sure?" I questioned her as if she could be wrong.
"Mrs. Wallace each pregnancy is different, you won't always experience the same symptoms."
"This time I'm gonna need my momma and my husband in the delivery room."
She exhaled, "Mrs. Wallace, we..."
I cut her off, "we've already discussed it. This is what I need! It's not open for negotiation."
My doctor didn't look happy but she did as I asked.
When I got to Katie's house the kids were outside having a ball. Little Malachi was doing his best to keep up with Kiah and Timothy. I looked at Katie and smiled, we did a celebratory dance then I asked her for ideas of how to tell Timothy. I told her the poor thing has had to quit smoking cold turkey just to get next to me. He's been a little grumpy and he's put on a little weight because of it.
Katie said she always imagined that she would cook a big elaborate dinner for Jeremiah and just before dessert she would lovingly give him the news. She exhaled and said the closest she's gotten to her dream is when she told him they were raising Kiah as their own. Then she shook her head; she said Hezekiah can't stand this arrangement anymore. She said he's been trying to convince Emma that they need to be a family again. She asked me why Emma was afraid of being a mother. I told her I had no idea as I watched my niece play with my boys. Kiah is such a good girl. Katie insisted that the boys sleepover so I could tell Tim the right way for once. I got excited, "this could be my little Lucinda."
Katie looked around the room. "I'm sorry, I have to ask. Why do you like that name?"
"It makes me think of innocence and goodness."

"It makes me think of that guy from your town when you write it down." I frowned at her; she put her hands out like she was weighing one name over the other. "Luther? Lucinda? You don't get it?"
I frowned at her, "no! No! No! He has nothing to do with that name." Then I got mad cause even though it wasn't true she ruined the name for me. "We are not family anymore!" I pouted.
Katie laughed and hugged me. "Cheer up honey, it's probably another boy anyways."
I gasped, "you are really hurting my feelings. I'm out numbered, I need a little girl."
I went home made a wonderful feast for my husband. Cleaned up the house spotless, and put on a pretty dress. I was standing in the doorway smiling when Tim came home. He was frowning when he walked in the door. Nicotine withdrawals, he sniffed the air then he looked at me with a question on his face. "What's going on? Where are the boys?"
"Tonight it's just me and you. I wanted to say that I love you, and I appreciate all that you do for me, for us."
Tim's frown melted. I served him his meal and his eyes got big with appreciation. I sat down and watched him eat. "You're not eating?"
"I was tasting and snacking while cooking. I'm not hungry."
"Annette you're losing too much weight. I need something to hold on to." He joked. I smiled but I didn't say anything. When he finished eating I told him to shower and I had his suit laid out for him. Tim smiled so big as he got up to comply with my request. Once he was dressed and looking like a million bucks, I kissed my man and I told him I loved him. I could tell he was eating the whole evening up. We got in my car and we went to "The Place Where Jazz Is Played". Gus had our table ready for us. We enjoyed our cognac as we listened to the house band light up the stage. Our favorite local artist Catfish Jones played a wonderful set, and then he brought the music down to a nice low hum. "You know ladies and gentlemen *LOVE* is a wonderful thing. Let me hear you clap your hands if you have love in your life." The audience clapped. "I don't think you heard me. Let me hear you clap your hands if you got *LOVE* in your life!" The applause was louder and people were testifying. "I'm looking out in the audience and all I see is love." He pointed at a few tables, "can't you see the love there!" The audience applauded again. Then he looked at our table, "let me tell y'all about Mr. T over here." He pointed to our table. "Take a look at this fine couple over here." Catfish walked to our table then he winked at me. "This man is so in ***LOVE*** with this woman sometimes it makes your teeth hurt cause it's so sweet!" Everyone applauded. "I know Mr. T has told me he's not passing but he's got so much soul it really does make you wonder. Not that it matters but sometimes one wonders." Then he looked at the house band. "I need you to give me something that sounds like love that I can talk to." Dun, dun, dun the baseline played like a heart beat. The wind and percussion instruments played behind the baseline. "Mr. T your wife called today." He smiled real big. "She ***SO IN LOVE***! With her man that she had to bring you here tonight." He said to Tim. "She has something to tell you."
Tim looked at me with a **big** smile, "I'm pregnant!" I said with a smile.
Tim stood up came over and kissed me. Then he made me dance with him next to our table while everyone cheered us on.
"Thank you for not throwing anything at me this time." He said as he kissed me.
"Just my heart."

We enjoyed the rest of the evening, as we stood to leave Tim froze for a second then he laughed. When I asked him what he pointed at Rudy and that girl who came with Tim to Katie's house all those years ago. It looked like Rudy was trying to duck out, but they came towards us once they knew we saw them.
"Congratulations," Rudy said like he was forced to say it.
"Is this your wife?" I asked.
"Yes, Mary Jane you've met Annette before."
"Yes, but barely. Nice to meet you. Is this your first baby?"
"No, this will be our third. How about you?" I asked.
"We have a little girl," she said proudly.
"Congratulations." Tim showed no enthusiasm to speak. "Ok, well we're going to get back to our celebration. I'm glad to know things worked out for you just as they should've."
Rudy looked me up and down, "Annette you look really good!" He said shaking his head.
Mary Jane and I gasped like, "**NO HE DIDN'T**!"
Tim let go of my hand, and stepped into Rudy's face. "You trying to provoke me?" I found my self completely turned on and quietly hoping Rudy would say or do something to make my man lay him out. Rudy backed away like the coward that he is. Tim grabbed my hand again, kissed it, and then he announced that I was his Queen!

Timothy

"Why are you so moody?" Jeff asked, "is Annette not performing her wifely duties?"
"Spoken like a true honeymooner!" I barked at him. "She's complaining about the smell of cigarettes. She's complaining about every smell."
"I thought you only had them occasionally?"
"Lately it's been a daily occasion." Jeff looked at me, "I've been a little stressed."
"If holding back stresses you out so much just let go and get them."
"Fine, I want Avery gone! He's come by the office one too many times. He's been seen too close to my house for my liking."
"I'll put someone on it." Jeff adjusted in his chair. "Have you talked to Franky, I mean Frank recently?"
"He told Raynel, she's devastated." I said feeling bad for him.
"Did he tell you that they spent the night together after he told her?" I blank stared at my brother. "Sounds like little miss good girl read a book or something. He said he couldn't believe it."
"She going to file for divorce?"
"He told her she couldn't, she tried it once. I think her parents were forcing that issue though. Frank brought so much legal resistance that I think they learned their lesson."
"They don't like Frank do they?"
"The only way I can kind of understand it is when I think about when I have daughters. If she wants to marry him, even if I know it's a mistake, let her learn."
"You know that's easier said than done."
"I know, but why cause my princess more stress than needed?" Jeff said calmly.
I laughed, "that's what you say now. All of a sudden mister hot head will act first and think second. RIGHT!"

We talked about business, and security on family. We called Frank before we went over so that we wouldn't walk into the middle of anything. Security was tighter at his house than usual. Frank said the newcomer tried to get to his house the other day. We asked him why he didn't say anything. He said it was handled before it began, as a safety precaution they put someone on Pops and momma's house as well. Christy came inside in her bathing suit with her pregnant belly big and swollen. "Are your boys going on the camping trip?" She asked me.
"Malachi is too little to go without us. Why are you thinking so far ahead?"
She shrugged, "I was just wondering."
I looked at Frank, "she's a thinker all of a sudden?"
"Christy please never be dumb enough to go against me!" Frank said.
I was greeted at home to the welcome of a King! My wife made all my favorites and she kept looking at me with so much love in her eyes. At first I thought she wrecked her car or threw away one of my tools by accident AGAIN! When we got to Gus's I realized she had something to tell me. When she announced she was pregnant I appreciated that she wasn't angry this time, I couldn't wait to get her home.
On the way home Annette and I debated about when we think this baby was conceived. She said she thought it was the night of the bachelor party. I said I think it was in the shower before the bridal shower. We smiled and got quiet for a minute cause we both forgot the other incidents until now.

****

Franky called me, "she's in labor." He said dryly.
"I'm on my way, are you at your house?" I said.
"No, I'll call you when the baby's been born. We're at the hospital already." His tone was flat and unexcited.
"Ok, cheer up! You're having a baby. You should be overjoyed." I said.
"Bye Tim!" Then he hung up on me.
I turned my attention back to Dale, "who was that?"
"Franky," I said.
He frowned, "Raynel's pregnant?"
"No," I said watching his eyes.
Dale whistled, "there's a nightmare I wouldn't want to have."
"So why chance it? Out of all of my brothers I thought you'd be the one who would be faithful to his wife."
Dale rolled his head slowly like something tasted nasty. "Blanche is a good woman. Don't paint the picture like I step out on my wife on a regular basis." I stared at him, he shook his head. "I don't know why. Its not like I do it very often."
"That doesn't make it any better. Does Blanche know?"
"Of course not." He said shifting in his chair. He was quiet for a minute thinking. "I love my wife, and it doesn't make you better than me because you haven't been tempted."
"I didn't say that, of all my brothers I thought for sure you would be the one to never stray."
"Tim I'm human, what you think there's nothing but goodness in me? I'm just as much a Wallace as you are. I may not have it in me to kill someone, but I will beat them until they stay down." He smiled, "I could never be as heartless as Matt or Franky, but Franklin Wallace Sr's blood runs through my veins just like yours. We all suffer from selfishness in one way or another. You may not cheat on your wife, but I know that there has to be at least one selfish something you've done through

out the course of the time you've been with Annette. Don't judge me or us for that matter like you're above us."
I sat back, "I got Annette pregnant with Timothy on purpose. She wanted to wait until after the wedding to get pregnant."
"And the truth shall set you free." Dale smiled.
"Don't tell Blanche about Franky yet. She'll tell momma and he's not ready for momma to know yet."
When we got to the hospital Franky was holding the baby and he had a pained smile on his face. He said it was a girl, and I knew how much he wanted one with Raynel. He gave her to me and I smiled at her, she's a pretty little thing. I looked at Franky and I told him to get excited about his daughter. "I'm happy about her, I just wish she was from the woman I love."
"Franky stop taking this so hard. It's going to be ok."
He exhaled, "Franky died when Raynel left. Call me Frank."

****

"Why do you have to do this today? It's supposed to be Beth's day." I said
"We saw Mrs. Epstein at the store. It's only a matter of time before she tells momma. It will be worse if I don't tell her." Frank said, "when are you coming?"
"Annette's moving slow but we're coming." I tried to warn Annette the best I could on the way to momma's house.

Annette

This pregnancy started off really well, but now... I'm tired and I have two little ones to look after. I used to glow, and now my skin lacks luster. Lauren and Jeff have started trying, but nothing's happening yet. She's getting frustrated and worried. Katie has been really good about talking her through it. Tonight we're going to meet the guy that Beth has been dating, she's really excited. Irma said the guy is ok, but he's weak just like Beth. She said they're going to have a bunch of tender foot babies. Tim said there's going to be another surprise tonight and that we would talk about it later. I wanted to know what he meant but Tim wouldn't say. I squinted my eyes at him while I rolled my long ponytail into a bun on the top of my head. Having all these babies has been great for my hair and nails. My hair is now long like it was when I was little before I started hot combing it all the time. I don't have the energy to play with it. So I wash it, comb it, and put it up. In the car I kept asking questions trying to get Tim to spill the beans. He said it was so bad he couldn't talk about it. Little Franky, Ethan, and Fernando were sitting on the grass out front when we pulled up to the house. "Does your dad know you're out here?" Tim asked them they all had sad faces as they shrugged at us. "I know it's hard to understand boys, but everything's going to be ok. Meanwhile let's have you guys go to the backyard."
The boys got up and did as they were told. Now I was concerned. When I walked in the door the first person I saw was Christy and I could hear Irma going off. When I walked in the door Irma was holding a baby and cursing Franky out so badly my ears were ringing. Irma looked at the baby and then she started crying. She told Franky he was making a mess of his life. Tim took the baby from my momma and he put it in my arms. "Her name is Gwendolyn." I looked at the red head little girl and I started crying for my sister. I thought I had done something for Raynel to pull away from me. Now I know the truth, my heart hurt for Raynel. Christy stayed by the door looking unbelievably guilty. Franky got up and walked away when I started crying, he left Christy standing there looking dumb. Irma screamed that she

didn't know what was wrong with the men in this family. A very unsuspecting Pops walked in the door right into the ring of Irma's fire. She blamed him for teaching his sons to be so selfish. I thought Pops would argue back or something, but he had no defense. Regardless this little girl is gorgeous and she watched me cry like she was trying to understand why. Christy watched Irma and I cry together with no empathy in her face. She could've cared-less that we were upset. As family arrived most of the women had the same reaction. This news put an ugly cloud over the evening; even the kids were looking hurt. "I know your family is going through a lot right now. However, I did come over with the intention to do something very important." Then Chevy got down on one knee and proposed to Beth.

Just as their love lightened the mood, Christy opened her mouth. "You all are too dramatic. It's not like Franky was ever going to be happy being married to a prude." She spit at all of us.

I slapped her so hard she hit the floor before it registered that I knocked her. My combination of words were not words I ever wanted to use in front of my children let a lone in Momma and Pops's house, but this dizzy broad took me there. When Christy got up like she was going to retaliate, Irma grabbed her by her hair and threw her up against the wall. She lifted her up by her neck and held her there. Irma was so angry she was shaking. "How dare you! I wasn't going to make this about you, and I was prepared to unleash my rage entirely on my son! You don't respect my family! My daughter in-law loves my son! No thanks to you that love may be lost forever. You are a bottom feeder worse than any white trash I've ever encountered. It's not enough to be pretty Christy; you need to have a heart. You are heartless and cold! You are not welcome in my house ever again! Get out!" Irma said still holding her against the wall. Christy started kicking her feet because she couldn't breathe. Pops gently touched her arm and asked her to release Christy so she could leave.

Timothy

One thing you can always count on is momma going completely off. What I didn't expect was my wife's quick reaction to Christy speaking out of turn, no one did. I know Christy deserved what she got, but it upset me that Annette would even go there while she was pregnant.

The car ride home was quiet; Timothy said his cousins were sad because their momma was sad. I asked him if Fernando was sad too, and he said yes. Fernando calls Raynel momma too, and he was upset that she was sad. Tonight was a disaster no matter which way you turned it.

Annette and I got into a big argument because of her fighting while she was pregnant. I know she's even more emotional during her pregnancies, but we can't risk something happening to the baby because she can't get a hold of her temper. Like I said tonight was a complete disaster. I had to lay down and turn off my brain. Neither one of us could back down.

Annette

"I didn't know, I'm so sorry!" I cried.

"You had nothing to do with this. And I don't want to hear about you fighting on my behalf or period especially in your condition." She scolded me.

I told Raynel in that moment I completely forgot I was pregnant. Raynel said after the wedding Franky told her he needed to talk to her. She said she really needed to talk to him too. She said she couldn't get that book out of her head and the fact that everyone was happily married except her and she was the one with an aversion to everything in that book. She cried as she said she was going to tell Franky that she wanted to work on it. She said they met at the bar in the Berkeley Claremont hotel. She said one look at Franky's face and she knew it wasn't an option. She said he kept apologizing from the beginning to the end of their conversation. She said she spent the night with Franky anyways. She said it wasn't the loving and freeing experience she hoped for cause her heart was broke. She said the experience was unlike any they ever had; she said it was better than that kiss that got her in trouble. She said only if her heart could've connected to that room they'd be together right now.

I told her that Franky's picked up more weight in the last few months. She nodded and said he's not happy. He finally has his little girl and although he loves her, having his daughter with Christy made him feel robbed. I smiled when she said that. I told her I was happy to hear that they still talk. She said they talk all the time, and sometimes he drops by the shop. I asked her if they were going to get back together, and she quickly said NO!

****

"We need to agree on names." Tim said excitedly.

"What's wrong with the names I have?" I said coping an attitude.

Tim sighed, "Annette please baby, let's agree on this. Jody? I don't like it."

"What's wrong with Jody?"

"Nothing, but that's a nickname. What about Tobias?"

"No! This baby is not a Toby." I said rubbing my stomach, making a face at him.

He laughed, "you look like your momma making that face."

All laughter left me; "ok so because this baby has made my skin black like my momma's you think that's funny?"

"Yes!" Tim belly laughed.

I blank stared at him, "fine! I want Jody then."

"Ok let's be serious, what about girl names?"

I smiled, "you think it could be a girl?"

"No, but we should at least humor the idea." He laughed.

"IF I HAVE A BOY I'M NEVER HAVING SEX WITH YOU AGAIN! I'VE BEEN AS PATIENT AS I CAN BE WITH YOU!"

"Well that's not fair, I don't control what I give you. Maybe your body rejects the idea of a daughter. You can't punish me for that." He said messing with me trying to make his face look pitiful.

I got up and walked into the kitchen where Timothy was doing his practice homework for school. There was a panicked knock on the front door. Then I heard Emma's voice, she was in tears and beyond reason. She said she needed to talk to me. Tim volunteered to watch the stove and we went to my room. Emma sat on the floor in Indian style. She put her hands out, "fix me!"

"What?"

"Annette! I don't know what's wrong with me! My husband loves me, and he wants his family together under one roof. I don't want Kiah back, she doesn't like me no how."

"What? Where did you get that from?"

"The way she looks at me. Katie gotta tell her to say hi to me. She's more happy to see you than she is me."

"That's just your guilty conscience. Kiah loves you even though you abandoned her."

Emma cried, "Hezekiah wants her back and he's not letting it go. I can't face her. She's going to hate me, what type of momma does this and is still loved by her child?"
"I can't guarantee that she's not gonna feel some kind of way about you, but you know it's not right."
Emma looked around the room, "maybe I should've stayed away from momma too. Your family is thriving and she's never met your kids."
"Every time I talk to her she's calling me and my babies names. She accused me of messing around with Whispers."
Emma moaned, "Whispers is so fine though."
I smiled, "I know. My man is finer!"
"Matter of opinion, there's no point in arguing about that one." She said, "I don't know what to do."
I rubbed my stomach, "after I have this one I can come over more. Take it slow; show her you're interested in her. Katie said Kiah is doing really well in school. Go with Katie to her school stuff, maybe when she's more comfortable with you, you can take her back home with you when you go for business."
Emma looked at me, "are you mad at Harriet?"
"Not for marrying Luther. I understand that, but she wants me to stay away because of it. That hurt!"
Emma leaned in, "he still goes to Hazel's. And more than once he's called out your name while they were getting it on. She's convinced that he had you, and you're lying about it. He tells her you guys never had sex but she don't believe him. Last time Hezekiah and I were there we switched to Claudette's place then Josiah's cause Harriet was doing too much."
"What do you mean?"
"You know how you can tell when someone is moved to a vocal range of oh my goodness?" I nodded yes, "she was faking it."
"Why would she do that?"
"I guess so I would tell you about it. I know Luther gives it to her good though. One time I came to the house in the middle of the day. That was different and more real than that show she was putting on. Her nose is so open for him that she does whatever he tells her to."
"Does he love her?"
"Enough, he could've remained her friend, but you know how money changes things. All those women around town mad that Luther not single any more. Harriet's business ain't the same since you pulled out though. She's having a hard time finding vendors. One took her money and never delivered the merchandise."
"Am I supposed to feel sorry for her?"
"I guess not I make money regardless."
"You should think about selling your interest over there. While business is good. I'd suggest you invest in Babydoll's store. Some of the stores over there will do well, but since Harriet is so worried about her store I doubt she's keeping up with advertising. She needs to keep that up, otherwise all that you worked to build will disappear."

****

"We're going to have another baby! What do we think this one will be? Boy or girl?" Irma said from the back seat.
"BOY!" My boys yelled betraying me.

I looked at Tim who was focused on the road and as nervous as he always is about this part. His knuckles turned white as he drove and griped the steering wheel. He had no jokes to share or insight to add, he just wanted to make sure I was ok. When we walked in the door Pops and Franky were waiting. When the nurse tried to wheel me in the back even though I was in the middle of a contraction I told her to wait for my husband. When she tried to give me a hard time Irma got in her face and told her to get someone else cause she was going to hurt her. Tim hurried in with my bag ready to go to the back. My doctor came out and said we made her nurse cry. Irma told her what happened and that we needed a new nurse. Tim held my hand as he nervously waited for instruction. While they took me for my shave and enema they took Irma and Tim to clean up. Tim sat with me shaking his leg. Irma took out the cards; she called the game, "gin rummy!"

Once we got into our game Tim relaxed. "This is what you two were doing while I was out there dying each time?" He said like he couldn't believe it.

Once my contraction stopped Irma and I laughed. I did one walk around the room and the baby was ready. When it was time to push, I heard Irma tell Tim to stay by my head. Two and a half pushes later the doctor held up a brown baby.

"Congratulations Mrs. Wallace it's a girl!" The doctor said.

Tim looked like he was in shock. "Did she say GIRL? As in like me?" I looked at Tim for confirmation.

The nurse put the baby in Tim's arms and he shook his head yes as he looked at the baby. "Annette, we have a girl!" Then he gave her to me.

“It’s really a girl?” I looked at her little face and she was looking at me. “Oh Tim! She’s so pretty!” I said as I cried with joy in my heart. I kissed her little face while she looked at me.

“She’s beautiful just like her momma.” Tim said with tears in his eyes. Irma was on the side taking appropriate pictures of our first moments with our baby. “I’m going to introduce her to her brothers and my everybody. I’ll be back.” Tim said holding her ever so gently as he walked away with her.

“MOMMA! It’s a GIRL!” I cried to Irma.

“I saw baby, congratulations.” She half smiled.

“What’s wrong?” I asked

“Tim took my job!” She huffed.

Timothy

When I walked into the waiting room holding my daughter I had the biggest smile on my face. Everyone was here and wanting to know, when I proudly said it was a girl everyone got excited for us. Frank was the first one with his arm extended to hold her. I wasn’t ready to share her yet, but I told myself there would be plenty of opportunities to hold her so I gave her to him. He looked down very proudly at my daughter almost like a father looking at his little girl. Pops had to go take her from Frank because Frank was completely aw-struck by my little girl. Frank put his hand on my shoulder and he told me she was beautiful, and then we hugged. Everyone came and hugged me and telling me how beautiful my baby girl is. I thanked everyone for coming, and then I told Pops Momma would be out as soon as Annette went to recovery. The baby watched my face as we walked down the hallway. I couldn’t stop smiling at her and kissing her. I told her I never have to smoke again; she brought me peace and calm.

Annette

Although it was important to me that Timothy and Malachi slept in their bassinet when they came home. Jade slept in the bed with us. In the morning we'd stare at each other. Whenever she ate, we stared at each other as well. Jade is my brownest baby and I think it's so perfect that she'd be so caramel colored. Timothy and Malachi come in, in the morning to say hello to her. Timothy reads one of his books to Jade and Malachi. Then Malachi asked Timothy questions about the story. Its so hilarious. Jade quietly watches and listens propped up on a pillow. Timothy reads, Malachi asks question after question. Some of his questions are so silly that Timothy just sits there and laughs. Both of my boys are little charmers, but Malachi has enough charm to give away to the less fortunate. When Timothy goes to school Malachi and I go over his lesson so that he can be ahead when he eventually starts school. I still have to keep an eye on Malachi cause he's so curious. He's such a little sweetheart though; he sings silly songs to Jade and performs all kinds of acrobats for her. Whenever he gets a little happy around her I remind him that she's a little lady and he has to be gentle with her. During my down time everyone comes over with the most adorable princess dresses for my baby. Emma stares at Jade, she asked me how Jade could be the same complexion as Kiah when her daddy is white? I told her it was genetics and I didn't care what color she was, I'm just so happy to finally have my little girl. Jade's hair isn't as full as Malachi's was but she has a lot of hair. She doesn't fuss much and she seems to love when I dress her up real pretty. Tim is so in love with our babygirl. He kisses me hello, rough houses with the boys for a little then it's his time with his babygirl. One time he showed her the gun he bought just to protect her from little boys like he was. "So now that you have your little girl do you want to have anymore?" He asked.
"I think our family is complete, don't you?"
"Yes, so now what? We use condoms the rest of our lives."
"I was thinking about signing up for that trial drug that Raynel is on."
Tim frowned, "what drug?"
"I'll get more information from her about it, but there's a reason he couldn't get her pregnant." I said watching his eyes.

****

Katie stopped talking and coughed really hard. Even though she wasn't feeling well she was in really good spirits. Emma took my advice and has been trying to get Kiah to warm up to her. At first Katie felt a little devastated understandably so. She thought she was going to raise Kiah all of her life. One day all of a sudden she was ok, happy and singing. I brought the kids over to play with Kiah like usual, and Katie was moving about in good spirits. "You went to the doctor today?" I asked with big eyes.
She smiled real big, "un huh."
"Come on Katie, spill it! What's going on?"
Katie put her hands up to her face and she excitedly whispered while giggling, "I'm pregnant!"
I screamed to the top of my lungs! "CONGRATULATIONS!!! WHY DIDN'T YOU TELL ME RIGHT AWAY? HOW FAR ARE YOU? WHEN ARE YOU DUE?"
Katie jumped up and down crying, "can you believe it? I'm with child? I'm going to have a baby? A baby of my very own. Coming from me and my husband!"
I continued to scream at her, Jade stared at me not startled by my screams. Timothy, Malachi, and Kiah came running inside to make sure we were ok. When I told the

kids we were ok both of the boys looked at us like we were crazy. I was in such a GOOD mood I told them to get out without getting on them for the way the were looking at me. Those boys know I don't play with them. I asked her how she told Jeremiah. She said he went to the doctor with her so they got the news together. She said the doctor told her that her situation is fragile and that she needed to take it easy. She said the timing with Emma and Hezekiah couldn't be more perfect. She said they didn't tell anyone in case they had to un-tell people later. She said the doctor said she's doing a lot better than expected. So Emma takes Kiah to and from school, and she's been spending more time with them getting to know them all over again. She said they haven't come clean with her about actually being momma and daddy yet. All I could do is smile at Katie, I was so happy for her.

Timothy

"What's wrong?" I asked my best friend, he held pleasure and pain on his face.
"My world has just turned upside down, I don't know which way is up anymore." I waited for him to say. He looked at me with a pained smile, "Katie's pregnant."
"WHAT? CONGRATULATIONS!" I erupted excitedly.
Jeremiah smiled through his pain, "thank you."
"Why aren't you excited?"
"Katie isn't well, it's no secret that she's been sick for some time. She's got a laundry list of health issues. The doctor tells us that she has a very delicate situation and she has to take it easy. All she focuses on is that she's pregnant. I tell her to relax and she does it." Jeremiah's lip trembled, "I'm afraid that if she miscarries I'm going to lose her." He said trying to hold back his emotion unsuccessfully. "Last night she wants to make love and I'm scared." He exhaled looking up at the ceiling. "I keep praying that we all make it to the other side of this ok. I don't want to lose my wife just to have a baby. I want children, but not at the cost of losing my wife."
"I understand, as much as I love my children. When I think of forever I think of Annette, eventually they'll go on and have their own lives. Then it will be me and her again like it was in the beginning."
"Right, what if having my child takes her away from me? I'm telling you now, I can't do it!"
"You know, Annette and I had that conversation. We agreed that we would hold on for our children, but we'd never remarry. So if something ever happens to me, feel free to remind that woman that she vowed forever to me and she needs to hold on to her word." I smiled. Jeremiah tried to smile but he couldn't. He was worried about his wife. "You gonna mess around and make yourself sick worrying about Katie. Then you'll be of no use to her. Katie is one tough cookie, stop worrying about her. You're going to have a healthy and strong child, and Katie's going to be fine."
"I hope you're right."
"I know I am, but you know what puzzles me?" Jeremiah looked at me. "How Annette hasn't said anything about this. I would think she would be crazy with excitement."
"Katie and I said we weren't going to tell anyone until she was four months, but I had to tell you cause I might need to take off."
"Understood, I'll start coming over to this office twice weekly so you can give me the run down of this empire that you've built for me. You can start taking more time off to be with your wife and enjoy your pregnancy. Jeremiah," he looked at me. "Katie is strong, and your child is strong like you. Everyone is going to be ok."

Chapter 21

Timothy

"Here's my reports, and where I got the information for them." Hezekiah said

I looked at them, "you've got maintenance down to a tight schedule I see."

"Yep, that's why you hired mechanics. Jeremiah said we can't afford to waste time on someone else's shop where our trucks could sit waiting for them to get to them. Jeremiah thinks of everything."

"So I see, you guys have done an amazing job."

"Is your company the most successful business under your family's umbrella?" Hezekiah asked.

"Nope, I think we all operate on the same level though."

"So I was talking to Jeremiah about retirement planning. He said I should go through a company he went through Cooper Financial, have you heard of them?"

I smiled, "yes."

"He showed me the plan they have mapped out for him." His eyes got big; they've grown his money so much in just a short period of time. I don't have money like Jeremiah, do you think they'll look at my pennies and turn their nose up? I don't want to be embarrassed."

"I'll give you the number of my financial planner. He won't turn his nose up at you. He'll work with you. Maybe you and Emma should go together." I said.

"Oh no! She can't even know about this." I looked at him, "that little girl likes to spend money. Now that Kiah is coming around more she spends even more."

"What about the money she makes from Kansas?"

"Tim, when I tell you she likes to spend I'm telling you she likes to spend. I have to have my own separate checking account to keep things afloat. I know they didn't have anything growing up so automatically she sees the newest and the latest and she has to have it. Clothes, shoes, home furnishings, think about it. Has my living room been the same any time you've come over?"

I thought about it, "no it hasn't. I didn't even pay attention."

"I want to retire with all my children grown, educated, and married off nicely. I can see myself working until the grave if this keeps up." He said like he was exhausted.

"She likes to shop and decorate." I said thinking of a way they could use that to their advantage. "How about this? How about you open a store, she can shop for the clothing you'd use in the store, and she can decorate the displays. Draw customers in and then her habits become an advantage to you instead of a handicap."

"Yea, maybe one day." Hezekiah said not understanding me.

"Brother in-law, I'll open the store. You can buy it from me now or later." I said

"But, we've got Kiah on a good schedule with us. We're going to tell her soon."

"It will have staff, Emma won't have to be there the whole duration of the day. She can do what she does best and then tend to your family. You'll have to talk to her about her spending habits of course, but working in this capacity should fill the void of reduced spending."

"Ok, sounds good." He said like he didn't exactly believe in my vision.

"So by the end of the week, I'll have the information together. By the end of next week we should be moving forward."

He looked shocked, "like that? You all don't waste time do you?"

"If it's a good idea why waste time dragging your feet?"

"True, I wasn't mentioning any of that to you thinking that it would go anywhere. I was just venting." He said embarrassed.

"Brother in-law, we family. We've been family even before the women. I appreciate all that you and Jeremiah have done over here. You've helped me out so much. Between the two of you, you've turned my business into some REAL money. How could I repay you?"
"Um, do you know how much money I make just to do all that I've done?" He joked.
"Yes I do." I smiled, "and I could still stand to do more. Annette doesn't have spending habits like Emma, and I think that's because she always had to take care of the little ones and she saw what happened when you spend recklessly today how that affects tomorrow. At least your woman lets you get the big fancy house. Annette don't want our kids to be spoiled little rich kids." I frowned, "and now she's talking about the example she wants to set for Jade. She says when my baby girl goes to school she wants to get a little job to set an example for her that she doesn't wait on a man to provide for her. I don't like it, but its not like she's saying something wrong."
"Your little girl's going to be smart, she will know better."
"That's what I said, but she says kids follow what you do more than what you say or show them. She got a come back for everything I say. So I've learned to pick my battles." I laughed.

****

When I walked in the door the women were spread out all over my living room creating girlie things for the shower. Jade was sitting up watching them, when she saw me she smiled and crawled really fast to me. I LOVE this greeting as I walk in the door. There's no better feeling than holding my little girl after a long day of work. I thought Annette was going to be mad, because I had to work later than normal and I got so caught up in work that I forgot to call. I was happy she was distracted with the baby shower so she hadn't noticed. All the kids were out back playing tag and having a good time. Momma said my dinner was in the oven still warm. Jade and I went in the family room and we ate my mashed potatoes together. Completely full she passed out on my chest and I fell asleep happy and watching something on TV. Annette woke me up by taking the baby from me; she said she bathed the boys and everything already. I didn't realize I was that tired. She put Jade in her crib and then she came to our room. She was so excited she was rambling like Emma telling me about all the surprises and treats in store for Katie's shower. She said everyone had to come here, cause our house was the only house that Katie wouldn't just pop up at without notice. I told her I would be happy when the surprise was over because its hard not to say anything about the surprise to Jeremiah when we talk everyday. Annette kissed my neck as she undressed me and said it would be over soon.

Annette

I was counting down the days until Katie reached four and a half months. As soon as she hit it we all sprang into action. By the time she turned five months we had the most amazing baby shower planned. Just before she reached six months we had the biggest and BEST baby shower slash party EVER! Everyone wanted to pitch in and make sure that this baby shower was **OVER THE TOP!** I think we hired every vendor we could think of for this shower. Flowers, balloons, you name it, and it was there.
For Katie, even though she hadn't had any babies of her own, she was always so happy for each of us. She made each of us feel like our child was the most special

child even if it was your third child it didn't matter she was there. Although I wanted to say she was like that for me only, I knew better. Even Stacy who Katie didn't care all that much for had her own special bond with her. Stacy surprised me and provided the most delicious food for the shower. I made my pies and a peach cobbler; I mean this party lacked nothing. Even the men came for a little while but then they eventually moved to the outside.

Tim was really into the whole idea of it as well. When we balanced the checkbook together over the past few months he'd ask about the different checks that cleared our account and he would smile so big. It didn't matter how much I spent, Tim was all for it.

The shower was a huge success and all of us were pleased with the outcome of our labors. When we got home that night, Tim and I stayed up late replaying the evening and how much fun we had. How satisfied we were with our gifts, and how happy we were for our friends.

Around three in the morning the phone rang and my heart stopped beating. It was Jeremiah, he said Katie started spotting and they rushed her to the hospital. The doctor said the baby was fine and that they wanted to keep Katie for observation, and make sure she was getting proper rest.

Timothy

I could hear how upset Jeremiah was and all he said was "hello." He said the doctor said that Katie needed to relax, she over exerted herself and it caused her to spot. He quickly followed with she and the baby were fine. However, the doctor wanted to keep her in the hospital for a little bit to make sure she doesn't have any episodes for a little while. Annette started crying immediately even though I assured her that Katie was fine. I had to talk fast to calm her and get her to come back to bed. I thought I was making love to her to put us both back to sleep, but when I woke up and her side of the bed was cold and she was on the phone I realized she was tiring me out so I'd leave her alone so she could do whatever she felt she could in the middle of the night. She said Katie asked her what took her so long to call me, and she told her she had to put me back to bed. I thought about how good I got it and did not complain about her tactic.

Annette and I have come down to the hospital as much as we can to see them. Katie as usual is in good spirits, and Jeremiah is worried. I told him he's got to calm down otherwise it was going to start affecting Katie. He gave his car keys to Hezekiah and he told him to take his car home. He was afraid something would happen to it if it continued to sit in the hospital garage unmoved. I asked him if he felt like they needed assistance while he was in the hospital, he said no. He just felt that the car was vulnerable sitting out there like that.

Annette

Lauren, Emma, and I were at my house. We'd just came from the hospital and Katie as usual was in good spirits and the baby was doing well. Jeremiah was right there by Katie's side practically living in the hospital with her.

Emma said that they came clean with Kiah since they've had her with them this whole time. Emma said she was expecting this whole dramatic scene or words full of hate and resentment from Kiah. However, Kiah is still just a little girl, so she barely had a reaction other than hugging and kissing Emma and Hezekiah. Emma was shocked by how well Kiah took everything. To me that said that Kiah may have known or remembered. I didn't have the heart to tell Emma that she probably

needed to wait until Kiah was older to really know how she truly felt about the whole thing. Emma told us that things were going so well with the three of them that she and Hezekiah were talking about FINALLY increasing their family. She said before she jumped in she wanted to get her momma issues resolved.
Since it was a rainy day out the kids and Kiah were in the family room playing. Jade has been trying to walk; I'm not ready for my baby to try to walk so fast. Everyone says she's trying to get out the way for the next baby. Tim and I keep telling everyone that this is it. Malachi is barely potty trained, and it was difficult with two babies in diapers. I would not willingly do that to myself again.
Our little princess is strong willed though, and once she sets her mind to something its difficult to change it. She yields to me like she knows better than to battle with her momma, other than that whatever she wants she gets even if that means she has to sit there and keep trying.
Jade had just crawled to me and I picked her up. She came to give me hugs like she does a lot. My baby girl is full of tender love and compassion. Emma was continuing on with her animated story about last night when the three of them were discussing their family and how grateful they were for each other when there was a knock on the door. Emma was still talking as she walked to the door, she opened it and her mouth fell open. Emma turned a little pale as she looked at me with panic in her eyes, then she asked the person what they were doing here? Lauren and I exchanged looks when a male voice responded to her. We stood up and crept to the door, the closer I got to the door the more familiar the voice and country manner of speaking was. Lauren said, whoa when she laid eyes on Luther. I was stuck and confused as to why he was on my porch. He had Lucille Harriet's oldest with him. Emma looked at me cause she didn't know what to do or say and neither did I.
"Annette!" Luther said with so much love and excitement to see me in his eyes.
"What are you doing here?" I asked rocking Jade, she didn't need to go to sleep or anything but I had too much nervous energy.
"You had another baby?" Lucille asked with a smile on her face.
"Hi sweetie, yes I've had two more babies since I've seen you all." I looked at the almost storm happening outside. "Come in," I said looking at Lauren like I didn't know what else to do. "This is my sister Lauren. Lauren this is Luther Harriet's husband and their daughter Lucille."
"Wow! Auntie Annette your house is down right fancy! I love all the gold. When I grow up my house is going to look just like this." Lucille said looking around in Aw!
Emma took their wet coats, umbrella, and hat. Then I told them to have a seat. Jade was looking at both of them really hard. She didn't frown but she stared. Luther would not take his eyes off of me. "Annette, you look.... so beautiful! Your baby weight suits you."
I rolled my eyes cause I didn't want to hear that. Tim said he liked it too, but I wanted it gone. It was just kind of hard to focus on anything else right now. "Thank you, why are you here?"
Emma clasped her hands and sat next to me. "My daddy's store." Lucille said.
I looked at Emma, "what about it?"
"You know how technology is these days, every six months to a year something newer and better is coming out. If you don't keep up very quickly your inventory can be considered old an out dated." Luther said not taking his eyes off of me.
He started to say something else, like he had rehearsed these lines before they came. "I'm not going to step in. I have nothing to do with the goings on out there."

"With Emma selling part of her ownership, things have gotten interesting. Since the store is not doing as well as it used to investors want to buy the store. They claim they can bring it back to what it used to be."
"So then Harriet should sell." I said like it was that simple.
"My momma wants to hold on to the store for us. So we can run it when we get big enough." Lucille said.
"What is the…" Tim walked in the door.
My heart fluttered cause I knew he would be mad about Luther being inside the house when he wasn't here, but the rain kind of took away my choices. "What is this? A family meeting?" He said looking at Luther.
"More like a business meeting." Luther said standing to acknowledge Tim.
"Who's idea was it for you to come all the way out here to discuss what could've been said over the phone?" Tim asked.
"Mine, you know she would've hung up." Luther said.
Tim smiled as he glanced at me, "yes she would've. How are you here instead of Harriet? You know better than to be in my house when I'm not here!"
"I decided to come, I brought Lucille as reassurance that I would be on best behavior."
Tim looked at Lucille, "how you doing darling?" He said extending his arms for a hug. Lucille happily got up and gave Tim a hug. I frowned at the little girl cause she seemed a little too eager in my opinion to hug him. "Sweetheart, can you do me a big favor?" Lucille smiled at Tim as she waited for instruction. He walked to me and took Jade from me. "This is our daughter Jade." He said as he handed her to Lucille. Jade frowned at her daddy like she didn't appreciate being handed to a stranger. "The kids are in that room back there, can you take the baby and make sure that the kids stay back there while we discuss grown folk's business out here?" She smiled real big at Tim like he just charmed her. I shot evil eyes at Tim then I looked at Lauren who smiled and shrugged as if to say he didn't do that on purpose.
Tim looked at Luther; "you came out here for Annette. Don't try to jerk me around. You wanted to see her, touch her, anything."
"That too." Luther said unapologetically.
Tim looked at me, "do you want to save Harriet's store?"
"How do you know about that?" Luther asked him.
"I know about everything." Tim said to Luther then he looked at me again. "Do you?"
"No," I said point blank.
"Harriet needs you." Luther said.
"She still owns the land, she will not lose your lifestyle if she lets the store go. If anything business could only get better and she could continue with the hotel project." I knew that Harriet wanted to build a hotel and build up the town. It was a good idea, and maybe she could focus on it if she let the store go. Besides whatever Emma told me I did my own checking up out there.
"Annette, she wants to leave the store to her children since it belonged to their father. You can understand that."
I nodded yes, "I can understand that, but what about **all** of his kids? Does that include Babydolls kids from Mr. Coleman as well? She knows Babydoll did not willingly mess with her husband or have those babies. They are just as much his kids as hers are."

Luther looked at me like he couldn't believe it. "So you made sure that Babydoll, your stepmom, was taken care of because of her kids? They're already taken care of. Harriet's thinking about her own kids."

"Was she thinking about her kids when she decided that our friendship was worth ending just to lay up under you? Why did I deserve that? She doesn't care, neither do I? That's the emotional Annette talking. Ms. Cooper says it makes no financial sense for me to get back in business with Harriet. I would never take her land rights from her, and unless she keeps the city name out there, the little town we built for her will go back to what it was. I'm sorry." I shrugged.

Luther focused on me, he didn't look mad, but he wouldn't stop staring. "Is there anything else to be said?" Tim asked.

"Can I talk to you?" Luther asked me.

Tim squinted, "get real!"

"Emma and, I'm sorry I forgot your name?"

"Lauren," she said as she stood up.

"Can you give us a minute, I need to talk to Annette alone for a minute."

Emma shot me a goofy look, "I'm only going cause Tim is staying." Emma said as she walked out like she was dying to know what was going to be said.

Tim put his arm around me and rubbed my back. Luther focused on me as if Tim wasn't there. "Are you mad that Harriet and I are married?"

"No, I would've been excited for her. She stole my thunder by ending our friendship. You and I both know that I am in love with this man." I pointed to Tim, "why would I care who you married?"

Luther looked at Tim then back at me. "That hurts, but I get it. I don't like it, but I get it. I had to come to terms with the fact that you aren't coming back. No matter how much I want you to, I know it won't happen. To look at you two together it's clear that you won't. I don't like that, but I get it."

"You have a big habit of saying the things you don't like." Tim smiled.

Luther looked at him, "stop making fun of my pain."

"You came to my house, you're sitting in my living room. Pouring out your heart to my wife and you think I'm not going to do something? Out of respect for her wishes I'll give you a measure of space. I can't sit here and not make you feel it."

Tim smiled, "you like our family picture?" Tim said pointing to the wall.

"I'd love it if that were me." Luther said staring at the picture. "I know what happened to my letter, my momma never mailed it for me like I asked her to. I gave her the money and everything." He looked hurt and angry. "She said she felt that you deserved better than me. She had no idea you'd end up with a white man. None of us did."

"Does it really bother you that I'm married to a white man?" Tim looked at me. I could tell he didn't want me to ask that question, cause really what does it matter if it does?

"He could be purple and it would bother me when you're married to anyone except me."

"I am married to the love of my life, and we have a family. I'm happy Luther, and I hope you're happy with Harriet. Cause only love should be the reason to let go of a life long friendship." I was speaking on Harriet's behalf.

"Harriet's a good woman, I get to be a father when I never thought I would be." Luther exhaled. "I kind of knew coming out here that you wouldn't change your mind. You've always been stubborn. Can I ask for financial advice? You all came

in savvied up the place and expect us to know how to maintain it? Come on! We're in over our heads."
Tim smiled at me. "Luther you can consult with my husband, but you will have to pay a consultation fee.".
"YES MS. COOPER!" Luther said, "Annette I'm sorry."
"For?"
"For being an immature child. I can't change the past, but I can apologize for it."
"And you can stop running, be good to Harriet. She needs the love of a good man in her life for once."

Timothy

"So the doctor said it's selfish of him to keep us here cause Katie and the baby are healthy and strong. We get to come home tonight, with the promise that we'll take it easy once she gets home. Katie has promised on everything that she will relax and prepare for the baby to come." Jeremiah said sounding better than he has in a long time.
"You sound good."
"I feel good. We've listened to the heart beat so many times I can hear the fighting spirit in my baby. To have made it this far and almost be at the finish line I feel pretty confident we'll be ok. Katie is doing really good, She's not letting anything hold her back from this."
"Would it be over stimulation if we were there when you all came home? I'm asking now cause you know Annette's going to demand to be there."
"Yes it's ok, the doctor said there has been at least three or four visitors daily and Katie has responded positively to it all. I told him that as soon as he released us our family was going to be stuffed into our house. I think Katie has been feeding off the love everyone has been showing us. I know I have." Then his voice got emotional, "thank you Tim! Thank you for everything! Because of you I'm not worried about this doctor bill or any of the others. I don't have to worry about anything except the things I can't control, but we're almost to the finished line and I'm ready."
"Stop all that sissy talk, you're my brother and my best friend. No matter what you will always be taken care of." I said, "now what time should I pick you two up?"
"Katie wants to wait until one of her nurses comes on so not until this evening, would six'ish be too late?"
"Not at all, it gives us time to wrangle everyone up." When I called Annette she reacted exactly the way I thought she would. She called everyone and everyone was breaking their necks to get over to Katie's house to welcome her home. On our way over Annette suggested that I park in their garage when I bring Katie so that we wouldn't have to walk out in the rain. I hadn't thought of that, and it was a good suggestion. When I picked up Jeremiah's keys, Emma and Kiah said they wanted to go. Hezekiah told me he was going as well. We didn't need the four of us to go so I tried to convince them why they should wait until I come back.
"I didn't want to have to do this but you leave me no choice." He pulled out an imaginary card. "I'm playing the brother card, and you can't tell Kiah she can't go. Let me go get them and then we'll be good." He said smiling at me. I let it go, cause its not like I wouldn't see them when they got here. Emma was talking about the store with Mrs. Barnes, as Hezekiah and Kiah were ready to go. "Emma, I swear woman. Once your mouth starts going you can't stop it, we're ready to go and you don't even have your boots on."

"Momma we will be right back ok?" Kiah said taking control of the situation and saving her daddy from the hot seat.
You could hear Emma's heart melting from hearing her baby girl call her momma.
"Ok baby, I'll have your hot chocolate waiting for you when you come back, its cold out there."
Kiah put her hands on her little hips, "Malachi. You better not sneak my chocolate either!" She warned him.
Malachi's face lit up, "there's chocolate?"
"Momma don't let him drink mine." Kiah said.
Emma laughed, "come on Malachi. I'll get you your own so you won't drink hers."
Malachi and Timothy are the little brothers that Kiah loves and also drive her crazy. Especially Malachi, he does stuff just to get under her skin.
I noticed that Mr. Barnes and I were walking in the same circle; they should've been back by now. I looked at the clock and it was almost nine. The hospital is not far from here; I called the hospital and asked if something happened that would've required them to stay longer. The nurse said they left with Hezekiah around six-fifteen'ish. I got a sinking feeling. Pops and I put on our jackets to go see if they were stuck on the side of the freeway with a flat tire or something. When we got on the freeway a few exits from the house on the opposite side there was traffic. We got all the way to the hospital and everything was fine along the way. My heart started racing and I drove on the shoulder of the freeway back towards the house. Traffic was moving slowly cause everyone had to merge to two lanes to pass the accident ahead. All I could see was a big truck that was jack knifed from a distance. I stopped breathing when we got closer and I saw cars all twisted up and I saw Jeremiah's car sandwiched between two of them. Police, paramedics, etc. were all there. Even though it was raining they had sheets over the bodies of the people who were thrown from their cars and worse. I recognized one of the officers. "Please tell me that the Barnes family is ok!"
He looked at me with sad eyes, "as in the family that was riding in that car?" He pointed to Jeremiah's car, the twisted metal screamed at me. "No one in that car survived." He said sadly.
"No! See you didn't hear me. Jeremiah, his pregnant wife, Hezekiah, and his daughter Kiah were all in that car. Are they at the hospital already?" The twisted metal screamed again.
"Mr. Wallace," he put his hand on my shoulder. "No one in that car survived. The father, daughter, and wife died upon impact. I'm assuming the gentleman in the back was the husband, he died before we could get him on the stretcher."
"She's pregnant!" I roared.
"I understand, but there's no way the baby survived. The truck jackknifed when a car cut it off, the trailer hit that car; the Barnes vehicle was hit from behind by the car, which slammed it into the first car. There are very few survivors from this accident."
"You're not understanding me!" I yelled at the officer.
"Tim!" I kept yelling, "Timothy!" Pops yelled trying to pull me out of my shock. I looked at him like I couldn't believe he interrupted me. "Come on son!" He said with his voice cracking.
I couldn't move, I sat on the ground and cried. Other heart broken families were arriving to receive the same traumatic news. Pretty soon most of us were sitting in the rain crying our eyes out.

Chapter 22

Annette

My heart is broken, but who cares. My sister and my man need me. At least I think he does. Tim hasn't said much, he hasn't done much either. I know that feeling, it's like sound is too hard to process, so you do what you know you're supposed to do. Even Irma was surprised when I said Tim went to work the next day. Tim cries in his sleep and wakes up screaming. I comfort him the best I can and then he tries to go back to sleep. He barely kisses me, I can't touch him otherwise.

I was at Emma's house trying to get her to eat something. Mrs. Barnes told Emma she couldn't lose her too. I hugged her and admired her strength. She lost two of her sons and grandchildren in one night and she was trying to encourage Emma to hold on. Not to let her grief consume her. When the doorbell rang Timothy called me cause he didn't know the person at the door. My momma stood there looking at the numbers, I guess trying to make sure she had the right house. This was the first time since I could remember seeing her without evilness in her face. She looked at me then she looked hard at Timothy. "This your boy?" She asked looking at him. I shook my head yes, she tried to smile but tears for Emma were in her eyes. My momma actually showed compassion towards Emma. The situations weren't the same, but they had the loss of their husbands and children in common. Momma apologized to Mrs. Barnes for all the trouble she caused their family. Momma was able to get Emma to eat, just like Emma had done for her all those years ago when our father died. Momma kept looking at my children, but she didn't say anything at first.

"Momma, I don't know what you want my children to call you? I don't know how to introduce you." I said feeling dumb.

"They can call me Grandmother Rose, after all that's what I am to them. What do they call their other grandmother?"

"Nana."

"Sounds like a white lady, Grandmother Rose works for me."

"Timothy, Malachi, this is your Grandmother Rose, she's my momma."

"I didn't know you had a momma." Timothy said surprised.

"I know baby." I said rubbing my baby's head.

As my momma was tending to Emma I looked at her feet. Her shoes were very worn which was unlike her. She normally kept her shoes in good repair and she kept nice ones. I couldn't let my curiosity go. I snuck downstairs and I went through her purse. She had coins and a dollar in her wallet. There was a paper with information about the local food bank, their hours of operation etc. I looked for a possible hole where she could've stuck money in the lining of her purse. I searched her coat the same way. She didn't have to pay rent, but if my brothers weren't giving her money I don't know how she was getting food. The thought of my momma going without food, soap, electricity, or the basic necessities hurt me. Cooper Financials was pouring money into my bank account; the least I could do was give my momma money for the basics. I decided that I would give my momma a little, and I do mean a little, more than she'd need monthly just to survive. Regardless of how she will try to convince me that she needed more I told myself the minimum will do. I put the little bit of cash I had in her purse, then I left.

When we got home Tim was in our bedroom going off cursing and swearing. I gave Jade to Timothy and I asked him to play a record for everyone, while I went in the

room to talk to their daddy. When I walked in the room the music came on and I closed our door. “Tim, what’s wrong baby? What are you looking for?”
Tim was sweating and red, he looked like he hadn’t slept in days. I immediately started crying when I saw him. “I can’t find my black suit.” He said returning to the closet.
“You only have one and its here on the floor.” I said picking up the pants.
“NOT THAT ONE! DON’T YOU THINK I KNOW THAT ONE IS THERE? THE OTHER ONE ANNETTE! The one I bought when we went to Francine’s that time. Jeremiah bought one just like it. I want that suit.”
I cried harder, “you threw it away. You don’t remember? That’s why you bought a new one, that one got a hole in it.”
Tim fell against the wall, “how could you let me throw it away?”
"I don’t know baby I’m sorry.”
“I can’t go tomorrow! I can’t do this!”
“Tim I need you tomorrow, our boys are going to need you tomorrow. Please don’t make me do this by myself.”
“By yourself! Woman stop being selfish!” He didn’t even sound like himself. “I can’t go! I won’t!”
I went to the phone and I called Jeff, I couldn’t think of who else to call. I told him that Tim says he can’t go tomorrow. Jeff couldn’t believe it either, he got to our house so fast. I left them in the room while I fed the kids and then bathed them. I put out their clothes for the funeral, and then I sat in the living room crying my eyes out. I wished Lauren would’ve come with Jeff, but she was with Irma finalizing the plans for the funeral tomorrow.

Timothy

I got to take care of business. The world doesn’t stop because I lost two of my brothers. STOP CRYING LIKE A SISSY! Suck it up! Man up! I’ve got work to do! Get it done, go home and try to get some sleep.
When I close my eyes, I see them all. Hezekiah and Kiah happy walking out the door for the last time. Jeremiah and Katie happy in the hospital making all the staff smile. I know I still have my flesh and blood brothers, but there’s nothing like the brother you choose. Each one of my brothers, blood and chosen serve a special place in my heart.
Annette keeps trying to comfort me I guess, but there’s nothing comforting about her touch these days. I shouldn’t have let Hezekiah go instead of me. Maybe I would’ve seen how crazy the freeway was and went another way? Or maybe I would’ve avoided the truck altogether? The driver should be grateful he died in the crash cause he wouldn’t be breathing right now either way. If I ever find out who cut the truck off it’s lights out for them! I need to blame someone, I need to hurt someone. I keep searching for a reason why this happened and why this happened in my family.
When I saw Jeff walking in my bedroom I got angry. I don’t know why it made me angry but it did. “What do you want?”
“I came to check on you, see how you’re doing?”
“I’m fine!”
"I can see that.” Jeff said looking around the room. “Why is your wife in the living room crying by herself?”
“I don’t know, maybe she wants to be alone!”
“What woman wants to be alone when they’re this upset?” Jeff said calmly.

"Annette does!" I barked looking around the room.
"How are the kids dealing with all of this?"
I plopped on the bed, "they don't understand. How am I supposed to explain to them what I don't understand?"
"What did you tell them?" He asked me watching every movement I made.
"Annette told them." I said feeling frustrated again.
"Hold on Tim! This is too much!"
"What? How you gonna tell me what's too much for my wife? This whole situation is TOO MUCH! If you want to go there! I lost my best friend, my brother in-law, my sister, and my niece! This is too much for everyone!"
"So you gonna let Annette dangle out there like that? She's got to be a wife to you, sister to her sister, and a mother to your children? While you shut down from everyone and only deal with your pain? Don't leave your wife hanging; Annette's a good woman. All of this is too much pressure for one person. She will snap and you won't like the way she breaks. It will devastate you!"
"Jeff this is too much!"
"Go hug your wife, don't shut her out. A hug won't change what has happened, but that hug will change how other things will happen. Annette needs you, and you need her. Stop thinking about only you. Your family needs you right now."

Annette

Tim and Jeff walked out of the bedroom together; Tim only looked depressed which was an improvement because at least his sense came back to his eyes. When he locked the door he started crying again, but at least this time he came to me on the couch. He said he was supposed to be the one to bring them home, my insides screamed at the thought of losing him. I told him I couldn't bare it if I lost him. He started crying harder when he said that Jeremiah was so worried about losing Katie. He said he thinks Jeremiah could've survived but when he saw that Katie was gone he had no reason to fight. Even though he rejected me all week, I offered myself as comfort. I didn't know what else to do, I needed him to feel good about being alive even if only for this brief moment. Tim didn't reject me this time; he just needed comfort from me. When I woke up cold Tim was awake lost in his thoughts. When I brought him back to life again, he took me into our bedroom and this time we made love together. He told me he loved me so much and he didn't think about how much I'm grieving as well. I told him about my momma coming to Emma's rescue and how I watched them bond all over again.
In the morning Tim and I stared at each other like we were trying to will the strength to move to the other person cause neither one of us had it. We stared at the tears that silently poured out of each other's eyes. There was a knock on the door, and the front door opened. I knew it was Irma; she knocked on our door as she slowly opened it. She moved my hair then she gently kissed my cheek which made me cry harder, then she did the same for Tim. "Babygirl you have been working hard all week, I thought you would conk out on me today, today is the hardest day. It's ok," then she started crying. "Momma's here baby, I'm going to help you." I started crying again. "Are the children bathed?" She asked through tears. I shook my head yes. "Good, I'll make breakfast, and we're going to make it through today."
Tim continued laying there staring at me. I don't know what was going through his head, but I couldn't fake strong anymore. Irma got us ready and then we road in her car to the funeral. Tim had on shades and he sat back not saying much. Irma took

Jade from me and told me to grab my man's hand. This mortuary was huge and all four caskets were up front. When Tim and I attempted to sit amongst the friends Mrs. Barnes demanded that we sat up front with the family. She told Irma and Pops to bring their entire family as well.

I saw my Uncle Rufus and Aunt Dorothy as we moved forward. Kathryn was there with her family as well. My momma had her arms wrapped around Emma tightly as they both cried. Tim squeezed my hand every time emotion washed over him. I couldn't take my eyes off of the little casket that held my niece in it. I saw family go up and look in each of the caskets. I couldn't do it; my niece was just getting on Malachi's case about her hot chocolate. I didn't want the last time I see her to be a lifeless body in a casket. I couldn't go, and Tim didn't want to go. It upset me when momma went up to Kiah's casket and she said something to her and then she kissed her. I buried my head in Tim's chest cause the whole scene upset me. I don't know how Emma felt about it, but I was upset. She never wanted Emma to have her, and now she kisses her probably for the first time when she's gone? Tim rubbed my back as he sat there taking everything in.

Timothy

At the funeral Jeremiah's family kept coming to me and hugging me as they broke down crying. They kept telling me how much Jeremiah loved me, and how he always talked about me as if I was just as much his brother as Hezekiah, and their oldest brother James. Josiah and Maybel came with Harriet and Luther. I couldn't even be concerned with the fact that they were there, when they offered their condolences Luther looked me in my eyes. I think he understood that I had nothing to lose if he decided to try anything. I did not have time to be concerned with them. I don't know if Annette even knew they were there.

My family kept an eye on me all day and night. Annette stayed within an arm's length away from me after the burial site. Mr. & Mrs. Barnes both hugged me with tears running down theirs faces. They told me they were going to pray for my family and me. They lost their family in one night and here they are worried about me? That didn't make sense to me. Katie's parents on the other hand were on the opposite end of the emotional line. Katie's momma tried to climb in the coffin with her daughter. Buckie and Stacy were crying snot running down their faces and everything. I wasn't gonna hug them like that, but I understood the feeling.

Annette

All I wanted were the pictures of our good times together. Tim agreed that was all he wanted as well. Everything else in the house was sold and then Emma and the Barnes sold both houses. I thought for sure momma would convince Emma to keep the house that she and Hezekiah shared. Momma was working hard on her, but Emma didn't want anything from that house, she said she couldn't do it. Emma sold the big house and she got a little condo, just big enough for her. Emma told me she went off on momma so badly she made her cry real hard. Emma was angry relaying the story; she said the whole scene at the funeral was nice for the people who didn't know. However, it was no secret that momma never liked Kiah, Emma said she called her out on everything. She even got on her case about how she's always treated me and how it was not right that the only time she called me was to beg for money as if I owed her anything. Then she even told her about herself and how she lies on me all the time. I sat there crying as I listened to my little sister defend me with the rage I thought only lived inside of me. Emma said she needed to get away from San Francisco for a while, and that she'd call me when she came back. She said she was going to spend some time in Kansas, but she was eventually going to get out and see the world just like she and Hezekiah had always planned.

Timothy

"Well hello stranger!" A familiar voice said.

I turned around and it was Natalie. I hadn't seen her in years, and she looked exactly the same. Looking at her I remembered a time when I used to smile. "Hey yourself!" She was standing there with her chest stuck out so I looked at it.

She poked her lip out at me. "Someone said you got married, I thought I'd never see you again."

I held up my hand to show her my band, "the rumors are true. I've got three of the most beautiful kids."

"No doubt about that, look at their daddy."

It had been months since I've felt like smiling and Natalie made me blush repeatedly. "Sit down, have a seat. What's new with you?" I didn't really care, somehow talking to her made me feel better. Talking to her all worries and issues vanished.

"Are you still a bad boy Tim?" She watched my eyes.

"Nope, I love my wife."

"My mother says once a bad boy always a bad boy. She was surprised when I told her you got married."

"Why was that surprising to her?" I asked.

"She's the one who told me you weren't the marrying kind. Looking at you today, you look like a bad boy who caught the love bug, but you're dying to act out again."

I sat back, "are you offering to free me from my cage?"

"Maybe." She smiled at me.

I don't know what else she said or I said for that matter. On autopilot I drove to the drugstore, I bought condoms then I went back to her place. Natalie laid there satisfied with herself and I now felt angrier than I had been before. I felt lost amongst other things.

Annette

My headaches are back, my hair keeps falling out, and I can't even deal with it. I can't be pregnant; Tim and I have been too busy mourning to make love. Lately Tim's so busy working and we hardly see each other, so I can't be pregnant. When he finally comes home he tries to sleep on the couch claiming that he doesn't want to disturb me. I tell him to come anyways, but he gets mad and tells me to stop bothering him. I tell him he needs to sleep, he looks bad, but he ignores me. I don't know where my loving husband has gone, but the guy occupying Tim's body is mean and hurtful. He's always angry, and very short tempered. "Mrs. Wallace you're pregnant," my doctor said gently.

"How?"

"How?" The doctor looked confused.

"Yes! How! Tim and I are done having babies."

"Yes I understand that, but sometimes when a man and a woman love each other very much they become very passionate towards each other. And that passion can lead the man's body to respond…."

"Thank you I needed that laugh. Tim and I haven't made love in months." I said.

“This is the longest you’ve gone before checking in with me. You’re almost four months give or take a week.”

Then I remembered, the last time we were together there was no condom. “Please tell me that the birth control my sister in-law is on is legal.”

My doctor smiled, “after this baby we can get you on the pill.”

“Good, cause I don’t know how we’re going to survive this. My family has been through so much, last thing we need is the pregnant Annette around.”

“As usual, eat healthy and get plenty of exercise.”

Reality hit me again as I sat in front of Katie’s house preparing myself to go in. When the new family came home, I realized I drove there on autopilot. By the time I got to Irma’s house I was a blubbering mess. I could barely talk I was SO upset! Irma made me go lay down, I couldn’t even tell her what the doctor said. In my dream I was talking to Katie, and she was so excited for me. I started crying in my sleep telling her how much we missed her, and how much we needed her. I woke up to Irma holding me and telling me it would be ok. I told her I was pregnant, and I didn’t know how Tim would respond. I told her we both agreed that we were done, and that he’s been working so hard he comes home exhausted. I told her he lost all his pudgy weight from when he stopped smoking. She asked about the weekends, and I told her he takes the boys with him. He doesn’t stop working, he keeps going and going. She rubbed my arm and said ok. She told me she’s been trying to reach him all day. I told her, he moves around a lot more these days so its hard to catch him in one spot long enough to tell him anything.

Timothy

"What is this?" Mr. Barnes said frowning at the check.

"Jeremiah's wages for the rest of the year." I said trying to walk away.

"Uh! Son come back here." Mr. Barnes commanded, I came back out of my respect for him. I didn't want to argue about it. "Thank you? We don't need Jeremiah's money. I have my retirement and we get along just fine."

"With all due respect sir I'm not going to argue with you about this. I know Jeremiah was helping out around here. As long as I'm here you will want for nothing!" I said trying to keep anger out if my voice.

"Come in," he said walking away from the front door. I looked at the sky. All I wanted to do was drop off the check and get on with my day. I stepped inside the house the Barnes's have lived in my entire life. It was torture cause immediately I remembered running around this house even though we were told not to. Getting my butt beat for acting crazy, and eating good food and good times. "Have a seat," he said nicely. So I sat, "how's the family?"

"You know us Wallace's, we're always hustling." I tried to sound light hearted but I knew it didn't sound that way.

"I'm not going to beat around the bush with you. It's not my style. You look like crap! Are you sleeping?"

"No," I said watching his face.

"My boys loved you very much, one thing I've always admired about you was your ability to laugh and smile, even sometimes when I didn't particularly find anything funny. It's been months since I've seen the slightest hint of a smile from you. You're walking around mad at the world."

"Can you blame me?"

"Yes! You are a young man in good health, with a beautiful and healthy family. Stop focusing on what you lost and start appreciating what you have before you

lose it. Your wife hasn't been feeling well, did you know about that?" I looked at the floor. "I know you're hurting, but don't get so caught up in remembering the dead that you forget about the living."
I asked if I could use the phone. I called home and there was no answer. Annette was probably out picking Timothy up from school. I went to both of my offices, and then I dropped by Emma's store. Everything was running well, and then I went home. It was dark in the house. I called Raynel and asked if Annette was with her. She said no and that she hadn't seen her in a couple days. After awhile longer I called Lauren and she said the same thing. I knew Emma was in Kansas so she wasn't with her. One by one I called everyone and just as panic started to hit me I called my momma. Momma tore into me, she said Annette and the kids have been at her house for the past three days. When I thought about it I didn't go in our bedroom, or in the kids rooms. I came in late slept on the couch and left early. I was immediately angry with Annette for bringing my momma into our business. I told my momma I was coming and she told me not to come. I looked at the phone like my momma was crazy. I told her I was coming to bring my family home. Momma dared me to confront her! She said I needed to stay away until I could come and show my family the appreciation they deserved. I surprised myself when I found myself on the freeway defying her words. When I pulled up to the house momma was sitting on the porch with Pops. When I got out the car Pops stood up and momma marched towards me. She pushed my shoulders while she screamed at me. She told me I wasn't the only person hurting and she was disappointed in me! When I tried to walk past her she punched me in my jaw. That got my attention; I looked at her in disbelief. She told me to go home and not to come back until the Tim she raised was back. I looked at her and then I looked at Pops. His eyes told me I better listen to my momma. I got back in my car then I burned rubber as I pulled away.

****

As I started to pull out of my spot a car pulled up behind me blocking me in. I looked at the car, it was Pops and Jeff. Pops tapped on my driver's side window, "get rid of her. Meet me at the store."
"Natalie?" Jeff said looking at her, "where you come from?"
"I've always been around," she tried to say like she was somebody.
Jeff looked at me then he reached in the window and unlocked the back door. He got in the car and started talking to me like she wasn't sitting there. "You look like you're sick!"
"Whatever!" I said shaking my head.
"I don't know why you're doing this. I bet you, you throw up after you touch her."
"Not my finest moment." My comment wounded Natalie.
"Why are you doing this if it's not even what you want?"
"You're judging me?" I asked in irritation.
"YES! Whew! I thought you were going to miss the point in this state of craziness." He smiled as he sat back. "Keep going like you're going and you're going to end up like Frank."
I stood on the break! "WHAT?"
Natalie looked scared, "are you crazy?"
"Shut up!" I told Natalie.
"You're about to lose your wife. Unlike Raynel, you know Annette won't be single for long."
"You're telling me my wife is stepping out on me?"

"Well I guess you wouldn't know would you?" He watched my eyes in the mirror. "Wouldn't you say it was in her right if she did?"
I pulled over, "get out!" I told Natalie.
"Tim?" She said with tears in her eyes.
"Don't make me push you out."
Natalie got out of the car in tears. "Where's her car?"
"Around the corner!"
When we walked into Pops's office he had the chessboard set up. He told me to play Jeff. We were moving fast and Jeff beat the pants off me three times. Then Pops sat down, he told me I'm falling apart. He said I'm lashing out angry and no matter what I keep setting up the board against myself. Then we started our game, which only brought home his point. I told him we play again as I set up the board. When I got tired of losing I threw the board across the room. Pops said nothing, he watched my face. "You're not the only one hurting. Your family needs you. Go clean yourself up and then beg your wife to forgive how you've behaved.

****

Momma was on the porch watching me get out of the car. She met me on the sidewalk and she looked up at me with sad eyes. "Where did you go?"
"It was supposed to be me." I said trying to hold back my emotion.
"With the way you've behaved it might as well had been you. That poor girl has been going through a lot and I will not let you run all over her you hear me. If it were up to me, I'd send you away again." She looked me in my eyes. "I can see the guilt all over you. You don't have to do everything like your father would." Then she popped me upside the head.
"DAD!" Timothy said as he ran out the front door top speed, with Malachi right on his heels.
My boys tackled me then they asked question after question as they had me on the ground. Momma walked inside then she returned to the front with Jade who was now walking on her own. It hit me like a ton of bricks that I missed her first steps. She looked at me with questioning eyes just like her momma was going to. "How's daddy's baby?" I said as I put my hands out. Jade's little face lit up and she ran to me and placed her head on my shoulder.
"You determine the type of man she will have in her life." Momma said then she walked inside.
"Can you take us to the park?" Malachi asked.
"That's where you want to go? Sure. Go grab a jacket for your sister. Tell your momma we will be back." I said stalling going inside.
When we got to the park the boys stayed by my side instead of running off to play like they normally would. Timothy had his protective man stance on as he asked me where I've been. I didn't expect Malachi to understand what was going on, and I underestimated Timothy. I didn't try to make it pretty or give him a false sense of security. I told him point blank that I got so caught up in what I was feeling, that I didn't consider what I was doing to him or our family. Timothy looked at me with pain in his face as he told me he's needed to talk to me. He said his Uncles tried but it wasn't the same. When he said his Uncle Frank has been coming by everyday an alarm went off inside me. I hadn't spoken directly to Frank in I don't know how long. As I drove I started plotting Frank's death in my mind. He better not have even thought of pushing up on my wife. Is this what Jeff was trying to tell me without telling me? That FAT... FOOL! Was going to die a quick and painful death!

HE'S HERE! His car was parked outside. I put Jade down so she could play with Gwen. Then I went from room to room looking for my wife. When I got to Pops's office he and Frank were talking. I didn't care that they were talking I interrupted. Pops waved me off saying they went to the market. I parked next to momma's car and then I went inside. I combed the entire store. They weren't there, but momma's car was still parked next to mine. I sat in my car waiting for them to appear. I exhaled, why momma gotta make sure Annette plays these games? Time kept passing and I was dying! Frank would die, but I would forgive Annette. It was dark, it was cold, and I was hungry! The market had been closed for an hour when Pops's car pulled up. Jeff got out while Frank drove back to the house. Jeff asked me why I was sitting out here? I told him I was waiting for momma and Annette. He smiled and said they've been at the house for a long time. Irritated I burned rubber on my tires back to my parent's house. My momma plays too doggone much! I thought about running the red light, but I decided to wait. I pulled all up on the curb with Jeff right behind me in momma's car. Jeff smiled really big at me. "What's with all the smiles?" I snapped at him.

"I'm gonna be a daddy!"

That fast I forgot about all my irritation and self-pity. "Congratulations!" I gave my big brother a hug.

"Thank you! Thank you! I was starting to question what was wrong with me. I guess our time wasn't until now. My brains and Lauren's looks, I don't think the world is ready for my spawn." He laughed wholeheartedly. Momma looked out the door and his smile dropped. "You better go!"

"Am I walking in to something?" I asked him. He shook his head yes then he looked away.

I took a deep breath, all the women were in the living room looking at Lauren's barely there stomach. All smiles dropped as soon as all the women saw me. I knew Annette would be mad, but to see Martha look at me the same way as everyone else hurt. Annette's face was full and full of hurt and disappointment. I asked her to come outside with me. "It's too cold outside!" Martha barked.

Then I noticed that they were all sitting under blankets as they visited. "Can we go upstairs?" I said cause I wasn't going to sit in front of everyone and talk.

Martha told Annette to take the top blanket that she wrapped around her shoulders before she stood up. I followed Annette out of the room. As she started to walk up the stairs Frank called out to her. "Aaaa! Where you going?"

I stuck my head around the corner; Frank sat there staring at me. We went in the guest room. I shut the door then Annette slapped me as hard as she could! "I TELL YOU I HAVE ABANDONMENT ISSUES AND NOT ONLY DO YOU LEAVE ME! YOU LEFT ME AT MY WEAKEST POINT! BECAUSE YOU CAN'T HANDLE WHAT YOU FEEL! IT TOOK YOU THREE DAYS TO EVEN NOTICE I WAS GONE!" She slapped me again. "I DON'T EVEN KNOW WHY YOU'RE HERE! YOU SHOULD GO BACK TO WHERE EVER YOU'VE BEEN FOR THE PAST FEW MONTHS!" Then she stood up to walk out the room clasping the blanket around her shoulders. I grabbed her wrist as she tried to walk past me. Through clinched lips she said, "I KNOW YOU HAVE NOT COMPLETELY LOST YOUR MIND! LET ME GO!" When I didn't let go. She dropped the blanket and started hitting me.

The room spun and I fell on the bed. She was coming to hit me and all I saw was life growing in her stomach. Now I really wanted to crawl under a rock and die. I put my hands on her stomach while she kept hitting me and yelling at me. "I'm sorry! I'm sorry!"

Chapter 23

Annette

Since this is my baby alone, I don't tell Timothy about it. I refuse to go home with him or deal with him at all! He comes over everyday and follows me around the house. I won't speak to him, I don't want to look at him for fear I will grow a heart and take it easy on him. So every time he gets close to me I hit him as hard as I can. On the days I can't deal with looking at him I cry, then I get mad at my self for having a reaction or letting him see me cry. Jade gives him hugs and kisses as soon as she sees him. She's my cuddle buddy. Seems like that girl knows every time I need a hug cause here she comes. The moments I'm not cuddling with her then I'm cuddling with Malachi. My babies know how to give me the love their no good daddy couldn't.

I feel guilty about Pops getting up early in the morning to take Timothy to school all the way in Oakland. Pops told me to hush and he said it was not a problem. Pops takes him and Tim brings him home. Irma told me I don't have to go back to Oakland unless I want to. She said we could stay with them as long as we want. I thanked her, cause I was not ready to deal with her son.

Tim hurt me so bad, I can't even put it into words other than to say; his abandonment has felt worse than when my father died. If this baby wasn't so crazy I'd lay down all day everyday. If I lay down too long the baby starts kicking, like it knows my schedule better than I do. It has to be a boy, cause it's so bossy. Because I can't stand Tim so much right now I know my baby is going to come out looking just like him. More like him than Timothy and Malachi combined. I have no idea if it is a boy or a girl so Lauren and I have been going back and forth with names for our babies. Since the moment she told me she thought she was pregnant I haven't felt so alone anymore. Even though Peggy just had another baby, and Beth would deliver soon, being pregnant with Lauren was just what the doctor ordered.

I will say being in this house makes me see Poppa and Nana's (as the kids call them) relationship differently. There's no doubt that Poppa loves Nana, he will move heaven and earth if she moves an eyebrow at anyone or anything. Then.... He disappears for a while. Irma normally gets on his case real bad when he reappears. He has to work hard to get back in her good graces, but she let's him back in. I don't want to spend the rest of my life fighting with Tim like this. I'd rather call it quits. At this point calling it quits feels like the right thing to do.

Timothy

I sit here staring at paper with the pen in my hand. I need to make her understand, I need her to see things the way I saw them. No wait a minute that could be bad too. Annette walks around looking so hurt and I know that's all my fault. Being this upset can't be good for the baby, but who am I kidding? I'm not the one to cheer her up. Every time I come near her she has an extremely emotional response. I prefer it when she hits me, her tears hurt worse than her punch ever could. I know where those tears come from. I wish I could take it all back, but you can't undo what's been done. I'm worried about her and the baby. Since she's not talking to me, I'm hand fed the things she wants me to know from momma. Momma at first said I messed up badly, now she says she doesn't know if I can fix it.

Frank keeps coming around; he's here sometimes when I get here. He brings his kids to be with mine and our parents, but I also see him watching Annette. Wishing my daughter was his. Annette doesn't pay him any special attention, but he doesn't get the cold shoulder like I do. Frank and I have stare downs sometimes, and I tell him he's greedy. How he's always wanted what was mine. Frank doesn't say anything; he doesn't even try to deny it. He watches me back until someone else breaks up our love Fest.

"Dad?" Timothy said

"Yes son."

"Why do you carry a gun?"

"You never know where the day will take you." I looked at him. "It's about time I teach you how to shoot."

He stretched his eyes, "a gun?"

"No you're mouth! Of course! A gun!" I laughed, "as soon as momma has the baby we'll go."

He smiled real big, "ok." Malachi walked in the room with a milk mustache. "I thought they needed to buy more milk?"

"Mrs. Walker gave me some, and she gave me cookies too." Malachi said sitting on the floor.

"Why she always giving you stuff?" Timothy asked.

Malachi shrugged, "I say hi. I help her with her yard and groceries. She say I'm so cute, then she give me stuff. You should be nice to her too."

"Stop working that old lady." I said laughing.

Malachi smiled, "how?"

"You go over there charming her. Smiling at her and doing things so she looks at you like you're the greatest little man ever."

"Timothy does it too. Is it wrong?" He asked

"Depends," I said shrugging.

"Dad's going to teach me how to shoot."

"I wanna go! Can I? Can I?" Malachi begged.

"I don't know, you're kind of too little."

"I won't be little, I'll be big! I promise!"

Annette

"Momma," Timothy whispered. My eye popped open. "Dad is in the hallway, he has breakfast for you. Do you want him to put it in the oven to keep it warm?"

"No, it's fine." I said slowly sitting up. Jade woke up with all of my movements. Timothy opened the door and Tim brought in the breakfast tray. Malachi had the job of carrying the beautiful bouquet of flowers. I wanted to react to them cause they were beautiful, but I didn't. I said a dry and ungrateful thank you. When they left I smiled at Jade as her little nose sniffed my flowers. Jade and I ate like Queens then Tim came back for the tray.

Irma sat on the bed excited. "I keep having more and more grand babies. Each one is like a little treasure. I see another piece of me and Franklin living on in this world. All our babies gonna be educated and powerful!" She said with so much pride. "Look at Jade, she's so smart. Make sure she uses that to her advantage. Timothy reminds me of Dale with all his drawings. I hope you don't mind that I asked Dale to see if he's interested in architecture. Darren and Sharon say they want to be architects too, but neither one of them can draw as well as Timothy." I smiled. "Now Malachi," she laughed. "That little charmer, I took him to the market with me and he had women giving him money cause he's so cute. He acts like his daddy.

Tim always had old ladies falling all over their selves for him." My laughter subsided. She rubbed my stomach, "I wonder who this firecracker is."
"Your guess is as good as...." A contraction hit me hard out of nowhere. I bent over holding my stomach.
Irma's eyes got big. "This one wants to debut early I see."
I got up and went to the bathroom. As I was sitting another hard contraction hit me and it made me vomit at the same time. Fortunately I grabbed the trash can and vomited there cause I couldn't get off the toilet. Irma opened the door... I mean I know she's been there for all of my babies, but I did not want her in the bathroom with me. She said I didn't look good and then she felt my forehead. She told me as soon as I was ready she was taking me to the hospital. I could hear commotion outside the door as I sat there begging the room to stop spinning. When I came out the bathroom Tim was standing by the door waiting for me. He tried to touch me to guide me; I smacked his hands telling him to stop touching me. When the hospital staff was wheeling me to the back my contractions were coming in on top of each other so I couldn't tell them to send Tim away. The doctor said my baby was breach but there was still time to try to turn the baby around. The baby was being difficult until I told it to knock it off. To everyone's surprise the baby did as I told it to. It let the doctor guide it and then my labor changed to normal labor for me. The baby slid out porcelain white. I gasped when I saw it. "Congratulations Wallace's it's a girl!" When they put her in his arms he looked at her then he looked at me with red eyes. "It's me!" He said, and then he brought her over for me to see.
That girl belted out the loudest newborn cry I've ever heard. "No, she's me."

Timothy

Seeing how Annette won't let me near her, I know it's wrong. I'm grateful for the contractions that haven't allowed her to talk to tell them to kick me out. As my child changed colors and they called out that it was a girl, I was shocked that she was so light skinned. She looked at me and cried really loudly. Even though Annette corrected me and said the baby looked like her, momma said she looked like me too. I walked down the hall with her as she watched me. I proudly told them it was a girl, and I handed her to Pops. He said whoa when he looked at her. I could tell Frank was dying to hold her, so I made him wait until everyone else did. I held Jade and I showed her her baby sister. She smiled really big and looked at the baby with love in her eyes.
In her room Annette kept staring at the baby, she told her she knew she was going to look like me. She looked at me and told me the baby's name is Amber. The first words she's spoken to me on her own.

****

Amber is a little sweetheart; this one has Annette's fire. Jade has it too, but she focuses on kindness more than Amber. She's only a baby and I can see her momma all over her. She has a big heart, but don't make her mad. Amber is always looking for her momma, that is momma's baby for real. She's the only one to prefer her momma so strongly over me, and then I feel guilty. With all my other kids they heard my voice, they knew me before. I got no belly time with Amber; I could be an uncle for all she knows.

Annette

"Mrs. Wallace your stitches have healed nicely. It's ok to be with your husband."
"HA! He's not touching me!" I tried to laugh but tears came pouring out of my eyes.
"Oh honey," she said giving me tissues. "It's just the baby blues."
"I wish! Our best friends died a year ago, the only time he touched me is when I got pregnant. He forgot about us for a while. You saw how long it took me to realize I was pregnant. He didn't know until I was big. I'm in no hurry to give him anything that will make him feel good or loved! I didn't do anything wrong! He left me behind like I don't matter."
My doctor rubbed my back, "honey every marriage goes through something. What I do know is how much that man loves you. I'm not telling you to forgive him…."
I cut her off, "GOOD! Cause I don't! Now that the pregnancy is over I can try to get my whits back. I have to decide what I'm going to do." I said my mind was running a thousand miles a minute.
"Do you need the prescription then?"
"Yes, just in case I meet someone new. I'm done having babies! They get you pregnant to trap you. All these men talking about women using babies to trap them, and that's all my man has ever done. Each time he got me pregnant was to set me up for this! FOUR KIDS! I'm going to take my kids and run away. Let him feel the PAIN!"
My doctor was sitting there with her eyes stretched. "Mrs. Wallace, Annette. I know you're hurting! Don't react until you have a clear head."
"I LOST ONE OF MY BEST FRIENDS TOO! MY SISTER! His stupid buffalo head brother made things difficult with one friend. Then I lose another, and MY NIECE! SHE WAS JUST A BABY!" I screamed in anger! "He knocks me up and then leaves me to deal with the kids and their questions. I didn't know what to say to them; my son comes home from school talking about heaven. I'm not religious I couldn't tell him yes or no. My momma finally had to explain that they were sleeping. He left me to deal with that all by myself! I want to step on his man parts and make him bleed!" I said, "men are useless! All they do is leave you when you need them most. I'm not counting on them anymore. I bought the fairy tale, the idea that someone could actually love me. IT'S ALL LIES!" I cried angry tears!
My doctor tried but she couldn't get me to calm down. She doesn't understand my life. I asked Tim if this is what he was going to do. He should've been honest with me. Instead of making me believe I was a part of something real. Now I got four kids and stretch marks to show for it. Well money, a fancy car, and a nice house, but STILL! That doesn't make this ok. When I walked out in to the lobby Irma was trying to calm Amber who was always fussing. Sometimes I would pace the floor with her, this little girl is a lot of work. Jade was so mild and Amber's a little firecracker. Malachi normally makes her laugh, and Jade's kisses will stop her tears some times. Most times she just wants her momma. She got the nerve to not look black at all. I told Martha that Amber was her baby or anyone of her sisters. This girl is all Wallace when you look at her. Tim calls her little Annette when she starts fussing. I ignore him and go about my business.

****

"Look at my babies!" Aunt Dorothy said as we walked up the stairs to her door.
"Come in, come in!" She said taking Amber from me.
"Gentlemen, I made a seesaw just for your visit today. Let's go test it out." Uncle Rufus called the boys out to the backyard."

"How's my little Jade doing? You're such a sweet little lady." She said.
Jade smiled, "tank chu."
"Annette your children are adorable. It looks like you got one each color too." She joked, I didn't laugh. "Is Tim still acting up?"
"I wouldn't know, I'm not talking to him."
"You trying to push him back out there?"
"Auntie I don't care what he does. I didn't do anything but try to be there for him. He can go run the streets and have four more for all I care. I'm DONE!"
Aunt Dorothy looked at Amber and Jade, "you've got some beautiful girls. It would be a shame for them to grow up without their father, for them to end up victims to some no good no life idiot. Passed around from guy to guy."
"That could happen whether he's there or not."
"But doesn't that kind of seal it for them. Isn't that what happened with you?"
"NO! I see what you're trying to do. It's not going to work!"
"What am I doing?" She said trying to make her face innocent.
"You're trying to make me defend Tim in hopes that that will make me see something that isn't there!" I rolled my eyes.
As we talked Aunt Dorothy cleaned an apple then she gave it to Jade. Amber wanted some, and Jade was happy to share with her. Amber doesn't have teeth so I told Jade to enjoy her apple and not to share with Amber. Amber got so mad her little cheeks turned red and she started to cut up. I popped her and told her to cut it out. She cried and then she wanted me to hug her. Aunt Dorothy told me I didn't want to deal with Amber alone.

****

"Lauren, she's beautiful!" I said holding her baby girl. Little Sophia was a combination of her momma and her daddy just like Jeff said the baby would be.
"Doesn't she look just like me?" Jeff said proudly.
"Yes, but she looks like Lauren too."
"Thank you Annette, she wouldn't be beautiful without me!"
"Forget all of you! My grandchild gets her looks from me!" Pops said touching her hand.
Lauren smiled at Tim who was watching Frank as he held Amber. Frank comes over all the time, and every time he has to hold Jade or Amber. Since Jade is on the go now with Gwen and the rest of the children he gets Amber who isn't mobile yet. Sometimes Gwen pitches a fit and she wants her daddy to hold her and put my girls down. He tells her she can share for a minute as he refuses to let my girls go. When I talk to Raynel she says he tries to tell her they could agree to have a little girl together and that she could have whatever she wants in return. She said she reminds him that he has a daughter and that she doesn't want to have anymore kids. I told her she should see him with my girls and she said she hears about it from him and from the boys. Then she asked me what Gwen looked like, cause she's never seen her. Fernando comes over all the time; he even spends the night with his brothers. Raynel said that's because they bonded when she and Frank were together. Gwen on the other hand was never brought around her. She's a smart little thing, but I see a whole lot of her momma in her.
Martha walked in the door followed by her clan and with her baby on her hip and pregnant again. "Moving takes forever!" She yelled.
"Come sit down baby." Irma said taking her to the couch and giving her a pedestal to put her feet up.

"Momma feel free to keep them a little longer if you like. I can get more unpacking done without them in my way." She said.
Sebastian came in the door whistling, "that camper is NICE! You gonna take her out on the road and open her up?"
"That's for our family trip. I might take the misses away, but that won't be in that camper."
"Annette!" Martha said like she was angry, "HOW ARE YOU SO SKINNY? The baby isn't six months yet."
I blushed cause everyone looked at me. "Four kids will do this especially when the baby is strong willed and tries to out stubborn you." Martha rolled her eyes at me. Does it help that I've lost a lot of hair? I plan on cutting it again this weekend. Well Raynel's going to cut it for me."
"That helps," Martha teased.
Couple by couple the parents left after they dropped their children off. The house was crawling with kids Malachi's age and bigger. Uncle Tim was the hit of the sleepover nights, and I helped Irma during the day manage all the kids. Pops and all the boys took the camper to the Market and loaded it up with food and supplies for their trip over the weekend. Irma told me I didn't have to go home while they were gone; she said we could stay just like last summer. I didn't know what I was going to do, I told her I would play it by ear. Malachi was torn, he didn't want to leave his momma, but he didn't want to miss the fun either. I told him to go have a good time and that his sisters and I would be waiting to hear all the fun. I held Amber while Tim held Jade and we waved goodbye to everyone as they drove away down the street. Tim stood there staring at me. I rolled my eyes at him and walked back inside. I went up to my room and I shut the door. Amber watched me like she was taking notes. Tim knocked softly on the door. "Are you hungry?" I rolled my eyes, then I got the brush and started brushing Ambers curls.
Tim slowly opened the door and Jade came running in. "Mommy hungry?" She asked me as if I didn't hear her daddy.
I smiled at her and shook my head no. "Do you know what you'll want for dinner? I could go to the market."
"I WANT YOU TO LEAVE ME ALONE!" I yelled then I threw a shoe at him. Jade and Amber looked at their daddy like they didn't know what to expect next.
"Annette we need to talk."
"I DON'T WANT TO TALK TO YOU! I'M DONE WITH YOU, JUST LIKE YOU'VE BEEN DONE WITH ME! WE DON'T HAVE TO PRETEND!"
"Who's pretending? This is the longest conversation we've had since I came back."
I picked up another shoe and threw it, "THAT'S BECAUSE YOU LEFT ME! GET OUT TIM OR I WILL LEAVE!"
"I'm trying to be patient with you but you keep pushing me!" He said trying to get a hold of his own temper. I could see in his face that he was seconds away from snapping. The girls were looking with big eyes. I got up, hit him, grabbed my purse and headed for the door. "Annette take Amber wherever you're going. I can't feed her."
"You'll figure it out!" I said then I marched out the door.
I found myself driving to Oakland. My poor little house was all closed up and abandoned. I called Raynel and I told her we were kid free and we were going out. Although I doubt that Tim could follow me with the two little ones I got my clothes then I went over Raynel's place. Frank bought the house next door to her parent's house for her. Partly because he wanted to be able to come over when he liked and

mostly because Raynel needed her own space away from her parents. All the way next door. Raynel asked where we were going and I told her we were going to *The Place Where Jazz Is Played*. I told her we'd have dinner and drinks, and if we felt like dancing later on, we'd decide where to go after that. As we were enjoying our meal, drinks, and the music the host was showing someone in. Raynel immediately became annoyed as the host sat Frank and Christy near our table. When Frank saw us he smiled, then his smile disappeared. I told Raynel he was going to send Christy home. Frank wouldn't take his eyes off of our table. Eventually Christy saw us as well. I imagined her remembering the last time she saw me and how I smacked the life out of her face. I smiled at her then I returned my attention to the stage. Sure enough after the first set finished I saw Frank call someone over and he told them something. Christy turned red just like her hair as Frank dismissed her. I pointed at Christy when she stormed out. Frank walked over to our table, "you coming ladies?" He said putting his arms out for us.
"Where are we going?" I asked grabbing my purse and standing up.
"You'll have to come along and see now won't you." He said waiting for Raynel to get on board. Raynel exhaled and stood up. "Neither one of you has ran with me all night have you?" He said as we walked out of the club.
"You're scaring me," I joked.
"Let me have your car key." He said putting his hand out.
"As in take it off the ring?"
"Hurry up you're wasting time." I gave him my car key. He waved a guy over from the shadows. When he got close I realized it was Eugene. "Take her car to my parent's house. Park it in front and put the key in the mail slot on the door."
"Bye Eugene," I said feeling a little tipsy already.
"Who is Eugene?" Raynel whispered to me.
"He works for Tim. Do you remember Whispers?"
"Girl! Who doesn't?"
"That's one of his many kids."
A car pulled up to the curb in front of us, and Franky held the door open. He told the driver to take us to *The Red Door*. I asked what that meant, and he said it was the name of a club. We pulled up to a restaurant called Scott's. Frank held out his arms and we walked with him as he walked so proud. People were looking at us trying to figure out who Raynel and I were. We walked through the restaurant to the red door next to the bathrooms. Frank knocked a specific knock and then the door opened. This club was packed with people, people who were dancing and then people who were all over each other. Frank stood still and let us take in everything. Raynel was definitely out of her element. She was looking all over the club at everything cause she never seen anything like it. If Hazel's was in a big city like San Francisco I imagined that it would be just like this. Frank asked us if we wanted to go behind the *GREEN* door. My curiosity was peaked but I looked at Raynel, Frank told us to watch him and we didn't have to try anything if we didn't want to. As we approached the *GREEN* door someone opened it for us. There was a green light and the room was very cloudy. It didn't smell like cigarettes though. It smelled more like my father's pipe. A woman came over and told Frank there was a private couch over to the side for him. When we sat down Raynel looked around with big eyes. There were six hand rolled looking cigarettes on the table. Frank picked up one lit it and then inhaled. He started choking then he asked me if I wanted it. I asked him why I couldn't have my own cigarette. He smiled and told me to inhale. I took a big inhale off of the cigarette and I immediately started choking. It wasn't

like my first cigarette though. The feeling was different. I gave it back to Frank and asked him what was that, he said it was grass. He offered it to Raynel, but she declined. Frank shrugged and then he finished the cigarette. My lips felt numb like I had been drinking. Then the woman who showed us to our couch came over, she asked Frank if we wanted a brownie. He said he needed one for us to share. Raynel said she loved chocolate and she wanted her own. He smiled and said he doesn't know why he never thought of this. I didn't know what he meant by that. The girl brought us each a half of the moistest and delicious brownie I've ever had in my life. Raynel sat back on the couch like she was thinking. She looked at Frank and asked him what was in that brownie. I raised my eyebrow at him and he held up his cigarette, then he told us we needed to relax. Every time Raynel tried to sit up she fell backwards like a magnet was pulling her down, that made us laugh. "Now, let's talk." Frank said smiling. "Raynel, do you still love me?"
"Franky you know I do!" Then she slapped her hands over her mouth like she couldn't believe she just said that. I laughed so hard I felt like I was going to be sick, but it felt good. "Why did you cheat on me?"
Frank looked at her, "cause you wouldn't work with me. It was your way or no way. Your good girl speech was KILLING me!"
"I didn't know." She said like she was explaining. "Why didn't you tell me?"
"I thought my asking was telling you. Come home Raynel."
"I'm not that drunk! NO! You need that big ole house. I don't want it. You have another woman living there."
"I'm not going to divorce you." He said watching her face.
She smiled, "until I get old and wrinkly."
"We are not getting a divorce! If I have to play boyfriend the rest of my life so be it."
"Then so be it! Glad that's settled." She smiled.
Frank grabbed her thigh with his big hands. Raynel smiled back at him, then he looked at me. "How long you gonna leave my kid brother in the doghouse?"
"I want a divorce!" I said nonchalantly.
"You really think you're going to find someone who loves you more than Tim?"
"Probably not, but I don't believe he loves me. Who treats someone they love like he treated me? I'm tired of men!"
Franky lowered his head, "meaning?"
"Meaning, I think I'll just go it alone with my kids and call it a day."
"Oh," then he looked around. "So you want Tim to man up and win you back."
"No," I said shaking my head yes.
Frank started laughing as he tried to mimic me. "NO?" He said shaking his head yes.
"Stop trying to confuse me!"
"You did that one on your own." He laughed, "Tim is in love with you! He's not going to let you go."
"I'm already gone."

****

In the morning I was in pain, I needed to breastfeed Amber quick fast and in a hurry. I grabbed my clothes that were spread out all over the floor and quickly put them on. I told Raynel she could NEVER tell a soul about what happened last night. She smiled and then she asked me why would she EVER tell? I took her pillow and I hit Frank with it, he shook his head yes as he hurried back to sleep. The driver took me to Irma's house. Amber had just woke up and Tim was about to make her a

bottle. I took her and happily relieved myself, I was hurting. Amber was so full she went back to sleep. Tim watched me as I got my things to get in the shower. I kissed Jade then I went to the bathroom, I got in the shower and then as I stepped out Tim was standing there. “You have fun last night?”
"Of course! Hand me my towel.” I said not hiding.
“You don’t love me anymore?”
“No!”
Tim stared into my eyes, “what do you want me to do?”
“I want a divorce.”
“Is there someone else?”
“Maybe, it’s none of your business.”
Tim stood up in my face, “none of my business? Who you think gave you business worth having? If it weren’t for me you’d still think you were broken! All these years of you throwing your little fits and acting like a crazy person. The first time I go off the deep end you want a divorce?” He said calmly but very angry.
“I go off when you deserve it. I did not deserve what I got. I may be emotional and high strung, but you NEVER wondered where I was, if I still loved you. You knew you had me. I don’t know how many women you were with but I know there was at least one. You didn’t even try to hide what you were doing. I don’t know what you thought was going to happen, but I only knew you. I was waiting on you. You violated everything, and went against everything you vowed to do. You said you’d never, and here we are. **YOU ABANDONED ME!** You know everything there is to know about me. You know better than anyone else how that affected me. I want a divorce, you don’t get to be my husband.”
“No one will ever love you like I do!”
“And look where your love has gotten me? You might be right, but there will always be some man waiting to get his hands dirty with me. I won’t be lonely, in case you’ve forgotten I’m beautiful. Men will always come, They may not love me, but all the guys who’ve claimed to love me couldn’t be any worse than the dogs who will come and piss on me. I don’t even care anymore.”
"I wasn't trying to hurt you."
I stared at him, "wow! Really? So what you were doing was supposed to make me feel good? Excellent job! Well done! I feel so loved and valued. I lost my family too! You don't care! All you care about is what you were going through. How you were hurting!"
"At the time I couldn't see past what I was going through. I didn't do any of it to hurt you."
"But you did! I don't care why anymore. Tim I don't want to be married to you. I will never let anyone hurt me like you have ever again!"
I could see Tim teeter-tottering between his emotions, but I didn't care. "You have fun last night?"
"A blast thank you for asking. Let me know the nights you can afford to take off from your whores so that I can go out again."

Timothy

"That's good son, but you gotta hold it like this cause the recoil on the gun can hurt you." I showed Timothy how. Malachi sat patiently on the side taking notes.
I love that Malachi sits on the sideline listening as if I'm talking to him. He takes mental notes then he applies them. When it was Malachi's turn, he stepped in like a professional. Jeff looked at us with pride, and then he paid attention to the rest of

the nieces and nephews. Momma feels it's important that the girls learn almost everything the boys know. Pops says it isn't necessary exactly, he said there would be no *Candy Men* in this generation. He tells little Franky that he's going to be a great man and not just because he carries his name, but he sees it in him. Then he tells Ethan and Fernando that they will be great as well. None of us know what Fernando will be good at though. He's such a tender foot, too kind, too gentle, too gullible, and too naive! Ryan always talks Fernando into doing the dumbest stuff just for the amusement of seeing him get in trouble. One day Ethan is going to get tired of defending his big brother.

Frank walked up to me, "why are you acting funny?"

I took the gun and I told Timothy I'd be right back. Jeff jogged up to us and took my gun from me with a smile. "No accidents, carry on." Then he jogged away.

Frank and I sat against his car. "Explain to me how my wife goes out with you and your wife then she comes home talking about she wants a divorce?"

"The matter of fact way she said it that night suggested that she's said it before. I assumed she had said it to you." He said watching my face.

I slumped, "where did you go?"

"The Red door." He watched my eyes.

"Tell me you did not take her in the *GREEN* room?"

He nodded, "Annette went behind the *GREEN* door."

"DON'T TAKE MY WIFE THERE!" Then I looked at him, "did she hit it?"

"Once," I threw my hands up. "She didn't like the choke, so I gave her half a brownie."

"SHE ATE IT?"

Frank nodded yes, "then Raynel and I cleared the air some, but you'll like this part."

"I doubt it!" I said blowing air.

"I asked her a very important question and she answered like this. No!" He said shaking his head yes.

"What?"

"I asked her, you want Tim to man up and win you back? And she said No!" He said as he shook his head yes.

"How high was she?" I asked with an excited smile.

"Right after that she was completely gone. Life of the party, a guy asked her to dance and she came right back saying he couldn't dance and how she wished you were there. Then she went on and on about the things she misses about you. She's pretty mad at you, you hurt her, but she still wants you." He watched me process, "are you going to give her a divorce?"

"No, and especially not now!"

****

"Someone attempted to break in last night. The dogs took a bite out of someone," he pointed to the blood and bloody paw prints. "If they were professional they would've been prepared for the dogs."

I looked at Whispers, "Avery?"

"More than likely," Detective White said. "I'll go by his house and check him out. Before I go, I told Franklin and Frank already, but I wanted to let you know as well. Maureen Wallace ran away from the hospital last night. It looks like she may have had some help, but we don't know who."

"Honestly her mother is too depressed and unhealthy to walk out the door. She has a sister, but she's in England. Unless she's cultivated friendships I don't know about, it could be anyone." I said

"The hospital is going to give me her visitation log. Your brother wants her back in the hospital. However, he feels we should keep an eye on you cause she may try to reach out to you."
I frowned, "put someone on my house. I got a bad feeling about all of this."
"My man will coordinate with your man." Whispers said to Detective White.
"Take Avery out, I don't have time for these games." I commanded.

****

Momma touched my hand with sad eyes. "I don't know what to tell you son. I don't think you can fix it. Annette is so hurt. If she knew you were talking to me like this she'd pack those babies up and leave. She say she don't want you back and I believe her."
"Momma love doesn't vanish into thin air. She loves me."
Momma sighed, "no it doesn't son; but now that love has taken on the form of hate. One of these days she's going to successfully push you down the stairs."
"Well it's not like I don't deserve it." I exhaled, "momma will you watch the kids for us? I gotta try."
"It's not that I don't want you to try. My fear is that you will make things worse and she packs up my babies and leaves me too."
"She's not going to leave her momma."
Momma looked at me like she couldn't believe it. "After she had Amber she was about to get on the train. She was angry and hurt talking about she didn't have anybody. She was going to leave me too! Your wife is hurting, I think you've done enough."
I looked at my momma in disbelief. "Pops has never given up on you. How could you tell me to give up on my wife?"
"With everything your father and I have been through I never questioned whether he loved me. Your father is selfish and entitled, but I know he would give his life for me. Our relationship is different, I have my ways. Sometimes your father needs me when I can't do it. It's not easy to be married to someone like me. Annette has pushed herself to be there for you regardless of everything. You were her everything." Momma shook her head. "She hasn't even grieved properly and you keep pushing at her."
I sat back and thought about it. "Ok, ok. I won't trick her. I'll invite her, but if she says yes will you keep the kids for us?"
"Of course."
I kissed my momma's cheek then I let her walk out of the restaurant first. I walked down the street to Pops's store. I knocked on the door and it was locked. I heard my father tell me to hold on. I heard movement then he opened the door, when he saw it was me he opened it. A woman was fixing her hair, sitting in the chair. I looked at my father and I asked what happened to Mae. He said she expired and it was time to move on. He started to tell me the new woman's name and I told him I didn't want to know. I told him I came by because I just had lunch with momma a block over. He told the woman she had to go. He couldn't get her out of his office fast enough. He sprayed air-freshener and then I left out the back door. As I pulled away I saw momma going in the front of the store.
When I got to the house Annette was out back with the kids. She was sitting on a blanket facing the kids with a story she was reading them. Timothy was holding Amber. "No chipmunk stay with me." He kept telling her as she tried to get up. When the story was over Annette asked Timothy to summarize the story she just read him. My son did an excellent job of relaying what he heard even with the

distraction of his baby sister. She asked Malachi questions about the story, and he answered correctly. Then she asked Jade if she liked the story. I was sitting on the bench smiling at my children. Annette turned around when all of them looked at me. She turned back around quickly. I kept making silly faces at the kids, which made it impossible for them to focus. When she gave up she sent the kids on their way to say hello to me. As she walked past me I grabbed her hand. She snatched her hand away and told me not to touch her. "Annette you're coming with me."
She sucked her teeth, "no I'm not!"
"I have to go over the Barnes'."
She froze then she rolled her eyes and went inside. I said hello to my children and played with them until my momma came home.
I held Annette's door open for her. She wouldn't look at me the entire car ride. I let the radio fill the silence. Mr. Barnes was watering the grass when I pulled in front of the house. He called out that Annette was here when we got out the car. Mr. Barnes pointed for us to sit on the love seat even though I know Annette didn't want to sit that close to me. "Tim! That's very slick bringing Annette." He said trying to pull back his anger. "I told you we don't need it!"
I leaned forward cause this fight was getting old. "Every month it's the same fight! Why Mr. Barnes? Why? You are the last person I want to fight with."
"Then stop fighting me. You got a family that needs you. Look at how skinny Annette is! She needs your attention more than I need anything from you."
I glanced at Annette and she rolled her eyes at me. "Mr. Barnes I'm at the end of my rope. Annette doesn't love me anymore. It's not her fault; we all know what I've done. The only thing I can control is where this check goes, please let me honor my brothers." I said swallowing my emotions.
Mr. Barnes looked at Annette long and hard. "I heard about it." Then he looked at me. "I never thought it would've been you." Then he called out to his wife, "bring the box when you come." Then he looked at Annette, "how you doing babygirl?"
Annette exhaled, "I'm just doing what I have to so that I can survive."
Then Mrs. Barnes brought a box and her bible in the room. She gave both of us hugs and kisses hello. "I've been thinking about you two." She said as she sat down. "Remember when you asked me to hold all these love notes and poems for you when you were in trouble, wouldn't you say that was now?"
Annette put her hand up, "Mrs. Barnes the man who wrote that left me. I don't want a reminder of what I used to have."
"Annette, baby, grief will make people behave differently. It's not like you to be so bitter and hardhearted. Just like my baby lost his mind as well. Are either of you familiar with Job?" Both of us shook our heads no. She touched her bible then she told us about his story. "This man had everything just like us, happy life, good friends, children, wealth you name it. He lost everything in a matter of minutes. Then he got sick, there was a lump in my throat and Annette was shaking her leg as she listened. When she said Job's wife couldn't take it anymore and she told her husband to curse God and die, Annette started crying angry tears. Mrs. Barnes explained that Job's wife grief caused her to act out of character, but she got it together and came back around. Annette pushed me and screamed at the top of her lungs at me. Everything she said didn't exactly have anything to do with me. I had to take her wrath for every man who's hurt her. Mr. & Mrs. Barnes cried with us. I told Annette she was right, I forgot that we were in the same pain. She said she refused to go through this kind of pain the rest of her life. I told her I'm here now and I'm not leaving. She said it was too late! She held on to the point that she

wanted a divorce. Mrs. Barnes told her she was right. Annette looked at her like she was trying to trick her. Mrs. Barnes said she was angry and she was hurt and it was only fair that Annette hurt me like I hurt her. Annette got madder. Then Mrs. Barnes explained that Annette had every right to every emotion that she was feeling. She asked her to work through them and not to let them fester and be her motivation to do anything. She warned her that decisions made in anger did not stick. Annette didn't want to listen but you could see that she was. Then… Mrs. Barnes told her… "I don't want you to end up like your momma. Mad and hurt at the world, your children deserve better than this. Jeremiah and Katie would be so hurt if they saw how you two were falling apart over here." That made both of us cry, I kept telling Annette I was sorry.

We sat there talking for a long time, then Annette said she was ready to go home and I could come for a little while, BUT! I had to sleep on the couch and it was only temporary until I found a house near by so the kids could see me regularly and she wanted me to file for divorce. I didn't want to agree to that but I did. Mrs. Barnes gave Annette the box of my love letters and poems. We said nothing in the car, and I pulled up to the pump. When the attendant came out I tipped him and told him I would pump my own gas. I was trying to see the silver lining; my wife and children were coming home at least. It was a step closer in the right direction. Out the corner of my eye I saw Annette reading and it looked like she was crying. I felt horrible.

"Tim! Why haven't you called me?"

I looked up to the heavens, could this night get any worse? "Go away Natalie!"

She looked in the car, "YOU MARRIED HER!"

"GO AWAY NATALIE!" I didn't look to see if Annette was looking cause I knew she was. I tried to keep any indication that this was the female out of my body language.

"Tim, please…."

"What do you want?" Annette said getting out of the car.

"Never mind you, its none of your business!" Natalie snapped at Annette.

Annette looked at her then she looked at me. I didn't know what to do, if I snatched this girl up she'd think I was trying to cover something up. "I told you to go away!" Natalie stepped like she was going to touch me and I swear it looked like Annette's eyes turned red. She grabbed Natalie by her shirt and swung her around to the opposite side of the pump from me. Natalie squared off as Annette came at her. When she hit Annette you heard it, but it didn't stop Annette. Annette hit Natalie so hard you heard it and you felt the vibration. Natalie was screaming for help as Annette beat her face like a punching bag. Maybe Natalie thought she could fight, but no matter how good you think you are, there's always someone better. ALSO, she knew what she did and Annette let the comment slide moments ago. She should've backed away when she had a chance. It wasn't a fair fight so I picked Annette up. Annette was kicking and screaming telling her to never look in her husband's direction again or she would kill her. When I put Annette in the car, she cursed me so badly until her voice literally started going out cause she had been screaming all night. When we came home momma asked what happened cause Annette looked wild. Annette used the little bit of voice she had left to tell momma as much as she could. The last thing she told her was that we were going home in the morning.

Momma waited until Annette was sleeping them she came in the room with the boys and me. She told me this was my last chance and not to blow it. I told momma she didn't want me. Momma said if she didn't want me she wouldn't have agreed to come home with me, and she wouldn't waste her time reading the letters. Momma popped me upside the head and told me not to blow it.

****

I took a deep breath as I got in my car. Annette isn't making this easy, but why would she? I keep telling myself I made my bed I gotta lay in it. When I got to the house Timothy was waiting in the window. Since Annette refuses to do anything that I might confuse as a loving gesture I know better than to expect dinner when I come home. So today, I told the boys I'd take them on a "picnic" when I got off work in the park. I went by the deli and picked up the packed basket they had waiting for me. Rita put apple juice in the basket for the kids, and wine for me. The bottle made me sad, she had no idea my wife wasn't coming. Timothy held Amber as he excitedly but carefully walked down the steps. "Come on momma." Malachi said assuming his momma was coming.

"No baby, I'm going to stay here." She said standing in the doorway watching Jade very carefully walk down the steps.

"Momma? You're not coming? Dad said it's a family picnic." Timothy said hitting her with big brown eyes.

"Momma please come, I'm going to be sad without you." Malachi said making his face pitiful.

"Peas mommy!" Jade said

I held back my smile; Annette cut her eyes at me. "You put them up to this?"

I put my hands up to say I was innocent. The boys made their faces really pitiful, and I thought about the trucks I was going to bring them from the toy store. Annette sighed; she went in the house and got her purse. She took Amber from Timothy and then she got in the car. All of the kids got excited and they laughed excitedly and talked the whole way to the park. I opened the wine and the juice and we ate and drank first. Annette's eyes didn't look as mean towards me, but sometimes she would be softer then she'd flash. I gulped two glasses of wine then I ran around the park with my children. Annette stayed on the blanket watching us for a while. Then she turned her back to us as she read. I assumed she was reading a book, but when we approached her to pack up to go she put the paper back in her purse and then she wiped her eyes.

****

"Have you filed yet?" Annette asked me as I approached the door.

"Hello my love, how was your day?" I said sarcastically.

"When are you going to move out? You can go buy that big monstrous house you always wanted. Live like Frank with your whores." She barked.

"My day was long, I'm tired." Then I looked at her, "you make it all worth while with your talks of divorce and mistresses." I kissed her cheek as I passed her.

She punched me. "Keep your lips off of me!"

"You ready for me yet? I'm waiting on you."

She frowned at me, "you will never touch me again!"

I stood there looking at her. She's been drinking, and the kids are in the bed already. She wants me, I told myself not to get too excited and blow this. "Ok." I said as nonchalantly as I could. When I walked in the kitchen she followed me. I grabbed a glass and then I went to the bar and poured a tall glass. "Have a drink let's talk everything out."

"I don't need a drink to do that."

"You need a drink to stop yelling at me. I'm being as patient as I can be, but since you don't want me anymore it's difficult to deal with you."

Annette poured a drink and sat on the far end of the couch. When she hit halfway through her glass I got up for a refill and I refilled her glass as well. "I only agreed to move back home because you said you would do whatever I wanted."
I sat down next to her, "I stay away as long as I can. Isn't that what you want?"
"I want you to move out." She slurred a little.
I took her glass from her and I put our glasses on the coffee table. "Annette, I don't want to move out. I love you! I want to be here with my family. Tell me what to do to make it up to you. I promise on my life I will never leave you again!" I moved closer.
Annette started crying, "you don't mean it! You're just going to do it again."
I kissed her lips, "no! No! I won't! Never again!"
"Get away from me Tim! I don't trust you!"
"That's fair, I will work to get your trust back. Please let me back in, I'm dying without you!"
"You're always getting me drunk!" Then I kissed her deeply like my heart has been begging to. "Don't kiss me like that!" She said with her eyes still closed. I pulled her legs, which made her lay down, and I gently laid on top of her. I looked her in her eyes and I kissed her deeply. "Get off of me!" She said as she opened her legs and rubbed my head.
No one feels like my wife! My body was made for her, and hers for mine. I needed to make sure she knew this happened in the morning, I went in as deep as I could which made her gasp like she couldn't take it. I need her to know no one could ever make her feel like this other than me. I put in my best work ever!
When Annette woke up, she started crying. Not the reaction I was hoping for. I pretended like I was sleep while she tried to quietly escape to our room.

Chapter 24

Annette

"Annette what's the problem?" Aunt Dorothy asked.

"I can't believe I did that! He didn't deserve it!"

"Did you enjoy it?"

I unwillingly shook my head yes, "but he didn't deserve it."

"Forget about all of that. He's still your husband and you made love. You needed it, did you use anything?"

"No, but I'm on the pill."

"Does he know that?"

"No."

"Good! Watch what he does. If he's not truly sorry he'll show his butt again."

"Does it make me weak if I give in? I miss him."

"No! You married him because you love him. When it's your husband you can be as weak as you need to be. Remember, if you're going to forgive him you can't drag this on and on."

I keep telling myself to stop reading those doggone letters, poetry, and notes where Tim has poured out his heart to me over the years, but they keep calling me to read them. I always knew my man has a romantic soul, but reading some of them moves me to tears. I've always known that he's written me love notes when the spirit moves him. Sometimes Tim would come home with love letters, flowers, and an expensive bottle of liquor. Looking at these letters reminds me of how things were before the accident. I keep thinking about what Mrs. Barnes said about Tim acting unlike himself due to grief. It's a lot easier to believe that he was trying to hurt me than to believe he was hurting so badly that I got hurt in the process. The other day I woke up missing the feeling of being in love. I read my favorite letters and poems that day; I could feel forgiveness washing over me. I sat in the middle of the living room feeling crazy. Normally I'd call Katie when I couldn't put my finger on something with Tim. Between the two of us we had him nailed down to what he would and wouldn't do. I fed the kids and put them down for bed. Then I had a couple drinks trying to get Katie out of my mind. I miss my sister, I miss my brothers, and I miss my niece. Katie, Lauren, and Emma were my circle for a little bit. Katie would always make things beautiful. The things that would drive me crazy about Tim she would paint them with love and then hold them up for me to see and appreciate. Katie and Jeremiah would be so angry if they knew how we've fallen apart. This whole thing is traumatic cause I lost so much in one night. I was ready to be there for Tim to try to help him any way I could, forget about me, and what I needed. I guess I expected him to have the same feelings towards me and when he didn't put me before himself for the first time ever it devastated me. It was like my father left again, and there was no Luther, no Hazel's to drown my misery at, no Harriet to run to. To try to stand on my own.... Wow! I needed love when he got there, but I was still mad at him. I'm tired of fighting. I want to feel loved again.

Timothy

"What do you mean you couldn't find him?" I barked.

"It was definitely him at the office. He dressed his wounds at home and then he disappeared. I've checked the hospitals, and everywhere I can think of and I can't find him."

I looked at Whispers, "please protect my family."

"Eugene is on your house as we speak. I've also got people looking for this guy. If they can't find him we will."

"Why don't they call you Raspy instead of Whispers?" Detective White asked.

Whispers blank stared at him, "you better be happy I like you."

When I got home I could see Annette battling with herself. I hired enough help to do my best to be home by dinner. No one would ever be as good or trust worthy as Jeremiah and Hezekiah with my business. However, I found decent fill-ins for now. Most times I bring work home with me, but Annette needs to see that I'm trying to be here. She's been running hot and cold on me since that night. At first I thought she might've been pregnant and I feared that she would think I did that on purpose. I was the most relieved when I noticed she was on her period, even though I think she was trying to hide it from me like she was testing me. She could test me all she wanted, I'm standing firm in my conviction to NEVER be this blinded by pain again.

It wasn't even like I was enjoying being with Natalie. Jeff was right, I looked sick and I think I was trying to die. I wasn't thinking about how I was hurting Annette or our children. All I could see is that I should've died that night in the rain. I felt so guilty to be a live breathing and feeling loved. I should've let Annette help me, but I felt like she was going to take my pain away as if it would make me forget my BEST FRIEND! Our lives together until that night. The pain in my heart from losing my family doesn't go away. I'm still angry that they're gone, but none of it is Annette or my children's fault. It's not wrong for me to continue to live without them.

The other day it started sprinkling on my way home. Annette and the kids weren't home when I got home. As it started to rain, I couldn't stop myself from freaking out. I called everyone until Raynel said they just left and should be home in a minute. As I hung up the phone they were coming in the door. Still panicked but relieved that they made it home I hugged and kissed each one of them. Annette watched me with big eyes and when I got to her I squeezed her tight and I wouldn't let go. At first she let me hold her. Then she put her arms around me and she said I was trembling. When I put the kids to bed that night Annette was waiting on the couch. She had tears in her eyes and she said she thought she was the only one who freaked out about driving in the rain now. I told her that normally she's home when it rains; this was the first time that she wasn't. Annette said she still hated me and she wanted a divorce, but she invited me back to our bed. I wasn't going to read anything into her invitation, but I was happy to sleep in our bed again after all this time apart. When Annette started crying I asked her if it was ok to hold her. She called me an idiot and then she said yes. I didn't realize how much I missed holding her until now. The rain hadn't let up and she couldn't stop thinking about Katie, how big the baby would be by now, etc. she missed them all. She said Timothy was scared to get in the car to come home, and he didn't calm down until he saw that I was home already. She said my reaction to them walking in the door was exactly what Timothy needed to completely calm down. She said in that moment she felt like the old Tim was back. Not the monster who broke her heart. In the morning when I got up to get ready for work, she cleared her throat. She thanked me for not assuming that her invitation meant that she was inviting the revolving door of sex between us, but she was looking for more comfort than cuddling. I was late or as late as the boss could be to work that day.

Ever since then I've been more open about my daily pains. Sometimes I've found that we're going through the same thing on the same day. I think we're on the road to recovery.

Annette

"So.... I got a call from Christy." Lauren said slowly. "She wants me and Truvy to go to lunch with her today."

"Ok?"

"This is so random. Can I bring Sophia to your house? That way I can come directly to your house afterwards."

"Of course, I wanna hear everything."

Lauren brought Sophia over a little after that. I put on records and Amber and Sophia sat on the blanket bobbing to the music while Jade stood there rocking. These three were the easiest to look after. I put on music and they would dance and entertain each other. Jade would smother both of the girls with hugs and kisses as if she was so much bigger than them.

When Lauren and Truvy came over after their lunch, they said Christy is weird and she's up to something. Truvy said that Christy was trying to dissect her or something. Lauren called Jeff to check in. She frowned as she spoke to him. When she got off the phone she said Jeff told her we were all going out tonight. Tim and I weren't exactly back on good terms, but he was sleeping in our bed again.

Timothy

"Francine's is going out of business. We have to go!" Jeff said

"I don't know, Annette and I aren't there yet."

"How else you gonna get there? You want me to have Lauren talk her in to going? Martha and Sebastian, Matt and Truvy, Frank said he wants to bring Raynel. It's going to be a good night."

"Raynel? What about Christy?"

"Frank put her out, he's tired of her and all her drama."

"Where did she go?"

"Don't know don't care, Frank said he's keeping the kids."

"Really?"

"You know those kids would be worse off with her. She'd raise them to be racist idiots."

"Racist?"

"She don't like our family and the only reason she clings to Frank is because of his money."

"What would the odds be that she knew Avery?" I said thinking out loud.

Jeff was quiet cause he was thinking about it too. "Let me make some calls. I'll call you back."

My phone rang when I sat it down, "Ace Trucking."

"Tim it's Detective White. Listen the hospital got back to me. The only visitor Maureen had outside of your brother was a Christy Bailey. That's your brother's girlfriend isn't it?"

I looked up at the ceiling, "yes."

"That's what I thought. I'll keep looking."
"I think that might be our answer. Something's wrong, I'll call you back." I hung up, and then I called home. Annette answered on the second ring. It sounded like she was talking to someone. "We got company?"
"Lauren and Truvy are here, they had lunch with Christy. I kept the baby for them."
"I need you all to pack up and calmly go over my parent's house." I said.
"Lauren said something about going out tonight?"
"Did you want to go?" I asked sounding surprised.
"Raynel said she'll go if I go. It'll be hard to be there, you know." She was referring to Jeremiah and Katie, "but I think it could be good for us. Only if you want to?"
I exhaled, "I want to be anywhere you want to be."
I could hear Annette smile, "good. So go to your momma's house? What should I pack for you?"
My heart screamed, MY WIFE! "Whatever you think is best, but I need you all to get going."
"Ok, see you soon, I love you." She said for the first time in what felt like forever.
"Annette! I love you so much! I... I..." I couldn't find the words.
I could hear her smile through the phone, "we'll talk later ok?"
"Yes! Yes, we will. I love you! Talk to you soon." My second line started ringing, my heart was pounding. I took a breath to get a grip, and then I answered the phone.
"Ace Trucking."
"Detective White just called me." Frank's voice roared through the phone.
"I'm on the line as well." Matt announced.
"Hold on I'll call..." Jeff walked in the door. "Where did you call me from?"
Jeff shook his head, "not important." Then he sat down.
I put Frank and Matt on speaker. "Lauren and Truvy are at my house. They had lunch with Christy."
"WHAT?" Frank and Matt said at the same time.
"Avery is Christy's cousin." Jeff informed us.
"WHAT?" We all replied.
"Frank you've been slipping."
"Are the girls staying at your house?" Matt asked me.
"I told Annette they needed to go to momma's."
"What about Raynel?" Jeff asked.
"She and the boys are already in route to momma's." Frank said.
"Do we think Christy busted Maureen out?" Jeff asked.
"Looking at the board fellas. Secure your women. I'm calling everyone and telling them to go to momma's. It don't look good." Frank said.

Annette

"I haven't worn this dress in years, do you think it will be too much?" I said holding my red dress up to me.
"Good choice, Lauren do you have a red dress?" Truvy asked.
"Of course I do. The question is which one fits? I've got a little more to go before I'm back completely."
There was a knock at my bedroom door. "Momma Eugene is at the door." Timothy said peeking his head in the door.
As I walked past the kitchen I caught a glimpse of Sophia sitting on the kitchen floor. While Jade was telling Amber to get down as she climbed up on a chair. I stood there and folded my arms. Amber is worse than Malachi with the stuff she

gets into. Her little fat legs were kicking until she got completely on top of the chair. Her victory was short lived when she saw me standing there. "Get down!" I said, she almost fell trying to get down. I popped her little leg. "How many times I gotta tell you to stop climbing up on stuff? You are so hard headed!" I sat her on the floor in the hallway as she cried. Jade and Sophia came to hug her.
When I got to the door Eugene's face was very serious. "Mrs. Wallace I need you all to get going."
"We were packing, and we'll be ready..."
He cut me off, "Mrs. Wallace! I need you to get going now!"
"Alright."
"Go through the garage to get in your car. Everyone needs to ride with you. No matter what happens keep driving until you get there." He said firmly.
"Alright." I closed the door and I told Timothy and Malachi to get their bags, which I had already packed. I went in my room. "Eugene says we have to go now!"
Lauren sat up, "ok!" She ran to get her baby.
"You're riding with me, and he told us to go through the garage." I said loudly. I grabbed my dress, Tim's suit, shoes etc. I threw everything in the garment bag. I picked up Jade and Truvy grabbed Amber. Timothy opened the garage door and closed it when I pulled out, he got in the car and I drove very paranoid over the bridge. I could see Eugene following me. Fortunately the kids were quiet and unaware that anything was going on. Timothy kept watching my face like he knew something was going on. I parked behind Irma's car in the driveway. Martha and Beth pulled up at the same time. Eugene came over and helped everyone get their things inside. Blanche arrived as we were going inside. Eugene told us to go in and he'd help her. Peggy and Raynel were already here. Eugene went through the house securing it. He closed all the curtains and even though it was daylight he turned on all the lights in the house. He told us to leave all the lights on and to stay out of the windows. When Irma walked him to the door everyone stared at her gun in her waistline of her skirt. "Momma what's that?" Lauren asked.
"Honey, I know you've seen a gun before." She looked at her like it was a dumb question.
"Why are you wearing it like that? We have children here."
"I don't know what's going on but I'm ready." Then she looked at Blanche. "Both of your kids know how to use a gun, all of your kids do." We all, and by all I mean Lauren, Blanche, Truvy, and I gasped.
"What do you think all the men were doing when they took all the kids?" Martha asked.
"They said they went to the park." Blanche said.
"Yes, and they've learned a few other things there as well." Martha said.
"Why would Sharon need to know how to shoot?" Blanche asked mockingly.
"For the same reasons I do." Irma said, "your children are Wallace's and everyone doesn't like us. Boy or girl, our children need to know how to defend their selves. Your kids know that guns are not toys. Think about it, when have you seen any of them playing around like they have guns? They know!"
"Our children are not being groomed for the *candy* business are they?" I asked.
"No, I've told you our plan for our grandchildren. Unfortunately they're all still connected to this family so we can't afford to have any weak links." Then Irma looked at all of us. "Just so we're clear if Christy or a Christy type randomly invites you anywhere question it. That girl has never cared about anyone in this family and

suddenly she's inviting you out to lunch. There's a lot that happens in this family. I don't expect you all to keep up with everything, but be smart for crying out loud."

"What are you saying? How would we know anything is going on one way or another? For all they knew Christy could've been planning a party for Frank or something. I would've been suspicious if she invited me, she still mad about me hitting her. Is there something going on with Christy?" I said defending Lauren and Truvy.

Irma chewed back irritation, "sometimes I forget that I didn't raise you. You have to pay attention."

Peggy took the big kids down to the basement and created some games for them to play. The little kids and babies played in the family room. Beth made tea for us as we sat in the kitchen. When Irma walked out of the kitchen Martha leaned in and whispered, "am I the only one who still brought a dress for tonight?"

Everyone except Lauren and Truvy brought their clothes. Lauren said she thought she was going to be able to go home to get clothes. Martha said all this was more than likely just a safety precaution and then we'd be able to go out later.

Lauren and Truvy replayed their lunch with Christy for everyone else. Irma sat next to Raynel and listened. Irma told us that Frank kicked Christy out and he wasn't letting her see the children anymore. She said Fernando didn't seem to notice, but Gwen cries for her momma. Irma said Christy was just as removed from Gwen that she has been from Fernando, but Gwen was a momma's girl and wanted her anyways. Raynel didn't say anything but she listened closely. We asked about Christy's family, Irma said they were working class people. They didn't make serious waves one way or another. We asked if they ever met her family. Irma looked irritated when she said no. She said Christy's parents felt we were beneath them on account of them being convinced that Irma was passing and they felt the way Frank and Tim married showed proof to that fact. They were livid with Christy when they found out she was still messing around with Frank, and they disowned her and her colored kids. I asked why she wouldn't fix her attitude if Frank was all she had. Irma shrugged and said maybe Christy thought she did.

Timothy

"Dale we need you to go to the house as back up for Pops. Even though Sebastian, Chevy, and Thomas would be there Pops would need backup. In case anything happens." Frank said

"Ok, I'll get going now. I'll see you all when you get there." He said

"Let's go," Frank commanded as we headed out the door.

I told my staff to go home, the dock walkers were making their way around so my guys were excited. Frank said hello to my dogs. He said they were his leaders at home, and their pups were growing up to be just as good as their parents. We locked up and let the dogs run free around my space.

We went to the hotel that Christy was staying at. The guy at the desk said she checked out this morning. He said she left with another girl; Matt showed him a picture and asked if that was the other girl. The guy said yes.

I told everyone to look at the imaginary board. Maureen and Christy being together was only a threat of ridiculous emotions. Jeff begged to differ he said, "Maureen is mad cause Matt had her falsely certified as crazy. He took her kids, locked her away, and moved on with his life. Then Tim has the nerve to be in love with a black woman. Christy, you kicked her out, you're in love with a black woman. Tim fired her cousin and replaced him with a black guy. Oh and don't forget that Annette hit

her and she didn't get to retaliate. If they didn't have Avery I'd say they were non-or minimal violent threats. So we need to decide now, do they go down?"
"Any threats to my Queen go down!" I said
"Raynel is my Queen."
Matt threw himself backwards in his seat. "Maureen is my Queen!" He said in pain.
"THAT'S HOW YOU TREAT YOUR QUEEN?" Jeff yelled
"She's the mother of my children, my name sake! I do love her." Matt said
"Our direction has to be clear."
"I know! I know!" Matt said like he didn't want to deal with it. "I want her back in the hospital."
"Matt come on you can't whimp out on us now. You know she's not going to go back willingly."
"That's my wife!" Matt said in pain.
"I thought Truvy was your wife!" Frank roared.
"She is!" Matt said angry.
"Now how is it fair that you get two and I can only have one? Pick one! Man up!" Frank said.
"No!" Matt said weakly.
The whole car was in an uproar. "You know stuff like this is what gets people killed. Tim pull over!" Jeff barked, so I did. "Mr. Wallace you can't have Maureen. She's now a threat to our family thanks to you. If anything happens to my wife because of yours not only am I going to kill her in front of you, but I'm gonna shoot you no matter how much your momma begs me not to!"
I turned around and looked at Matt. Softness was all over him, "you take it this far to back down? What did you think would happen? You should've never gone behind me, stuff like this never works. Maureen and I didn't just hold hands and drink sodas. She was depressed when she wasn't carrying me inside of her. Where do you think those feelings go? You think they turn on and off just like that? We were in love once upon a time. I don't know what she could've said to you to make you so stupid to believe she was over me, but she lied to you. How do you think it makes her feel to see me with Annette? Living the life that she and I always talked about living. She's an imminent threat to my Queen! They can ask you to choose all day long, but I know you won't. So let me tell you now, when she bucks up at my Queen! MY QUEEN! I'M TAKING HER HEAD OFF! I DON'T WANT TO HAVE TO PUT YOU DOWN TOO! BUT HONESTLY RIGHT NOW YOU'RE NOT SHOWING YOUR LOYALTY! They can ask you all day to choose, but there's no choice here other than whether you die with her!" Then I put the car in gear and drove on.

Annette

"How many men you got out here?" I asked Eugene.
"Eight."
"Take these two and we'll have more when you come back." I said handing him dinner plates.
He smiled at the plates, "who made this?"
"Lauren mostly, Blanche is making dessert so save room."
"Thank you!" Eugene said smiling at the plates.
I looked at the clock it was just after five. I thought Tim would be here by now, I told myself to calm down cause whenever he's had things like this in the past I didn't see him like clockwork either.

We made sure everyone ate including the men outside. Then Irma made drinks she told us everyone only got one because we needed to be alert.

Timothy

We went every brilliant place we could think of. Frank said we would not hide from them, we needed to look alive. When we got to the house the women were relaxed with cocktails not the tense scene I imagined. Annette smiled at me and I forgot about the day I was having. She asked me if we were still going to Francine's. I told her we would do whatever she wanted. Annette excitedly announced that we were still going all of the women cheered. Jeff and Matt took their women to go get dressed. Annette led me by the hand up the stairs my heart was pounding as I followed her. She showed me the gray suit she brought for me. I smiled with approval. I saw a flash of sadness in her face and I asked her what was wrong. She told me that she still loved me and she wanted no one but me, but she was still mad at me. She said she felt like she couldn't trust me, even though she wanted everything back the way it was. I sat and I took it, what else could I do? I told her nothing could ever excuse what I did to her. I was selfish, and trying to justify dying cause I couldn't stand living without my best friend. I told her I forgot about my other best friend in that moment. She exhaled, she said she told me she'd kill me if I cheated on her, and she was mad that she failed the test to prove to me she wasn't playing. She said almost everything about Amber is different and she wondered if that was because I wasn't around. I thought about everything I missed while having my own pity party. Jade was running, she was barely crawling when I clocked out. My sons needed me, my wife needed. Our child didn't know my voice like the others. I told her Amber was the most like her out of all of the kids even though she looked like me. Annette said that was only true to a point she was never outright bad. I smiled and said she got that from me. I asked Annette if this meant we were going to work things out? When she said yes I hugged her as hard as I could. Then I kissed her as deeply as I could. When I kept going with the kiss she told me to save some for later. I didn't want to, but I did as I was told.

Annette

When we got dressed we stood in the mirror together like we were posing for a picture. Tim's handkerchief matched my dress and the whole look of everything popped. Tim looked at me like he wanted to tell me to stay in. I was looking at tonight as an opportunity to finally say goodbye to our friends together. Tim pulled me in close as he watched our reflections in the mirror, he sucked his teeth. He said we looked good together, I agreed. When he kissed me he looked in the mirror, then he sighed and said he couldn't see how good we looked kissing. I laughed; I told him I missed his silliness. That made Tim smile bigger then I told him we needed to get going. His smile dropped and he hesitated. He asked me to sit on the bed and then he said he needed me to understand something about tonight. He said Frank kicked Christy out, he said they think Christy got Maureen out of the hospital and someone saw them together. He said Christy's cousin used to work for him; he didn't know it was her cousin. He fired the guy and every since he has been a serious problem. He said Whispers and all his men were going to be at Francine's tonight as well. I asked him why we would be afraid of Christy? Or Maureen for that matter? He said that it's better to be safe than sorry. He said he needed me to be alert and to stay with the group at all times.

Timothy

We sat at our table and the women were very good at being normal and relaxed. I was on edge, and I kept making eye contact with every person I could. I kept looking around the club and the vibe wasn't right. True it was a going out of business party, but it didn't feel right. I looked at Jeff and his eyes were searching the room as well like he was thinking the same thing. "Everyone grabbed their glasses." Frank commanded so we did. "To Jeremiah, Katie, Hezekiah, and Kiah! We miss you! We love you!"

The owner approached our table and he was sweating profusely. I did not get a good feeling. I touched Annette's hand. I told her we were going to be leaving soon and it was a good idea that they all went to the bathroom before we left. She looked at my eyes then she said ok. She stood up, "ladies. Will you join me? I need to go to the powder room."

Martha looked at me, and then she looked at everyone else. I nodded at her and then she stood up and grabbed her purse. She nodded at Peggy and Beth as well. All of the women excused their selves and went to the bathroom. "Franky! I'm so glad you could make it." Dale looked at the sweat glistening on the owner, he sat up, and then he looked at me. Frank looked at him taking in everything. "I hope you like your table, everything to your satisfaction?"

Frank cocked his head to the side, "really? I never thought it would be you!"

The owner wiped his forehead, "Franky! I don't know what you mean! I…."

Frank pounded the table, "you let me bring my wife here for this! I liked you! Furthermore I trusted you! You're going to die a painful death!"

The owner stood up and gave Frank a "yea right look." He straightened his tie. "I might actually be concerned if I didn't know who was here. Marcos is here and he's here with a surprise guest." The owner stretched his hand towards the other side of the room.

Christy was sitting with Marcos, Maureen, and a few of Marcos' men. Marcos was trying his hardest to get in our territory. We don't sell to the poor, we are not poverty pimps. Everyone knows we have high-in clientele. Marcos and his family hustle for nickels, and they've been trying to get at us for a while now. Frank waved Marcos over. Marcos laughed and then he said yea sure why not. He called Frank a dead man anyways as he and his brother walked to our table. "I see you've been going through my trash again." Frank said to Marcos.

"You can not be referring to that beautiful flower that I found on the roadside where you left it. Why on earth would you ever let someone like that go?"

"I would tell you that you would find out, but seeing as how you're going to die tonight I might as well tell you." Marcos laughed like Frank just told a joke. "She isn't loyal! She uses sex as a weapon to try to get ahead. She's looking for money and support." Frank looked at her then back at Marcos. "She brought your men to my house?"

"Little good it did me though. I was very impressed with your set up, I lost my men and didn't get in at all." All of us looked at Christy, she looked a little nervous. "So," he clapped his hands together. "Wallace's and men married to Wallace's you're all going to die tonight. Ok? We can't afford to let any of you go." He leaned in, "the brunette thinks we're going to save her kids though."

"What does Christy think?" Dale asked.

"She doesn't." He looked at her, "she's not the motherly kind." Then he waved Christy and Maureen over. "Ladies do you have any last words for these men?"

"I wish you a slow and painful death you fat pig!" Christy said.

"She's so lady like." I said smiling at her.
"You're smiling now, but when your wife dies in front of you lets see how happy you are then." She said.
"Matt how could you lock me away like that? I'm your wife!" Maureen screamed at him.
"You know why and how." Matt said
"Tim I will always love you, locking me away doesn't change what's in my heart Matthew. Loving him didn't mean I loved you any less than I did before, but you were never first. Why would you be? I've always known about that woman, why is it ok for you to love someone else but not me? You even slept with my sister." We looked at Matt in shock. "You are so wrong!"
"Doesn't matter, you are my wife. I told you that you only had one chance to make it up to me and you failed me. Why are you with Christy?"
"She's the only person who cared enough to break me out. She's the only person who cared what happened to me." Maureen cried.
"Did you ever stop to think why? She's only using you, and you let her." Matt said. You could tell Maureen hadn't thought of that, "because the Wallace's have done her in too."
"You do realize that after they kill us, they're going to kill all of our children as well." Matt said burning her with his eyes.
Maureen shook her head no, "No. My children will be safe."
"So they're going to hold each child up to you one by one before they kill them to make sure they don't get yours? They don't need you other than to handicap me. Why would they protect your children?" He asked.
Marcos clapped his hands. "This is good but very boring." He gave Christy a gun. "Shoot her first."
Christy very clumsily held the gun up towards Maureen. "Christy?" Maureen said as she cried.

Annette

When we got in the bathroom Martha shut the door and put a chair under the door. She told Peggy and Beth to check the stalls. Martha opened the supply closet making sure no one was in there. Lauren, Raynel, Truvy, Blanche, and I stood in the middle of the floor looking alarmed. Martha said this is a setup and we needed to wait in the bathroom for the men to come get us. Then she pulled her gun out of her purse and her sisters did the same. They made sure their guns were loaded, and then the put everything they could in front of the door. Martha said we needed to move as far away from the door as possible, in case someone shot at it. Martha used the pay phone and she called her momma. She told her that tonight was a setup and that we were in the bathroom. She told them to secure the children and we would be there as soon as we could.

Timothy

My eyes darted around the room, Whispers nodded at me to say he was waiting for the word to take Marcos and his brother out. I was looking for Avery, he had to be here. Dale told me to look up with his eyes. I looked up slightly and Avery was watching from above the stage area where he thought he was undetected. My next question was where were Marcos' other brothers? Paulie kept looking at his watch, which probably meant they were waiting for someone. I can only imagine that was

why all this talking was happening. They hadn't expressed interest in the girl's sudden exit yet, they were stalling.
Frank stood up, he said he was bored with this whole scene and he was leaving. Christy took her gun off of Maureen and put it on Frank as her hand trembled. Frank stared at her with hatred as she proceeded to go off about him making her play second fiddle to a colored woman, and for not defending her when the other one attacked her. Frank looked at her in her eyes and told her she deserved everything she got and what she was going to get by the end of this night. Marcos told her to put her gun back on Maureen, and that he was going to shoot Frank. When Christy didn't listen I slowly reached for my gun as I saw all my brothers moving to do the same. Marcos yelled and as he moved too quickly towards Christy, her shaking hand pointed at him and shot. Marcos looked completely shocked and I wanted to laugh because his dumb behind put the gun in her hand, but now it was go time. Paulie shot Christy which spun her and she pulled the trigger again and that time Maureen collapsed. Everyone was on their targets, Dale shot and Avery fell onto the stage. As bodies were falling Frank executed the owner of Francine's. A couple of the men charged the women's restroom, Jeff and I took off.

Annette

My heart started pounding when I heard the first shot. Everyone looked like they wanted to scream, but we couldn't. I looked to Martha to tell me what to do. I could fight, but they had guns out there. I don't know how to shoot, or the first thing about a gun. We all squished our bodies into the last stall in the bathroom. Martha told us not to scream, I was scared but I did as I was told. Sure enough someone tried to open the bathroom door. When they couldn't open it they shot at the door. Then you heard more gunshots. I covered my mouth as I cried. The door forced open then we heard tap, tap, and then a distinct whistle. Martha called out that we were in the back of the bathroom. Jeff and Tim told us to come. They told us not to look around, to look straight forward, and to keep going. Tim said we were getting in the car with Whispers, and they would come to us when it was safe. The air smelled weird, Jeff went out first and then he told us to come. Tim followed behind us. Jeff told the girls to put their guns away and that we were going to a safe house. When Jeff said it was ok, we hurried out to the car that Whispers was waiting inside of. Jeff told Raynel and I to ride in the front so that the car wouldn't draw attention to us. We looked like drivers and attendants if nothing else. Whispers drove away calmly as his eyes scanned everything. We drove up a hill to an alleyway, and then into a garage where the house was completely lit up just like Eugene had lit up Irma's earlier in the day. "Where are we?" Raynel asked.
"My house." Whispers said as he got out of the car.
"What about our children? I thought you were taking us to Irma's!" Blanche said.
"My men are at the Wallace home, your children will be safe." He said.
"I want to go there, I can't stay here!" She said.
"Your men will come for you when it's time. My assignment at this point is to keep you safe."
"Honey is that you?" Someone called out from the top of the stairs.
"We have company, come say hello." He watched our eyes. A light skinned woman came down the stairs and into the kitchen. "This is Verna, Verna this is everyone. I had to bring work home tonight."

Verna looked at all of us like she was trying to figure out which one of us was messing around with her man. She didn't wear a wedding ring and I saw her look at each of our rings. "Who are they?" She asked him.
Whispers looked irritated, "don't irritate me. I will kick you out and have no problem with it." He warned her. He showed us where the bathroom was and then we took seats in the family room where the television was. Whispers brought us water and he looked irritated that his friend didn't offer us any. She stood in the doorway dissecting us one by one.
"Whispers, your house is so clean. Do you have someone come?" Raynel asked looking around.
"No."
"You clean this place yourself?" I asked.
"Yes." He said sitting in a chair.
"Where do you find the time?" Lauren and I asked in unison.
"There's always time for the things that matter to you."
"He's pretty crazy about neatness and order. I guess that's why I can't move in." Verna offered, Whispers didn't respond.

Timothy

When Jeff and I returned, Matt was on the ground holding Maureen's lifeless body crying his eyes out. Christy wasn't dead but she was in a lot of pain. When the chief of Police walked in. Frank told him that Christy shot Marcos and Maureen. He told him to book her and her cousin for murder in the first degree. Matt screamed that he wanted Christy dead. I couldn't look at Maureen; I stayed behind Matt as I told him we had to go. Matt kept crying and saying that he couldn't leave Maureen. Dale put his hand on Matt's shoulder and he told him that she was gone and he had to finally let her go. Matt shook his head no as he kept kissing Maureen. Dale said he had to let her go for the children's sake. He said we had to go secure the babies and we needed him to pull it together. The children were the only reason Matt let her go, that didn't stop him from crying a heart felt cry as he said something in her ear. I waited with Jeff by the door, when they put her body on the gurney I couldn't look. I told myself I didn't know the person and to keep moving. Jeff heard my pep talk to myself and he patted my shoulder. Two blocks away from the house we separated. We covered the four corners up to the house to sweep the neighborhood. I met up with Eugene and he said Vito and his men have been talking for the past few minutes like they were waiting for a signal to move forward. Eugene said they were just about to get their potatoes and move out if I wouldn't have showed up. I told him any minute now they'd realize their brothers weren't coming and they would recklessly storm the house. I reloaded my gun and grabbed a bunch of potatoes and put them in my pockets. We didn't want to wake the neighborhood with gunfire so we used the potatoes to silence our gunshots. Common courtesy for our neighbors. We quietly took down Vito and his men, then we connected with Jeff and his men and they took down a car as well. As we got to the house Frank was fighting someone. This idiot thought he was going to successfully rush Frank. Frank grabbed him up and slammed his body around like a rag doll. When he was unresponsive I tossed Frank a potato then I went inside the house. All the kids were sleeping upstairs blissfully unaware of anything that was going on. We loaded up the bodies then we tossed the fish food into the bay. Matt stayed at the house with Momma, he was trying to get a grip on his emotions but he was pretty messed up.

When we went to Whispers' place he was sitting in his seat and the women were all sitting around talking to him. His friend looked annoyed standing over to the side. Whispers asked if we needed him for clean up, and I told him it was handled. I kissed my wife deeply and I apologized for the ruined evening.

Chapter 25

Timothy

Matt was sitting there taking it as momma went upside his head. He told her that Maureen died and she lost it. Momma didn't agree with the way Maureen conducted herself, but she did not like the way Matt ran over her. She told Matt this was all his fault and she would not go easy on him. Momma wouldn't calm down until Pops came to save his son.

Annette

Tim explained that Christy was beyond angry with Frank for beating her up. She started conspiring with the Torino family against the Wallace's. He said that she busted Maureen out of the hospital as a guarantee that they would come looking for them. Tim tried to tell me I couldn't go to the courthouse while Christy and her cousin were undergoing trial for the murder of Maureen, and Marcos Torino. I told Tim it wasn't up for negotiation. So he told me to go to the right and he would go to the left. He told me not to look around in the courtroom to focus straight ahead and to take notes. He had me dress up like a reporter since a lot of reporters would be there. He told me to blend in because the remaining members of the Torino family would be there as well. He told me to meet him at the car when it was time to go. He stepped back and looked at me. He said he liked my outfit and he didn't want me to change before he got to enjoy it.

During the car ride to the courthouse a song came on the radio. Tim got excited and turned the song up. He said this song makes him think of me and when he first laid eyes on me. The music in the beginning was pretty, and then it started. "AT LAST! MY LOVE HAS COME ALONG! MY LONELY DAYS ARE OVER…" I smiled and scooted closer to Tim while he sang along with the words. I listened to the words and they were so pretty. When the song was over I kissed his cheek, he told me this was our song. Every time I heard it he wanted me to think of him. I assured him I would.

When we approached the courthouse Tim was behind me. I followed his instructions and blended in with the other journalist. Christy's arm was in a sling and her red hair was pulled backwards into a ponytail. Her skin was even paler than usual. Matt was sitting in the audience behind the prosecution. Christy stood with her public defender that appeared to be shaking in his boots. Everything moved quickly, Christy tried to explain that it was all an accident. Of course Matt made sure every book was thrown at her. The prosecution painted the picture of Christy as a cold-blooded killer. It was no surprise when the jury deliberated over lunch and came back with a guilty verdict. Down the hall the same verdict was given to Avery.

Timothy

"Christy Bailey you have been sentenced to death by lethal injection."

Avery got the same sentence. Christy reached out to Frank a few times especially when I guess the death penalty wasn't good enough for the Torino family and they had Avery violently killed in prison. Frank went once; I can imagine what he said to her. She overdosed while in jail a short while later. When I told Frank what happened, he didn't look surprised or shocked.

Raynel and Frank sat down and had a heart to heart in my backyard. You could see the love they have for each other all over them. You could also see their pain and hurt. At one point Frank was yelling and I had to hold Annette back. Raynel is a big girl and she held her own against Frank rather nicely. I recognized the heartbroken kiss they shared. Raynel walked out the gate, got in her car, and left. Frank sat in his chair like he was frozen. Frank stared off while tears poured down his face.
"Franky? How come whenever Raynel is involved you turn into a girl with tears and snot?" I tried to lighten the mood.
"What did you say to get your woman back?"
"At first it wasn't so much of what I said but what I did. You have to remain persistent."
"I've been persistent." He said in defense.
"You've been persistently distracted." Frank glared at me. "I'm being honest. You said if Raynel won't someone else will and that's how you've been living. If you want Raynel, stop all this nonsense. She loves you, it's not too late."
Frank shook his head, "I've got moves I need to make. She still wants me to downgrade and I can't do that. The Torino's are not the last to try to get at me."
"You could walk away from it all take your wife and start over. Fernando doesn't care, and Gwen could forget Christy."
"Gwen refuses to forget her. She stares at all those old pictures constantly. Raynel will not live without her parents again, and if I leave who fills in for me? Matt?" We laughed. "I told her if I have to play boyfriend then so be it."
"Can you believe the moxie on that guy? He slept with her sister!"
"I thought you knew about that. Why you think she left the country?"
"Her job naturally."
"Um yeah! You leave San Francisco to live in England where you know no one and have no friends."
"Emma lives in Paris most of the time."
"Exactly to get away from here." Then he looked at me. "How are you handling Maureen's death?"
I couldn't help it I know I turned red. "I..." I took a deep breath. "I don't handle guilt well. I've been talking to Annette working through it."
"You talk to Annette about Maureen?" I nodded, "what does she say?"
"Annette and I discuss EVERYTHING!" I looked him in his eyes, "everything!"
Frank exhaled, "I was drunk, I was high. A lot of things were said and done that night."
"So what do you call this? A crush? What is it?"
"Tim you're my kid brother. I love you and....." He exhaled. "We talked it out that night."
"She told me, you were so heart broken over Raynel that you kissed her all those years ago. I might've believed that was all in the past if I didn't see how you look at my girls."
Frank looked me in my eyes, "I love Annette very much. I'm in love with Raynel. You are my brother, and my name is Franklin not Matthew."
"Un huh!" I eyed him, "not even Matt is crazy enough to kiss my woman."
"He married Maureen and had kids with her. I think that qualifies as kissing your woman. Matter fact he took her before you officially broke up. Matt is a bad boy!" Frank laughed.
I hadn't looked at it that way. I laughed too.

Annette

"I don't mean to stare, but why didn't you name her Annette? She acts just like you." Emma said

I frowned, "that girl is a handful. I can't just tell her to stop. I gotta pop her and if it don't hurt she don't respect it."

"Malachi was like that too. Remember I had to take off my shoe and chase him that time."

We laughed, "I guess I expect her to be like Jade."

Emma looked at me, "I'm glad you worked it out." She said talking about Tim and me.

"Thanks," I said taking a deep breath. "We're still working on it."

"Thank you for inviting me."

"It's perfect that you're here. If you would've said no I would've understood."

"You have to come visit me in New York sometime."

"You're hardly there or here."

"I really like being in Paris. One day you have to go with me. It's different there, so much love everywhere you look. Hezekiah and I were going to bring Kiah as our first family vacation. I pretend they're there with me." She cried a little. "I have a friend out there, but I doubt I'll ever be ready to move on."

Then my phone rang and I excused myself. "Hello?"

"Annette, it's me."

"Hi momma," I said waiting for her next story for why she needed more money.

"Hi, the doctor said I need to come in once a month, and I'm going to need medicine. So I'm going to need more money."

"Hello momma, how are you momma? I'm doing fine momma. My kids are doing well as well." Emma frowned.

My momma sucked her teeth. "Annette this is important."

I shook my head; she's never going to change. One of these days I'll learn to accept that this is who she is. "Look momma, you're wasting your breath. I can't give you more than I already do."

"But I have to go to the doctor. You must want me to die! I bet that's what you want."

"No I don't. Tell the hospital to send the bill to me, I'll ask Tim to pay it." Knowing she wouldn't want that.

"No! I don't want that white man in my business."

"But you want me to ask him for money for you. We'll drop by in a little bit to bring your money, but I cannot give you more."

"Fine! Whatever! Bye!" Then she hung up.

Emma stared at me, "I give her money every month. Well I mail a check actually."

I shook my head, "I don't give her much. Just enough for food and utilities."

Emma looked mad, "I give her only half of her rent cause I had a feeling she was getting money from somewhere. She just knew I was going to let her and the boys move into Hezekiah and I's house. She cried hard when I told her I sold it. Out of guilt I just send a check. How did she get you?"

I told Emma about her shoes when she came over her house that time. Emma shook her head and said no matter what she always seems to get over on us. When Tim and the boys came home from their Sunday morning work efforts we loaded up in the car. We went by momma's place and I gave her the normal change that I give her. She tried to look pitiful and sickly. She lost the act when she saw that Emma was with me. She barely said hi to Tim. She touched both of my girl's hair like it was going to turn around and bite her. Timothy and Malachi watch her, but they don't say much to her. When we drove away I took a deep breath. When we got out of the car Timothy went to Emma and put his little arm around her. Emma was in tears as she looked around. I gave Tim Amber's hand and then I hugged my sister as we cried together. Malachi and Jade held hands excited about the carousel. Tim put his arm under Emma's while Timothy held her on the other side. We came to Playland where we first met Hezekiah, Jeremiah, and Katie. Tim said he's been talking to Timothy and he needed to say goodbye to his cousin, aunt, and uncles as well. Playland isn't like it was years ago when we came before. As Emma and I sat on the bench, Frank came out of nowhere. "Take this money and shut up!" He tossed money at me, and then he smiled a painful smile. Emma and I stood up and hugged him. Then he took all four of his kids on the carousel with Tim. One by one families arrived until we were all here. Even Buckie and Stacy's family came, with the Barnes. Mrs. Barnes cried for the first time when she saw that Tim and I were still together. She told us to NEVER scare her like that again. Poppa and Nana bought out the carousel and stayed on with all the little ones who were too little to ride anything else. Everyone else ran all over the boardwalk. Tim and I walked over to the side. I rubbed his back while we stared at the water. I stood there quietly while Tim had a conversation with Jeremiah. I tried not to laugh as he listened to Jeremiah respond to him. He looked at my face and he laughed. So I interjected in their conversation. Then I had to speak for Katie. Tim and I were laughing so hard we couldn't breathe. We held on to each other and we promised to never neglect each other again.

.

Timothy

Now that we're back, WE ARE BACK! Seems like everything is better than I remember. I keep telling Annette I want to give the doctor or doctors who invented the pill almost everything I have. We are spontaneous and there's nothing like being skin to skin. Some of the side effects are some pregnancy like symptoms. The doctor said the occasional headache is one of those things that we'll have to deal with if she stays on the pill.

"I've been thinking." Annette looked at me, sweat glistening on her skin looking heavenly. "Are we absolutely sure we don't want to have any more babies?"

"Positive! We're done!"

"I'm willing to sacrifice my man junk. I'll get snipped so you don't have to deal with those headaches anymore."

Annette sat up, she kissed me deeply. "I can't believe you'd do that for me."

"So I have an appointment at the end of the week. Will you take care of me?"

"Tim don't do it. It's only an occasional headache it'll be fine. The doctor said as they make advancements the pill will continue to get better and I may not have them anymore. What if for some reason we change our minds tomorrow? I can handle the occasional headache." Then she kissed me. "I can't believe you'd do that for me."

"My whole purpose is to make you happy. To make sure that you have everything that you need. I want to do this for us."

"Yeah, but that's permanent. I like the option of changing my mind. I don't want anymore babies especially with Amber as the youngest, but I don't know what tomorrow holds and I may want or need another one." I didn't say anything. I was disappointed; I thought it would be completely romantic. Painful but romantic. Annette looked at me. She kissed my neck then she kissed me deeply. Then she got

on top of me. "I know! I know! You're not a machine." She laughed, "thank you for loving me that much. You are very rare, most men would tell their wife to suck it up."
"I'm not most guys! Your happiness and good health are important to me."
Annette kissed me again. "You think we'll be like this when we're old?"
"It will be my pleasure to push you around in your wheelchair. Help you find your teeth, give you sponge baths." I said raising my eyebrows at her.
Annette laughed, and then she kissed me again. "I know you're not a machine, but I need you again right now." Then she massaged me back to life.
"Woman you are draining me of all of my life force." We laughed.
"Tim, I love you so much! With all of my heart! Forever and ever!"
"Annette, I love you so much! With all of my heart! Forever and ever!"

MORE FROM THE AUTHOR

Thank you for allowing me to entertain you. I hope you have enjoyed reading Volume I in the Wallace Family Affairs Series. If you have not read Volumes I - VIII, please do so. Stay tune for more to come shortly. Follow my Author Page to keep up to date with my new releases Carey Anderson.

Volume I Tracy's Complications (Click here)

Beyond The Wallace's ~ Distorted Mirrors (Click here)

Volume II Part 1 Sometimes Love Isn't Enough (Click here)

Volume II Part 2 Love Is Just Enough (Click here)

Volume III Invisible (Click here)

Volume IV Look Beyond Your Eyes (Click here)

Volume V No Regrets (Click here)

Volume VI First You Laugh Then You Cry (Click here)

Beyond The Wallace's ~ A Heart That's Taken (Click here)

Volume VII At Last

Beyond The Wallace's ~ Abandoned (Click here)

Volume VIII Just A Friend (Click here)

Beyond The Wallace's ~ Last Words (Click here)

Once you've enjoyed all of the background stories for our lovely Wallace's and Latour's. Please tune in to the "**Together We Are Strong**" Wallace & Latour Family Seasons and Episodes (Release TBD) on Amazon.

Made in the USA
Charleston, SC
17 June 2016